GRADISIL

Also by Adam Roberts in Gollancz:

Salt
On
Stone
Polystom
The Snow

GRADISIL

ADAM ROBERTS

GOLLANCZ

LONDON

Copyright © Adam Roberts 2006
All rights reserved

The right of Adam Roberts to be identified as the author of
this work has been asserted by him in accordance with the
Copyright, Designs and Patents Act 1988.

First published in Great Britain in 2006 by
Gollancz
An imprint of the Orion Publishing Group
Orion House, 5 Upper St Martin's Lane, London WC2H 9EA

A CIP catalogue record for this book is available
from the British Library.

ISBN 0 575 07587 2 (cased)
ISBN 0 575 07631 3 (trade paperback)

10 9 8 7 6 5 4 3 2 1

Typeset at The Spartan Press Ltd,
Lymington, Hants

Printed and bound in Great Britain by
Mackays of Chatham plc, Kent

The Orion Publishing Group's policy is to use papers that
are natural, renewable and recyclable products and
made from wood grown in sustainable forests. The logging
and manufacturing processes are expected to conform to the
environmental regulations of the country of origin.

www.orionbooks.co.uk

The moment he began to concern himself with such questions, the primitive thinker must have asked himself why the heavenly firmament, with its sun and stars and the waters above it, did not fall to earth like everything else within his knowledge.

JH Philpot, The Sacred Tree in Religion and Myth (1897)

Part One
KLARA

nothing

Take this printed page, the very one you are looking at now. Take away all the letters, and all the commas and the dashes, and take away the apostrophes, and leave only the full stops, the colons, the dots over the 'i's. You will have a star map, cartography that describes precisely the sky of my imagination. *I want to go there,* you'll say. So do I.

I'll tell you about my father. In the, let's say, *1970s* he would have been the sort of man who played with model aircraft, building and flying in miniature, because the technology in those days was too expensive to allow anything but that. In the, let's say the *2030s* he would have been the sort of man who built and flew real aircraft, propeller planes, primitive slow-jets. Indeed, it so happens that my father was such a man, before he married my mother, before I was born. That was his hobby in those distant, impossible days before my own arrival in the world: he flew his own aircraft, little one-seater jets. But by the 2060s, when my story begins, he was the sort of man who flew into orbit as a hobby. But of course it was more than a hobby.

I have reached that time in life when the need to fix one's memories becomes more urgent than it once was. A person has more time, more empty gaps in their life. This is also the moment, passed, when the prospect of personal extinction becomes more real, and it comes to a person, one cold blank morning, that if they do not scatter the words upon the blank sheet, grain on a ploughed field, then they will leave no harvest at all except their own nerveless body to be decomposed or turned to ash. But I want more than that. So I shall look back, though that perspective is as vertiginous as looking down a great distance, a tremendously long way down. Many things have happened in my life, and it has been a long life, and it has gotten me to the point where I can think things such as: am I in orbit about my life now, my past that great planet, pulling at me with its crushing gravity? Or would it be fairer to say that it's my life that is in orbit around *me*? Something of ego in that, I suppose. I suppose that *something* has tied me to this life, like one of

Newton's cords with which he used to illustrate the inverse square law: such that if four strings hold an orbiting body at distance x, then at distance 2x only one string will hold it. You know about that, but there are things you don't know. In all that shrinking perspective of history, it matters less than once it did that I killed her, that it was I who killed her; but that before I myself die I want to claim that glory to myself. So—

one

This is where the story starts: in the spring of 2059 an American woman called Kristin Janzen Kooistra came to my father and offered to pay him a significant sum of money. In return, my father agreed to hide her in the uplands, a country, unique in our world, in which there are no extradition treaties to the USA or Europe; a country without policemen and without taxes. This agreement between my father and Kristin Janzen Kooistra was where our difficulties began.

She was, of course, in some sort of official trouble. She was on the run from one set of authorities or another. Why else would she have wanted sanctuary in the uplands? But we didn't enquire too closely.

My father took her to the uplands. She paid him a fee of 35,000 euros beforehand, and agreed a rental of eleven hundred euros a month whilst she was up in hiding. We didn't ask her any questions. This was clearly a No Questions sort of deal. Dad said to me: 'This will clear us for the year. She'll schlep us the *purchasing power* to do tremendous things with Waspstar.' I was as excited as he was. I was sixteen that spring. Waspstar was a craft that I called 'our spaceship'. My dad was more restrained. He called it an 'orbital plane'.

Here is my dad, talking about NASA: 'That was the problem, right there, right at the beginning. Is where the rot set in, with the initial premise, and everything subsequent was poisoned by it. If your premise is faulty, then *necessarily* everything that follows is faulty. Oh, NASA. After the Second War last century, the Euro-Asiatic-American war, the Nazis were defeated, but one Nazi, called von Braun, he was given sanctuary by the Americans: he lived in the US the rest of his life, and changed his name to von Brown. And because he had been in charge of Nazi military missiles, he steered the America space programme in the direction of rocketry. He became head of the programme that developed enormous liquid fuel rockets to shoot men into orbit – can you imagine it? That was the only way into orbit in those days – on the apex of these great rockets, like a fairy on top of a Christmas tree. Great rockets, big as the Giza Pyramid. The waste! Then the Russians copied the Americans, out of a spirit of envious emulation, and soon the world was spending twenty to thirty billion euros a year building these rockets!' My father would shake his head in great, mournful motions, left to right, right to left, as if full of pity for the idiocy of twentieth-century humanity. 'And because von Brown was so influential, nobody explored other means of flying to space. And the irony is that the twentieth century was the *great century* of fixed-wing flight! All the great advances in *actual flying* happened then. But oh *no*' (emphatically sarcastic emphasis), 'for fucking NASA it was rockets, only rockets, always rockets. They're still committed to fucking rocketry. A hundred years later and they're still launching their junk and their robots by *rocket*.' His tone of voice was eloquent with his contempt. I learned to hate rockets early. When I was eleven I went to live with my father full-time. At the beginning of that period, I did not understand his hostility to rockets.

I would say: 'But what's wrong with rockets, Father?'

He would roll his eyes, and tug at his doughy earlobes. 'Oh, *very* pretty fireworks they make!' he would say. 'Oh such bright lights! What's wrong with them? Wrong? Klara, I'll tell you what. Or, better, let me *ask* you. Is there a *more* expensive way of moving material into orbit? No. Throughout the last century, it cost as much to move a kilo of anything into orbit as it would have done to build a replica of the thing in solid gold. Imagine that! Imagine it. When NASA planned to fly a hundred-kilo man into orbit they could have taken the money they were going to spend on doing that and instead spent it on building a replica of the man in solid gold, that's what the costs were. This century the cost has come down a little, it is true; but that only moves the metal from gold to platinum, to silver. It is wasteful – oh! Wasteful. So, here we are, and how few people travel into space? Tell me – how few?'

I didn't know.

'Two men last year,' he said, disgusted. 'This year, nobody. Nobody from NASA, at any rate.' Father had various cod-names for NASA. He would refer to them as 'No sir', as 'Nil-ascension sad-acts' and '*Nada*' and other such waggishnesses.

My father was always asking me questions of the following nature: what is the most expensive way of raising a person to orbit? What is the escape velocity? How much heat must a shield process to withstand re-entry? When I was a very small child I did not know the answer to these questions. But I was not very old when I knew as much as he did of the technicalities of fixed-wing flight into space. I worked with him on Waspstar, converting an old Elector private jet into a spacecraft, which was simply a matter of mounting a generator and running the Elemag coils the right way around the wings and under the belly. Soon, I was seeing the world in a different light, as he did. The curve of the horizon around me, when I occupied a vantage point, seemed to me to trace out a ballistic trajectory, an arc rising from the left and falling away to the right. I'm thinking of a particular vantage point when I say this: specifically, the west coast of Iceland where we stayed for a year. It was a beautiful land, though bleak, very hard compared to what I had known as a child. I remember a storm; the weather was such that we had been unable to fly, I think, and so my father stomped off on a walk in the foul weather, and of course I tagged along behind him, like a faithful dog. His temper swirled up from nowhere when he was frustrated, and raged all around him like thunder and lightning; but, equally, he could be so very tender, so very loving. Nobody knew him as I did. I remember that walk very precisely. We walked the cliff walk. The Atlantic wind was enormous, a pressure on the skin like gravity, with sparkles of rain on my face and the sound of distant but tumultuous applause on my waterproof. The sky had turned purple and black, the clouds were great clusters of plums and grapes, great undulations of black cloth, great bulging muscles of black cloud flexing and flowing. As we walked back towards our home the weather worsened. It was as if the wind was trying to pull the sea up by its roots, the water moving in heavily shifting masses and shouldering up against the rocks at the shoreline. And the sky much closer, so low I might almost have reached up my hand and touched it, the ceiling of clouds heaving like a great upside-down flood.

Back inside our ground house, Father was calm again, as if the weather had effected a catharsis upon him. He tinkered with a canister of lithium hydroxide catalyst, and hummed to himself. 'The problem with this place,' he said to me, twitching his head a little to the left to take in the whole of Iceland, 'is that it doesn't have forests. Where I grew up,' (he meant in Hungary-EU), 'there were great conifer forests, hundreds of acres.' I didn't say anything, because I was thinking of the forests of my own childhood, on the southern coast of Cyprus.

'Do you know what a tree is?' he asked me, another of his many rhetorical questions. 'A tree is a seed that wants to get into orbit. Its trunk is evolution's strategy for overcoming gravity. It is rocket-thrust solidified as wood, much more efficient than ballistic flight. If it grew tall enough then we could climb it to space.'

This was one of his favourite themes. After I left home to be with him he took over my schooling, in an erratic sort of way, and made sure I read many books on space flight. 'Only,' he would say, 'ignore the equations for ballistic flight. That is humanity's great wrong-turn, right there. If it hadn't been for NASA, and von Brown, and Korolev in Russia, and their mania for rockets, mankind would have colonised the planets by now. Instead of, what? Two men in space last year, and both of them on three-day repair missions. Nobody scheduled to go up this year, nobody at all. We fly robots up there these days, and precious few of those. Man has turned his back on space. Why? Because they were fooled,' (he was riffling the pages of one of my school books, from the last pages back towards the first), 'because they believe *that*.' He pointed to a passage about escape velocity. 'Eleven kilometres a second, that says. Ignore it! That only applies to free ballistic flight. Ignore it! Imagine a space elevator – imagine a tree tall as orbit – imagine a great tower, like the one in the fairy tale, with a princess at the top. Imagine it reaching hundreds of miles into the sky!' (I was eleven; I'd read plenty of science fiction; I knew that such a structure would have to reach up to the geostationary point above the earth, and up beyond it as far again). 'Imagine a staircase winding up and up inside that tower,' my father continued. 'Like stone DNA, curling and curling all the way to the top. With such a prop, we wouldn't need to reach eleven km a second – would we? We could *walk* into space, slow as we liked.'

'It would take us a terrible long time,' I said.

'It *would* take longer,' he conceded. 'That is not the point. Speed is where all this went wrong. Humanity became hypnotised by *eleven kilometres a second*, and all its space research was oriented towards achieving that ridiculous speed. Only rockets could do this, so rockets were what the space programme became. But the tower – that's a thought experiment, you see? Eisenstein used to do thought experiments.' Father was never very precise with names. In this case he meant Serge *Einstein*, the physicist. '*We'll* use them. What does the tower teach us? That the key to getting into space is not speed, but having *something to climb up* – having somewhere to stand, having what the Greeks call *pou sto*. That's the key.'

'Building a space elevator would be as costly as the rocket programmes, wouldn't it, though, Dad?' I said.

'Oh, building an elevator would certainly be costly – certainly. Too costly, certainly. Yes. But why not grow a tree? A great tree, like the Yggdrasil itself, its branches reaching into space. Then we could climb, up, couldn't we?'

'No tree would grow so high,' I said. I was thirteen, and my mind was logical. 'Higher up its branches would die in the vacuum. And what's *gradisil*?' I had not heard the word before.

'It,' said my father, 'is a mighty tree from Viking myth. But don't worry about that. We don't need to grow such a tree. The Earth has already provided for us. The Earth possesses something called a magnetosphere, created by the differential in rotation between the Earth's molten core and its solid mantle. Really – think of it like a bar magnet, though on a huge scale. The lines of magnetic force run out from the North Pole in a great sweep through space, and in again at the South Pole. Ions from the sun stream down the branches of this tree, my princess, at the north and the south poles, to create the auroras. Better, we can climb up the same branches to space.' He put down what he was doing and came to hug me. Can you genuinely take this as a symptom of disintegration? Naturally not.

That night I dreamt about forests. There is a great deal of pine forest on Cyprus, and it is very lovely. Calm and fragrant. You should go there, visit it. Inside a pine forest it is cool on a hot day, and silent. The tall trunks, like the masts of ships, stand in stately congress. It shrinks you to the size of an ant amongst grass-stems without diminishing your spirit. You're walking between them now: close your eyes. The sound of your footfall is muffled by the spread of pine needles under your tread. The air is aromatic and soothing. The storms of northern latitudes are fine, almost sublime, but I prefer the blue skies of the Mediterranean. Now that I am an old woman I prefer blue skies to any other. I can point up and say *I've been there.*

We were almost a year in Iceland. At the end of that time Father was summoned to appear in an Icelandic court to speak to a case brought by my mother's family, and rather than face that judge we left for Canada.

two

In 2059 my father and I flew Kristin Janzen Kooistra into orbit in Waspstar. We had a small house up there. I was the one, actually, who settled her in there, showed her how everything worked: how to turn the house around on its axis when the sun was on it to stop it overheating; how to vent waste; how to cook; how to recognise and plug leaks, how to scrape and spray the mould that kept growing in the danker corners, and so on. I was a child, but that was alright because it's a very simple procedure, maintaining an upland house. A child can do it. I did it often. The house was, in effect, only a large metal cylinder with a window at one end. We dragged it up empty to orbit one flight in '58, emptying everything possible out of the plane to reduce weight and even then it was a strain. Father thought of hiring a friend of his to tow it up for him, a man who operated an adapted 777 to the uplands, with a more powerful pulse motor that generated more amp; but that would have been expensive. Uplanders don't do things for free, even for good friends. They've got to make a living, after all.

In the end we managed it, although only into a very low orbit. We had to fly down straight away and load up with solid burners, fly back up, fit them to the outside of the tin can, and shoot it up to a higher, slower, safer orbit. After that, my father pressurised the house himself. As with most of those sorts of early-day colonial upland adventures (read the history books) it was a hand-to-mouth, see-how-it-goes procedure. He chatted with friends, checked the web, but in the end he just flew up and did it.

This is what he did: he rendezvoused with the orbiting object, by hand and eye rather than any fancy space-tracking or -docking software. I know that everybody uses the software now, but manual docking isn't as hard as you think, after the first couple of times, after you get the *feel* for it. I've done it many times. He nosed into the hole at the end of the tin can until it was a tight fight. When he first bought his jet he'd sawn off the nosecone and refitted it so that it opened outwards three ways, and then he had fitted some retractable spikes so that he could lock Waspstar into the hole.

Then he opened some nox cylinders inside Waspstar until the air pressure inside the plane was much higher than usual. Then he just opened the nose. I'm sure he was bashed about as the air rushed through and the pressure equalised; in zero gravity it doesn't take much to rattle you around like a dried pea in a maraca. But you can strap yourself down if it's a thing you're worried about. Then he opened some more cylinders until the pressure was comfortable again, and drifted through.

The next task was to seal all the holes and gaps in the tin can, which Dad did by puffing a little mist into the air from a hand-held perfume atomiser filled with water and watching the directions in which it was drawn. Seal the larger holes with patches and sealant; seal the smaller ones with rubber, with cycle-repair-kit components, with whatever you have. The far wall of our house was one great circle of reinforced glass, and provided a really super-splendid view. The only problem was that the frame leaked air very badly, and Father spent a long time sealing all along it, and then repairing his seals, and then fixing his repairs. This process was, doubtless, made much harder by the fact that venting gas into space can cause the house, and the attached plane, to rattle around like a rodeo horse. It's not easy to apply glue to a patch, or to press malleable rubber sealant to a crack with such wild bucking about. But Father managed it all 'without hiccough' as he put it in English, a phrase he had picked up in Aberdeen, UK-EU, where he had lived for several years. Finally he fitted the airlock, bringing the pieces one by one from Waspstar and assembling them around the open nose hatch. After twelve hours' constant work he was done, and our house was airtight. He slept.

Ours was, perhaps, the fortieth house built in the uplands. We were not the very first people to move there, but we were amongst the very earliest settlers and that is a fact of which I am proud. In those days it was like a small village. Everybody knew everybody else. Forty houses in many billions of cubic kilometres of clear space.

It took, I suppose, a dozen flights, over a month and a half for us to fit out the house properly. The trickiest task was strapping the various solid-fuel sticks to the outside, which we did with a radio-controlled waldo (the most expensive piece of equipment of the whole project, apart, of course, from Waspstar itself). I tried to hold the plane in a stable position whilst Father fitted the rockets: the two large ones, initially, to repair orbital decay; and then on subsequent flights the various smaller ones used to move and roll the house. But the waldo's gusts of directional gas kept nudging me out of alignment, and it took a long time. Later, as Elemag technology became more sophisticated, uplanders would rig their houses with Elemag coils and position their houses by riding the turbulent electromagnetic medium. But these were early days. We positioned heat-transfer piping to generate some electricity. Then we rolled metal tape around the whole house; or, rather, we rolled the house beneath us spooling out metal tape, like a spider cocooning its kill in myriad reflective structurally-binding strands.

Furnishing the *inside* of the house was easier: some plants, some air scrubbers, some cylinders, some canned food, some dried foods, some lights, a microwave, kegs of water, radio equipment, microwave transmitter, three pumps, books, clothes, all the paraphernalia of a house.

It was cosy. It was home.

We lived in the house together for several weeks, just to settle in, just to experience upland living for that length of time. I was happy then. After that we flew down, and restocked, and Father flew back up alone and lived there for two months by himself. He didn't like to leave the house unoccupied: without somebody inside to turn the house in the sunshine the temperature differential outside becomes too great when-ever the house orbits in sunshine, and the whole warps. Cracks can appear, and the air can all drain away – not a fatal eventuality because a house can always be re-aired, but a circumstance that kills all the plants and might damage the more sensitive electrical equipment. I was worried about the window – if that broke, then everything inside would be sucked into space and we'd lose all our stuff. But Father was never worried by this. It was a special weave-glass, not cast like traditional glass but woven of transparent square-profile strands, and so it had more flexibility than conventional glass. 'It's tough,' he would say. 'It'll hold.'

But over the following year we were not able to spend as much time in the house as Father would have liked. We came and went as much as we could, but it was never enough for Dad. He fretted that the house was wracking and ruining as we sat around at the plumb of the gravity well. He was happy, therefore, to acquire a tenant. 'She'll look after it for me,' he said, '*and* she'll pay for the privilege.' At that time I agreed with my father. I suppose I had notions of us turning the house into a extremely lucrative form of hotel, with guest following guest, paying us riches, and stringing our income generation out indefinitely into the future. That was wrong. Of course, looking back I would rather we had never been introduced to Kristin Janzen Kooistra. I would rather our house had fallen out of the sky and crashed into the ocean. Such is the wisdom of hindsight.

three

I have said that there were forty other householders in the uplands when we first moved there, and I'll now say something more about them. Some of these forty were very wealthy. Some were moderately well-to-do, technophile middle-classers, retired businessmen or stockbrokers. Only one of them was a woman. None of them were poor. Twentieth-century Apollo had cost NASA eighty billion euros over two decades – huge wastage of money, as my dad would say. The uplanders got into space for a tiny fraction of that enormous cost, but that tiny fraction still meant – [item] enough money to buy and convert a jet, [item] enough money to buy such expensive toys as solid-fuel rockets to attach to your plane, [item] to buy cylinders of nox and canisters of lithium hydroxide, [item] to buy jet fuel, [item] to buy waldoes and other devices. My father was one of the poorest of the original uplanders. One of the richest was Giangiacomo Spontini, heir to the energy baronetage and one of my father's friends. It was he who suggested to Kristin Janzen Kooistra that we might be able to offer her the sanctuary of an upland house.

'She's a friend of mine,' he said, 'and she needs a place to hide away for a little while. She'll pay rent.'

'Great!' said Dad.

We flew from northern Canada, the three of us squashed into the cockpit. Waspstar was packed with luggage and supplies. The plane was sluggish on the runway, lifting off uncertainly and climbing more slowly than usual. She reached her flight ceiling at a lower level than was usual too, and when Father got out of his pilot seat to go aft and switch on the conductor relay he put his elbow, inadvertently, into my face, 'Sorry sorry'. Kooistra looked on, amused. It didn't help that she was such a large woman. She seemed to fill the already crammed space to the point of popping the rivets and bursting the compartment. She was a conspicuous human being, obese, extrovert, with a shotgun laugh, and creases and folds in the flesh of her face and neck that seemed to chew when she moved, as if the skin of her body were devouring the space around her.

We flew due east, Father turned on the current through the wing resistors and I squeezed a few seconds of burn out of the side rockets to give us the necessary upward inclination. Then, cutting into the lines of force of the magnetosphere, our counterfield gave us purchase, and the phenomenon of magnetohydrodynamics (I had spent a whole evening at age eleven learning how to spell and define the word, to please my father) kicked in. Without wishing to bore you, I will explain a little: the added torsion caused by the interaction of our wing current and the magnetosphere creates this effect at relatively low speeds. The aerodynamics of flight become an electromagnetic phenomenon rather than a matter of air currents, but the *effect* is the same. Our wings mark a differential of electromagnetic potential, beneath and above; or, if you like, think of electromagnetic fields as fluids – for they are like fluids: not compressible, true, but flowing, variant in intensity, and (with electronic fields at any rate) drawn into sinks and expelled from sources. So we dug our fins into this tenuous medium by firing rapid pulses of lightning-strike intensity through the cables of our wings, and flew upwards. Or, if you prefer to think of it this way, we jagged ourselves into the branches of the Yggdrasil, we stuck our heels in and we clambered up through the sky.

And so we climbed, and climbed, circling in great arcs through the magnetosphere, each rotation bringing us higher than before. We flew no faster than four hundred klims-an-hour, one hundredth of NASA escape velocity, but fast enough to move us up. And the sky darkened and darkened around the cockpit, like a late winter afternoon, until it was purple-black and the Earth below us showed a lens-shaped curve. 'Hell,' my father called from somewhere in the back of the plane. 'There's a new leak. I can hear it hissing. I can't hope to find it with all this junk back here – we'll need to open a new canister until we've emptied the hold.'

He was speaking English, for the benefit of our passenger, and so did I, turning towards her and reassuring her: 'It's OK, we always discover new leaks when we come up. It happens every time. It's nothing to worry about.'

'I wasn't worried,' said Kooistra, smiling broadly.

Father was trying his best to locate the leak by pulling items out from the wedged mass of objects, cursing and having no luck, so I was the one that lifted us to our house's orbit, picking out the radio beacon and accelerating towards it. I had done this on several previous up-flights, but it was always an exciting thing. The sky is black and unimaginably vast, and the Earth turns its face as if spurning you, which means you are free. Then you see the bright star in the distance, and you give the plane another double burn and the star grows brighter and brighter and thickens in brightness until you can make out its shape. The trick with docking is not to try and do it all in one go. Fly up until the house is big enough to fill the cockpit windscreen, then stop applying the bursts. Without thrust you won't accelerate, and because both you and your destination are hurtling in the same direction, you won't get any closer without acceleration. Then it's just a question of orienting yourself at the right end, and nudging forward until the nose slides in and you can release the clamps. Father had fitted a manual release, and it was hard work tugging the lever that brought out the spikes. I wanted a hydraulic release, which would have been easier on my skinny arms. 'So do I. I want lots of things, my princess,' he told me. 'We can't always get what we want.'

We opened the nose, and there was immediately a breeze in the cockpit, air blowing from behind us through the hatch. You always lose a bit of air from a house if you leave it unoccupied, but it's not usually anything serious. Pressure equalises when you redock. So we waited for the breeze to settle. Then we unclipped the seats and stowed them, and Father started hurling great packages from the hold with that illusory super-strength that zero g gives you, those bizarrely straight trajectories that the objects follow when you chuck them, that ant-with-a-leaf disjunction of your small arm and your huge burden. I slipped into the house and took the luggage and tried to stow it, but there was too much stuff for the storage straps that Father had installed so I had to leave various things just floating around. Kooistra squeezed through the nose into the house – she only just made it, I remember, because she was so fat. Father, in the plane, was squirting gas from a coloured aerosol into the air, following the curls and draws it made to the leak. 'Found it!' he yelled. 'Got it. It's one of the bolt holes.' He meant the holes he'd drilled in the fuselage to fix the pencil-rockets. They hadn't taken very well to resealing afterwards. We'd often had trouble with them.

Then what happened? It's a long time ago, now, and my memory's not what it used to be, but I want to get it right because it's so very important. Father fixed the hole in the Waspstar, and we all had some food together. Then Father flew back down to Earth, riding the electromagnetic surf, ducking and squirling down with his metaphorical hands and feet firmly on the branches of the Yggdrasil, never accumulating enough speed to overheat the fabric of the plane. He went down below, leaving me to settle our tenant in.

'Oh, it's spartan,' she said. 'But oh, it's got a marvellous view.' She floated her bulk to the window, where the sun was lining the Earth's nightside horizon with white, as if a great arc-shaped lid were about to be levered off that side of the globe and the light inside was spilling free. 'So these are the uplands?'

'First time up?' I asked, nonchalant in my sixteen years, as I squeezed some water into the base of the plants that were fixed to the wall. She didn't look at me.

'First time. I must say, this lack of gravity is very pleasant indeed. For a woman of my weight. I mean, of course, *mass*.' She laughed with disconcerting vehemence.

'It'll make your hands and feet cold,' I told her. 'Even when it's real warm, you never quite get warm in your feet. But you get used to that. Also you'll feel heady to begin with, the blood will swell in your head until your body sorts itself out. That takes a day or two.'

I showed her how the house worked. 'In about five minutes,' I said, 'the sun'll come up. We can switch off the lights then, it'll be bright enough. I usually wear shades, actually. But when we're in the sun you got to turn the house, which you do by firing the jets a bit, for a second, or less. You do that with little *little* turns of this handle—' showing her '—and it'll tumble.' A little jarringly, it did. 'Catch hold of something. You get used to it, it's only a very slow turn, you get hardly no g out of it, but it stops the wall getting too hot on one side.'

'Does it get hot in here at all?'

'Yeah-huh,' I said, with that inflection of voice that conveys teenage disdain of another's ignorance. 'It'll get hot. You might want to undress, it's up to you. You get used to it after a little while, leastways I always do. It does cool down after you go into shadow again, but not much. Vacuum's the best insulator and we're surrounded by it. More-or-less vacuum.'

I suppose, if I'm honest, that my English was not as good as I'm here reporting it. It was school English, not the decades-familiar day-to-day idiom I use these days. But it was good enough to communicate.

'I'm surprised,' she said, in an absent voice, 'you don't fit a cooling system.'

'Sure we'll do that,' I said. 'When we get round to it. When we got the money. It don't really matter, *I* think. The heat don't bother *me*.'

She didn't reply, because she was watching the art-deco splendour of a sunrise from space, the smile-shape of light widening and then the spearbright sun – not yellow up here, but blue-white – pulling itself

17

clear from the Earth's body, and all the stars dimming, as if in homage. I fumbled for my shades.

I showed her how to vent waste, by putting it in the airlock, pumping as much air out as the puny little pump we owned could manage, and then hauling the lever to open the outer hatch. When I did this, the house trembled and shook, bucked a couple of times, shuffling free several items of luggage inside. 'It's best not to do that too much,' I said, 'or you can mess up our orbit.'

'I see,' she said.

Later I plugged in the microwave and we ate some hot food together, and drank some water. She spilled a fair bit, but all the crumbs made their gradual way to the corners as the house slowly turned. 'I had no *idea*,' she confided in me. 'I mean, I heard of the uplands of course, on news shows and such. But it's *quite* another thing to actually come up here. I really had no idea how – liberating a feeling it is.'

'I like it,' I told her, ingenuous. 'Yeah, it's free. It's a free land. Give me liberty or give me death.'

'No police,' she said, musingly.

'None of that. No government, no taxes.'

'Except that you have to return to the Earth from time to time. For supplies.'

'We do,' I said. 'But a friend of ours called Olsen, Åsa Olsen he's called, he lives up here all the time, don't ever go down. His house is on a similar orbit to ours, and he just pays people to bring his food up. Pharmaceuticals, I think. I mean, that's how he made his money. HIV medicines, Dad says. But he always was a space nut, so he lives in a big house in the uplands and people make money bringing him food and things. He's got enough money to just live up here all the time, you see.'

'Really,' said Kooistra, excessively interested. 'Have you seen his house?'

'Last month Dad and I brought him up some water, some scrubbers for his air, some hams. His house is five times our size – it's got different rooms, and everything. Heating and cooling. A gym. *Very* nice. He gave us tea. He said he was getting another room flown up in the autumn.'

'He must be wealthy.'

'Oh – loaded, yeah.'

'Doesn't he get lonely?'

I shrugged. 'He's in touch with everybody by radio and webline and such. He gets visitors from time to time. He likes his own companionship, Dad says, or he wouldn't have moved here in the first place.'

We finished our meal. After a long pause, Kooistra asked me, with a sly tone, 'Aren't you curious why I'm here?'

'Dad told me,' I said carefully, 'not to pry. You're a customer, you see. In Europe they say *the customer is always right.*'

'In America,' Kooistra said, 'we say *the customer might have a gun.* It amounts to the same thing. Well, you can guess that I'm in trouble with some governments.'

I shrugged again. Shrugging in zero g is a different experience from shrugging on the ground. It shuffles the whole body. If your shrug is lopsided (not something you usually think about on Earth, but space is different) it'll even rotate you a little.

'There's no need,' she said, smiling and showing her enormous twin rows of perfect teeth, 'for us to be coy with one another. I'm your guest. We can be friends. I'll be frank with you: I'm what the European government calls *a political undesirable,* and the American government calls *a defined person within the counterterrorism act.* I'd more or less run out of countries on Earth in which I could safely have stayed. But up here, they can't get at me. Up here I'm untouchable. Aren't I!'

I stared at her. I'd seen enough action films to have preconceptions about what terrorists looked like, and they didn't look like her. They looked like slim men with sideburns and expensive plastic suits of black or purple. They were bald or had dyn-stripes. They wore shades and moved with drug-enhanced rapidity. They said things like *the best place to crack the ribs of the state and get at its heart – is from within, hah! hah! hah!* They certainly didn't look like a one-eighty-kilo white woman with a massy tangleknot of blonde hair on her head and creases all over her body as if she had originally been an even larger balloon woman who had been partially deflated. She didn't look the part at all. But I kept my cool.

'Oh,' I said.

'It's alright,' she said, turning from me again to watch as the Earth – majestically rotating in our window now, as if we were looking into a cosmos-sized clothes drier and the globe were being slowly tossed – came between us and the sun. 'I'll be no inconvenience to you. I'll stay a few months, until the police who are looking for me are properly confused, and then I'll go down again. No more than a few months. Three months at the most. But I'll tell you this, my dear. I'm *seriously* thinking of buying a house up here myself.' The sun went behind the Earth, and it darkened abruptly inside the house. I lit up a bulb. 'How beautiful it is,' she said, still facing the window. 'I could watch it for days!'

Perhaps I should have taken her more seriously when she said she wanted to move to the uplands. You're thinking that, now, as you read this, because you can view the scene with the benefit of hindsight. But I naturally didn't see it that way. I was tired after a long day, so I said to her: 'There's a thing about sleeping.'

'A thing?'

'Yeah – when you go to sleep you need to make sure your own breathing-out-gas (I knew this was CO_2 but in my teenage arrogance I wasn't sure *she* would know) doesn't pool around your head. Here, you need to wear one of these sleeping tubes, like this – you wrap the elastic bladder around your chest and fix the tube's end on your cheek with its sticker, then when you breathe in the bellows action will puff spurts of air over your mouth. It's enough to stop the build-up.'

'Why, thank you, my dear.'

'Everyone wears them up here,' I explained. 'When they sleep.' I unrolled a sleep-bag; it was warm in our house and the sleep-bags were made of silk. I fixed it to the Velcro patches on the wall, put my elasticised eye-muff on (the sunlight would wake me otherwise), climbed in and went to sleep. I woke a few hours later, because our spin had slowed down, the loose baggage knocking against the walls probably, and we were getting too hot; so I sponged myself with cool water and took a long drink and gave us a little more spin and tried to get back to sleep. Kooistra was snoring in her sack, her arms and her breasts – (she was naked) – hanging over the lip of the material and floating in front of her, so she looked like a stationary sleepwalker. Or like Frankenstein's monster. But, when I say so, maybe my own hindsight is colouring my impression of her.

In the morning I upped the air pressure inside from a cylinder and checked the scrubber. I didn't really need to do this, after only one night, but I wanted to show Kooistra how it was done. The new air cooled us a little. The two of us had breakfast and made more smalltalk. Soon Father came on the radio, letting us know that he'd cleared the auroral zone and would soon be with us. I pumped the lock and opened the outer hatch so he could fit the nose in. Then we waited for his arrival.

About an hour after this, the whole house shook as violently as if we were experiencing an earthquake (*space*quake, I should say). Both Kooistra and I were flung lengthways and smacked into the bales of supplies that were stacked loosely at that end. There was the loudest noise, as if the whole house were breaking in two and we were being spilled into space. This was the Waspstar hitting the docking hole. There were more cracks and bangs, and soon enough there was a little breeze, a taste and smell of different air, and after a few moments father came floating through.

I don't want to dwell on the recollection of this time, because it still hurts, so I'll hurry along a little. We stayed, all three of us, in the house for another day. Then father flew me back home, to Canada. There was little point in me staying in the house up there, consuming supplies, breathing out carbon dioxide, getting in the way. Besides I was taking a university course (distance learning) in web topography and geography, and some term papers were due. I'd pestered my father to help me gain a little more education, seeing as how my schooling had been so heavily interrupted up to that moment. This particular college course had been my idea. I mention this, I suppose, to explain why I stayed downside, when my father flew back to the upland with more supplies and some trading cargo he hoped to sell to some of his neighbours and make money. He could have stayed on the ground with me, I suppose: there was no pressing need for him to go back up to the house. Kooistra was settled in alright. But he loved flying up and down; loved doing little trades with upland neighbours. He felt good doing it. He felt free. So he went.

I spoke to him that night; a brief and crackly five minutes conversation on the radio phone, curtailed by him passing over the horizon. We didn't say anything very much. I didn't say 'I love you, Dad'. I was sixteen, and that wasn't the kind of thing you say when you're that age. Anyway, I was going to see him in only a few days.

For several years afterwards I used to have a recurring dream about that conversation. Presumably my subconscious was trying to rerun my life, to make things better. To make it work out all right. I had the conversation again and said different things. But the odd thing is what I *didn't* say, in this dream – I didn't say 'I love you, Dad', or 'Quick, get in the Waspstar and fly home!' or anything like that. Instead I said 'I've got to play the violin in front of the whole school later, Dad.' And he said, 'You can't light a candle up here, but you can play the violin all you like. Light doesn't propagate the way sound propagates'.

A strange dream.

The next day I tagged my term papers and emailed them to the tutor. It was about internet geography – tree-locations, and web-leaves – old-fashioned terms, now, to today's youth, I have no doubt: but that was where the subject was in 2060. Then I radioed the house, because I knew it would be in the sky over Canada. The radiophone buzzed and buzzed, and that was odd – strange that he didn't pick up the phone straight away. There was no way out of the house, except by the Waspstar. You couldn't pop out into the garden; you couldn't go to the east wing and not hear the phone. It was right there, beside you, all the time. I wondered if Dad had flown away from the house for some reason, and if Kooistra, feeling herself a stranger and a guest, was reticent about answering the call. After a little while the receiver was picked up and I heard a woman's voice say 'yes?'

'Hi, Kristin,' I said. 'It's Klara.'

Without pause she replied: 'How lovely to hear your voice again, Klara. I wanted to say how much I enjoyed our little time together. It was like a slumber party. The two Ks, yes?' Her voice was perfectly warm, perfectly natural-sounding.

'Yeah,' I said. 'Great. Could I speak to my dad?'

'Oh, I'm afraid he can't come to the phone.'

'What you say?'

'There's been an accident, I'm afraid.'

I coughed with surprise. 'What? Is he hurt?'

'Oh, yes, I'm afraid so. In fact, it's worse than that.'

'Are you joking? Are you making a joke? This isn't a very funny joke.'

'It's no joke, I'm afraid,' she said in her fruity, thrumming voice. 'I'm terribly sorry, of course. You know, I'm not sure I can pilot the plane without him. Is it a plane? Is that what uplanders would call it? Or is it a spaceship?'

'What? What? Tell me what happened. What's happened? Put my dad on. I want to speak to my dad.'

'Oh, he can't speak, I'm afraid. He's dead. It's a shame. But accidents will sometimes happen, even in the best regulated homes.'

'Let me speak to him!' I was crying, suddenly, with the shock and the fear of it.

'My dear,' she said, her voice never varying its balanced, melodious tone. 'I'm not sure you've been listening to me. He's dead, as I explained.'

'Did you hurt him?' I said. 'Put him on the *phone*, you fuck.' My voice was high-pitched and unsteady. 'What did you *do* to him?' I was almost shrieking. You can imagine what I was like.

'It's unfortunate, I know,' she said. 'But everybody dies, you know, eventually. Oh, did you think he'd live forever because he was your father? Is there a manual or something?'

'What?'

'A manual – for the plane, you see. I *have* flown a plane before of course, but never,' and she laughed a little self-deprecating laugh, 'in space you know.'

I put the phone down. My head was burning. I couldn't believe it. I walked round and round in a tight circle. I couldn't believe it. I phoned again, thinking 'This time Dad will answer the phone', but once again I got Kooistra. 'Hello again, my dear,' she said warmly.

I howled.

I didn't know what to do. I called some friends, an elderly couple called Eric and Deborah de Maré who lived half an hour away. Eric had been an upland-traveller, flying up a few times, although he never built a house there; but then he'd had a cancer in his sinus and the treatment had left his head too sensitive to pressurisation and depressurisation to allow flight. I called their house in tears, and they drove straight over and comforted me. At first they didn't believe it. They called the police for me, and a squad car came over, and a policeman took a statement, two policewomen tried to comfort me. They gave me sedatives and I slept eighteen hours. When I woke a different set of policepeople were in the house. They wore the dark blue uniforms of UP. 'Tell us everything,' they said. 'From the start.'

I repeated everything.

They seemed surprised that Kooistra had given us her real name. 'That was bold of her,' they said. 'Usually she uses a false name. Didn't you recognise her name?'

I told them that neither of us had recognised her name.

'I guess you don't follow the news too close,' one of them said.

One of the UP officers said to me: 'You shouldn't worry that he suffered.' By *he* he meant my dad. 'She usually kills quickly, cleanly. She doesn't make her victims linger.' I think he believed it would make me feel better to hear this.

It didn't make me feel better.

Later, maybe a month or so later, another UP officer during another interview told me how lucky I was, to have spent a whole night in a small room with Kooistra and to have lived to tell the tale. 'I wonder why she didn't kill you?' this one mused, aloud. 'Maybe it was because your father hadn't brought up the shuttle, so she was worried she would have been stranded. But he would surely have come up anyway, even without hearing your voice on the radio?'

They asked me how she had come to contact us. I told them, again, that the billionaire Spontini had given her our name. She'd called us, she'd told us that Spontini had recommended us, that she needed a little help, somewhere to lie low for a while. 'Spontini,' they said, knowingly.

'He doesn't come down from orbit any longer. He's got plenty of contacts in the world of crime and terrorism.' I thought of saying *he's our friend*, because he was. But, after several weeks of close contact with them my sense of hostility to the police was a continually growing thing, and I was behaving in an increasingly uncooperative manner. At one point I threw a tantrum. It wasn't exactly play-acting, because I genuinely was upset: but it was partly a set-piece because I was bored and wanted to rattle them and wanted an excuse to get out. I screamed, 'My dad's dead, and you don't care a bit, I hate you all, I hate you all,' and I ran out of the house.

The irony was this: Dad loved the uplands because they were free from the police interference and harassment that had plagued his earlier life. He believed in individual liberty, he disbelieved in organised government. I believed the same things; but there were fewer and fewer places on our overregulated planet where it was possible to live as a free human being. He was drawn to the possibilities of the uplands for that reason. But, now that he had been killed, the police disclaimed all capability to help. They couldn't apprehend the killer unless she came down again, and more or less presented herself to the authorities. 'Our squad cars don't fly that high,' they told me, as if it were a joking matter. They were worse than useless.

four

Let me tell you a little about my father, Miklós Gyeroffy. He was born in Hungary-EU. But he had come to Cyprus as a young man when he was travelling around the world in his restless way. There he had fallen in love with a Cypriot woman, and had married her in the teeth of her family's disapproval. I was born six months after that wedding, in May 2043. In '46 Dad wanted to move to Scotland, but my mother's family would not permit her, or me, to accompany him. He flew planes he'd built with whatever money he could accumulate, but there was never enough money, and my mother's family hoped, I think, that he would crash and die, and then Mother could fast-forward through a decent period of black-clad mourning and marry a nice Cypriot man. But he did not die, and when he was offered a job as a satellite consultant in Aberdeen, my mother did not go with him. So he gave up that job, and stayed in Cyprus, poor. Late in 2046 my mother died of what my family call 'an infection', but which may have been a hangover from terrorist bio-weaponry of the '20s, one of those phage-plague things. It was sad that she died, but, of course, I was only three and not much affected. I do not remember my mother. I do, however, remember my father arguing with my Cypriot relatives, a few years later. I remember a court case when I was seven (or thereabouts; I think I was seven), a case about custody, in which a Cypriot court awarded me to my maternal grand-mother, and her multitudinous relatives and allies. So I had to go and live with them. Instead of calling me Klara, which had been my name all my life, they called me Kassandra. My grandmother wanted to call me Eleni, after herself, but I was registered in school as K. Gyeroffy. My violin (I used to play the violin in the school orchestra) had 'K. Gyeroffy' written into the varnish with a heat pen. I had labels holo'd into my clothes that said 'K. Gyeroffy'. So, rather than go to the bother of changing all that sort of thing they kept my initial. But they changed my name. Grown-ups understand the importance of names.

My dad went to Finland to work and I did not see him for four years, although he emailed me frequently. After that, from time to time, as I grew up, he would come visit, and my grandmother would tolerate him: but he would stay in a hotel, never in the guest room; and he would take me out for a meal to a place with plastic seats and plastic tables. He was never invited to join the family at their evening meal at home. As I got older and had all the fantasies that children have, my father became a talismanic figure to me. I did not resent the fact that he was away so much, but I loved the weekends when he came to stay. It's funny how perfect he was in my secret imagination – I say *funny* because my Cypriot family did their best to poison me against him, telling me how terribly he had acted towards my mother, how you could never trust a foreigner and such stories. It puzzles me, in fact, that they failed to persuade me. They were persistent and eloquent, and sometimes I found myself half-believing what they said. But some inner part of me held back; and that inner space opened fractally before my closed eyes, and there was my father swooping and flying on wings of chrome through the blue-painted immensities.

My father came back to Cyprus for my eleventh birthday, and the day after the birthday he took me out for a drive in a hire-car. He drove me right across the island, from Greek-EU into Turk-EU. In the car he said 'Klara, you are my daughter and I love you. You are my whole life. Will you come with me?'

Understand this: I had not been unhappy with my Grandmother Eleni. Life had been *ordinary*, and ordinariness is what a ten-year-old most craves, even if she does not realise it. But I was tugged by the gravitational pull of my father's love. He moved in his orbit about Europe, finding work where he could, and he drew me after him, I moved in an orbit about him. He was the most important being in the world to me. I said, 'Of course, Dad.'

We flew from Cyprus to Ankara, and then to Roma, where we lived some months; then to Bristol in England-EU for a year, then to Lille in France-EU for six months. Then we left the Union and moved to Reykjavik, where we lived two years or so. We only left in '57 because Iceland signed a new accord with the EU granting more extensive co-legal access, and that brought Father under the same legal jurisdiction as the Cypriot judge who had awarded me to my Greek family. So we moved on again, in '57, to the Canadian Republic.

I loved Canada. There was a large community of uplanders living there – twenty, or more – flying from the northern counties, from airstrips at high latitudes, up through the magnetosphere and into a North-Pole-inset orbit. The only ground-based orbital community of comparable size lived in Tierra del Fuego and flew from a privately maintained base on the Antarctic coast. What you must understand is that these people were all amateurs: men of moderate or comfortable means who had grown up watching SF screenshows and reading SF stories, men who were in love with the idea of flying in space. A particular friend of ours, an American called Jon Snider who was living in Canada at that time, pursuing his space flight hobby, told me: 'I applied to join NASA, you know. I wanted to be an astronaut ever since I was a kid. Couple of decades ago I thought, "I'll be like John Glenn, I'll be like Piper Harrows, I'll join the government agency". They strung me along, strung me along, until eventually they owned up. "Hey it's really really unlikely you'll get any flight time." Hah! They barely send up *any* people these days. They're too busy trying to make a profit selling launch opportunities and fine-tuning comsats. You know for how much money the EU government sold the latest mobile netlink rights? Bandwiths were going for a billion euros, minimum. Thirty billion euros for the whole bag! That much! I'll tell you,' (he was getting quite heated now, his bald head blushing damson from cheeks to crown), 'I'll tell you, they'll make that money back from consumers in two years. That's just from EU consumers, never mind the rest of the world – spending so much on mobile netlink that companies can clear *more* than thirty billion in profit, in profit alone, over *two years*. Think of the gross! So *you* tell *me* – is that the best way of spending humanity's money, webbing friends, playing games on the bus? A *fraction* of a *single per cent* of that money, we could have bases on Mars in five years. Destiny – possibility – glorious – but, no, we'll keep frittering our money on games, on cosmetics, on flim-flam, and we'll turn round in five hundred years and still be right here where we are now.'

As you can see, Jon was very much like my father. Most of the original generation of uplanders, including my father, and including Jon, shared certain traits: they revelled in their technical competence and curiosity, independence – sometimes to an antisocial degree – and in a kind of restlessness, a refusal to simply take what fate had given them. Gather together three or four uplanders in a room drinking whisky, and the conversation would be about sixty per cent technical discussion of the practical problems of space flight (swapping stories and ideas, passing on corner-cuts and good practice, cackling over the incompetence of some third party), and forty per cent rants about the stupidity of the world, similar to the speech I have just put into Jon's mouth.

I don't want to give the impression that my father and these others had a grand plan for the colonisation of the solar system. They didn't. Not at all. They were really only interested in getting themselves into space; theirs was a fundamentally selfish dream. But their DIY culture was in part created by a sense of the futility of state-sponsored space flight. 'DIY' was a one-syllable word in their patois, 'die-y'. You may remember this: in 2055 EUSA put together a solar probe, with complex and weighty magnetic shielding to enable it to penetrate a fair distance into the Sun's penumbra. They paid a South African company to launch it, on a rocket (of course), and fired it towards the Sun. It stopped transmitting data two days into the mission. It was barely out of Earth orbit. Nobody knew what had gone wrong; some malfunction, screw-up, random accident, impossible to be sure. But the whole enterprise was a dead loss. The EU news media roasted their own agency for this: money thrown into a black hole, they said. The cost of the mission was 45 million euros, and it was indeed wholly wasted. But, worse than that, EUSA suffered permanent harm: their funding was cut, their mission schedule reduced, their chief executive sacked. The same year *Cosmos II: The Void* was produced, starring Jenny Open and Pablo Stilmandole. It cost 90 million euros, an average budget for an A-league movie in those days. It earned back five million. It wasn't even the biggest flop of the season. The studio shrugged their shoulders, and went on to commit a budget twice the size for *Swimming in the Mainstream* the following year, which also flopped. As my father said at the time: 'it's like a punch in the face, the stupidity, the aggressive stupidity of it all.' *Think* what the space programme could do with a fraction of the money spent on media entertainment – on teenage cosmetics, narcotics and communication – on clothes that are designed to melt off the body after one wearing – on specialist food. Billions and billions wasted every year on these pointless nothings. A fraction of this money would give humanity a genuine future.

I hear myself. It's arresting: I sound exactly like my dad.

When my father died I was sixteen years of age, two years beneath legal majority for EU and therefore two years shy of Canadian legal jurisdiction. I applied to stay with Eric and Deborah de Maré, who were kind enough to agree to take me on – solidarity between uplanders, I suppose. They were good people. In fact, I did live with them for nearly two months, until a Canadian court ruled (Eric and Deborah and I were present virtually) that I must return to my mother's family in Cyprus, and so I had no choice, I went back. I hated it. I was placed back in a Cypriot school, two years below my ability level because I had not been following the official syllabus. I had to share a room with the Somali maid my grandmother had hired to help her around the house, although there was a spare room in the house ('we must keep that for guests', grandmother said). I had no friends, and the family were chilly with me because I had, in their eyes, deserted them to follow my father. There was no sympathy expressed by my Cypriot relatives for his death. As far as they were concerned it was, as they say in England, a 'good riddance'. I was miserable. I stayed nine months, and took to cutting my arms with a sharp knife. I can no longer remember why I did this, except that it proceeded from a deep and nebulously suicidal sense of misery and self-hatred. I used to curl up under the duvet and score red lines into the skin of my forearms, not minding the pain, in fact darkly welcoming the hurt of it. Then I would wrap my wounded arm in loop after loop of tissue paper and try to go to sleep. Sometimes when I woke the mattress would be sticky and wet beneath me with my own blood. I failed the year's school classes and was re-entered the same year. I had visions of repeating the same miserable cycle in my life forever, of being stuck and trammelled. I was possessed by the hopelessness of it. I wept for my father every day. Sometimes I would lie in my bed weeping and, simultaneously, I would think how astonishing it was that a person could be so profoundly unhappy and not simply expire of the sensation. It was unhappiness as acute as the pain of a newly broken bone, as consuming as influenza, a grey and utterly devouring affliction.

My grandmother soon became alarmed at the scars on my arms, and took me to an expensive clinic where they fitted drug-release sacs into my scalp. This eased the acuteness of the mental distress, but did nothing to relieve the blankly oppressive underlying pressure. I moped. 'Cheer up!' my grandmother exhorted me. 'It won't come easily, but you must work at it – you must make the strenuous effort to be cheerful. You think happiness comes to people like the leaves to the trees? It doesn't – it's work, not nature. You say *I'm unhappy*, and what I hear is: *I'm too lazy to cheer up*. Don't do it for your own sake, but for other people.' But I did not cheer up. Perhaps it was indeed a sort of emotional idleness, as she said; sinking into the quicksand rather than trying to pull myself out, but there was no fight left in me, no fight of that sort at any rate. I shaved my head, which was the fashion in those times, and fitted plastic carbuncles into the skin to mimic plague symptoms. Many teenagers across Europe were doing this sort of thing, listening to atonal thrash music, wearing clothes made of black strips that sagged to reveal more than they concealed. I didn't like the music, but then *liking* wasn't really the point. I hung out in bars downtown with scary teenagers. My grandmother despaired. 'I despair,' she said. On a few occasions she hit me, slapping me on the face or across the back of my legs, but this had no incentivising effect upon me. It was only a small pain, and a larger humiliation, and I believed at that time that pain and humiliation were my proper due. I pulled the drugsacs from my head, breaking the skin of my scalp to get at them. I took to smoking a tobacco pipe, as was the fashion for women at that time, and sometimes I would dip my fingers' ends into the glowing bowl of the pipe and burn the skin. My fingers' ends acquired thimbles of scar tissue.

Grandmama, yielding to advice from other branches of the family, paid for me to attend a psychotherapist. This was a last resort for her. She didn't believe in the practice, because (as she put it) psychiatry had been so thoroughly exploded as a medical science, exposed as mumbo-jumbo. But what else could she do? There were still small groups of believers, cadres of Freud-enthusiasts (or is it spelled 'Frued'?), and there was a practitioner in our town. So I sat through a dozen sessions with a stocky, craw-bearded man in a blue hoop-suit who dipped his head, as if in respect, every time I spoke. Some of his questions were fatuous: 'why do you cut your arms with a razor? Why do you burn your fingers?' Others were more thought-provoking. He had a theory, something I came to understand over several sessions, that I had suffered a psychic trauma because, in effect, my 'mother' had killed my father. Of course, Kooistra was nothing at all like my mother: home video showed a small, precise, dark-faced, black-haired woman with a clear laugh like a door-chime. Kooistra, in contrast, was an enormous tent of a woman with snow-pale skin and yellow hair like a tangle of cloth offcuts. But this did not deter the psychotherapist. He said: 'Of course, you must have recognised her name when she first introduced herself to you – she used her own name, after all.' I said: 'But we didn't recognise the name.' He refused to believe this. His theory was that I must have recognised the name of one of the world's most famous serial killers, but that I had repressed this information in my subconscious, and that this was now making me feel responsible for my father's death. I don't think it had, until this moment, occurred to me that I ought to feel responsible for his death, but once the psychotherapist had put the idea in my head, of course I started to believe it. 'It's natural,' he murmured, 'for a daughter to feel both love and murderous hostility towards her father. You resented him for taking you away from your Cypriot family, and dragging you all over Europe, for disrupting your life, for flying you up into space when all you wanted was to keep your feet on the ground.' This, I now believe, was almost exactly the opposite of the truth, but then, seventeen years old, crying, picking at my skin with dirty nails, slouched in the therapist's chair, I half-believed it.

He said: 'Once you acknowledge your sense of responsibility, your aggression towards your father, your sense of complicity with the woman, Kooistra, then you will start to feel better.' I made this acknowledgment, or I tried to. Genuinely I did. But I didn't feel better. I was aware of no sense of complicity with Kooistra. I fantasised about spiking her onto the metal spire that was on top of the school tower, impaling her, of running her through the heart until she spat out her own blood from her mouth like vomit. I didn't tell the psychiatrist this violent fantasy. I assumed he would misinterpret it.

One day my psychiatrist made this little speech: 'The essence of good mental health,' he said, 'is to be found in a *grounded* existence. Too many people seek constantly to escape their unhappiness by running away, by flying away, but no matter how rapidly you fly you will not escape your unhappiness, because it is carried inside you, inside your head. Instead of the pathological urge for escape, instead of the restless compulsion to travel, you must *root* yourself in one spot. You must confront your demons, purge your subconscious conflicts, and centre yourself.' So many theories of happiness! As I look back, after a long life, this theory seems to me to possess less merit than my grandmother's theory. But I thought about it a great deal at that time.

I thought about it. I lay in my bed that night, with the maid snoring in the other bed, and I thought about it. I thought about flight, and about stasis. I thought about escape, and acceptance. I shut my eyes and imagined the video image of one of those great rockets from the 1970s, hurling out millions of kilos of thrust from its tail and rising into space. You know the image? It's kind of a famous one. It seemed to me, as I thought of it, that it was not so much that this building-sized rocket was rising, but rather that it was the still point of the world of flux, that the cosmos was moving around it. As if the power of the rocket was forcing the universe out of shape around it. Then I thought of Waspstar, floating up like a leaf in an electronic hurricane, and it seemed to me a more natural mode of travel altogether. A more natural mode of travel.

I got out of my bed then and there. I dressed without waking the maid, stole some money from my grandmother's chip, and left the house carrying a loaf of bread and some cheese. I walked five miles to the station, hired a cab to take me to the airport, and flew to Italy-EU. From there I used the de Marés' family name, address and co-don card (I'd memorised the number when I'd lived with them) to borrow money for a flight to Canada. I justified this to myself by telling them that I'd pay them back when I got to Canada. I'd get a job or something and pay them back. I lied to the airport staff, telling them I was nineteen. I was going to say 'eighteen', but then I thought to myself that a bigger lie is a more believable lie, provided only that you don't go too far.

The de Marés were kind, and, frankly (it seems to me now) they deserved better than the angry, graceless teenager who descended upon them. They explained, patiently, several times, that they couldn't take me in: that the police would simply return me to Cyprus. There was nothing they could do. I cried, howled, shouted at them, called them appalling things, but they were quietly adamant. So I calmed myself, and went to see Jon Snider. He lived sixty klims away, and to get to him I took the de Marés' energCar, without asking their permission, and without ever returning it. So selfish! I look back on my seventeen-year-old self and I think: she is another person to me, a stranger. Am I really connected to her? A mere chance of timelines. But there was an animal drive for self-preservation, a strength of will, in me then.

The energCar only ran on state highways, and Snider – like most of the uplanders – lived away by himself in the wilderness, with his own runway and his own adapted farmhouse. I left the Car sitting in a two-hour-maximum siding and hiked across country. When I reached his house, I must have been a sight: mud and dead leaves glued to my shoes and calves, wearing one of Eric de Maré's too-large overcoats, my head covered only with a layer of black fuzz where the baldness had grown out a little, the petite constellation of scars from my old treatment still visible through the suede of it.

'Hello,' said Jon, as he opened the door. 'It is Miklós Gyeroffy's girl, as I live and breathe.'

He took me in, suggested I had a shower. After I had cleaned up he found me some fresh clothes, gave me some food. After I'd finished eating, with him sitting opposite me watching, I told him my whole story, and he sat silently throughout it. In fact he said very little; he only sat and looked at me with a quiet intensity. I was not so jeune that I didn't know what it meant, and not so innocent that I didn't think I couldn't exploit it. But I didn't think I could simply come out with it and ask, so I said. 'The psychiatrist – my grandmamma sent me to him – said that happiness was finding your roots in the ground, and not running away from your fears and anxieties. My grandmamma, though, she said that happiness is in making the effort to be happy, for the sake of other people. What do you think it is?'

He sat for a long while, thinking about this: a fifty-five-year-old man taking this teenage girl's question as seriously as if he were testifying before the House Committee on Terrorist Activities. His head, empty of hair except for two pale beige eyebrows and two rows of filigree eyelashes, was crossed and marked all over by a higgle of creases. These didn't follow the normal pattern of old people: laughter lines bedded in where the person had been wont to laugh, worry lines huddled in at the brow where the person had been wont to wrinkle their brow, that sort of thing. Jon's lines went seemingly in defiance of the process of ageing: two deep ones running diagonally across both cheeks like duelling scars, making a great V across his face; lines horizontally and vertically on his brow and head, lines on the back of his neck. He looked, I used to think, like Callisto, his skin like the cracked and refrozen ice-skin of that Jovian moon.

'Happiness,' he said eventually, with his soft Missouri accent. 'Only one place I've found that, and it ain't on this planet.'

'Take me upland,' I urged him, grabbing his forearm with my two hands. 'Eric and Deborah say the police will take me back to Cyprus, and I can't go back there.'

He thought about this. 'You could live in my house for a little,' he said, slowly. 'Sure. Would you mind it? It's only a bachelor pad, but it's bigger than your dad's place.'

'Oh yes, oh please, oh please, yes.'

He nodded, and stood up. 'We'll go up tomorrow morning,' he said. 'I'm too tired to pilot tonight.'

'We can go straight away. I'll fly,' I told him, in my eagerness.

He considered this. 'You only flown your dad's old Elector, I reckon,' he said. He meant I had never flown a modified Flight Master, bigger and more powerful, and he couldn't trust me with it. He was right, of course. Then he said, 'I was sorry t'hear about your father.'

'Me too,' I said, uncertain how to respond to formal expressions of condolence.

I didn't think I was going to be able to sleep that night, I was so excited, so keyed up with the thought of returning to the uplands. But I must have been more tired than I realised, because I fell asleep as soon as I saw the bed, not even undressing simply flopping onto the mattress, I woke once that night, sometime after three a.m. There was a strange cooing noise, very distant and eerie, audible through the open window-casement. I thought to myself that it was probably one of the ferals, as they were called; domestic dogs and cats adapted by animal rights activists to grow bigger and act more savage and predatory, and then released into the wildernesses. Have they all been culled now? I don't

33

know. There had been a craze for these things in the mid '50s, but now they had been mostly rounded up by the authorities as a danger to civilians. But a few still lived out there, I think; and their calls were strange and otherworldly, because although their bodies were hormonally enhanced many of their internal organs, including their voiceboxes, were still original size, giving them a falsetto edge to their calls. I fell asleep to the music of it.

five

The following morning I helped Jon load cargo into his plane and then, as he went through the pre-flight checks, he told me the latest news about Kristin Janzen Kooistra. She was occasionally seen by one uplander or another, he said, but mostly she was a mysterious figure. Presumably she had learned to fly Waspstar, and settled herself into our house – *my* house, it was now, as my father's sole heir. But she had changed the transponder, so that the old signal was no longer heard, and had moved the building into a different orbit. Despite the fact that the uplands are all open space it is extremely easy to hide there, hurtling round at thousands of klims an hour, in whatever orbit you choose, from less than a hundred to many hundred klims high. There's a mass of junk up there: old satellites and systems, new devices, other uplanders' houses, debris, waste, chunks of ice, all sorts. In a few hundred thousand years, people say, much of it will settle into an equatorial orbit and Earth will have its own ring system, like Saturn, only smaller and more tenuous and made of crap. As it is, it's all but impossible to scan the sky and be sure of finding what you're looking for – say the few tens of square metres of metal-tape-wrapped house that used to be my home. I had the frequency of our homing beacon, but of course she'd turned that off. In effect, flicking that switch made her invisible.

'She comes down to the ground from time to time,' Jon said, as we strapped ourselves into the cockpit seats.

'How do you know that?'

'You don't follow the news?' he asked, checking his instruments.

'Not much,' I said. I never liked the news; it pretends to be all different, every day, when in fact it is all the same. It's so eager to generate anxiety and fear in its viewers, to get them hooked on it; but it is the definition of ordinary. The definition of everyday. I avoid it as much as I can.

'Well,' he said, 'security video taped her killing three people in Kuala

Lumpur. Hey,' he added, looking shyly at me. 'I'm sorry. I don't want to upset you or anything.'

'It's OK,' I said. 'It don't upset me as much as it did.'

'She killed these three, people don't know why, money the police say. Then she vanished. Then she flew upland again.'

'Kuala Lumpur's a long way from the poles,' I said.

He shrugged. 'You know Bert Felber?'

I knew him: he owned an especially large upland house, four rooms and a multiple docking port so several planes could nose in at once. He sometimes held parties.

'Bert traded with her. Says he was scared, says it didn't really sink in until after she was gone. Somebody called him, asked him if he wanted some water-ice. He said, sure, of course, who wouldn't. She said she'd fly it over, and barter it for some food, a few knick-knacks. On the phone she said her name was Carter. Big fat blonde woman came through the hatch. Bert had his boyfriend over, Tam, you know Tam Entzminger?'

'Oh,' I said, gossipy-fatuous in the midst of this terrible anecdote. 'Are those two dating now?'

'Sure, for months now. Which I only mention because Bert reckons if he'd been alone she'd have killed him. But I reckon, no, it wasn't that. If she'd wanted to kill them both she would have done so. But then who'd trade with her?'

'You mean people'll trade with her now?' I demanded, outraged.

'Well, naturally. I mean, you're right, it's somewhat shocking, but – you know,' said Jon. But what he meant was, *of course they trade with her, trade is what uplanders do.*

We flew up from Jon's Canadian strip and into the huge, forgiving sky. It was a smooth passage up, and as we pulled up into a first orbit the sun came round the curved wall of the Earth, spreading light all over the broad uplands. The light came as a giant and luminous smile that poured through me, that world-spanning U of transcendent shining. I'd forgotten how beautiful sunrise is from space. Cyprus, and needles in my cranium, and cutting my arms with sharp knives, all that fell far beneath me. That life seemed suddenly to belong to somebody else.

Jon's house was nicer than ours had been. Two rooms, and a separate attachment for docking that could act as a man-sized airlock if you wanted, and had the equipment, to space-walk. Jon had even acquired an old NASA EVA-suit, complete with the fishbowl helmet and metal hoops set into the cloth at elbow, shoulder and knee. The Nasty-Suit, I called it. But he said he hardly ever used it: unscrewing a screw took hours in it, he said, because the fingers were fat as cushions, and you could hardly move your limbs; you got overheated quickly because you weren't rotating, it was worse than useless. 'I use a waldo,' he said, 'for most anything now.'

I lived with Jon in that house for more than a year. We slept in the far room, where the gym equipment was. Exercising in those elasticated pulleys and pedals took up a great deal of our time when we weren't working. After exercises, we used to work together in the near room, where Jon taught me many useful things about electromagnetics, about repairing machinery, and about medical competence. For the first six months we made repeated trips down and up, collecting the tradeables of the upland world: water, food, jetsticks, new technology.

There was at that time an upland craze for cladding, and panels of lead or compacted asbestos became very widely traded. Money could be made on those products. People were realising that they were spending longer and longer in the radiation-rich atmosphere of the uplands, and more and more people wanted to clad their homes, or at least have one cladded room into which they could retreat in the event of solar storms. Jon mocked the craze; he said most orbits were still inside the Earth's field, protected, as it were, by the upper branches of the Yggdrasil, and that solar storms were crazy things to worry about. He mocked the craze, but he earned a lot of money supplying it. Of the two determinants of cost in the upland economy, the *dead weight* of the commodity was by far the more important. Its original price, downside, was of less significance than the fact that somebody had had to lug it up the trunk and branches of the Earth's polar magnetic tree and put it into orbit. So sometimes Jon by himself, and sometimes the two of us, would fly down, buy up used lead panelling, load it, fly it up, and then sell it to various uplanders at a smart profit. Some customers even paid us to fit it using our waldo. Imagine that! That was laughable to us, you see, because uplanders were *above all* self-sufficient. Self-sufficiency was the key defining quality of our people. Paying somebody else to do a job you could easily do yourself was a flat insult to that ethos.

And yet, I suppose, for those wealthy enough it was worth shirking the tedious, pernickety chore of manoeuvring the waldo, removing whatever was affixed to the outside of the house, taping panel after panel down, and replacing positional jets or sat-discs. Six months of this and Jon had earned, he told me, more than he had taken in the whole of his life as an uplander before. He mocked these people for buying expensive lead panels, however. 'Lead's not the way,' he told me. 'Water is better – better because, a)' (and he ticked the reasons off on his fingers as he spoke) 'everybody trades it anyway, so it's cheaper; b) it's a better insulator against radiation, and c) it'd encourage people to cover their houses in water, instead of cluttering up their insides with hundreds of stupid little bottles of the stuff.'

He followed his own advice, too: he brought up water and poured it out through a special hose in his plane, parked up against the dark side of his house, in the coign where his two rooms made an L shape.

Jon didn't need to rotate his house, as Father and I had been compelled to do, because his was fitted with an expensive cooling system. That meant that the shady side could store a great mess of water. I pointed out to him that this provided no insulation from solar radiation, and he pooh-poohed. 'I'll put another room that side,' he said, 'make my mansion Π-shaped, and then that far room'll be our bolt-hole in the event of a radiation emergency.' He did this, too; using his money to hire Tam Entzminger's adapted 777 to fly up another empty accommodation cylinder, and positioning it behind the mass of ice. He and I cut a door between the bedroom and the new room, and sealed it, and decorated the space on the far side.

You'll have guessed that Jon and I lived as a couple during this time. It was remarked upon in the close-knit community of uplanders. Of the, maybe, 120 people who lived there now, eighty or more were in continual contact with one another. The other forty were, I suppose, too reclusive, too shy, too grumpy, or – like Kooistra – too wary to join the village. They existed on its outskirts, contacting the others only in emergency, or for occasional trade. But amongst the eighty, Jon and I became a fixed feature of gossip. He was *old enough to be my grandfather*, they said. *The shock of my own father's death had unbalanced me*, they said. I know they said these things because they told Jon so when he was alone with one or more of them – 'You understand,' they told him, 'we're concerned for the kid, she's only a kid after all. We gotta to look out for her – we gotta to look out for one another. Make sure she's not being exploited.' Jon would come home in agonies of remorse and repeat all these comments to me verbatim, begging for reassurance that he wasn't exploiting me. I cradled him and stroked his head and told him it was all alright. I told him – which was the truth – that they didn't know the way our relationship worked, that I was much more the mother to him than he was the father to me. That was the truth.

Was that the truth? Oh, I think so.

To be honest, I didn't think much about it at that time. It was just the way my life had arranged itself. We cohabited easily, because neither of us was an overly emotionally demanding individual. We did not require constant attention or endorsement or validation from the other party, which is, as I later discovered, often the logic of adult relationships. Also, both of us were interested and involved in the practical, the day-to-day problems of maintaining a house in the uplands. That aspect of our relationship was the easiest part. Sex was the most difficult. It was not frequent, and when it happened it was, whilst not unpleasant in the moment, always awkward afterwards. Now I tend to think, looking back, that Jon felt guilty doing it with so young a girl. He desired me, that was plain; but he hated himself for desiring me, and I suppose he half believed the opinions of the others, that he was taking advantage of me. I told him he wasn't. I didn't mind. For me, sex has never been too big a deal. I have a theory and here it is: sex runs according to a generational sine wave. For one generation it is a *terribly important thing*, the most profound connection, something that must be regulated and controlled with countless codes and rules and restrictions because, unconsciously, people believe that unregulated it is so powerful that it would tear society apart. Then for another generation it is simply no big deal, just one of the many things bodies do, more or less pleasurable depending on how skilfully performed, but otherwise not any more significant than the other bodily functions and appetites, eating and shitting, drinking and pissing, scratching yourself, stretching, luxuriating like a cat. And so on. Jon and I straddled that generational gap. He thought, for instance, that I must be a virgin, at seventeen, and was so shocked by my laughter and my blasé account of my previous sexual connections that I had to stop talking about them to avoid upsetting him. He apologised if I so much as winced during the act; he was a cautious, attentive, rather dull lover. Here's another thing: whilst I loved living in the uplands, I never much enjoyed zero-g sex. The positioning can be fun, but good sex needs a degree of purchase, something to push against, something to make you feel the pressure, the force, the weight of the other party. In zero g you tend to bungee around the room, sometimes banging your head or your shin, rarely getting a good run at it. Or else you strap yourself side by side, and then you're much more restricted than you'd be on the ground. Another turn off: after sex Jon would sometimes cry. I don't know why he did that.

Sometimes he'd say, 'I love you, Klara,' and I would never know how to reply. Sometimes I would reply: 'That's great', or 'That means a lot to me'. Sometimes I wouldn't say anything. Then we'd fall back into our more comfortable non-erotic rhythms, cooking, exercising, mending, making, trading. We made four consecutive trips down and up for Åsa Olsen, each time bringing up nothing but water that we collected from the pump on Jon's land. Åsa was accumulating an enormous supply of uplander water, wisely. He paid us well for that.

'I guess,' Jon would say, as if to console himself, 'that sometimes the oddest folk end up together as a couple. I guess that's just the way life is.'

'Sure,' I agreed. 'This is life,' I said. That was the difference between us. His phrase, *that's the way life is,* was, as it were, the statement of somebody standing outside life, observing it with a degree of dispassion and disengagement. My phrase, *this is life,* was spoken from the heart of it. Perhaps all I'm saying is that a man nearing sixty does not live life in the pulse and in the gut the way a teenager does.

An uplander called Billy Season had a structural failure and an explosive decompression in his house, and was dragged suddenly the whole length of the room, catching his leg on his comm equipment as he went and cutting it very deeply. He fixed the hole in a daze caused by lack of blood, working through a sticky red mist that filled the room. He could barely bandage himself. He called a neighbour two days later, but by the time he'd gotten himself transported down to a hospital on the ground his wound was infected, and doctors amputated. I heard this story first from Teruo Nakagomi, and when I told it to Jon he shook his head, and said, 'That's terrible. But you shouldn't have sharp objects fixed to the walls of your house – there are too many jolts and jars up here liable to smack you against them. Oh, that's terrible, Billy lost a leg. But I guess that's the way life is.'

I said, 'Yeah, this is life.' I knew what it was to be pushed by forces too strong to resist such that my body scratched itself along sharp objects – knives, say. I knew what Billy experienced. Jon only observed it from a distance. I'm not saying that he was a cold man, not a distant man, I'm not saying that exactly. But – well, put it this way: he was a *little* further away, as it were, than many men I have known in my life.

Still, we settled into a comfortable period of upland living in which I was, I am tempted to insist, *happy.* I had left my misery behind. I was *up.* I was living where my father's spirit still spun, soaring round and about the globe in forty minutes and trailing photons and invisible radiation. We went about the day-to-day business of living in an upland house. We exercised a great deal in stretch and push devices, to stop our limbs from whittling away like polio victims. We maintained the house. We flew the plane down and brought it back up again, coasting on the broad leaves of the polar World Tree. We stared out of the window at the world turning below us. If you stare long enough at the image of the world you begin to see fractally, and greater and greater depth of detail

40

starts to uncurl in your field of vision. Clouds like crumbs, details of glimpsed land masses like jewellery worked tightly into fretwork and checkerboard fields. Little brooch-like cities, pewter-and-lead coloured, like scabs on the buff. The improbable smoothness of the oceans from which reflected sunlight would smear into brightness.

Six months of happiness. My future was as open as the view from our upland window. Life circled on its orbital rhythms.

During that time I had a number of conversations with Giangiacomo Spontini. When he first heard I had moved up to live with Jon he called, and asked to speak with me. These were the first words I exchanged with him since my father's death. He said: 'Klara, Klara, I'm so sorry, I'm so sorry, I feel responsible.'

'That's OK,' I said, and although the sentiment was nonchalant my throat was tight and there were unshed tears at my eyes.

'I never knew her, I never met her, I'm so sorry,' he said. He spoke English and Greek with me, interchangeably, and with a bad accent in each. 'A business acquaintance recommended her to me, and I passed on your father's details. She used a false name with me, I never knew who she was. Can you forgive me? Can you forgive me?'

'Sure,' I said.

'I have cut my business acquaintance, he should have known better. I'll help you find her – you must have revenge upon her, it is truly terrible, truly terrible.'

'Goodbye, Sponti,' I said, because now I was crying, and I hated to cry.

After this time, Sponti and I had other conversations that were not so fraught. He gave a party one Christmas and had five separate planes, not counting his own, docked at his mansion. We ate fine food and drank wine and schnapps and played poker and sang songs, all of us as close and hot as badgers in a sett, and I cried again, but happier tears this time. 'I'm sorry,' Spontini said, 'with my crazy talk of revenge and all, only it's the way in my tradition, you see. But don't listen to me. Don't listen to me! Only, I loved your father, he was beautiful man, I loved him so.'

'I swear revenge,' I said, my brain thrumming with alcohol and the stimulation of company. 'I will listen to you, Sponti. I'll find her and kill her if it takes me all my life.'

There were twelve in the party, I remember, and all of them cheered and clapped at this. Uplanders love a violent oath, a promise; it appeals to the romantic dimension of their souls. But I knew that nothing would come of this. It's easy to talk of melodramatic quests for vengeance when you're drunk and amongst friends who egg you on, but people can't actually live their lives that way, outside Viking sagas and Shakespeare plays. It's not the way the grain of life runs, to dedicate yourself wholly to such an aim. Nevertheless my oath freed up the conversation. People had been inhibited from talking about Kooistra in my presence for fear of upsetting me; but my fire and determination gave them licence. 'I met her,' said Teruo Nakagomi. 'She's not alone now, I think. She lives in Miklós's old house, in your house I mean Klara – lives there *with* a companion.'

No! people said. Wow! Who?

'I don't know,' said Teruo, rubbing his palms over his close-cropped hair vigorously, as if trying to strike a spark from his scalp. 'I didn't get a good look. A small, shifty little fellow, like a lapdog. A sidekick, you reckon? A lover?'

'She never needed a sidekick down on the ground when she was killing people,' somebody said.

'I guess not,' said Teruo. 'But a lover? She's the size of the Moon. Ugh, ugh, no. I docked with this house, didn't know whose it was except that they'd called mayday, and when I opened my snout she called through "Don't come in, don't come in, we've got flu". But by then my head was most through the hatch, so I could see her, stark naked – not nice, not a nice sight. And behind her this little weedy fellow.'

'What did she want?' Jon asked.

'Medicines,' said Teruo. 'She wanted these new-style pharmakos, or failing that conventional medicines. Said she had a terrible flu, all her body aching and her head giving her hell.'

'Good,' I said.

'Sure,' agreed, Teruo. 'Good.'

'Did you sell her medicine?'

Teruo looked nervous at this, and rubbed his scalp double-hard, such that flakes of skin lifted off and flew slowly through the air. 'Well, I did,' he said, embarrassed. 'I did. I saw who she was, and I got a bit scared, to be honest. So I hurried back, and shouted through that if I gave her some red-cross she had to promise to undo the docking hooks. She promised, so I threw a green box through and she undid the hooks, and I got the hell out of *there*.' What's interesting to me about this, as I recall it, is that Teruo did not lie. He could have said *I didn't give her anything, I pulled the lever from where I was and I left*, but he didn't. It's a feature of uplanders, like the ancient Persian nobility, that they do not lie. I'm not sure why it is that way, but it is. It's not a point of essential principle with us, this telling the truth at all costs. It's just something we do. In this case, it brought Teruo much hostility. 'How could you!' 'You didn't even sell it her, you just gave it away?' and so on. He turned his face away, and people flicked chunks of bread at him.

That night I had bad dreams, unsettled by Teruo's tale of sticking his head inside Kooistra's house – her house that used to be *our* house, used to be *my* house – and seeing her inside with her new companion. I hated the thought of it, but couldn't stop thinking about it.

six

After a year I left Jon, broke up with him and moved in to the house of Teruo Nakagomi. It was not an easy break-up. Jon refused to accept it. He wept. Teruo had been, you might say, *courting* me for several months. Women were still, in those early days of the uplands, a rare commodity, and many of the men I met would look at me in a way I could hardly interpret as anything other than lust. I was neither repelled nor excited by these circumstances, but I was self-aware enough to plan how best to use them. What did they see when they looked at me? I was skinny and tall. I wore a pantshirt and some feet-gloves to give me purchase on the walls as I moved around. My hair had grown back black and lustrous, and I did not cut it, but because long hair is an inconvenience in zero g I wore a headscarf most of the time. There were old sunken scars on my forearms, two rows of paler lines in the skin like tiger markings. Was I desirable? Or was I only desirable because there was so little choice for the heterosexual men of the upland population?

Teruo had made it plain he wanted me. On several occasions when I was still 'with' Jon I would take the plane and fly out and up to Teruo's orbit, and park and go in. Once, when Jon flew downside solitaire, Teruo came over and we had sex then and there, in Jon's house. Isn't that shocking? But I had no more remorse than a bitch on heat. It was exciting, to be honest. We had a number of those secretive little meetings, fox-like couplings, the thrill and shame of it. Finally I decided I should move out, and I did. I decided to end it with Jon and afterwards leave his house.

After a meal I told Jon that it was over between us, and that I wanted to move out. He stared at me for two lengthy minutes in complete silence, and then started crying with strange little yelping cries, like a puppy. 'I couldn't bear that!' he said, as if I had only been rehearsing the possibility of a split, instead of announcing it to him as something that had already happened. 'I love you! I love you! I love you!' He went on

44

and on. Finally, after hours of crying, and clinging to me, he said 'Let's talk about it in the morning.' I said, no, I was going now. Either he could fly me to Teruo's, or I would fly myself and Teruo would bring the plane back in the morning for Jon to drop him off afterwards. These complicated games of permutation were necessitated by the fact that Jon's house had only one port. More and more of the upland houses were fitting multiple docking chambers (they were known as 'porches') but Jon had not gotten around to that.

In the end, after hours of wrangling, and several phone calls, I flew Jon – still weeping and calling out loud denials – to Sponti's house, where Teruo was waiting to collect me. And that was how I left Jon, except that he refused to accept that I was going, and kept phoning Teruo, shouting at him, threatening, cajoling, begging. It was embarrassing. At first I felt guilty for his pain, but his persistence was so forceful and so annoying that soon I could do nothing but despise him for his weakness. It was a shame our relationship ended that way. It had been fun, for a while.

I stayed with Teruo for less than a year. Our relationship was much cooler than had been the case between Jon and myself – on Jon's side, at any rate. Teruo never declared his gushing love for me. He was in his early forties, a shrewd businessman with a childlike side, a man who had *revered* space flight from a young age. There was much about him with which I could not connect. He was, for instance, a news junkie, and I have always hated the news. He had three viewscreens in his house and they were on all day, in the background, churning out three different news channels, two in English one in Japanese. I told him I couldn't understand how he coped with the noise, the interference. I couldn't concentrate on any one of the programmes because the other two jabbered in my ears and distracted me. He claimed to watch all three at once.

He was a fairly handsome man. He kept his body in trim, and had a neat-featured face, although he had a series of nervous mannerisms. Amongst these were: rubbing the palms of his hands vigorously back and forth over his close-cropped hair; pulling his eyelids out from their eyeballs, one after the other, and running the tip of his finger inside the lid; yanking out eyelashes and eating them; pulling on both of his earlobes at once; and squeezing his lower lip between two fingers and rolling the bulge of flesh left and right. He was twitchy. He had set up a commercial company in Japan as a young man, and it had prospered, and he had sold it to a bigger company and with that money he had bought an old commercial JapanAir jet, and had adapted that for magnetosphere flying, and had fled the world. 'I was never comfortable down there, not as a man, not as a child,' he told me. 'Don't think me crazy, but when I was on the ground I got to feeling that my actions were not my actions.'

'How do you mean?'

'I used to think – you'll think me crazy – I used to think that somebody had an effigy of me, like a voodoo doll, and was making me move my head this way or that way, or making me raise my hand. I got in trouble with the police sometimes.'

'Jesus,' I said. 'What did you do?'

'I had some trouble with schoolgirls,' he said, obscurely. Later I learnt that he had manhandled these schoolgirls on the subway trains, pulling at their skirts and pushing himself against them. He had been arrested. His defence in court had been that his actions were not under his conscious control. This was a real psycho-medical condition, or so he insisted, but the vogue for psychiatric explanations of criminal behaviour had passed, and he was sent to a correctional institute. 'I hated being locked away. I couldn't bear it. I paced and paced the cell, and threw myself against the wall, and broke all my fingernails trying to open the unopenable window. I went a little mad. It was horrible, horrible.'

'How long were you inside?'

'Oh,' he said, dropping his head and pulling mournfully on his earlobes. 'Three days, three nights. Never again.'

When he came out he poured all his nervous energy into making money, working all the days of the week and many of the nights, and even in the hyperactive money-making society of Japan he had done well. This was in the late '40s, when Japan was rearming, and Teruo's company supplied a number of essential devices for the air force. When he had what he thought enough money he sold out, fled to the uplands. 'Up here,' he told me, rubbing his pate with his palms, 'I never feel like somebody else is controlling me. I always feel in control of my body. Isn't that strange?'

'I know that nowadays everybody disses psychiatry and such,' I told him. 'But I think there's something in it.'

'Is that the explanation for my behaviour, do you think?' he asked me, with his ingenuous face. 'Was it psychiatric?'

'Sure. What else?'

'I don't know,' he said, turning round and round in the zero-g like a dog settled into its bed. 'Maybe I was just crazy. Sometimes I thought so – sometimes I wondered if there really were – you'll think me crazy – mind control rays, or something. The military have some weird things.'

46

'I find the first explanation,' I said, 'more likely than the second.'

'You're probably right.'

He had excellent powers of concentration, Teruo, and although he was a little unhinged in various eccentric ways, I never felt unsure or uncomfortable with him. The sex was better than it had been with Jon: less hamstrung with guilt and anxiety, much more a straightforward physical thing. Here's one good thing about Teruo in that respect: if he made sexual advances towards me and I wasn't in the mood, and I turned him down, he accepted the rejection blithely and went and did something else. With Jon, and with some other men I have known, such a rejection seemed to crush them, leaving them despondent or angry for days, as if I were denying their essential worth. With Teruo it was no big deal, he just tried again later. That's an attractive feature in a man.

I taught him some Greek phrases, and some French ones. He tried to teach me some Japanese phrases, but they were too hard for my tongue. I told him, 'That! I can't say that! It'll break my jaw coming out!' He laughed at this, and tried to catch me and kiss me, and we pushed and flew around the house laughing.

Teruo was not much of a trader. He made occasional flights down, but he preferred to stay in orbit. Although he exercised with an admirable regularity he had been downside so infrequently that he was starting to worry that his bone mass was reaching an untenable state. 'I don't want to go down and try to walk and break my legs,' he said. 'I don't want to go *down there* at all.' Personally I think his animadversion was more psychological. His associations with the ground were all bad, and so he preferred not to go there. When I was with him he made a few more trips down, and I went with him. He kept a prefab room in a settlement in Asian Siberia, in the northern territories, up near Magadan, a miserable and freezing settlement near the Arctic Circle. But otherwise Teruo had no links with the Earth. Since he didn't really trade, he had little income, and was still living on his savings, which gave him a more frugal attitude than many uplanders. 'Savings don't last forever,' he said.

One day he woke up with an idea. It came to him, he said, in a dream. 'I dreamt of spaghetti trees,' he told me. So then he ordered a huge reel of fibreoptic sheathing, tens of kilometres long, over the ethernet from a Russian company. Then he emptied his jet of all it didn't need, and flew downside, to Asian Siberia. He wouldn't even let me come with him on the flight: even my skinny body might compromise his lift, and prevent him bringing his cargo back up with him. 'I don't want to have to hire Tam's big plane,' he said. 'I can't afford that.'

In the event, he'd underestimated the power of his plane, of magnetohydrodynamics, of the broad branches of the Gradisil tree, and he lifted his cargo easily. It was an enormous wheel of spooled-up microcable, the passage inside the pipe less than a millimetre thick. 'What are you going to do with this?' I asked him.

'Watch,' he said. He was giggling, he was so excited.

Teruo's house was three rooms, not spread out on the same level as most houses but arranged as a stack, like three can-shaped rooms stored one on top of the other two. This is what he did: he drilled a hole in the lower room, sealing the hole with a new brand of sealant, a semi-liquid vulcaniser – a kind of jelly held in a grid, very dense but minimally malleable. Because his cargo, this great wheel of cable, was too large to fit through the nose of his jet, he had to unspool it inside the plane by hand and feed the piping through into the house, round the corner and into the lower room. It took all day, and I quickly got bored with the task, but Teruo persisted, pushing the pipe through the new hole he had made and feeding it down and down. I exercised for two hours, came back and he was still methodically doing this. I went off, ate, slept, read for a while, exercised again, came back and he was still doing it. 'What's this about?' I asked.

He was too excited to hold it back. 'It'll revolutionise life in the uplands,' he told me. 'It'll bring air and water. At the very least, it'll bring fresh air. Pump it in this room, pump it out through a capillary pipe in the airlock, a constant supply of fresh air – no need for canisters, for scrubbers, for any of that. Imagine it! We'll be that step closer to self-sufficiency.'

'Is that pipe going to dangle all the way down into the atmosphere'

'Sure is.'

'How long is it?'

'Fifty kilometres.'

'Jesus. And you're feeding it all out by hand? It'll take a week.'

'Maybe,' he said. 'But what else would I do with that week? Just hang about, eat, sleep, and at the end of it – nothing. But, at the end of *this* week, I'll have my own free air. Free air!' He'd been paying Emmet Robles to run up and down with canisters and scrubbers, and I guess the cost of it had been preying on his mind.

In the end, even Teruo with his unnatural ability to concentrate on a dull task for lengthy periods of time, even he grew bored. He slept, and then he rigged up a little motor and some runners and automated the process, spooling the capillary pipe out and out. It was slow, and the motor was noisy which made life in the house less pleasant, but eventually it was all done. We anchored the pipe firmly inside the room, and fitted a small pump to the end of it. Then we set it running. I complained that, if he intended running it all hours of the day, the pump was too noisy. He insisted that we wouldn't hear it after a while, but he knocked up a housing to go around it and muffled the noise some. Several hours later he shrieked with glee. 'Klara! Klara! Come see, breathe the free air!' And there it was: a tiny stream of new, cold air, coming out of the pump.

'I must name it!' he said, very excited, and so we debated what to call his invention. He wanted 'periscope', but I told him that the Greek meant 'about-seeing', and his device was nothing to do with seeing. I suggested telepsuche, the far-breath, but his Japanese-trained mouth couldn't get around the pronunciation of that. In the end, after several uplanders had adopted the technology, refining it in various ways, it indeed became known – illogically – as the periscope. He was so excited with his invention that he called everybody he knew on the phone. Several people came by, had a look at the thing, and were suitably impressed. Teruo called Jon, and invited him over, but Jon was curt and didn't come.

Another time, at one of Sponti's parties, we ran into Jon. He blushed, and was silent, whilst Teruo – drunk, and excited at his invention – gushed and chattered. People asked him questions. 'Won't it snag?' 'What's to snag on?' Teruo insisted.

'It's fifty klims long,' said Bob Newman. 'It's a hazard to flying, surely.'

'But it's a millimetre across! The hazard is to me, not to a plane – if a plane hits it it'll snap like cotton thread. *I'm* then the one inconvenienced, I'm the one who has to get more capillary pipe. But it's so wonderful, having fresh air. Everything in the house smells clean!'

There was a great shudder, and Sponti's house jolted. 'What's that? What's that?'

It was Jon, leaving the party early without telling anybody. The shudder was him backing out of the porch, rattling the walls with his departure. We pulled ourselves to Sponti's windows, and watched his jet dwindle in the black sky, marking its departure with little cigarette-end dots of light under each wing as he put out controlled bursts.

I suppose I did feel a little bad. I had gotten slightly drunk myself, and perhaps I had been draping myself over Teruo a bit, like a trophy girlfriend. I didn't do it deliberately to upset Jon. I don't think so, anyway. But I was proud of Teruo and his new invention – the house was indeed cleaner-smelling, and it was nice to think that we were breathing fresh air. Keeping the house pressurised had become an automatic thing too: no need to open a canister in the morning, or to wave air from one room to another. We'd fitted a pressure-sensitive capillary pipe at the airlock; when the pressure rose beyond a certain point it opened and vented air. Because the pump was always bringing in fresh air, keeping the house pressurised was a simple matter of arranging the setting on this valve at the level we wanted it. Of course, we kept some canisters of air for emergencies, but we hardly ever needed to use them.

seven

Here's a version of a media editorial I saw at Teruo's. Because he had the news on all the time I fell into the habit of watching it, even though I disliked doing so. It is an addictive thing, news-watching, which was always a reason for not doing it, it seemed to me. It's never a good idea to court addiction, I think. The news at this time was not good, by and large. America and Arabia were squaring up to one of their occasional military fights. This time, though, matters looked worse; America was lining up the newly militarised East Asian states in an anti-Arab alliance. They called it an anti-terrorist alliance, but most of the world saw it as anti-Arab. With the covert aid of the Japanese league – at least, without their opposition – Arab nationals and Muslims were being forced out of Malaysia, Borneo and some other locations. There was a great pother about this in international forums. Ethnic cleansing, they called it, although nobody was actually being killed, just turfed out of their homes. But there was a great scandal, and talk of World Court charges and so on.

Commentators talked grimly, but with a glint of excitement in their eye, about the approach of war. News reporters love war. War makes for lots of news. Especially worrying, they said, was the position of the Union of Europe. Several member nations had high Muslim populations, especially UK-EU, Allemand-EU, Espana-EU and Morocco-EU. There was pressure in the Bruxelles parliament for the Union to ally itself with Arabia, or at least to sign a non-aggression pact with Arab states. America was furious at this proposal, furious at the very thought of it. US diplomats blustered and threatened, and although there were significant voices within Europe against such a move, nevertheless (said the smug newscaster) the prospect of an EU-America war grew ever more likely as time went on.

'It's crazy down there,' said Teruo, hugging himself and spinning over and over in front of the tvs. 'They're mad. Nation states, nation-state-conglomerations, they're all crazy-insane.'

But Teruo had some unreconstructed views with respect to Arabs. 'I never saw one,' he told me, 'in Japan. No Arabs in Japan. I met one in Asia-Siberia, but he was a civilised man, a flier.' He pulled a face. 'Mostly they are not civilised, the Arabs.'

'Teruo,' I cried. 'Are you a racist?'

'Everybody in Japan is racist,' he said. 'Everybody in Japan hate Arabs. Hate all foreigners, howsoever not? – except maybe Americans, Elvis-style Americans. I'll tell you,' he said, smacking the wall with the palm of his foot to propel himself over to me, grabbing me in mid-air and hugging me as we tumbled over to where the bedding was stowed, 'I'll tell you a secret, if you promise not to think me crazy. Sometimes I think you look a bit like an Arab. I think maybe Greeks have that Arab look about them, and that excites me, that *turns me on* baby.'

'You're disgusting,' I said, but I was laughing.

Here's another media editorial I saw at Teruo's. This was a talk-to-camera piece from Lyn Whitney, one of the most respected opinion-formers on ENN. This is what she said: 'In these days of political tension, of possible military conflict between those two great power blocs – America and Europe – that have done more to shape the world in the last three centuries than any other . . . when every other nation in the world has to decide with whom to ally themselves . . . run the risk of ignoring a small but threateningly placed nation that has grown up over our very heads. They call themselves the *uplanders*, a rag-bag of eccentrics and criminals who eke out a primitive living in patched and dented tin cans hurtling round the planet. Estimates suggest their population is no more than four hundred, but they are growing, growing all the time. When they started, there was a rash of human interest news stories about their adventures, but as time has gone on many people have forgotten that they are there. But we forget at our peril! They have reached a crucial stage in their development as a community. For the first time, companies down here are manufacturing equipment specifically designed for this new, exclusive market. The uplanders fly up and down regularly, taking up supplies and equipment. They trade with anybody, promiscuously. They have no loyalty except to themselves, no sense of honour or worth, except for money. What if there is a war? Might one of these *uplanders* not decide to take the yankee dollar, haul up ordnance or dirty bombs, drop them down upon European targets? I say the time has come when the nations of the earth stop turning a blind eye to this growing threat! It is time for EUSA to be given the mandate to police these people. If they appear in the skies over Europe, I say they *are* European! If they are European, then they should be compelled to obey European law, to pay European taxes, and to ally themselves with the European cause of racial and religious tolerance and diversity, against the monolithic McDonalds imperialism of the USA!'

McDonalds had gone out of business in 2056, after a cattle phage had pushed the price of beef too high for their plastic restaurants to cope. And nobody had bought their beanburgers, so they'd gone belly-up. But when I was a girl people still used the term as a shorthand phrase for all they disliked about America – this was before the establishment of the MakB franchise you see. I had lived in Europe, and I had lived in America (or Canada, which is the same thing), and I liked things about both places, and disliked things about both places, but that wasn't the way ground-dwellers were thinking in those days.

This newscast caused a deal of debate amongst us uplanders. Some were worried. The follow-up newscasts, and various ground traffic, suggested that Lyn Whitney had hit a chord with ground-dwellers. American networks started carrying similar opinion pieces, that if uplanders appeared over American skies (as we all did, as we all did over European skies) then we were American, and we should be compelled to obey US law, to pay US taxes, and to ally ourselves with the US cause of freedom and peace against the religious fundamental-ism and civilian-murdering terrorism of Islamic states and their mis-guided non-Islamic allies. And so forth. And so on. Some newscasters tried to speak to uplanders, and some uplanders gave interviews – I saw Piper Harrows, Bert Felber and Åsa Olsen on shaky image-capture talking about our point of view. They said what was on their minds, and mostly it was sensible – how we were our own people now, how we felt less and less interested in the continual round of politics and war on the ground, and how it increasingly struck us as simply batty. But Bert also said he felt like a god, looking down on puny mortals, which was not a politic thing to say, and was widely reported amongst the groundbased media. There were calls in the Euro parliament for police action against us. 'Threaten to shoot them from the sky unless they capitulate!' MEPs yelled. Opinion in America was similar.

'Maybe they'll invade,' I said. 'Send up troops.'

'But how,' said Teruo, 'are they going to do that? This is our land.'

'Land,' said Julie, scoffingly. But Teruo was adamant.

'No,' he said. 'We own this land, they don't. EUSA still uses rockets, they got basically no access to us up here.'

We were having dinner. Åsa Olsen and Julie Spelling were with us; in fact Åsa, who was the wealthiest uplander of them all (probably) had brought the food with him. He could afford to be generous in ways that the rest of us couldn't, could afford to stand other people meals and wine and such. Julie was a relative newcomer, coaxed up by Åsa and his money, but she seemed nice enough. So they were round having food, chez nous, and the discussion naturally turned to the news.

'I agree,' said Åsa, in his slightly wheezy voice. 'But several states now operate Elemag plane-ferry services up to orbit, placing satellites and such. It's so cost-effective, it's only a matter of time before EUSA and NASA switch from rockets and embrace the better technology. Then they can flood the uplands with their bases, with their people – with soldiers, maybe.'

'Not them!' I said, remembering my father's opinion on the subject of NASA. 'NASA is nothing but rockets, rockets for a hundred-twenty years now. If they stop using rockets then they're nothing. And as long as they keep using rockets, they'll be too inefficient as carriers to do much more than lob up a satellite or two.'

'I saw a rocket come up the other day,' said Teruo. 'Made a nice picture, long foxbrush of light moving very rapidly across the dark of the earth, and swooping up and round to the lightside. It left a sort of residue behind it in the atmosphere, and even up into space, a little bit. A trail. I didn't know they did that. In space, I mean.'

'Huh,' said Julie, unimpressed.

'I still warn against false optimism,' said Åsa, helping himself to more pasta. He was a flabby man, and he had more or less given up exercising, so his legs were skinny dribbles of flesh. Had he flown downside the gravity would have snapped them like wax rods; but he said he had no desire to go down ever again, he was happy to stay up here until he died. He seemed positive about this, but his manner was melancholic, and some of his friends called him the knight of the doleful countenance. 'Eventually NASA will adapt, or die. If it dies, then another agency will be formed, and they'll use the planes. It's not that I *worry*, you understand. Because,' he added, with grim satisfaction, '*I'll* be long dead. But eventually you younger uplanders are going to have to work out what to do. Should we band together, form an army, repulse invaders? Or should we let whichever government exploits us first, Europe or America, just annex us?'

'It won't be Europe,' said Teruo, with a little flush of anti-EU Japanese pride. 'They ran down EUSA after the sunprobe went wrong. They haven't the impetus to invade the uplands.'

'America then,' said Julie, in a soft voice.

'They won't bother,' I said. 'Three hundred people? That's not even a village. It's not worth their while.'

Abruptly, suddenly, there was an absolutely massive noise of buckling metal and shrieking, and a great rush of air threw the food parcels and the wine sachets and the bits and pieces and us into the air and slammed us against the walls. It was like the world ending. I was not hurt, because I happened to hit a place where there was some padding. Julie flew through the air, hit the radio casing and broke her nose. Åsa hit Teruo, who had hit blank wall and bruised himself quite badly. The air was howling all around us, and pressure was dropping, and the house was bucking and swinging about and about. Julie was shouting something, but the air pressure was shrinking and my voice was tiny and my ears felt plugged. I could see Teruo struggling to brace himself, looking around for the breach. It occurred to me, given what we had been talking about, that America, or Europe, had attacked us. I half expected to see space-suited stormtroopers crash through a hole in the wall.

Teruo was pointing. Through the hissing, and the lurching spinning of the wall, I could see a pole sticking out of the floor that hadn't been there before. We pulled ourselves over towards it, my grip impeded by something slimy and loose that had got smeared on my hands – later, I discovered that it was Julie's blood, from her nose. Pearls and balls of red were floating in a sticky string from her face as she span in the middle of the room.

The spike was loose in the floor, and air escaped past it where it had punctured the skin. But it was tapered, and by grabbing it and pulling it inwards Teruo was able partially to seal the hole, and I found some sealant and smeared it all around. Then, because my ears were popping and my sinuses were hurting, and because I felt breathless and very cold, I located a cylinder and emptied it, filling the room with bottled air.

For a while everybody simply hung, recovering. Teruo swore from time to time. Julie clutched her face and rotated.

'Was that war?' Åsa asked nobody in particular. Obviously he'd been thinking along the same lines I had. 'Are the Americans attacking us? You see how vulnerable we are?'

The phone rang. It trilled three times before I roused myself and pulled over to answer it.

'Hello?'

It was Jon.

He said: 'Are you alright in there?'

'Just about,' I said.

'Who's there with you?'

'Where are you, Jon?' I said. 'Are you outside?'

'Yes I'm outside.'

'Well, come and dock, there's room in the porch. We need some help, this is mayday, we've had a breach. It was *scary* stuff.'

He paused for a little while, and then said: 'I know. That was me. I'm sorry, Klara. I'm sorry.' He was crying, I could hear it in his voice. 'I'm so sorry.'

'Oh, Jesus,' I said. 'Oh, Jes*us.*'

Jon wouldn't come to the porch, no matter how I coaxed him, even when Åsa came on the phone and begged him to come in. I felt a strange mixture of intellectual alarm at the thought that I had been near my own death (although this did not move me very much) and concern for poor old Jon, fear that he might be about to do something stupid, something suicidal. I went over and helped bandage Julie's face, and I could hear Åsa on the phone losing his temper. 'What you want to do that for, anyway? That's just crazy, you could have *killed* us all, you could have *killed* us all.'

I didn't say what was going through my mind, which was that of course he'd been *trying* to kill us all. He cried on the phone to me, to Åsa, to Teruo, even to Julie. Then he hung up. Then he called again, and cried again at us over the phone. Finally he said 'I'm going, I'm going' and hung up. I watched out of a window as he pulled his jet away and slipped up out of view.

What happened next was that, the following day, we got a call from Sponti, telling us that Jon had fetched up at his place. He invited us over. I for one was not eager to go. I was disinclined to meet Jon. I felt a degree of responsibility for what had happened. 'You're *stupid,*' said Teruo, unhelpfully, 'to say so. Responsibility? You nineteen – he's sixty, near enough. You break up with him, of course you do. You'll break up with me in time. That's only natural. We gotta accept that. He couldn't accept that, this is his problem, not yours. That don't give him the right to get crazy-murderous. This is a dangerous land, you can't go bashing people's houses. He's a crazy cannon.' He meant *loose cannon.*

We flew over to Sponti's, and Åsa and Julie came with us. When we got there his porch was packed with planes; we took the last available docking point and climbed through. Sponti's house was filled with uplanders; there must have been twenty people inside. Because I had been at the heart of the incident, it hadn't really occurred to me how *exciting* a thing it had been. It was, after all, attempted murder. It was a crime of passion. Uplanders love passion, though they are usually reticent about it themselves. And of course it was rare for something so melodramatic to happen in the narrow world of upland life. The gossip went around the houses at lightspeed.

It was a much, much more interesting thing to uplanders than the prospect of war downbelow.

Jon was there. He caught my eye guiltily, and then looked away. He looked, somehow, smaller. I felt no animosity towards him. I suppose my nineteen years carried with them a certain elasticity of character. Events did not dent me out of shape then. Perhaps they do, now, more, now that I'm in my eighties.

Sponti pulled himself to the ceiling and we all oriented ourselves in line with him. 'I thought we should talk about what happened. I figured it could go like this: let Jon say what was on his mind when he did this thing, and then decide what to do next. We ought to decide. We have no courts, no police, no gaols, nothing like that. What happens in a case like this? What do we do? Do we *want* courts, police, gaols? I don't think we do, I don't think that's what the uplands are about, but then we got to decide what to do when something like this happens.'

People murmured, chatted, and Sponti pulled an uncomfortable-looking Jon up to the ceiling by his sleeve, pulled him into a place where we could all see him. He started talking softly, and his first words were lost in the chatter, but people quieted down when they realised he was speaking.

'I want to say,' he said, 'that I'm real sorry. I went a little crazy. People here know that Klara and I used to be together. Maybe they don't know I,' his voice caught a little, carried on in a slightly higher register, 'loved her, I still love her, it fills me completely that I love her. When she ended it I couldn't bear it. I got nothing against Teruo personally, he's a nice guy, but I couldn't bear it. I sat at home just thinking about it, thinking about it over and over and thinking about nothing else. You can imagine. Can you? It went round and round in my head until I think I went a little crazy. So I fitted some harpoons to my plane, just metal spikes with a short-push booster on the end. I mocked them up in my house, fitted them to the plane by waldo, and then I sat at home for a further week. I sat at home doing nothing but going round and round in my head about Klara, Klara.' He caught my eye again, and started crying. 'Oh Christ I'm sorry,' he said in a loud voice, hiding his face in his hands. I don't know if he was apologising for trying to kill me, or for crying in front of us all. Maybe the latter. Eventually he got his tears under control. 'I thought about it for a week, and then I just got in my plane and flew round to Teruo's. I fired all my harpoons, but only one of them hit. It's hard,' he said, the tears drying as he explained the technical problem of propelling missiles in zero g, 'to target correctly, because the short-burn stick throws the plane a little off whack, and

57

your targeting goes with it. I targeted, and fired, three times and missed with each of them. Then I fired the last three at once, in a spread, and only one hit.'

Whilst Teruo and Åsa and Julie and I had been chatting blithely away about earth politics, these harpoons had been silently hurtling past our house, perhaps only feet away. It was a chilly thought.

'After I saw one hit I was glad,' Jon said. 'Then as soon as I felt that, I felt ashamed. I felt terrible. I'm real sorry. I'm real glad I didn't actually kill anybody. All the hate and desperation went out of me. I felt like I'd done something stupid.'

'You *did* do something stupid,' said Teruo.

'I'm sorry,' said Jon. 'Only, maybe you don't know what it's like. To sit all by yourself, crazy for somebody you can't have, so that the thought of them goes round and round inside your head. It's hard.'

There was a pause.

'You got any questions for Jon?' Sponti asked. 'Anybody?'

Somebody at the back said, 'So, you're admitting that it was pre-meditated? You made these missiles with malice aforethought, and had them in your house for, like, a week?'

'Sure,' said Jon, covering his head with his hands. 'I'm sorry.'

'I only figured,' said the person in the crowd, 'that it being premeditated maybe made it worse.'

'Oh I reckon,' said somebody else (I could see it was Tam Entzminger), 'that it's a *crime passionelle*, for all that.'

'What?' somebody called. 'What was that about cream?'

'A crime of passion.'

'Yeah, yeah,' said a couple of people.

'I'm sorry,' said Jon again.

'I don't see what we can do,' said Bill, in the midst of the crowd. 'I don't see we're a properly appointed court. How did you pick us, Sponti? Just call a score of folk at random? Is that a way to appoint a court?'

'I couldn't invite everybody,' Sponti objected. 'My house is not big enough for that.'

'We're like a jury,' said Tam. '*They* get appointed at random.'

'But the judge don't,' countered Bill. 'Judges sentence, juries don't.'

'Maybe up here it shouldn't be that way,' insisted Tam. 'Maybe up here juries should sentence. Hey, Jon, do you accept the, uh, what's the word, the *authority* of this court?'

'Sure,' said Jon. 'I'm real sorry for what I did.'

'What are our options?' somebody else called. 'We can't lock him up.'

'Take away his plane,' somebody suggested. 'House arrest.'

'I think exile is a better punishment,' said somebody else.

'Permanent exile? Or temporary?'

'What do you think, Klara? Teruo? It was you he tried to kill.' said Sponti.

'And me,' said Åsa, a little petulantly. 'And my girlfriend. Hey!'

'I think,' I said, 'that maybe exile's the best thing.' Leaving somebody in their house without a plane for long periods of time seemed to me unusually cruel.

'Maybe that's it,' agreed Sponti. 'Down to earth for a while. Do we think?'

'Well,' said Jon, shifting, and blushing all over his face and bald head, 'I could suggest something else. I tell you: I was thinking of going away, but not downside. I was thinking of going to the Moon for a while.'

That shut everybody up. There was silence for a full minute. Finally, Sponti said:

'Seriously?'

'Yeah. I was thinking of it anyway, but maybe I should go now, just push off up there, and get out of everybody's way.'

What happened next was that this new plan of Jon's squeezed out the pretence that we were a constituted court of law. The primary interest of uplanders (which is to say, the fascination with technical aspects of space flight, problem-solving and science-fiction dreams) came to the fore instead. 'How will you power the flight?'

'Well the magnetosphere is dipole to about six Earth radii,' said John eagerly, for this was the sort of thing about which he could be immensely fluent and eloquent, 'though it gets pretty weak so far away; but I'll climb, and try looping round, slingshot to give myself momentum. When I'm fast I'll fire a single tube rocket. I've done some back-of-envelope calculations, I reckon that will get me there.'

'But the Moon doesn't have a magnetosphere . . .' somebody objected.

'It'll have to be conservation-of-momentum venting,' said John. 'I was thinking, water. I've got a great mass of water, in the coign of my building. I was thinking – I don't know what you guys think – I could run a wire out through it, insulated except for the end, heated wire that would bore through it easy. Then if I applied current, I'd steam off a little portion of the block, and that would give me some jet power.'

'Wouldn't be enough,' said Ben, immediately. 'Not just a wire. Maybe a spread of wires . . .'

'Or a tube, with a heated element at the end.'

'Do you have *more* than the mass of the house in ice, Jon?'

'Bout the same.'

There were some murmured conversations, people solving equations in their heads. Sponti called a calculator to his screen and put in some equations. After twenty minutes of discussion, unanimity was reached. By putting out a series of wires into his ice block, in such a way that the wires were pointing towards a focal point two metres behind the back of the block, Jon could generate thrust. With a long enough burst to slow himself, and a bit of careful piloting he could manoeuvre himself over the Moon, maybe even drop down. He said he'd buy a spring-frame with six legs and fit it to his plane. With a little care he should be able to land on the Moon. He'd take some solid packs with him, too, so that he could lift off again when he wanted. 'It's only point one six g,' said Sponti, several times, with an exaggerated brightness of tone.

'I'm sure,' said Jon, looking brighter, 'I'm sure I'll be OK.'

'It'll take days to get there – maybe a week.'

'I know.'

'But,' I said, uneasy at the speed with which this topic had taken over the discussion. 'How will you navigate?'

'I'll keep the Moon in my left-hand window all the way up.' There was general laughter at this. Of course!

'Man,' said Sponti, excited. 'The Moon! Nobody's been since Apollo. Nobody's been in a *hundred* years.'

'But what?' I asked, because it was bothering me. 'But what will you do there?'

'Sit,' said Jon, looking at me with cow eyes. 'Think about stuff. Maybe wander about . . . I've got an old NASA suit, you know. Maybe play golf.'

People were crowding round Jon now, laughing, congratulating him. 'You tell me what it's like when you get there,' one booming voice announced. 'Maybe I'll come with you. Be your neighbour.' It was ironic: the meeting had started as a court of law, condemning Jon Snider. It ended celebrating him as the new Apollo hero. When Teruo and I finally got home, he was furious. 'He tried to kill me, crazy man, and now he's celebrated all over the uplands.'

'Well,' I said. 'I guess he's still being exiled. I guess that was the point.'

Teruo banged from wall to wall all up and down the house. 'Crazy people up here. Murderous crazy-men up here, murderous warmongers down there. What a people! Oh the humanity!' He calmed down eventually, and we went to bed together. After the sex, I was thoughtful: 'do you think I could get Sponti to convene another court?' I asked. 'We could convene another court, and condemn Kristin Janzen Kooistra. Condemn her as the murderer of my father.'

Teruo pulled his arms out of the silk bag we were both in, and rubbed the top of his close-shaved head very vigorously with both palms. He considered. 'I guess so,' he said. 'Why not? Condemn her how, though. To exile?'

'To be executed,' I said, my belly turning over with the excitement of the thought. 'Why not? Eye for an eye. To have her executed.'

'Off with her head,' said Teruo. 'Stab her with a harpoon. Sure, but how we going to catch her?'

'I guess we set up a posse. Search her out. Follow the next lead, whoever runs into her.'

'I'd say she keeps herself to herself mostly,' said Teruo. He turned away from me and went to sleep.

eight

Jon left the uplands and went higher up. He fitted his plane up, and climbed into the highest orbit he could, where the magnetosphere gets tenuous and turbulent, and then swooped through a slingshot orbit – decelerating the Earth a tiny bit in its solar orbit, accelerating his house a great deal in its Moon shot – and spun away into a quicker orbit. He did this half a dozen times, picking up speed each time, depriving the Earth of a fraction of its speed so miniature it would be impossible to calculate it. He did it another dozen times, and then he was able to fling himself moonward.

The flight lasted seven days, and he was on the phone to various people almost the whole time. He called Teruo and me quite often, the first time with tears in his voice, but as time went on in a more controlled way. He kept apologising, every time he spoke to me. He was clownish with apologies. It was embarrassing. After Jon entered lunar orbit, Bert Felber hooked his phone line through a transmitter, and we were all able to tune in to his descent. It was clumsily done, Jon angling his plane so that it was orbiting sideways, as it were, and then blowing off a targeted stream of water to bleed off his velocity, and he started curving in to the Moon. Once he was committed to a landing his voice got very panicky. He was familiar with the ease of manoeuvring a plane through the sticky medium of the Earth's magnetosphere where Elem pulses slowed you as much as you liked; but this was different. 'Oh god,' he gabbled, 'I don't want to come down on those mountains, oh god, this lump of water is not equally spread on my belly. Oh god, I shouldn't have committed to landing when I did – another twenty seconds of orbit and I'd have been over the plain, Jesus, no, I'm going to splinter onto that rock, I'm coming down too fast, I'm going to crack my plane open on the rock.' There was a pause, with nothing but buzz. This was what was going on in my head: I had a mental picture of him smashed and decompressed, his body lying frozen on a lunar mountainside. Then we heard him again, 'Burn,

burn, Jesus', presumably exhorting his solid packs, because the buzz on the line rose in volume. Then, after a heartbeat's pause, his voice came through exultant, 'Jesus, I'm hovering over the Moon', I can see the dust running away from me all around the plane, below, and – *ugh* – I'm – down. *Jesus*, there's a leak. *Jesus*, there's another one.' There was a minute of static as he hurried about fixing the holes in his house. We learnt later that he had landed beautifully at the foot of the Mons Lunaris, and that he had a lovely view from his right-side window over the lunar plane. The mare, he called it. He pronounced it like *mary*.

Some Earthbound receivers picked up the broadcast, and there was some media interest in a new Moon landing, but NASA came out early on to deny the validity of the story. Uplanders, said Earth media, could only manage a low earth orbit. They had neither the power, the know-how nor the equipment for a lunar journey. It was a hoax, probably perpetrated by the Europeans to discredit NASA. EUSA and the EU government officially denied this slur, intimated that they thought NASA was behind the hoax, condemned the whole affair as an attempt to distract the world from their own racist religious intolerance. Jon took a walk in his second-hand suit, having established a video camera at the airlock, and a downlink with Bert so the images could be dis-seminated. He opened his door, and hung on whilst the last of the air blew away, and then he stepped out. 'I'm on the fucking Moon!' he said, the first words spoken by a moon-walker in a hundred years.

That's true, that part. People sometimes say that it's an urban myth, but I can vouch for the fact that it's true. He was very lucky, was Jon. He really was. In the years that followed many people tried to land on the Moon, and later on to land whole houses up there, and several died in the attempt: I don't have the actual numbers (why would I have the actual numbers?) but it was a fair few people. Or, to be more precise, several crashed; but most of those who died did so because they crashed at high speed and broke their bodies. For those who managed to get their speed right down – and that's easy, so they say, in the one-sixth g – even a poor landing, and rupturing of house walls and so on, was not likely to prove fatal. Once you get used to explosive decompression, it's much easier to deal with than you might think. The trick is not to panic. Keep your head, fix the hole, even if the air pressure goes right down. Go straight to the hole and fix it; don't try to repressurise until the hole is fixed, even if, as I say, the air pressure goes right down.

Jon's new Moon landing made headlines in the websheets and newscasts, but the headlines were all 'NASA implicated in moonwalk hoax', 'Fraudster wearing NASA spacesuit' and so on. Not that any uplander cared what they thought downbelow. We knew what Jon had done.

What about downbelow? The situation downbelow got much worse. This is what happened: war planes flew over the Atlantic. Dozens of new military satellites were rocket-launched into orbit – into our uplands. Lots and lots of them, sharing our space. We tried not to get involved, to keep out of the way (and there's a lot of space up there in which to keep out, so it wasn't hard). But this remilitarisation of orbit was so thorough-going, the rockets coming up were so commonplace, that we couldn't keep entirely out of the way of them. I saw two launches myself, and once we actually saw one of the new breed of 'dumper' satellites up close. It happened this way: I noticed something glinting in the sunlight from our window. It's true to say that, by this time, the uplands were busier than they had ever been; but nevertheless it was a very rare thing to see anything man-made from the window. The space up there is so vast. I really can't overstress just how big the uplands are. Very bright in the acid sunshine, very wide-horizoned, curved like a longbow and enclosing all the blue of sky impossibly below you, scribbled and laced over with folds of cloud-fronts, or the intricate sketch-threads of coastlines, and all that is your *basement*, all that is your footstool, and you've ten times the cubic space to live in as they do down there – and there are only a few thousand of you. You very rarely see anything up there but the overspill of black.

So, one day, when I saw something glinting I didn't know if it was a satellite, or a piece of junk, or another house. I thought, perhaps, it was Kooistra's house – *my* house, I should say. So I jollied Teruo into starting the plane and flying towards the bright light, hauling up into a higher orbit until it swelled in the cockpit window. We could see it was a piece of military ordnance because it was bristling with downward-pointing shark-teeth missiles, and blistered with chaff pods and com-discs, and it had 'USAF: Private Property' painted in white letters on the side. Teruo thought that a specially nice touch, the private property notion: this object chucked untended and untenanted into space. But, on the other hand, the uplands *are* a private sort of place. Then Teruo checked the radio, and sure enough the ground was cycling through a wide range of frequencies trying to reach us. 'Intruder! You are violating US air space. Move away from the satellite, or we will be forced to shoot you down.'

'Do you think they could shoot us down?' I asked.

'From the ground, I doubt it,' said Teruo, pressing his face against the window to see more detail. 'We'd see a missile coming, and we'd avoid it.'

'Would it be heat-seeking?'

'We could shut down our heat. Turn off our electronics. How would it trace us? But I'm more worried about the chaff pods on the satellite itself. If they decided to blow one of those off, we'd get chaff-shrapnel all in our fuselage. No, let's not risk it, let's go.' So we flew away and returned to the house.

nine

It was a few weeks after this that something big happened, and everything changed abruptly: I discovered I was pregnant. Teruo went to pieces when he heard the news, slapping his head, pulling at his eyelids, jabbing his thumbs in his mouth, sticking his fingers in his ears. 'This is terrible!' he said. 'Terrible! I don't want children! You should have told me there was the chance!'

'I didn't realise that there was a chance,' I replied.

'This is terrible!'

'I've got a contraceptive chip fitted in my uterus. How was I to know that zero g was likely to dislodge it?'

'Is that what happened?'

'Jesus, I don't know. I don't know if that's what happened. I guess it was something like that. Maybe it malfunctioned.'

He rubbed his head feverishly. 'I *never* agreed to children,' he insisted, sounding himself more and more like a tantrum-possessed child. 'You didn't discuss this with me.' He was spinning in the middle of the room.

'I didn't *discuss* it,' I said, getting angry, 'because I didn't know it was going to happen. I didn't plan it. I don't want children either. Leastways, not now. And not with *you*, that's for sure, you immature idiot.'

'Anyway,' he said, coming up to face me with wide eyes, grabbing the fixtures with one hand to steady himself. 'Anyway, you *can't* bring up a child in zero g. It can't be done. The uplands are no place for a child. They'd never grow properly. They'd grow all deformed. You wouldn't want our child to grow all deformed, would you?'

'It's *our child* now, is it?' I snapped. 'I know that I couldn't bring it up here. I'd have to go downbelow to have the child. But maybe I'll have it aborted. Sam the Clinic has all sorts of pills; he'll surely have some pills to terminate the pregnancy.'

Teruo beamed, as if the idea had not occurred to him before. 'Yeah,' he said brightly. 'You could do that!'

66

'I could,' I said, infuriated by his selfish, grinning face. 'But I won't. I'll have the child. I'll go downbelow to do it.'

'Where will you go?'

'I don't know. Canada. Europe.'

'How will you live? You can't live down there like we live up here. You need money, money. Where will you get it?'

'You'll give me some,' I said boldly.

'No child-support police will ever knock on *my* door,' he said proudly. 'They can't reach me up here. You can whistle for your money.' But then he added immediately, 'Although, I will give you some money. Sure, you can have some money. Only I don't have too much money, you know, I'm not rich any more.'

'I've got some money of my own,' I said, trying to act proud and disdainful, but actually thinking that the money – my Dad's Canadian assets, some few dozen thousand euros in a Canadian bank – was probably inaccessible from Europe, given the heightened tension between the two blocs. And then thinking that if I went down to bring up my child in Canada I might get interned, as technically being a European national. Then I thought, I could fight through the courts for the right to be declared an uplander citizen, although that was not a category that existed in law, and although I doubted whether any court would give my claim any attention if – when – war broke out. But the prospect of a fight, any kind of fight, buoyed me up for a while.

After a night's sleep, Teruo said, pulling at his eyelashes with pincer-fingers, one by one, 'Are you really going to have the baby? I mean, are you sure you don't want it terminated?'

'I'll keep it,' I said, sounding decided. The truth was I had no strong urges either way. If I came down on any side, it was on the side of keeping the baby, but I felt no special maternal bond.

'It's hard to believe it's real,' Teruo said. 'Me? A dad?' He snorted, a ridiculous laugh. 'Crazy.'

'I guess so.'

'Should you go down straight away?' he asked, a concerned expression on his face. 'I mean, would it hurt the baby to grow – in your uterus – in zero g?'

'I don't know,' I said. 'I don't think it's ever been done before. I can look online and see if there's anything published about it, but I don't see how there can be. But I don't see it'll matter to the baby. Babies are weightless in the womb, aren't they? They float in that fluid. It won't matter to them if I'm weightless as well as them.'

I knew, in my heart, that all I was doing was deliberately postponing going back down to Earth. I didn't want to go. I had no good memories of being down there, and I couldn't see how I was going to make a life there that was in any way half-happy. It was, as Teruo said, unreal. I stayed in the uplands for three months, four months, until my stomach was unmistakably pregnant, and my belly button became thorn-shaped. It was *easy*, being pregnant in weightlessness, much easier than those poor human milch-cows lugging their double-weight through the treacly gravity of Earth, but my exercises – which I increased in frequency and effort to prepare my bones for Earth's gravity – became harder, I became more tired more quickly. I felt changes in temperature more acutely than I had done before too. I was not nauseous, though: either because zero g nullifies pregnancy nausea, or else because I just wasn't. Teruo withdrew from me. He didn't like having sex with a pregnant woman, and became more fidgety and more eccentric around me. 'You look fat,' he told me, baldly. 'I don't like the look of you.' 'Thank you,' I replied, sarcastically. He bunched up his face, rubbed his bald pate with great energy. 'I'm only being honest,' he said. 'You wouldn't want me to be a liar. You wouldn't want that.'

'Save your honesty,' I said.

'We should sort out where you're going to live, when you're down,' he told me.

'Yeah,' I said. 'I guess.'

Then another significant thing happened. Tam Entzminger called on the phone. 'Hi, Klara,' he said. 'You'll never guess where I am.'

'If I'll never guess,' I said, 'why should I try?' I was feeling flippant, skittish.

'I'm outside Kristin Janzen Kooistra's house.'

Away went my flippant mood at once. 'You're kidding,' I said.

'Not kidding. I was chasing some junk, thinking of salvaging it, and I saw a light. I got curious, so I flew over. It's your old house. I'd recognise it anywhere. It's been augmented.'

I called Teruo from the other room. 'Tam's chanced upon Kooistra's house,' I told him, and then said into the phone, 'How do you mean augmented, Tam?'

'Two more rooms. A porch. She's fitted a periscope, I think. Difficult to see, but something's glinting in the light, like a thread going down to the Earth. She's put some powerful-looking com dishes out of one of the rooms. It looks like she's keen to keep in contact with the ground.'

'Jesus,' I said, excited. 'I can't believe we've found her after all this time. Is she home?'

'There's a plane in the porch,' Tam said. 'It might be her. Difficult to say.'

'Can you set your transponder?' I said. 'We can fly to you.'

'Sure,' he said.

So we hauled ourselves into the plane, and flew round from the dark side into the night side in a lower, faster orbit, and then climbed up on a line to Tam's transponder, bursting out into the sunshine again. There was a bizarre multi-layering of cloud in the blue of Earth below us, like rips and patches of white-bread pressed into a great mass. But the sky was its same black purity hammered by the shining tentpeg of the sun. Tam's plane was a speck, then a smudge of white, then a chevron-and-stick, and then we were right by it, large as life. We pulled gingerly alongside, so close that we could see Tam's face peering at us through his cockpit windows, and we waved to him. He waved back.

He was right. There was no mistaking the taping around the left-most room, nor the corner dents. This was my old house. Kristin Janzen Kooistra had augmented it a great deal, and Tam had not been exaggerating about the mass of communication equipment piled, seemingly precariously (although, of course, in fact not so), on the right-side room. The plane that was docked in the porch was not my Dad's old Elector jet; whether that had been discarded and this new plane was the replacement, or whether the Elector was off flying somewhere, it wasn't possible to tell.

I stared at my old home for a long time. You know that uncanny feeling, that *unheimlich* feeling, you get when you see an old house that used to be your home and isn't any more? I had that feeling. It was intense. I could sense Teruo sitting next to me, fidgeting with nerves, watching my reaction. He kept jiggling and jiggling his legs, trilling his feet against the floor of the cockpit and bouncing his knees up and down, pushing his body up against the restraining harness. I stared at my old home.

Then I looked at the Earth. All the time I had lived in the uplands it had never stopped fascinating me. Like almost all the uplanders I loved staring at it, watching through a window for, sometimes, hours at a time. The size of it, and the detail. The way familiar shapes of coastlines and the crumpled spreads of mountain ranges are overlaid by the unfamiliar, ever-changing shapes of cloud formations. The polished blue-steel effects of the sun reflecting from exposed ocean; the wadded and stringy stretches of cloud. The impression of inlaid precious materials, of golds and browns, yellow and ochres, of creams and greens, all fitted mosaic like in a ground of blue and then draped over with shredded cotton. It looked, to my eyes then, beautiful but strange. It didn't look like home either.

'Should we see if anybody is inside?' Teruo suggested.

Tam came over the radio. 'I flew round. The docking ports are all shut. We could try calling her? We could use the mayday frequency.'

I picked up the phone and sent out. There was a thirty-second pause, and then the sound of the connection being made. I heard a woman's voice. It was her voice. It said: 'hello?'

'Kristin?' I said. 'This is Klara. This is Klara Gyeroffy.'

'Klara,' she said, with apparent warmth and ease, 'how lovely to hear from you. How are you? It's really been too long.'

'It's been too long,' I said. I felt removed from myself. My voice sounded oddly in my own ears, a controlled and rather taut voice, somebody else's sound being relayed to me. My head seemed, strangely, smaller than it usually did. My senses were playing tricks with me.

I said: 'I like what you've done with the house.' I think I was trying for an acidic and withering wit, but she took my words at their face value.

'Do you? I'm so pleased to hear that. It *was* a little cramped, wasn't it, before. Are you outside now?'

'Yes, we're outside. We've got you. We've got you in our sights.'

'You'll excuse me for not inviting you in,' she said, blithely.

Then, I'm sorry to say, I lost it a little. 'That's my house, you murdering psycho, you killed my father, you killed my father, I hate you, I'll kill you, you sent me to hell but I'll reach up and stab you to death.'

Teruo's hand was on my leg. I ranted some more, and then I bit my lip and made myself stop. There was static for a moment, then Kooistra's voice.

'You *do* sound upset, my dear,' she said, smoothly. 'I am sorry to hear you so upset.'

'Did you ever lose a father?' I asked. 'Did you ever *have* a father?'

'Everybody has a talent,' she said, and for a moment I wondered if she had misheard me. 'You do, my darling. I do. Your father had a talent. His talent was to build this house, for me. His talent was to die at the right time. And if that seems like a poor sort of talent, well, it's exactly as important as everybody else's. Your talent? I don't know, my dear. Oh, maybe it is for revenge, maybe that's where your talent lies. But I'm not sure. Now *my* talent . . .'

I interrupted. I'd bitten a piece from my lip, and blood was moist and earth-tasting on my tongue. 'Who cares about you?' I snarled. 'Who gives an iota about *you*?'

Her voice in reply was mild. 'Oh, I think you do care about me. Why would you be so upset, otherwise? Why would you have come looking for me? Oh, I think you do care.'

'You arrogant miss,' I said, but I didn't say any more because I could feel tears coming in the back of my throat and behind my eyes, and I didn't want to give her the satisfaction of hearing me cry. I didn't want Teruo to see me crying.

'Now,' she was saying, 'my talent is particular. It has to do with a certain cast of mind, a certain way of thinking – clarity, the ability to see through to solutions, of a certain kind. An uncluttered mind is how I sometimes like to think of it.'

'The ability to kill,' said Tam, cutting in to the conversation.

'Why thank you,' she said, ingenuously. 'Whoever you are, sir. I'm pleased you recognise that it takes *talent* to do that. To know when to do it, and to do it. Oh, my talent is not more important than yours, sir, or yours, Klara, or your father's, but it has certain material advantages. There are people who pay well for its use.'

'I'll kill *you*,' I called. I grabbed the controls. I believe, truly, that I would have rammed the house there and then if Teruo hadn't wrestled me back. He held me with one arm, undid my webbing with the other, and hauled me out and away. I was crying, sobbing, swearing. He cut the phone connection.

'Don't be crazy,' he said. 'You want to kill yourself?'

'I don't care!' I screamed.

'You want to kill *me*? And what about your *baby*. You want to kill your baby?'

'She's mocking me,' I cried. 'She's baiting me. She's tasking me.'

'*I* don't want you to kill me,' Teruo insisted. 'I don't want you to damage this expensive plane that I converted to space flight with my own hands and with my own *money*, god damn it. I don't want you to kill baby either.'

'She'll get away. We've got to stop her. We've got to get her,'

He had me in an embrace, although I struggled, and we were spinning in the main body of the fuselage now, knocking the walls from time to time, literally bouncing off the walls. 'Say you crash into her house like kamikaze,' he said. 'Say you do that. How do you know which room she is in? What if you get the wrong room, and she seals her doorway, and then you're dead and I'm dead and the baby's dead, and *she's still alive*. Is that what you want? Is that what you want?'

'What else can we do?' I sobbed. 'What else? We don't have weapons. I can't fire one of Jon's harpoons at her, we don't have it. What else?'

'There's nothing we can do now,' he insisted. 'We must go home, and plan it more carefully.'

Eventually his reasonableness wore me down, penetrated my hysteria. I calmed down a little. Ten minutes later we took up our seats in the cockpit again. 'I want to scare her, though,' I said. 'I want her to think I'm going to kill her. I want to ruffle her feathers.'

'Take it easy,' Teruo advised.

I called her again. She picked up after two rings. 'Hello?' she said, as if she really didn't know who was calling.

'Hello,' I said.

'My dear,' she said, with instant warmth. 'You worried me. It sounded like you had a funny turn.'

'You're insane,' I said. 'You're a sociopath. I feel sorry for you.'

'Are you still upset over your father?' she asked, with genuine bafflement in her voice. It was as if she were talking about a finger cut yesterday.

'Yes,' I said, in a heavy-voice. 'I'm upset about my father. Perhaps you don't understand.'

'Oh,' she said. 'When we had our slumber party – do you remember? Happy times. I'll tell you what I liked about you then. You seemed a very *unsentimental* individual. I admire that in people. Too many people lived their lives poisoned with sentiment. I do hope you haven't gone that way. I hope you haven't lost the ability to see more clearly. Some people live in the valley, and they are conformist and they are sentimental. Some people, though, live on the mountain-top, and they are the future-humans, the higher-humans, the above-humans. That's where we are. Oh, what is there to be sentimental about anyway? Everybody dies, after all. Your father died, I will die, everybody.'

'You'll die sooner than you think,' I said, and pushed two spurts out of the strapped-on solid sticks. The plane lurched towards the house, and Teruo's head and mine snapped back. In a second we were past, and speeding away. I puffed side jets and brought the plane about, by which time the house was a speck lost against the backdrop of the Earth. I had to pick up Tam's transponder to find my way back. It was sloppy flying. But this time I came in more slowly, and deliberately nose down, and nudged forward. I was aiming for her comm set-up, and this time I caught it. The plane's nose went under the main dish, and with a painful, metallic wrenching sound, that made Teruo squeal with fear that the nose was breaking open, I pushed on and ripped the dish away. I hope that it sounded like the end of the world inside Kooistra's house, and that she was scared, if only for a moment. I hope I at least rattled her for a moment.

72

We flew home.

It turned out that I had indeed warped the nose a little, and Teruo had to open the hatch from inside with a crowbar, which made him grumpy. 'You were lucky not to break the seal,' he said. 'Then we'd have explosive-decompressed, and that would have shoved us backwards, and you wouldn't have been able even to break off her precious comm disc. Not to mention, putting us to con-sid-er-able inconvenience.'

'I didn't break the seal,' I pointed out.

'You were lucky,' he said, as he fetched a hammer to knock the nose back into a better shape. But I didn't feel very lucky.

I spent a week building some harpoons, like the ones Jon had used on me. My hope was that Kooistra would stay more or less where she had been. If she was using a periscope to bring in air – more and more uplanders were doing so – then she couldn't fly to too high an orbit; it limited her range. I told myself that it would be easy to find her, and that this time I would break open each of her rooms one by one. I told myself that the mistake Jon had made, when he had attacked me, was in not coming close enough to the house before firing. I told myself that I wouldn't make that mistake. Teruo refused to come with me, and indeed tried to talk me out of going. 'You'll waste solid sticks,' he said. 'These things aren't free. They cost, you know? They cost money. Somebody's gotta schlep them up from downstairs, and everything.' But I didn't care about that.

The old model of bubble-set sticks, solid fuel shot through with bubbles of oxygen like the old chocolate bars, had been replaced by a newer model, longer thinner sticks of solid fuel with a spiral-shaped detonation thread running along it. They were more efficient and much easier to fly, but they were also more expensive. Nowadays, of course, almost nobody uses solid sticks; electrical generation is so much more sophisticated, it's easily possible to generate the amount of energy you need to manoeuvre through the magnetosphere in space as in the atmosphere, and solid-state fuels are a thing of the past (or so they say: I never go upland these days). But then these accessories were a drain on upland finances.

But I was in no mood to listen to Teruo whinge about money, something he did all the time these days. I snapped at him, and took the plane, and flew round and round the Earth looking for her. But of course she had pulled in her periscope and moved off to another orbit. I was looking for a needle in a great, black sea. It was hopeless.

ten

The time came when I could no longer postpone returning to the Earth. My encounter with Kristin Janzen Kooistra had upset me, and I could feel my upset as a physical symptom, because when I was angry the hormones upset my baby, and it kicked and jiggled inside me. It was the physical manifestation of my agitation. I neglected my exercises. I was sour when Teruo told me he'd been in touch with somebody he knew in UK-EU, and had set up a flat for me to live in in London. But my biology compelled me along the path.

Teruo flew me down to a private landing strip outside Reykjavik, complaining all the time that he had had to pay for its use. I told him I was happy for him to drop me at his usual place in Japan-Siberia, and then pay for a conventional flight to London, but, as he knew very well, that would have worked out more expensive overall.

I had to be taken from Teruo's plane in a wheelchair. In fact, I spent the rest of my pregnancy in a wheelchair. I had not anticipated just how heavy a pregnant belly is: the baby, the fluid, everything. It was agony. I caught a passenger-charter flight to London Barking Airport and took the train across the capital to the flat Teruo had rented for me. Ah, but that first night on Earth was one of the hardest I have known. I could not sleep, because the sheer weight of my bones kept me awake. It was not possible to lie in a comfortable posture: the huge tug of my planet-shaped belly, the bruising downward pressure my ribs seemed to exert upon my lungs, the feeling my newly large breasts gave me of hauling my skin out of shape. It was all painful, everything was painful, every breath and every single movement. The baby didn't move very much inside me. I thought, at least it's happy. Then it occurred to me that perhaps the lack of movement signified the reverse of that; that maybe it meant that the baby was very far from happy. Maybe the baby simply did not have the musculature to move its new gravity-laden limbs. Maybe it was being crushed, maybe it was dying. I panicked. I rushed to a doctor.

I spent almost all the money I had in my chip over the remaining three months of my pregnancy: I was in the hospital much more often than would have been normal for a pregnant twenty-year-old: checking my health, checking my baby's health. It all cost money. My daughter was born in the summer of 2063. Had she been a boy, I would have called him Miklós, after my father. I thought of Mikla, but didn't like the sound of it. I thought of calling her after my mother, Nikola, but that sounded too much like Mikla. Instead I called her Gradisil. 'What kind of name is that?' the registrar asked me, checking the child's vital signs. 'Is that a Greek name? You're Greek-EU, aren't you?'

'It's a Hungarian name,' I lied. Then, because I felt weirdly uncomfortable at the lie, and because I associated the name with my dad, I added: 'My father was Hungarian-EU,' as if that explained and justified it.

'It's pretty,' said the registrar, 'What does it mean?'

'It means,' I improvised, 'road to the stars. Or, rather, it means Beautiful Tree,'

'Lovely. A pretty name for a pretty baby.'

But Gradi was not healthy. I should not, it transpired, have spent so much time pregnant in zero g. Calcium had not fixed in her bones properly. She broke her legs being born, and cried and cried. She fed hungrily from my agonised breasts, but for two meals out of three she would immediately vomit up all the milk again. Doctors gave her a nutrient implant, in the wall of her duodenum, to prevent her becoming malnourished. I had to replenish this through a plastic duct in her belly. Her poor belly, stabbed through with this plastic implant.

After a month she stabilised, and after three months more the casts came off her legs. I went back to living in my tiny flat in Putney Common in London, and for six months or so, it was very hard. I begged Teruo for more money, but he whined and whinged and said he hadn't any more money. I called Sponti, almost with the last money I had in my chip, and cried and cried, and begged him for help. I was not so upset, although I was crying, that I didn't tweak the guilty spot in his conscience by mentioning my father. He still felt responsible for Dad's death, even after all this time. He was very supportive. He emailed me some more money at once, and arranged for some business contacts he knew in London to come and see me, to introduce me to some people downside, with a view to finding me some work.

It transpired that we uplanders were followed by a large community of Earth-bound fans. Especially in Europe and the US, it seemed, there were specialist webgroups, media channels, conventions and the like devoted to following us. Telescopes tracked out trajectories across the sky. Receivers listened in to all our open-band communications. One of Sponti's Earthside friends set up a number of paid interviews, and I talked about my life as an uplander. The questions followed a certain pattern. Groups were interested in the Moon landing, and almost always prefaced their questions with 'Personally, I absolutely believe that you guys went to the Moon, I don't believe the EUSA bullshit about it being a hoax'. They really did. They *more* than believed. They seemed to think that we had a whole community living on the Moon, that we flew back and forth all the time.

'Have you been to the Moon yourself?' they asked.

'I haven't,' I said. 'I'm sorry. But,' I added, 'I know the guy who did go.'

They knew some features of our gossip, of our interpersonal relations, but not others. When I mentioned Jon's name, they said 'oh, right' in a knowing voice, as if they were all aware that he and I had been an item. But they did not seem to know about Teruo.

They all asked this question: 'Will you go back there? Will you go back to the uplands?'

I always answered it: 'Yes, absolutely, as soon as I can.' This was what I believed.

I did half a dozen European interviews, three of them face-to-face. I did two US interviews, by virtual connection. The European interviews were, all of them, interested in my dad. 'Your father,' they would say, sometimes having the grace to look sheepish about asking so intimate a thing, but sometimes looking only avid and intrusive, 'your father, he was – if you'll excuse me – killed, murdered, wasn't he?' 'Yes,' I would say. 'I hope you don't mind talking about it,' they would say, looking understanding and concerned, but still hungry for all the painful details. 'He was murdered by the Crystal Killer, wasn't he? She's now officially the world's most wanted serial killer, Kristin Janzen Kooistra. Did you know that? Did you know that she's now the world's number one most wanted?' No, I said, I didn't know that. 'She's an American, of course,' they would say. 'She's been hiding out in the uplands for years now. The best intelligence says that she is secretly being funded by NASA, as a fifth columnist, living amongst you, an American spy in effect.' I said that sounded unlikely to me, but my opinion was insufficient to discourage them from their conspiracy theories.

Neither of the American interviews mentioned my dad, but they both – to my surprise – brought up the long gone subject of my mother's death. 'That was a long time ago,' I told them. 'I was very young when it happened. I really don't remember it.'

'But isn't it the case,' an American interviewer pressed, 'that she died as the result of Arabic terrorist action? Another civilian casualty in the ongoing Islamic war or terror against peaceful civilians?'

This was tricky, and perhaps I should have been more diplomatic. But I still thought of myself as an uplander, not as a European living in a continent on the brink of war. 'Oh,' I explained. 'It's not certain, but I guess so, I guess so. There was that terrorist campaign in the '30s, of course, when some fundamentalists poisoned a large number of breweries and distilleries. It was a way of striking at the decadent Western addiction to alcohol, they said, seeding our beer and wine with a genetically mutated yeast that acted as a gut poison, and adding those, what-d'ye-call-them, those *neuropoisons* to spirits. Most of that alcohol was intercepted and destroyed, but in some parts of the world some supplies slipped through, I think my mother was just unlucky, she happened to take a bottle of beer that was from an old crate, and she got a gut rot that killed her.' I surprised myself, as I was saying this, by how little moved I was. Why should my father's death churn me up, and my mother's not move me at all? Weren't they both equally my parents? Weren't they both equally dead?

That's genuine equality, right there.

But the Americans ran my interview under a 'Mother Slain by Islamic Terrorists' banner, and the Europeans ran it under a 'Father Murdered by US Spy' headline, and only then did I realise how naïve I had been. I earned less than nine thousand euros from all those interviews and picture rights, and I created, inadvertently, a great deal of fuss. In my defence I think I really didn't understand how close to war the downbelow world was.

War came, of course. I lost touch with my friends in the uplands, because I could no longer use radio communicators to talk to them: the use and even possession of such transmitters was declared a prisonable offence. I ran out of money. Life became much harder. I could not stay in my pleasant London flat, and had to wheel myself in my wheelchair, with Gradisil on my lap, all along the west road and out to less salubrious parts of the capital. I was walking a little now, with difficulty even after six months, but I used my motorised wheelchair for longer journeys. I travelled twenty-five kilometres at three kph an hour; and I had to stop frequently to soothe or feed my baby; it was a ridiculous way to travel.

Then the European armies were mobilised. This meant, at least, that work opportunities opened up for those of us not in uniform, as the regular workers left to travel to the Atlantic front. I took some work as a data manager in an office in London-West. There was an office crèche, and free medical attention for my still tiny, still ailing baby, and that was more of an incentive for me than the meagre salary. I had an affair with the manager, a one-armed man with a tender face, but he was married and he broke it off after a month or so. German troops were stationed in our buildings, prior to being moved out to the Atlantic platforms, and I had a brief affair with one of them, a man called Matthias Henke. He was a beautiful young man, and was, in fact, the first of my lovers for whom I myself felt an overwhelming physical attraction – the swoon of that physical infatuation, the *tug* of it. But he went out after a few weeks, and I believe he died in the fighting. There was, as you may know from the history books, a two-month period of intense combat, and then a year of very little other than sporadic raids. Then there was a period of heavy bombardment, and I lost three toes from my left foot when my leg was crushed by falling masonry. My foot is still misshapen today. After that there were several months of uneasy peace between the USA and the EU, and finally the Treaty of Tenerife was signed and we were no longer at war. Europe remained under military dispensation for a year, or longer. That's all common knowledge, and I don't mean to bore you by rehearsing it here.

At the end of this period I was living in Cambridge on the UK-EU East Coast with a new man, called Thomas Baldwin. Thom is still alive, and I have asked him whether he has any objection to me writing down details of our life together, but he always was a secretive, suspicious man – although not without a generous side – and he has refused me permission. I have checked with lawyers. They have an obligation to go through my manuscript after I have completed it and make sure it complies with the Decency and Privacy legislation of 2122, so they have promised that they will make sure that what I write here complies with the legal right of my ex-husband for privacy, whilst enabling me my constitutional right to self-expression. It's a balancing act. I don't know, actually, exactly to what extent 'the right to privacy' is defined under the legislation. I am an old woman now, and the doings of governments seem remote to my life. It seems to me that the legislation does not prohibit talk of sex, provided it is not in more than a certain degree of detail, and provided certain forms of words are avoided. As far as the privacy legislation goes, I may talk about material relating to my ex-husband that is undeniably in the public domain, and that means his business success, his name, his nationality and so on.

His name was Thom Baldwin – that much is undeniably public domain. When I met him he was working in the clinic to which I was obliged to take Gradi. She was two now, and was walking with the help of motorised callipers on her legs. But she was tiny for her age, and had little appetite, and was often ill, and sometimes her skin tone was unhealthily yellow-green. Thom was working a paediatric term. He attended to Gradi. He prescribed drugs that I couldn't afford because Gradi needed them, and when he realised the level of my impoverishment he filched the drugs from the hospital supplies and gave me them free. He smiled at me as he handed this illicit plastic package to me, and I sensed the possibility of another partner. And so it proved; within a day we were rutting – a word I use deliberately, because there was a slightly frantic, animal flavour to our sex. We fucked at every opportunity, and in every location, until my knees and the small of my back were scratched and bruised from cramming myself into cars and cupboards. After two weeks of that I moved into his place. By the time Gradi was three she was calling him 'daddy'. We were married the year of her third birthday.

It was hard living to begin with, and the Army Council was spending most of Europe's wealth on reconstructing the bomb-ruined western cities and on building up Atlantic defences. There was talk of the need to build an Asian shield wall, fearful speculation in the media that the Americans might launch a land assault from their Japanese bases and sweep through Russia. Eastern-EU nations, who had largely escaped the destruction of the recent war, were most worried by this, of course. But in practical terms all it meant was that there was too little food in the shops, too few clothes and shoes. Nobody seemed to have any money. Even doctors like Thom earned next to nothing. Our clothes became ragged. I was even grateful, in a way, that Gradi was so small of stature. Because she grew so little it meant I did not have to buy her too many suits of new clothes.

But even in these early days Thom had plans to make himself wealthy. 'I won't go for it now,' he confided in me, 'because the taxes are still too high, it's still war-level taxation and I'd lose most of my wealth to the government. But in a year or two, when things settle down, I'll make us a fortune. I'll be rich, you'll see.'

This he did. He had invented a drug regimen when still a student, and had been able, in between his official medical work, to refine it down to a single implant. This is before the ubiquity of today's *pharmakoi*, although Thom's work was, I suppose, part of that climate out of which they were developed. This was how it worked: the metabolic systems that take excess food and lay it down as fat are governed by hormonal and chemical pathways. Slimming treatments that had been developed in the late twentieth century had simply blocked the uptake of the fat in the gut, but this had the unavoidable and unpleasant side effect of creating loose, malodorous and sometimes uncontrollable stools. Thom's drugs had a different effect. They rewired the body. Fat was still laid down, but it was only stored in one place in the body. A woman could eat as much as she liked, and she would only get fatter in her breasts.

Thom marketed his drug for the first time in 2067, and it was an instant hit. The austerity of the war years was changing, giving way to a voluptuous cultural styling that emphasised female breasts as desirable objects. More and more food was coming on the market from the oceanic farms. People started celebrating more, eating more, dressing more showily. Women bought Thom's drugs in enormous quantities. It was a craze. It crossed the difficult Atlantic boundary and became a craze in the Americas too. Female breasts assumed wholly new sizes and dimensions. The effect was completely unlike surgical breast enlargement, for the new breast matter was ordinary body fat, and the breasts felt and moved in wholly non-plastic, realistic ways, excepting only that they were huge. There were side effects of course: many women suffered backache from the unusual weight on their chests, and some tried to sue Thom's company, but the lawsuits were unsuccessful. Worse, if the breasts became too fatty, the texture of the flesh could deteriorate, leaving the skin of the breasts deeply dimpled and pocked. But although all this was well known it did not deter many hundreds of thousands of women from taking the drugs. Fat women took them in order to slim; skinny women took them to enlarge their breasts; and so it was something that Thom could sell to everybody. The market grew and grew. In commercial terms it was a glorious success. Thom became one of the wealthiest EU businessmen in the postwar boom.

An irony was that Thom did not much care for breasts. My own breasts, once the milk went out of them, were small, and he told me this was how he preferred it. I have always been skinny, regardless of what I eat, so I have never needed slimming regimens. But I did not complain about Thom's business, or about our large Cambridge house on the Anglian coastline, or our London townhouse in the central section, with a roof garden, or the cars and planes. I did not complain that Gradi got the best medical interventions money could buy, and that she finally discarded her callipers and walked free and strong with only minor internal prostheses to help her knees and hips carry the weight. I did not even complain, although I felt bad about it, that Thom began relationships with a succession of women he called 'muses', which is as good a euphemism for 'mistress-prostitute' as I know. It was, I told myself, one of the consequences of his great success, one of the perks I suppose, and a natural follow-on of the many new people who thronged around him all the time. He had met me when we were both poor. Now he was not poor, he was wealthy, and he was a different man.

Gradi was at school when the Short War happened. She watched the news reports of the destruction of Paris by those dumper-fired shark-teeth missiles, and she was very upset. If you're too young to remember that, then there's little I can do to convey the sheer shock of it. There had been several years of peace, and then, suddenly, this enormous destruction. It was not that we had forgotten the war, but it had assumed the marmoreal other-ways distance of history, anecdotage, tv-docs, memoirs. Peace was the new medium in which we lived, and we got used to it. Then, from nowhere, a diplomatic storm blew up, and then we dumped on Atlanta and they dumped on Paris, or perhaps the order of those two events was the other way around, I can't remember. The consequence was that everybody seemed to stop, abruptly, in the middle of their frivolous spinning lives and look around them with, as the poet says, wild surmise. Could everything end so quickly? It seemed to spring on us from nowhere, a tiger tumbling from the high heavens. But the Short War lasted only three weeks, and the Peace of Madrid that followed seemed to us a more permanent footing for world relations than we had ever had before.

Thom and I were living in separate apartments now, although he was still supporting me financially, and still took an interest in Gradi's development. He was courteous, and distant, and sometimes he was sentimental, particularly when he had been drinking: then we would have sex, and he would sometimes coo into my ear how he loved me, only me. But he didn't. I saw less and less of him, these awkward occasional reheatings of our former relationship notwithstanding. His love was directed elsewhere; it found another woman.

He offered to pay for me to have the scar tissue removed from my arms, but I refused. I think I was still attached to my past, even the painful portions of it. I think, also, that I wanted to spite Thom for separating from me, to snipe at him about his new relationship with a younger woman, whose name I cannot recall. I was bitter that I was now a single parent. Thom did not stint me financially, and with his money I lived a pleasant, leisurely life; but I was ungrateful, telling myself he could afford it, that he was *buying me off*, that it was my entitlement.

It's strange to recall it now, because the world has changed a great deal and such petty racism seems very dated, but Gradi was bullied at her first school. She had a rather Japanese look about her face, it is true, and immediately after the war there was a deal of anti-Japanese, and anti-American, hostility. She was taunted, smacked, locked in a cupboard, she had her lunches stolen. But even as a little girl, she was a fierce creature, and I did not realise what was going on until several weeks later because she did not tell me. She was too proud and too solitary to come crying to mummy. She tried to fight her bullies, despite the fact that she was small and relatively weak. She would launch herself at them in class. I only learned, belatedly, that things were wrong when I was called to speak to the three-person headmaster panel.

'She bites,' they told me. 'Now, it is true that the other children sometimes call her names, but she *kicks* and *scratches* and *attacks* them physically. She interferes with the balanced dynamic of the classes. Perhaps it would be best to remove her to another school?'

'Are you expelling her?' I asked, becoming angry.

'No,' they said. 'We only make the suggestion of transferral.' Their faces might have been carved from ivory, so inexpressive they were. They sat, three people in charge of one of the most expensive schools in Europe, behind an ebony desk in a tall room lit only by lines of clear glass windows high up near the ceiling. Light fell in interlocking parallelograms on the polished floor, on the clear table top, and fell across their grey jackets and their impassive faces. There was a suggestion of dust in the air, but barely a suggestion. The room smelt of lavender and musk. Only the presence of a folded-away ordinater in the corner revealed that it was ever a workroom.

'If my daughter is being bullied,' I told them, 'surely it is because you are failing in a duty of care towards her.'

'Is it true,' one of the headmasters, a woman, asked, 'that Gradisil is half-Japanese?' Her voice was insinuating.

'Is Gradisil a *Japanese* name?' asked a second.

'We only ask,' said the first, 'because there is still a legal duty to register all Japanese Europeans with the authorities, just as it is with American Europeans.'

This was too much. I told them that I knew *my* legal responsibilities. 'I thought we fought the war *against* racial discrimination,' I fumed. 'I thought that Europe stood for diversity and cultural respect, and not for a foul, ingrained racism.' I told them that they did not have the legal right to expel my daughter, and I threatened and blustered. But, when I took Gradi home that evening, I couldn't get her to open up about the bullying. She seemed embarrassed that I would even ask. 'It's alright, Ma,' she said, in her ten-year-old way. 'I can handle it. Don't go on about it! Leave it alone!' She was small as a bird. I hugged her with a sort of desperation. I didn't know how to get through to her. She was so self-contained.

The following week she bit one pupil, and stuck a broken calculator-chip into another one's eye. This latter child had to have surgery. Causing actual bodily harm constituted non-contestable reason for expulsion, without refund of fees, and Gradi left that school. I decided to teach her myself, at home, but after two months of that I gave up. I had gotten used to being a woman of wealth and leisure, of morning lie-ins and lengthy alcoholic lunches, and it was too much of a shock to my system to have to stick to school-teacher hours, and to enforce a school-teacher timetable, and to have to discipline my wilful, passionate daughter. I arranged for her to go to another school.

It was shortly after this that Thom lost his fortune. The vogue for enormous breasts passed, as all such cultural fashions inevitably do. Sales of the drug fell away. New implants that burnt fat in situ, giving over-eaters an all-over slim physique and a constant supply of energy and vigour, became the fashionable way of treating obesity. Thom had diversified his portfolio in a range of separate investments, but he was unlucky. The Euro economy suffered one of its frequent depressions, and he lost all his money. By this stage Thom and I were divorced, and his financial ruination had little impact on my life, except only that the monthly payment for Gradi ceased, and this was inconvenient. I took work as a hair artist, a skill I had picked up in my years of leisure. The fashion at this time was balloon hair – all out of date and hopelessly old-fashioned nowadays, I know, but *all the rage*, as they say, once upon a time. It went like this: I coated each strand of hair of my subject with a special gel, that hardened in seconds; then I attached a micro-nozzle to the end of each hair, and inflated it with various gases. You would do this regularly over the surface of the hair, varying the effects, and the result was a floaty arrangement, or tangle, of lenticular expanded hair-strands that bobbed and rose and gave body and shape. It was a time-consuming and therefore an expensive process, but I was good at it. For a time I had enough money to send Gradi to another school, but the company I worked for went out of business and I was unemployed for four months. Gradi had to leave the school, and we lived on the handouts of one of the welfare charities. This, financially, was our lowest period. We shared a large but nevertheless single room with two other single-mother-daughter families in Kent. After this, my life improved.

eleven

I did not entirely lose touch with my uplander friends during this period, although I did not stay in contact as closely as I perhaps should have done. But from time to time I spoke to one or other of my old neighbours; and from time to time I sold interviews to the media about the uplander life. This became harder the longer I stayed down on the Earth. Editors began to think, with reason, that my first-hand experience of the lifestyle was out-of-date.

It was 2075, thirty months after the devastation of the Short War. This was the time when Paris was declared the capital city of the Union of Europe – the arrangement superseding the unwieldy shared-rotating scheme, whereby a northern, southern and eastern city shared the status of capital for two years. Nobody could object to Paris becoming the centre of the Union, since Paris did not, properly speaking, exist. Some of the banlieues, and some of the old twentieth-century suburbs (which had their own historic charm) had survived the bombardment, but much of the housing from the river to the peripherique had been flattened. By '74 there was a comprehensive regeneration scheme in place, and Paris was to be rebuilt as Paris-Centreuro. By chance, I was at this time dating a building manager, a specialist in the then new technologies of aerated-concrete, who won a lucrative contract to work on re-covering glassed ground with stone for roads and foundations. He was keen on me, I remember, and he suggested that Gradi and I come with him.

So we moved to Paris. We stayed in builders' quarters, which were comfortable but noisy with the comings and goings of sky-cranes, buses, energTruks and the like at all hours. Here I gave an interview to *Builder Europe* magazine that changed my life. It was, naturally, about my time as an uplander, and it was more interesting than many I had given before. Instead of the usual prurient interest in zero-g sex, or in my father's murder, or things like that, this interviewer wanted me to speculate on the possibilities for the building trade of the new community in the sky.

'There are,' he said, 'well over a thousand people living permanently up there, and another six hundred who own little huts and boxes up there and fly up for weekends.'

'Is it so many now?' I replied. 'When I first moved up there were no more than forty houses in the whole of the uplands.'

'Planes are more powerful now; the pushjets can operate on a small reservoir and provide vacuum thrust equivalent to the old solid sticks you used to employ in your day.' The interviewer enjoyed displaying his technical knowledge.

'Really!' I said. 'How fascinating.'

'War always results in advances in technology,' he said with false blitheness. 'The new Civilian UltraJet has a range of two thousand klims, and can fly from pretty much anywhere above the Tropic of Cancer to polar orbital entry in under an hour.'

'Marvellous,' I said.

'The new elec-generators can maintain high-amp pulses for much longer stretches. It's possible now to use Elemag not only to climb into orbit, but to manoeuvre, to perform quite intricate manoeuvres.'

'Marvellous,' I said again. But I couldn't see the point in interviewing me about new developments, when the interviewer clearly knew more than I did. I was expecting to be asked to reminisce about the historical earlier period of upland colonisation. But this was not how the interview proceeded.

'Now,' he said, 'my question is: given the continued expansion of the upland community, and given the fact that more and more industry down on Earth is producing specialist material for these uplanders, can it be long before they start hiring builders to fly up and work for them?'

'Well,' I said, carefully. 'All of the uplanders I know pride themselves on their self-reliance. Very few of them would be happy contracting work out, especially to ground-dwellers. It's a specialist environment, you see, and a very unforgiving one. You mention the companies down here who manufacture for the upland market. To take them as an example: I don't know any uplanders who would be happy to buy their stuff and use it without modifying it, checking it, rejigging it. There's a company, I know, called Belius, producing expensive vacuum suits – but only a fool would put one on straight from the shop and jump out of an airlock. If you haven't made it yourself, you don't really trust it.'

My interviewer did not seem very happy with this; I don't think it was the answer he was expecting. 'Still,' he pressed, 'houses in the uplands are getting larger and larger. Surely there will be some demand for building professionals to fly up and work on these properties?'

'I suppose so,' I conceded. 'Perhaps the weekend uplanders you mentioned might be more likely to employ contractors.'

'And then there's the Moon,' he added. 'A dozen people are living there now. A man called Åsa Olsen has been, it seems, voted mayor of the Moon. These mooners fly down to Earth orbit – to, that is, the uplands – during the lunar night, and fly back up to the Moon for the lunar day.'

'Åsa Olsen,' I said, smiling, 'is a man with ample independent finances, and can do what he wishes. But how can a village on the Moon become anything other than a rich man's folly? How could it become economically self-sufficient? I don't see it.'

The truth is, my years living downside again had altered my perspective on the uplanders. I tended to see them now as foolish sorts, living an impossible life, which was pretty much how the ground-media presented them. How could it ever become a real country? It was so hostile to life, so difficult and expensive to live in. But despite the awkwardness of this interview it had significant consequences for my life.

For the time being, however, I could not foresee this. I was living in the builders' village, and Gradi was going to a France-EU school, and hating it. 'Only half the lessons are in English,' she said. 'The rest in stupid French. I hate my teachers, and I hate my schoolfellows.'

'Are you being bullied?' I asked, anxious, and she looked disdainfully at me, as if I had mentioned something embarrassing. 'Oh no,' she said. 'I just hate them.'

'Just because your daddy was originally from Japan,' I told her, 'doesn't give anybody the right to make fun of you.'

'It's not *that*,' she said, her tone of voice inexpressibly dismissive of my foolish notion.

'Isn't it?'

'It's because I'm an uplander's child. They all say so.'

'What?' I was shocked to hear this.

She set her mouth in a thread-thin line and looked at the floor.

'Do they hate uplanders so much?' I asked.

'They say the uplanders killed Paris. I'm glad they did – if Paris is full of people like that, they deserved it.'

I rebuked her for this savageness, but only mildly. It startled me, in fact, that there could be such hostility towards the uplanders in a European school. 'It was the Americans that bombed the city,' I told her, but she only shrugged, and went off to play with her ElectroInsect, flying it round and round her room with her control glove. That was her toy of the moment, I remember.

I became a little paranoid, in fact. I began to think that it had been foolish of me to give so many interviews, to broadcast the fact that I was an uplander, if they – if we – were to become the new hate-figures, the scapegoats, the new Jews, the new Arabs. I found myself walking past knots of people on the shopping boulevards, overhearing or imagining that I overheard disparaging comments. It was almost certainly nothing but my imagination. When the commissioners contacted me, I assumed at first that it was to arrest me for being an uplander. I nearly fled.

They approached me, all three of them in EuroCivil uniforms, when I was standing at a coffee counter in the market boule of Paris-Est.

'Ms Gyeroffy?' one of them said.

'Who are you to ask?'

'We also have you on file as Mrs Baldwin,' said the second.

'I no longer use that name.'

'Are you, though,' said the first, 'the Klara Gyeroffy who used to live in the uplands?'

That was when I nearly ran off; nearly dropped my shopping and left my coffee and limped-ran away. But I didn't. I swallowed deeply, and tried to calm myself. 'It is true,' I said, 'that I used to live up there.'

'Have you had lunch?' the second one asked. I said no. 'May we take you to lunch? We have an officially sanctioned proposition.'

They took me to a very expensive and exclusive luncherie. My then-boyfriend, the builder, was fairly well-to-do, but he had never bought me food at so expensive a place. 'Let me ask you one thing, Ms Gyeroffy,' they said. 'What do you want?'

'What do I want?'

'Yes.'

I thought about the question. Perhaps it is a strange thing, but I had not thought about that question for many years. You become caught up in the day-to-day when you have a child. 'I want,' I said, 'a house in the uplands.'

The commissioners smiled at me, and looked less like policepeople. 'We can help you to that.'

As soon as I said it, and as soon as they replied, I knew that this was truly what I wanted, and that I wanted it more than anything else. Gradi was twelve. In a few years she would be an adult and would leave me, and then what would I do? Pass from boyfriend to boyfriend until I became too old? Work at one or other menial job? I would never earn enough money to be able to afford a plane, to be able to buy a house, to be able to do nothing but live in the uplands. Like the overwhelming majority of the people who lived on the skin of the Earth these things would always be beyond me – above me. Saying *I want this* is, in part, articulating what you do not have, what you may never have. We desire unattainable things with an intensity we cannot muster for the attainable. How else could it be? It was the gap between me saying *I want a house in the uplands* and these policiers replying *we can help you to that* – it was the little abyss of unattainability between those phrases that gave such piquancy to my excitement. It was fireworks in my belly and my brain. I said: 'Can you. Can you really?'

'Sure,' said the commissioner.

'We read your interview in *Builder Europe*,' said the second commissioner. 'You really know the upland community, don't you? I mean, you know the core community – the people who have been there for decades. The key players. Maybe you don't know the *new* people so well, the parvenus, but you know the important people.'

'Sure,' I said.

'This mayor of the Moon, for instance,' said the first commissioner. 'You know him?'

'I know him well,' I said, and I did not add *although I have not spoken to him in many years.*

'What we want, Ms Gyeroffy,' said the first of them, '– and by we I mean the People's Government of the Union of Europe – the thing that we want is an ambassador.'

Here it was that my life changed about again. The restaurant was called *Potalovo*. It's still there, I believe, in Paris-Est. A long, low-ceilinged new building. Its tables were made from marble, and it was lit by droning artificial flies that circled over the tables and mazed their way through the girders up by the ceiling throwing a variable pale-orange illumination below them. There were hardly any other diners in the place. The inside was fashionably murky, dark corners in which diners could feel they were enjoying privacy, but the broad frontage windows were shimmering and bright with daylight. When waiting staff passed before these windows on their way from the kitchens to the tables at the back they became, as silhouettes, spectral, blur-edged, dark smudges.

'An ambassador,' I repeated.

'Let me ask you not to repeat this outside this restaurant,' said the first commissioner. 'Europe is on the verge of recognising the uplands – recognising them diplomatically, that is. We want to go further, we want to establish a specifically European enclave in the uplands themselves. Naturally we want good relations with the existing uplanders. Ideally, we want a treaty, an alliance of one sort or another, but more important than that – that may come, in the fullness of time, but more important than that now – is that we establish *friendly relations* with the uplanders.'

'You can help us to that aim,' said the second commissioner. 'You're an EU citizen, born and living in Europe. But you are also an uplander, with many friends.'

'The father of your daughter,' put in the third, 'is an uplander. Is he not?'

They didn't need an answer to that. They knew that already.

'As ambassador,' said the first, 'you would live for a while in the European, uh, in the European *enclave*. But eventually, after some years, we would be able to help you towards a house of your own – a private house, in the uplands. If that is, indeed, what you want?'

'That is what I want,' I said. I was slightly dazed. I took another sip of wine.

'Then I'm delighted to say it is settled!' said the first commissioner. 'You will agree to work as acting ambassador. You will not be granted actual ambassadorial rank; it's a quasi-appointment. But it will help you on your way to a house of your own. And your brief—' he trailed off.

'My brief?'

'To establish friendly connections with the uplanders.' There seemed to be some unspoken problem here. The commissioners looked one to another as if egging one another on to say something to me. Finally the first of them spoke. 'Let me put it this way,' he said. 'We would like the uplanders to be *well disposed* towards Europe, rather, say, than towards America-Japan. Do you understand?'

'I see,' I said.

'I can say,' the second commissioner announced, 'that EUSA is changing. The old order vanishes, yielding its place to the new. NASA, you see, is still wedded to rocket flight, but EUSA, and Europe as a whole, is now committed to flying planes through the torsion of the magnetosphere. A new breed of space plane is being developed right now – as we speak. Six large carriers, bigger than any plane that's flown into space yet. A dozen smaller jets, fast deployment. And that's just the start. We intend to establish a large-scale European base in orbit; the first national presence in the uplands.'

'There are, naturally, worries,' interjected the first, 'that the present inhabitants will not be – ah – *pleased* with this development. We need to find ways of assuring them that our intentions are in no way hostile. Not hostile towards *them*, at any rate,' he added.

'You are building dedicated space planes?' I said.

'Oh, your old techniques, adapting conventional jets, that's no good for a proper project,' said the first commissioner, with easy condescension. 'The safety margins are too narrow. No proper government could run a space programme on patch-up-and-mend the way you people, the way your uplanders, have been colonising the area. No, for us it's got to be design-from-scratch, great gleaming spacebirds. I've seen the tenth-size model . . . a beautiful design. Curves by Stilnoct, you know. Some of Europe's most exclusive designers are being included in the project.'

twelve

In this way my life changed. I began to think realistically of returning to the uplands. I had several meetings with European officials, and signed a number of documents, including secrecy documents. According to my lawyers those documents had a fifty-year statute of limitation. It didn't say so on them when I signed, but apparently a recent court case established the half-century principle for most government binding contracts; of which legal decision I am glad, because without it I would not be permitted to tell you anything of what followed.

I used official facilities to call all the uplanders I had once known. I had fallen out of the habit of talking with them over the previous few years, because the cost of the calls tended towards the prohibitive. But the Union government was content for me to call all the uplanders I liked. I couldn't reach Åsa Olsen, Emmet Robles or Bert Felber, but I spoke to Tam – he was pleased to hear from me, I think – and to Sponti. Then I called Teruo, and with him I had a much less pleasant conversation.

'Hi,' I said. 'How are you?'

'Who's this?' he said, and his tone of voice was worrying, like a senile old man's. 'What? What do you want? What?'

'It's Klara,' I said. 'Don't you remember me?'

'I've no money!' he shrieked. 'No money at all! Leave me alone!'

I tried to remain calm. I told myself to get into the diplomatic idiom I would soon be using as quasi-official ambassador. But it wasn't something that came naturally to me. 'Teruo,' I said sternly. 'I don't want your money. Don't be stupid. Let's talk.'

But he only said, 'I've no money! No money at all!' and then he started to cry. I began to wonder if he had gone a little mad, or a little *more* mad, and this thought, oddly, made me angry. What right did he have to lose his sanity in my absence? How dare he not *remain the same* whilst I was away? It seemed to me that the least he could do was to stay as a fixed point in the background of my life, like a star, so that I could return to him and things could be as they always were. Of course we all treat the others in our life this way. We don't see them for, say, two years and then we resent the fact that, on meeting them after all that time, they've grown, they've changed. If we leave our house in the morning we don't wish to return to it in the evening to discover that it's grown an extra storey.

'Stop that crying,' I shouted. 'Shut up! I don't want your money! Will you be quiet? Don't you want to know how your daughter is doing?'

This made him cry more, and he became incoherent. I caught 'my daughter' and 'oh, humanity!' and 'crazy', but the rest was garbled, some of it in Japanese. I thought of calling off, of trying again another time, but suddenly Teruo stopped crying and his voice came through very clearly.

'It's a shock to hear you, Klara, actually,' he said. 'My skin is all bubbling off me.'

This was such a weird thing to say that I almost didn't register it. I decided to ignore it, thinking Teruo was just acting goofy, or just overplaying his reaction to hearing my voice for the sake of sympathy.

'I don't mean to shock you,' I said. 'Has it been so long since we last spoke?'

'Three years,' he said. He sniffed. 'No, four years. More than four years. Such a long time. How are you? Are you well?'

'I'm well,' I said. 'I've got some news.'

But he didn't seem to want to hear my news. 'And how's Gradi? How's my daughter? The daughter that I've never seen?'

I didn't say, *the daughter you didn't want to see, couldn't wait to get rid of*. 'She's well. Doing well at school. We're living in Paris now.'

'Paris,' he said. 'They're rebuilding Paris. It's to be the Euro capital.'

'I know,' I said.

'It was on the news. Paris was destroyed during the war.'

'I know,' I said again, worrying that Teruo's mental faculties were so loose. 'Are you alright Teruo?' I asked. 'You're not making a whole lot of sense.'

His voice, when he replied, was stiff with anger. 'Didn't you hear me earlier? My skin is all bubbling off. It's coming off my back in sheets.'

'You're *joking*,' I said. 'Really?'

Now he was crying. 'It's been this way for months now,' he sobbed. 'I'm dying, Klara, dying. I'm going to be dead, and I'll never have seen my own daughter. How I wish I'd come down with you, lived with you in London! Don't it sound stupid to say so? Leave the uplands – me? I was never happy down there. And yet look what it's done to me, cancer, carcinoma, neoplasm, all over my skin and under my skin, and I look like a freak. I'm so glad there's no picture on this phone, or you'd faint to see me. Fucking uplands, they've boiled me with their radiations.' He snorted, sniffed, and then, abruptly and rather shockingly, he laughed very loud. 'When the war started and I knew you were in London, I said to myself, *at least I'm up here*. Can you believe that? How selfish I was! I had visions of you and Gradi being smashed to atoms by the American bombs in London, and I thought I was safe up here. Safe? Safe?' He was sobbing again, now. 'It's fried me, living up here. I got cancer, and I'll be dead before the end of the month.'

It was heartrending. Uplanders still live within the protecting curtain of the magnetosphere, of course, but they're much higher up than groundlings: the protection is less and the risk accordingly higher. I spoke to Teruo for hours. I said to him: 'Fly down, come down to Europe. Or if you're too ill to fly, get somebody else to fly you down. Come and spend some time in a hospital down here, maybe you can get cured.'

He was dismissive. 'I'm already dead,' he said morosely. 'I'll be dead in a week.' Then he started crying again. 'I haven't exercised in nine months,' he whined. 'My legs are like a doodle-man's. They'd snap if I came down, snap like they were made of breadsticks. There's no hope! There's no hope!'

It was extremely upsetting. But I must make a rather shameful admission. During the middle of this conversation, when Teruo was sobbing and telling me how much he regretted, and how he didn't want to die, and when I was commiserating with him and reassuring him as much as I could – right in the middle of this, I thought to myself, *if Teruo really is going to die soon, then maybe I can get his house. I used to live there, after all. It should come down to his daughter by the laws of inheritance – and then I'll have my house in the uplands again.* I felt bad that I could think such a thing at such a time, but that didn't stop me bringing it up with him.

'How's the house, Teruo?' I asked.

Immediately he was suspicious. 'What do you mean?'

I got a little angry to cover myself. 'I was only asking,' I snapped. 'Have you added to it? Is the periscope still working? I'm only trying to distract you from your misery, you selfish cuss. But don't tell me, I don't care, I don't want to know.'

'The house is fine,' he said, sounding cowed. 'I haven't added anything, but it's good. The periscope is fine. Most people have them, now, up here. That was a good invention, I think.'

'And you told me you didn't have any money!' I said, mock-chidingly. 'When you've got a perfectly good house of your own.'

This made him cry again. 'But it's not mine,' he said, between gulps. 'I borrowed money from Åsa. It's his house now. It's mortgaged to him. But I needed the money to live on! I ran out of money, Klara.'

'Oh,' I said. 'I see.'

'When I – when I – when I—' he said, as if he was having trouble putting the words out, 'when I *am gone*,' he said, finally, 'Åsa's going to take my house to the Moon.'

'No kidding?'

'He's got a little ranch there. That's what he calls it, a little ranch. He wants more living space, up there. He says the lunar gravity agrees with him better than no gravity at all. They've got an inflated tent, there, now, you know. Inflated. They're putting their shit in it, their shit mixed up with lunar dust and so on. They're maybe going to grow some lettuce or tomato or something, in a couple of months.'

So that was that.

I had medical tests with EUSA. They scheduled me for a flight up to the new European station. It was all going ahead.

I had to broach the subject with Gradi. It wouldn't be possible for her to come and live in the uplands until she had stopped growing, assuming that she even wanted to. But she needed to know that I was going back up, and she needed to know that her father was dying. I hadn't discussed it with anybody in the government, but I wondered if it would be possible to fly her up to say hello-goodbye to her father, and then fly her down again and put her in a live-in school. As I look back on it now, it seems to me that I was almost monstrous in my self-obsession on this issue. Perhaps I should have put my daughter first, and told the government to go fuck itself. But, you must understand, firstly, that Gradi was an unusually self-reliant child, so much so in fact that I had gotten out of the habit of thinking of her as a child at all and thought of her as a little adult. And secondly, you must understand that I wanted *so very much* to return to the uplands. If that latter reason does not sound convincing or weighty to you then I can only think that you have never been to the uplands. Go, look through the window, then you'll understand.

I went in the car to collect Gradi from school. She looked so beautiful, in her tiny coat and hat, sitting entirely alone and apart from the other children in the drop-off lane. 'My darling,' I said, embracing her. She let me embrace her, but only briefly. 'Did you have a good day in school?'

'No,' she said, and climbed into the back of the energCar next to me. When some other children climbed in after her, she shuffled along, pressing into me to ensure that there was clear upholstery between her and them. I squeezed her hand.

'I've some news,' I told her, 'I spoke to your father today.'

'Daddy,' she said, and momently her face brightened. 'Is he coming to see me?' She meant Thom Baldwin, of course, when she said daddy.

'I don't mean daddy daddy,' I said. 'I mean your biological father.'

'Oh,' she said, the interest draining instantly out of her. 'Him.' She looked out of the window as the half-rubble, half-built-up streets rolled past.

'He's not very well. In fact he's very ill.'

'I don't care,' she said.

I tried to be shocked. 'Gradi!' I said.

'He's a stupid uplander,' she said, savagely, and twisted one of her coat tails in both her hands. Her reaction nonplussed me; it didn't bode well for my other piece of news. But the energCar had pulled up and this was our stop.

We went in the house, and I cooked some food, and Gradi did some of her homework, which seemed to consist of callisthenic gestures and movements – nothing like the sort of homework I used to take home when I was a child. But times change, I suppose. When we sat at the table to eat, I tried to raise the subject again.

'Don't you like uplanders, Gradi?' I asked.

She munched, moodily, and then turned her face away. I thought she wasn't going to answer me, but then she said, 'The other children at school have daddies, most of them. Some of them don't have daddies, but then their daddies died in the war, and that's better. But my daddy is a criminal.' She meant Teruo when she said this. 'Uplanders are all criminals and bank robbers and murderers, and they've run away from the world, and it's proper to despise them. The teacher said so.'

'The teacher shouldn't have said so,' I returned. 'You shouldn't believe such things. I know many uplanders, and they're not any of them criminals. I used to be an uplander myself,' I reminded her.

She looked at me, with a tender expression, and suddenly dropped down from the table and ran around to me, hugging me about the waist. 'But you came home, Mamma,' she said. 'But you came home!'

I was surprised by my own tears when I hugged her. I don't know why I cried. It was the mere pressure of emotion, I suppose, the sudden intimacy with my chilly daughter, the fact that there was at least one small thing I had done which had pleased her. The steam coming out of the kettle's spout doubtless doesn't understand its own relationship to the heating element inside the device.

It was not easy. I hadn't the heart to raise the subject again that evening, and when I tried talking about it the next day Gradi seemed to blank me out. She didn't want to hear it. She had no room in her feelings, and perhaps no room in her mind at all, for her dying father, or for the idea of her mother returning to the uplands.

'But,' I tried, the next day, or the next week (because it went on and on), 'but wouldn't you like to live in the uplands? To live amongst the stars? You're weightless up there, you know. You can float, and fly. We could go to the Moon.'

'The Moon,' she said, with deadpan twelve-year-old intensity, 'is all desert and vacuum. Why would I want to go there? There's nothing there but emptiness.'

I tried to find a way of communicating to her that I had been happy in the sky; that my life on the ground had never been as satisfying or fulfilling. But I didn't have the language. Or, more precisely, she and I did not have the language in common.

It was a time of tears and tantrums.

I remembered how I had been at her age, when my father came to take me away, how eager I had been to go with him. Now I was offering to do the same with her, to take her away, and she wasn't interested. She didn't want it. As I write this down I feel how foolish it is, or to be more precise, how foolish were my unspoken assumptions at that time. What was I thinking? I was thinking, at some subterranean level: *as I was at twelve, so must my daughter be at the same age.* When I state it baldly, like this, of course I can see how foolish it is. But this belief, in some unmined, unrefined form, was certainly inside me at that time.

I moved out of the builder's house, not particularly mourning the end of that relationship, and I took an apartment in the Government development of Paris-Nord. Gradi resisted this also, because it meant moving schools. 'But,' I told her, rather baffled, 'you always said you hated that other school. You said the children were cruel to you, and that you hated the lessons in French. All the lessons in this school are in English, you know,' English being the language of governance.

'You don't know *anything!*' Gradi shrieked. 'You're taking me away from all my *friends*. I'm never allowed to settle *anywhere!* I've been to a thousand schools, and they're all *awful*. And now I've got to leave the only school I *ever liked*. All my friends are there!'

It was hard. She sulked, and banged doors, she refused to eat. Once she threw the food I had prepared for her from the table to the wall. I tried to discipline her; something I had never done before. I tried grabbing her and smacking her. To be honest, I was very angry myself. But although I am a relatively tall woman, and although Gradi was a girl of small proportions, I did not have the strength. She wriggled free easily and ran off.

Eventually I made some sort of peace with my daughter. One night, as she lay in her bed I came through and sat on the edge of the mattress. We talked for a while, and she surprised me. 'What do you want, Gradi?' I asked her, and she replied without hesitation: 'I want to join the military.' Imagine it! 'You want to be a soldier?' I asked her, taking care not to load my voice with any tone of dismissal or contempt, trying to ask the question in a neutral way. 'The teacher told me,' she said, 'that I was probably too small for the army, but that my stature would be a positive asset in the air-force. I could fly planes. I want to fly. That's my dream. I'll be thirteen in five weeks, and then it's only four years until I can join up.'

'You never mentioned this before,' I said, suspecting it was a whim of the moment.

'You never asked,' she said, with a hint of sulkiness. 'Anyway, you hate the military, you always said so. But Daddy was in the army.' Now she meant Thom Baldwin.

'He was seconded to the medical corps,' I said. 'During the war. But that was during the war, when lots of people went in the army who wouldn't normally. He's not in the army now. There's no war on now.'

'It's always war,' she said, simply. Those were words that stayed with me for a long time; that blank wisdom, that unstudied eloquence that children sometimes achieve. I sat in silence on the end of her bed. She sang to herself for a little bit, and I realised that she had been conducting the conversation with me at the same time as listening to some of her music through a single earphone. She liked a very different sort of music to the sort I had liked at her age: hers was softly melodious, with multiple harmony and echo effects and a soprano vocal line trembling above it. It seemed insipid to me, but it was what she liked. She sang: *fire light, fire light, fire little, fire light,* or something like that. Then she said: 'It's alright, Mamma. I know you want to go to the uplands.'

'Well,' I said, shortly. 'I do.'

'It's OK. You can go, if you like.'

And with that casual permission, she stopped fighting me. It was as simple as that. She stopped her tantrums, and became a much better behaved, if slightly distant, young woman. At her birthday five weeks later she invited friends from her new school. By then it was apparent that she was much happier. I had the sense, only nebulously available to my conscious mind, that some great obstacle that had been blocking my actions as mother had been rolled away; indeed that, in some sense, I had completed my duties as parent, that at twelve Gradi had moved into adulthood.

thirteen

The new EUSA spacebirds test-flew for the first time in late '75. By '76 the cargo birds had carried several hundred building components up to a high orbit. Just as the journalist from *Builder Europe* had predicted, scores of specialist builders were contracted to assemble a platform. A hangar, a dozen chambers, generators, heating and cooling, solar panels for energy, hundred-klim-long periscopes to siphon-in clean air. It was to be the largest house yet built in the uplands. The cost was estimated at a hundred and twenty million euros. By the time it was finished this price-tag had risen to nearly three hundred million euros. My father had built our first house for a little over 6000 euros for the major parts, another 2000 for essential components, and maybe 900 for fuel (this is not counting the original cost of Waspstar and of father's various modifications of the original jet). Of course, the government's house was much bigger. But to be involved in the manufacture as I was, even in a relatively minor position, was to see how much money was wasted, how much was scooped off by corrupt operators, how much was spent unnecessarily. It reawakened my father in me. I found myself sounding off to people in the staff bars, about the wastage, about the inefficiencies of government. One time I got too drunk, and I said 'The more I think about it, the less I think that colonisation of new lands should be in the province of government at all – government should never try to colonise, that's just oppression. People should do it themselves.' The following day I was reprimanded by my superiors. 'You work for the government now,' they told me. 'You can't simply mouth off every thought in your head. What if a journalist had been listening? What if a spy had been listening?'

There was a great deal of talk of spies in those days. Suspicion and what was called 'hot peace' existed between the American-Asian alliance and Europe. Nobody expected the peace to last. The only question in the media was: what form will the war take? Will it be a lengthy and casualty-rich war of attrition? Will it be a short war of sharp-shocks? To think of it now . . . to think how blasé we became in contemplating mass death.

I was on the government payroll, it is true. I spent my days in my office doing the *Times of Europe* crossword, or reading, or staring through the window. That's what it's like to work for the government. Sometimes I spoke to uplanders, and I filed reports on what I said. Here is a conversation I had with Åsa. I checked the transcripts, which recently became available under the fifty-year rule.

'I have missed you, my dear,' he said. His wheeze had gotten worse. 'There are so few people from the old days left. Not that I'm lonely. More people have houses up here than ever before, you know. But I miss some of the old faces. Did you hear that poor Teruo died?'

'I heard.'

'Poor fellow. He got very ill. We all tried to encourage him to go downbelow for some treatment, but he was always stubborn. Stubborn to the end. But how are you, my dear? I have missed you. You always had such life, such energy. You were working your way through the available men up here, do you remember? First Jon, then Teruo, poor Teruo. I always used to hope that you'd work your way round to me in due course.' He laughed, amiably. 'Times weren't so bad back then, were they.'

'How is Jon?' I asked.

'He's very well. I'll tell him you were asking after him. He'll be pleased by that. He has a house on the Moon now, and a house in the uplands, and he goes from one to the other. Sometimes he digs out interesting things from the Moon, and hauls them into lunar orbit – rocks and crystals and things. It doesn't take much to get them into orbit, and when they're up then it's downhill all the way to Earth. He had an arrangement with some American universities, I think, to provide them with raw material. It doesn't pay much, but it's something.'

'Is it true that you're mayor of the Moon?'

'What's that?'

'I heard this story that you'd been voted mayor of the Moon. It sounded a little bizarre to me, but that's what I heard.'

'Ah, the Moon!' said Åsa. I think he was getting a little bit deaf in his old age. 'It's a splendid place. You really should come and visit. Although,' he added, with a certain snideness in his voice, 'I hope I'm not being insensitive. I sometimes forget. It's a privilege, isn't it?'

'A privilege?'

'Living up here. Being able to fly to the Moon, to live in the clear unfogged sunshine of the uplands. Not everybody can do it. It's such a long time since I was on the ground, since I had to work for my money. I didn't mean to – what's the expression – to rub your nose in it.'

'You didn't rub my nose in it.'

'I'm glad to hear it.'

'In fact,' I said, and as I said it I felt a joyous little contraction in my chest, a knot of euphoria and hope tying itself there, 'in fact I may be moving back up to the uplands fairly soon.'

'Really? How marvellous.' He sounded wary. Perhaps he thought I was about to ask him for some money to buy a plane and to build a house.

'I've taken a job with the European government,' I explained. 'They've promised to establish me in a house.'

'Your own house? Or government accommodation?'

'The deal is I work for them for some years, and afterwards I'm allowed to retire to a house of my own. Isn't that wonderful?'

'Wonderful,' Åsa agreed, in a bland voice.

Eventually I got to fly back into the uplands. The EUSA Station was complete, and had been staffed with scientists, all of whom held senior ranks in the European military. I was flown by low-air flight to Norway, and there boarded into one of the new spacebirds. She was a beautiful-looking craft, silver-skinned, sweeping lines running from the cup-nosed cockpit down to fretted wings, serrated, or 'metal-feathered' as it was termed, on the trailing edge. Two large cargo doors were inlaid into the spine of the fuselage. This was one of the smaller spacebirds too; the larger, freight 'birds were simply enormous, the size of ocean liners, able to haul incredible amounts of stuff into orbit.

I took my seat inside the spacebird and simply gawped at the fixtures and the fittings. They were signed with the logos of half a dozen of Europe's most celebrated design companies: JaF, Stilnoct, Charles-Pierre Dutoit, Daysign, Adidas. It was undeniably *chic* if rather oppressively opulent. They served me luxury food, dainties, fine wine. My seatbelt had a platinum clasp.

The actual experience of flight, however, was less pleasant. I chatted with an aide as we rose, and I couldn't stop myself clutching the armrests. Through the windows the air darkened from pale blue to lavender, to a prune-black speckled with random blinks of ionisation, and finally to the authentic black of space itself. Stars shimmered into visibility. But instead of a continuous rise the plane lurched and tumbled, stuttering in its upward momentum before catching again and rising. These drops wrenched my gut nauseatingly.

'I guess you've flown up plenty,' said the aide, a West-Russian called

Natalya Shelikhova. 'But not in such confort!' Her English grammar was excellent, but her vocabulary sometimes let her down.

'Confort,' I repeated. 'No, I haven't. But I don't like these sudden little drops.'

'Clear turbulence,' said Natalya, with a shrug of her shoulder. 'I have been up thrice. Each time this has happened. It does that.'

'It shouldn't happen that way,' I said. 'Not once we've cleared the air, not when we're running on mag-aerodynamics. There shouldn't be any turbulence up here. There's nothing to – uh, to turbulate.' Her bad English was infecting mine. I was, in fact, very nervous. The plane was stuttering in flight, dropping, climbing sharply, leaving your stomach above you and below you in a nauseous manner. The only time I had felt that before was when I had taken a ride down in Teruo's plane, one time, long before. He'd painted on heatResist enamel to the belly and underwings of his plane, as was necessary, but he'd done a poor job and it had cracked. On the way down the heat had seeped through, although we didn't realise it at the time, and burnt out some of the electro-magnetic spread of the left wing. So we unloaded, and reloaded, and trundled back down the runway. But when we tried to climb again to the uplands the bite of our field into the earth's magnetosphere, our purchase on the branches of the Gradisil, had not been complete enough and we had gone into a tumble and a spin. We were lucky: we weren't too high; we levelled out, flew back to Teruo's strip, and rewired the wing.

In this gleaming new craft I got the impression that the spread of underpinning was poorly laid out by design.

I tried to explain all this to Natalya Shelikhova, but she was blasé. 'Oh I believe our designers know what they're doing,' she said smugly. 'They're the best in Europe. They know more about magnetic flight than a bunch of – if you'll forget me – rag-tags like your *uplanders*.' When she said *if you'll forget me*, she meant *if you'll forgive me*.

'They do have *experience*,' I began, but she raised both her palms to me.

In the event we got safely to the uplands. I filed a report, actually, warning of the dangers. I said that my feeling was the wings were not properly in-pinned with the necessary spread of electromagnetic con-ductor cable, and that the plane's purchase on the magnetosphere was too tenuous to be safe. I said that loss of the correct altitude in flight resulted in complete loss of power, since the planes only flew up on their electromagnetic friction; and that without that friction planes were liable to tumble disastrously from the sky, to go into spin, that there was a strong chance that any such plane could crash. I have no idea whether my report was ever read by anybody other than my senior officer. I don't believe anything came of it. I tried calling it up, recently, to see if it were still on file; but certain military documentation is subject to a longer-than-fifty-years legal interdiction and I could not gain access to it.

On the Station I was met by my new superior, a tall man called Gar Murphy-McNair. He showed me to my chamber. 'Eventually you'll share,' he told me. 'When we carry our full complement of crew. But at the moment you've got the place to yourself.'

He had to shout, to be heard above the noise of blowing.

The Station had been designed with a simulated gravity. The walkways were metal grids, and the ceilings were fitted with huge expelair fans that blew a constant stream of warm air downwards. The effect was to press you gently against the floor as you moved along – to provide a *floor* and to enable you to *walk* – but it felt nothing at all like actual gravity. At first the sensation was deeply strange: your body felt the push downwards, but your limbs tended to float. The oddest effect of this design was that, should you try to walk naturally, the pressure changed markedly. You might lean forward into a step, and expose a greater angle of your back to the ceiling, and suddenly the pressure would increase suddenly enough to wrongfoot you and send you sprawling on your face. Similarly, if you straightened up the area of your body exposed to the downdraft would decrease and you might find yourself leaping inappropriately through the air. But after half a day you developed a form of habitude that enabled a sort of progress around the Station in a weirdly dancing-zombie style of perambulation.

I never saw the point in this pseudo-gravitational artifice. The main disadvantage of zero g is not that it impedes progress around a house – quite the reverse, in fact. The main disadvantage is that without the natural stress of one g your bones lose calcium and your muscles waste. This blow-air pseudo-gravity did not apply anything like enough pressure to keep your bones strong, and if anything it made moving around the Station more, not less, difficult. But I think it reveals something of the government or the military mindset (as I get older I tend to think of those two things as one and the same). The government-military thinker is happiest if he or she can plan everything on a grid, on a map. They like the idea of the familiar. Rather than design a space station according to the constraints of the uplands, they build it as they are used to building a military base, and then try to orient the natural conditions of the new environment around their design. It is the same as the old rocket technology: forcing the world around the machine, rather than adapting the machine to the world.

So, these fans were tiresome. They were noisy (although Murphy-McNair boasted that they were a new design, the quietest fans ever built), so they made talking and concentrating hard. They consumed a great deal of energy, because they had to be run all hours of the twenty-four. Worse, the constant passage of air dried out your skin, dried out your mouth and nose. If a new arrival came up to the Station incubating a cold, then everybody in the Station caught that cold in a matter of days. Bits of fluff and rubbish were forever swirling through the air; grit and smuts were always getting in my eye, catching on the back of my throat.

Still, there were aspects of the Station that I did like. I liked my spacious chambers. The Station was in a geostationary orbit, so my view was always of the same shield-shaped spread of the Earth, and I spent long and happy hours simply observing it. I became very familiar with its geographical features, with the dozen-or-so varieties of weather-fronts, with the occasional flashes of rockets (rockets were still some-times launched), or with the scratchy lines scored in the atmosphere by approaching spacebirds. I stared at the painterly splotches of white cloud, or the miniature etching effects of landmass geography, or at the way the line of darkness did not mark a clear crescent, but rather a grey scythe-shaped area that varied in depth depending on whether dusk was sweeping over clear air or cloudy sky.

Otherwise I had little to do. I tried to persuade Murphy-McNair that I ought to take one of the docked 'birds and so visit some of the uplanders. He discouraged me. 'You can surely just talk to them, radio them.'

'I could have done that from the ground,' I said. 'What's the point of my being up here if I'm not actually going to go face-to-face?'

He looked evasive. 'There's a problem with that. Our 'birds are all designed with side-fuselage docking tunnels. Your uplanders all have nose-hatches, don't you? I don't think our 'birds can actually dock with any of your upland docking hatches.' He grinned, like a boy who had done something naughty. 'It's a design flaw,' he said. I was going to agree with him, when I realised that he meant that the flaw lay in the uplanders' docking hatches. I scowled. 'Perhaps,' he said, as a parting shot, 'you might talk to them on the phone, persuade some of your uplander contacts to fit more up-to-date docking features?'

fourteen

I kept myself calm by telling myself that this was all only a means to an end. I would serve my term as European ambassador, and then I would make sure I received my private upland house in which to retire. I was thirty-seven. I had no official career plan, no contractual obligation to work a certain amount of time, but I assumed that by the time I was in my mid-forties I would have completed any diplomatic duties the government might have required. Perhaps it seems naïve to you now, but this is what I believed. I thought to myself: at forty-five I would still have half a century of living as a private citizen in the uplands before me. I even countenanced the possibility that the Europeans might want me to come out of retirement from time to time, to liaise between up- and downlanders. That would be alright, I told myself. I saw myself, hazily, as a sort of elder statesman, a grand old woman of the uplands. Settling disputes, chatting to the younger generations. Things like that. Foolish, of course, but my wanting had infected my thinking.

In the event, I was – mostly – bored. The upland hostility to the European base and the incursion into upland territory that the government had anticipated did not materialise. Perhaps the government had simply underestimated the potency of the upland live-let-live philosophy. *Vivre et laisser vivre.* Or perhaps they had overestimated upland bellicosity. In the event the Station was just another house, one among many hundreds now circling the earth. Nobody gave it much thought.

I tried to find work for myself. I pestered Murphy-McNair. 'I feel I'm useless,' I told him. 'A fifth wheel.'

One day he took me on one side. He put his mouth close to my ear so that others could not overhear his words; but he still had to speak up, to be heard over the noise of the fans. 'You don't *get* it,' he said. 'It's obvious you're not used to working for the government. There's no hurry. Fill the time any way you like. Think of it this way; you're waiting until you get your guaranteed government pension. Do you know how impoverished non-government workers are, generally, nowadays, when they retire? The government pays the best pensions, and you don't want to do anything to jeopardise that. Just put in the days, the months, the years, and do what you're told. You're on the gravy-plane now.'

He told me this as if he were imparting the secret of life. Perhaps, from his point of view, he was. In my head I substituted *my own house in the uplands* for his phrase *pension*, and then I started to see wisdom in what he said. But still I pestered him for things to do. I couldn't help myself; I was bored. I spent more time in the Station gym than anybody else.

I persuaded him to have an airlock converter fitted to the Station, so that uplanders could – if they wished – come by. He agreed to this only after my repeated nagging, and then it took three months before the component arrived. It was newly designed, a smart-gel technology that morphed itself into one of a hundred shapes, and that fitted as a prosthesis to any European airlock. I was inordinately excited. As soon as it arrived I called round all my contacts in the uplands and, effectively, invited them to the Station. But they were all reluctant.

'It's nothing personal,' said Sponti. 'But I've learned to become more and more suspicious of governments the longer I have lived up here. I'll have to decline your invitation.'

'No thanks,' said Åsa. 'No thanks. Not even the pleasure of seeing you again could compensate for the peril of walking into the European den. I'm not *well liked*,' he added, mysteriously, 'not *well liked* in Europe.'

The only person who was in any way open to the suggestion was Jon Snider, which surprised me. I had not spoken to him very often since coming up to the Station. There was, I suppose, a residual embarrassment there on my part. But when nobody was prepared to come visit me, I called him. I waited three days until the Moon was in a position of sight-line radio conjunction. I could have bounced the call off a military satellite, but then I would have had to clear the call with my superior first and I didn't want to do that.

'Hi, Jon,' I said as he picked up the phone.

There was a pause. Then he replied, with a dawning warmth in his voice, 'Klara? Klara? Hey, is that you?'

I felt a clutch of affection in my gut for him, this man in whose house I had once lived. 'Hi Jon,' I said. 'How are you? How's things on the Moon?'

'Good,' he said, after reflection. 'Yeah. And you? You're a government woman, now?'

This sounded to me a little like a rebuke. 'Yeah,' I said, apologetic. 'It seemed the only way I could get back up here. The only way I could get back up to the uplands. I don't have the money to build my own house up here, you know.'

'Jesus, Klara,' he said, the faintest popcorn crackles speckling the connection. 'Why didn't you say? You could have come lived with me again. You could come live with me still.'

I surprised myself when he said that, because my eyeballs were prickling a little, as if tears were not far away. I was touched. 'That's kind of you, Jon,' I said. 'Come live on the Moon? What's it like up there?'

'In the day it's good,' he said. 'They last a fortnight, the days, and it gets warm. In the night it's not so good. The equipment doesn't last so well. In the cold, I mean, outside. It tends to break down. We've two tents here, now.'

'Really,' I said. 'Two tents?'

'Sure. We put all our waste there, mix it with the lunar soil. Vegetables grow pretty well, in the day. To think how we used to just chuck our waste out the door in the uplands! That seems such a scandal to me now, such a *waste* of *waste*.' He chuckled at his own joke. 'Waste is too precious to chuck away.'

'But surely you're not self-sufficient there now,' I said.

'No, Jesus, no,' he agreed. 'Not by a long long way. But it's not bad. It's easy taking off from the Moon in a regular plane, and then easy to coast down to the uplands. That's down all the way, you know, down the gravity incline. Hauling stuff up is harder, and landing on the Moon is always a little tricky, killing orbital velocity *just right*, and dropping down *just right*. But Tam has a plan.'

'Tam?'

'Sure. Ever since Bert died – did you know Bert died?'

'No,' I said, feeling sorry.

'Well, he did. He went down, Earth-down I mean, and crashed on his runway. Maybe he had a stroke or something as he flew; maybe his plane just malfunctioned. But he died. Ever since then Tam's been at a loose end without him. You know what he said? You know what he said to me? He said *I thought of killing myself, but I've a better plan now.*'

'What's his plan?'

'He's going to fetch some water. He reckons it'll be easy to find, in amongst asteroids.'

He had to say this last sentence twice, because crackles on the line meant that I didn't quite catch it. When he repeated it I still didn't believe it.

'You're kidding?' I said.

'Hell, no. He's bought up some big sticks, some of the new power sticks. He reckons he could pull over half a g acceleration to Mars, slingshot round, and be in the belt in three months. He says, what else would I do with those three months? Sit on my ass? He might as well sit on his ass in his plane, and get somewhere interesting, as sit on his ass at home and go nowhere. I reckon he's got a point.'

'So what's he going to do?'

'Find something with plenty of water, and then just push it back downhill, down towards the Sun, and bring it to us. With a big chunk of water and lots of clear solar light we could grow plenty, I think, in our tents. The longer we stay, the more of us there are, the more waste we get, the more we can grow. None of it is thrown away.'

'Jon,' I said. 'This sounds pretty bizarre.'

'I know,' said Jon, with glee in his voice. 'Doesn't it, though?'

I invited him to come to the Station. 'So, do you come down to the uplands much?' I asked.

'Sure,' he said.

'Come and visit,' I said. And he said he would.

I thought about Jon's invitation to go live with him. It was tempting, but not realistic. I wondered how it would work out, practically. In my mind I had grown attached to the idea of having my own house, of living in my own space by myself. The older I got, the more I valued my own company. I clung on to that ideal.

I returned to the Earth for Christmas, and spent a distant two weeks with Gradi in Paris. She had enrolled in the University of London on a military scholarship, and was due to begin her studies in the spring. At one point she said to me: 'When you were my age, Ma,' and I put down the book I was reading and looked at her.

'Yes?'

'You were pregnant with me, weren't you?'

'I guess so. More or less.'

She looked at me, hard. 'That must have been awkward.'

'It was alright,' I said.

She went back to the music to which she was listening. The fashion at that time was what they called neo-celibacy. Teenagers spent as much time together as they ever had done, but it was not cool to have sex. Instead one or other of them exerted themselves on elaborate chivalric rituals – it might be the male or the female who undertook these, but they absorbed as much energy as the older courtship rituals had used to, and more. I looked at my daughter in that Paris apartment, and I realised that I had no idea whether she had a sex life or not, whether she had a boyfriend or not. More, I had no idea how to frame the question to ask her that without offending her. I did not feel especially senior to her. Looking back, with my hindsight, I suppose I was feeling out of place in a broader sense. The cultural climate was changing, and the new morality was starting to make itself felt. It was my daughter's generation, and most especially *their* children, that has shaped the cultural idiom in which we all now live. I think I had an intimation of the way things were changing.

In January I flew up again to the uplands, and again I clutched the armrests of my seat as the plane wobbled and jerked through a dangerous upper flight. As soon as I arrived at the Station Gar Murphy-McNair came up to me. 'You'll be pleased to hear this, Gyeroffy,' he said. 'We've some work for you to do. You always complain that you've not enough to do. Well, we've got an important assignment for you.'

We went through to his office, and he strapped himself into a chair. I found the corner of his room with the least downdraft, where I felt most comfortable.

'What do you want me to do?' I asked.

'You'll be working with a contact of ours, an uplander.'

'Oh?' I said. 'Who's that?'

'Woman called Norma Fryer.'

'I've never heard of her.'

'She's not as well-connected as you, though she's a longstanding uplander. But she's been living up here for *quite* a while. She's coming to the Station tomorrow. You and she, you'll form a team. For our purposes,' and by this he meant the purposes of command, 'you'll be senior, but I don't want you bossing her around.'

'And what will we be doing?'

'Listen to me, Klara,' he said. 'I'm serious about this. We have certain public relations victories to win, do you see? Polls say there's still a widespread hostility to the uplanders in Europe. I'm not giving away any state secrets when I say that the *hot peace* may soon get a little *hotter*, do you see? That there may soon be a development with regard to the Americans. When that happens, the uplands will be an important arena. We need to show our people that we're in control of the land up here.'

'But we're not in control of the land up here,' I said, mildly. It was a simple statement of fact.

He overreacted to this. 'I'm not standing for your insolence, Gyeroffy,' he bawled. 'You're under my direct orders, and I'll put you on a charge soon as snap my fingers. You'll fall in behind me and do as you're told.'

'OK,' I said. 'I didn't mean to be insolent. I was only saying . . .'

'*This* is the way it'll go,' he said, still yelling, and clicking his fingers in front of my face. 'There are a lot of uplanders now. The population is well over three thousand, and most of them still feel more of an attachment to the ground than the sky. But the old guard, the people you know, carry a great deal of weight in the – for want of a better word, the community. They're respected. They're the pioneers. If we make a gesture with them, it resonates far and deep. Do you see?'

'Not really,' I said.

'There have always been two sorts of uplander,' he said. 'There have been wealthy eccentrics who just like living up here. And there have been people who came here to get away from the law downbelow. OK? Millionaires and criminals. But *money* has changed, OK? Since the war, old-fashioned chips have been largely replaced by these new bearer-chips. We don't like this development – by *we* I mean the authorities. The old bank-tied chips were easy to keep tabs on, and very hard to steal. Or, more exactly, they were very hard to use once stolen. But these newer chips are negotiable. They're like cash, you see? But people won't trust bank-chips since the war, since those insurgent attacks collapsed half the banks in the world. So now there's a great fortune floating around in bearer-chips.'

'I don't see . . .' I started saying, but he cut me off.

'There have been a number of large-scale robberies. People in the uplands have been handling the stolen chips. In effect, laundering them. Some of your old-timers think they're beyond the law, think they've nothing to lose. Criminal gangs send the chips up here, and they're kept out of circulation, or re-entered someplace else, or else traded against other commodities. It's a scandal. It is illegal.'

'You want it stopped ?'

'Ms Fryer, who you'll meet tomorrow, is what you might call *grey* uplander. She's not white like you.' There was a hint of sarcasm in his voice as he said this. 'But she's not black, like some of them. You and she will sting a number of old-timers, arrest them, and we'll have a big PR celebration. We'll splash it all over the Euro media. We'll win hearts and minds downbelow. Cleaning out the upland Augean stables.'

'The *what*?' I asked.

'Don't you know any mythology at all?' he snapped at me. 'I thought you were Greek?'

I took a deep breath. 'If you think I'm going to betray any of my friends . . .'

'Don't get all high and mighty,' he said, waving his hand and making a sour moue with his mouth. 'Please, please. You won't have to betray any of your friends. There's a list of people, you can vet it in advance. We only need, say, three high-profile cases, enough to convince our people that we're bringing law and order to the uplands, clearing out the outlaws. So that it'll look, in the media, as if we're taking the uplands under our wing, building a land fit for Europeans to live in. You might have a word with your friends, of course,' he added, 'let them know that things are changing. That it'll benefit everybody to live under the rule of law. That's true, after all. Don't you think?'

'Under the rule of European law,' I said.

'Of course.'

There was a silence. The white noise of the fans seemed louder in my ears. I said: 'Show me this list.'

He handed me a piece of paper that flapped and wriggled in my hands as I took it. On it were a dozen names. I recognised four of them. At the top of the list was Åsa Olsen. This was a shock. I remembered him saying to me on the phone 'I'm not *well liked* in Europe', and now I understood his reluctance to pay me a visit. But I had always thought of him as a man of bottomless wealth. It had not occurred to me that he might have been driven to money-laundering as a means of financing his life in space.

'You only need three?' I said.

'Three or four. Provided they're high-profile enough.'

'Åsa Olsen is a friend of mine,' I said. 'I'll not betray him.'

'Then pick four other names,' Murphy-McNair said.

I chose four unfamiliar names, and went to my chamber. I was sharing it now with the West-Russian aide, Natalya Shelikhova, but she was asleep, so I lay down in the dark on the mattress-grid under the blowing pressure and thought for a long while. It seemed to me that my dream of reacquiring a house in the uplands was becoming morally compromised. Then I scolded myself: surely you didn't think that they would just *give* you a house, did you? You'll have to earn it. And, I told myself, there is some justice in what Murphy-McNair had said. It was better to live under the rule of law than to live in an outlaw community. Eventually, I told myself, the uplands would have to grow, to take on for themselves the trappings of civilisation. It was inevitable.

In this way I reconciled myself to my new work. I persuaded myself that I was not *only* being selfish – that there were good reasons for my actions apart from my own selfish reasons. I persuaded myself that I was helping the land I loved become a better place.

In the morning I washed and put on my uniform, ready to meet this grey uplander, Norma Fryer, with whom I would have to work. I waited by the hangar as her plane nudged into a lock. Murphy-McNair and Natalya Shelikhova were with me. The docking seemed to take ages. Finally the gate opened and Fryer pulled herself through.

Stupidly, perhaps, I did not recognise her at once. She had lost weight, although she was still enormous; but her skin was saggy now and curled itself in patterns of cellulite and pock-marking that seemed, under the dual forces of downward-blowing air and ambient zero g, to move and flow with an oily fluidity. Her hair was as massy and tangled as ever. She stood, unsteadily, under the fan blast. As her eyes fell on me she beamed a great smile, and her two great dolphin-like rows of teeth became all visible.

'Klara,' she said. 'How delightful to see you again.'

I was dumb. I said nothing. I didn't launch myself at her, I didn't scream, I didn't try and throttle her. I simply stood, unsteadily, as Natalya Shelikhova advanced and shook her hand. It felt as if I were still dreaming. Is it a cliché, to say so? But that was exactly how it felt – actually as if the timbre of reality had, somehow, slipped out of focus. I could still hear the susurrus of the fans above me, but now they seemed almost to be speaking to me, hushing me, telling me to hush, to hush, to hush. Murphy-McNair was saying something, his mouth moving, and I clicked my eyes from her face to his.

'May I introduce,' he was saying, 'Norma Fryer.'

'I've met Ms Gyeroffy before,' she was saying.

'Kristin,' I said, my mouth dry. But my mouth was often dry in that place. 'How do you come to be here?'

'Oh,' she said, turning her great bulk about and about. 'I flew here. As, I suppose, did you.'

fifteen

At no point during that first meeting was I alone with Kristin Janzen Kooistra. There was an official briefing chaired by Murphy-McNair and attended by half a dozen others. Then there was a period when I was alone. Then there was a second meeting. Finally Kooistra retired to her guest chamber. By this time my mind had returned to me, at least in part. I was fizzing.

As soon as I could, I demanded to see Murphy-McNair alone.

'What is it now?' he said, grumpy. 'You're a very awkward woman, Klara. Why can't you just accept what we've agreed? A week's work and it'll be done.'

'That woman,' I said. 'That Norma Fryer, as she is calling herself. That's not her real name.'

'Yes,' he said. 'We know.'

'Her real name is Kristin Janzen Kooistra,' I said.

'We know.'

'You know? How can you know? She's a killer. She's the most wanted killer in the world.'

'No,' he said, blankly.

'What do you mean *no*?'

'She has got a criminal record, yes, that's true. But if you check the web, the world's most wanted killer this week is Yakov Znamenski. Fryer's name doesn't appear even in the top twenty most wanted.'

I was silenced by this. My mind was burning. 'Are you crazy? Don't you *know* what this woman has done?'

'She hasn't killed anyone in years,' he said. 'We don't have her down as suspect for any European killings at the moment.'

'I can't believe that you're so blithe about this,' I said. My voice was high pitched. 'I can't believe that. Is she working for you for a pardon? Is that it?'

'Not at all,' he said. 'If you listen, you'd hear me. She doesn't require a pardon from us. She's not wanted for any crimes by the European police at this moment in time. She's working for us for money. What else?'

'She killed my father,' I said.

He looked at me. Then he said, 'Really?' It was as if I'd just told him *my favourite colour is blue* or *the canteen overcooked the eggs this morning.*

'Is that what you say? You say *really*?'

He blinked. 'What else do you want me to say?'

'I want you to say that you'll arrest this woman and prosecute her for the murder of my father.'

'Well now,' he said, folding his hands together. 'I don't see how we could do that. When do you allege she committed this crime?'

'I say she committed it in '58,' I said.

'That's a while ago,' he said.

'It's under the statute of limitations for murder,' I said.

'Well. Did you report this crime to the police at the time?'

My face went into a sort of spasm. My eyes closed and my mouth fell open. I couldn't believe I was having this conversation. 'Of course I did,' I said. 'Of course I did.'

'Then I'm surprised your complaint doesn't appear on our police records.'

'It wasn't the European police who dealt with it,' I said. 'I reported it in Canada.'

'Oh,' he said. Then he made a sort of *'hhh'* noise, an exhalation. 'That explains that.'

'You can call up the Canadian records,' I said.

'I very much doubt it. Really. Relations between America and Europe are in a dip at the moment. There's about to be a war, you know?' – spoken as if to a child.

'Are you crazy?' I said. 'Are you insane? For something like this an exception would be made. I'm not asking for state secrets. It's a humanitarian, a criminological requirement. Ask them, they'll send the evidence file over to you.'

He looked at me for a long time. 'Do you know what?' he said. 'I don't doubt it. Ms Fryer is *a significant asset* to the European agency. A significant asset.'

It took me a moment to take this on board.

'What on earth do you mean?' I said.

'What do I mean? I mean she's an asset to us, I mean she's a thorn in the side of the Americans. I don't doubt they'd be happy to concoct some file or other to get her into trouble. I don't doubt they'd be very happy for us to lose her – ah – special skills. Her contacts. She's a major player, Klara. She's a big cheese. Do you know what? It's *very good of her* to help us with this current project. Rounding up a few delinquent uplanders, that's small beer to her. She's doing it for a very small fee, relatively speaking. We're *very grateful to her.*'

My ears appeared to be ringing. My face felt hot. 'I can't believe I'm hearing this,' I said.

'Believe it,' he said. For a moment his face creased with an expression almost of humanity. 'Look, Klara,' he said. 'Perhaps this isn't easy for you.'

'Isn't easy for me,' I repeated.

'Will you listen to me for a moment? Will you take my advice?'

'Advice.'

'Let it go, alright? Do this thing I'm asking you to do. Let it go. In a week she'll be out of the way again, you needn't bump into her any more, you can forget about her.'

I considered this sentence. 'Forget about her,' I said.

'That's right. My advice is, to consider your options very carefully. You can't touch her. You can't even embarrass her. There won't be criminal proceedings against her. *Will not be* – do you understand? Not unless the Americans invade the uplands and arrest her, and we're here to make sure *that* doesn't happen. That's why we're here after all. She's helping us make sure *that* doesn't happen, and she's doing a tremend- ous job. She's an immovable object as far as you're concerned, alright? So your options are clear. You can do what you're employed to do. You can let her go, and then – eventually – you'll get your own place up here. Then you'll be a private citizen. Then you can do what you want. Come that day, I will no longer care. Or—'

'Or?'

'Or you can make a fuss. But you won't be able to get to her. What would you do, try and punch her out? She'd break your neck like a cigarette. Or what? Listen to me, Klara. If you so much as embarrass her, if you so much as *incommode* her, you will be sent back down to the Earth. You will be dishonourably discharged. You'll go to prison. You'll live the rest of your life afterwards in poverty on Earth, and you'll never see the uplands again. Do you understand?'

I was stunned.

'I'm trying to make it easy for you,' he said. 'If you cause any harm to our agent, you will be prosecuted. You wouldn't like it in prison, believe me. The choice is a simple one. Roll with it, and you'll get what you want, eventually. Resist, and you'll lose everything. Which is it to be, Klara? Roll with it, or resist?'

'That doesn't sound like a choice at all,' I said.

'I'm glad you see it that way,' he said. He was smiling.

I spent the rest of that day in a sort of daze. I slept, for about twenty minutes. When I woke the whole encounter had the friable, out-of-focus feeling of a dream; but, limping awkwardly down the main corridor there was Kristin Janzen Kooistra, taking cautious little steps underneath the constant downward gale, testing her new artificial 'weight', coming along the corridor towards me. I turned and fled. I couldn't bear it.

It was the reality of it that was unbearable. The reality of it. I was jammed, now, and there was no way out of the choice that Murphy-McNair had placed so lumpenly before me. I tried to think it through, like a chess game. Make this move, that move will follow. Make the move after that, and find yourself in the place you wanted to be. I told myself, a private citizen again, my own house in the uplands – not dependent on anybody else, not living on anybody's sufferance, but my own person.

And then what?

This was what was most disorienting of all. I tried to be honest with myself. I sat eating government food in the poky little Station galley under the constant downward gale, and I tried to think the possibilities of the future through. If I became a private upland citizen, then what? Would I devote my retirement to trying to kill Kooistra? One voice in my head said yes! yes!, but it was a high-pitched and juvenile voice. Other voices in my mind had greater weight. *No* is a weighty word. No, I wouldn't. Of course I wouldn't. Human beings don't devote their lives to killing other human beings unless there is something wrong in their heads, some fused circuit in their skull. I had lived many years in the uplands, and they had been my life's happiest years – and all through those years I had cohabited with Kooistra, in the sense that I had shared the uplands with her. Once I had knocked her communication satellite dish off her house in a fit of anger, but that was all that I had done. Had I spent every day consumed with the appetite for revenge? – of course I had not. I had been too busy, most days, to think of anything other than what my hand fell to, what jobs needed doing, my three-hour stint in the gym. This was the choice, then: to plan to live my life for me, or to plan to surrender my life to this abstract 'revenge', to the hope of killing another.

It was hard. I'm not trying to suggest it was easy. Kooistra left the Station for two weeks, and went about her own business. Murphy-McNair arranged for her to return at a certain date, and thereafter for she and I to fly out together to round up some sacrificial victims to the new idol of European Law and Order. Murphy-McNair seemed pleased with my restraint at the final meeting, but the truth of it was that I was not restrained, I was stunned. I even shook Kooistra's hand.

Jon came to visit four days after that. He had returned to the uplands to pick up some supplies, before returning to his Moon house, and he phoned me from orbit. I cleared it with the Station, and he nosed his streaked, grubby plane into the docking attachment that I had fought to have installed.

I was excited at the prospect of seeing him, in fact. It had been years since I had seen any of my old friends. But when the lock opened and he pulled himself through, looking startled at the great wash of air pushing him down from above, I was struck by how *old* he looked. He had always been much older than I, of course; but now he was a broken-down and aged man, a great-grandfather rather than a fatherly figure. The lines on his face were deeper, his limbs were stick thin, his back seemed curiously bowed: not weighed down by gravity, obviously, but something the reverse, buoyed up and out of human shape into a simian curve. The last of his hair had gone, and splattery liverspots were all over the crown of his head. A series of unpleasant-looking red moles with black bases spotted his neck and the side of his face. But when he looked at me, and smiled, I saw something of the man I had once had a relationship with, and I hugged him.

'What's that breeze?' he asked, looking up over my shoulder.

'The artificial gravity,' I said. 'You like?'

He pondered it for a little while, and rubbed a smut out of the orbit of his eye. 'No,' he said, eventually. 'What's the point of it?'

'The point of it,' I said, taking his arm, 'is that we can walk together down this corridor, even in zero g.'

We walked. 'It's an odd sensation,' he said.

He stank: a coarse, chemical smell, and a mist of dust, like grey pollen, was being blown from his clothes, from his skin. I tried to identify his stink, and placed it eventually as gunpowder. 'Jon,' I said. 'You smell of gunpowder. Have you been building fireworks?'

'No,' he said. 'That's the moondust, that's the way it smells. It gets everywhere in the house. I don't even notice it any more.'

I showed him round the inside of the Station, and he was suitably impressed by the grandeur of the scale, and the gorgeousness of the design. 'But what's it all for?' he asked me. I wanted to say, *to annex the uplands for Europe*, but of course such honesty would not sit comfortably with my new role as diplomat, so I said 'Who knows? Big governments like big projects.'

He harrumphed softly.

I took him to my chamber, and we drank some whisky that he had brought with him. For a half an hour we chatted. I wanted him to tell me about Tam's trip round Mars to the asteroids. 'A guy called Crisp says he's been to Mars already,' said Jon. 'Opinion is divided.'

This was news to me. 'You're kidding?'

'He's a relative newcomer, this Crisp. Walter Crisp is his name. He says he flew out on one-tenth g acceleration the whole way, made it to Mars and back in four weeks. *William* Crisp. No, Walter. No, William. I can't remember.'

'Four weeks?' I boggled.

'The conjunction is right, and if he really did pull one-tenth the whole way then the time factor wouldn't surprise me. He took some pictures of Mars from his window as he circled it, and they're very pretty, but I guess it would be child's play to mock those up with the right computer software. There's no other proof, nobody tracked him. But it could be true. One tenth gee the whole way would be some achievement, but these new motor sticks are extremely efficient, and he claims he had a great stack of them, and his plane is only small.'

'He went in his *plane*?'

'Yeah, not very comfortable, must have been cramped. Me, I wouldn't go except in my house. You need that extra bit of leg room.'

'Does that mean you're thinking of going?'

He twinkled at me, but didn't say anything.

The conversation moved round, inevitably, to the one topic that was most on my mind. 'I saw Kooistra again,' I said.

Jon didn't say anything, but he dropped his head a little. He looked even more tired. 'Where?'

'Why, right here. Right here. Can you believe it? Jesus. She walked down that corridor that you've just walked down.' I explained the circumstance. 'Jon,' I said, 'I've a very important question to ask you. Do you remember a party that Sponti held, years ago? He was guilty because it was through him that Kooistra came to stay in my dad's house, and he prodded me into a vow of revenge.'

'I remember.'

'Well,' I said. 'Now I've met up with her again.'

He nodded slowly. Eventually he said, 'And?'

'Tell me,' I said. 'What should I do?'

He pondered my question for a while, as he always did with my questions, no matter how goofball. 'You mean,' he said, eventually, 'with respect to this question of revenge? Hmm. Hmm.'

'If I attack her at all, or even try to get at her, they'll send me downbelow. I'll never see the uplands again.'

'That's hard,' said Jon.

'But can I *not?*'

'Can you not?' he repeated. 'I see.' He sat in silence for a long time. 'It may be,' he said, meekly, 'that you're asking the wrong guy, Klara. I have nothing good to say about revenge. You remember?'

He was referring to the time he tried to kill me, and to kill Teruo. I squeezed his hand. 'It's OK,' I said. 'That's OK. That's different, that's alright.'

But he was agitated now, and I was worried that a great flow of apologies was going to come tumbling from his lips. 'No, no, it's *not* alright, it's not OK. I was out of my head, sure, but is that a defence? I don't think so. I didn't do you any harm, OK, but I *might've.* That's where revenge got *me.* Sitting in my house all alone, just thinking of you, thinking of you all the time, running my imagination over the memory of your body, turning it over and over. It wasn't good. It wasn't healthy. You're talking revenge. Shouldn't you vow revenge on me?'

'That's just stupid,' I said.

'Is it?' he wanted to know. 'Is it? Why is that stupid? If you can forgive me, you've the strength to forgive her. Haven't you?'

That clarified it for me. It struck me, with a sense of belated revelation, that this was the issue. Could I bring myself *to forgive?* Did I have the emotional competence to achieve such a mighty thing, to forgive the murderer of my father? I remembered when I had been a child back in Cyprus, and my grandmamma had sent me to one of the old psychiatrists. I remembered that for that shaman Kooistra had been my mother in some strange way. I hadn't believed it then, and I still didn't really believe it, but it made me think. My mother died, but I vowed no vow of revenge on her account. Why was it so easy to forgive the fate that killed her? Why was it, accordingly, so hard to forgive the fate that killed my father?

'I forgive you,' I mumbled, not sure what I was saying. Then I focused my gaze, saw Jon's puzzled face. 'That goes without saying, Jon,' I added, to give the impression that I had been talking to him. 'Of course I do.'

'Well,' he said, pulling away from me a little petulantly. 'Maybe you shouldn't do,' he said. 'Forgive me, I mean.'

'Is it as clean as that, though?' I said, suddenly pulling myself together. 'Is it actually forgiveness? – civilisation – all that? Or am I just selfishly pursuing a house for myself in the uplands, am I masking my egotism and self-interest under fancy terms?'

But Jon had lost interest in the conversation. He wasn't looking at me. I noticed, with a start, that there were tears in his eyes. 'I shouldn't have come, Klara,' he croaked. 'It was stupid of me to come.'

'Jon! What's the matter?'

For a moment his bleared old eyes caught mine, and then he pulled his gaze away again. 'You don't even see it,' he said.

'See what?' I said. And, genuinely, I didn't understand.

'There's a cruelty in your soul,' he cried, and put his hands over his face. 'Can you really not see? I guess I shouldn't be surprised; you were like this before, you're like it now.'

Perhaps I had some shadowy intuition of what he was saying, but I shied away from it and adopted a matter-of-fact tone. 'I'm starting to think you're going a little ga-ga, Jon. What is the matter? What won't you tell me?'

He made a little percussive grunt in his throat, and then pushed with his legs, bouncing high in the windy air of the chamber, dropping down near the door. With his back to me he said, 'When you were younger, when I used to say, sometimes, that I loved you, you always got this *blank* look on your face, like I was speaking a foreign language. No, no, that's not it. It was the look of a kid who hears the adults talking, hears them using a certain word, and doesn't really know what the word means, but doesn't want to admit that they are ignorant, doesn't want to give the impression that something has gone over their head. That's what it was like.'

'Jon,' I said.

'But because *you didn't know* what that term meant didn't mean that it wasn't real.' He was facing me now. 'It *was* real. I really felt that way. It's not easy for me to say so, it's not in my nature to go on, to open myself, but I did with you and you always mirrored back this blankness, as if my love for you were an empty term. And it wasn't. It wasn't. OK?'

'OK,' I said. 'I'm sorry, Jon, but—'

'You know how I could tell it was real?' he said. It was so unusual for him to interrupt me, to chop across my sentences with his own like this. I can't tell you. It was very much out of character. 'You know how I could tell it was real? How I knew it was something more than just a crush, more than just the sex? Because of how it hurt. Because of the

120

hurt of it, the way it stopped me thinking about anything else, because I could only have you in my head, like a migraine. The not sleeping was real, and hurting was real, and love for you was real.'

He stopped, embarrassed at his own outburst.

'I don't see,' I said, speaking slowly and trying to put sincerity into the words, 'what there is about me that is so loveable.'

He thought about this for a while. That was more like the old Jon. Finally he said, in a low voice, 'Neither do I. Neither do I. But what can you do? I was in love with you then, and I'm in love with you now, and there's no chance that anything can happen between us and that is painful to me. And you don't even see it, and that makes the pain worse. You can look right at me, and not even see it. There's a dead part in your heart, you lack something.' He was speaking in a calmer voice, but his face was flushed, sunset-coloured blotches on his cheeks and forehead. 'You left your kid on the Earth and hurried up here. Your mind is caught in the orbit of itself, round and round itself. I don't know. You break my heart. You have always broken my heart. I gotta go. I gotta go.'

He fumbled with the door, and loped out of the chamber down the blowy corridor. I limped quickly after him. Better used to the artificial gravity I caught up with him quickly despite my malformed foot.

'Jon,' I said. 'Wait. Look, I'm sorry. I've been insensitive, I can see that.'

But he would only say, 'I gotta go,' and he clambered back inside his plane and sat in the cockpit. Then there was a bathetic coda to our meeting, because he couldn't fly his plane away until the gel-clamp was released, and I couldn't do this without the watch officer's permission, and the watch officer was, would you believe it, in the toilet. So I hung around for ten minutes, and Jon sat stiffly in his cockpit looking straight ahead at nothing, for all that time. Finally he was released, and I told him he could go, so he puffed his plane back and then juddered a brief burst and pulled away into a lower, faster orbit. That was the last I saw of him.

The meeting did upset me, but – if I am honest – only a little. I pondered what he said. Not to sound banal, but there seemed to be so many points of connection between human beings over the course of a life that involved hurting them. Had I really broken his heart? Say I had. He had tried to kill me, but I found that easy to forgive. I had broken his heart, and he couldn't forgive me that. Which was the greater crime? My thoughts went round and round, all the time circling the empty centre. I did think about Jon a great deal. Truly, I did. It bothered me. It buzzed at me mosquito-like. Of course, if I'm being honest – *since* I'm being honest – I'd have to say that I only thought about this question of Jon and me as a way of avoiding thinking about Kristin Janzen Kooistra. I knew that even then, even as I was doing it.

sixteen

Down below us, on the ground, there was an incident. The Eastern Siberian government declared itself in alliance with Asian Siberia, which is to say in effect with America-Japan. At a single diplomatic stroke the American border had moved, effectively, from Khabarovsk to Irkutsk. The European media went into a frenzy of outrage. What next? Would America extend itself as far west as the Urals? Eastern Europe would be next, and then – shadowy, unspecified, but newsmonger hints of rape, pillage and disaster. The political situation seemed so much more intransigent than it had done in my own youth. Troops were rushed from Atlantic defence to the middle of the Asian continent. Shots were exchanged in the Sayan mountains. It looked as though full-blown war was on the very edge of breaking out; but then, tensely, nothing happened. For a month nothing happened. The month grew into three, and the prospect of immediate war began to seem less real. The media called it the Autumn Tension, because it was autumn in the northern hemisphere. But we had no sense of the passing seasons in the constantly blowy, continually monotonous existence on the Station.

For those three months the routine on the Station changed. More people flew up, and the corridors were crowded. I found myself sharing my chamber with three people in addition to Natalya Shelikhova. I don't know what all these people were for, or why the government thought to pack the Station with armed men and women. Perhaps they anticipated a gun battle in space – an absurd notion, of course. But there they all were. Murphy-McNair called reveille, drilled us in safety procedures, prepared everything for crisis. The crisis did not come. Or, to be more precise, an unexpected crisis came. This was it: one of the spacebirds, ferrying up some supplies and three medical orderlies, fell out of the sky shortly after entering magnetohydrodynamic flight. It crashed into the bronze-coloured forests of the northern Norwegian coastline. The pilots died, and although three passengers successfully ejected, the wind blew them out to land in the sea and, in a grimly absurd twist, only one of them survived the cold. They were still dressed in summer uniforms despite the fact that it was late autumn.

I tried to tell Murphy-McNair that I had filed a report of the dangers of the spacebird design many months before. Perhaps I did this insensitively, for he bawled at me, yelled that nobody liked an I-told-you-so queen, and suchlike phrases. I gave up. I felt removed from it all, anyway. I felt less and less like a European, more and more like an uplander. Only the prospect of my own house in the uplands buoyed me up. I could not identify, for instance, with the atmosphere of heightened media hysteria that followed the crash. Downbelow news agencies and press went on and on about it: it was exaggerated to the point of multinational disaster. The political tensions threw the spotlight on the military, accusations flew that the military were not even able to fly a plane straight. All spacebirds were grounded over a forty-eight-hour total overhaul, and after that the military flew three up to the Station as soon as they could, in quick succession, to demonstrate their confidence in the technology. But everybody was edgy.

'We need good PR now,' Murphy-McNair told me. 'Above all now. I'll called in Norma Fryer. You and she will go out and round up some sacrificial victims. I want the media tomorrow celebrating our firm hand up here. I want some good news in the news.'

I saluted. I told myself that this was my moment of testing. I would endure my time with Kooistra, and thereby earn my reward. I told myself that soon it would all be behind me. I would be the better person for forgiving her. I was not sure what form my forgiveness would take, but long afterwards, when I settled into my own house, I would be able to look back and think I did the right thing.

Rectitude is a form of gravity, I think. The humanitarian duty to act properly, to do the right thing, is a sort of immanent pull on every person. It can of course be overcome, by criminals and psychopaths, but only with great effort. It's simply easier to do the right thing, just as it's easier to fall from the sky than it is to climb up into orbit. Or so I thought.

seventeen

My tale comes to its moment of forgiveness. Kooistra came on board, and greeted me with her usual, cloying warmth. I smiled at her, and she smiled back. We consulted with Murphy-McNair, and as the world moved round and around the pivot of my head I found myself, only three-quarters-awake, climbing into a EU spacebird with Kooistra behind me.

'Well,' she said, settling her saggy body into one of the cockpit seats beside me. 'Here we are, my dear. Shall we?'

She took the controls, edged away from the Station and accelerated fuel-inefficiently into a fast high orbit. I watched the Station shrink to a star standing on a tangent from the great swell of the Earth. Some voice in my head told me, *here you are, sitting next to Kristin Janzen Kooistra.* It was a disorienting thought. I recalled all the hatred I had known in my life towards her. I thought of all the hurt she had caused me, but it seemed a long way away. I thought of what it would achieve to kill her, and it didn't seem to me that anything would result. My father would still be dead, as he had been dead for these many years. More, I didn't see that I would derive any satisfaction from killing Kooistra. I tried to throw my imagination forward in time, but all I could picture was a worn-out feeling of emptiness. And yet! Here she was, sitting right next to me!

'Oh,' she said, brightly, and turning to face me. 'You do look rapt in thought, my dear.'

'Yes,' I said.

'What's on your mind?'

Without premeditation I said, 'Revenge.'

At this she laughed, a chirpy little arpeggio laugh. 'I have *always*,' she said, 'found room in my large heart to admire consistency. You are wonderful, my dear. You continue to impress me.' Why did she say *large heart*? Or did she only mean that she had a large heart because every part of her body was so big?

'Haven't you ever,' I said, with a sharp sense of the surreality of the conversation we were having, 'felt the impulse for revenge?'

'Oh,' she said, checking the transponder signal. 'No, of course I haven't. Or if I have, I have overcome the impulse. Revenge enslaves. Don't you think? And of course the effort of life must be *not to be a slave*. Don't you think?'

I tried to think about this concept, but it seemed to slip from my mind. I kept trying to pick at it with the fingers, as it were, of my thoughts, but it kept slipping and falling out of my apprehension, like an oiled pebble. 'I don't think I understand,' I said.

'There we go,' she said, and we lurched downward towards the Earth, picking up speed and hurtling towards the dark side. A star twinkled, swelled to the size of a pebble of quartz in the sunshine, and abruptly – with, I must admit, a skilful series of manoeuvring jerks on the jets by Kooistra – we were hanging before a patched and glinting house. Before us the line of morning divided the Earth dark from light, the land creeping inexorably from shadow into light, always, always. The land-mass down there was glinting as myriad mountain-tops caught the new light and refracted it away white, yellow and pink. Honey-coloured plains, moss-green forests, little maggot-shaped lakes of polished brass, puffs and puffs of cloud like patchy snowfall, all inched continually into the light. Nothing stopped that progress. Nothing stops that progress. Nothing will stop that progress.

Kooistra called the house on the mayday. A man answered, his voice crackly with fear even though the connection was clear. 'Who's that? Who's that?'

'You know who it is, my dear,' said Kooistra.

'Norma?' said the man. 'Is that you? Not today, OK? Come next week. I got a run-down to make, tomorrow or the day after. If you come . . .' He trailed off.

There was a pause.

'Let us in,' said Kooistra, smilingly.

'What's that you're flying?' he said. I imagined him peering through his window. The sunlight had frozen it white from our point of view, but he must have had a good view of the sweeping curves of the silver spacebird.

'Oh, it's *government* business, my dear,' she said. 'You must let us in. Don't make me huff, and puff, and blow – this 'bird carries four different sorts of offensive weaponry, you know.'

He let us in. He clearly had no doubt in his head that Kooistra would be happy to experiment with the destructive capacity of the plane upon his house. His name, Robert Yuille, was not on our list, but as we inched the 'bird towards the house Kooistra turned to me and said, 'Oh, a bad man, have no fear. A deserving case for the police. A deserving case.'

We had fitted a smartgel docking converter to the hatch on the 'bird, and – apart from the fact that it was more difficult to sidle the plane up to the port than it was simply to fly the nose straight in – the connection was smooth. We opened our door, and Kooistra called through for Yuille to crawl in. He obeyed as meekly as a puppy: a froggish, unshaven man with sallow skin, yellow cheeks marked all over with irregular black patches of stubble, like banana-skin on the turn. He was wearing a T-shirt and shorts, an outfit that displayed how fat was his belly and how very thin his legs and arms. He seemed genuinely afraid of Kooistra, who smiled at him, and smiled at me, and smiled at the walls. She positively beamed as she turned her head. Her smiles went everywhere. I watched as she bound his hands with plastic cuffstrip, and strapped him into one of the cargo seats of the 'bird. 'You stay there, my dear man,' she said. I watched him flinch every time she came close to him. What I was thinking was: how strange that he is so afraid of her, and that I'm not. Perhaps surrendering the impulse to revenge means surrendering the reasons to fear?

Is this what my life story amounts to? A giving up of the impulse to revenge? A tale of giving something away, a gift, a donation. To give, to for-give: is fore-giving a pre-emptive sort of gift? I really haven't thought about this stuff for such a long time, and these observations only just now occur to me, now that I am old. I don't know.

There is a difficult with giving, as I'm sure you can agree. If somebody gives you something it obligates you to them. If you give them some-thing, then they are obligated to you. No matter how freely and bountifully you intend the gift, the recipient becomes in a small way enslaved to you. Is there a gift that breaks this bondage of obligation? Kooistra's gift to me had been the death of my father; how could I repay such a gift? Or could I short-circuit the connection that bound us together, her to me, me to her?

What would my father want?

If I try to recall my father's face I can picture it easily; but if I think more carefully about it I realise that what I am recalling is – always – a photo of my father that I possess. If I try to recall some natural memory, some image, I cannot do it. This, I believe, is simply how memory works. Try it yourself. Try now.

You see?

Kooistra floated through into this man Robert Yuille's house, and returned after only five minutes, carrying a pillow-case full of stuff. 'Evidence, you see,' she said. 'This will please the government people.'

'Good,' I said.

It was all very odd. It felt almost dreamlike.

We took our cockpit seats again, and disconnected from the house, dropping into a low orbit and sweeping round through the dark for ten minutes. The cabin lights switched on. The black Earth below us was dusted with lights: street lamps, lit house-windows, cars, all the paraphernalia of human night-time activity. Those lights have a distinct orange shade to them, and they form strange random swirls, patches, spirals. The Earth-constellations are interrupted again by the blank spaces of clouds moving across them, black soap-flakes and rags.

Our passenger, or prisoner, spoke only once. He said: 'Norma, where are we going, where are we going Norma?'

'You be quiet now,' Kooistra called back. Then she spoke to me: 'You continue to impress me, my dear. Impress me very favourably. I'll confess I used to wonder if you were ever going to become *competent* enough to handle your feelings of anger.'

'Handle them,' I said.

'Oh,' she said, sweetly, 'there's a talent there, don't underestimate yourself. There's a talent in recognising the force of necessity. Necessity is a *terribly* important feature of our lives in this cosmos.'

'How do you mean,' I asked, interested despite my disgust, 'necessity?'

'Well, look at you, look at me. If you tried to assault me I would easily overcome you. Am I not more powerful than you? Am I not more skilled in combat?'

This was too close to my own thoughts for comfort. 'What makes you think,' I jittered, 'that I want to—'

She chuckled, and it sent zero-g shudders through her fleshy chin like waves in treacle. 'A lesser woman would hurl herself at the blank wall, crack her head against it like an egg. But you sense the pointlessness of that. We get on well together, you and I,' she said, and favoured me with another smile.

Then she said: 'Would you like to see my house?'

'*My* house,' I said.

'A house is only a thing,' she insisted, putting up her right index finger in front of her rather pedantically. 'Things pass from person to person. But, yes, it was once yours. Is now mine. Would you like to see it?' She fixed a new transponder signal, pulled the jet up, slowing it

128

down. 'I need to make a stop before we return to your government's facility.'

'Very well,' I said.

I was curious. Or, perhaps, curious does not properly express the feeling I had. I was drawn to that house, the primal scene, the house in which my father and I had lived. To be able to say I have come back. My stomach seemed to be pulsing, expanding and contracting with light. It was sparkly, and buoyant, I kept dabbing at the corners of my eyes with the coarse cloth of my sleeves. We came through the line of shadow into the light again. The blue-white sun was, suddenly, there in the sky, bursting continually with its great light. Kooistra sat beside me, her arms hovering at her sides the way limbs settle in zero g, and the light pushing through the cockpit and enveloping her, washing all around her, giving her great bulky body a luminously spectral edge. We jerked in our seats, shoved forward by deceleration, shoved again.

'Here,' she said, and I realised we were at her house.

We were at her house.

I should say *at the house. The* is a better word than *her.*

Carefully she pulled the 'bird round, bringing the docking excrescence on its side up to the porch. 'There,' she said, as a shudder of contact passed through the fabric of the plane, gel-suckers latching onto the metal of her house. 'Home.'

We left Robert Yuille cuffed in the body of the 'bird, and Kooistra hauled herself easily through the air, through the hatch, and into her house. She was carrying her pillow-case, the goods she had pilfered from Yuille's house, and I realised that it wasn't evidence at all, that it was booty. I pulled myself through after her. Through the porch, and into the first of her rooms. This was the space that had once been my father's house, but I did not recognise anything. The clutter that floated, or was strapped to the walls, was her clutter, not ours. The window at the far end could have been anybody's window. A new door led through to a wholly new room.

'Home,' Kooistra was saying, with her back to me, 'is such a bittersweet concept. Don't you think?'

'Yes,' I said.

I grasped the frame of the doorway and my right hand fell on something blocky. I started fiddling with the strapping. I did this much as a person fidgets with a pen, or a cigarette, or picks their nose, or rubs the top of their skull. I did not do it with any clearly defined intention in my head. I wasn't even sure what the thing under my right hand was, to begin with.

As the strapping slipped free I was able to hook a thumb underneath it and lift it level with my eyes. It was the size of an old-model television, and for a moment I thought it was a television, but then I saw that its screen was blank, its controls were dials rather than buttons, and I saw that it was a microwave oven.

Kooistra was looking through her window. Her attention distracted for a moment by the sight of the world in the sunshine below her. But it would only last a moment, and then she would turn back to me, and the chance would go. 'Oh,' she said, without turning to me. 'I *never* get tired of that view.'

My hands had their own minds, their own consciousnesses. My brain was thinking, *we'll be back at the Station in a quarter of an hour and I can take a shower.* I remember having that thought. I thought of the shower, of cleanness. But my hands had undone the webbing around the microwave, and freed it from the wall.

I grasped the door-jamb more firmly with my left hand, pulled my knees up to my chest, pressed the face of the microwave against the palms of my feet with my right hand and kicked out with all my strength.

The block of metal and plastic flew in a perfectly straight line. It flew with surprising speed – *surprising* because I had become so used to a sort of dreamy slowness that always surrounded Kooistra. By chance, it started to turn in flight such that it presented one sharp corner to the back of her head.

With the impact the whole of her body tipped around in space, and her face bounced against the floor, her limbs starfished in surprise. Her fat body wriggled, and she twisted round, and I could see that the microwave was still sticking into her head. Its sharp corner had actually dug into the flesh of her head, and as she turned it turned too. Then it caught on the wall and broke free, floating off and still turning. Pearls and balls of blood were stretching out from its corner, drawing a rough line through space to the back of Kooistra's skull.

My heart was thudding. I thought to myself, *what have you done?* If the microwave had hit Kooistra's head flat on it would probably only have jarred her, it would barely have had any effect. Oh, what an insane risk I took! By chance the corner had struck her, not the flat, and now she was wobbly, now she was hurt and bleeding. But her eyes were still open, looking at me. She raised an arm, and kicked out with a leg, probably to launch herself at me, but her leg struck the wall at an oblique angle as she flew off to my left and collided with some rolled packs of cloth – clothes, sleeping bags, I didn't know what. She trailed a beaded string of red through the air after her.

She scrabbled with her hands, tried to get herself in the same orientation as I. Then her limbs went loose. Her eyes seemed to lose focus. Then she scrabbled again, and a great fear seized me. I felt it pour into my innards, like molten metal. I felt her physical proximity to me as intolerable. The conviction was in me that she would reach me and tear me to pieces with her bare hands. She would reach me and kill me. I entered a less than rational state of mind.

I pulled myself back into the 'bird, and heaved clumsily through to the cockpit, banging my limbs as I went, jarring my shin on the expensively designed metal expanse of flight-deck. I hooked my feet together around the stalk of the pilot's seat, charged up the drivestick and put excessive acceleration through the pushjet. My fear exaggerated my surroundings. It seemed as though I was not moving. I was jiggled in my seat, but despite leaning the control all the way over, we were hardly shifting. Then, but only slowly, we started picking up acceleration. I tried to angle the jet down, to sweep into a lower and faster orbit, but the directional jets were as sluggish as the main powerstick.

The world was starting to move past my window, but Kooistra's house – the thing of all things that I was trying to leave behind – remained stubbornly in frame. I realised of course that we were still connected, the house and the 'bird, she and I. Looking back, it surprises me that the gel connection did hold, but it was a tough sticking point, it was designed that way.

Plane and house moved together. I couldn't shake her off. She was the albatross.

We were travelling faster now; half a g, more than half a g, and I could hardly pull myself clear of the back of my chair. I expected to see Kooistra's grinning head rising up into the cockpit space beside me. The path was open for her to come, to crawl along the wall of her house that acceleration had turned into a floor, to slip through the porch and through the open hatch, into the 'bird. I expected to see her face appearing at my shoulder any moment, to see her wide grin, her man-killing hands. But I did not see her face, or her grin, or her hands at my neck. To this day, I do not know whether she was still too dazed from the semi-concussion to co-ordinate her own movements, or whether it was the sudden accel-gravity that baffled her, or whether she simply decided to stay in her house. I accept that this last belief is unlikely.

I was panting, making little singsong *ah! ah!* noises. I couldn't help myself.

I angled up, the 'bird's pushjet juddering and whining as I kept it fully firing, trying to build up speed. My fear had alchemised inside me into a sort of elation, a sense almost of jubilation. I was punching away, riding a rocket-jet, pulling higher.

Then a shiver of panic trickled through my sensations at the thought of the open path from her to me, from the house to the 'bird, and without premeditation I yanked the lever to seal the hatch in the side of the 'bird; and then I pulled the gel-connection that held the docking pathway open. There was a great shudder, and the house swung suddenly, rotating past the cockpit and starting to dwindle, like a house in a hurricane, like that scene in Wizard of Oz. It was venting from the open airlock in a sparkly, snow-storm patch of glitter, and the outpour of gas was pushing it away and turning it slowly.

I look back, and I try to calculate its trajectory, but I cannot be sure. This is what I like to think: I think it was angled fast and high along the same orbital pathway that the Earth itself follows, in true with the elliptic. We were travelling, at the point of release, much faster than eleven klims a second, and anyway at such a height even a slower velocity would have resulted in escape. I assume that the house swung very wide and high around the Earth and slingshotted away from the sun, hurtling out towards nothingness, darkness, the cold, the black vacuum. More than that, I cannot say, and neither can you. Maybe Kooistra was able to co-ordinate her actions sufficiently to close the door to her porch, to keep some of her air inside the house. Maybe she survived the initial departure. But if she did she was – I like to think – only reserving to herself a more lingering and less pleasant death: because there was no plane in her porch (she had flown hers to the Station), and because her house was fitted only with tiny directional jets, so she was locked into her escaping trajectory and was unable to do anything about it. I'm sure she had some supplies on board, but even if her house were packed with supplies they would eventually run out, and she would die of thirst, or die of hunger, speeding at a constant velocity through nothingness towards nothingness. For her sake – and I can say such a thing – I hope she was too disoriented by the blow on the head to lock up, that her air all flowed away, that she asphyxiated before she froze. I like to think that her body is now frozen in vacuum for ever. I like to think so, as I write this. That was the manner of my forgiveness, and of the death of Kooistra.

eighteen

Oh, but I wasn't sure what to do next. I killed the pushjet and for an hour or so I simply sat, circled the world, watched darkness turn into light and light into darkness. Forgiveness is all very well, but it can have indigestible consequences. I had no house to fly to. There was only the Station, and if I returned there I would be arrested and expelled, or sent to prison, or (I didn't know) shot as a traitor. I considered flying the 'bird down through the air and landing it – perhaps in America, a defector, bringing key European technology to the enemy. I even pondered the likelihood of my being able to make a deal with the Americans, somehow still obtaining a house and a plane of my own. But it was pipe dreaming. I knew it.

In the end what persuaded me was the fact of Robert Yuille, still cuffed and strapped into a seat behind me. During the sudden acceleration, and after all the crashing and jerking about of the disengagement, he was silent. I suppose he was terrified. But after things quietened down, he began calling through from the back. 'Hey! What's going on?' 'Hey!' 'Look, you guys, I need to go to the bathroom,' and so on. I pulled the Station's signal on the dash and flew directly there.

Murphy-McNair was furious when he realised what I had done. He detained me, confined me to my chamber, and I was content to stay there. He arrested Yuille, deported him down to the ground, but there was no evidence to convict him of any crime: I did not have the location or the transponder of his house, I had no material evidence, and I lacked Kooistra's knowledge of his activities. He was taken down the following day, whilst Murphy-McNair spent an hour fuming and raging directly into my face. Debacle! Waste of time and resources! Where was Kooistra? Where was she? I lied: I told him that she'd asked me to drop her at her house, and then sent me on my way. I assumed, I told him, that the Station possessed her house's address. He didn't believe me. 'Her plane is still docked here,' he raged. 'Why would she leave her plane here?' I didn't help my case by getting details of my story wrong.

She told me to drop her at the house. I suggested to her that she stop at her house. She told me she had some evidence to pick up. She took the evidence from Yuille's, and stowed it at her house. I wasn't careful to be consistent. I didn't care.

I spent a week confined to my chamber. The people I shared with were moved out – much, I'm sure, to their discomfort, and certainly to more cramped Stations. I was brought my food. And then, one morning, the door was opened by a stranger, somebody wearing a uniform I did not recognise. The Americans had captured the Station. That was that.

I slept through the whole thing. Can you believe that?

They had flown up in their new design space planes, stormed the docking hangar, swarmed through with glue-guns that fired great sticky gobs of stuff and disabled the enemy. The European troops had been unwilling to fire their conventional weapons, for perfectly common-sensical reasons, and apart from some shudder when the American planes connected with the Station, and apart from some shouting and running around (which was masked by the noise of the fans, I suppose), the whole operation was bloodless and rapid.

From being alone in my room, I was again sharing with a dozen people, including Natalya Shelikhova. We were prisoners. It was a form of house-arrest. 'War has broken out below,' said Shelikhova, darkly. 'The Americans stormed a dozen fronts in surprise attacks. They stormed us too, up here. I'm sure they're broadcasting to the world that they have captured and "liberated" the uplands.'

This is what later became common knowledge: the Americans had been developing their new design of space plane for over a decade, and had held back their invasion and the outbreak of groundwar until it was ready. Later, of course, I discovered the physics behind the design. At the time it was bewildering, like a piece of magic. It could take off from any place on the Earth and fly straight up into space! It did not need rockets or pushjets to fly through the vacuum, it simply glided through, apparently infinitely manoeuvrable, infinitely supportable. It was still a plane, of course; it still carried wings, and its main motor, set into the nose, still turned internal blades like a jet engine. But it works like this: it is a quantum wing. It divides not air, as does a conventional wing, but instead divides the constant background fizzing of particle and anti-particle that defines spacetime at the quantum level. The lead edge of the wing is inset with a thread of quantum disturbance agents, and a field sweeps an excess of particles below the wing, and an excess of anti-particles above. The difference is very slight, but it is enough to create what amount to aerodynamic effects, and the plane flies. The leading edge of the five-bladed jet propellor works on a similar principle, pulling the plane through the vacuum. It is a most elegant design. And, what is more, it can accelerate at three-quarters g through clear vacuum. It can fly to Mars and return in two weeks. It changes everything. Everything has changed.

I had of course assumed that the European government would return me to the ground and incarcerate me. I did not know what the Americans would do. I was still wrapped around by the near-mystical bubble of my forgiveness, buoying me up.

We were kept on the Station by the Americans for three weeks, and mostly we were treated well, although circumstances were certainly cramped. Before the month was over we heard that peace had been reached between the US and the EU.

I was interrogated by a colonel in the room that had previously been Gar Murphy-McNair's office. He was a tall thin man with a shaved white head and a beard made of dreadlocks. 'Gyeroffy,' he said, looking at me, looking at the screen open in front of him, looking back at me. 'Gyeroffy. Yes, we have intelligence on you.'

He said it in a knowing, rather spooky voice, as if he were a priest and could see inside my soul. I said: 'What do you mean?'

'We came across your daughter,' he said. 'In an EU military cadet uniform.'

'Gradi?' I replied. 'What do you mean, you came across her?' I felt instant nausea. My guts felt slippery, suddenly, as cooked noodles. 'What about her? What are you going to tell me about her? Is she alright?' I had, obviously, not had contact with her during the American occupation.

He looked at me coolly for a long time; perhaps a minute. It is hard for me to convey how cruel it was of him simply to look at me for that time.

'Ms Gyeroffy,' he said. 'We'd like to talk to you about Kristin Janzen Kooistra.'

My gut spasmed again. 'What about Kooistra? Tell me about my daughter. Tell me about my daughter first.'

'Your daughter is fine. We picked her up in Paris. She was at a cadet school, but she was too young to be a combatant. She's fine.'

I breathed harshly for a while. My face felt hot. 'Why did you pick her up?' I insisted. 'Do you normally pick up schoolchildren? What would an occupying army want with schoolchildren?'

'Since you ask,' said the colonel, putting his head a little way on one side, 'we did it at the specific request of somebody important to us. Somebody who wanted us to guarantee that she would not be hurt. Now, if you'll accept my assurance that she is fine and well, will you please tell me what you know about Kristin Janzen Kooistra?'

'Somebody?' I pressed. 'Somebody? Who? Who?'

'Ms Gyeroffy . . .'

'Somebody important to you insisted that you pick her up, my Gradi. Who was this?'

The colonel sighed, a slight noise. Then he said, not loud but distinctly: 'Your father.'

This clicked into my comprehension like a magazine snapping into a weapon. I allowed my eyelids to rise, slowly. The colonel's American-Prussian face and knobbled white skull blurred a little. I tried to reply, but only a hushing noise came out. He leant forward, an enquiring expression on his face. He said: 'Ms Gyeroffy . . . ?' in a softer tone.

'That's not possible.' I said.

He sat upright at this, 'Isn't it? I assure you it is.'

'He's dead,' I said.

'Dead?'

'He's dead,' I said again.

'I can see from your file,' he said, looking down, 'why you might think so. But I assure you he is not. He's been working for us, actually, for a while now. I can believe it's a shock to hear *that* – some might call him traitor, quisling. But that's not how he sees it.'

'He wouldn't,' I said, breathily. Then I said: 'Kristin Janzen Kooistra killed him.'

He was too military a man to laugh at me, but his eyes sagged a little with amusement. 'I'm afraid you've been misinformed, Ms Gyeroffy. Why would she do so?'

'Serial killer,' I said.

'No,' he said. 'No, that's only her cover. Her cover story. She's been an agent of ours for a very long time.'

'Gar Murphy-McNair hired her as an agent for the EU,' I said. I was only able to take shallow breaths. My throat felt prickly.

'With,' the colonel replied, putting a finger on his screen, preparatory to writing something, as if the conversation had finally lighted on the topic in which he was most interested, 'with our cognisance, of course. Of course, I . . .'

'She *told me* she'd killed him,' I insisted.

'Told you that? I don't think so. I really don't think so. She's not a killer.'

136

'You're saying she's never killed?'

'I'm saying,' said the colonel, 'that she's not a serial killer. That was her cover story.' He repeated this as if speaking to a child. 'Her cover story. She may have killed, I suppose, in the line of her duty. We've been at war. But your personal animosity against her has no basis. Didn't I just tell you she was working for us?'

'Why,' I said, feeling a desperate sorrow and a frantic unease building inside me, 'why didn't he contact me?'

This seemed to puzzle the colonel. 'According to your superior officer,' he said, ignoring my question, 'you went on a mission with Kooistra some weeks ago, and returned alone. Your report seems contradictory. Please tell me what happened.'

I told him. I recited the story in a monotone, all the time thinking *why did she tell me she had killed my father?* I tried to recall whether she had ever actually said those words, or whether she had only ever used phrases such as *he died* or *he passed on.* But I was sure she had boasted of killing him. I tried to imagine the circumstances, my father still alive somewhere in America, helping them with their war effort. Perhaps, I fancied, designing their marvellous new spacecraft, for he was still, to my thirtysomething mind, the magician with machines that he had seemed to my girlish eyes. Why had he abandoned me? It hollowed me out and bent me to think he would abandon me. And to use a subterfuge, so hurtful a fiction, to slip away from me. Could he not have simply said *I'm going to America and you can't come with me* – could he not say that? And why could he not take me with him? I had followed him faithful as a dog to whichever country he had gone. I would have gone with him to America. Had he thought I wouldn't be prepared to throw in my lot with the Americans, had he assumed my loyalty would be to Europe? I would have been prepared to throw in my lot with the Americans, if he had asked. And then, as the words I was speaking to the colonel mumbled and knocked against the words in my head, an interference pattern started to emerge. I should not have killed Kooistra.

But I found it hard to feel sorry for my action, nonetheless.

'You killed her?' the colonel repeated, in poorly disguised disbelief.

'I threw a microwave at her,' I said. 'It caught her with one of its corners at the base of her skull and this stunned her. Then I climbed back into the jet and flew away. I flew off with the house attached, and jettisoned it as I was accelerating. It would have voided of atmosphere. Even if it didn't, it would have slingshotted around the Earth, and it'll be halfway to Mars by now.'

The colonel tutted and shook his head. I was taken away, and locked up in a room by myself. After weeks of cramped co-existence with other Station staff this was almost a relief. I could not think of myself as a criminal.

I tried out thoughts, gingerly, like touching the flat of an iron to see if it is hot or not. I tried out: I'll see my father again. But it was too painful. How could he leave me? How could he justify his deception? And so painful a deception – he could just have slipped away without telling me, that would have been less cruel. My whole life, I thought, had been bent out of shape by this one act, and it turned out my father had been the agent and not Kooistra at all.

I was interrogated again, by a team of military lawyers. I replied that I had believed Kooistra to be an enemy agent, and that I had believed my life in danger. 'She never once so much as suggested she was other than what she appeared,' I said. 'How did she appear?' they asked. 'A killer, a killer,' I said.

At night I found myself unable to shake the certainty that my whole life since my sixteenth year had been a wrong-turn, a false narrative; everything that had happened to me since I was a teenager had been a sort of ghost life, an alternate reality pathway, as in the science-fiction tales, that had diverged from the true path – the true path, I felt, was me growing old with my old father, like Cordelia and Lear. In that frame of mind it was easy for me to slip into adolescent habits of cognition. I allowed dark thoughts to circle and swoop through my head. I pulled a screw from the base of my bunk and tried to cut my wrists with it. The screw's-end was too blunt to cut my skin, but it scored and scored the flesh so that red shooting-star trails marked the white. The soldier who brought my breakfast in the morning could not help but see the wounds I had made on myself.

Later that day I was flown down to the Earth in one of the new American planes – the first and the last time I have travelled in such a machine. It was a smooth flight, smooth all the way down.

On the ground, near Biarritz, I was given a new pharmoneurological treatment and kept in a bed in a secure room. The urge to hurt myself was lost in a weltering swell of lassitude. I watched the high window throw a perfect square of graph-paper on the white wall opposite, and watched as that square moved smoothly along to the folding together of wall and wall, where it folded itself slowly and inexorably into a fat shining tick shape, a *very good* marked against the copy book of life. And then it moved on, until it faded and died, and I slept, and in the morning there it was again, ready to begin its journey.

'Very good,' said one doctor. 'These new adrenoinhibitors really are the most sophisticated medication yet devised for personality disorders. You're doing very well.'

'I want to see my father,' I said. 'Can I see my father?'

'Not right now,' said the doctor, distractedly, writing something on his screen, which he was cradling awkwardly in the crook of his left arm.

'If he'd have been made head of NASA,' I said, 'we'd have cities on Mars by now. Princesses on Mars and mistresses on the Moon.' I think the medication, by taking away the sharpness of my aggression, took away the sharpness of my focus too. Had you ever considered that you are only able to focus, to concentrate, because of your anger? That's the truth of it, you know it, you've known that for a while now. Without my rage I meandered, I free-associated. Perhaps when I asked the doctor if I could see my father he assumed I was only meandering, free-associating. But I wanted to see him very much. I wanted to see him before they stopped the drugs, before my anger came back, because when that happened I wasn't sure that I would be able to prevent myself from hating him.

A lawyer visited me in my bed. 'Your case is going well,' he told me. He had dark black skin and sharp green eyes, a striking combination that may have been artificial, or genetically induced. He was a handsome man, but I was too droopy even to flirt with him.

'Going well,' I said.

'You can imagine there are tens of thousands of court cases happening all at once. It's always that way when a war comes to an end.'

I snorted a little out of my nose at this, but the earnest young lawyer said: 'No, no, it's best that way, believe me. It prevents governments from waging war for too long a period. If there are tens of thousands of lawsuits after a three-week war, imagine how many there'd be after a year-long war! It would bankrupt any government. It's a force for good, it's a force for peace.'

This had the smack of a prepared speech, but I didn't much care. They were reducing my dosage, and occasional flickers of anxiety would curl at the edges of my consciousness.

'Who's paying you?' I asked. 'I can't afford you.'

'Don't worry about that,' he said, smoothly. 'Your ex-husband's paying me. He's pulling strings, too.'

'Pulling strings?'

'He has some powerful friends in the American military,' said the lawyer, but didn't say any more.

The lawyer told me: he'd offered a plea-deal to the Staff Office of Military Prosecution. They could prosecute me for killing Kooistra –

assuming, he added, that she is even dead – but if they did (he said) we'd have 'a hell of a good shot' at prosecuting them for incitement, arguing that their agent's cover story, 'serial killer', was too well handled, that 'any reasonable individual' would have believed her a serial killer, and would therefore be justified, 'on grounds of self defence' in killing her. 'We'd probably win that. It might not keep you out of prison, but it'd reduce your sentence, and make you rich – psychological damage, that kind of thing. Sue, sue, sue. My sense is that, to avoid that, they'll let you take prisoner-of-war status, which means you'll be released as soon as the General Command releases all the other prisoners. 'StOMP don't like me,' he added. 'But, hey, it's not my business to get StOMP to like me. I'm a defence lawyer, I've got to do the best by my client.'

My brain was too slow to be able to work out who StOMP were. 'They don't like you?' I asked, hoping for more clues.

'Hell, no, but they don't like any defence lawyers, methinks.' I was struck by his use of this odd word. 'They're annoyed, we might say, because Kooistra was a valued agent. That's what they said to me – a valued agent.' He shook his head.

'She was working with my father,' I said.

He put up his hand. 'Stop. Don't tell me. The less I know about your case the better for you. Just leave me to do my job, Ms Gyeroffy, and you'll be fine.' He left.

From my bed I watched the square of light process across the blank wall again.

nineteen

I was eventually released. Technically I left American custody with a criminal record for 'war-related manslaughter', but I have not found that this, in my later life, has ever been an encumbrance. European employers were not, in the last two decades of the century, liable to pay any heed to US-sponsored criminal records. So I was released by the Americans in southern France-EU. I had to find my own way back to Paris. I had no money, but there were many military transports threading back and forth across the newly cratered battlefields and through the newly shredded towns, and soldiers are usually happy to help any not-bad-looking woman, even if her arms are marked with scars old and new. In three days I was home.

And now I am an old woman, nearing ninety. I am grateful to Fate that Gradi was too young to be in the military at the time of that war – the space war of '81, it is sometimes called, although seizing the Station was a very minor portion of the hostilities. I am grateful to Fate and to Thom, although he cheated on me and cheated on me because deception is in his heart. After that war Gradi served three years, and got out as soon as she could. By then she had a new dream, which she pursued with the doggedness that is part of her nature, with her ability to concentrate on close detail for long periods that perhaps she inherited from her father, and with the ability to keep in view a longer-term aim that, perhaps, she has inherited from me. She had met a bland but wealthy young man called Paul, and she set about using his money to further her dreams – something he connived in, with that sacrificial blankness in his eyes, like the Tollund Man, glad to be throttled by this young woman with whom he was so besotted. It's not for me to judge, of course. Gradi is a forceful personality, and perhaps that is what men really want. All that erotic side of life seems irrelevant to me, mostly. The time of one's life when sex, or indeed politics, government, war and such, all seem vital and worth sacrifice and worth even dying for – that time does not last, for most, beyond their forties.

I remember the '80s as a terrible decade. I had breakdown after breakdown. To have grown habituated to the fact that my father was dead, and then to have that certainty yanked away from me. His return to life, in my head, was more shocking in its way than his original death. To live, and die, to be brought back to life, to be shuffled off into death again, it was too much for an ordinary person to handle.

I was in Paris for two weeks, after my release from US custody, before I got through to Gradi. It was very hard to find out where she was. Nobody in the US occupying administration would talk to me. I was, I suppose, one of thousands of suppliants. I tried to trace her through her new school, her cadet college, but few of the original staff remained, and nobody seemed to know anything. I tried net searches. I thought of paying for advertisements in likely media. Then she contacted me herself.

'Gradi,' I called, when I saw that it was her on the phone. 'Where have you been? I've been sick with worry. Sick with worry.'

'I'm fine, Ma,' she replied. Her dark little face looked embarrassed by my outburst. 'I've been with Dad.'

It occurred to me, vaguely, that it was odd for her to refer to her Granddad as Dad. 'Where are you now?'

'London.'

'Stay there. I'm coming there.'

'Don't, Ma. We're coming to Paris tomorrow.'

I thought of my father and my daughter travelling together to come and see me. The thought was inexpressibly unsettling for me. That night I stayed awake into the small hours writing a letter to my father. I kept writing drafts and then erasing them because they weren't right. *I am glad*, I wrote, *that you have been able to get to know your granddaughter. I am sorry that you must find me like this.*

When I said 'like this', I meant that I had lost weight. That when the drugs regime had finished, I had taken to cutting myself again, as if I were an unhappy teenager in Cyprus all over again. I cried much of the time. I woke myself up crying. I stood in line at the store, one of the few not emptied or destroyed by the Americans, and I burst into sudden tears. When the storekeeper told me there was no more meat, I offered – in a loud voice, so that the whole queue could hear – to have sex with him if he found me some chicken for my supper. I washed my feet over and over, scrubbing between my toes with a toothbrush until the skin cracked.

I have missed you, I wrote to my father. My voice was so warbly that the voice-writing programme queried one word in three on the screen.

The next day, at lunchtime, Gradi arrived at the door. Thom Baldwin was with her. I stepped onto the landing and looked around, half expecting to see my father standing in the shadows, but of course he wasn't there.

twenty

Can you believe this? It took me three whole days to understand the true state of affairs.

Gradi understood what had happened in my muddled head, early on, but no matter how many times she explained it to me, I could not grasp it. Something in my head prevented it from being true. So all the years I had believed my father dead, it seems, I had not really believed him dead at all. Or put it another way: perhaps I had *known*, intellectually, that he was dead; but in some deeper, squatting, toad-like, patient part of my mind I had known him alive. When I had fashioned my gift for Kooistra, my for-giving, I had on this level believed it would make my father happy. Why else would I do it? If Dad were dead, then whether I killed her or did not kill her would be equally irrelevant to him. But if he were still, somehow, somewhere, *alive*, then I could imagine him nodding with satisfaction at her paying-back. I needed him to be alive to give purpose to my revenge. I felt him to be alive.

When the American colonel had said to me, 'Your daughter is with her father' and I had heard him, genuinely, actually, literally heard him to be saying 'Your daughter is with *your* father', it was only because I felt the *truth* of the latter statement that I was able to perpetrate the mishearing. Is there so much difference between 'her' and 'your', spoken with an east-coast US accent? When I had insisted, slightly hysterically, that this could not be true, that he was dead, the colonel had checked his records and seen that Gradi's biological father was dead, her step-father alive, and he had replied 'I can see from your file why you might think so.'

Perhaps you understand how idiotic a small error can be. But the result of this small error, this banal mishearing, was that first I lost my father, and that then he was reborn to me, and then taken away from me again. I expected him to come back to me at some later stage in my life. And then taken away again. Isn't that how it happens? Round and round we fly. The orbit is the trope of living. We have all the space we could possibly need, and yet our lives are cramped. And yet we keep coming up against the same people, over and again. Now that I am an old woman I can contemplate this in a more sanguine fashion, but at that time, exiled from the uplands never to return, it was more than I could stand. I cried.

Gradi said, for the twelfth time, 'But I didn't say I was with my *Grand*-dad, I said I was with my *dad*.'

I cried, again. You can understand, I hope, how heartbreaking a statement that is. If I were my daughter, and she were me, and we were together to say that statement *I was with my dad*, then my father would be alive again.

There were several difficult years at that point in my life. Drugs were effective when I could get them, these new 'pharmakos' treatments that were just then coming onto the market. But I could not always get them. When I stopped the spectres returned. I thought death was the gift that short-circuited the push-pull economy of the gift. I was wrong in that. It is too easy to summon up ghosts from the grave, and then they are more demanding than living beings. A simple mishearing of 'your' for 'her' will do it, and then the ghost is there, and it is quietly and insistently demanding. *I gave you everything*, it seems to be saying. *I gave you everything. I presented you with life. How can you make me a gift that balances out such a present?* I don't know the answer. Do you?

If you know, what would you require to tell me? What would the price be?

I am now an old woman, but I still do not know the truth of what happened between Kooistra and my father. She may have killed him, or not. If not, then I have heard nothing more from him during all the many decades of my long existence. From time to time I have tried to trace him, but without success. She was supposed to be a killer, but I was told she was not a killer. But she may still have killed. Who can say? I, in my turn, may have killed *her*. Or not. If not – if she were retrieved by the Americans in their vacuum-rapid space planes – then I have heard nothing about it. But I daresay they would keep that kind of thing secret. But, I tell myself, surely that cannot be the case. Surely when I left her, wounded and bleeding, her air was moments away from leaking out altogether. Surely she asphyxiated, shortly before she froze solid. Surely she has not been retrieved by the Americans, but is still up there, somewhere, falling in her Newtonian trajectory. A gentle kink in an infinitely long line.

It is all travel, travel, it is all only travel.

Once, many years later, I was travelling on a ground-effect train across North West Russia, a journey from Moscow to Helsinki. There is no need for me to go into the reasons why I found myself in that place at that time, or for me to reveal the identity of my (still living) travelling partner. Only that I went to the upper floor of the car to look about and noticed that the world all around had opaqued, misted, and that we were isolated, apparently motionless even as we swept ceaselessly onward. Far behind the motive car hummed invisibly, shrouded in the mist. Ahead the body of the carriage in which we were standing faded after a few metres. From time to time a pylon would materialise out of the mist, hurtle past over our heads and vanish behind us. Apart from that, there was no sensation of motion at all. It was a spectral, ghostly medium. My companion said to me, 'Isn't this exactly like life? Rushing on, but feeling motionless, no sense of where we go or what we do.' But, although at the time I said 'Yes, you're right', I am not sure, now, that he *was* right to say so. Some people travel surrounded by a mist, wrapped in the ghosts of their past, unable to see past the spectral material of that fact. Of course that is true. But for many their destination is too clearly, *too* sharply defined. There's a kind of vertigo looking forward in your life, for that sort of people, as there is in looking backwards into the past when you are old. On a clear night, when the stars are distinct and multifarious over my head, I look up and think in fact I am looking down, at the jewels embedded in the furthest, deepest, abyssal floor. It is a long way to fall. Somewhere in that same sky, Kristin Janzen Kooistra is in the process of falling that long distance. She can see exactly where she is going, it is all spread out before her with the inevitability of gravity and the terror of falling. But it will take her millions of years before she reaches the black rocks and occasional sparkles of that deep downbelow ground, before she and her cold dead house crack and splinter on the rocks. Millions of years. At least, I think so. I have no certain knowledge one way or the other.

The news this morning was presented by a young man from the US base on Mars. They've established a base there, at the northern ice-cap where most of the water is. Today is June 21st, 2132, and my name is Klara Gyeroffy.

Part Two
GRADISIL

one. Slater

Fort Glenn

Here is Lieutenant Slater in the main corridor of Fort Glenn, walking with a snap and a twang.

In one of the rooms off the main walkway is Colonel Philpot, Slater's superior officer but yet his friend. Philpot has his arm hooked round a handle to keep his body steady for a moment, and is squeezing himself into an all-body elastic skin. This piece of total underwear is designed to put resistance into every ordinary bending and flexing motion of his human limbs, with the very creditable aim of thereby reducing bone loss. Everybody wears them on Fort Glenn. They are wearisome, and not especially effective at preserving bone mass, but those are the orders. 'Hi, Slayer,' Philpot calls. 'How you doing?' Slayer is the nikname by which Slater is known.

With a snap and a twang, Slater comes to a stop.

'd'up Jean, doing *good*,' replies Slater. This mutual greeting is a sort of joke between them. Because the habitation portions of the Fort are so very small, the staff bump into one another a hundred times a day, at least, and so these elaborate social interchanges are redundant. Which is why these two men perform them, of course.

'Where you going?' asks Philp. 'We're going to *war*,' says Slater. This is also the standard exchange.

'Hey, don't let the man keep you,' says Philpot. *The man*, in this context, is their commanding officer, General Niflheim. 'You tell him that you-me got time booked to go outside, try the new rifles out.'

'And I have not forgotten that,' says Slater.

And with a snap and a twang he is off.

During this conversation Fort Glenn has travelled several hundred kilometres. It's a hurtling place. Its speed is not apparent to those on the inside.

The rear-wall motor barks, chugs, and pulses for twenty seconds. Air circulates. The motor ceases, and it is quiet again.

Slater knoks at the general's door, and the metallic door rebounds against his meaty knukles. Not only the door, but the metal frame that holds it, and the metal walls in which the frame itself is set, and which angle away ninety degrees to enclose the general's room and the corridor – all these surfaces act as a sounding board, and Slater's knok booms mightily through the whole Fort. Everybody knows that Slater is knoking.

'Come,' says the general.

These niceties, the hello-goodbye, the knoking-at-doors, these are all holdovers from the ground. The Army is by its nature an organisation that clings to its routines and rituals as far as possible. You might think that, given the space limitations of the Fort, it is an unnecessary extravagance of space for the general to have a personal cabin, a storage cell *and* a private office, as well as a cabin for his subaltern. But he is a general, after all.

Slater pulls the door open and with a snap and a twang steps into the general's office. The window behind the general's desk shows a good stretch of the world, sunlit and glorious. *It's the* whole *world, you believe that? Wat a view! Wat a view this man has from his office window!*

A storm front, curled around a low-grade hurricane, has drawn a spiral galaxy of cloud over Siberia. The eye of this weather-cluster sits south of the Earth's pole like the nubbin on an orange the size of the world. Through the cloud tatters at the outer rim of this storm front brown and olive landscape is visible, and the little tin-coloured scabs of industrial parks or cities here and there.

Slater clunks his booted feet onto the metal dek smartly and salutes. One thing about these elastic boot tethers; if you bend your knee up far enough they enable you to really clunk your boot hard down, which makes the whole military, stand-to-attention, *yes-sah!* thing so very much sharper.

'Sir!' says Slater.

The general himself is working at his desk; but he is standing, since in zero g standing is precisely as easy and comfortable as sitting. For this same reason Slater does not take a seat.

The general and the lieutenant have a conversation. Implicit in the things they say are certain facts, known to both of them and unneedful of repetition between them, but things which make sense of the exchange. Amongst those facts, the most salient are as follows: that the upkeep of this Fort is costing the American taxpayers a great deal of money, and increasingly people regard this expense as a waste of cash, for many politicians do not see the need for a military presence in the Uplands, *now* (which is to say, after '81) that the EU has been thoroughly beaten and has withdrawn itself from those territories. It is true that the civilian population of the Uplands has continued to increase – exentrics, millionaires, wealthy criminals looking for a hideaway, cranks, plane-nuts, space-nuts, hermits, libertarians, romantics, a *real* mixed bag. But, in the opinion of the most influential groundling politicians, these people do not constitute (in the quaint old phrase) a clear and present danger. Maybe they need policing. Surely they *don't* need a hugely expensive military operation, permanent base, billions of dollars annually, to keep them loyal to the USA, especially when loyalty to that monopower is only notionally required. For wat *is* there in the Uplands? How many natural resources are there to be exploited and shipped bak down to enhance the prosperity of ground-born Americans? None.

Wat are the strategic benefits of that territory? None that haven't been benefiting the USA for a century and a half already, without the need for an expensive military presence – which is to say, Clarke orbit slots for satellites, surveillance and communication and weapon bases. The satellites are there; they were there for a century before any garrison was posted to defend them, and they did very well, thank you. They are well defended with automatic systems. Uplanders stay away from them, which is easily done in billions of cubic kilometres of space. So why, exactly, precisely, do we need to maintain a garrison up there? *Precisely* wat are the American people getting for their investment? Nothing.

General Niflheim and Lieutenant Slater, of course, disagree with this assessment. So does the Army as a whole. The Army as a whole is unpersuaded by the money argument. It has never been persuaded by the money argument (for in the heart of every soldier is the unchallenged belief that – after all, why would any nation accumulate national wealth *in the first place* except to support a large and glorious army?). The top brass want more, not less, US military presence in the Uplands. It wants to expand the Uplands Corps, and create new corps for subsequent expansion into the solar system.

But new technology has rendered at least some of the older arguments redundant, which makes it harder for the top brass in their bikerings with the administration. Under the old model the idea was that a space installation was a necessary way Station to further exploration; that having hauled oneself out of the Earth's gravitational well it would be necessary to pause, rest and recuperate before launching further out, like a weightlifter propping the massy laden bar on his collar bone before the final jerk and up. But this is the logic of rokets! And rokets are old news. Elem planes sweep up so effortlessly into high orbits. Even more elegantly, the newer planes, fitted with their Quanjet motors, can glide through vacuum itself above and beyond the branches of the Yggdrasil – though they require quite enormous amounts of power to move themselves along, and are accordingly much more, so much more expensive to operate than the older Elem craft (though not quite as expensive as rokets).

And so the problem facing the military is this one: *how* to create a sense that a military base in the Uplands is an ungainsayable necessity for the security of the American peoples? And the answer that the military grope towards is the same as it has ever been, and the answer is war, it has always been war. The sort of destabilising questions that are aimed at the Army in peacetime become impertinences in wartime. War, once the initial momentum has been established, creates its own justifications. You know this. Just as they do. It's well known. But the difficult part is in establishing the proper grounds in the first place.

The general and the lieutenant do not rehearse these points; they have no need, for they both know them all already. Instead, the general says: 'Is it the midday plane?'

'Colonel Philpot and I have booked some time, sir, to go outdoors and try the new rifles. Booked last week.'

'That's right,' says the general. 'That's right.'

'At ten, sir. Outside at ten, so the midday plane is fine. I'll make that plane fine.'

'Hagen and Walsall are on that plane.'

'Yes sir.'

'So it's definitely – I only mean, lieutenant, that it *is* leaving at midday, it's a scheduled flight now. *Capiche?*' For his own reasons, ignorance or caprice, the general pronounces this last word as *kapitchy*.

'Yes sir, I understand.' Wat he understands is *don't tarry, for if you do not make the plane by midday you'll miss the plane.*

'And you got your – you know – ready? You ready with your . . . ?' The word the general is groping for and not finding is *presentation*.

'My presentation, yes *sir*, I got it all in my thumb.' By *thumb* he means not flesh-and-blood, he means his data storage device, tagged to his shirt just underneath his uniform jaket. He pluks this out to show the general.

'Just run it past me again. Not the specifix . . . just the . . .' This sentence does not come to an end.

The general is a big man, his jowls and his nek-fat slak in the no-gravity which gives him a weirdly bulbous look. His head is shaven, which makes plain a single thorn-shaped scar on his temple. His plump eyes, his nose with its golf-ball tip, his ω-shaped chin, his toothbrush eyebrows, all the furniture of his face seems uneasy without the arrow of orientation that gravity provides, taking wat might be a rather handsome and distinctive visage and muppetising it, giving the impression that the various facial elements do not belong intrinsically to that skull but might be attached and detached at whim. But although he personally dislikes zero g, although he is not personally enjoying his posting, the general nevertheless believes genuinely, believes passionately, in the rightness of the Upland Corps *being there*. 'Run it past me again,' says the general.

The sun comes into the window, painful-bright, and the smartglas darkens automatically. Slater can see his own reflection, floating there. He is a handsome man. He likes the way he looks. He really has no problem with the way he looks.

'It's pretty much wat we've discussed,' he says. 'The threat, to play up the threat, yes, but above all the *strategy*. It'll be a house-to-house operation, just like a ground city; and our guys are tiptop-trained in house-to-house. The Uplands have unusual features, of course. If you said to me, sir,' Slater is warming to his topic, 'to take a ground city I'd take the key features first. I'd send in shok troops to seize the airports, the TV studios, the parliament buildings, and so on. I'd drop troops to grab the high ground, to give us a commanding perspective. Then I'd work street to street, moving up the river and outwards. But—'

'But,' repeats the general, who knows all this, but wants to make sure his subordinate has it all ready for the downbelow meeting.

'But there are no such features in the Upland. There's no airport, TV studios, parliament buildings, no river, no hills, nothing. Just a whole bunch of empty space and a couple thousand houses . . .'

The general holds up one of his rectangular forefingers. 'Precision *plays*, lieutenant,' he says. 'Precision always plays downstairs.'

'Twenty thousand and ninety houses,' says Slater, 'supporting a population that varies, at any given moment, from fifty to ninety thousand. But it's a fundamentally itinerant population; almost all of them have ground bases to which they go regularly, to reverse the bone loss and avoid radiation. Only a few hermits stay up all the time, and they're not healthy. Plus, of course, it's a population without a standing army, without a centralised government, so it has no unity. Militarily, it'll be an easy business occupying and subduing the population.'

The general nods. This is good. 'And if they ask: hek soldier! haven't we already sub*dued* this population?'

'It's true that we have no ground rivals for this territory. But the Uplanders have proved disinclined to accept our dominance.'

'So we want to insist.'

'We want to make them accept that we're in charge, yes, sir.'

'And if they ask, so why should *we* pay for this little adventure?'

Slater grins. 'If we treat the Uplands as a country, then it has the highest proportion of billionaires anyway. They'll pay for their own military occupation – for their defence, I mean.'

'Defence,' says the general, a little severely. 'Defence is always the word.'

'They'll pay,' says Slater, 'and hardly notice it. But we *can't* enforce a proper regimen of taxation without a more robust military presence. At the moment they're legally required to pay a minimal tax on property held up here, but almost none of them do and there's no enforcement to make it happen. A two-week military operation, the public capitulation of the two dozen most prominent Uplanders, and a sweep through the whole area fitting state-registering transponders, and we can enforce a legal tax sweep. It'll pay for the operation, and our presence here, tenfold.'

'Stress that,' says the general. 'They'll like to hear that. And wat else – Moon?'

'The Moon base is a folly,' says the lieutenant. 'It's dying already. It's practically dead already. The thing is, Uplanders are really wedded to Elem, which means that they're much more comfortable in the Upland shell of space. None of them have Quanters. Travelling away from the Earth means using some really primitive propulsion, and it's time-consuming, and it's expensive, and it leaves them feeling vulnerable. The founder died last year, moonbase-guy I mean. People go less and less, which means the greenhouses die, it's all going to wrak and ruin. So we can disregard the Moon.'

'Stress that too,' says the general. 'The Moon would require a force of Quanters, and that's pricey, they're pricey, so stress that we can conduct the whole campaign Elem, in the Uplands themselves.'

'Sir.'

The general is nodding. 'Very good,' he says. Behind him his window is clearing, to reveal the nightside of the Earth glinting and sparkling and rotating like the most titanic bauble ever fashioned; a million points of yellow and white light spekling its broad, coally, rotating torso.

Slater's New Gun

Slater and Philpot strip, peel off their all-body elastics, and suit up. Their suits are striped red and white, their helmets white-stars-on-blue, but the white is reflective and the red a lumine colour, so a spacewalking US marine is visible hundreds of klims away, and when the sun hits them just right they can be seen as tiny pink asterisks in the sky, even from the ground.

Inside the fabric of the suits an Elem wire is coiled around legs and torso, and powered from a pak in the small of the bak. It would slosh under gravity, since the envelope formed by the two main layers of plascloth is filled with water, but in zero g this is equally distributed and moves slik as oil. The water is insulating, and the water is drinkable, and the water is breakdownable to supplement the oxygen-wedge situated across the small of the bak, should that becomes necessary (which it won't, on this occasion, because they're only going out for an hour or so). The water provides some small protection against radiation too, though it is only a thin layer, so not much. And the antifreeze makes it taste funny, should the drinking thing become necessary.

They step into the porch together. They are laughing together.

And it's *ssshhh* as the air is pumped bak, the air is suked into the Fort, and the suits become a little stiffer in the arms and legs, just a *little* bit stiffer, but the elbows and knees and the crotch and the armpits are sewn-in with smart cloth that makes flexing and unflexing just that tiny bit easier than it would otherwise be.

Slater and Philpot both take a rifle from a rak fixed to the side of the porch. These are two of the new batch of rifles, long bore and Very High Speed projectile ordnance. Vacuum rifles can fire bullets at a much higher speed than rifles in air; a very minimal magnetic charge keeps the bullet from scraping the sides of the barrel as it flies along, the lak of air means that the bullet does not deform or bang or get slowed down by air resistance.

These new VHS-rifles have a refined mag bore, and a more powerful explosive in the bullets. According to the manufacturers they can fire projectiles at extraordinary speeds.

Slater and Philpot want to try these new guns out. The door opens, and a little dust and glitter (from the minimal residual air in the porch, don't you see) flutters through the door into the great dark outside. Slater and Philpot float through the door, being careful not to bang their rifles. That's one problem with these VHS-rifles; the slightest knok to their two-metre barrels and they can become kinked, much less effective, or even wholly ineffective.

Both Lieutenant Slater and Colonel Philpot are tall men; but on a shorter person these red-white hoops are fattening, can make a person look *stumpy*.

Dam. *Fuk!* It takes the breath away. The world is simply larger and more real than screen representations ever suggest.

They can see the whole Fort now, as they float away, great cylindrical and elliptical components fitted together like supercost Lego, with spiderweb wing work of braided wire to manoeuvre and to preserve it against orbital decay. They move away from it.

They are talking to one another via a direct-sight laser, which, providing it strike the material of their suits, enables them to communicate without having to broadcast – since howsoever well encrypted, broadcasts are not private: they can be pikked up by Uplanders and maybe decoded, they can be piked up by the whole wide rainy-stony Earth which is just there, which is right there, fuk, it's fifteen miles away, it's closer than Boston is to Harvard – there's the *whole world* and they might be eavesdropping on you, you don't know.

Not that they have anything confidential to say. It's just habit.

'Hey Slayer,' says Philpot. 'You want to fire up? Or down?'

Slater grins, although Philpot can't see it behind his darkened visor. To fire down is to watch bullets flare briefly as they burn up, but there's always the chance (who knows? millions-to-one but you don't know, do you?) that you'd hit a jet, a space plane in the upper stages of its journey to the Uplands, and cause some real damage. The chances may be millions-to-one, but it's not zero. And that thought makes Slater grin. He can't help himself.

'Up,' he says, conscientiously. 'Or along.'

'Could try *hit* one-nother,' says Philpot mischievously.

'Kill my best friend,' replies Slater. 'Sure. Yes.'

'And I figured *Marina* was your best friend?'

'Sure,' agrees Slater. 'I do indeed prefer having sex with her.'

And Philpot barks a laugh. 'Marine,' he replies, mok-severe, 'I am obligated to warn you that sexual harassment is a potential court martial offence, and I may be having to have to report you to the Legal corps.'

'I can only apologise, sir, apologise,' says Slater, and then: 'your transp on?'

'Yowsir.'

'Yow.'

'*Well* then, let's untether this little,' says Slater, turning the laser off. He unhooks their target from his belt (for, of course, they have brought an official army target with them) and tosses it like a baseball pitcher (which causes him to rotate about his centre of gravity, which motion he stills with a twitch of his glove). It disappears into the dark, flying rapidly and with a perfectly straight trajectory away.

Slater is able to steady himself with a twitch of his glove because inside the finger is where the primary controls of the Elem lining to his suit are located. Now he activates the whole grid, and – small though the charge is, relatively tenuous though the foliage of Yggdrasil is at this height – it sets him straight, with a slight shudder. Philpot has already used his grid to move away from his comrade until he is a small red-white doll in the distance. He is practised with the Elem suits, with generating *just enough* differential front-and-bak to surf the lines and move himself along. Slater is good too, but not so good as Philpot. But then Philpot is a colonel, and Slater only a lieutenant.

Slater fits the VHS-rifle to his armpit, the exhaust over his shoulder. His visor software connects with the dwindling, near-invisible target, blows it up for his eyes.

He wobbles as the twigs of Yggdrasil brush through him; he waits until he is steady again, aims, fires.

There's the sensation of a hand squeezing his shoulder hard; the recoil from the bullet matching the opposite-and-equal recoil (calculated by the rifle's chip) from the exhaust. And in his visor he sees a schematic, and sees that almost as soon as he fired the target registered a hit. He sees a momentary cloud from Philpot's rifle, dissipating as soon as it emerges from the rifle-mouth, and another hit registers.

In his head he, Slater, is thinking: that's a rebel house, and that's put a fist-sized hole in their wall at two klims, and all their air is going away. It feels very good, it does feel doubleplus good. He can't wait for this war to start.

On the Plane Down

Hagen and Walsall are on the plane down with Slater; the three of them in their purply-blue dress uniforms, three of them belted into the circular seats in the middle of the plane. It's an Elem plane, much cheaper to run than Quant types. The pilot undoked Fort Glenn at precisely midday.

'So,' Hagen is saying, conversationally, to Slater. 'You going down to make the case?'

'Make the case?' echoes Walsall.

Wherever Slater moves, howsoever he shifts in his seat, whichever way he leans against his straps, Hagen's eyes follow him. Each of Hagen's pupils is like the bubble in a spirit-level, leaning left or leaning right with Slater's every move. Slater has, in the past, wondered if Hagen has the hots for him. But then again, he has no idea whether Hagen prefers the masculine of the species or the feminine of the species or the bivalve, or *wat* he likes. He's known Hagen for two years now, and he doesn't know even this basic fact about him, no. He's a comrade-in-arms, and he's prepared to die next to him, and yet he doesn't know *the first thing* about him. It's because he doesn't like him, of course.

'I'm giving a presentation,' said Slater.

'So, this war about to start?' asks Hagen, watching cobra-fashion as Slater shifts in his seat. Slater fidgets, unused to the sensation of gravity created by the plane's deceleration (as it hurtles into the foamy leaves and brush of the world-tree and slows for descent). 'This war about to start, is it? I only ask – it's not I'm indifferent to the need for secrecy and the . . .' But perhaps he is tired, because the repetition comes, 'the secrecy and all.'

'And so on,' agrees Walsall.

'I respect of *course* the need for secrecy, chain of command, and so on. But you know wat *I'm* working on. You know *my* brief.'

Hagen's job is liaising with the civilian contractors who are, slowly, putting together a new project, a wheel-shaped spinning platform in orbit, a real *2001-Space-Odyssey* style USUF space station. A great rim of a station with real simulated gravity, none of your snap-twang elasticated imitations, no sir. This has been tried before, of course, but it's never been got to work, no sir. The problem with those retro *2001-Space-Odyssey* style space stations is the vomiting – you see? Stand on the dek and it's not too bad, but start walking and you feel sik. Turn right or left, or (god forbid) turn right around and trying walking the opposite way, and your inner ear has its conniption fit. Jesus, shake your *head* to answer a question 'no' and you'll like as not throw up. They're bad. The first USAF-Dev wheel, only a small one (forty metres across) was niknamed The Vomorama by its staff. The designers had assured the military that initial disorientation would go away, that the inner ear would get used to it, that it would only take a day or two – that was proven wrong, wrong, and the puking went on. 'The only good thing about this,' said Colonel Ash Ederdidge, in notional command of this eternally spinning bicycle wheel, 'is that the puke does fall to the ground, so it's not too difficult to clean up.' Puke in zero gravity is an unpleasant thing.

The first wheel was abandoned. It's still up there, it's used as a storage facility.

But the USAF and the fledgling USUF have not given up on using centrifugal effect to simulate gravity. They've been working on some new models, some new concepts, a mucho-mucho *bigger* wheel for one thing, so that a considerably relatively slower rotation will still generate a palpable seudo-gravity; and a system of moving walkways that provide sharp centrifugal differentials. But this is a big project; a big money project, and a major investment of men and material. This is Hagen's problem.

'This war comes along next month, or month after, then my ferris wheel gets bumped bak in the schedules. You gather? So I'm only asking, do I get my pet project sooner, or later. That's wat I'm asking.'

'Later,' says Slater. 'That's wat *I* hope.'

'We know wat you hope for, Slater,' said Hagen, grinning.

'. . . hope for,' echoes Walsall.

And the strange thing is that Hagen hopes for the same thing. Even though it would muk up his own schedule, even though it would push his pet project bak by many months, nevertheless he's a soldier, and soldiers in peacetime always look forward to wars. Fish need water t'swim-in, roots need soil t'grow-in, soldiers need – but you don't want the platitude.

The two soldiers sit in silence for a little while.

'Shall I tell you wat I heard?' Hagen announces. 'I don't know, this might just give you something to work with, downbelow . . . maybe Niflheim already told you this?'

'Niflheim didn't tell me anything,' says Slater, intrigued despite himself. 'Niflheim told me nothing. Wat?'

'It's about Madame Gradisil,' says Hagen. 'You have heard the latest Gradisil rumour?'

'I heard she's pregnant again,' says Slater. 'That wat you mean?'

'I don't mean that,' said Hagen.

'Not that,' repeated Walsall.

'She *is* pregnant though,' Slater says again.

'Yes, yep, third time, number three, but better than that. I heard she had a meeting with the EU ambassador. That's a treaty-breach by the EU, right there.'

Slater thinks about this for a while. 'An official meeting?'

'Well a secret meeting of course. But not a *local* official, you know. One of the three EU ambassadors.'

'EU ambassadors,' says Walsall, knowingly.

'And most of all, a meet, a political meet. EU is plotting something. Uplanders are plotting with EU.'

'Plotting wat?'

'Saint Christ alone knows!' barks Hagen, for some reason *very amused* by this question. He grins, the grin in his big round head like an axe-cut suddenly in the side of a honeymelon. 'I don't know *that*! How would I know that?'

'But you can use your imagination,' says Slater.

'We can all use our imaginations,' agrees Hagen. 'Something's cooking. Upland is a glass bowl, you know? EU can't really have thought that they could send an official to neg-o-t-iate with Gradisil herself and it not be *noticed*.'

'So it's a deliberate EU play?'

'We can all use our imaginations,' says Hagen again.

'Yep,' agrees Walsall.

'It's a pretty flagrant flouting of the terms of the eighty-one treaty,' says Slater. 'But they can't *want* a war, can they? We'd kik their ass. We can surely kik their ass if they want it, but they can't want it. I mean, less they got something up their sleeve. They got something up their sleeve, you think?'

'Me I'm liaising the space station, that's all,' says Hagen, sitting bak. 'I'm the wrong soldier to ask. But you got to wonder. Are they trying to precipitate a war right now, *up here*? That's the salient, no? Up here!'

'Yes,' replies Slater, meditative. 'Thanks for sharing,' says Slater.

The plane is shuddering now, as if cold, because it is into the atmosphere, and soon it is sweeping down and around, over the Earth that lies passively there below them, like Danae sighing in anticipation, and the sighs visible as little cotton clouds. And then they fly through the clouds and down.

two. Paul

Who I am

My name is Paul Caunes, husband of Gradisil. You've heard of her, even if you haven't heard of me, but bear with me and I'll get to her, as soon as I've sketched some conventional, uninteresting details about me. I was born into a wealthy EU family, and as a consequence I have never had to labour to earn my fortune. But I did need to labour, and earnestly, at spending it; finding an appropriate outlet for it. It was in the strenuous and not entirely joyous pursuit of this aim that I became an Uplander. And it is as an Uplander, as the husband and political consort of Gradisil, that I can now tell my story.

In fact my portion of this narrative is a simple story, and here it is: story of a woman who marries a man, but not for love, rather for his money, for the opportunities he can bring her. He is a branch for her to set her foot upon, a stepping stone on the path she wishes to tread; and her *wish* is a potent thing, her willpower can shake nations and win wars. And, perhaps, she does not even despise him. Weeks and, sometimes, even months pass when she is not even fully aware he exists. She doesn't even hate him, which is the worst of it, for in hatred there might be some sort of passion to answer the passion in him. But she is largely indifferent. When it occurs to her, she is even affectionate. She even uses the phrase 'I love you', although it tends to come up in phrases such as 'you know I love you', and 'don't be silly, of course I love you.' Which, I hardly need to tell you, isn't quite the same thing. And as for him, well, he *loves her*. He loves her wholly and hopelessly. He betrays her, he hands her to the enemy knowing that it will mean the end of her life (in prison, in execution); and knowing that, and loving her as he does, he betrays her. This, then, is the story of that betrayal, that's all.

Why does this man love this woman? Not for her political ambition, or the plan she has to shape by force of will a disparate collection of selfish, wealthy exiles and forge them into a nation. Not for her celebrity. Not for her faithlessness, although I concede that is a reason why some men love some women. Not for the 3nimation figure cultural historians are already sketching in clumsy sphere-and-blak characters. He loves the real her, the actual her; the her that generates the particular odour of her skin, the her that pushes the blak hairs from her scalp millimetre by millimetre. He loves her distinctive smell, which is hers alone, and which you can only smell by being close to her.

Here is a public Gradi

We were on the ground, in a pale wood-clad room. The room was in Finland-EU. The wall projections were fluid with swifts and alouettes. There was a green hatstand in the corner, shaped like a cactus. Gradi was there, a handsome woman, physically slight but enormously charismatic, compact like a jewel or one of those jade circuit-chips that has folded all humanity's cinema into its miniature whorls and dots. She was dressed in blak. She was a few weeks past her fortieth birthday. She was sitting slightly askew in a large chair, the desk at a forty-degree angle away from her, and I was sitting diagonally across from her. There are three other people in the room. This is late on in Gradi's political career. I suppose we can call it a career. The three other people, two men and one woman, are wat a more conventional politician would call aides or advisers, although it was part of Gradi's style that she did not use this sort of vocabulary.

One of the men is at a second large, polished-and-carpented plastic desk. The other man and the woman are both huddled intently over opened notepads. We are all discussing a certain matter: politics, diplomacy. The man at the desk is holding two telephone receivers to his head simultaneously, one each side, like an Amish beard. He looks very severe, very stern, this man. His name is Mat. One of the receivers goes into its cradle. 'It's viable,' he announces. Gradi looks sage. 'He near as had a nosebleed when I suggested it,' continues Mat. 'But it's viable.'

'Viable,' says Gradi, a verbal nod.

'Wat is it?' I ask. But she shushes me, since the man is still talking on the other phone.

'We've set up a meet in Gallano's house.'

'He changed his transp,' says Gradi.

'I've got his complete cycle,' says Mat. Gradi nods, nods, uh-huh.

I get up and I walk out of the room, and I believe, and I still believe today, that the others did not even notice that I was gone. I walked through the rest of the house. I had bought this house myself; I had used my money, and searched the housing sites, and met with the vendor, and furnished it; I had lived in it for longer stretches than anybody else who lived there, for they were often away in the Uplands or moving restlessly about the globe. And yet it was not my house; it was Gradi's house, since everything was hers.

Here is a flight to the Uplands

I flew ground-Up and Up-ground so many times that, now as I cast my mind bak, all those many flights coalesce into one: a single hypertextish 'Flight'. Sometimes I flew up with Gradi and nobody else, or with only a small group of people; but more often I was in a plane with a large crowd. People wanted to come and go; seats were traded and bought, people hopped aboard when it was clear that there was a flight upward. It is one of those sorts of flights that is, for my purposes here, my Flight.

The plane is paked with people, blithely disregarding the straps and even the seats as we thunder along a runway and climb into the air, with that distinctive lurching sense of inner rearrangement that comes from kissing-off the ground and trusting to the invisible medium. The judder of flying through the treacly lower atmosphere. Wat do I do? I look out of the window.

Here we are, *in the sky*, fancy! But the ground is only a few metres below us; you could fall from here and not hurt yourself too badly. But now the ground is much further away, the ground is a spread of toy buildings and toy cars on diagrammatic roads. Then roads and rivers are threads, towns ragged-edged scabs of blak and brown. Then swirls of smoke, quikly blanking out the window as we rise into the whiteout of the clouds.

And up again out the other side, into the upper sunlight. The brightness stings in my eyes.

Gradi has come to sit alongside me. 'You're sure?' she asks. 'You're *sure* they want to meet? I met with them—'

'Yes,' I said.

'—not long ago, you know? We met with them not so long ago.'

'I'm sure,' I said.

'It's kosher? It's a real meet, you trust them on this?'

'It's concessions, that's wat I heard, only they want to be a bit secretive, they don't want EU media knowing that they're granting you concessions. You know?' This was all a lie. There were no concessions. They only wanted Gradi, to imprison her, to try her as a terrorist. My heart was quivering as I spoke this lie, as if it was fitting. I loved her so much it resembled epilepsy, or Theresa's religious ecstasy. It was not even especially sexual; it was much more thoroughly bodily than that.

'Is it,' she asks, her brow still furrowed, 'your usual source? Your guy – wat's the guy?'

I squeeze up a broad smile. The guy. 'It's him, it'll be fine.'

'We only met a month ago,' says Gradi, distracted, peering at the brightness that plunges through the window. 'Why do they want another? So why *do* they want another meet?'

'Maybe they want you to run for the Presidency when Veen steps down. Maybe they want a real leader running the US this time!'

Gradi laughs at this. She has many laughs. Her laughter is almost a language in its own right, and this is one of the many, many reasons that I love her. She can laugh with her heart and her chest; she can laugh so hard she wees and loses control; she can laugh with a charming sparkly fullness; she can laugh politely, pointedly, generously, precisely. She can laugh with an official reserve, a diplomatic laugh. This last one is the laugh she uses when I jocularly suggest that the Americans want her to run for President. She is looking past me at the group of people lolling and fidgeting at the bak of the plane, like a true politician. For a politician never need doubt her spouse's vote *of course*; whereas a group of half-friends and strangers might well be potential supporters. For a true politician, the unknowns, the as-yet-unaligned, are the most fascinating human beings in creation. Not that there was anything as antiquated as voting going on in the Uplands; but support for a politician is support for a politician, whether it's registered by democracy AIs in the polling booth or not. I am looking at her, as the bright sunshine illuminates her face, and I am thinking how sharply and totally I love her. It surprises me almost into tears; but it shouldn't surprise me. Of course I love her. How could I betray her to the Americans if I didn't love her?

'And where's the meet?' she asks me, not looking at me.

'I've sorted it, it's in hand,' I assure her.

'Where's the meet?' she presses, her eye moving over the crowd.

'Gallano's.'

'Same as last time?'

'Same. We'll fly there from hub.' But she is already moving away, she is already ignoring me, and I move my gaze bak to the window and the sunlit sky outside. I can hear her, hullo, hullo, behind me. I can hear the buzz of the hoi polloi behind me rise as she comes over to them. They are excited to meet her. She is an Upland celebrity; she is known all around the world. Of course! The antiphonal interphase of conversation, Gradi's voice, some man's voice, the words not clearly audible. A child suddenly shrills *Parky's got a nosebleed! Parky's got a nosebleed!* and a gush of laughter swells through the group. Then, gradually, Gradi's voice grows more and more audible, as she takes control of the conversation, as she pulls these new people around the orbital tether of her charisma.

I put my face closer to the glass. We are not going to Gallano's. I shall fly her to an American facility and hand her over to the enemy, and this will be my betrayal. People have died for lesser betrayals. I've seen that with my own eyes. The enormity of wat I am doing excites me almost exactly as much as it terrifies me.

I look not through but at the window. The high sunlight casts all the myriad scratches and buffs on the plastic window into brilliant relief, as if they are burning hieroglyphs from some mysterious language written on the plastic, the plangent significance of which is only just out of my mental apprehension. *Up*, the strange symbols say. Light—Space—Freedom—*Up*——*Up*——they say. They look like the uttermost twig-ends of the luminous world-tree itself. *Grimoire* means grammar, the arrangement of words, nothing else.

The clouds below us span the great arc of the horizon. Looking down upon it is like looking along the top of an immense white forest; albino oaks bleached like bone; enormous coralised florets of white. Then we have moved higher in the sky and the clouds look more like a snowfall, a snow-covered landscape. Sound shrinks in my ears, which removes me further from the scene I am observing. I might glance bak and see Gradi in animated conversation with the other passengers, but it's all dumb show, a front with nothing behind it. Then, hold my nose and close my mouth and blow hard and ears pop, and the words become audible again.

We fly on and the cloud cover below us breaks into cumulus, fragmenting into innumerable islets of white isolated against the deep blue of the Arctic Sea far beneath. It looks like the edge of the pak ice. Then the cloud vanishes, we are over clear sea, the blue unlittered with cloud. For long minutes we fly on over the unmarked sea, and then, slowly at first but with gathering haste as we move onwards, the cloud gathers again, like patches of foam on an immense and immensely blue bath of water. Then there is nothing but cloud beneath us: we are over another horizoning bank of cloud, the white below us covered in odd striations and grooves running for hundreds of miles, scored into the white bubblewrap bobbliness of the whole. The engines roar louder, for we are piking up speed.

'Elem two minutes,' calls the pilot from the open-plan cokpit. 'Everybody get ready,' and we are supposed to bukle up, like landing and take-off, for Elem represents a middle sort of take-off, or perhaps a landing of a different sort, a landing onto the colossal branches of the great tree. Nobody really bothers with the safety. Then the pilot says 'OK, OK.' And he fliks the switches.

The Elem motor hums, its generator coils running underneath our floor and out along the wings. The wings start shaking like the terrors are in them. The cabin jiggles violently. I hate this part. I always hate this part of every flight. An *ahh*, half moan and half exhalation, is vibratoed by the shaking. The *ahh* is from my throat. It just comes out, I can't control it. The blue looks a long way down now. Little clumps of white afro cloud.

'Little faster, hold on,' the pilot announces, over the noise, his voice tremulously bright. 'Hold on, folksies.' The whine of the Elem motor increases in pitch and, suddenly, *schoom*, we are flying level and smooth. I have been holding my breath and now I release it. But I keep my eye on the view below. It is my suspicious terror that hints to me that by merely looking down as we enter this bizarre magical mode of flight I can exert some magical pressure upon the ground and thuswise hold us up, balanced, as it were, on the invisible shaft of my eye.

There are a few sparks coming off the leading edge of the wing. This is one of the things that happens in Elem flight, sometimes; and it goes away when the air gets thinner. But that knowledge does not reassure me. Sparks, they glitter into existence in irregular clusters along the leading edge of the wing, like luminous crumbs of disaster, and the spirit of fire, and the promise of love, *for do we not*, sonorous voice, echoing in the echoey head, *do we not fly through the medium of love?* Like a ten-euro preacher, very not-good cheapskate preacher-man, very very not-good-at-all. Perhaps he had moved to the uplands to be nearer to God, this nonexistent preacher, who knows? *Does not love strike sparks from our leading edge, and give us the gleam in our lives? Did you not, yourself, collide with Gradi herself as a flint upon granite, and strike up the sparks of love? And did those sparks not fall on the tinder of your heart and flame up in passion?* So now the inner preacher is addressing me directly, and that is the most not-good of all – *by – golly – oh – fuk*. I am sweating a little. I am panting a little. I can't take my eyes of the sparks hurtling off the leading edge of the wing. Perhaps a fellow passenger will lean over and try to reassure me, 'that often happens, it don't mean shit, don't fret over that' or something like that. Perhaps not. I am scared.

Once, observing my twitchiness, a fellow passenger, some skinnyma-link fellow, asked me, 'If you hate flying so much, why do you keep going up?'

'It's not so bad up,' I replied. 'Properly *up*. You don't feel like you're continually on the edge of falling when you're actually *up*. It's – peaceful. It's the getting that is so – stressful.' But all the time I spoke I was looking, not at my interlocutor, but at the view below.

And then, miraculously, a purply darkness thikens around us. Blue shrinks to a sedimentary layer of paler shades pressed down against the horizon by the much greater weight of blak, and stars distil out of the sky like droplets of luminous condensation. Finally I am able to relax a little. I breathe out.

I breathe out.

I concentrate upon breathing out. I'm not even sure where the breath is coming from that I am breathing out so thoroughly. I am purged of air. My lungs are as vacuum filled. But it's alright, it's alright, *we're here*, and the babble of people chatting around me becomes audible again, and I look out of the window at a land of wonders, a blak and three-dimensional sink of a land, and the view.

Look down now. What see you? The dunes of the West African desert crowd together like ripples in yellow sand at low tide. The white peaks of the mountain ranges, running through central Asia, or running along the bakbone of South America, blend into the broken cloud formations which they so strongly resemble.

The spekly, sugary look of the high white cloud that covers most of the visible demihemisphere. It looks like sand has been trailed over a curving blue surface.

The globe looks so vivid and sharp directly below, yet the horizon-arc is so misty viewed as it is aslant, looks so air-brushed, a 2-D ring of fuzzy blue ringing the bulging 3-D world. I remember wat it is about this place that I love so. My relief and my love mingle, and I find that I am crying. Gradi has come bak, and kisses me on my cheek. 'Soppy,' she says, kindly. 'Crying again?'

Since certain recent events, I have been crying all the time, it is true. There are deaths it is possible to learn to accept, because there are structures society provides that help us work through the grieving process. There are other kinds of grieving, such as the sort I have been enduring, for which these structures do not exist, such that the grits of grief precipitate out of the miasma as teary rain for months and months. Her acknowledging it makes me cry more.

The in-the-chest urge almost overwhelms me, to level with her, to tell – her – the – *truth* – in all its horror, to throw myself on her mercy, to beg her not to stop loving me. I can barely keep it under control. 'I just love this place,' I say, feebly. She is strapping herself in the seat next to me to stop floating off. 'And I love you,' I add, even more weakly, feeling vulnerable and stupid as I say it.

'I love you too,' she replies, but her voice is automatic, it's not real, and the bulging urge to confess curdles and sours in my breast. She is not even looking at me. That's the truth of it.

Here is a Gradisil speech

This speech, like the previously described flight up, is also is from late in her career. In the early days (which we will come to in a moment) she sometimes gave speeches to mere knots of people: three people in a tin can whirling round the world; a mere seven people on one occasion, I remember, in an empty storage facility, also in the hurtling Uplands. But usually, in the early days, she would not give speeches as such. She would engage in conversation. She would visit, like a good neighbour. This was so old-fashioned a political strategy it was almost modishly novel. Groundling politicians never 'just' met; and how could they, when their constituencies were counted in the millions? Instead, they interacted only with people preselected, these meetings being streamed out to much larger audiences. But it was thought of as almost dishonest, certainly disingenuous, for a President to pretend he was 'just out there, pressing the flesh'. How could a groundling President, stroll amongst all his people and stare them smilingly out, face-to-face? Upland was different, of course. When I first moved there, before knowing Gradi (and how strange a phrase that is – as if there could truly be a before) my first Upland house took its place in a population of no more than 50,000. That's not even a city, nor even a town; that's a village. It became a more populous place later; but I'm talking about the beginning.

So through canvassing Gradi could meet a significant percentage of the total population she was working towards representing. It was a unique political environment. Here is one of her speeches. They've all been preserved for future historians:

Upland is a new country. But more than this it is a new kind of country. In the past when new territory was opened up it was – America, Australia – largely colonised by the poor. Indeed, the first stage of colonial history is largely wealthy nations deliberately offloading their poor upon the wide open spaces. Those poor did not, many of them, stay poor for many generations: there were indigenous populations to press into servitude, people who had developed the natural resources, hus-banded the land in various ways, whose labour and resources the settlers could steal. When they were plagued and slaved into abeyance, there was also the new poor, settlers from other lands, who also could be harnessed. This has been the logic of colonisation on Earth for centuries.

Not in Upland. We have no poor. We supplant no aborigines.

There were no previously existing indigenous peoples here. More significantly there are no poor people amongst our population. Most are wealthy; some are super-wealthy. Think of that!

It is not that Uplanders are somehow better human beings than previous settlers of previous new worlds. If we had happened to be poor – and if we had happened to find a population of technologically bakward little green men living amongst the space junk – then we would probably have exploited them. Stolen their habitats. Made them slave for us. But we weren't poor. And there wasn't anybody here before us.

And so we are in a unique position. We can build a nation that – for the first time in the history of the world! – is not founded on conquest, oppression, on human misery. To build a fair nation! To build a strong nation.

To build a guiltless nation, a beacon for the future. That is our challenge – and our glory!

I remember that speech particularly well. I remember thinking at the time how typical it was, and indeed its very typicalness made it memor-able. There were hundreds of speeches like that. Perhaps seventy people were present, not counting myself, Mat, Liu and Georgina.

We were inside wat they used to call a house, a structure that was in fact an enormous tube, a fifty-metre-long cylinder schlepped Upland filled with some tradeable (milk, wine, who knows) strapped beneath one of the Leviathan-class Tanker jets FowenCo developed specifically for the Upland traffic. First, the pilots sold the contents, mostly to middlemen and middlewomen. Then the pilots sold the tube, and some enterprising Uplander cleaned it and sealed it and fitted an open access porch that could accommodate scores of planes at once; they could then rent it out – or live in it – or do watsoever they chose.

This tube was paked with enthusiastic Gradiphiles. How they loved her! How completely they loved her! People had hooked themselves onto the floor-straps, and the wall-straps, either side of the ceiling (isn't it tiring having to deploy those inverted commas, that prissy pedantry, the 'ceiling' yes, the 'floor' yes, we know). They listened to her every word. Most had recording buttons, so as to be able to replay it over and over.

As she finished her speech, the applause started. People clapped and clapped, the sound like summer rainfall against a stone tile roof. Gradi had the knak of smilingly acknowledging applause without ever looking smug.

From the far end of the tube she looked small. But, then, she *was* small. Of course, the people in that tube were not applauding her as such, the small-framed, slightly plump, dark-haired woman, they were applauding the sense of hope she brought them, the possibilities, she sparked in their minds, the frigid brilliances of the dream she was peddling. They were applauding the vision of themselves as citizens, stakeholders of a new world power. In other words they were applauding their own egos, and the self-regarding indolence of it made me scornful; but privately scornful. I kept my scorn to myself. And, naturally, I clapped too. I was the Husband, the Husband-in-public.

I fixed my gaze upon a curiously-shaped patch of mould growing up against one of the strip lights. The applause went on and on.

As it finally died, Mat unhooked his foot and floated up. 'OK,' he said, brightly. 'Questions?'

Later, bak in our plane (we weren't leaving, but space was tight in the tube and this was the best we could do by way of an anteroom) – bak in the plane with Mat and Georgina and Liu and me, Grad was glowing, beaming. She was wide-eyed and buzzing, flashing smile after smile from her dark little face. She often got that way after a successful rally. 'To our next gig!' she beamed. She panted the question. 'I think it's time to spread a little more love.'

At the beginning of our marriage, at the beginning of Gradi's career, we visited widely amongst the peoples of the Uplands, canvassing, meeting, growing networks and making as many friends as we possibly could. This, for several years, was our main occupation. And I say *our* occupation, but it was Gradi, it was always Gradi. At the beginning she had only one assistant, other than myself: a general political factotum called Mat Chang (*Mat* being short for *Mohammed*) who followed her out of an unquenchable belief in her manifest political destiny as the saviour of the Uplands. He loved her. We all loved her, of course. He was a young-middle-aged businessman who had made a fortune out of banknote design – software to design it, machines for printing it out so that it looked exactly like the actual antique product (dollars or euros), something that enjoyed a worldwide vogue in the early '80s just as the major powers finally retired their last foldable exchange. Frat houses, Reading Tribes, gangs, families, all sorts of groups made their own banknotes, really beautiful things; people traded unique designs; collectors assembled huge collections. There were many imitators, but Mat's company was first in, and claimed the Vogue, and he sold up and took a considerable fortune and moved Upland. When Gradi moved Upland herself, as my wife, and slipped so naturally into her unique hand-shaking and face-to-facing political career, he got to know her. He fell under her spell. Everybody falls under Gradi's spell sooner or later; Mat was just one of the first.

And so, in those early days, we three flew from house to house; we chatted with old friends, and made new friends; we radio'd or phoned from our plane to speak to householders who were too suspicious, or too hermetic, to agree to allow us in. We started visiting as many houses as we could. 'Wat do you want?' people would ask. (They would only ask this at the beginning, of course; after a while Gradi's fame grew large enough such that this question became superfluous).

Gradi would introduce herself. And replies:

'Who are you? Wat do you want? Leave us alone, we have a firearm.'

– *or* –

static, nothing, no reply, which was another way of saying *fuk off*.

– *or* –

'Never heard of you. You trying to sell something?' which at least left the door open.

– *or* –, perhaps, a more welcoming conversation, or even an invitation into their house. During the first year the former responses were more frequent than the latter; but in the second and subsequent years the latter became more typical.

We met many people this way. It was not that we were making friends, for politicians – I mean true politicians, not amateur committee-sitters or school-board makeweights – must not expect to make friends. But we were establishing a good network of positive contacts.

– we piked up a new transp signal and swooped down for speed and up to bank and slow outside a three-room house of spacious proportions linked together in one long line, with a large bulb on the end, the porch, with two planes doked. The side of this house was inscribed in a flowing magenta script of sikles, half-moons, rice-grain dashes and marks: Arabic. We phoned in. 'Hello! How are you?'

After a pause, a man's voice, with no visuals: 'Who are you? Whoever you are we request that you leave us in peace.'

'My name,' said Gradi, 'is Gradisil. We were just passing, and were hoping to introduce ourselves.'

Another pause: 'why?'

'To make friends. We are all Uplanders together, and I believe we need to know one another – to help each other out if need be, to leave people alone otherwise.'

Another pause, and then a different male voice, deeper and with more of an undertone of anger: 'the name of this house is *daru'l-ridzwan*. This house had been established by the People's Islamic Republic of Brunei as a retreat, for contemplation and the Will of *Al'lah*, the wise, the compassionate.'

'Well,' said Gradi, finding in her voice that extraordinary ingenuousness and innocence of tone that served her so well as a politician, 'as a European, and somebody who fought the Americans in the last war, I can understand your caution upon encountering a stranger here in the US-occupied Uplands.'

The voice coughed a few phonemes of scornful laughter. 'We are not afraid of the US, up here or below. US occupation in this region, this is only a joke. Please leave us in peace; we wish to have nothing to do with politicians, orbital or ground-based. We are a religious retreat.'

I could tell from the expression on Gradi's face that she had immediately cloked *daru'l-ridzwan* as a lost cause. She had the politician's instinct to know when to persevere with a possible convert, and when to abandon the case. 'I understand,' she said. 'I myself have no desire to receive the infected title of politician. We shall of course leave you in peace. Only, before we go, please allow me to tell you – we believe the Americans are planning military occupations in the Uplands, with a view to registering all transponder codes and levying taxes upon them. Our advice is that you keep a number of transponders, with different codes, and that should the Americans visit you appear to accede to their demand, register your transp and then jettison it into orbit and start using a new one.'

There was no reply to this, and soon Gradi nodded to Mat and we dropped into a lower orbit and sped away. The sun stretched two arms of light around the curve of the Earth, lazily, before blinding us with its face.

– we piked up a new transp signal and swooped down for speed and up to bank and slow outside an aggregation of rooms, linked in so disorderly a manner that it took a while before we could count them: five, a power-bloc connected, and a mantle of ice spread like tendrils over the whole. There was only one plane parked at the porch.

Gradi phoned in, and the people inside were delighted to hear from us. 'This is so great,' said an excitable voice, and an excitable smooth face on the tiny phonescreen, it being impossible to tell whether either was male or female. 'I've heard of you – I really approve of wat you're doing. You wanna come in?'

'Thank you very much,' said Gradi, sombrely.

We doked at their porch, and pulled the hatch to float into a hot wet dishcloth atmosphere flavoured with something sharp and offensive to the palate, ammoniac. There were lights on in every room, and a heater in most of them, and the air was blurry with smoke. Smoking in an Upland house is a stupid thing to do, but some Uplanders do it; and although they pollute their air and strain their scrubbers they enjoy (apart from the chemical input into their bloodstreams of course) the sight of smoke in zero g, which is something weird and beautiful: pooling out from a cigarette end, dissipating into a perfect haze, like a drop of oil spreading entirely to cover the surface of still water. There are none of the ribbons and strings of smoke you get from smoking downbelow: instead a slowly expanding oval as you draw the cigarette through the air to prevent the accumulated smoke snuffing the lit end. It makes for a hypnotically sculptural sense of ease.

There were half a dozen people in the house, men and women, and more than half a dozen more (we were told) downbelow at the moment. They were all young, or youngish, and welcomed us with disarming openness. We all hitched ourselves to wallstraps or furnishings and passed around a globe of weak, warm beer. 'It's a cost-share thing,' one of the householders, Brendan, explained. 'We're none of us rich. I'm a schoolteacher. Aziz there is a software specialiser. Lyn and Kate both work for the government' (the EU, he meant). 'But we all love it up here; so though we're none of us rich we've pooled our money with a dozen other people and bought a plane, bought this house. We spend as much time up here as we can.'

The source of the ammoniac smell became apparent as a cat came floating through the doorway. It was a large, overfed domestic cat, with fur the colour of a tiger's eyes. The expression on the creature's face was that of furious non-comprehension, an animal that did not understand and implacably did not like the experience of weightlessness. He scrabbled at a wall, trying to get a purchase, but there was nothing for him to sink his claws into and he only succeeded in propelling himself into the middle of the room. Urine beaded in a kinked string of noisome pearls from his hindquarters.

The householders laughed joyously at this, and did not seem to mind the slow floating trajectories of the miniature fluid asteroids, inevitably due to intersect with the walls, or with the occupants, of the house. I found it distasteful, and although I tried to hide my feelings I'm certain my distaste was only too obvious. But Gradi, though fastidious and clean in her own space, seemed genuinely not to care. She laughed with them all, chatted, and had an involved private conversation with Georgina, a turf-headed violet-eyed girl with a permanent *femme-qui-rit* rictus on her face and the slightly loose-skinned slenderness of the drug-enhanced slimmer. Whilst they talked, Brendan and Aziz showed me round their communal house.

Later, Gradi generated an ersatz but wholly convincing enthusiasm of her own, to chime with the messy enthusiasm of this house. 'Georgina wants to help,' she announced, with her arm around Georgina's skinny shoulders. Georgina's grin was even wider than before, if that were possible. 'Georgina wants to join my staff. I've told her we can find a place for her.'

'Many hands make light work,' said Mat.

'Welcome aboard,' said Gradi.

'Thanks, I'm really excited,' said Georgina, a nervous trill in her voice.

'Shall I tell you where we are, and when we are? Guys?' said Gradi, addressing the whole room. 'We're here at the *birth of a nation*.' Half a dozen wastrel weekender Uplanders, I thought to myself, and she sounds as if she's addressing the Congress and Senate of the United States itself. But that was part of her genius; to take each and every person as if they were the crucial contact that would make her political career. Never to slak. Attention to detail. 'We're here at the birth of a nation,' said Gradi, 'and we have the chance, almost unprecedented in world history, to shape the development of that nation. To make it a place of justice, equality, a shining beacon for the world below. Georgina is going to help me make that dream come true.'

There was applause. Applause followed Gradi wherever she went.

At Gradi's prompting I bought a house in Helsinki. This was early on, a year or more before we met with Georgina, several years before she addressed houses crowded with adoring followers. This was in the third year of our marriage when she was pregnant with her first child.

Finland-EU, in common with many countries above the 70th parallel, had found in the Uplanders an economic asset. Between the 70th and the 79th parallels the lines of electromagnetic force branching down from the pole were at the optimal angle in sky for the flight into space, and myriad little specialist suppliers had set themselves up in the countries in between those magic lines. Of course it was possible to climb the branches of the Yggdrasil from an inset point further south, or further north; it was simply more energy-expensive, requiring the generation of greater charge along the wing-cables. The Americans had the Quantwing and could fly straight to orbit from anywhere on the planet they liked; but that was much more energy-expensive than Elem, and only marginally cheaper than roketry, so those two bands of geographical serendipity, 60-68 north and 60-68 south, gleaned their little economic booms. Suppliers of new and second-hard hardware; little communities clustered around airstrips; the large and the small cargos that Uplanders needed, ready to be ferried up.

It was for this reason, I suppose, that Finland-EU was the first groundling nation to establish semi-official links with us. They had appointed a local minister for air economy, which was to say, for Uplander-related trade and monies, and his name was Aleksandr Smouha. The office of Smouha made surreptitious approaches to the office of Gradisil, which is to say Mat, and we flew down to Helsinki to meet with him.

We had been Upland for a couple of weeks, and it took us a day and a sleepless creaking night to begin to acclimatise to full g again: Gradi, me, Mat and a man called Liu Chuanzhi. We were taxi'd to a central Helsinki hotel where we did nothing for twenty-four hours but lie on our respective beds watching TV, or moving painfully and complainingly to the toilet and bak. But Gradi was the most resilient of any of us; more motile sooner, a better sleeper, and the following morning she was a walking, smiling picture of vigour when we were still using autocallipers on our legs to help us walk.

'You're amazing,' said Liu, to Gradi. 'It's like you just *shake off* the gravity.'

'I'm small,' said Gradi. 'That's the key. Small, and strong bones.'

But the truth was that she didn't have strong bones; she had suffered various serious and concurrent ailments as a child, and she retained, beneath her bullish exterior, a physical fragility. She simply refused to let this show. She acted *health* and *strength* with utter conviction during our first official diplomatic meeting, with Aleks Smouha, in a pine-clad room with December's sunlight falling coldly lemon-and-white through the tall windows in the far room. It all smelt of cleaning products, of polish. The sunlight made gleaming parallelograms upon the polished ebony of the tables.

'You understand,' said Aleks Smouha, 'that we cannot *officially* acknowledge the Uplands as a separate nation. Officially you're a territory of the US. And naturally we are, after '81, in a tiklish situation as far as the US is concerned.'

Gradi had adopted a thoroughly convincing facial expression of concerned understanding. It almost fooled me, who knew it to be an act. It must have made a good impression on Aleks Smouha.

'Of course,' she replied. 'We understand how difficult the Americans can be. And,' she added, with the most perfectly understated smile, 'might I compliment you on your English? It's fluent, perfectly idiomatic and almost wholly accentless.' And Aleks Smouha was flattered by this clumsy praise, because Gradi was able to put it over as convincingly ingenuous and appropriate.

'Thank you,' he replied, his pleasure too evident. 'But let me tell you wat the local government of Finland . . .'

'Not the EU,' said Gradi, nodding sorrowfully as if she perfectly understood the regrettable limitations of his position.

'No, not EU in entirety, but Suomi-EU, and, believe me, I can speak for the whole of the Finnish population when I say that we had long wished to establish a bridge with the actual Uplanders. Not the puppet American Upland representative, but the individual who most accurately and democratically represents real Uplanders . . . you, Madame, are that person.'

Gradi nodded. 'Thank you,' she replied. 'Although our system is not exactly democratic in the sense you mean.'

'I did not mean to give offence,' said the diplomat, smoothly and immediately, 'I only meant to contrast the . . .'

Gradi nodded again, and smiled, and he stopped. 'You're quite right. It is just that our system is much looser than is implied by the term democracy. We might call ourselves an anarchy, the ideological principle of no government, only the affiliation of Uplanders when and if they face common threats, or common opportunities. But anarchy is a word . . .'

'I'm not sure I'm familiar with the word . . .' said Smouha, smiling.

'An archaic term. When pressed I usually describe the government of the Uplands as a Liberty. It suits the population, and the landscape. So, for example, I have never been formally elected as Upland President . . .'

'We are aware of this, of course,' said Aleks Smouha. 'And I must report that there are members of the local government a little troubled by your status. But talking to actual Uplanders, many of whom have bases in Finnish territory, it seems clear that . . .'

'Don't make the mistake of underestimating my authority,' said Gradi, her voice gleaming with it, summoning charisma out of nowhere in that way characteristic of her.

'Of course,' demurred Smouha. 'Of course.'

'Let us be honest with one another, Minister,' said Gradi, leaning forward and somehow filling the room with her presence, with an infinitely expandable charisma. I don't know how she did that. Everybody waited for her words. 'We are here, in this room, discussing possible futures. There's little benefit, here and now, for Finland-EU or for the Uplands, in an official treaty between our two small nations; but in the future . . . who can tell? All we can offer you right now is that rather nebulous thing, the goodwill of a good proportion of Uplanders, which may or may not translate into economic benefits for your country. And I appreciate that all you can offer *us* is an under-the-table friendship, nothing that will arouse the annoyance or even notice of the USA. All you can offer us is the possibility of future flowering.'

'You put it,' said the ambassador, 'very well.'

'Then we understand one another.' She stood up.

Aleks Smouha, who had clearly been expecting some bluster, or more resistance, now found himself pouring out concessions that he had clearly intended to yield slowly, after long negotiation. 'Of course we cannot,' he said hurriedly, standing up also, 'sign anything, and we must ask you to keep these meetings secret, but I am authorised to give you my personal assurance, and the personal assurance of the whole Finnish government, that we regard ourselves as bound to you in a treaty of amity in all but name . . .'

'Excellent,' said Gradi, briskly. 'Thank you.'

Another night, slightly better sleep, and another day's rest, then the four of us were well enough to explore Helsinki a little. And so we wandered in the late afternoon through the broad clean streets of the city, past many posters announcing *Helsinki Pour Vous*, which (we debated amongst ourselves) was a festival, or a tourist advertising campaign, or a perfume, it wasn't clear. The sky was blank and bright, but its light was muted, like white neon filtered through fog. Our breath made ectoplasmic sallies out of our mouths in the winter cold.

It was my first visit to those Helsinki streets, though I came later to know them very well: the yellow-fronted monumental architecture with grids of blok-fringed windows; chain-mail sheets of Christmas lights hanging very prettily from the department storefronts; the humps of gritty snow amongst the slush; the grumbling of trams; posters announcing *Bakkonaalit* and *Kotimaan Matkailuneuvonta*, and none of our party prepared to take off our gloves to spell these words into our palmcomps and find out wat they meant. Every Helsinki man woman and child was wearing woollen hats. Nobody sported the sorts of enhancements – hair, or metabolism adaptations – popular as defences against the cold of the winter in other northern hemisphere countries. A distinctly old-fashioned feel. Every other store sold ski-wear, puffed-up multicoloured sports jakets, huge boots.

We walked past the harbour where the authorities subsidised an antique market as a draw for tourists, and we saw shrimps blak as beetles piled on beds of ice, and fish astonished at their own death lying row upon row also upon ice, and rusty-looking crabs the colour of autumn leaves. 'Are all these fished from the local seas?' Mat asked the *kioski* man.

Everybody spoke English. We didn't bother with translation chips.

'Of course,' the stallholder replied.

'Shall we buy some?' asked Liu, excited.

'I wouldn't know wat to *do* with them,' said Gradi, a little hyper after her successful diplomatic encounter (that went well, I think? she kept saying, as we wandered the streets of the city). 'Eat them raw? Microboil them? Christ knows wat.'

But the stallholder winced at her obscenities. 'Madame,' he said, a little severely. 'Excuse *me*.'

Gradi looked wide-eyed at him. 'I'm sorry, did I offend you?'

'As a Lutheran I find your swearing offensive,' he confirmed.

'I apologise again, but – if you don't mind, for I find this very interesting – is it only religious swearwords, or all swearwords? The word *fuk* for instance . . .'

'I would not use that word myself,' said the stallholder stiffly. 'But it's hardly as offensive as the citation of the Lord Saviour's name.'

'A hundred years ago *fuk* was considered far more offensive than Christian terminology,' she observed.

'That's as may be. I'm not interested in that. I can only say, if somebody said, eh, that f-word, or damn, or something, I would not take offence in the same way.'

'I understand. Thank you – I'll be more guarded in wat I say in future.'

The guard took her proffered hand and shook it seriously, nodding his head. As we walked away Mat whispered, in a thrilled *sotto voce*, 'if you were in a Finnish election he'd fuking vote for you!'

'You *are* a marvel,' Liu agreed.

We wandered about some more, and made our way to a bar not far from the hotel. *Bar Tartary*. Here, on orange plastic settees, under strings of glowing bulbs like luminous onions hanging from the ceiling, the four of us drank beer together. Mat and Liu were, I think, giddy. I'm sure, like I did, they felt like kids playing grown-up roles, like amateurs who were somehow, miraculously, managing to con the professionals. We were diplomats, weren't we? We were ambassadors, and politicians, and the proper representatives of tens-of-thousands of Uplanders, a whole new nation? It was exciting and giddying and slightly alarming for us; but not for Gradi. She was completely at home in this world. She was born for it. But there was a ruthless quality in her. I think I have already mentioned how ruthless she could be. Have I already mentioned that I'd loved her since the very first time I saw her? That I worshipped her, I revered her, I loved her so much it was a physical pain to me?

'Paul,' she said, in that Helsinki bar, rotating her beer glass slowly on the low table, as if its disc top were a blonde planet circling. 'I want us to buy a house in Helsinki.'

'A house in Helsinki,' I said. We owned a large house in France, and a smaller one in Iceland. But if she wanted a house in Helsinki, then I would buy one. Of course.

Mat and Liu were silent. 'OK,' I said, after a short while. 'I'll find a house here, I'll buy a house – central, is it? A central city location?'

She nodded.

'You're sure?' said Mat. 'I mean, you want a house as . . . ?'

' . . . as a diplomatic outpost?' Liu overlapped. 'Are we that *far*, yet? I mean . . .'

'Liu's right,' Mat cut in. They were both suddenly high with excitement, like schoolkids. They couldn't contain themselves. 'Obviously eventually we'll want a proper groundling base, an *embassy*, but is Finland really the place?'

'And is the time really *now*?' said Liu.

'I'd say France-EU,' said Mat, looking at me, for no other reason (I think) than that I was born in France-EU. As if that had anything to do with it.

'France, or Russia, but not yet surely,' said Liu.

They were practically bouncing on the settees. It was *look at me! notice me!* It was like toddlers, and Gradi was calm as any mother. I sipped beer and it caught a little in my throat, a heartburny sensation. I think I had an intimation of wat was coming, but perhaps that is merely the narrator's hindsight.

'It will be a private house,' said Gradi, firmly. 'A private house, that's all. We'll see wat happens down the line when we're down the line. I'm not thinking politics. Not for this one.'

'You're thinking?' Liu egged on, leaning forward.

She stopped revolving her beer glass on the table and took my hand. This was it; it was coming. 'Well,' she said. 'I'm pregnant.'

The world stopped turning. The twenty thousand houses of the Uplands fell out of the sky like rubble. The world folded over in half like a paper circle. I breathed in deeply. I breathed out.

My first thought, wide-eyed, was: *I'm to be a father!* Gradi was still speaking, 'It's early days yet, so don't go announcing it to the whole world, since I know from my mother's experience that you need to be very careful with pregnancy when you're in the habit of spending a lot of time Upland. In fact I'll be spending no more than a day or two in the Uplands at a time for the next nine months. We need a base, and I like it here.'

Liu said 'that's fantastic news, Gradi! That's, like, the *best* news!'

I thought: *I'm to be a father.* My heart, I realised, was moving faster than normal, the fibres of its muscles vibrating like strummed guitar strings. The beer had all cleared out of my skull. The decor of the bar resolved into abnormal clarity and vividness: the foul bright orange of the seating, the paisley walls, the white plastic straps fitted to the windows, the bulbous glowing ceiling lights.

'Congratulations!' Liu was saying, lifting his glass. 'C'mon everyone, a toast, to Gradi's coming motherhood. A toast!'

'We'll need serving staff,' said Gradi, to me, and squeezed my hand. 'And a house with a garden.'

'Of course,' I said, still feeling a little numb. *I'm to be a father.*

She lifted her glass, and clinked its cold rim with Liu's. I raised mine with an automatic hand, and chinked her glass and Liu's before it occurred to me to say 'Should you really be drinking in your condition?'

She smiled, and then I realised that Mat had not joined the toast. I looked over at him. He had on his face the stunned, almost-smiling expression of the druggy. And, as Gradi smiled at me and released my hand, I suddenly knew, I suddenly *knew*, that the child in Gradi's womb was not mine at all, but Mat's. And I saw that he knew too.

Wat? But of course, of course, parenting a child is not ownership, for that would make the child a thing, a plastic lump of raw immaturity. From the first assertive labial grip of a teat, the first furiously ecstatic eyes as the milk goes down, children are beings not belongings, curiously dense and branched little knots of *will*, and so, and so it does not matter that it was this spermatozoon or that spermatozoon, of the more-than-galactic trillions being generated daily in the conker-hanging testicles of the various men who surrounded Gradi, that chanced to pierce the egg. But the Paul inside the Paul sulked, bristled, despite my very best efforts – and I urge you, as you read this, sons, to believe me how strenuously I tried – to convince myself of this. I wept, although I managed to reserve the tears for my private use. This is the considered judgment of hindsight: the truly salient feature of any of this phylum of depression (under which are arranged, in neatly-lettered legends, bereavement, existential sadness, rejection, wounded amour-propre and the nebulous grey blankness that sometimes swallows the most watchful consciousnesses) is the future-blindness that accompanies it. Unable to see beyond the malign tractor beam of gloom, the sufferer can see no end to his or her misery; just as I, throughout my wife's first pregnancy, when my insight about the true identity of the father was confirmed by a thousand little clues, just as I could not see a time when I would feel anything other than corrosive humiliation. But (to glance ahead in my narrative) it did not stay like this for ever. When the child was born I felt my bones warm towards him. And children have a strong magic about them, a verbal magic (*grimoire* means grammar and is therefore, after all, only an arrangement of words), and when the boy first called me Papa the mere utterance made it so, conjured fatherhood out of me, interpellated me into the relationship.

three. Slater

On the ground

It's early in the year 2099, it's downbelow, and the frost has made coral of the blak twigs of the trees. None of Lieutenant Slater's elasticated prophylactic garments have managed the trik of preventing a certain amount of bone loss, or have prepared his muscles for the feeling of dead obesity and dreary inertia of full gravity. He spends a day only lying down, or walking slowly in callipers, *like a fuking cripple*, as he puts it to his subaltern.

He calls his wife. She is in Florida with the children. She likes Florida. She insists (insofar as somebody with a personality as passive as hers ever *insists*) on living there, she really prefers living there, despite the fact that most of the military establishments at which her husband might conceivably be based are located further north, to take advantage of the Elemag effect. There are one or two Quantplane bases in the South, but only a few, for Quant flight is so expensive.

'Don't be nervous, honey,' says Marina. 'You'll do just fine,'

'Sure,' says Slater. 'Did Caz like the movie?'

Marina laughs. The phonescreen cannot capture her pollen-delicate beauty, the extraordinary and almost Native American blakness of her spreading hair; but Slater's memory is not screen-sized or screen-limited. He loves to see her laugh. 'I'll tell you wat Carrie said about the movie,' Marina says.

Carrie is their younger child, three years old.

'Wat did she say?' Slater asks, and the total anxiety of the imminent presentation has sublimed away.

'She said "Mom I liked all of the heads and all of the bodies and all of the *legs*", that's wat she said.'

Slater laughs. 'But wat does *that* mean? I thought it was a movie about horses?'

'Zebras, yeah, it was a sort of fantasy about the zebra republic,' says

Marina, beaming. 'I don't know wat she meant about the "all of the heads" bit.'

'I gotta go, love,' says Slater, because his aide has stepped into the room. 'I gotta get my presentation ready.'

And she wishes him good luk. She tells him she loves him. She wishes him good luk again. She assures him that he will do just fine.

Through the gateway into the compound, a flagpole, a blok of three-storey barraks, and behind it all the jute-coloured winter sky of Washington. Slater's callipers take him awkwardly across this little cardboard scene. The air is very cold. Those parched-coloured clouds are *plein* with snow. Some ashy intimations of the coming storm are starting to droop, dilatory, mazy, down through the air.

He walks through the first snowflakes. The winter air of Washington State smells distantly of cold apple. This, Slater knows, is the barraks odour, released by small motile automata on continual aerosol patrol to cover wat would otherwise be an unpleasant stench of petrol and the putrid organic-pit behind the mess hall and, above all, the weirdly persistent, hot-rubber-dust stench created by the Quant engines, separating the underlying logic of space to generate their special kind of lift. A wonderful invention, of course, but one that does something horrible to the sense of smell.

But here he is. He steps inside the building, and it is crowded with folk.

A very palpable buzz of excitement is evident, a thrill that might almost be measured on a static monitor. The Vice-President is going to attend the briefing. Nobody knew that the Vice-President was planning to attend. Everybody thought that this was going to be strictly in-house, a purely military briefing. But if the Vice-President is here, then maybe the whole administration is planning to get serious about the Uplands.

It makes Slater nervous. He brushed his teeth three times in his hotel room bathroom. Immediately before coming here he had sat at the little hotel desk and opened his palmcomp, extended the keyboard, let his fingers rattle and dart at the keys as he ran through his presentation one last time, as he cheked the latest web news, as he confirmed the truth of the rumour about Gradisil and her third pregnancy (and it does seem to be true). Usually working at a comp calms Slater, takes his mind off things, but on this occasion it was as if his fingers were plunging and dabbling in his own chest. It felt as if his heart had embarked upon its final drum solo, and was working itself towards a clattering climax.

His heart is still straining as he prepares to give his speech. It's only the effect of the gravity, he tells himself, just gravity making my heart tumble. This is true but this doesn't calm him.

Outside the window is Washington State and winter, and it is snowing in earnest now. A very great many white corpuscles of snow are floating and spiralling lazily in the air, as if disinclined to join the upholstered chill of the ground. The sky, insofar as it is visible, is pale grey and bright. Slater stares through the glass of the main door at this weather. There's no weather in the Uplands.

The hall is crowded, but as he walks through the door Slater knows it is too late to turn bak, and his nerves solidify into something more useful, something that approximates courage. This is one of the oldest soldiers' triks.

First coffee: then the presentation, Q&A, all that. Hagen is attending the briefing; the only face Slater knows in the crowd of people. He's there in the hall amongst all the other uniformed USAF and USUP officers filling the little room, holding the little cups to their chestbones and talking to one another animatedly. Hagen has created a little knot of people around him, interested in his plans to build a simulated gravity environment.

'If the radius is *large* enough,' he is saying, 'then we can reduce the effects of nausea. But that's only reducing, that's not doin' away with it altogether. I guess it'll just be one of those things. If you want to move under the influence of artificial gravity you're going get a bit queasy.'

'Wat we need,' put in a stoky female officer, 'is a *proper* artificial gravity.'

'Sho nuf,' agrees a dun-coloured officer with deep-set weathering lines on his elderly face The creases have enhanced and piked out the lines of his cheekbones, the contours of his mouth, and have left his eyes and forehead relatively line-free.

'Wat we need is, like,' continues the female officer, 'a grid we can charge up to *imitate* gravity, something to fit in dek floors to *draw* people *down*.' The last three words are accompanied by hand gestures, the right hand pushing the left down in three connected motions. It annoys Slater that the officer has said *draw people down* but acted out with her hands *push people down*. That sort of disparity seems to him an index of sloppiness of thinking.

'Yes, that *would* be good,' says Hagen, expansively, 'but until such time as a wholly new technology is invented, we're stuk with physics as we understand it, and it's acceleration, or centrifugal effect, or we're stuk with elastic straps tying our boots to the deking.' He beams.

'Still,' says the walnut-skinned old officer, 'they are inventing new stuff all. The. Time.'

'Actually,' puts in a thin-faced lieutenant, his beakish lips quivering slightly, 'I was reading a paper on this on-on hawknet, and they-they said, the authors of the paper that is, they said they surveyed the-the *rate* of technological innovation over four centuries and-and they plotted *two* graphs, one for technical advance, and one for underlying *conceptual* breakthroughs and-and,'

But the others have grown bored with his stammering prolixity. 'If we could throw out a wheel the size of the Moon,' said Hagen, opening his arms to indicate vastness, then it would need to rotate only very slowly, and the nausea would be next to nothing. Size is everything.'

The officers nod at this. The military has ever and always been enamoured of size.

'After a peak in the twentieth there's been a-a-a *steady* decline of both technical and conceptual innovation, with-with the conceptual graph descending steeper, which-which means that,'

Nobody is listening to the lieutenant, but still he keeps babbling on.

The room settles, and subalterns usher people through to the seats. Slater makes his way to the front of the room.

He gives his presentation, and waits for questions.

It goes well, but nobody puts any questions to him afterwards. Nobody is more status-obsessed than an army man, and they are all waiting for the Vice-President to kik it off.

But all the VP says is, 'Nobody got any questions?'

Nobody has any questions.

'Thank you very much, Lieutenant,' says the Vice-President. That's that, the end of the meeting. And at his words the room is filled with the rumble of many chairs being pushed bak, of many military officers standing up and filing out.

And, slightly dazed, his heart still working strenuously in his chest under the desperate weight of one full g and his limbs trembling slightly, Slater smiles, and nods, and pulls his thumb out of the projector slot and prepares to leave.

But before he can leave the VP comes over, and says 'A word in private? Walk with me to my jet.' And for the first time in his career Slater feels that heady sense that comes of being intimate, howsoever briefly, with the very powerful, that beguiling taste of proximity to the heart of things.

A conversation with Vice-President Johannes Belvedere III

The Veep walks with Lieutenant Slater to the door of the building but, looking out, stops there. 'Let's talk here,' he says, as one of his five-strong security detail sweeps the corridor (even though it's a military facility) and two more take up armed position fore and aft. 'No point in getting mouthfuls of snow as we *chat.*'

Slater is a little thrown by the peculiar emphases the Veep gives to the word 'chat'; but he says, 'Yes sir.'

'Good presentation,' says Jon Belvedere III briskly. 'The Moon?'

'I'm sorry, sir?'

'You didn't mention it?'

'No, sir. The Moon – still technically under international treaty, so the Moon, it's in a slightly different category from . . .'

'But we go there.'

'Yes sir, though not often. There's nothing there, pretty much. And as I say, we can't actually claim the territory without violating . . .'

'Uplands different?'

'Well, eh, yes, sir, the orbital treaties, such as they are, are a century and a half old. No one supposes they'd stand up to sustained legal challenge, so they've effectively fallen into abeyance. Leastways, no lawyers filed suit when we declared Uplands a US territory in eighty-one.'

'Lawyers,' says the Veep, drawing an enormous and rather intimidating smile out of his wide face. Slater's answering smile is wholly beta-male-mimics-alpha, nothing to do with pleasure of amusement. He is struck, stupidly, by how *very like the Vice-President* the Vice-President looks, this face that he has seen a thousand times on screen media and in the newsbooks now *here* in front of him, and some part of his brain cannot get past the thought, *wow you really look like the Veep of the USA.* The brambly hair only partly kept under control by his personal barber; the slightly goat-eyed intensity of his stare, the drug-perfected tone of his beech-coloured skin that doesn't – a frequent unfortunate correlative of drug-perfected epidermis – escape a certain staleness, a hint of the unalive. But certainly a strong face, a handsome face, certainly a senatorial face.

By saying 'lawyers' in that tone of voice, the Veep is laconically conveying the sense 'damn lawyers, they're a pain in the ass, now that the US is the undisputed monopower the closest we've got to an

186

international enemy is fuking lawyers and their endless antiGovt suits'. Not that he would ever *say* that, out loud. Of course.

'Yes, sir,' says Slater.

'OK,' says the Veep, the smile tuked away in his face again ready for another occasion, his mouth set sternly. Statespersonlike. 'Forget the Moon. Wat about these Uplands. They're ours, de facto *and* legally, yeah-yeah?'

'That's right sir.'

'And these Uplands are just crawling with billionaires, yeah-yeah?'

'Well I don't know about crawling, sir, but . . .'

'And we're *entitled* to tax their ass. So remind me why we're not getting a revenue stream?'

'Well, sir, the problem . . .'

'Remind me,' says the Veep, looking over Slater's shoulder, 'why the golden coins ain't simply *tumbling* down out of the high sky into our treasury coffers?'

Slater waits a beat to be sure the Veep has finished talking, and then says: 'Well, sir, the problem is with collection. We register all the house transponders so theoretically we can locate any tax avoider. But the Uplanders just change their transponders. They throw the old one out the door, and it continues in orbit, so our AIs think they still know where the house is, but then we send a team round to enforce pay-ment and they just find the box orbiting in blank space, not the house. The house has disappeared into billions of cubic kilometres of space.'

'So do another sweep. Make it illegal to switch transps.'

'We did that, sir, in eighty-five.'

'So do another sweep, *fine* the offenders, enforce the taxes, make a few examples.'

'It's,' says Slater, nervy, 'triky, sir. They're slippery. When we do catch up with them they deny they've ever seen us before. They're not who we think they are. They've changed accreditation, or papers. If we've got DNA on them they claim to be identical twins, that kind of manoeuvre. They're wealthy and their lawyers are good. There are, if memory serves, four thousand legal cases pending contesting individual tax assessments.'

'Four *thousand*?'

'It's very expensive for us, naturally. A greater net financial loss is due to legal contestation than to the brute expense of maintaining Fort Glenn and its staff, sir,'

'It's co-ordinated?'

'Sir, yes, in our opinion this is a very efficiently co-ordinated policy of civil non-cooperation and obstruction.'

'This Gradisil woman?'

'She's obviously the ringleader.'

'Calls herself the President of the Uplands.'

'Well, actually, sir, she's careful never to call herself that. But plenty of other people call her that.'

'Elected?'

'No, sir,'

'Remind me why we don't have her in custody?'

'Well,' says Slater, nervy again, 'it's not necessarily that simple, er, sir, er. It's. Partly it's just the problem of locating her. It's. Upland's a very big place and she has lots of friends who'll happily stash her in their bak rooms. And partly there's the legal question. At the moment it would be hard to make a charge stik, which could turn any arrest into a very costly jamboree for the lawyers, and a very embarrassing public relations snafu for us.'

'Right, but if,' says the Veep, unsheathing his enormous smile a second time for several long seconds, 'but if we're at *war*, a properly constituted and declared *war*, then the legal situation changes.'

Slater's straining heart does a gulping thrum; this is assuredly exciting. He can feel history about to turn, feel the say-so of the Powerful Man on the verge of moving events around a new axis. 'Yes, sir,' he says, quikly, 'that's exactly the point. Then she'd be a legitimate prisoner of war, and we could hold her as long as we like. In that case the tax cases go into legal abeyance, 'til the war is over, and we open up all manner of possibilities.'

'OK, lieutenant,' said the Veep, looking past Slater's shoulder and trying not to look like somebody who has forgotten his interlocutor's name, 'OK, lieutenant, let me tell you wat the President is thinking. The President is thinking we either have to be very discreet about this, or else we need to come out all guns blazing. Yes?'

'Yes, sir,' said Slater.

'My sense is that discreet has not worked. Is that your sense? Yeah? Tell me: is that the sense of the President's *good-and-faithful* General Niflheim?'

'Yes sir, I believe the general and I agree on that.'

'Then, guns-blazing it is going to be. You and I, Lieutenant,' the Veep says, pulling his collar up against his nek, 'are going to be seeing a lot of one another in the next few weeks. We need a pretext, we need a strategy, we need AI'd in-and-out dates, and above all we need a *proper* intelligence so we can grab this Gradisil as soon *as*, cut the head off of the chiken.'

His security detail have opened the door and cheked the walkway outside. Snowflakes are drifting in through the open aperture, and a fridge-door waft of cold air touches faces. Outside the snow has loaded the roofs and trees.

'Sir,' says Slater, 'just before you go . . .'

The Vice-President of the United States of America pauses, looks at Slater.

'One more thing, sir. She's pregnant.'

Slowly the Veep says, 'I think I'd already heard that rumour. Yes.'

'It's true. Which means she'll be on the ground, for the duration of her prepartum. That's very good for us. She's got two houses in the EU, though she'd be crazy to go there. Nevertheless it'll be much easier to apprehend her if she's on the ground.'

'Good.'

'Only – sir—' and Slater is increasingly anxious at how bad this looks, detaining the Veep as he is about to hurry through the snow to his jet, buttonholing the second most powerful man on the planet, 'only, sir, that means the operation *must* get a green-to-go within the next four months, five at the outside.'

One final glimpse of Jon Belvedere III's mighty smile. 'Lieutenant,' he says, turning away from Slater, 'we'll be at war long before that, I promise you.'

four. Paul

Here is another Gradisil speech

This also is from late in her career, not long before the war, when the killing efficiency of the American army was unleashed upon the Uplands and so many people died. She was in a house in high orbit with somewhere between forty and fifty people, almost all of whom were recording her Q&A for wider dissemination around the Uplands.

I was asked: how can you feel patriotic about empty space? It's the most deserted of deserts, 'a million times more barren than the Negeb' as the phrase goes. Wat is there to be patriotic about? A few free-falling foxholes in an immensity of nothingness. He was no Uplander who said this to me! [laughter] How to answer him? Perhaps by inviting him to see for himself? [applause] Or perhaps by challenging wat he thinks he means. Let's leave the patriotism *to the groundlings, to the little children downbelow cowed under the disapproving gaze of their Pater-Patriarch.*

Instead, let me suggest matriotism. *Instead, let me suggest that not a single Uplander owes a duty of obedience to this country, that not a single Uplander owes a duty of tax to this country, [cheers] not a single Uplander owes a duty of subjection to this country, that all we owe is our multiple-individual loves for freedom, as we circulate forever in the amniotic orbit. And if it comes to war [more cheers] then we will fight not because the father orders us to, but because the mother needs defending, because our freedom needs defending, against the enemy.*

Afterwards, in response to some question or other, she said: 'Well some people just love deserts, I guess.' That brought laughter of delighted recognition. People took that up as a sort of slogan. You'll find that in the archives of political quotation under Gradi's name.

The dangers of canvassing

In those early days of Gradi's political career we flew from house to house, meeting and getting to know and *getting ourselves known*, that was the most of it. People ask: but weren't you scared? Weren't you *sometimes* scared? There are a lot of criminals and sychos hiding in the Uplands, fugitives from downbelow justice, and you were walking unprotected into all these strangers' houses, were you *really* never scared?

The answer to that question is that I was frequently scared; and I believe Mat was often scared, and when he joined us, Liu was scared as well. Sometimes we would call in and people would be suspiciously eager for us to enter their houses. Though we went in together, strength in numbers, we did not go armed, though Mat sometimes suggested it. But wat sort of an impression would that make upon people? Gradisil objected. Hey, the President's come to visit our house, but she's coming through the door with a gun?

She began referring to herself as President early on, but only in private. She was too canny of the precarious *auctoritas* of her political status to do so in public.

So we might pik up a transp signal and swoop down for speed and up to bank and slow outside a four-room house made of hexagonal units, with a two-plane porch and get ourselves invited in. Inside would be (on this one occasion) a trio of dangerous-looking men; wearing static batteries at their neks to keep their long hair in a state of continual electric excitement, such that their drug-skinny bodies appeared to dangle from a massy dandelion explosion of hair. They were tattooed all over their bodies in sine waves of purple and gold, and their naked torsos were a knotty mismatch of bone-prominent skinniness and occasional drug-enhanced muscles standing up like elongated blisters. They declared themselves to be the Cannes Cannibals (though they spoke no French) and laughed aggressively and drank continually, and throughout the whole long hour of our visit I was in a state of heightened terror, a condition I was able to disguise only poorly. All three of them carried firearms, with which they played as they talked. There were many more firearms strapped to the wall behind them. I convinced myself that I could decipher their body language, and that language told me that they were going to shoot Mat and myself and rape Gradi and kill her. Or perhaps (I became increasingly convinced of this as the hour wore on) shoot Gradi and rape Mat and myself, torturing us perhaps for days before leaving us in their porch and opening the front door. Sweat beaded from my forehead clinging to my skin in the zero g until it was a bulging skin of water, and I wiped my palm across it scattering salt pearls of water in a promiscuous little shower.

'You sweating,' observed one of the Cannes Cannibals, leering at me.

'It's hot in here,' I returned. And indeed it was hot in there. But that was not why I was sweating.

But then the meeting was over, and the Cannes Cannibals were congratulating Gradi on her plan to snatch freedom for the Uplands from the USA, and cheering her, and promising to spread the word. I could not believe that we had escaped with our lives. It was thirty minutes in the plane afterwards before I began to believe that I was going to live. But Gradi was blithe. Were you not even a little bit scared? I asked her. No, she said.

I believed her.

On another occasion, in a two-room house with one inhabitant (a man called Denis, from Australia) there was Actual Violence. In the middle of our conversation he brought out a gun and told us he was robbing us. But Gradi was utterly calm. It was miraculous, it was *inspiring* to watch her. She did not move, and she did not give ground. I think he was called Denis, our attaker. Perhaps it was Dengbert. His house was painted mustard yellow on the inside, I do remember that: and I remember that the lighting was very bright. I remember thinking that a man might go mad in such a room, and when he brought his gun out I thought to myself, without satisfaction: you were spot on *there*, Paul. 'That's an ordinary gun. If you fire that weapon inside your house,' said Gradi, unruffled, 'you'll puncture the wall. You want to puncture your wall? How much air will you lose whilst you're fighting off my two associates?' She gestured towards us.

Mat pulled a face; I believe he was trying to look mean. I don't know how I looked; I'm sure I looked as terrified as I felt.

'Just give me your chips, give me your stuff,' the robber repeated.

'No,' said Gradi.

'I fuking *mean* it, guys. I'll shoot you.'

'No,' said Gradi, 'you won't.'

There was a long pause. Then the robber put his gun away, and looked pointedly past us at the wall behind. And then Gradi started talking to him again, skilfully drawing him bak into conversation, and by the time we left there was even a tear in his eye. He pledged himself to our cause with a tear in his eye.

Of course, the Gradi magic did not always work. On more than one occasion we had to surrender valuables; although, of course, we did not travel with much that was stealable. Once an elderly couple both drew knives, and when Gradi tried to talk them round the old man launched at her and cut her on the arm. On another occasion a man punched Mat calling him 'filthy Muslim, filthy Muslim' over and over, although it is hard to land an effective punch in zero g. We retreated with ignominious haste from that encounter.

But the single worst occasion was not a lowlife, not an obvious criminal or hermit or madman, but a wealthy man from Italy-EU called Stefan. We piked up his transp, swooped down for speed and up to bank and slow outside a six-room mansion of spacious proportions. We were invited on board, and we were met in the foreroom by a blak-suited servant, an actual butler, do you believe that? Very nineteenth-century. We were led through, hand over hand along a wall-ladder, to a gorgeously furnished room, at the far end of which a slim, hawk-faced young man was resting against a wall, watching a large scrollscreen. He killed the visuals and smiled at us.

'Hello,' said Gradisil, brightly. 'My name is Gradisil.'

'And I am Stefan,' he replied. And he talked pleasantly if rather distantly to us for a while. But he was a rapist, a man with a cruel and hateful aspect to his nature, and even Gradisil could not talk him round when he was started upon his attak.

Halfway through a conversation about the possible political complexion of a future Upland assembly, he waved to his servant, and the fellow brought out a gun.

Gradi was as unflappable as ever, but nothing she could say made a dent upon his purpose to do us harm. To do *her* harm most especially. 'You're doing this to the wrong people,' she told him, calmly.

'I disagree,' was his reply.

Mat and I were cuffed; the servant strapping our wrists behind our baks with tight plastic bands, and hooking us to the wall. 'And now you will take off your clothes,' Stefan announced.

'But this isn't the right way to do this,' Gradi insisted.

'And now,' Stefan repeated, evenly, 'you will take off your clothes.'

'I'd prefer not to.'

He raised an eyebrow at this. 'You'd prefer not to? But wat do I care about that? You are in my house. You are subject to my will, whether you like it or not, and – as a matter of fact – I shall enjoy it more if you *don't* like it. I shall find that more exciting.' He didn't smile. His servant seemed oddly detached from the whole scene, as if he were going through the motions of serving dinner or dressing his master rather than aiding and abetting this crime against a person.

'This really isn't the right way to do this,' said Gradi again.

At his master's command, the servant fastened a cuff around Gradi's wrists, pinning them to the wall above her head. Then he pulled off her shoes and trousers. She didn't struggle.

'You told me to get naked. But I can hardly take off my top with my wrists pinioned,' she pointed out, in a reasonable tone of voice. 'Please undo my cuffs.'

'No,' said Stefan. 'The cuffs stay on.' His voice betrayed no excitement although his eyes were in fidgety motion over my wife's body. The servant pulled off Gradi's knikers. She did not resist the undressing.

And now, with us both watching, he floated over to her, and brought a knife from out of his belt. With this he made numerous little cuts and shreds in the fabric of her shirt, until it was floating in rags about her torso. She didn't flinch. In her ever-reasonable voice she said to him 'I'd advise you not to go any further.'

'Would you?' he said, sounding amused. 'Would you really?'

'You won't be able to say you weren't warned,' she said, mildly, 'at any rate.'

This seemed to amuse Stefan even more.

All through this display Mat and I were silent, absolutely stunned by the swiftly horrible turn events had taken. I can't speak for Mat, but I could hear my inner voice inside my head repeating over and over *I don't believe this, this can't be happening, this can't be happening*. It felt like a joke, a scene from a drama being acted out, not real life. I couldn't believe that this man was holding a sharp-edged blood-hungry knife to the throat of my beautiful wife. I simply could not believe that he had taken his cok out and was pushing himself up against her body. When I was a child I had enjoyed fairy-tale vids, and in particular *Tom and the Fairy Queen*, which perhaps you know. But at that moment of horrible consummation I felt like Tom in that story, his voice taken by the Fairy Queen with her little finger placed against his lips, such that he cannot speak or cry out, and despite all the extraordinary sights she shows him he can tell nobody. I felt sik in my stomach, and I had the urge to shout out, a shout loud enough to shatter the walls of his house and kill us all, a panic shout, but I did nothing but hang there dumb.

As Stefan pressed against her, Gradi said, 'since I'm pinioned here you really don't need to hold that knife to my throat.'

'I have never,' said Stefan, in a voice of polite surprise, 'known someone in *your* position so wedded to the ideal of talking, talking, talking.' He pressed the point of the knife further into her nek and the skin sank tautly under the point of pressure, like those diagrams of the rubber sheet of spacetime under the influence of a massive object they show you at school. 'Of course I don't *need* the knife. But I *like* the knife. *Like* the knife, and very much I like it. And if you say another thing I shall *cut* you with the knife.'

The blank expression on Gradi's face did not change.

This was the point at which Mat's inner blok broke apart. 'Get off her!' he yelled. 'Wat are you doing? Get off her!'

And Stefan got off her, but only to float over to Mat's immobilised body, and press the point of his knife against his right cheek. The skin cut, and blood bulged out. 'If you interrupt me again,' said Stefan, in a focused voice, 'I'll kill you. If you interrupt me again I will hurt her badly – I mean, more badly than I intend to, anyway.' He pushed himself away and floated bak to Gradi. Tears were in Mat's eyes. A globe of blood the size of a grape had swollen from the cut on his cheek and hung there like a rubyglass ornament. He was gaspingly silent.

'You know,' said Stefan, repositioning himself and placing his knife again at Gradi's throat, 'you think to talk me round, but in fact you only enhance my pleasure by drawing out my anticipation.' For the first time his voice contained a sense of glee. With his free hand he pushed Gradi's legs apart. She did not resist. 'You will both watch,' he said to us, happily, as he pushed himself inside her. 'And you won't be able to do a *damn* thing about it.'

Then he was making this sort of retching noise, a mixture of dry coughing and a forceful groaning, an insistent series of *k'huh k'huh k'huh* noises. He had dropped his hand from the knife, which stayed where it was floating at ninety degrees from Gradi's nek with the point snagged in her skin. He was curling up and floating away from Gradi as if repelled by magic, his face clenched in pain and surprise, and a string of thik spheres and teardrops of red pulsing from his crotch.

I stared, amazed. But Gradi did not hesitate. She doubled up, pulled her legs together and, with a lifetime's experience of manoeuvring in zero g, and a practised lithe gracefulness, she grabbed the handle of the knife between her feet and pulled it away from her nek. Her toes were virtually prehensile, her spine was immensely flexible. She positioned the knife at the plastic crossband of her cuffs, and heaved with her thigh muscles. It was at this point that the device in her vagina ejected the severed member of Stefan, spitting it out such that it floated fast across the room and knoked against the far wall. It looked like nothing very much, except perhaps a shred of white cloth leaking red at one end.

Stefan had stopped making his strangled choking noise, and was now producing a low-pitched wail of distress and pain. He was doubled up on himself, still seemingly linked to Gradi by the thik beaded line of his blood reaching across the centre of the room. This blood – propelled by his pulse – was moving in a sinuous line, floating along, missing Gradi's body (because she was curled up against her own cuff) to splodge against the side of the room. 'Oh no,' he was saying, in a cowed tone. 'Oh no, not my little man, my little man.'

Every muscle in Gradi's legs strained once, twice, three times as she levered the knife against the plastic band in her awkward position. Then her hands were free, and she transferred the knife to her hands. I watched, unable to blink. I expected her to go towards her attaker, but instead she moved quikly to the doorway to our left.

Stefan suddenly found his voice. 'No!' he bellowed! 'No, it isn't true! Cavlos! Cavlos! Come here, Cavlos!'

The servant came hauling himself through the door with one hand, his gun in the other hand. Gradi brought the knife down in a curving and unflinching motion and cut through the side of his nek. His blood scattered into a wide arc of fast fat droplets that sprayed with a rainfall sound against the wall, and the man crumpled and died, his body angling and his legs knoking and holding him against the rim of the door. As he died his finger reflexed on the trigger and the gun spoke its single angry word, its *bang*. The bullet was a specialist charge, a wire-frame that expanded in air, a bullet designed not to break through an Upland house wall, but jagged and fast enough to tear into human flesh. We piked it off the wall afterwards, and I thought to myself *he wasn't bluffing* – he wasn't doing the criminal bravado thing, carrying a downbelow gun and brandishing it just for effect. He bought this gun fully intending to use it in the Uplands. He had thought to himself beforehand *I shall want to shoot people, but I do not want to damage my house.*

Stefan himself watched the death of his servant, and it seemed, oddly, to calm him down. He stopped yelling. Instead, clutching his red-pulsing crotch with both hands he put his head bak to look straight at Gradi. In a steady voice he said: 'You have killed him,' and when Gradi did not reply, he went on, 'listen, we need to find my member, to cool it, we need to keep the organ *cool*. My plane is state of the art, it's very fast and very luxurious, we can fly down to a private clinic in Canada where I have a VIP account, and they can reattach it. But we need to move *fast.*'

Gradi glided towards him, still naked from the waist down, still wearing only tatters on her torso, but with the bloodied knife in her right hand. She glided straight through the air like a vampire.

'You can help me,' Stefan said, earnestly. 'We can still reattach it. Of course I'll pay you, I'll pay you anything you ask, but we must act *now*.'

Gradi said, 'I would prefer not to.'

At this his eyes widened, and he started making a high-pitched whining sound, like a child denied a toy, or, perhaps more like a dog; but Gradi cut short his noise with the knife, and the singsong note ended in the spatter of blood against the wall.

I was shaking so hard when Gradi cut me down that I could hardly help Mat and her stow the bodies in a loker. There was blood everywhere throughout the air. Mat got a sheet from the next room along, and Gradi and he scooped it through the room, working from top to bottom (though in zero g we might as well say *from bottom to top*, or *from side to side*) until the blood was mostly moved away. Then we all three got naked and washed ourselves in Stefan's private shower; a spacious shower cubicle through which hot soapy water (incredible excess!) was sprayed ceiling-to-floor. Gradi took the device out of her vagina, a compact linkage of four white wires with shark-tooth serrations, and a motor and chip at the hinge; she washed it in the flow and put it bak inside herself.

Afterwards we dried ourselves on Stefan's large, clean towels. I saw Mat stealing several glances at Gradi's unselfconscious nakedness, her flat buttoks, her lithe legs and arms, her small breasts conical in the weightlessness. He was bent a little forward with the towel bunched about his midriff, and I knew he was hiding his excitement. I truly felt no sexual excitement myself. I felt only sik in my gut.

We ransaked Stefan's large wardrobe for clothes to wear. Mat and I found expensive smartfabric clothes to fit us easily, although there was nothing tailored for Gradi's small frame.

Mat said with forced jollity: 'I've seen those things advertised, from time to time.' By *those things* he meant the device that Gradi had carried in her vagina. 'But I never encountered one in real life.'

Gradi didn't reply.

'It's a very efficient piece of kit,' he said.

He stopped speaking.

We piked our way past the remaining hanging droplets of blood in the room with the corpses, out into the porch, into our plane and away. 'Maybe we should take his plane?' Mat offered. 'He said it was state of the art and—'

'No,' said Gradi. And that was that. But she took the pistol.

She did not seem ruffled by the encounter, she really didn't. I was drinking whisky from a bladder all the way home, and I was if anything more trembly and sik-at-stomach an hour later than I was at the time. But she seemed completely calm. She flew the plane, she doked at our porch, she unloaded stuff from the plane.

A little drunk, and a little hyper, I tried to lighten the mood with humour. 'I'm glad you take *that thing* out before we go to bed together!' I said, forcing laughter. 'That could give me a *nasty* surprise!' But my laughter was false, and Gradi replied in a serious voice, her little face creasing at the temples a little, 'But I would never forget to take it out, Paul. Of course I would never forget to take it out. I only wear it if we're visiting strangers.'

But this was ill-judged by me on two accounts. One because although she seemed very calm and in control, this episode must have hurt Gradi inside – hurt her emotionally, I mean. In such a circumstance, wouldn't you say that a husband's job was to comfort his wife, not to make snippy jokes and then retreat to his sleeping bag to shiver and have nightmares? That might be the more normal marital dynamic, although there was little normal in our marriage.

The second reason why this was an ill-judged joke is that Gradi and I had not been to bed together, and had not had sexual relations, for many months. That side of our marriage had always been troublesome, intermittent and awkward.

On the very first time we had gone to bed together I had been unable to perform. I don't know why. She took me bak to her Parisian flat, and we sat on the floor beside a flask of red wine and kissed. It was perfect; it was the perfect moment. There were lights in the sky visible through the broad glass of her eastward wall. We knelt in front of one another and kissed, and we kissed. But then she led me through to the bedroom, and there we stripped off and I found myself goggling at her tight young body, after which, for some reason, my stiffness left me altogether. Despite her best efforts it would not return.

Gradi was perfectly non-judgmental at my failure, accommodating, as if this were an everyday, take-it-in-your-stride sort of thing (I ventriloquise for her; that's how her younger self would have put it; that's her youthful idiom; the more properly political and rhetorical idiom belongs to the more mature Gradi). 'It's OK,' she told me, as the light reflected off the rich cream of her skin. Her eyes were looking kindly at me, but I couldn't shake the absurd, childish-paranoid sense that her two nipples constituted another set of eyes set in an unsettling torso-face, and that those eyes were scowling.

'It's not OK,' I said.

'I've got some Vig,' she said, reaching to the bedside cabinet. She meant to be helpful, but this stung me; for why would she have such a thing right there, beside her bed? Who else had required chemical stimulation in order to be able to stiffen it and insert it? Not only was I not her first sexual partner, I was not even her first sexual inadequate. Looking bak, I suppose it is possible that she bought the drug specifically for me, on the off chance (and, looking bak, it would not have taken a genius to deduce from my manner that I would be awkward in bed) that I would flop. But that was not how I saw it at the time.

'Don't like that Vig stuff,' I said, rather abruptly, trying to hide my mortification behind an assumption of priggishness. 'It does bad things to your veins, I've heard.'

This did not in the slightest erode her mood. 'I've got some conds too,' she said. 'Not the regular ones, the ones with the memform plastic? You put them over your wang like a sok, and pull the thread at the base, and they tighten and stiffen and—'

'Oh Christ, Gradi,' I said, burying my face in her stomach and willing myself to cry to maximise the dramatic effect (but no tears came. I am a poor actor). 'I'm sorry, I'm sorry.'

For the first time a little uncertainty was audible in her voice. This was because her can-do *let's-fix-it* come!-on! attitude had been doubly rebuffed. She did not know wat to do with the philosophical category of 'the uncertain' except reject it wholesale. Were she ever to allow it the meanest purchase on her own thoughts, it might corrode everything about her. She would avalanche from *everything!-is!-possible!* to an all-encompassing 'wat's the point'?

I have heard her speak so many times at rallies and public meetings, and even on screen, with that distinctive delivery that is so easily parodied, and yet which was so effective: as if every single word is given its own! exclamation! mark!, and the choppy little gestures with her small hands, like karate strokes. In private she spoke much less rhetorically (you'll say: *but of course!*) and yet she was never wholly removed from that pumping assertiveness. On the other hand, her body sometimes let her down. She would sometimes chew the inside of her cheeks. You know that spongy wet flesh on the inside of your cheek, where your molars like to slide-and-grind? She did that. You could see the bones of her jaw shifting slightly, regularly, like a pulse. Then she would pik at her eyelids, a nervous tic. Then her diction collapsed, her eloquence fled, she sounded like a teenager all through her life. Her small hands loosened into pikers and feelers and gently caressed my non-performing genitals. It felt very nice, but did nothing to rouse the member itself.

'It's OK,' she said, without exclamation-pointing the statement, which was the closest her voice could get to intimacy of understanding. 'Don't worry about it, love. It's alright.' She'd piked up that usage, calling me 'love' from her stepfather, who was English. She called him 'Dad'. Two days later, we finally consummated our relationship; and for several months after that we almost had a 'normal' sex life. But we could never have been entered in the sex Olympics. We did not make love three times a night every night after the manner of the porn vids. We did not make love every night, nor necessarily every week. You are not as interested in this topic, my sexual life, as you think you are. I shall stop speaking about it.

five. Slater

Slater

Slater flies bak up to Fort Glenn, up through the air and through the airlessness above it and all the way to the Fort which seems to stand in nothingness sixty miles above the seamless ground. Is that miraculous, when you think of it? Yeah? Is it, or not? A crew of twelve Quanjet pilots have been billeted at Glenn, encroaching on the cramped space in addition to the usual staff. They're there for space manoeuvres. To fly and zip and stuka their spacecraft away from the Earth, away from the usual orbit lanes; to test their piloting abilities and the limits of the craft. Ready for the real war, the shooting war shoot-shoot (*chute* means fall). It's not Slater who is falling; on the contrary *he* now knows the reverse! Ascension! Up and up!

Slater flies up in an Elemag plane, with that line of gleaming violet scorching along the cutting edge of the wing. He has to wear his spacesuit in this craft, which is less comfortable than his uniform. Blakness thikens visibly around the window he stares out from. The pilot takes the plane into a counter-orbital sweep until the Fort's transponder registers, and then flies straight to the base; and out of his passenger window he can see the extra porch that's been unrolled on the far side of the Fort, with the six Quanjets parked, wide-winged swans nosing at a tubular trough. 'They're something,' says one of his fellow passengers, a supply-side colonel peering out through her own passenger window. 'Those jets.'

'Something,' Slater agrees.

'I guess they're here for manoeuvres, testy, for test flights.'

'I guess.'

'I heard they can manage fractions of c, if the engines really let rip. They can turn the dial all the way up, that's wat I heard'

'Short haul, though. It's an expensive way to fly.'

The sun comes round the wall of the horizon and each of the white, birdsfoot-shaped jets shines suddenly, gloriously, as if lit neon from within.

'Tell ya something else,' says the colonel, conversationally. 'I happen to know that one of the things we carrying to Glenn is *blak paint.*'

'Really?'

'War paint. Come war, they'll paint those babies blaker than coal at night. None,' she adds, 'more blak.'

They dok at the main porch, but Slater smells something wrong in the air. There's the slightly margariney tang of the stuff they use to clean the walls, and the fug of recirculated air, and so much Slater knows well. But there's an added animal scent, alien testosterone, that raises Slater's metaphorical and wholly subconscious hakles. How little he likes having strangers in his fort!

He reports to General Niflheim. General Niflheim is excited at his news. They can start gearing up for war. General Niflheim hasn't been this excited since he sat in the belly of a Quanjet bak in eighty-one, with a dozen nervous marines, gliding up through the atmosphere and preparing for their nation's first ever official space war. That turned out to be the least bloody war in American history. But maybe this time it'll be different. We can but hope.

Slater takes a meal. The Quant pilots are all standing together, laughing together, unwilling to share their bullish hilarity with the regular staff. They're dressed in modish dark blue uniforms. Their heads are shaved bald, blue-smudgy pink skin or shining blak skin in a row like smooth pebbles.

'They're kings of the universe,' says the man Slater is standing next to as he eats. 'I do wonder wat we're going to do with those jets, though. Nobody else has got them. It'd be like flying Z-33s against propeller-driven planes, you know? It'd be like a Elemag plane fighting a biplane, you know?'

'*They* think,' opines a second party, also floating nearby, 'they're training to fight aliens. You believe that?'

Slater stops looking at the Quanpilots. They are boring him now. His eye rests on the ridged wheat-coloured wall of the mess room. 'But there aren't any aliens,' he says, half distracted.

'Sure. But they think they'll be fighting against them. They think that's wat their training is all about. In case aliens suddenly appear in the solar system with, like, really zippy fighter starships or something.'

'There are no aliens,' Slater repeats, perfectly correctly.

The US has been to Mars by Quanjet: two separate expeditions, with suited explorers stumbling about in the autumn-coloured dusts. There was even talk, for a while, of a Mars base; but that seems to have come to nothing. The American attention is now on the Uplands, their solar gaze focused on the shiny-carapaced Upland houses, as if boys were focusing the midday beams through a lens onto silver-bodied ants and burning them up, for their sheer delight.

Busy busy busy. So much to do, *too* much to do, but he'll *do it*. Slater is walking up and down the length of the Station, with many a snap and a twang, briefing people individually, compiling reports and requisitions, cheking out how close to combat readiness the Fort is, deciding how many extra rooms need to be flown up to accommodate how large a strike force. So much to do.

He stops at one of the Fort windows on his way somewhere else, and looking through he notices that the new Quanjet porch is empty. He loiters, peering through the small window. The porch is there, but every single one if the craft is away in outer space somewhere, flying somewhere, moving at greater speeds than any other craft is capable of, performing zags and zigs of unprecedented agility. He strains his nek, wondering if he can see their white forms whooshing across his field of view; but there's nothing to see. And then the sun comes up, and in the half-second before the glass reacts to the sudden brightness Slater's retinas are branded with persistent little blots of blindness. He swears.

He briefs and briefs. Sometimes he thinks that he must be briefing every single soldier of the assault force personally.

'Supply lines,' he says, to three weightless people and, via a vidlink, a dozen more on the ground. The ones on the ground have weight, which they have distributed into various chairs around a table. 'We hold all the cards. We can supply our troops at will; but better than that, we can cut off the Uplanders' lines of supply. They're flying up all their supplies, everything, food and water, everything. A lot of them drape these lines into the upper atmosphere for air, but that's vulnerable too. Cut them, stop the food, water getting through, it'll be the most rapidly effective siege in the history of war.'

'You're sure, Lieutenant?' asks a lugubrious-looking general on vidlink, the screen image, which Slater can only see at an angle, flattening his angular face into a series of pink polyhedra. 'You are sure we can cut them off?'

'Absolutely. That'll be one of the easiest interventions of the war, General, believe me.' (*Be! Leave me!*) 'They can only fly up from a narrow band of latitudes, much of which is ocean, and almost all of their bases are northern hemisphere. In practice, the infrastructure for supplying the Uplands exists in a dozen places only, in northern EU, Canada, Iceland, Siberia. There are one or two sites in the southern hemisphere, but most of it is northern. We can isolate those.'

'Treaty terms would make a military occupation of northern EU difficult . . .'

'We wouldn't need to occupy, simply to monitor, intercept planes when they got above a certain height.'

'By intercept,' says a female general, floating to Slater's left, 'you mean . . . ?'

She doesn't need to complete her question; and Slater doesn't need to answer it. That's obvious. Boom!

'But this is only applying pressure. Cutting off their supplies, and a few high-profile military interventions in the Uplands themselves, and we predict the war will be over within one week. Certainly no more than two weeks. Worse comes to worst we can grab the ground bases and deal with the legal fallout later; but I do not believe it's going to come to that.'

'Good,' says Slater. He likes the sound of this word, and says it again, resays it. 'Good, good.'

Busy busy busy. With a snap and a twang Slater marches up and down the Station. He has a meeting with the senior propaganda officer Tchang. Tchang has bluebell-blue eyes in his sharply handsome Tibetan-US face, and these eyes see everything. Oh, you'd have to get up very early in the morning to get the better of Tchang. 'You'll excuse me if I seem ignorant, Lieutenant,' he says, smiling, as they sip luke-warm coffee from two globes, floating together in the otherwise empty mess. 'Only I need to know wat we're dealing with, to start setting up the strategies for managing and spinning the war to downbelow media.'

'Of course.' The coffee tastes too bitter on Slater's tongue; too strong perhaps. Dirty-tasting, too sharp and bitter. The coffee tastes funereal. But it at least contains caffeine, and the caffeine at least perks him.

'We're looking at a short war?' Tchang wants to know. 'You'll pardon my ignorance, Lieutenant, but nobody's told me otherwise; for all I know the war is scheduled to last *years*.' He laughs at the absurdity of his own speculation, but it is shortlived laughter. Once it has served its indicative purpose the laughter stops.

'Weeks at the outside,' says Slater. 'One week is our best guess.'

'Good. With the new century coming up, it would be better for us if the war did not go over into the new year. We can spin it as a new start for the Uplands, the Twenty-Second will be a New Age for the Uplands.

These symbolic markers play really well downbelow. So you can guarantee me that the war will not last into the next century?'

'Guarantee.'

'Excellent – only, if I set this up as a new century for the Uplands and the war is still being fought Jan 2100 then it'll look bad,'

'Guarantee,' repeats Slater. He is *so* bored by this meeting. He hates this side of the war-making process. He's the inheritor of Vikings and samurai and here he is jaw-jawing with law-lawyers. He takes another sip of the ashen-flavored coffee.

'Now, Lieutenant,' Tchang continues. 'You'll excuse me if I seem ignorant, only I *must* ask about the EU. My office thinks that the EU is the *biggest* problem we face, *both* legally *and* in PR terms. They won't like it, you know. They won't like us going to war with the Uplands.'

'You didn't get my briefing file?' Slater asks, bored. 'Intelligence is that Gradisil has been meeting secretly with the EU. Spin that, embarrass the EU, press them on that, and the war will take a bak-seat.'

Tchang smiles at him, a hard-cornered smile that says *stik to your own job, Lieutenant.* 'Right,' he says, as the smile falls away.

In the corridor behind him there's a rapid drumroll of snap-twangs and Hagen touches his shoulder. 'Slater,' he says. 'Lieutenant. A word?'

'Hagen, I'm really busy,' says Slater.

'It's mission-related,' says Hagen, with an air of self-important, reptilian *superbus.*

'I thought your big nineteen-oh-one spinning wheel was bumped bak in schedule.'

'That's *two thousand* and one,' corrects Hagen, puffing his chest up, although of course Slater knows that, and Hagen knows he knows. 'And I've got new orders. They want to bring it forward. They're talking about garrisoning the Uplands after your war. Rumour is your war will be a seven-days war.'

'Is that the rumour,' says Slater, uninflected, uninterested.

'So my wheel might be on in construction sooner than we'd thought.'

'Post-hostilities,' says Slater, walking on with a snap and a twang. 'That's not my department. I'm strictly conflict. You need to talk to post-conflict people.'

'But there are things I need to talk to *you* about.' Hagen hurries after him, with a snap and a twang.

'I'm late for a meeting now, Hagen.'

'Let's eat lunch.'

'My lunches are all booked up, Hagen,' he says, thinking to himself: I so *do not* want to luncheon with this lizard. He quikens his (snap! twang!) pace.

He steps briskly to his meeting. This meeting is with three USUF lawyers. It is the first of wat will be a great many meetings with lawyers. Meeting with lawyers, swearing antebellum affidavits, establishing rules of engagement, filing anticipatory bloking suits, setting in place the whole elaborate superstructure of legal war-making. There are, for legal purposes, eight different varieties of war that can be declared, and they need to establish which is the most legally advantageous declaration to them in this instance. They need to map out the legal parameters, plot the best path through the legal landscape.

'Good morning Lieutenant,' says the Captain-Legal, a small-featured, snow-coloured, lilac-eyed young man, good-looking in a childish sort of way, neat and handsome features but very young. Slater thinks he looks very young to have achieved the rank of Captain, even in a corps like Legal, but he smiles, and returns the Captain's insinuating handshake. 'Shall we get started? We're going to be seeing an awful lot of one another over the coming month or so.'

'I guess we will,' says Slater.

six. Paul

Our first child, a son, was born in Helsinki in '91. We called him Hope, and his full name was Hope Gyeroffy Baldwin-Caunes. This is a spectacularly uneuphonious hyphenated surname, I know very well; but we agreed upon it, nevertheless. In practice he was called Hope Baldwin (for instance, when he was registered at his first school in '95), and so my own name was extinguished in him. He later decided *aet* 21, or 22, I forget, to take on his great-grandfather's surname and became Hope Gyeroffy. Old Man Gyeroffy, long since dead, had been killed by the Americans. He was a folk hero of sorts to some amongst the Uplands, and by the twenty-one-teens he had acquired talismanic properties.

The last few months of the pregnancy I began to consider the possibility of happiness again. For the first time in our marriage Gradi was tied by her sheer sloshy weight to one place, and I had uninterrupted time with her. I woke up with her in the morning, I went to sleep in her bed at night. I became habituated to the intoxicating smell of her skin. There were consolations to being a cuckold, a tendency for the deceiving wife to pay various little attentions to the husband.

I bought a house in central Helsinki, in the Rödbergen district: a pleasant, four-storey manor built several centuries before out of some purplish Scandinavian stone: a granite, perhaps, which darkened to crow-blak in the dusk, and warmed and sparkled to violet in the early morning. The windows had been replaced with weave-glass and the internal technics were run by an AI, of course, but otherwise it was an actual old-fashioned house. At the bak and at the front, symmetrically aligned, were two square lawns, perfect as pressed green sheets, each surrounded by a pathway of pink sand. To sit in the garden, in the weakly bright Finnish sunshine, whilst Gradi sat beside me, earnestly absorbed in a screen on her lap, was exactly like happiness.

But Gradi was not happy, because she wanted to be Upland very intensely. She kept complaining that there was *so much to do*, and she didn't mean to do downbelow. Soon she was too large to move with any comfort; her stomach as curved as the world itself, her belly-button a tiny fleshy beak. She hated her very corporeality. She fidgeted herself out of bed, propping herself round the bedroom by hanging on to the furniture under the unforgiving gravity. 'I wish I were up,' she said. 'I wouldn't be weighed down with . . .'

'I wish you could just forget about the Uplands for a little while!' I complained.

But the Uplands were the lines of force around which our lives were oriented, for good or ill. I had my part to play as well. I was expected to accompany Gradi from time to time, to attend the more important Upland group meetings. I was part of her inner Council and sat through many tedious discussions of strategy. Now that Gradi was confined to Earth, prior to her confinement, I myself flew up in her place,

The pregnancy swelled to its bursting conclusion, and I was present in the Helsinki clinic as Hope emerged. Wat an extraordinary planet a baby's head is, a whole moving world! I remember being moved to tears by the sight of the squeezed conical skull, the cross little face with its bulging eyes shut, and I remember being rather startled by how unfleshlike the umbilical cord looked, bright blue, ropey and plastic. I was rather unsettled by the smell of the experience too, unsavoury and bloody. But the joy of the father at birth is too conventional a topic; you're not interested in that, even though it's your birth I'm describing.

Gradi was bak Upland less than a week after giving birth. I stayed with Hope and the nurse in our too-large house. It was all very strange to me. I would wake in the night when Hope cried his hoarse little cry, even though it was the nurse's job to attend to him; and I would lie there listening to the sounds through the wall of him being soothed, or chatted to whilst his diaper was changed, or fed. He was not my child.

But how beautiful he was! His face was so fat it looked inflated, and yet it could crumple in a moment as if the air were suked through, and the skin would fold complexly at eyes and mouth, and he would disclose the various vowels that communicated feed me! change me! hold me! do something to make me stop crying! – and that was the whole of his universe, all of the rainy-stony earth shrunken to that world. The pleasure of holding my son in my arms whilst he sukled strenuously on his bottle-teat, eyes scrunched, milk making traks down his chin, that pleasure was the most intense I have known. He was not my child. My DNA did not shimmer in its minuscule woven threads in his cells.

O.

His face with its button nose and its great round cheeks pressing together his fuchsia-shaped mouth, like an old drawing of the god of the blowing winds, was so beautiful. I was simply unprepared for the surge of love that would rise in my throat and scatter through my chest when I piked him up and hugged him. He wasn't my child, I loved him.

I am tall, pale-skinned, with sand-coloured hair that would be thinning were it not for the intervention of pharmakos. I have the look, I think, of the Saxon French: a large-featured, open face, a long yet still stoky body, slightly over-sized limbs. My eyes are a dilute grey-blue colour. Gradi, of course, was half-Japanese, half Cypriot, and so she was small and dark and compact, quite different to me physically. Then there was Mat: a naturally skinny, thin-baked man with close-cut dark hair and skin the colour of a clear-sky dusk, and dark eyes like dabs of wet paint. When Hope was first born he had the blue eyes of the generic baby, but in a few weeks his eye colour darkened. I could see Gradi in his compact fat-cheeked little face, but when I gazed in it, and even at that early stage, I could see Mat too. Once noticed it was unmissable. But I saw Gradi in you too, that was the important thing. My love for her lighted hungrily on you as well, as a glorious doubling of the object for my emotions.

I would put him in the chest-saddle, so that his little goblin face buried itself in the soft wool of my sweater, and his arms and legs in their padded jaket would dangle. Then I would walk out with him along the Bulevarden and up the hill of the Unionsgaten to the Lutheran Cathedral, and round the building and bak down the hill home again. The small weight of him against my torso was only a token, of course, but nevertheless it was gravity's greatest gift to me. It was early autumn, but already cold, and bright clouds clustered together in the sharply blue sky, piling igloos and snowdrifts in mid-air.

Gradisil's mother came to stay with us. She was a crazy, spiky old woman was Klara: only just fifty years of age, yet giving the impression of somebody much older. In part this was her sheer physical exentricity; the weird little fidgets and jerks she wrung out of her body; her way of speaking, as if she could not gauge in her head the volume at which her utterance would emerge, or the proper balance of profanity and respect. It was also that she had that early-century disdain for the various pharmakos products available, so her skin was as wrinkled as might be expected of any natural-living fifty-year woman, rather than wrinkled after the taut, tugged manner of the actual fifty-year-old walking the street. She limped slightly; there was something wrong with one of her feet.

I had met her several times, of course, since marrying her only daughter, but it was not until Hope was born that I properly got to know her. She arrived on the doorstep of the Helsinki house like a fairy godmother, wearing a blue puffy overcloak ripped to rags at the edges, whether by design or accident was not clear. Beneath the cloak was a thik-cloth dress, the cloth a centimetre or more thik, though buoyant. Beneath the dress she wore an all-body suit, from which her lengthy, bony wrists and her ankles like knots in silver rope were visible before they disappeared into fat gloves, and large oval shoes, respectively.

'Hello *Pa-owl*,' she said, walking directly past me as I opened the door. Sometimes she called me *Pa-owl*, sometimes *Poll*, sometimes *Pall*, indifferently. 'I have come to see my grandchild, and perhaps to bless him.' She chortled at this, a weirdly birdsong-like series of chukles.

She was a storyteller, was Klara. By this I mean both that she told good stories which amused children and adults, and also I mean that she lied. When she spoke she scattered words like a dog shaking itself dry, and the emission of words was far more important to her than the truth or otherwise of those words. Many people are like this.

'It's up the stairs, Klara,' I called, 'first on the left. And,' (this spoken at greater volume as her slender form vanished up the stairway) 'it's lovely to see *you* again, mother-in-law.'

I shut the door and made my way up. The nurse, a girl called Kirsi Heikura, was giving Hope his afternoon feed. His little arms and little legs worked up and down, their clokwork motions of ecstasy; his little eyes were tight shut; the white cylinder shrank in realtime, leaving behind a ghost-cylinder of transparency. 'Hello,' shrieked Klara at the nurse, startling her and making Hope open his eyes. 'I'm the kiddy's grandmother. Hello, little Hope. Hello! Hellow! Helloo!'

'Klara,' I said, catching her elbow. 'Don't frighten the child.'

'Which one?' she asked, nodding at Kirsi Heikura, who was no more than eighteen herself. Then Klara laughed again. Then, in the middle of the room, she did a weird twisty little dance, holding her feet on the floor but wringing angular shapes out of her body and lifting her skinny arms over her head. Her hair was a very dense mass of blak, fastened on the top of her head with a clasp, and this she now unfastened so that her hair fell, a mass of cords and threads like wet weeds.

'He is a very beautiful child,' she announced, not looking at Hope. 'He is worthy of being my grandson and I bless him – his life will be full of marvellous things, he will achieve marvellous things, he will be marv—,' and she broke off to laugh at herself.

'I hope,' I said, politely, 'that you can stay with us for a while?'

'Is Gradisil here?' This was spoken almost sharply.

'No. She's Up.'

'I'm staying, Pa-owl, I'm staying at least to the new year, at least 'til the summer, and maybe more.'

This was more hospitality than I had been hoping to extend, but I smiled and nodded.

'He's a beautiful child,' she said to me again. 'But he looks nothing at all like *you*.'

'Oh,' I said.

I don't believe that she was trying to hurt my feelings by saying this. Such considerations would, almost certainly, simply not have occurred to her.

Klara never flew. She travelled everywhere by train, preferring ground-effect trains when possible, but happily taking the slow-crawl antique variety when not, sitting in the single passenger car with a few like-minded exentrics behind hundreds and hundreds of cars of bulk cargo. She had arrived at Helsinki after a series of train journeys across Siberia and northern Russia. She could easily have contacted us to let us know she was coming, but she chose not to.

She never went Upland.

In her youth she had spent a lot of time in the Uplands, and she was happy to tell richly embroidered and implausible stories about her adventures. But she had not travelled in an airplane or spaceplane since the war of eighty-one, and vowed melodramatically (she repeated this vow whenever the subject was raised, sometimes raising her arm over her head and booming the words forth) that she never would return. Of the precise reasons for this disaffection she was unchar-acteristically reticent, but from time to time she would drop hints of some calamitous encounter with the forces of America. 'I have always taught my daughter,' she would say, 'about the grievous harm America has done to our family.'

'I see, Klara,' I replied.

She took possession of a room at the top of the house, and spent several days wandering around the city, before growing bored with it. 'Everybody speaks English,' she complained to me at dinner. 'I'm trying to learn the language, hazarding some Finnish here and there, but everybody replies in English. I spent hours and hours on the train here listening to teach-by-induct Finnish language files. You—' here she directed a piercing shriek at Kirsi Heikura who was sitting on the other side of the table with her boyfriend (she was living in the house, of course, and often joined us for dinner, and sometimes her boyfriend joined us as well). 'You,' said Klara: '*etteko puhu englantia?*'

Kirsi looked startled. She glanced at her boyfriend, and replied 'Of course I speak English.'

'Everybody here speaks English,' I said.

'Music off!' boomed Klara, speaking in the general direction of the ceiling, her face creased with annoyance. Some caressing music was playing in the bakground; something by Michelle Kokel, I think. 'Music off!'

'Klara,' I said, 'you have to *clap*.' I clapped once, sharply, and the music stopped; but she seemed to take my intervention as a personal affront. The rest of the dinner took place in silence.

I would not have been surprised had Klara, the following day, announced that she was leaving; that this was no place for her – perhaps even simply vanished. But on the contrary, the following day she was hyperactive with joy, singing little snatches of song to herself, fussing about the baby, piking him up and cuddling him, laughing, handing him bak to the nurse, only to swoop him out of her arms again. She stayed, as she promised, the whole winter. The snow fell very powdery for several weeks, accumulating in the garden like volcanic talc. The city was duvet-covered in snow.

Snow falling through the dirt of the city air gathered in drifts that looked like heaps of cold ashes.

Gradi returns

She called me to say that she was coming home for a week. 'Do you hear that?' I cooed to Hope. 'Mamma is coming home. You're going to see Mamma.'

And then, late one afternoon, as the sky was blushing in the west and darkening above us, I was playing with Hope in the front room. She let herself through the front door, walked in upon us, kissed me on the cheek, piked up Hope and set him on her lap. 'Well,' she said. 'I'm bak.'

My heart was instantly alive with my love for her. Light fell through me, and I felt holy to my bones with my love for her. I almost cried; tears were pressing in the tiny channels at the corner of my eyes and building. 'Gradi,' I said. 'It's so good to see you!'

'It was a tough week,' she said, exhausted-sounding.

Then Mat came through the door after her, and the force of my love for my wife burst into electric disgust, and I closed my eyes. I had not seen Mat since the birth of Hope, and I had not thought about him

212

more than I could help, but here he was, grinning his stupid grin, and even though he had just spent many weeks with my wife, closely confined with her, enjoying her all this time, yet still now I was not rid of him, not purged of the thought of the two of them together.

'Gradi,' I said, turning to her, 'your mother's here.'

'Now?'

'She's out now. But she's here, staying with us. She came visiting whilst you were out.'

'Klara,' she said, enunciating the two syllables very clearly to the baby in her lap. 'Kla. Ra. Klaara. Klaaara.'

'I'll bring in the bags,' said Mat, disappearing round the door.

Politics

Politics went on. There were many more meetings than in the earlier days, because the demand by Uplanders was more acute. Word would go round, or be announced on newsnets or some other form of information dissemination. From giving speeches to half-empty houses, Gradi was soon filling Upland venues completely, and we had to turn people away.

We met a man called Alexis Wadenström, who styled himself the Upland's first farmer. He was, of course, a very wealthy individual; absolutely a dilettante gardener rather than a farmer. But Gradi was very aware of the PR possibilities he represented. The first step towards practical independence for the Uplands; no longer dependent on flying up fresh and dry supplies from downbelow. A meeting was set up by the Upland Council who liaised between Gradi's team and Wadenström himself. We flew round and closed in on his dumbbell-shaped house.

'I'm very excited to meet you,' said Gradi, floating through the porch-door with her smile completely convincing, even though it was manufactured purely for that occasion. Nobody but I could tell her simulated smiles from her real smiles. No. No. I'm not sure even I could tell them apart. Wadenström was a classic example of a fat man kept thin by pharmakos drugs; his body was too long, somehow, his limbs connected to the torso with not-quite-right fluency, his face had an elfin, almost monkey keenness to it. But he was very excited to meet the great Gradisil in person. 'The honour's *mine*,' he said. 'I'm a big fan. I'm very excited by wat you're doing for our people.'

'You are the future of the Uplands, Mr Wadenström,' said Gradi, shaking his hand so hard he started to rotate in air.

'It's just a hobby,' Wadenström insisted. 'I made my money in the law, made more than enough. It was a childhood dream to be an astronaut. I always told my wife I wanted to take up farming . . . but she didn't realise wat I meant by that!' Richly amused by his own sentence he repeated it: 'She didn't realise wat I meant by that!'

Gradi was expert at precisely judging the appropriate level of delighted laughter.

He took us around his house: two central rooms in which he slept and ate, and at each end a globe. Each was a metal gridball inset with two dozen fat plastic windows, and each was full of green.

'They grow well,' he says. 'It's not enough to live on, 'course. I ship most of my food, and all the water to grow these things,' and he paddled his fingers in the foliage of his plants, 'but it's satisfying.'

'If we can come up with our own supply of water,' Gradisil said, with a serious expression on her dark little face, 'then we can start on the long road to becoming independent of the Earth. If we could, for instance, snag a comet . . . ?'

We dropped into a lower, faster orbit and swung up again to slow before a large seven-room house, with a centrifuge at one end: this was the House of the Tragic Poet. He was famous in certain groundling subcultures, a very flamboyant figure in a very messy three-room house.

'I have come here to write,' he told us, and through us the watching audience, for our meeting was being recorded on screen. 'I have come here to escape from downbelow and write the poetry out of me, the way Thomas Mann's invalids went to their high place to sweat out their fever. I wake, make myself coffee, pull the tab on a croissant to heat it, and sit at my window watching the world. In the old days I had much more *peace*. Poets must have peace. But now people are constantly pestering me. Is this a consequence of fame?'

'Fame is the enemy of art,' agreed Gradi, and the Tragic Poet smiled, pleased.

His phone was chirruping. 'There it goes! Go on, interrupt the inspiration, the working of the muse within me—'

He snapped the screen on. 'Wat? Wat? Wat is it?'

A dark, tentative face on the little screen. 'Er, hello?'

'Who is this?' The Tragic Poet may have been acting up because he was on screen; or he may have been like this all the time, observed or unobserved.

'Hi, my name is Antonio. I'm a neighbour.'

'Wat do you *mean*? Wat do you mean by *that*?'

'Hey, I'm a fellow Uplander, you know? C'mon man, we're all in this together.' He was peering out of the screen, trying to see past the face of his interlocutor to see who the people were in the bakground of this house.

'All in this together? In wat?'

'Look I'm outside your house now, in my plane, yeah?'

'Go away, I'm working! Wat do you want? I don't know you!'

'I'm just being neighbourly, man. I'm paying a social call. Also, I was wondering if I could borrow a chunk of water, y'know?'

'You want water? Go away. You want to buy water? Chek the web for transp locations of water sellers. *I'm* not a water merchant. *I'm* a poet.'

'Thing is,' said Antonio, scratching his beard-bristled chin (the phone screen made him look dark and untrustworthy) 'I'm sure you can understand, I'm in financial difficulties, y'know?'

'Poor? If you're poor then wat are you doing up *here*?' This, he clearly thought, was clever of him. He turned to smirk at his audience. His expression said, very clearly: Upland is the rich republic; everybody knows that. Poor people have no place up here!

'It's a temporary financial embarrassment, I got things lining up, next month there's the prospect of solvency, you know how it is, next month.'

'I don't understand how you could afford a house up here in the first place if you're *poor*,' the Tragic Poet said, pressing his perceived advantage.

'My house was kind of an *inheritance*, y'know? My plane too. But I'm short of water and I thought I'd ask a neighbour to, y'know, lend me some—'

'Lend it?' He laughed at this, high-pitched pipping laughter. 'I'm not sure I'll want it bak after you've finished with it! Wat would you do, borrow my water and bring bak *urine*?'

The face in the phone screen folded into a pained expression. 'C'mon man, don't be like that, I havn't had a drink in a day. I'm real thirsty. Can I just . . .'

'No!' he said firmly. 'Fuk off, leave me alone. Go downbelow if you want water – it falls out of the sky down there. Leave me alone!'

'C'mon man,' pleaded this stranger, this Antonio. 'It's not like there's a communal Upland drinking fountain or anything. I'm desperate, man. I can't go downbelow, not right now, I got personal reasons for avoiding—'

'Communal drinking fountain!' he shrieked, laughing. 'Fuk off. Leave me alone.'

After he had dispatched his mendicant caller, the Tragic Poet turned to us, but actually looking a little past us at the screen, and said 'I shall recite a poem.' He was holding a strap with his left hand to steady himself, and was holding the flimsy of one of his poems with his right, and he recited in a boomy high-pitched voice.

Sea-bred cattle slaughtered   *their bodies pharmakon magnified*
Their deaths magnified   *without magnificence*
Their bodies as helpless   *floating, as the most expensive houses*
Until the blades
In the mudsink at the centre   *a slurry of lights,*
O baboon-populated cities   *O! disembowelling themselves*
into metastasising suburbs   *each scab of light a*

It's awful, it's very awful. But Gradi had created on her face the expression of somebody rapt, captured by the beauty of the verse. That was the true work of art in the room; Gradi's control over her expression.

As we left the Tragic Poet nodded ponderously, dolefully, and took Gradi's hand and then my hand in his limp right *manus*. 'It has been an honour to this house,' he declaimed, 'to have the President of the Uplands visit.'

'The honour is ours,' said Gradi, seriously. She never used the expression *President of the Uplands* in reference to herself, but others were starting to use it.

The Tragic Poet held up his right hand, its creased palm and twig-like fingers almost as long as his horse-long face. 'As I said in my first epic, *Felicity of Paking Face-folds and Wire-thin*' he announced: 'Realising that nothing changes changes everything.'

'Beautifully put,' said Gradi with a straight face.

seven. Slater

Slater

Busy busy busy. So *much* to do, marching from meeting to meeting with a snap and a twang. And here, at last, is a friendly face. 'Colonel Philpot, sir!'

''d-up Slayer,' booms Philpot.

'Howdy doody.'

'Now here's wat I hate,' says Philpot, grasping his friend's shoulder: '"*howdy-doody*".' He wrinkles his face and falsettoes his voice in approximate impersonation of Slater, and Slater laughs loud.

'Man, it's good to see you,' he cries. 'You on a war footing?'

Oh, they are *grinning*, the pair of them.

'We are *all* on a war footing,' says Philpot. 'It's *all* about to pitch off.'

'Amen.'

'It's *all* about to kik off.'

'Amen to that.'

'I was downbelow to sign, to sign this legal documentation shit,' says Philpot. 'I wished I lived centuries ago, in one of the golden ages of warfare, before all this legal shit heaved in to make our lives complex.'

'I've been doing the same, signing the anti-torture and the hazing contracts. It's just all the hoops we got to jump through.'

'Let's get the lawyers over and done with and get the war *going*,' exhorts Philpot. 'Let's *get* this party *star*ted.'

Strat has been piecing together an intel map of the Uplands, but it's slow and patchy work, and since transp signals cannot be trusted it is in large part guesswork. But mostly it's gathering wat intelligence can be gathered.

Slater briefs Strat: seven young officers in preternaturally clean uniforms, all paying very, very close attention to all the words coming out of Slater's broad-lipped, well-proportioned mouth. He thinks of his own lips in motion as he speaks: worms writhing, seaslugs in ecstasy, pygmy snakes arching their baks in a mating dance.

'You've heard all this before,' he says to them. 'So I shan't dilate.' And he smiles at them. They smile bak. Their faces look a little bloated. There is a pharmakos to deal with that, but the military doesn't approve of it, since it needs to be inserted every time the individual moves to zero g and altered every time they return to one g, to prevent blood pressure rebounding. The army prefer people to adjust to zero g blood redistribution naturally so they can perform their duties without that dependency, which means that people tend to be bloated in their first few days up.

'Intelligence is the way wars are won, it's as simple as that. There are a thousand examples for US wars fought in the last two centuries in which a thousand dollars of intel has been more effective at saving lives, or at killing the enemy, than billions of dollars of ordnance.' All of them looking at him. 'The main difficulty of the Uplands is the high average net-worth of the citizenry.' Only in a military briefing would you find a word like *citizenry*. 'Hard to bribe billionaires; they already have more than enough money. Other forms of pressure need to be brought to bear. And given the *organised* nature of the resistance we are facing here—'

He pauses to clear his throat, and in the instant before the noise gravels in his throat he catches the awestruk whisper from one or other of the officers, '*Gradisil*', and it's a recognition, almost a charm. King Arthur, Prester John, Johnny Appleseed. Fuk that. He barrels on: 'Nevertheless, we don't anticipate lak of intelligence being too big a problem for our purposes. In fact – I'll tell you this – in fact, one of the problems we *are* facing is making sure we don't win the war too quikly!' He beams at them here, which is to say it's OK to laugh at this juncture, and they oblige him with a row of wide mouths and trikly laughter.

'As you all know, we need a short war, with minimum casualties – casualties on their side, I mean: we're not anticipating any casualties on ours – minimum enemy casualties is wat PR are asking us for. But we also need the war to be more than forty-eight hours so that it falls into the right legal category. Once war is declared we will be acting quikly to take advantage of the *lex bellorum* window of opportunity; and ideally we'll need at least seventy-two hours to accomplish all that, though forty-eight is doable. After that we need a transition to the right legal category of peace deal, the right sort of surrender. So when I give you your various intel targets, this is wat I'm looking for: not so much the conventional military objectives, but things like high-profile houses, certainly the banking net they've established.'

He has lunch with Philp, hanging by the window in Fort Glenn's mess. The Ganges Delta is visible directly below them, those tasselled fringes of Indian and Bangladeshi coastline where the Ganges and the Brahmaputra rivers mesh with the sea. It looks, in its intricate weave of channels of islands, like a sheet of china smashed with a hammer upon a blue ground.

'Beautiful up here,' he says.

'Oh, nice *view*, Slayer,' says Philp, not looking through the window. He laughs, as if he has said something funny.

eight. Paul

The war began in 2099, but you know that, you know when the war started. Step bak in time a few years.

Here: our second child was born in the summer of '93. It was in part for political reasons that Gradisil called him *Sol*, a name that meant not 'sun' (though many people have since assumed that was the referent) but was rather short for *Solidarity*.

By '93 the mood of the Uplands had truly begun to coalesce. Disregard the thirty per cent of Uplanders who wanted nothing to do with anybody else, neither Gradi nor the USA nor EU, who wanted for myriad reasons only to be left alone – disregard them, and the remaining two thirds had discovered something extraordinary, an apprehension of what *unity* might feel like, a joy in being Uplanders. Solidarity was a reality. There was no way a single house could contain all the people who wanted to attend Gradi's speeches now; so all the members of the audience filmed the speech and disseminated the files to other Uplanders. Everybody knew that war was coming; it was simply a question of when. Any one of that audience could have made money, or curried favour, by passing those files on to the Americans. But of two dozen speeches so recorded and passed around the Uplands, as Uplander visited or traded with Uplander, as people bumped into people, or gathered for other purposes – of two dozen speeches the Americans got hold of only two.

I loved my new son, Sol, but his face was dark and strange to me, his eyes slim, his cheeks big. People said *he looks like his mother*, but they meant *he looks Far Eastern*, and I knew that he looked like Liu. A year before, Gradi had seemed to grow tired of spending so much time with Mat, and although he had grown clingy and erratic she had squeezed her time away from him, and in his place had begun arranging one-on-one time with Liu. He was a handsome young man, attentive, with a rather daring self-sufficiency which both Mat and (obviously) I laked, puppyish as we both were, wholly addicted to the little tablets of attention Gradi passed us. Over the course of a whole year Gradi would announce reasons to fly off with nobody but Liu in attendance: visiting Upland houses, addressing meetings. When she told me she was pregnant I, naturally, made the calculations in my head. During that month in which conception occurred she and I had experienced physical congress to emission of seminal material on two occasions. I debated with myself, anxiously, wat the odds were on my being the father. But then Sol was born, and the question was put beyond doubt. He looked like Gradi and he looked like Liu; he looked unlike me.

My life became unbearable, stuk in a narrow channel, scraping me along a rough-scratch groove. But, saying so, I recognise the overstatement straight away. My life was clearly bearable, because I bore it. And wat was my life? Months in the Helsinki house with my sons, and the staff; the shops, the sports-domes. Months in France-EU when the sun was hot down there, swimming, drinking, reading. From time to time Gradi would be with us; from time to time I would mount up the branches of the world-tree and join her in some hurtling house in the blak sky. But I was more alone than not alone. My life was *bearable*, barely, but very close to the territory of unbearable.

And wat was my life? Portions of humiliation and alienation in interference pattern with the joy. I was always afraid, I didn't particularly know *of wat*. When I spent time with Gradi I could not bear to see her. When I was away from Gradi I missed her so powerfully that the clok of my brain *stopped* at its sheer brink, and I existed in a dead dimension of loss and lak and acute misery. It was impossible. It was impossible. Gradi was still affectionate. I would float through and there she would be, head leaning in with Liu, whispering words together *as if* they were discussing a war-strategy. But they were whispering something more intimate than that, I knew it, I knew it. They were about to fuk, or they had just finished fuking, or they were laughing together about the many things that only they shared, things – in – which – I – had – *no* – *part*. And Gradi would look up at me as I came through, and beam her perfect simulacrum of a smile at me, and would float over to me and kiss me on the cheek, or snake her arms around me. But I knew. The whole scene was lit by that pure sharp light of the Uplands, everything was illuminated and bright and clean.

I was trapped. There was nothing to be done, and everything to be endured. Twice-cukolded, which naturally meant cukolded an infinite number of times, which naturally meant tear-stained sessions entirely by myself, private, in which I imagined precisely what Gradi and Mat were doing together, precisely where he was inserting, precisely how she, on hands and elbows, put her head back and cried out, sessions of internal TV that were excruciating to me and yet which I revisited frequently, like a fool who cannot resist probing the agonising tooth when he should let it well alone. But then again, there were two beautiful cukoos to hug and nuzzle and change nappies and cry over.

'We're going on a PR blitz,' Gradi told me one day. 'Upland. We need to be working together in the Uplands for a few months – Kirsi can take care of the boys for that long. Hope's starting school anyway. We need to do face-to-face with a dozen of the most important Uplanders. We need to do it now. Events are starting to come together.'

'We?' I would ask, and my voice sounded distant in my head, a scratchy piping sound buried beneath an avalanche of tearing, tumbling, rending inner sound, the noise of my blood as it slurried around my body amplified a million times.

'You, me, Liu.'

'Not Georgina?'

'She needs to be fielding downbelow calls. I got her fielding calls all day, heading up eight or nine folk. There's a lot of people down there, they're excited, they want to pledge, to support, to enquire, you know.'

I waited a beat, and said: 'Not Mat?'

'He's not here. Mat?' (as if he were some figure from her distant past). 'No, no. I have,' (gesturing vaguely) 'other plans for Mat.'

So the three of us went; it was just *the three of us*. We climbed into the little plane, and Gradi and Liu laughed and chattered with one another. He piloted and she sat up front, and I sat at the bak like the illustration for *Brooding* in a visual dictionary. They did not notice my mood. They were caught up in themselves, and the glorious and manifest destiny of their land, and meeting after meeting with important people, wealthy people, good meetings, 'That was a *good* meeting' Gradi would say. That brief golden era between Gradi forging the collective sense of *nation* out of her pure will, and the fast approaching moment when the American military would clout us and shut us down in a war it was quite impossible for us to win. But the candle that burns briefly burns more brightly, or so they say, or something like that, or something. Gradi knew that her slot was narrow, and so she worked with fanatic energy. Me? It swayed no yarrow stalks for me. But I was drawn along in the sinuous tourbillons of her wake, as her curious-shaped and -bladed mind cut through the element of my living.

We visited a faceless succession of wealthy Upland men and Upland women. It all happened a very long way away from the centre of my head, even though it happened within inches of my face. In the centre of my head was sunk a needle-thin but v-e-r-y deep gravity well that hooked round, like a fish-hook, and snagged the constant thought of my wife parting her legs and receiving into her body the flesh of some other man – worse, of *this* other man, this man who was saying: 'Thanks, Mr Bran, that's perfect, that's wat we want.'

And Liu looking at Gradi with this completely transparent *you-me-love* look. And even the thought that he was only the latest of Gradi's pretty men, that in time he'd be discarded and a new beau acquired, couldn't leaven my despair and hurt. And Gradi would swoop a little at the broad, red, sweating face of this Mr Bran, and pek at his right cheek, snatching a *tiny* kiss from his fat cheek, and pek at his left cheek, snatching an equally *tiny* kiss from that one. 'Thanks,' she would say, breathy.

We were bak in the plane.

We swung round the horizon. Gradi undid her scarf and fluffed her lustrous blak hair out with her hands. She was complaining of an itch in her scalp, so she buried her hands in her hair and rummaged, rummaged. Liu said something and her face bloomed into a full smile, the real variety, not the simulacrum that she used on political supporters or donors or me. She brought her hands out and clapped them together, that's how delighted she was with Liu's witticism. Watever it was Liu said, I don't remember, except that it delighted her. She duked her head a little and looked round at Liu in the pilot's seat. Since we were in zero g her hair did not move as her head duked down, so that it appeared to rear up around her face like a snood.

Then she gathered her hair together, tied a knot in it, and fastened her scarf about her beautiful head.

We swung round the horizon again and the sun buffed mother-of-pearl scintillations upon the scratched plastic of the pilot's window.

We swung round the horizon again and it was dark.

We swung round the horizon again.

We visited rich person after rich person. 'Money is the key,' she told them each, in turn.

'You can't have *my* money,' they all replied, laughing. Of course they said many different things, but this is wat, in essence, each of them said. And Gradi handled their suspicion in many different ways, but in essence she said this:

'I don't want *your* money. The Uplands is not a *taxing* nation: this is a new kind of country we're building here. The Americans tax, we don't. The EU tax, we don't. Your money is yours.' That's the kind of statement that you can't say too many times to a wealthy individual. 'But,' she continued, smoothly, 'I want to make sure that when the Americans declare the war that they are shortly to declare – next year, or the year after – I want to make sure that they cannot seize your funds, or freeze your bank accounts. We are trying to set up a new bank with Vijay Singh. In part it will be based in Bangladesh, and in part it will be based in excusive datafiles kept in multiple locations up here.'

A bank in the Uplands? Our own financial system? Some sooner, some later, but all eventually saw the danger:

'If the Americans declare war, they will seize this bank, and our money will become theirs. My fortune will then depend upon the vagaries of legal challenges to this seizure . . . and wat if that game of legal roulette does not end in my favour?'

And Gradi reassured them all the same way. 'If your bank data is kept in files in American banks downbelow then they will be seized. If your bank data is kept in EU banks downbelow then they will be frozen. This is certain. I'm not talking about building a bank in the Uplands with Doric columns in space and a neon sign saying Bank. We shall encrypt the data in two dozen linked machines in two dozen houses. The Americans may seize one or two, but not all. We will choose the most trusted Uplander of all to supervise this arrangement. Your money will be safer as Upland money than if you leave it in the EU.'

'I don't know,' they would say, only partially convinced.

'Look,' she said. 'Keep your money in downbelow banks if you want. That doesn't make you any less the patriotic Uplander. But do you know who I am putting charge of the first Bank of the Uplands? Bill Bran. He's putting his own fortune in the bank, and he'll be Official Treasurer. You trust him, don't you?'

Of course they trusted him. Bran was one of their own, one of the wealthiest Uplanders. He had made his fortune in investment. He had practically invented Investment Variables, and had helped create the Beliefs Market, upon which cultural capital was traded on various religions, and later on pop music and screen stars. Then he had followed the familiar Upland path: cashed in a large fortune, built a house in the Uplands, and transferred the emphasis of his day-to-day away from the Earth. He quikly became a famous member of the Upland community; tireless visitor to others' houses, and hospitable arranger of parties and get-togethers. He was committed to the new country yet distanced from Gradi. My belief was that he hoped, one day, to challenge her for the Presidency, when the nation was placed on a more established basis; and that, with this in mind, he was keeping a careful distance from Gradi, not alienated yet not a too-close ally either. Treasurer was the ideal job for him; power and prestige without being in Gradi's poket.

'He'll be responsible,' Gradi said, to each of the forty or fifty billionaires we visited during that time, 'for keeping your money safe. It'll all be Bran. There will be no fees, no interest charged, it will be purely a question of keeping your funds out of American hands.'

She persuaded many.

Georgina took many calls of support, promises of money, of personal assistance. She received many invitations for Gradi to come talk at the University of Cathedral-Major, address the finalists; to be interviewed by a dozen multimedia news outlets, to talk to the management and executives of Porplic.Inc about leadership qualities (fee negotiable); to receive the freedom for the city of Danzig; to meet all three Popes (Catholic, New Catholic and the anti-Pope Petrus II); to model for a mote-sculpture by the celebrated Garten-Hagen, commissioned by the National Gallery of Modern Sculptural Art at Barcelona, to be present at the (multimedia-televised, anticipated audiences in the billions) initial tasting of the latest vintage of *Les Ruffes La Sauvageonne* in Languedoc (a non-alc red available for those who chose not to imbibe intoxicants), to come visit here, to receive honorary doctorate there. In the EU she became a very famous figure indeed.

'There's money to be made in this sort of thing,' she would declare, smakking her hands together and rubbing them so hard that the friction of skin against skin made a rusty squeaking noise. 'But we need to be selective – or I'll wear myself out running hither and thither downbelow.'

'You're certainly flavour of the month in the EU,' I observed, intending the comment to be witty and *la-mode*, but instead sounding even to my ears only bitter and envious and petty.

'Flavour of the *year*,' put in Mat, in an over-enthusiastic voice, to override the negative energy with which I might otherwise be contaminating the proceedings.

'Flavour of the *century*,' added Liu.

'Which century?' asked Gradi, laughing. 'The next one I hope? The next one?'

And there, unexpectedly, was my face, reflected in the polished metal of a wall-strut, sandy hair floating as if charged with static, and the eyes collapsing in on the face in anger and sadness, the mouth mapping the hopeless ballistic trajectory that drags rokets bak down to the ground. I could hate that beautiful face, I thought. I am not worthy of her love. I am not worthy to be with her. She is so high above me.

A flare of light through the window of the descending plane. Gusty lights of purplish silver, a fatter, less fiery form of sparking caused by Elemag field meshing with the outer branches of the world-tree to slow us down.

And *down* we go.

And that rollercoaster feeling of tugging sikness in my stomach makes me close my eyes in misery. I will myself not to be sik. There's a worse thing than this lurching-sinking trajectory-induced nausea, I realise. The worse thing is the realisation, in my very marrow, that this sensation of sikness in my gut is no new thing to me. The most remarkable thing about this nausea is its familiarity. This is how I feel all the time. Something has gone very wrong somewhere.

The skin on the bak of my hands was dry, eczematic. I had little shallow scabs on my elbows. There was soriasis on my scalp. I required pharmakos to sleep, and although it was the best drug available and had no side effects I knew I depended upon it, and made a little fetish out of its sliver-shaped dispenser. I carried this container everywhere, and fiddled with it, and played with it.

There was one form of downbelow invitation which Gradi always accepted. She never turned down an approach from properly-constituted downbelow diplomatic authorities. She was a politician before she was anything else.

Three years before the war, Gradi met secretly with the Finn-EU local ambassador, and with the Cypriot-EU ambassador. Two years before the war Gradi met secretly with the Finn-EU local ambassador, the Cypriot-EU ambassador, the Polish-EU ambassador, the Italia-EU ambassador, the Czech-EU ambassador and the UK-EU ambassador. The year before the war she met with local representatives from most EU nations, in secret little confabs, meeting in wood-lined Suomi rooms, three times on board jets flying up or flying down or even – amazing! – flying along.

She never met with any of the Federal officials, the actual power-players. Nevertheless she received official instructions from the US embassy to the EU to desist. In return she filed suit against the US, arguing that there was no peacetime international legal ruling that should prevent her from meeting with local EU officials. She was careful never to approach, or to be caught being approached by, the EU Presidentiat. And the case sank into its years-long process.

There was another kind of invitation that Gradi never (or very rarely) turned down: invitations from fellow Uplanders. And they came in all manner of variety; invitations to dinner from wealthy men and women; 'come talk to our commune – we're dedicated Uplanders, and many of us have foresworn the ground altogether'; invitation to come try our peaches ('Upland-grown, in a perspex diving-bell-shaped conservatory appended to our house!'); invitation to come play 3-D Twister (the only game for zero g!); invitation to address our political meeting, the Upland Nationalist Party (the UNP was one of several dozen similar political groupings. I once asked Gradi why she didn't form her own political party. Her reply was: 'Isn't it obvious?').

Gradi on War

A meeting in a long narrow room, hurtling through the hurtling Uplands. A bakers-dozen of people, including Bran, the individual recently appointed Official Banker-Treasurer of the Uplands Bank. Since his appointment, and the establishment of an independent bank, Bran had begun a strategy of distancing himself from Gradi, establishing himself as the, you might say, natural opposition, playing the long game, manoeuvring himself to succeed her, to become President in his turn. In large part this consisted of him opposing Gradi's position on the impending war. I forget how this particular meeting, filmed of course, came about – but watever the putative reason for calling it, Bran turned it into a platform to attak Gradi.

'You're steering us towards war,' Bran was saying, visibly angry. He was a relatively old man, with the slightly mummified look that pharmakos can give older skin: two umlaut eyes over a fat nose and a broad, slightly drooping mouth; a furze of close-trimmed hair over his head and down his sideburns like black turf. His was a muscular, compact frame, which alternated periods of preternatural calm with interludes of rapid, strenuous agitation. 'Ms Gradisil,' he said, deferring sarcastically to her, '*President* Gradisil' (a self-deprecating expression on Gradi's face as he addressed her with this last title, a sweep of the right hand to brush this vainglorious title away, but Bran continued) '*Madame President,* the one thing I don't understand is – you can't expect to win a war. We simply couldn't beat the Americans in a fight. We don't even have an army. So *why*? Why would you goad the shark? Why would you push the US into declaring war, into moving the conflict into an arena where they are clearly superior?'

'They are clearly superior,' aknowledged Gradi.

There was a crowd of about three dozen present, watching Gradi and

Bran talk. Gradi had requested that no recordings be made, so we dozen were the only witnesses as the newly appointed Upland Banker and the unofficial Upland President debated the folly, or otherwise, of leading the Uplands into war.

'Wat do you think you are doing?' asked Bran, looking at the crowd. 'I don't think you know *wat* you are doing. It's a game of chiken, is it? It's all a giant bluff, a hope that the US will bak down at the last minute, is it?' Bran was shaking his head sending countershakes through his body as he dangled in zero g. 'Because I'll tell you wat—'

'Wat?'

'I'll *tell* you wat. They *won't* bak down. They're itching for war. They're uncomfortable in this debatable political land they're in at the moment, all lawyers and court challenges and countersuits, all public opinion and media coverage, and the incremental movement of sympathy away from them and towards us. They hate that. Once they get a war started, once they get a legitimate, legally sanctioned war started, then they'll be much happier.'

'I believe they will,' said Gradi, blandly.

'I don't think you *understand* wat I'm saying,' said Bran, becoming more angry, his face-colour shifting chameleon-like to match the dark pink-painted wall behind him. 'At the moment we can keep them tangled up in innumerable lawsuits, and they're tied down, they're Gulliver and we're Liliput and we have the innumerable little strands and cords of law. But when the war starts, when the war that you're doing everything in your power to *hurry along* starts, all that changes. Gulliver snaps all his fuking little threads, you see?'

And suddenly Gradi came alive, her furious energy focused as delight, her eyes shining. Her *nova* charisma filled that space. 'That's it! That's exactly it! Once the war starts the legal status changes . . .'

Bran barked, 'And you want to *bring that on*? Is it a *death*-wish?'

'You need,' she said (and she was no longer really addressing Bran, though she was looking at him; she was addressing us, her followers, her disciples), 'you need to understand wat war *is* in the twenty-first century, in the soon-to-be twenty-second-century. You absolutely *need to understand*. War is not wat it once was, the arena for masculine bravery and heroism, killing the enemy. Wat is war nowadays?'

This was obviously one of her rhetorical questions, and nobody answered.

'War nowadays is a mode of changing the legal protocols. And that's *all it is*. For complicated historical reasons we have evolved two separate, if intertwined, legal systems: one for peacetime and one for wartime.

The premise behind this, once upon a time, was that peacetime law was the norm, and that on the infrequent and extraordinary occasion when war happened a different set of laws was introduced. This is still the unspoken premise behind the legal superstructure of contemporary life. Of course, it is a lie. Human history has never been long stretches of peace interrupted by the occasional short war. The opposite would be a more accurate description. In practice, law for the *pax* and law for the *bellum* have always existed side by side. And so they do now. Historians insist that the court martial, and the whole of the *lex bellorum*, began life as a means of enforcing discipline within the ranks. So it did. But war is never just limited to soldier killing soldier; it always begins to involve soldier killing civilian, soldier capturing and torturing civilian, soldier stealing civilian's house, money, belongings, and so on. So the *lex bellorum* became more and more complex, made a series of connections with *lex pacificium*, roots and fibres from each discourse nosing their way under the soil and inter-tangling with the other. And now law is the dominant force in modern international relations. Not justice, of course not, but *law*, but the structures, the documentation generated by lawyers, the competing claims for relative jurisprudence of the many many courts.'

Everybody was silent. We were like attentive schoolkids, every single one, even Bran. Imagine listening to so tedious a lecture! Her words were holy to us.

'That's wat war *means* nowadays. It means a shift to a different code of law. And that's *all it means.*'

'Rhetoric,' objected Bran, weakly. 'Wat I mean is – that's one way of putting it – but, actually, there *are* such things as actual armies. The US trains actual troops, with actual guns. People get actually killed.'

'Killing somebody is a felony,' said Gradi starkly, '*unless* it is justifiable homicide. War invokes a different legal discourse for defining the justifiable.' Without waiting for Bran to reply, she went on, 'War used to be England and France at the time of Napoleon, squaring off, each pretty much the military equal of the other, and hammering away until one side or another reached victory. Not any longer! The military outcome of any war is, nowadays, always certain before the war begins. Wat nation would be so foolish as to commit thousands of men and billions of euros to a war where the outcome was uncertain? Strategists and AIs and officers for the Legal Corps work it out down to the last hour of every day of planned action. The last war that did not go the way the planners planned it was the South East Asian War of the 1960s! Since then *every war* has gone the way of the strategists' plans – there's too much money at stake for it to be otherwise. Everybody knows as much! Bran is right. When the US declare war on the Uplands—' (I drew a breath in at that moment, because Gradi had never before aknowledged that this was a *when* rather than an *if*) '—when they declare war, of course they will win. How could it be otherwise? They have thousands of highly trained troops, they have all the weaponry, all the spacecraft, all the experience. We don't even have a *militia*. We have nothing but a hundred thousand mostly wealthy people, most of whom have no intention of dying for the Upland cause . . .'

From the bak of the room, somebody shouted out: 'I'd die for you, Gradi!'

Suddenly the whole room was cheering, people clapping, a confusion of voices, 'so would I!' 'I would too!' 'Gradi, Gradi, I believe in you!'

It took long minutes for the mood to settle; it was cheering and babble and a slowly re-emerging quiet.

'Gradi,' said Bran, his voice calm and his face clear of anger, speaking slowly, 'please take me at my word when I say I *believe* in wat you're doing. I believe in the cause of the Uplands. I believe in your dream – the Uplands free. And if my dying would advance that cause, then I would be glad to die. But I don't want to die a *pointless* death.'

The whole room was deadly silent now. You could hear the creaking of the walls as the house moved again into the bright side, and the metal warmed, and the sun came in a solid blok of light through the single window at the bak, falling irregularly on the bodies of people hanging there.

'Nobody,' said Gradi, in a low, intense voice, 'wants to die a point-less death. And I promise you all this – nobody will die a pointless death by following me. But we must all die, sooner or later. And a death in a downbelow hospice bed with drugs soaking through your scalp to blot out your consciousness, *that* is a pointless death. And a death in the struggle for a truly free Uplands – that is a death worth something.'

Here the cheering broke out again. Bran seemed to lose it, his face blushing with wrath, and his limbs becoming marionettish with frustrated twitching. 'You're not making any *sense*, Gradi,' he blurted out. 'You're not making any sense! That's all very well – but if you provoke the US into war, you've admitted yourself that they *will win*. How does that help the cause of Upland freedom? That only takes away the little breathing space we have now! That will only lead to a full-scale military occupation, and proscription, and the seizure of our funds, not to mention Uplanders being killed, actual deaths – how does that help us?'

I heard all that because I was close to the old banker. But the noise in the rest of the room was raucous, and nobody was paying much attention. It was too much for Bran.

'Silence!' he bellowed. 'Will everybody *shut up*? Will Gradi *answer my question*?'

The hubbub died. 'Of course I'll answer your question, Bran,' said Gradi, in a tone of voice perfectly modified to express polite bafflement at his rudeness. He saw his chance, in front of this small audience and the much larger audience watching on screens. 'Why are you so dead set on leading the Uplands into a war *we cannot win*?'

'Why?' replied Gradi. 'Because I'm not interested in the war, I'm interested in *after* the war, it's after that counts; after the war when we can win independence for the Uplands. I'm interested in freedom. Freedom! Svoboda! Liberté! Eleutheria!' The cheering started up again. It was remarkable, and irresistible, to watch. Spittle and sweat beaded and floated through the air. A parallelogram of light moved, slowly but clearly, over the ceiling towards the bak, as if it too was moved by Gradi's rhetoric.

Of course there were times when, like Bran the Banker, I doubted her. When I was not around her, it would occur to me, as it occurred to him, that she might be simply and purely insane. She was fearless, but the lunatic who stands in the path of a groundeffect train is fearless. She talked of the future, planned for Hope and Sol to go to school, to university, to live lives, and yet all the time I was thinking *you want a war before the century's end*. This war would destroy the Uplands, kill many Uplanders, perhaps kill her; at the very least it would put her in an American prison for decades. Could she not see that? Was she wilfully blind? And the Uplands had no army, no training camps, no weapons beyond a few privately owned guns and explosives. The imbalance was obscene.

It was the *energy* with which she worked towards this end. She slept perhaps four hours a night (I needed twice as long). She was able to read 100KB documents in half an hour and then be able to argue expertly about the detail within them. She remembered thousands of people's names, and token details about their lives ('Tim! Alex, isn't it? Your son? Is he still at school?' 'Boöpis! How's your little Pharaoh?' 'Last time I saw you, Gennifer, you were starting an Illumination course, right? How's that going?' 'Hao-Chu, still dead set against the pharmakos? My mother's like that!'). She was able to go from dead tired, depressed, sunken, down-and-out, to perky and beaming in a fingerclik, and she could maintain that powerhouse charisma no matter wat was going on inside.

We no longer needed to go blind-canvassing, flying to random houses and introducing ourselves as we had done in the early days. She was well enough known now. But we still travelled through the Uplands a great deal, because she so rarely turned down an Uplander invitation.

She never took a vacation. I used to beg her: take a month off, come down to the France house, relax. She could not comprehend the concept 'relax', like an atheist contemplating God, or a blind man wondering about blue and red. She never took a month off. I went by myself, took Hope and Sol and four servants and spent the month stewing and miserable in the Provencal sun. Meanwhile she buzzed about her nation, far over my head, accompanied by Mat or Liu or Georgina-the-Grin.

Sometimes I saw her on EU screen media.

'Hi, I'm Gradisil!'

'Of course I know who you are. I'm honoured and proud to meet you ma'am. My name is Kentucky, like the state, though I weigh less.' (Gradi made her laughter sound real, polite but not forced or artificial. I don't know how she did that). 'I'm honoured and proud to meet you, ma'am. I was born an American, but I consider myself an Uplander now. Seems to me the US are the redcoats here, and that we're overdue a seventeen-seventy-six. That's how it seems to me. Anything I can do – anything at all I can do—'

'Thank you, Kentucky,' shaking his hand in front of the cameras and looking serious and sincere. 'Every Uplander can do something. In this country, in this new kind of country, *individuals matter.* That's the nature of true freedom – everybody means something important, everybody has a part to play, one man or one woman *makes the difference.*'

I saw that on one of the EU news stations. Gradi was a popular heroine in the EU. Downbelow I could stroll through the town market with Sol in a chair and Hope running to and fro round my legs, and there would be all manner of Upland merchandise: cheap vids and books of her life story (I sometimes had a bit part in those, but more often I was simply omitted); flags, maps, clothes, cut-downs, meadhres, all with her face, or some other Upland logo on them. The sunlight was as palpable as if we were submerged in hot, bright water. The shadows were sharp-edged, purple and blue and blak. Touristas and residents strolled, or lolled in the heat. The mairie, built of vanilla-coloured stone, projected onto its exterior wall images of the mayor herself meeting her constituency, shaking hands, smiling. The energy of it seemed dissonant with the heat and sluggishness.

'Can I have a ice cream?' asked Hope, tugging my trouser leg. '*Pwee-zhe* icecream? Icecream? *Pwee-zhe un-e* ice cream?'

'OK, my love,' I said, my heart dense in my chest as tungsten. It was not drawing in and discharging its blood as smoothly as it ought. Just looking at my son made my eyeballs prikle. We left the market and made our way through the summer streets. The maid was pushing Sol, who had now fallen asleep in his chair, along the lime-shadowed pavements, down the tall, shadowed alleys. We settled at a café, and the maid got Sol's bottle ready, and I tried to keep Hope sat in the aluminium-tube seat as he bounced excitedly going can-I can-I in French, and then shouting *choko! choko!* as if we were bak in Helsinki. And I thought to myself, shouldn't I be here with my wife, rather than with this sullen maid? Shouldn't wife and husband be sharing this time with our children? But they were *her* children, and they were not my children at all. That thought always struck home like a scalpel poked into my chest; an actual, palpable, feel-it-on-the-nerve-endings pain. Despair clanged brassily upon the shell of my being. I was dissociated from human community and family. I was a simulacrum-father. The waiter took our order, and I sat bak in my chair and stared straight up, at the sky, which is where she was. The sun put heat and light down through the high summer haze as if it were the biggest zero-g candle flame in creation. There was a thin smoky quality visible in the high air, the sky blue like tobacco fug, nothing like the sapphire or blue water the poets talk of. Passers-by moved listlessly along the pavements. Hope had already smeared dark brown all about his lips, over his chin, on his nose. The tik and scrape of his spoon on his bowl. I was drinking Opium-and-Vitriol, and it added to the heat and the stupor of my soul; it dulled me, made me sleepy, but it did not take away the sharpness of my misery.

Sol woke, in his chair, suddenly, and glared straight at me with the innocent fury of the just-woken infant. My love for him made a knot in my throat, made me cough. Fumes of Opium-and-Vitriol and the hot summer air caught in my gullet. Unless you have experienced it I do not believe I can convey to you the anguish a father feels when his child opens its eyes and another man peers out innocently through them. But I don't want to dwell on – I don't want—

On this question of the war she was consistent, and perfectly truthful. The one occasion when we met, officially (I mean in a diplomatic capacity) with the Americans, they were baffled by her absolute readiness to concede that the Uplands could neither defeat the US militarily, nor resist the military might of the US. I think they were expecting defiance, a rebel yell, a speech for the benefit of the world media.

'You cannot seriously expect, Ms Gradisil,' said the leading American representative, 'to take on the US in a military conflict and *defeat* them? You can't be so deluded as to believe that?'

'On the contrary,' said Gradisil. 'I completely accept wat you say. It would be foolish to deny the superior military might and expertise of the US.'

The American representative looked left at the various cameras, worn in the hats or on the lapels of various media reps present. 'I have to say, Ms Gradisil,' he said, 'that's a pretty *crude* play – you're angling for *sympathy* from the world's media – you're trying *pity-us, we're the underdog.*'

'Mr Representative,' Gradi said smoothly. 'Please don't misunderstand me. For I'm only stating the facts. The US are a great military force. The Uplands lak even a civilian militia. In the event of war, there is no doubt in anybody's mind who would be the victor. I wouldn't expect any such war to last much more than a week – for how could it?' She smiled at the media. 'The US outgun us, outnumber us, have better strategists and AIs, have a clear achievable goal, control *all* supply lines for their own and our supplies. They have the determination and the military will and the political will of a great nation. We are a near-anarchic assemblage of millionaires and billionaires and a few less wealthy enthusiasts, all of whom are too canny to hang around whilst their homes get boarded or even destroyed – they'll be in their down-below mansions, I can promise you that. War between the US and the Uplands? If there were to be such a war then we will lose it, then we have *already lost* it.' And the US did not know how to take this blithe admission of our national ineptitude.

nine. Slater

In Fort Glenn

General Niflheim, with Slater and Philpot and an officer from the Law Corps, have all just finished viewing a recording of Gradi's meeting. General Niflheim's face, slak in zero g, manages a bizarrely oxymoronic expression of angry stupor.

'Wat is she getting at?' he demands. 'Wat is she getting at? Like she's got some kinda death-wish? Is that it?'

'The best guess of our strategy team,' says Slater, 'is that's she's hoping for a Gandhi-style victory.'

'A wat?'

'It's a historical term. The idea is that she simply sacrifices her people, lets us kill them, destroy their houses one after the other, until the number of the dead starts to mount up and erodes public, eh, confidence in the rightness of the, eh . . .'

'Yes, yes,' (crossly), 'I see wat you're getting at. But she can't be that stupid, can she?'

'Well, we think that, *if* that is her strategy, then she's miscalculated her population base. These aren't peasants whose lives are so oppressed they'll shout "liberty or death". These are real wealthy men and women, most of them. Real wealthy. Since wat we want from them is only a tiny fraction, a tax, leaving them most of their wealth, they'll surely prefer that to throwing it all away following this woman.'

'The AIs agree?'

'They do, sir.'

'I don't like it, though. I don't like it. She's up to something. Wat did you call it?'

'Sir?'

'The kind of victory for which she was hopin'?'

'A Gandhi-style victory, sir.'

'That's a weird kind of name. Has she styled her name on his, do you think? A Gradi, Grandi, Gandi kinda thing.'

'I was wondering,' puts in Philp, 'whether it's a *legal* play?'

'How do you mean?' General Niflheim asks, and everybody looks at the officer from the Law Corps. Her name is Evans.

'Go on,' asks Evans. Philp nods.

'Well, maybe she thinks that conceding defeat before war is even declared gives her the legal grounds to challenge the war when it comes?'

'Say more,' orders Niflheim.

'In the sense, sir,' says Philpot, 'that – well, maybe she'll argue "there can't be a war, I've already conceded the war to the US", which means that we can't shift things to a war-legal footing, which means we lose one of the main reasons for going to war in the first place.'

'Well,' says Evans, her face the puffy pink of a first-time-visitor to the Uplands, 'that's not going to wash, sir. I assure you of that. That's plain *not* going to wash. Precedent is very clear on that one, sir. You can't admit defeat in advance, and neither can you do it retrospectively, for that matter. You can only do that when a war has actually begun. At the moment, in the eyes of the law, there is no war – so a surrender means nothing. Only once we've made the declaration . . .'

'Yes yes I see,' says General Niflheim. 'Still, she's up to something. Wat's she up to?' Then, turning to Slater and changing the subject without breaking his flow, he added, 'Got a complaint from Cristof Hagen – you know him, Slater?'

Philp chukles.

'I know him, sir,' says Slater, deadpan.

'Says you been deliberately ignoring him?'

'Certainly not, sir,' says Slater, glancing a little nervously at Officer Evans. 'It's just that I'm pretty doubleplus *busy*, wat with all the preparations for – you know.'

'Talk to him,' says Niflheim, bluntly. 'Downbelow has decided his gyrostation gets immediate go ahead. It's going to be ready, or leastwise ready enough, to billet the majority of troops for the war.'

'It's going to be built *before* the war begins?' repeats a dumbfounded Slater.

'You heard me soldier. It's wat the brass want, right now, downbelow. Don't antagonise Hagen. That's my advice. It's for your own sake but more importantly, for *my* sake. He's promised them that the shell will be up in a month, and the whole thing pressurised and katherine-wheeling in *two*. Capiche?'

Capitchy, thinks Slater, sourly. *Cipatchy.* 'Yes sir,' he says.

'Excellento,' says the general. 'Now, if you guys will excuse me, I have a long session about pre-declaration suits with Legal-Officer Evans here.' His words are jovial, but there is a strange sluggishness in Niflheim's manner that Slater can hardly read except as dislike. It puzzles him.

ten. Slater

Lawyers

With something as fine-tuned and delicate as planning a seventy-two-hour war, the *little-littler-littlest* thing can completely throw the timetable out of whak. Slater went bak to his people with the knowledge that there was to be a delay of at least two months whilst the U is welded to the U and the great wheel, to be called Fort Freedom, is assembled. Two whole months! It pushes the war closer to the end of the year, yet the ground are adamantine in their insistence that the war be over well before the new century celebrations. They don't want an American military episode spilling over into the new century; everything is to be neatly tied up by then. But they also want this huge spinning base, this eighty-billion-dollar installation, and five hundred highly trained troops billeted there. So Slater shunts the plans bak two months.

But everything is coming together, despite these impossible criteria.

He meets with the Veep. He is flown, by Elemag and even (on occasion, spacesuited up as if in fancy dress) Quanjet. Lawyers lawyers lawyers. There is no end to the lawyers. Even though he has nothing more than a minor in law, just like the majority of school graduates (his major was in War Studies – something less usual amongst military men than you might think) he is nevertheless expected to peruse a thousand legal documents. The precise wording for the declaration to be lodged, when the time is judged absolutely right, with the appropriate International Belligerent Court, probably either Washington (which has strategic advantages but will perhaps make the whole escapade look parochially American) or London, it has yet to be decided. There are half a dozen of variations for each possible submission. Then there are additional suits, countersuits prepared for every possible Upland retaliatory lodgement, summaries of precedence compiled both by AI and – Slater had to insist upon this, for it was very expensive – by real, breathing human beings. There are affidavits, copies made and witnessed on the proper legal standing of all American warriors liable to be involved, testifying as to their status as properly constituted belligerents. There are two thousand death forms, on which the enemy casualties must be logged (within the usual rubrics of reasonable search and notice).

The meeting at which the number of death forms is debated lasts a whole afternoon at Fort Glenn, the light swelling to brilliancy in the meet-room window every forty minutes, flowering in a swift sliding trapezoid along the floor and up the wall for twenty minutes, and then wilting and cliking out to reappear twenty minutes later at its starting place. It is some kind of loom-shuttle of light.

The meeting is between Slater, a listless General Niflheim, and four officers from the Legal Corps. Something's gotten into Niflheim, he's pissed, or restless, or something ('Wat's up with Niflheim?' he asked Philp yesterday, but there's no answer). Slater doesn't know wat's wrong, but he can't fret about it. He's got a war to plan.

They debate numbers. Slater's professional estimate is casualties (Upland) between 250 and 350, casualties (US) zero-5. It is always a good idea to have more death forms prepared than will be thought necessary – nothing more fiddly, and fraught with potential snafu, than having to rustle up additional death forms actually during the conflict. But 2000? That, Slater opines, is overkill. If the number is leaked ('and how could it *possibly* be *leaked*?' booms Niflheim, crossly, – *if,* Slater presses, *if* by some mischance this number is leaked, then it'll tend to suggest that the US are intending widespread butchery. It'll be bad PR. 300 tops, is all'll be needed. No but – yes but—

They argue it bak and forth. Finally they agree on the larger number. It is not, of course, really a discussion about forms; it is about the degree of confidence each party has in the US Army's capacity for restraint. Slater (as if his nikname weren't *Slayer*!) believes he knows the soldiers better than the more alienated high-brass, believes they'll *hold bak.* But he is outranked.

Slater has been given a week's leave to spend with his family before the war starts. Everything is in a high state of readiness. All the possible eventualities of Upland resistance have been stochastically appraised, these being:

[1] No Upland resistance, and immediate surrender, the problem here being the need to keep the war going for more than forty-eight hours. They have a dozen schemes for this necessary prolongation.

239

[2] No Upland resistance, but surrender delayed because of lak of national coherence and leadership. This would be very good; enabling the US to secure their territory before piking up a national leader and encouraging them to utter the crucial words.

[3] No Upland resistance, but Gradisil refuses to surrender. Much Legal time has been devoted to listing which other prominent Uplanders would have the necessary legal plausibility to offer surrender. Since she has never been officially elected, it is arguable that Gradisil's actions are a legal irrelevance anyway.

[4] Some limited Upland resistance. This is the best scenario of all, because it would justify US action, enable them to prolong the war as long as they wanted, and give the troops something of a workout. With *any* military resistance the game becomes mainly military, and that's where Slater's confidence is highest.

[5] Significant Upland resistance. However unlikely this is, given the lak of Upland resources, the lak of a national will to fight, and the precariousness of Upland supply lines, it cannot be entirely ruled out. Gradi is the wild card. It's conceivable – just – that she will inspire at least *some* of her people to an heroic stand against the Americans [*shout defiance in the maw of*—!]. And this, number '5' is wat Slater, in his truest heart, yearns for: a *useful military target*, a task to stretch the troops a little. The more military resistance they encounter, the stronger the US position; for they are, wholly, the dominant party in military terms. Nobody denies that. Slater has promised a seventy-two-hour war; but there is a great deal of leeway in this. Anything over forty-eight hours and less than one solar year is legally optimal. And there is simply no way the war could last as long as a year: for one thing, without food or the ability to travel downbelow the entire Upland population would starve to death before that. Which would not be ideal PR, but would still be a military result.

He flies down, and there are no clouds in the bright blue sky through which he swoops. It is the same inside his head. Through the window of his Elemag transport he watches the land come up towards him, as if some paradoxical solid flood of matter were filling the cosmos, pouring in from a fountain of land. There is a shudder as the wheels kiss the running ground.

He cheks out of the barraks, and takes a personnel jet to Florida, and then he signs a car out of the military pool to drive to his house. Six days of furlough. He calls Marina from the car. 'Honey,' he announces. 'I'm ten minutes out.'

She squeals in the screen with pleasure. 'I thought tomorrow!'

'Today,' he says. 'Are the girls at school?'

'At school.'

'Then I'm very pleased to announce,' says Slater, fumbling the automatic with his thumb so he can take his hands from the wheel and direct his attention more closely to the screen, and the image of his beautiful wife, 'that I'll be home in a few minutes. I must announce to you I am declaring martial law in this house – marital law, in fact. You must remove any unauthorised personnel from the house. Only you are to remain, and you are confined to the house – in fact, you are confined to the bedroom.'

She is giggling. 'How long?'

'Six days,' he says.

'Oh honey, that's fantastic—'

'Get yourself ready, ma'am,' he says, in his mok-stern voice. 'Estimated arrival window, in a *few* moments.' He is already imagining her body naked in bed, the dark wellspring of hair and the way her body flows, palely, down from her face in shallow sines of perfect desire. He is already imagining kissing her.

Family

Later that day Slater lies in bed with his beautiful young wife tuked under his arm, both her hands resting flat on his broad chest She is either asleep, or in that state of satisfied awakedness that lies still and calm like sleep. The walls are painted blue, and the ceiling white. The curtains, thinweave, green-blue-dyed and lit behind by the afternoon sun, move like two unhurried *aurorae boreales*. He is searching his mind, applying some of the methodical thoroughness that army train- ing has given him, looking for reasons to be unhappy, or anxious. But there are none: a beautiful wife, two beautiful children, a world- spanning job that has been time-demanding and stressful but in which he has acquitted himself very well. If he handles this war as well as he knows he will – if he brings the victory in within the parameters he has specified to the top brass – then a promotion will be a certainty. He'll be a colonel in months and a general before he's forty; by retirement he could well occupy a senior political post. He is loved and loving, he is working and useful, he is fit and happy. He is, indeed, very close to being the optimal human product of his age. He has a sense of almost painful satisfaction in his chest.

Later, the girls come home from school, ferried by the maid, a pug-faced little woman from the Republic of Bass Strait in her early twenties. This maid uses a conversational enhancer, worn looped over her ear, to augment her patchy English. Slater has forgotten her name, if he ever knew it.

'Daddy!' cries little Alice, and littler Menya, both hurtling themselves at Slater's body and swept in his broad arms upwards and around. 'Daddy! Daddy!'

'My princesses,' he booms. 'Have you been good girls whilst I was away?'

'Are you bak for *ever*, Daddy?' asks Alice.

'For a few days,' says Slater, kissing them both, and depositing them on the carpet again, where they fidget and jig about him. 'Daddy! Daddy!'

The following day Slater takes both girls out of school for a day, and drives the whole family over to the GWB Public Park, with its undulating perfectly manicured green spaces, with its award-winningly designed play areas, and its motorised dinosaurs of purple and gold that stalk clumsily in and out of the little copses of tamarind trees. The girls howl and whistle their delight and run and run. Slater links arms with his wife and they stroll together, like an antique couple. Their girls orbit them in ragged loops of sprinting and shouting, and then run off together giggling.

'Do I got any reason to worry?' she asks, when it is quiet enough for them to hear one another. The perennial question of the military wife.

'Given wat I *can't* tell you,' he says, slowly, and pauses, 'though you'll guess a bunch of that, I know.'

'I watch the news,' she says, laconically, looking past him at a hill in the middle distance topped with growing bamboo, like pins in a green cushion.

'Right,' he says, and they walk on for a while. 'Yeah, given wat I can't tell you, I can at least say that – no, you got no reason to worry. Maybe something will happen, but I've been involved in the planning, and it'll be the best planned something in the history of – somethings.'

'Still,' she says. 'There's always a risk.'

'Really and truly,' he replies, earnestly, 'there's no risk, not in this case. In this case I'll be as safe as if I were with you, down here. I'll not be frontline, and anyway it's all planned most carefully.' The clouds above them are being conveyed quikly across the bright blue sky. Some of them are edged with grey and purple, like white fruit just starting to grow mould at the edges. 'Maybe it'll rain,' he says, inconsequentially.

'Is that military code?' she asks, ingenuously.

It sometimes surprises Slater that he never gets tired of looking at the loveliness of his wife's face. 'No,' he smiles. 'I mean real rain, down-below rain.' He calls. 'Girls! Girls – we're going over to that shelter, 'kay? By the little river.'

'OK, Daad,' come their voices bak, distanced, gleeful.

Slater and Marina sit hand in hand on an oak bench under a plastic canopy, and for a while they do nothing more than both stare at the creek slipping past them down its stepped channel, the continual flow of its rain-cold solution washing gold-painted pebbles, and yet never washing the gold paint away. There are little green fish, like leaf litter, swirling and darting in the water.

'There's something,' Marina starts, and Slater sits bak a little. *Something.* His warrior sense tingles, the instinct bred through a thousand generations of anticipating dangers before they become threats. When one's wife says *there's something*, it could be the preliminary for a marital disruption, unhappiness; illness; confession of affair. Wat counts as *something*? After a night and a day, is this going to be the first flaw in his otherwise flawless existence? He readies himself, inwardly.

'Wat?' he asks, calmly.

'I was going to tell you earlier, only I figured I'd be better telling you face-to-face. Not through a screen, you know? Only—'

He doesn't feel too anxious. Watever it is, he feels competent to handle it. Accordingly, when he says 'wat is it?' his voice is neither urgent nor angry.

'I've seen the Pastor again, just a couple of times.'

'I see,' says Slater.

'It was only a couple of times,' says Marina, rolling her shoulders as if to remove a tightness in the muscles there, 'and he said I should tell you, that there should be nothing underhand about it.'

'Just the two of you, was it?'

'No!' Marina is blushing a little. 'Of course not – a group.'

'I didn't know he was in Florida,' says Slater, in a neutral voice.

'He travels around.'

'I'm sure he does.'

'It was a small group, Olivia arranged it – you remember Olivia? When he was going to be in town, she set up a worship group. So we met a couple of times for prayer and – and such.'

'With the Pastor.'

'That's right.'

The girls are approaching with scurrying legs. The girls are running over the green, towards their Mommy and Daddy, which is not a fair race, as Alice is older than Menya and therefore faster. Their faces are ecstatic with the hurry of it, the play of it, and the fact that they are coming closer and closer to the perfect location of their parents together.

'Did you,' asks Slater, 'talk about it? About that whole thing?'

'Yes.'

Slater looks away. The kids will be on them in a moment and he needs to press the point. 'Does he still feel the same way about all that?'

'Well, he does,' says Marina, as if this is the prelude to some longer speech, but she doesn't say anything more.

There's a question Slater wants to ask, but he doesn't ask it. He is weighing up whether it is a good idea to put it into words – whether it mightn't ruin the mood of his furlough, whether it would suggest distrust. He wrestles with it for a while, until Marina rescues him.

'You want to ask whether he's been trying to talk me out of my pharmakos.'

'Honey,' he tells her. 'You know the only thing I care about is your happiness – you and the children—'

'The answer is no,' she says, in a hurry, as the noise of the children's delighted yelling swells and they hurtle in towards the shelter 'The answer is, he isn't. I'm still taking my pharmakos.'

Then with a clatter and thud the girls land in the laps of their parents, laughing and sweating. 'I saw a *di*nosaur,' shrieks Menya. 'I saw him. He was *purple*. He was coming to get me but I ran away.'

'I'm a dinosaur,' says Slater, in a large play-voice to cover this sudden awkwardness with his wife. He gets to his feet and tries out a few roars, and his daughters squeal with delight again and wriggle free and leap the creek to run away, as he lumbers after them with his arms out – more like Frankenstein's beast than a dinosaur (as Marina later says) but happy.

Supper is Barachos-brand patties, and a special soup, and four different kinds of fresh vegetable. The kids are so excited they cannot sit still on their chairs. Afterwards they all watch the Bedtime Channel altogether, as a family. It's Tibby-Cat (*'gimme a kissy-cuddle!'*) followed by Prairie-Song of the Buk-Hare, which is edutainment. The girls go to bed exhausted-delighted. Marina prays with them, all three females knelt together in the girls' room, whilst Slater loiters atheistically in the hall outside, a misbeliever who is still weirdly touched by this little ritual, this verbal escort for the tremulous little souls through the darkness of the night. 'I love you, girls,' he hears Marina say, in a muffled voice, perhaps because her face is kissing their hair. 'We love you too, Mommy,' says Alice, and then in a louder voice, 'love you too, Daddy!'

'Goodnight, girls,' says Slater, in a slightly too loud voice from the hall.

That night Slater and Marina make love again, and then talk about the Pastor some more, and then make love again. But it's not a matter that can easily be resolved. His wife is entitled to hold religious beliefs, after all, entitled by national law and perhaps by natural law too. He does not share these beliefs, but he appreciates the freedom that permits them to her.

The girls are bak in school the following day, and Slater does nothing more than exist in his own house, breathing in each of the rooms, feeling his way bak into a domestic life. Marina doesn't mention the Pastor again. She sits in the front room reading, and eventually Slater comes and sits beside her. He wants to start a conversation with her, but can't think how to commence it.

The maid, haunting the room with her surly diffidence, asks 'Shall I cook lunch, Mrs Slater?' The words are prompted to her by Conversational Aid.

Wife and husband take lunch together, in the dining room, the whole of the bak wall glass, looking over the sloping emerald lawn to the row of silver beeches at the garden's extremity. This is his lovely house. This is his beautiful wife. He can afford as many fresh vegetables as he wants, and have them cooked by his servant to succulence. His job is going tremendously well; though only a lieutenant he has – in effect – been trusted with organising General Niflheim's war; and, given the wide-spread knowledge of the general's lassitude, this means that everybody knows he is really in charge of the campaign. When the victory is declared he will surely be promoted; it will launch a diamond-glittery career. And yet, he has to admit that the mere fact of the Pastor has dulled the gleam of his perfection. He can remember the first night of his furlough, that dazzling almost heroin-pure sensation of perfection in his head, in his body. He looks inside, and it is not there any more. He ponders whether it is the fact of the Pastor, meddling in his perfect marriage; or whether it is the fact that Marina has kept something from him. She had always been (or he had always taken her to be, which amounts to the same thing) transparent as a windshield, open-hearted, incapable of deception. If one is distracted by (let's say) 'other things' for a time, it can be a jolt to return attention to the homebase; the hypothesis that things can change, suppressed by inattention, asserts itself more alarmingly than it otherwise might. She had told him: *I figured I'd be better telling you face-to-face, not through a viewscreen.* But was that the truth? Or was this symptomatic of a broader series of mendacities? He looks at his wife as she forks spinach salad to her mouth. He smiles at his wife, and she catches his expression and smiles bak.

'I love you,' he says, suddenly, although wat he was thinking was, how can I have such complete access to your body, so that there is nowhere on its perfect surface hidden from me, no point of entry denied me, and yet be so loked out of your mind? It is on his tongue to ask 'Wat are you thinking about?' but instead – surprising himself – he asks: 'Does this Pastor guy have many skizophrenics in his congregation?'

Her eyes widen, and then shut completely. 'Wat?'

But he's started now, so he can't bak down. As he continues, he is thinking, I shouldn't have said that; but the subject has been broached now.

'I mean, does he *specialise* in skizophrenia?'

'Not at all,' says Marina, meekly.

'I mean, please tell me' – and Slater can hear a kind of ugliness in his own tone of voice, and he wishes he weren't speaking, but still he goes on – 'you don't want to go *bak* to being – being the way you were?'

'Of course not.'

'I guess, you see, from *my* point of view – you see, I don't know wat it feels like from the inside, only from the outside, but the way you were looked pretty bad.'

'It was terrible.'

'And you don't want to go bak to that?'

She shakes her head. She looks mournful.

'So tell me,' Slater presses on, although he is now urging himself, internally, to stop. But he can't seem to help himself. 'So tell me about this Pastor. Is he opposed to *all* pharmakos? I mean, some religious people *are*, aren't they. Refuse to have any in their systems. Is that his bag?'

'Why are you being so hostile all of a sudden?' she asks, her voice low.

'I was just curious whether this was part of a crusade this Pastor guy's waging against all pharmakos. Or if it was just the stuff that keeps your skizophrenia—'

Marina flares up at this point. 'Since you're so insistent,' she snaps, 'then the answer is no, he's cool with most pharmakos. Since you ask.' She is blushing, and stops abruptly.

Her anger calls forth a proportionate emotional response in Slater. 'Then it's just *your* fuking pharmakos he opposes, is it? He's just got a plan to wrek *our* marriage, is that it?'

'Don't shout at me!'

'I'm not shouting. I'm asking a . . .'

'He's a *man* of God.'

'Asking a question.'

There's an agonised pause in the exchange. But then Marina doesn't do anything other than repeat, sulkily, 'He's a man of God.'

'Like that excuses anything,' Slater urges, straining to keep his anger hot. 'He's fuking irresponsible, is wat he is . . .'

This sparks her up again. 'Don't swear at me!'

'Am not swearing at you, if you wanna know. Actually I'm swearing at *him.*'

Things are getting out of control. The level of rage is escalating. Slater catches a glimpse of the maid slipping from kitchen to front room, just the briefest sight of her sour little face. Was that a smile on her lips?

'I'm sorry,' he says, putting both hands on the tabletop. But he doesn't sound sorry. 'I think we need to bear in mind that he's a preacher, not a doctor, and that for him to recommend . . .'

'He's a man of God!'

'Mar, we've been through this,' Slater says, sounding exasperated. 'We've been over this a score of times. Yeah? The visions and voices and all that, those were the disease, they – were – *not* God. You thought they were God, but they were just, you know. Brain malfunction.' Her face tightens. 'Or not malfunction precisely . . .' he tries to correct, but she cuts across him:

'He disagrees, you know? He thinks that science doesn't understand skizophrenia and he's *right*.' With that last word a flame of passion flares up from her, red as her flushed face. Slater wishes, wishes, wishes that he hadn't started this whole thing now. 'He thinks that the pharmakos muffles and distorts my soul.'

'Oh,' says Slater, with automatic scorn. '*Soul* . . .'

'Shutup!' his wife cries, her voice needles and broken glass, the command compressed into one sharp word. 'Shutup! You shutup! You can't understand it, because you've never had a connection to God. But I had one, he lived in me, and now that's gone, because of the pharmakos. All the Pastor says is that I need to think hard about wat

God wants. Not wat my doctor or my legal adviser or my husband want, or even wat I want, but wat *God* – but wat's the use? Why should I – wat is the point?'

'Now look, Marina. Look. We went into all this, we've been through all – look. Some reduction in the immediacy of religious mania, I mean religious experience – it's listed as an effect of the pharmakos. But you still go to chapel? You still pray, and all that?'

'It's all mumbo-jumbo to you, isn't it?'

'I don't mind the religion. You be as religious as you like, honey. I mind the mental illness, and the mania, and all the stuff with that sword you made from a walking stik and a kitchen knife with the tape around—'

'You think you really need remind me of that?'

'That's wat he wants, for you to return to *that*!'

'No he doesn't. All he says is that it's a shame I've lost my intimacy with God. And – he's – right—' She's standing now, preparing to storm from the room.

He's faster and stronger than her; he's trained. Even though he's spent a good long time in orbit, and his body's not as strong as it might be, he still catches her easily, and holds her easily as she thrashes at him. He carries her upstairs, careless of wat the maid might see or think, and kiks the bedroom door shut behind. Then, like it used to be in the bad old days, he holds her on the bed whilst her eyes roll white in her head and she kiks and hisses out her tantrum. And then, when it starts to abate a little but there is still fire in her eyes, he pulls her clothes off and grapples with her, loosening her arms so that she can finally strike him, scratch him, all the stuff that can only enhance the sexual act.

Afterwards she sleeps, and he stares at the bright window and wonders if he provoked her on purpose. But the sex, alas, has not been cathartic. Rust has started its munching crumbling work upon his once cleanly metallic happiness. When he had first known Marina there had been a dangerous purity about her, a wild spiritual enthusiasm that had excited him even as it frightened, and even to an extent repelled, him. Sometimes she was calm, demure; and her lovely face would be haloed by her blak hair, and Slater could actually *feel* his heart in his chest *breathe in* with love for her. But then, on other occasions, her talk would become a clamour of excited words, and gestures, trying to catch the eye of invisible spirits, beings, angels, sometimes demons, and a blaze would almost emanate from her. For fractions of her time this might even be numinous and wondrous, times when it was impossible for her to see that there even was such a thing as an *ordinary* rainbow; times when the mere presence of rain in the air, or the texture of brikwork, or the visible signs of currents in flowing water, could move her to tears and a sort of mental orgasm. But this was only a small fraction of the time. More usually, during one of her episodes, she became fidgety and paranoid, her eyes in constant nervous movement, her fists clenching and unclenching, her darting gabble becoming soaked through with aggression and accusation. She spoke to God, in a pillar of cloud, or a smoky cloud of flies, or in the roar of the freeway. And God returned the communication, commanding her with sub-bass roar and elongated vowels to *rule* to *kill*, or *believe*, simple imperatives given awesome and alarming weight and heft by being boomed across the coastal freeway and echoed off the soundboard of the Atlantic. She strained to do wat God told her. She heard and tried to obey detailed, bizarrely *particular* commands from angels (*take a shovel, but it must be a shovel with a wooden handle, and cook twelve plain blak beans, and take them to the stretch of grass behind the schoolyard and dig three feet down, and lay the beans in the shape of a cross and fill in the dirt . . .*). Sometimes the commands were violent (*you must score the word putas in the flesh of the belly of the woman who works in the water-machine shop . . .*). On three separate occasions she cut her mother with a knife, and faced legal sanction, despite her mom's refusal to press charges. Her mother was a deeply religious person, and was in fact rather overwhelmed, even secretly impressed, by her daughter's confident assertion that she spoke to angels, and even God Himself. Because of this, and in common with many of the more intensely religious Americans, she denied her child pharmakos, regarding such drugs as theologically interdicted, although she did eventually, worn down by the relentless intensity of her daughter, countenance some varieties of the older anti-sychotic drugs. They had not worked very well. But earnest entreaty from Slater, besotted with this beautiful woman, had persuaded lucid-Marina to try the pharmakos that banished crazy-Marina forever.

Slater wooed lucid-Marina, and won her, and married her; and a daughter was born, and then a second daughter. And even Marina's mother admitted that pharmakos might be God's will, so complete and harmonious was their result. Marina was happy. She had never, she assured her husband (usually at his specific prompting) never been happier. But *God* had been banished from her personal acquaintance, and now she was only going through the motions of religion, in the same way that everybody else in chapel was, she realised, going through the motions. Like them, she was actually praying for the possibility of connection only.

And that was the way it was; until Marina met this Pastor man, who hinted to her that perhaps her skizophrenia – for all its unpleasantnesses – had been God's way of opening the possibility of His communication. And she began to fret that she had lost something more important than all the things she had gained, which is a dangerously persistent meme.

Slater's last day with her ends at 4, when a military car drives itself to his door to collect him. By dusk he is in a plane, climbing through a sky that seems to him to have gone into mourning over the loss of – something, he's not sure wat. Below him the western stretches of the Atlantic are becoming less and less distinct under the drawing crescendo of encroaching night. The water has taken on the appearance of tarmac. He stops looking down. Wat is ever the point in looking down, when up is so filled and fulfilling?

eleven. Paul

'I came up here, to the Uplands,' said Ustinov, 'to be closer to the stars. I am an astronomer.' He smiled for the cameras. The cameras simply stared their fish-eye stare, but downbelow a million people smiled inwardly bak.

'Not *just* an astronomer, my friend,' said Gradi, looking concerned and attentive. 'One of the most famous astronomers in the EU!'

Ustinov did not deny this. He showed Gradi, and the trail of attendants with their camera-headbands and globe-viewers, around his house: three large rooms, very well appointed, and then an even larger annexe in which three different types of telescope were mounted. Of all the wealthy individuals who had bought themselves a house in the Uplands Ustinov was one of the wealthiest. Indeed, one of the things that distinguishes the truly wealthy from the lesser fry is the adoption of a modulated form of humility: no parvenu showiness of conspicuous display for him. He seemed genuinely smaller than life.

'No, Madame President' (the cameras were catching all this, so Gradi made a self-deprecating gesture with her hand with a smiling shuffle of her head to disown the title), 'no, just a humble astronomer, an amateur.'

'An amateur with some of the most sophisticated telescoping technology outside the military!' said Gradi, laughing kindly.

'It is my life,' said Ustinov, simply. 'I spend more time in the Uplands than I do in Moscow. I consider myself an Uplander – one of your citizens, Madame President.'

'One of my friends,' she countered, suavely, putting her hand on his shoulder. Personal contact like bak-slaps and hugs and handshakes are a delicate business in zero g; you don't want to send the other person spinning or lurching or knoking their forehead against the wall. It's too easily done.

'And *now!*' said Ustinov, with tremendous Russian dramatic emphasis, 'the Americans! Tell me that my telescopes must be *confiscated!* But why? I ask you: *why?* Because they think I'm using my scopes to spy on their idiotic military force-of-occupation up here? A moment's thought reveals that as absurd. I am examining the Kuiper Belt. I am traking nearby star systems with planets. My gaze is set far away. As if my scopes could even see their ridiculous blak-painted Quantum-jets! As if I could even focus them on ground-based installations!'

'How absurd,' agreed Gradi.

'They harass me, they seek to take away my life's work, to beggar me.' Since Ustinov could, without exaggeration, have bought several small nations entire, this seemed to me unlikely. But I looked sober and nodded thoughtfully every time Gradi did. I was barely in shot, but it would not look good if I was caught rolling my eyes at the ceiling.

'They are the mafia of this land,' said Ustinov, fiercely. Since he had made much of his money via organised crime downbelow this was a clever comparison to draw in many ways.

Later, as we flew down and up to a new house, to meet some further Uplanders, I challenged her directly. 'I wish you'd include me.'

'I include you,' she said.

'You don't include me. I don't understand why you're pushing so hard for war. We can't win a war against the whole armed might of the USA.'

'No.'

'The whole of the EU, with air force, army and weaponry, didn't last two days against the US in eighty-one!'

'I know.'

'All I'm saying. There are many Uplanders with – concerns,' I said. 'You're pushing things along to war.'

'We cannot win this war.'

'But Gradi I really don't understand, I really wish you'd explain to me, I really don't understand how you can *say that* and still . . . you know, keep applying the pressure that will *shove* the nation along the groove to conflict.'

'The path to true victory lies through the road of defeat,' said Gradi. She was moking me? I turned and looked through the window at the blakness.

My last trip downbelow before the war

I spent a month with the boys, in Helsinki. Gradi was with us for only a few days. If I raised this matter, implying without having the courage actually to accuse her of neglecting her family, she looked at me as if I had sworn at her, or accused her of some crime of which she was manifestly innocent: a sort of hurt surprise that flowered from the unexpectedness, for her, of the rebuke. She genuinely did not, I think, comprehend any delinquency in her attentions. An only child, raised by a stiffly self-controlled English stepfather and by a mother, Klara, at best only semi-connected with the real world, I believe the truth is that Gradi's heart was so soaked through with herself that she was beyond seeing so abstract a concept as selfishness. It is not that she laked a sense of her role as mother; it is only that an entire nation of discontinuous houses and similarly self-absorbed, monkish billionaires fitted her notion of 'child' better than her own flesh and blood. 'Mother of the nation' meant more to her than actual mother to Hope and Sol and less still to the as yet unnamed presence in her belly.

We spent one last day as a complete family; Gradi, myself, Hope and Sol, with Kirsi along to help us. It was a cold late autumnal day, and we walked, as a family, down by the doks. Sunset came early in that latitude, at that time of year, and the boys ran bak and forth with Kirsi shepherding them away from the water's edge. Salt-halos shimmered into existence in the bay, reflecting the lights on the hill behind us. The water and the airy horizon blurred in magenta purple, the sun just round the world's corner, but slipping further, the sky darkening continually. The white and yellow lights of the town were assuming more and more solid definition. It was 5. 'Let's go eat,' said Gradi. She was, I remember, very nervy that evening, constantly looking over her shoulder, cloking every passer-by. 'Do you expect the Americans to kidnap you, here in Finland-EU?' I joshed. But she was terribly and dramatically serious. 'This would be the optimum time to nab me,' she told me, as if confiding a great secret. 'If I were them, and faced with a threat like me, I'd act now.'

I tutted. 'You're growing paranoid. Listen to yourself! Kidnap? That sounds so very twentieth century.'

'Practical,' she corrected. 'Although, kidnap is a less good idea than a quiet assassination. If it were me, I mean, that's wat I—' but she stopped machiavellising abruptly. 'Boys!' she yelled, sharp. 'Time for food!' And, cheering, they rushed at us to takle us both round the waist, Hope grabbing me and Sol her. This latter collision brought out a rebuke from Gradi.

'Be careful,' she scolded Sol, disentangling him from her midriff, pushing him away until he was at arm's length. He was only just six years old, a slender and rather jittery child, with eyes the colour of coffee-without-milk and his pinkish-yellow skin quite literally thin. Running as fast as he could, at that age, he could never have accumulated the momentum to damage even the small pregnant frame of a woman like Gradi. Indeed, I felt a prikle of anger at my wife for overreacting, and hurting the feelings of my little prince needlessly. But I said nothing, of course I said nothing.

'Sol, Leave Mommy Alone,' scolded Hope, with audibly capitalised earnestness, happy for the opportunity to pull rank on his brother.

'I'll tell you why,' said Gradi, stopping, and dropping to her haunches to bring her face a little below the level of her younger son's. 'Shall I tell you for why?'

Sol, wounded by maternal rejection, replied only with an intense and wordless stare.

'It's because I've a baby inside me. Inside my body, just underneath my tummy, I've a womb, and inside the womb is a baby. Have you done babies at school?'

'No,' said Sol, sulkily.

'We have,' cried Hope, gleeful. 'We did it in the summer. I know *all* about babies.'

Gradi took Sol by the shoulders and drew him to her. 'The baby is very small at the moment,' she said. 'He's curled up in my womb, and if you smash into me you might hurt him. OK?'

'OK,' said Sol, even sulkier.

'I know you didn't mean to hurt the baby, and I'm not angry with you,' said Gradi. 'But we all need to take care of him. One day he will be born, sometime next year—'

'After Christmas?' put in Hope, whose perspective of the future was closed off by that glittering imminence, crowded with those presents to which he was looking forward.

'That's right. And then you'll have a brother – a younger brother for both of you. You'll be *three* little boys, instead of *two* little boys.' Sol perked up at this a little, as if anticipating wat it might be like to have a new-printed member of the family, releasing him from the burden of littlestness. But Hope bridled. '*I'm* not a little boy,' he objected. 'I'm nearly *nine*.'

The sky overhead had blakened with unnatural suddenness, even for a late-year Suomi dusk. It was a raincloud, crow-coloured and wide as the sky, and it straight away began to unload on us; irregular splotchy drops at first, sounding in the darkness like an impossibly quik succession of eggs being broken in a pan, but then, without crescendo, a torrent. Shrieking and laughing we all ran through this nailstorm, along the lamplit street and into the first restaurant we encountered. In seconds we had become soaked. The staff brought us hand towels as we occupied a table by the window, laughing and padding ourselves dry. The boys ordered gammon. Gradi and I had real vegetables, a spread of six different sorts, steamed and boiled; we urged Kirsi to have the same, but she insisted it was too extravagant, and instead ate a nondescript shed-grown hotpot. The quik dash for shelter had perked a buzz out of our group, and we talked excitedly about this and that, Kirsi included. There was an antique piano being discreetly played in the corner of the restaurant, its enormous lid propped at forty-five degrees like the rudder of a sea-ship: Bach and Mozart and Boettcher, melodies and arpeggios weaving sine-cosine through the air. It was delicately digestive music. The waiting staff came and went. Rain chattered at the windows, passed off, then chattered bak against the glass. The lamp over the restaurant entrance put a tiny golden crescent on every raindrop clinging to the outside of that window, and after their food the boys crouched down against the glass and followed the trembling descent of a hundred drops, tracing the downward wiggle with their fingers.

This was our last time together as a family. But wat does that phrase mean, precisely, I mean, *as a family*? We were rarely familiar, in all the times we had been together. There was a single decade – less than a decade, at the fag-end of an exhausted century. Then came the war, and everything changed. But the tightness of chronological focus simply failed to generate a correlative tightness of familial focus. Nor have I the right to accuse Gradi of being an absentee mother, or neglectful. I, like her, was an only child. Perhaps I have spent too much of my life looping round and round the density of my own self, insufficiently attentive to the needs of others. More, I find it hard to see inside the minds of other people, to watch the world as others watch it. Most of all, even the many years of marriage to Gradi has not gifted me the ability to see through her face into her mind. She is as much a blank to me, her husband, as she is to the millions who have followed her career on screen, through news and doc and dramaticonstruction. Her manner, her breathtaking self-possession, her charisma, the sheer now! and now! and now! of her presence, working a room, flashing from person to person, the ability to mould people around her, to anticipate: all that is generally accessible. But do even I know wat swirled through the vesicles of her brain when she lay, tight in a sleeping bag hooked to a wall, in that interlude between wake and sleep? Doubts, anxieties, uncertainties, second-thoughts; perhaps she had all those. If so, I never saw them. And perhaps she was truly without even the most minor self-reproach;

perhaps the inside of her mind truly was smooth and flawless and pure. Much of the practical process of raising the boys was subcontracted to a series of childcare professionals; that's frequently the way with the wealthy. But I was not as absent as was Gradi, and that simple fact gives me more solace, now, than you might think. I did play with my boys; I did take them to the monster-theatre, to the cinema. We did watch 3nimations and share buckets of sweets together. I did go to at least some of their school events.

And, looking bak, I remember a seeming unending series of conversations with my boys. That was the period of parenthood I enjoyed most; between the frustratingly dumb and maladroit period of the baby years, and the insolently self-reliant period of teens, there was a glorious summerish flowering of years when the two of them were old enough to talk to and play with, but when they were still unthinkingly reliant on the mere existence of *parent*, that object without which they would be unable to work through the stiky medium of existence, day by day.

Sol developed an early interest in sports, particularly sports of which statistics were a part. But the earliest conversations I can remember with Hope were always about the Uplands. Both of the boys had been up a few times, but never for more than a day at a time. But Hope wanted to be there all the time.

'Why can't we live in the Uplands?' We had this conversation often.

'Because you and Sol are too little.'

'I'm nine, I'm nearly nine.'

'That's still too little.'

Hope had a distinctive inflection of the generic *aow* of childish disappointment, which he now deployed. 'But *I* want to live there all the time!'

'I know you do. But your bones are still growing. Growing bones need gravity.'

'Madame Hakkunen says that bones need calcium.'

'They need calcium too. But they need gravity. If you lived up there all the time, your arms and legs wouldn't grow properly. Your spine, too. You'd grow up to be a cripple.'

'I wouldn't mind.'

'But you would mind, if it happened to you! And anyway, *I'd* mind. It would mean I'd been a bad parent.'

'*When* can I live up there? Next year?'

'No, not next year either. You need to be fully grown: sometime in your late teens.'

'When's that?'

'It will depend, won't it? But late teens means eighteen, nineteen, maybe even twenty.'

Hope contemplated this impossible-to-imagine stretch of time with a sweetly beautiful look of genuine astonishment on his face. 'But that's ages! I'll be *dead* by then!'

'Time goes quiker than you think,' I said. It was one of the reasons I loved talking with the boys at that age, the way they absorbed even my rankest banality as a distillation of the wisdom of the ages. Although on this occasion Hope's mind was in combative mode. 'No, it doesn't,' he said, with finality. 'Time takes *ages.*'

I hugged him, because (I think) his words had magically reconnected me, momentarily, with that childlike slow-motion of existence, when single afternoons were deserts to drag oneself wearily across, or jungles to be fought excitedly through, and *hours* and *hours* and *hours* was a criminal sentence as long as decades. It is formed, perhaps, of the indiscrimination of childhood, that elasticity of time. Children have not yet learned the adult habits of selection and on-the-hoof editing, the dismissal of ninety per cent of our lives as not relevant to the task in hand. To a child every atom of existence is swept into the broad net of their senses, relevant or irrelevant, and the pressure, like solar wind, functions as a kind of palpable drag, slows them to a pace of time-known like a leaf uncurling. 'Time gets faster as you grow up,' I said, trying, in my clumsy way, to share this great truth with the boy. But of course this was a concept beyond his ability to understand.

Sol, all through this exchange, was absorbed in watching a rollball game on the screen. He was so much more curled up in himself, mentally speaking, than his brother. If the positions had been reversed – if it had been Hope watching the screen whilst Sol was talking to me – then Hope would have been unable to restrain himself from butting into the talk, eager to straining-point to share his opinion, to know wat was going on, fidgeting and hopping. But Sol was uninterested in things that did not directly impinge on him, and his concentration was such that very little did impinge.

Sol's mode of being in the world, his natural, unlearned hermeticism, would often catch me unawares. He was small, sheathed like an atom in tight little layers of indeterminacy which the external observer could not expect to penetrate. Hope was a completely different style of youngster; more sprawling, out-reaching, arboreal. Hope sprouted upwards in height with an almost brutal suddenness and, unused to his newly extruded body, seemed forever to be falling over; such that the ground, with a barber's practised firmness and swoop, was always scraping grids of skin off his knees and elbows. Whenever this happened, inside or outside, Hope had no compunction about bursting into hysterical tears. Even into his late teens, in fact; at a time when most children have learned to handle their emotions with *some* circumspection, there seemed to be no border between wat Hope felt and wat he projected to the world. A thumb caught in a door or a heavy lid, say, would bash out promiscuous tears and prolonged little yelping cries that combined physical anguish with a hopeless sort of sense of betrayal, as if he couldn't quite believe that the universe had been so cruel to him. This reaction was as common at eighteen as it was at eight; it pained me, to be honest, to see a young man bursting into childish tears at trivial causes. That is my most enduring memory of Hope – even now. He was forever rushing about, skidding or banging himself; forever running to Kirsi or to me with his face blotchily plumped and reddened with tears.

Sol was quite different. Do you remember the fashion for power-bikes? They were everywhere in the EU during the '90s, and I believe they were popular in the US also. Parents bought them because the advertising assured us the motor could only be charged by the pedalling of little legs, and charged therefore only up to a modest level. But naturally children found ways to circumvent the inbuilt safety features. They quikly discovered that leaning the bike at about forty degrees whilst someone took a portion of the weight of the bak wheel, and pedalling furiously so that the wheel half-slid and half-stuk, could charge up the little cablewire motor to a considerably enhanced level. Then, instead of moving along a fraction above normal cycling speeds, the intrepid child could zip about at twice, or even more, the usual pushbike speed. One summer Sol, with some of his schoolfriends, supercharged their bikes using this method, and Sol went caroming along the traffic-free Helsinki streets, scaring pedestrians, his face a mask of silent concentration, until the inevitable collision. The bike was bent in the middle through nearly ninety degrees; it looked like a 3-D model of some notional 4-D hyperbike. Sol himself came limping home, supported by one shamefaced friend. Kirsi was cross with him for putting himself in danger, and for wreking the bike, which relieved me of the dutiful need to pretend anger when all I felt was a cowardly relief. I asked him if he were alright and, through lips that kept snapping shut between words, he insisted he was fine, and limped upstairs to lie down. His colourless face should have alerted us as much as his demeanour – because, in fact, his thighbone was broken, a very nasty fracture we later learned. But his childish reticence meant that we did not take him to the hospital until the following morning. It still astonishes me; he lay on the bed in agony all night without coming to me. Wat went through his mind? I have no idea. Did he expect the pain to go away? Did he think he could conquer it by sheer childish will? When he was still white-faced in the morning, and unable to get out of bed, I called medics; and rode with him to the hospital, more amazed than guilty. He was in a thigh-sheath for a month whilst the pharmakos prompted his healing.

Klara

When the boys asked after their mother, as they did often (before, as teenagers, they learned a more studied indifference to their maternal origins) I tried to be truthful. I told them she was very busy, in the Uplands, working hard. I told them that she loved them, and saw them as much as she could, but that the work she was doing was very very important. When they asked, 'Wat work?' I said that she was helping create a new nation, a whole country up in the sky. The boys were relatively unimpressed with this.

But Klara, a frequent guest in the house, knew how to hold the attention of her two grandchildren. Her version of Gradi's life chimed with their understanding of wat a life should be. This is wat she told them:

'Have you heard about America? America is a big country, over the sea. Now, a while ago, before you boys were born, this country committed a crime against our family. They sent an assassin – do you know wat an assassin is?'

Wide-eyed shakings of the head.

'An *assassin* is a person who kills other people for money. Well, they sent such a person, and she killed my father – your great-grandfather. Murdered him in the Uplands, above the sky. It was a terrible crime, and it has scarred our family. All of us are duty-bound to revenge ourselves upon this crime. Do you see?'

'How did the sassin do it?' they asked.

And she told them the story, and they sat circle-eyed in amazement. She must have told them the story a thousand times, and it sank very deeply into their childish beings, their fluttery little souls, their intensities of excitement and resentment and sorrow. It occurred to me sometimes that it was ill-advised of me to give my boys (not *mine*, I *know*, must you remind me?) so largely over to their grandmother. She was a mad old woman in many senses. But I was distracted, and Gradi was absent almost all the time, and Klara loved her grandchildren: she

259

spent whole days with them, entering into the spirit of their childish games perfectly, her own childishness (something she had never outgrown) serving her so very well. The boys loved her.

On the rare occasions when Gradi was in the house as well, Klara would try to provoke her. 'She always seems to be leaving, doesn't she, your mother?' she would say to the boys. 'Always leaving! Running away to the Uplands.'

'Don't tell them that, Mother,' Gradi would say, crossly.

But the boys were snuggled on Klara's lap, all three of them settled in the sofa with the screen showing a 3nimation, and they egged her on. 'Tell us, Granny! Tell us!'

'I'll tell you something that not many people know,' said Klara, with each of her arms around a different boy, 'When she was a girl, not much older than you are now—'

'Do you mean not much older than me?' interrupted Hope, 'or not much older than Sol? I'm older than Sol you know.' Sol didn't say anything.

'Not much older than both of you,' said Klara. 'Do you know wat she said, about the Uplands? I'll tell you, she hated that place. She told me *Uplanders are all criminals and bank robbers and murderers, and they've run away from the world, and it's proper to despise them.*' Klara cackled, and taking their cue from that the boys shrieked with forced hilarity. 'She used to hate the Uplands!' Klara continued. 'And now she can't stay away from there!' Gradi returned her attention to the flimsy she was reading, contenting herself with tutting at Klara's foolishness.

'Mummy's silly,' said Hope, overexcited. But this was too much for Sol. He disengaged himself from Klara's arm and left the room, silently.

'You've upset your brother,' I said – mildly enough, I think.

'He's stupid!' said Hope, flushed, his mouth a ∩. All the hilarity had flipped into distress and accusation. 'He always spoils everything. He'll make my life horrid now – he will. He'll get at me all day now, I know he will.'

'How do you mean, get at you?' asked Klara.

'He'll say,' said Hope, with tears starting to brim from his eyes, 'that I shouldn't call Mummy silly, and he'll go on and on about it, on and on. He doesn't think Mummy is silly. He loves Mummy.'

Gradisil got up from the table and came over to the sofa and collected the boy from Klara's lap. 'But you love Mummy too, don't you?' she said, in a soft voice.

'Of course I do, Mummy, of course I do. But not like Sol does.' And that was when the tears really started pumping out of his little eyes.

twelve. Slater

War

The war begins. You know how war goes, its *bang-bangs* and its periods of lassitude. The declaration is lodged in the Washington International Belligerent Court at o-four-hundred on November eighteen, in the year of continuing grace and growth twenty ninety-nine. At precisely o-four-hundred every available warplane is in flight.

This is a war that runs precisely along the electromagnetic grooves spaced so carefully out by its planners. The Uplands, of course, have no chance. The war is won in the first three days, precisely as Slater said it would be. The USUF has purchased excellent intelligence, and moreover they own a man 'on the inside' ('though there never was a country,' Philp declares, drawling, 'that had less *inside* than these fuking *Up*lands'). This mole identifies the seven crucial houses, the ones in which expensive banking hardware is lodged. The military seize Upland assets, occupying this seven-house bank. They have also been provided with the secret transp locations of several of the more prominent Upland citizenry, including Alan Liu and Ardelion Sylvana; although they do not have the transp for Gradi herself, or her husband, or her second-in-command (as intelligence reports style him) Mat Chang. Which is to say, their mole – their crucial insider figure – he provides them with wat he *assures* them is this crucial transp; but in the event it leads them only to an empty tin-can house.

This is the only blip on Slater's otherwise perfect chart. The war goes so perfectly that it is being recorded *as it happens* by textbook-compilers for the Space Marines, to be used in future training of Upland assault forces. The troops are efficient, focused, they do their jobs and do not overstep their legal restraints. The territory is seized with minimal casualties: seventy-seven Upland planes and thirty-nine Upland houses are destroyed, a very small percentage of the many thousand in orbit. On exactly the chiming of the seventy-second hour the President

261

himself declares victory. There is only one thing needful: a formal statement of surrender by some Upland official senior enough for such a statement to have legal force. This is the triky part, because (and it is something many lawyers will argue over for many months) there doesn't seem to be anybody, apart, of course, from Gradi herself. Liu and Sylvana declare themselves to be private citizens, nothing more; they stik to this line with impressive tenacity. It is not true, of course; but it is a claim that has courtroom plausibility. Senior officers from Legal Corps decide that there is no mileage in pressing either party to a statement of surrender. 'We need Gradi herself,' insists a Colonel-Legal named Updijk. 'Of course, once we grab her, she might try the same trik – claim to be nothing more than a private citizen—'

'She's always been careful,' Slater agrees, 'never to refer to herself as President of the Uplands.'

'But that won't cut it in court,' says Updijk, confidently. 'Everybody *knows* she is President. It's de facto. That's common knowledge. Other people, including any number of Uplanders, use that title in reference to her. Uplanders follow her, some with remarkable fanaticism. No, take *her* – then we'll extract a statement of surrender from her, and the war will be finally over.'

'Soon as we locate her,' Slater says. 'We will grab her as soon as we can.'

Upland is a very spacious country, with many houses, so locating Gradi and bringing her in is not an easy matter. But Slater is confident. He flies down to report to the Veep in person.

Jon Belvedere III's broad, statesmanlike face does not betray any pleasure at the smoothness with which military operations have been completed. But Slater reasons he must be glad, inside. He was at the President's side during the announcement of Military Victory, looking similarly stern. Now the sternness is focused on Slater. 'Can you find her?'

'We'll get her, sir.'

'Wat's the timescale?'

They are in the Veep's office; a very wide, very tall room furnished with elegant antique chairs and desks, and rows of antique books in uniform binding, like a legal library from the twentieth century, although in fact the books are novels. Presidential sponsors this year are MakB, and their logo, a large red M with a small blue B pendent from the central spar, is tastefully evident about the walls.

'It's hard to pin it down to hour, or even day. But we'll get her.'

'Upland is pretty spacious. There are a lot of houses up there. She could be in any of them.'

'That's true, sir. That's true. But we've got a number of factors in our favour. For one, the blokade has proven itself watertight . . .'

The Veep unsheathes one of his scimitar smiles at this, and then stows it away again, all within a second. 'I'll confess I had my – anxieties on that front,' he says briskly.

'Yes sir, it *was* untested. And some of the Uplanders are pretty experienced pilots. But they simply can't outrun the Quanjets, so we can take the blokade as tight, sir. Tight. So she can't go downbelow. She's stuk Upland. And there are two problems with that, for her. One is food. Two is, she's pregnant. So she'll get to starvation quiker, with two bodies to feed; and she can't – our medics assure me of this, sir – she can't stand more than two-half, three months top in zero g. More than that, she'll risk losing the baby. Or even if she doesn't lose it, it'll be born deformed, deformed in the bones. So the clok is tiking for her, if you see. The clok is tiking.'

The Veep nods. 'Three months, then?'

'That's completely the *outside* estimate, sir. My estimate is that it'll be over long before then. We'll keep broadcasting terms on which we'll take her in, medical assistance, guarantees of safe passage, negotiations, one President to another. And then either we'll find her during a house-to-house, which—'

'Which are continuing, are they?'

'Continuing, yes sir. It's a continuous sweep. It's a big job, sweeping so many thousands of houses all in space, but it's going on, house by house. So we might pull her out that way. Or, if not, then in a month or two she'll come to us.'

'And when you have her, you're confident she will surrender?'

'It's negotiation, then. She'll want to negotiate. She'll gain nothing by holding out. Legal Corps tell me there are three varieties of surrender, at any rate: actual admission, tacit admission, or denial in the face of overwhelming evidence. Any of those will suit us, sir.'

For almost a minute, the Veep does nothing but look at Slater. Then he sits bak in his creaking chair.

'You have done well,' he announces. 'Keep me abreast.'

thirteen. Paul

Unluky number. So the war came. Most of the Uplanders who died perished not in their houses but in their planes making sudden runs for the downbelow. Gradi warned people that this is how it would be. The Americans put into swift execution the obvious strategy: blokading the band of latitude through which an Elemag plane gains the greatest purchase against the branches of the Yggdrasil as it descends. It is a huge stretch of sky, of course, particularly if one is anticipating desperate Uplanders risking ripping their wings off by rushing at the poles, or risking using all their fuel (and, simply being in the sky much longer, putting themselves in fatal peril for much longer) by flying a series of looping paths to try and shed speed in tropical skies. But few Uplanders were so stupid; most of us had years, or decades, experience of flying to and from orbit. Those Uplanders that made a dash for ground relied on speed, and threw themselves into that narrow stripe around the chest of the globe, which is where they were killed. They should not have trusted to speed.

Gradi had stressed this point again and again. Once the war is announced on the news media, *stay home.* Don't try the dash downbelow. Don't try the sparrow-flok dash past the kestrel, for this particular raptor had the capacity to pik you *all* off. Many heeded her words, but a few ignored them, either through exaggerated self-confidence or perhaps with sudden panic.

The first action of the war, then, was the shedding of seventy-seven (American numbers; they counted them) leaves from the topmost branches of the world-tree, to flutter, pause, swing groundwards: a near simultaneous hurry for the ground by seventy-seven planes. This simultaneity was a remarkable thing: for it was not coordinated, or planned; the various pilots had no communication with one another. But as soon as the EU News reported the lodging of the declaration at the IBC in Washington, seventy-seven Uplanders hauled themselves into their jets and dropped straight down into the high sky.

There is footage of wat happened next, although it is not very *visually* satisfying: shot from the noses of Quanjets, or USUF Elemag warplanes, it mostly shows the same sight over and over again. You can just make out a tiny white asterisk, just visible against the blue-blak, or moving against the deep bakground of cloud, sea, and darkly wrinkled landscape. This insect-like trajectory is a straight line, but then suddenly there is an almost imperceptible crumpling, a slight spasm in the tiny shape, and the trajectory slides into a spiral, or darts abruptly left. It has the wrong *shtam* about it, as the phrase goes. We want to feel that something so cataclysmic as the crushing out of a life (and watching another die is, in its way, entering into a dramatisation of our own mortality) is more than a tiny shiver of one detail on a sky-broad canvas – we want, rather, to believe that it is a spasm of the whole cosmos, that it is the walls and the ceiling and the floor ripping and shrieking to shreds all around us, a maelstrom of fire, a huge shout in the throat of the dying pilot. Not a curiously-shaped asterisk twitching a little in the far distance.

When documentary makers want to illustrate this first engagement, they usually concoct their own sfx, or borrow some imagery from *Scheherezade at War* or *High Sky II* or *Upland Conquest: One American Hero's True Story*, or one of the many other successful movie versions of the conflict. I've seen these, just as you have: darting Elemag planes flown by grim-faced swarthy Upland pilots, swerving and jinking silently through space with firework displays of sparks pouring like shower-water off their wings and blowing in neon crumbs into the plane's wake, whilst the Quanjets close for the kill (it is always Quanjets in these films), cutting the air sleek and turbulence-free as a shark. The climax is as it must always be in the movies, with the spectacular fiery detonation, standing in (as ever) for orgasm. I cannot tell you to wat degree this is a realistic representation. I never saw one of these destructions with my own eyes; like you I only heard of them at second hand, reported on the news.

I know, again only through downbelow-reporting, that the USUF used a number of strategies for 'downing' the planes. It was sport to them. Target practice. They used Elemag torpedoes, guided bullets, and even magnetic disruption detonations that broke the plane's purchase on Yggdrasil and sent them into fatal burn-up tumble. Every single one of those planes that dashed for the ground was intercepted and destroyed. Over a hundred people died, and all within a few tens of minutes of the declaration.

When people ask me wat my experience of the war was, I generally say *claustrophobic*. Like any Uplander, I was accustomed to frequent journeys between the Uplands and the ground: to give my long bones their regular gravity stresses, to collect supplies, to visit friends. But it so happened I was Upland when the declaration was made, and I was therefore trapped Up. I was in a certain house (not our own) with Gradi and Mat. We stayed in that house for seventy hours or more; simply sitting, watching the news feeds, barely even talking. We watched the reports of the first engagement; seventy-seven Upland planes engaged and destroyed. Then we watched reports of the Americans deploying their troops to wat they said were 'crucial strategic positions' in the Uplands. Gradi watched with particular intensity. I don't think any general, or any president in human history, ever had less command of their forces during a war. She was a wholly passive being, simply watching and watching. She did not even, during those first three days, phone anybody.

The Americans destroyed forty houses during those first three days. They occupied another twenty. They seized the majority of Upland assets. I was staggered, I was crestfallen, I was despondent. 'Our bank! They took *precisely* the seven houses they needed to take to claim the bank, to close it down! My money . . .'

'Inside information,' said Mat, darkly.

'It's over! They've beaten us.'

'Yes,' said Gradi, simply.

'I want to call down,' I said, for the umpteenth time. 'I want to chek the kids are alright.'

'The kids are fine,' said Gradi, not taking her eye off the newscreens. 'We don't call them yet. One thing they'll be monitoring is our kids.' She smoothed her pregnancy bump with her right hand as she said this. 'If we call we put at risk the—'

I swore at this, and pulled myself hand-over-hand into the bak room. The house we were in happened to have three rooms, and I was to become very well acquainted with those three rooms. It was far too small a house to sulk in. Within twenty minutes I came bak through to the central room, where Gradi and Mat were hanging on the wall watching the newscreens. 'We might as well let them know where we are,' I blustered. 'It's over.'

'Try to keep a grip,' said Gradi distractedly, watching the screen.

I was straining for *tantrum*. I was trying for *freak-out*. But it was more than half an act; and my performance skills have never been very convincing. But I felt I had to make my points, and I felt that I was entitled to a massive emotional upset, even if I didn't actually feel it. So I snarled and twisted in space, flinging my hands melodramatically about, O big baby, sniping at the leader (lead-her, lead? her?) 'It's over,' I nagged. 'This war you've been pushing for is over, this war you wanted so badly. You got the war, and now we've lost it. How long do you intend to sulk in this tin can, now that you've been beaten? How long will our supplies hold out? And I don't need to remind you that you're pregnant? How long until—'

'Paul!' she said, firmly. 'Control yourself.'

'I won't control myself – it's my child too – and I . . .' But the simulated passion was a thin and unconvincing thing. Wat was the point? She was stroking her four-month bump again, but her hand was automatic, and her eye was all the time on the screen.

I went through to the bak room, and strapped myself into a sleeping bag, and tried to sleep. But of course I couldn't sleep.

After three days the Americans declared their victory. This was less an occasion for triumph, and more a legal requirement, a staging-post in the process of wrapping up the conflict in the downbelow courts. But it was, as the EU media commentators repeatedly reminded their viewers, a declaration that had complete courtroom plausibility. No lawyer would be able to persuade a court that the Americans had *not* won. They controlled the Uplands completely.

After the initial interception of fleeing Upland planes (none of which had so much as returned fire) there was relatively little actual fighting; although there was a little. Famously, there was even one American casualty: Trooper Alton Haskell, about whom the popular movie was made. Perhaps you have seen this. Not every Uplander copied Gradi's passivity. When troops stormed the seven key houses, to seize the banking hardware, occupants in many of them fought, fired at the incoming troops with handguns, wireware, watever they had to hand. One American was killed, three wounded; fourteen Uplanders lost their lives. There were also sporadic unco-ordinated attaks on American planes, always when docked (it was futile even to try when they were in flight). A few enterprising Uplanders flew their planes close to occupied houses or military installations and fired makeshift roket tubes. No significant damage was done. And after the three days most of the Uplanders with any fight in them had been captured or killed.

After this the population settled into a sort of stupor. We had all been expecting this – I mean, expecting not only war, but defeat – but experience is different to expectation. It is a hard thing to do to live in defeat.

On the fourth day Gradi, Mat and I left that house and began our cat-and-mouse travels about our own country.

The American occupation meant a change in our mode of travel. The best way to move from house to house in the Uplands is to drop down into a lower, faster orbit, and then sweep up to approach one's destination on a decelerating curve until velocities match and one can nudge one's nose into the porch. But the American blokade was concentrated on the lower orbits, and any plane that flew within their ken risked being destroyed.

On the other hand the space of the Uplands was so enormous it was quite impossible for them to monitor all of it. And so the daring pilot might start up his or her plane, fly up into a higher, slower orbit, and wait for their destination to come hurtling round beneath them. Then they could accelerate down towards it. This was a much more tiresome process; not only did it mean that flights took considerably longer, it was more dangerous. It is much safer to decelerate up to a target than to accelerate down towards it, for there is much less chance of catastrophic collision. But, having no choice, this is wat we did. Gradi piloted, and we flew up and hovered, and flew down, following a transp signal. When we doked we sat before knoking at the door, not wanting to be shot for Americans. I have seen it reported that we had a secret knok, but we had nothing of the sort. The way we distinguished ourselves was simply by patience: Americans always doked and came straight through. We would dok and wait fifteen minutes before gingerly opening the door.

So we moved around. Here we were: in a large house, but it was paked with people so it seems claustrophobically tight. These were real Uplanders, and they were scared. They clustered around Gradi like piglets around the momma pig, yearningly snouting for the nipple that reassures.

And Gradi spoke to them, spontaneously, without notes. She told them that the war had begun, and that the Americans had achieved their military objectives, as everybody had expected them to do. But she said, but, but, the Americans had underestimated the Uplands. The Americans had underestimated *her*. For now, the Uplands would lie still. We were the branches of a mighty tree; the Americans were a great wind – a mighty wind, she conceded – but they would pass through the branches and pass on, but *we* will still be here. She made this speech, or variants of it, a hundred times.

At the end of this speech their faces were all, every single one, beaming. She had fed them on actual, honey-flavoured *hope*. A woman called Grays Bikta gave Gradi a new transp signal, and Gradi thanked her earnestly.

We took to our plane again, with this new transp location; Mat and I and Grays and a man called Barabas Stottlemeyer; and we unsniked the plane and flew up, to wait, to wait.

'That was some speech,' said Mat. When he was nervous he became high, prone to little scratchily-voiced interjections out of nothing. 'A great little speech.'

He and Gradi were sitting in the pilots' seats side by side. Mat kept casting dubious little glances over at her, like a beast sipping stealthy little slurps at a waterhole ready to bolt before advancing predators. He was trying to drink from the sight, the physical presence of Gradi. His hopeless has-been passion for her was as earnest and consuming as it had ever been; and he knew that I was right there behind them, floating by the wall, watching the two of them. He was being almost operatically surreptitious; and Gradi was wholly unnoticing, staring through the blankness of the windscreen at the nothingness outside.

'It was a good speech,' I said, glancing in turn at Grays and Barabas behind me. 'I almost believed it.' I added, in case my implication had not been clear enough, 'almost.'

'*I* believed it,' said Mat, overeager. 'I *believe* it.'

'It'll be a century before this wind blows away,' I said, with self-conscious sourness. 'Longer. The Americans are here to stay.'

'There we go,' said Gradi, as if to herself. Our destination was sweeping round the world beneath us.

We flew another ski-jump undershoot down, up, settle. It was another Upland house; and we nudged our way in, and loked the nose into the porch.

Inside this house was Bran, the Official Treasurer of the Upland Bank. He was there with a dozen other people, and they looked grey, tired, scared.

'Well,' boomed Bran, as soon as Gradi emerged through the door. 'I hope you're *happy*, Madame President. I hope you *are happy* – you pushed for this war, and now you got it. The Americans pushed straight through us, like we were made of paper, like we were made of wet paper.'

The mood in this large, crowded house was not welcoming. I recognised the faces of the dozen; some of the wealthiest Uplanders, people who had been persuaded by Gradi to shift most of their funds to the

Upland Bank. We had come straight through into an ugly scene. 'The Yanks have my money,' shouted one of them, a billionaire called McManus.

'They do,' agreed Gradi.

'How did they do it?' called somebody else, from the bak of the room. 'How did they know precisely which houses to seize? We were set up.'

'You *prom*ised,' yelled McManus. 'I trusted you – put my fuking money in your bank, and now the Yanks have seized all our funds.'

'I told you, Gradi,' said Bran, pitching his voice loud enough to cut through the hubbub. He was very cross-looking, his eyes popping. 'We had a *dozen* meetings in which I said – many of you were there, you heard me. I said it was a fool's mission, pressing on towards war the way you were. But Gradi was *so certain*,' (addressing the crowd now), 'and now she's brought disaster on us individually, and disaster on our nation.'

Everybody in the house was murmuring their agreement. Everybody was glowering at Gradi. She floated up a little, and hooked her left hand round a strap to steady herself.

'Clery,' she said, in a voice of extraordinary calmness.

This was unexpected. Clery?

Clery was a stubby-legged property bigwig with a slightly twerpy manner. His face was wearing the same wrathful expression as all the other billionaires in the room, although on him it looked comical rather than intimidating. He was one of those patently in love with Gradi – by which I mean, of course *we were all* in love with Gradi, but one or two Uplanders nursed a painfully obvious *tender passion* for her, and he was one of those. Nobody took this seriously. Clery, for all his money, was the clown of this group; he was a scragga, a schlemiel, a boyo.

As she addressed him directly, his face folded into pained delight. 'Gradi,' he replied.

Everybody was looking at Clery. Everything had gone quiet.

'Clery, come out from behind Bran, would you?'

Clery was floating a few feet behind the Official Treasurer of the Uplands.

These words of Gradi's, seemingly *non sequitur*, had a strangely potent effect on the little group of people assembled there. Written down there, they don't seem to be very striking words; but they were delivered with such complete calmness and control that they straight away soaked up some of the anger in the room. Everybody was looking at Gradi, which is how she liked it – or, no (of course) how she *required* it. Everybody look! Over here!

That's better.

Clery reached out and grabbed a strut to pull himself from behind Bran. 'Gradi,' he said again. 'Wat? You want to talk to me?'

'No, Clery,' she said, again with her commanding calmness. 'I just don't want you hanging behind Bran.'

'Don't play games with us, Gradi,' snarled Bran, trying to whip up the mood again. 'It's your fault we've lost all our fuking money to the Americans. You think we want to play games here with you?'

'It's not,' said Gradi, deadpan.

'It's not? It's not?' echoed Bran, scornfully.

'It's not my fault,' she said without raising her voice, 'that we've lost all our fuking money to the Americans.'

She had a gun in her hand, pointing at Bran.

I'm not sure whether it was this understated brandishing of a handgun, or the fact that Gradi had uncharacteristically used the word *fuk*, that caused the chill to run through the room. The latter was almost as shokingly unusual a gesture as the former. The rage in the room had sublimed away into astonishment. Everybody was looking at Gradi now.

'Hey!' snapped Bran, his face blushing darkly and his brows creasing together. 'Hey, wat, hey! Wat do you *think* you're – Gradi! Hey!'

She did not say anything.

'Are you threatening me, Gradi? Wat's with the – gun?'

Nothing. Bran folded his arms, matching her stare for stare, saying nothing.

But Bran couldn't hold the silence. 'Look,' he said, putting his hands in front of his chest, 'if you're trying to imply something – look, why not come out and say it, OK? Wat are you implying? Are you accusing me of something? Is that the reason for the gun? That's pretty heavy-handed, Gradi. It really is. C'mon, there's no need for that. If you've got an accusation to make, you should make it. There are witnesses here.'

Gradi did not say anything. She held the gun steady, pointed at Bran's chest.

Again the silence priked Bran into speech. The colour had flushed into his face and then, almost as rapidly, drained away. 'Look, Gradi, let's *talk* about this, shall we? I'll admit I'm angry with you – we're all angry with you, here, but with *cause*. You know? Cause. It doesn't mean I'm any less committed to the idea of the Uplands. It doesn't make me any less *patriotic*. I know money's not life and death – and you know that too, yeah? But, fuk, don't you think we've *reason* to be angry? The bank was your idea, Gradi, you know it was. All we're saying is that . . . look, if you want to accuse me of collaborating with the Americans, will you – please – just – come – out – and – *say* – *it*—' He spoke these last words with enormous, strenuous emphasis, his eyes seemed to bulge and pulse. He floated a little to the left. Gradi's aim with the gun followed him.

The silence swelled, and for a third time Bran had to fill it. 'You've no proof,' he said, urgently, and his voice contained real fear now. 'You've not a single atom of proof. Think of all the people up here who could have provided them with the transps for the bank buildings. Think – look. This is wrong. Gradi – a gun? Really! Look at yourself!' He glanced round the other people in the room. 'C'mon, guys, time out. You don't believe that I'd sell you out to the Americans? Why *would* I? It's not as if I need the money!' He tried a laugh, but it didn't come out right. 'Gradi, Gradi,' he went on, speaking more hurriedly now. 'Are you really going to murder me, in cold blood, here, in front of all these witnesses? Is that wat you want to do?' He paused, waiting for Gradi's reply, but she was silent. 'I don't know wat ideas you've got in your mind about me, Gradi. But shouldn't we *talk*? Doesn't the condemned man,' another failed attempt at a laugh, 'get a trial? Look, if I wanted political authority up here there are better ways of going about it than selling myself out to the Americans. Do you really think anybody in the Uplands would follow me as President, if they knew I'd sold you out to the Americans? I'd be a fuking quisling.'

'If,' said Gradi, in a quiet voice, 'they *knew*. Which, I guess, is why you're here, and not in Fort Glenn.'

Her words were like a magical charm. They compelled our attention. Everybody looked at Bran. Sweat was coming so prolifically from his face that it was pimpling into pearls and breaking free of his skin. Dots of fluid hung in the air about his face.

'This is a crazy conspiracy theory. This is *crazy* conspiracy talk, Gradi. Listen to yourself! I didn't sell you out to the Americans. I swear I didn't. Believe me, I—'

A wireware gun makes a distinctive sound when fired, a sort of snare-drum pop. A bubbling, red-beading hole opened in Bran's chest, and a snap later in his bak. The projectile cliked into the wall behind and stuk there. If you've never seen a wireware bullet, I can tell you that it looks like the spindly metal frame in which champagne corks are corseted.

I hiccoughed with sheer astonishment. I had not expected Gradi actually to shoot him. Nobody in that room, at that time, had expected Gradi actually to shoot him. Bran twitched and threw his arms out, but otherwise made no sound. His body drifted bakwards and lodged in at the coign of ceiling and wall, and a tremendous amount of blood gushed out of his chest, squash-ball and pool-ball-sized globes of bright red, like giant marbles spilled from a bag. Everybody was staring at this body.

Then Gradi spoke. Her voice pulled all our gazes bak to her, and I saw that she was no longer holding the gun. 'Quikly, people,' she said, and clapped her hands lightly together, as if commanding a genie. 'Somebody grab a sheet and net this blood before it goes *everywhere*.' People twitched. 'Lau,' she said, addressing R. R. Lau, the famous screen compositer, who had (famously) amassed a fortune and retired to the Uplands. 'Fetch a sheet, please?'

'Sheet? Paper?'

'No, cloth. A sleeping bag or something.'

Lau moved, and the weird tension that had held that group of a dozen weightless people in unnatural stillness sagged. People moved away from the corpse, manoeuvred to avoid the spilling baubles of red, people were chattering rapidly and nervously amongst themselves. Two went with Lau and came bak with one large sheet that they held between them to scoop up most of the blood. Some gore had already splotched onto walls or floor, but in moments the air was mostly cleared. They wrapped the body in two sheets and tied it with a plastic rope.

'Everybody,' said Gradi, and the chattering stopped. All eyes were on her again, and all faces pouring their focused attention onto her. I thought to myself: she's gone too far this time. I thought to myself: people think of her as a sychopath now; she's traded their love and admiration for their fear, they'll never trust her again – when this gets out she'll be a pariah in all the Uplands. I was wrong about that, as I so often was about Gradi.

'Everybody,' she said, and (impossibly) her voice was warm, her face sincere. 'You've all just witnessed something shoking. I'm sorry about that, but it could not be helped. This is the Upland's darkest hour – it's happening now, *right* now, *right* here. Our nations' darkest hour. We're all a part of it. If we hold strong, our nation will emerge stronger and better. But if we *waver*,' (her voice trembled on that terrible word), 'if we *give up*, then we might as well stamp ourselves as citizens of the fifty-third state of America.'

All eyes were on her; but nobody spoke.

'Let's go through, all of us,' Gradi said. 'Let's talk about wat's happened here – and about why it had to happen.'

'You shot him,' said Clery, in his twittish high-pitched voice. Because it was Clery who spoke, it struck the comical keynote. The group tension was at that precise pitch and resonance that it started tumbling over into frank laughter, the sort of laughter that people try to stem as it comes out, knukles-between-lips laughter.

'Are we at war?' asked Gradi in a clear voice.

The laughter died. Nobody answered. Gradi looked pointedly at Clery. 'Yes,' said Clery.

'We are at war,' said Gradi. 'And that was an act of war. Do you want to know why?'

'He was a traitor,' said Lau, as if the pieces were fitting that moment together in his brain.

'I did that because I wasn't prepared to ask anybody else to do it. But we *are* at war, and he *was* a traitor,' said Gradi.

'He was a traitor,' said somebody else; and then another person repeated the phrase. They said it almost wonderingly, the way the audience to a particularly well constructed mystery who, upon hearing the unexpected revelation of the criminal's identity, whisper the name almost with awe: *so that was the missing key! That explains everything! With that one word everything coheres!* And the weight, on the one hand, of a single human death, and the weight on the other hand of the whole decade-long accumulation of belief and faith, the weight on the other hand of Gradi herself. Which way would the beam tip? To ask the question is to answer it.

Bran's body, wrapped in a blotchy red sheet and tied about with string, was shoved into a porch and taped – with one stripe of ordinary stiky-tape – to the nose of a plane. Then one of the party (I don't know his name) flew the plane out, pulling slowly bak, angling slowly down, and then engaging Elemag for a flik forward that broke the body away and sent it tumbling. With the exception of the bloodstains inside the house (and they were easily bleached and cleaned), every last crumb of Bran's DNA would burn up in the atmosphere, the very molecules stripped and shredded and oxidised. This is one version of the perfect crime.

After the return of the pilot from this body-disposal run, we all went through to one of the bak rooms and had some food, had something to drink, all together. With unseemly rapidity it became an upbeat, even triumphalist gathering. People chattered excitedly, saying sentences that existed in a curiously quantum state between truth and lie – things like 'I always suspected Bran was up to something', or 'I think I knew in my bones that he was a traitor' – things that were not *correct* (for everybody had loved Bran! Everyone had trusted Bran!) but which, by repetition in this social context, became *the truth* in a perfectly genuine, unhypocritical sense. People loved Judas once; but love is something that only exists in the mind, and therefore it, and its history, is more malleable than gravity or momentum.

'He betrayed our money,' said Gradi. 'He's been in league with the Americans for nearly a year now.'

Nobody replied to this, caught between the obvious retort (if you've known this for a year then why have you only acted now, after his actions have gifted our money to the US?) and the disinclination of those present to antagonise Gradi. This, I suppose, is *respect*, which is to say, plucking a synonym from the political lexicon, fear.

'It's his doing,' said Gradi, and she knew exactly wat people were thinking. 'I wish I could have acted sooner – I wish I could have prevented this. But I needed proof. The most essential part of being an Uplander is liberty. Who dare take away that liberty, for anything short of blatant treason? I had to be sure.'

'Of course,' muttered Lau. 'You had to be sure.'

'You did the right thing, Gradi,' said somebody else.

'If we hang together,' said Gradi, her voice suddenly fierce with a rhetor's passion, 'then we can get through this! He wanted the Uplands defeated, and me in prison, so that he could set himself up as the US puppet-President. But I will not let us be defeated!' I thought: but we've already been defeated, although of course I said nothing.

And I was as susceptible to the mood of the meeting as anybody. People were grinning. Some had tears in their eyes. It was extraordinary – I don't think I can convey to you just how extraordinary it was.

'We'll get the money bak, I swear it, I promise you all,' said Gradi. 'It's tangled up in the weedbeds of the lawcourts, the groundling legal system. That's exactly where the Americans are misunderestimating us. Maybe they have more guns and bigger guns, but wars are not fought on battlefields so much as they are in courthouses. And we have one advantage on the legal front: nobody has ever fought a war such as ours before. I will get our money bak.'

The next day we left: Gradi, myself, Mat, just us three. We scanned the vacuum landscape before decoupling; our naked eyes were too crude as optical instruments to spot Quanjets, but we looked anyway, habit, and of course saw only blackness and the glinting nail-heads of myriad stars. So we unsnibbed and climbed through the magnetic medium to a waiting position, and turned all electrical equipment off, and became the same thing as junk, hollow and vacant.

Mat kept looking at me. I did not return his gaze, unsure wat sort of intimacy he was trying to establish, although in retrospect it is obvious enough. He wanted to reassure himself that Gradi, whom he loved, was not a cold-fleshed killer. He hoped by conferring with me, who also loved Gradi, to reaffirm his precarious sense of Gradi as (to pik only a few of the relevant words) tender, warm, loving, fleshly, yielding, sensual, climactic, sleepy – or, to put it another way, he wanted me to help him somehow balance the two variables of this complex quadratic, whereby Gradi could be the same sensitive love-making human being and simultaneously this pitiless being with its slaughterous will. But, frankly, why would he want to ask *me* to help him in this? I didn't know. I was no good to him.

After half an hour, Gradi turned on the console briefly to chek for the transp; but it had not yet emerged from round the shield of the whole world, and so she turned the equipment off again.

'That,' said Mat, abruptly, 'was something else.' He was speaking a little too loud; he was not entirely in control of himself.

Gradi looked at him.

'I can't stop thinking about it,' Mat conceded, in a hard and bright voice. 'Why didn't you warn us, Gradi? Why not—' He stopped.

'Why not wat?'

'I just don't,' Mat started, and again stopped.

'Boys,' she said, with infuriating condescension. 'Don't you know wat politics *is*?'

'I'm sure you can tell us, Gradi,' said Mat, but the sarcasm was ill-judged. I almost winced. I reached out and grabbed the wall to pull myself a little apart from him. I didn't want to be associated with him if he was going to antagonise Gradi in this manner.

'It's a show,' she said. 'That's all. You need to make a splash. C'mon boys. Tell me this: Why did I insist on you *not* telling anybody about the incident with Stefan?'

I could not, at first, remember Stefan, and from his expression neither did Mat. Then I remembered; the wealthy house, his butler. 'The man who tried to assault you,' I said.

Mat's face bloomed in distress. 'Him?'

'The man who tried to rape me,' said Gradi calmly. 'I killed him.'

'That was self-defence.'

At this Gradi shouted: 'So was this!' She almost never raised her voice. It was worse than a blow; we cringed, we really did. But she carried on smoothly, adding in a level tone, 'Do you know why I insisted you not tell anyone about that? Why that had to be a secret?'

For seconds we were both too scared to answer. But when Gradi repeated her question, and it became apparent that an answer was required, Mat said, in a low voice: 'I supposed it was because it was too distressing for you to . . .'

'No, that's not it. You really *don't* understand.' From his face to mine. 'Either of you.'

'It's strength,' I said.

'Yes—' in an exasperated teacher's *at last* tone of voice. 'That's it. Stefan, Stefan, *that's* a story would paint me as victim. The leader cannot be victim; people do not believe in and people do not follow the victim. Now, on the contrary, this execution of Bran – this is a different matter. This paints me as strength. Do you see?'

She said: 'It is sometimes said that politics is about will, but it's not; really, I can't imagine how so ludicrous a misapprehension has entered common currency. Strength of will correlates to strength of character, but people have always found it hard *wholeheartedly* to follow the strong character because his or her own personality intrudes too distractingly into the popular fantasy. The ideal politician is somebody upon whom the people can impress their own ideals, and because everybody's ideal is slightly different (for this is the joy of human diversity) the ideal politician must be someone whose surface is specular enough to match a wide variety of fantasy-projections. Politics is about people seeing, about the best show, about the *eye*. That's wat's wrong with weakness, not the ethical, purely the practical consideration. The weak personality, like crumbly half-wet sand, will not take the signet ring impression of the public's gaze. Show strength to the people and they will see themselves strengthened. That's all. But you – must – organise the *show* properly.'

Of course she didn't say any of that. Can you imagine Gradi making a speech like that? I am extrapolating from several conversations, much less obviously aggressive on her part, over several occasions. I am trying to capture not the canny, considered mode of her speaking, but wat was in her mind. That mode of flat assertion, that wasn't really her conversational style at all. Even her public speeches tended to be more balanced, seductive.

One thing she did say, during that conversation in the hovering plane. She smiled, and asked rhetorically: 'After all, who's going to come after me?' she murmured, more to herself than to us. At first I thought she meant, who will pursue me? – perhaps Bran's family, perhaps the Americans. But then I saw that, on the contrary, she meant *who will succeed me?* She did not trust any of her inner circle with the responsibility of political leadership. Perhaps she was right to be untrusting.

This became the subject of everybody's conversation, over the weeks that followed. Some were shocked, said that it corroded their trust in Gradi. 'I've met her,' said a man called Juniper; 'I'd have never thought her capable of something so – violent, violent.'

'She's capable of it,' I said.

'So cold-blooded.' But there were three other people present, on that occasion, and they all immediately disagreed with him.

'Downbelow leaders kill people all the time,' said a woman called Irrawaddy. 'Only they do it hypocritically; they deny they do it; they employ others to do their dirty work. Gradisil's not like that.'

'He was a fuking traitor,' said a man called Smith, speaking with heat and absolute conviction. 'Wat – he should have been allowed to just go? Is that wat you think? Go scot-free?'

'No! No!'

'Gradi's no hypocrite, and she's not a leader to hide behind her subordinates.'

'She's certainly no hypocrite,' agreed Juniper.

'She has the strength,' said Smith, firmly. 'She's got wat it takes.'

fourteen. Slater

It is a cliché that war is much more frequently a waiting than a shooting game. Where do you stand on cliché? Its relationship with reality? I see, I see. The war goes on, and there's little shooting, and there's a great deal of waiting. The year 2099 folds over into the year 2100, with worldwide celebrations downbelow, and even some modest hoo-haa and military-sanctioned yawps aboard American military bases in the Uplands. It seems an auspicious date: no longer tip-toeing in the waters of the third millennium, humanity has now unambiguously taken the plunge.

Once victory has been declared, and the game becomes a waiting one, Slater is granted several furloughs; each for a couple of days at a time, and always *on call*, such that he might be dragged back Up at a moment's notice. The first of these he spends at home, with his wife and children. They invite Philp and his girlfriend to dinner, to stay over (it's quite a flight bak to DC).

Philp is on fine form at the meal, and his girlfriend is (as Marina whispers to Slater, whilst they both loiter five seconds too long in the kitchen disposing of the plates and fetching the blue jug of hot chocolate) '*a peach!*' Her name is Daria, and she is a tall, wand-slender, almost translucently white-skinned young woman whose broad hammerhead skull, with wide eyes, her petal-like broad nose and full lips, are unconventional enough to prevent her looks being merely insipidly pretty. Her eyes move a fraction more slowly than the rest of her body, giving her gaze a dreamy belatedness, as if she is always just catching up with the rest of her corporeality. She speaks with a fairly pronounced Creek accent, very prettily pluking her vowels up short, 'this foo[*uh*]d is ju[*ah*]st delee[*i*]cious!' Philp's pride in his beautiful companion is comically blatant.

'She's a catch, isn't she?' he booms. 'Catch, yeah?'

'Oh, stop,' she says, laughing.

The following day, the four of them go for a walk around Newport.

The sun is warm, despite the season. New Year decorations have been cleared away. The wide streets are relatively empty, except for the ubiquitous shapes of advertising mannequins, those automata standing with weird plastic stillness until such occasion as a pedestrian walks within their ambit, when they start up with their spiel. 'You hardly see those in DC,' says Slater, gesturing towards the nearest. 'A judge threw out a case for criminal damage against these guys who kiked one to pieces, on the grounds that they are intrusive in personal space when they spark up without being specifically asked. So after that the local youth went on a culling spree, knoking arms and legs and heads off.' He laughs at the thought of it.

'I feel sorry for them,' says Daria, tenderly. She is walking arm looped in arm with her beau, like an eighteenth-century couple.

'Sorry for them? They're nought but *things*,' says Philp, dismissive.

'Even so,' says Daria, dreamy (*'e'en so[uh]'*)

'Wat are you two planning?' asks Marina, ingenuously. 'For after the war I mean?' She is angling for *we're getting married*, but Philp, canny, only puts his head on one side. 'War's already over,' he says.

'The victory's been declared,' corrects Slater.

'M'learned comrade is quite correct, war isn't over, though victory has been declared,' pronounces Philp in an hilarious, hypercorrect legal accent. Hilarious insofar that Daria laughs, at any rate.

'Very well,' says Marina, humouring him. 'So wat is it, *precisely*, that marks the end of a war?'

'That's not something can be answered straightforward, like,' says Philp, gambolling around his girlfriend like a wolf about a fawn.

'There are several stages to it,' says Slater, more soberly. 'There's the victory declaration that means that the military campaign is over. There's the enemy's surrender, which means that they've accepted the fact of their loss. Then there's the tying up of legal loose ends – that can go on for years. But that's not our problem. That's for the lawyers to sort out. The surrender is our problem.'

'So how long until the surrender?'

'Won't be long now,' says Slater.

'Gradi has to surrender soon,' agrees Philp. 'She's got a *fish* in her *tank*.'

'And *wat* on earth does that mean?' asks Daria, in a strangely distressed voice, as if this phrase were somehow upsetting to her.

'She got a loaf in her oven,' says Philp. 'She got a chiken in her bucket. She got a frog in her standpipe. She got a acorn in her soil.'

But they have strayed too close to one of the advertising automata, a vividly pink and yellow model with a cartoony smiling face. He stirs into ersatz life and starts speaking: *Not all vatgrown and seacultured foodstuffs are revolting! Talk to me for further information on an exciting new development in food technology and—* the four of them run, giggling, away from this pronouncement.

That evening, sitting together playing TrixPoker with the house AI at midnight, Philp confesses to Slater the nub of the matter, the thing he had shied away from admitting to Marina earlier that day. 'I've fallen for her, man. I love her. After the surrender, when the Army gives us a month, we're getting married.'

'Congratulations, man!'

'Thank you, Lieutenant. I'm pleased you're pleased, I truly am.'

'She's a lovely woman.'

'Isn't she, though? *Isn't* she, though? My daddy would like to meet her. I may even set up that rendezvouz,' (he buzzes that word on both zs) 'I truly might.'

Slater has never heard his friend talk of his parents before. He says nothing, only ponders his cards with unusual attention. And after a pause Philp continues: 'never told you this, Slayer, my da, but he was involved in the albino riots, bak in the sixties – yeah?'

'Oh,' says Slater. Then, because that sounds a bit stark, he adds, 'No kidding?'

'I know. Had that pigmentation pharmakos, everything. He was white as greasepaper. But wat people don't understand about those rioters . . .' He is wagging his forefinger as if about to make a serious point, but the sentence laks a conclusion, and he looks around puzzled by its non-completion. He's been drinking.

Slater prompts him: 'Wat *is* it that people don't understand about those rioters?'

'They weren't racists,' Philp barks. 'Leastways, not *all* of them. It's possible, *is* possible to think . . . you know.'

'I wasn't accusing anybody of racism,' says Slater. Philp gives a *I-know-you-weren't* shake with his head. The walls all around are curtained in shadow. The circle of light on the green baize is like a diving bell on an oceanfloor of obscurity.

'I only mean,' says Philpot, selecting a card and laying it on the table just outside the circle, such that the AI must wheedle in its electronic voice, *I cannot see this card*, and Philp must reposition it inside the circle, 'I only mean that it's possible to think that *really white skin*, to think that just *no* pigmentation in skin, is just beautiful, you know? It's

281

possible to think that without necessarily believing all the racial purity stuff as well. I mean, I got nothing against more richly coloured people. I have dated them, people, er, like that, in the past. I could have married a more richly coloured person. That could have happened. But when I met Daria I just thought . . . I thought, phew, you know?'

'Sure,' says Slater. 'I'm proper happy for you, I really am. Marriage, eh? And then, children?'

'Why not!' says Philp. Then: 'I haven't spoken to my da in eight years, you know, you know.'

'No kidding?'

'He was arrested after the riots. Did you follow the riots?'

'There was stuff on TV.'

Philp nods. 'They didn't report it too good. It wasn't so much about race. It was about the local – the local—' the adjective is firmly in Philp's head, 'about the local—' but he can't seem to bring forth a noun for it to qualify. 'It's Missouri,' he says, finally. 'It was about ways of doing things, about the. Anyway, so Da got arrested after the riots, spent some time in a correctional fluid.'

'A correctional *fluid*?'

'A correctional facility, yes. I had to concentrate on my career, you know? But I may make approaches now. After the surrender – I'll have some good news for him. Da, hiya, remember me, war is over and *I'm* getting a-marriéd.' He laughs. 'Time for bed,' he adds, 'time for bed, time for bed,' getting clumsily to his feet. His physical dyspraxia is provoked by the superfluity of alcoholic compounds in his metabolism: he jars the table with his hip upon rising, and leans left before stepping right. 'Time for bed, time for bed, time for bed.'

It occurs to Slater, as he paints his teeth with PurePaste in the bathroom later, how easily intimacy can grow between men who know, really, nothing at all about one another. He had not known that his best friend was alienated from his father; that his father had been involved in those ugly albino riots (a particular use of pharmakos which had divided the community between religiously-inspired anti- and pro-racist); or that these factors, roots in the dirt of Philp's past, were still determining the choices he made decades later – this almost pharmakos-white bride! This strain towards military glory! Slater moves as stealthily as the whisky inside him permits into the darkened bedroom, where his wife's breathing susurrates in the blakness, and inserts himself between the smartcloth sheets with a fizz.

He cuddles into his wife's back, and she shifts in bed. She is whispering something to herself in her sleep, muttering, and Slater settles, listens, and can just make out thine is the kingdom the power. It annoys him. He pulls his eyes closed and tries to force himself into sleep, but it doesn't work that way. So he lies awake, crossly, and thinks about the Pastor, about the malign ecstasy of revealed religion that lies, black-hole-like, just to the left, just sinister to the path through life his innocent, passive wife must follow.

But the next day the warriors must return to active duty. Philp goes where his orders instruct him. Slater flies to DC.

Slater is briefed on developments in the war (and there have been *none*) and reviews the blokade. He has half a dozen meetings with lawyers in a spacious office, but he finds it hard to keep his attention on the matters in hand. His eye is drawn, pulled by the optic magnetism of beauty, to the view through the floor-to-wall window opposite him. Across an empty drill square, a hectare of pink sand, to a broad bar, perfectly rectangular, of bright green foliage – a row of tightly-intergrowing giant bushes. As clouds slide in front of the sun, and then pass on, the intensity of light builds and fades regularly, swelling the green with gorgeous brilliance and sinking it to more shadowy dun, for all the world as if somebody is tinkering with the brightness/contrast button on a screen.

The following day he meets the Veep again. 'I want that surrender,' booms Johannes Belvedere III. 'You promised me that surrender!' 'Yes sir,' he squawks. 'Don't "yes sir" me, Lieutenant,' says the Veep. 'Just get me the surrender.'

Yes sir, yes sir, yes sir, he can only think of yes sir. 'I'm on it,' he says instead, and instantly thinks *that sounds pretty feeble.*

He flies Upland again, in the same EleMag plane as the lizard-like Hagen. There's no escaping Hagen on this trip; he has been ordered to accompany him.

The spinning platform is ready now; an enormous construction of plastic and metal, painted red and white, with the hub blue-white-starred; all the paints lumine. It is visible from all the way down on the ground as a pale pink star, a new star that moves hurriedly through the sky at dusk and dawn. Niflheim has warned him of the perils of wanting to micromanage a war, but at the same time there are two potential niggles it would be best to address right away. In one of the searches of an Upland house a Marine had discovered a windowbox, or transparent porch, or some annexe (the report is not very clear) filled with growing things. In accordance with the statutes of war, and in consonance with suits 3990 and 3991 filed with the Washington International Belligerent

Court in pursuance of the legitimate American military and post-victory targets, the Marine had destroyed these growing things. The householder had reacted very poorly to this, and had threatened the Marine with a weapon. There had been, it seemed, a great deal of shouting and threatening, but (and this is one of the problems Slater must address) the corporal – the only one of the party with helmet camera – had been called bak to his ship to answer a call. The Marine, feeling threatened, had shot the Uplander once in the chest. This was within the parameters, and perfectly legally defensible, of course (provided the Marine was being genuinely threatened); except that the projectile had passed through the Uplander's chest and happened to strike a porthole. The projectile was wireware, sanctioned for firefights inside pressurised vacuum habitations, but it so happened the porthole was weakened, or substandard, or something along those lines, for it blew out. In the resulting depressurisation storm the contents of the house had been mightily disarranged. The Marines, trained in depressurisation protocols, had loked the leak down in minutes; but afterwards they discovered that the pistol with which the Uplander had threatened the marine must have blown into space with sundry other items. This was an unfortunate development.

Now, so far no legal countersuit had been filed. The Uplander had been alone in the house, and it was not clear who his next-of-kin even were, let alone where they might be. The contents of the house were being examined now. It wasn't clear wat was going to happen next. One possible outcome was that no next-of-kin was identifiable, which would mean that the possibility of countersuit would recede considerably. If a next-of-kin did emerge it was also possible that they would not lodge a suit, particularly if they hoped to inherit from the deceased and wanted the money sooner rather than later (for all inheritance monies would of course be held over until the settlement of any such suit). But on the off chance that suit was filed it was important that Slater could show that the US had followed all appropriate avenues, and one of those was that the testimony of the Marine in question be thoroughly determined, with multiple separate interviews. Slater has come up to conduct one such interview.

It is his first time aboard the completed station. And wat a strange experience it is to stride down the sharply curving corridor, his boots actually clanging on the grille-flooring underfoot. Walk this corridor in one direction and get heavier; walk bak the way you came and get lighter. Pe-cu-lee-ar. There is an unmistakeable tug and churn in his gut as he walks, and through the portholes equally spaced along the U-bend corridor the distracting sight of Earth falling and turning bothers the corner of his eye. But it is also a pleasantly rooted experience, walking like a hamster in a gargantuan wheel, always at the bottom, with the pull downwards so similar to earthly gravity as to be indistinguishable.

Here is Hagen, lizard-like, puffed up with his superb pride. 'Lieutenant,' he says. 'It looks good, don't it? Turn your head – go on. Tell you wat: spin right about, do a twirl.'

Ponderously Slater does so.

'Feel sik?' asks Hagen, leaning in towards him.

'Not much,' Slater admits.

'See! It's all a question of diameter! If I had the chance I'd build a wheel kilometres across and spin it real slow, it'd be just like walking on the ground!'

The war goes on, but it's a waiting rather than a shooting game. Their mole, their inside-guy, has stopped reporting to them, Maybe he's just gone deeper undercover, maybe he's shifted his allegiance, maybe he's dead. Slater finds it hard to care, except that – if he doesn't get back to them soon – he may have to write that operation off, which can only postpone the capture of Gradi.

fifteen. Paul

Boredom prolonged is exhausting in a way nothing else quite is. The occasional moments when the war was actively stressful could not leaven the lump of its overwhelming tedium. That which does not kill us makes us weaker; but because the sub-brain does not believe it can ever die, we can mistake the fact that we have not yet been killed with the belief we *cannot* be killed; we can confuse this weakness with a new sort of strength.

I reacted to confinement poorly. I could not get out – that line from the *Lord of the Rings*, the one that always most thrummed my heart with dread, *we cannot get out we cannot get out.* It speaks to a claustrophobia that transcends space (for we could always leave whichever Upland house we happened to be in and fly to another); the active claustrophobia of the human being unable to escape the prison house of his breathing, the bars of his own ribs, the shakles that strap the heart into its one restless position. The odiousness of the circumstance was made much more acute by the continuity of fear. Through portholes we sometimes saw Quanjet planes slipping through the dark, like oysters down a gullet, minnow-sized far below us, darting and surging forward, death in the shape of a spacecraft.

They are at the gate.

We did not spend our time stuk in any one single house. We flew up, being miserly with our jets and trying to get as much manoeuvrability from EleMag alone. We hovered, kites or kestrel. Then we rolled down the gravity hill again and slotted ourselves into some new house's porch. The plan was laughably simpleminded. The Americans worked methodically through the Uplands, knoking on doors and pulling themselves inside house after house; they came inside always grim-faced, always in threes or fours, always with guns primed and pointed. They logged the house's transp, looked through all the rooms, all the storage space, and left only when satisfied that Gradi was not lurking Anne-Frank like, in some architectural interstice. They never doubled bak and undertook a surprise immediate re-search: had they done so, they would have captured Gradisil early on in their campaign. But they never did. Gradi's absolute assurance that *they never would* amazed and rather disconcerted me – I couldn't share it, I was nervy and anxious, certain that my capture (and who knows? my torture – my execution) at the hands of the Americans was only hours away. Had I been in charge of the American operation that would have been the first thing I would have done. But, Gradi said, this was not how the military mind worked; and events proved her right.

So, soon after the military had been through, a householder would call us with their transp number. This information was passed to us in code, but our codes were laughable simple – so simple as to be overlooked by the five-AI trillion-bit-a-second network of prime-number-based codecrakers owned by our enemy. Gimcrak things like – numbers which were page references to a previously agreed book, in which the first sentence would be read for the number of vowels (or consonants, depending on whether the day had a 't' in it). Schemes like this generated transp locations.

We flew up, we waited and then we picked out target below us, and lodged for a week or more in another house. This was how we spent the siege.

There were other ways in which our warmaking blundered like a bumble-bee through super-rapid American detection webs designed to capture atomic-finesses. No American discussion of military strategy took place inside a room with only one wall between the interlocutors and vacuum – because a properly aimed laser device could read the vibrations of the fabric of the house and convert it into a remote account of the conversation. Nor did American soldiers discuss sensitive matters online or over the phone, for fear of the messages being intercepted and decoded (as if we possessed the capacity to do either thing!). So they gathered their personnel into physical proximity, within shielded double-walled cells deep inside their forts, with interference patterns drumboxing into the fabric of the building to be on the safe side. It didn't matter. Gradi knew wat their strategy was going to be anyway. It was always going to be the only strategy it could be: to continue the blockade and starve the Uplands into a suitably abject surrender; to continue the house-to-house searches; to seize the monies of all combatant Uplanders – and that was all of us – and freeze it, pending proper legal settlement of reparations and tax contributions, which would in turn follow a proper surrender. That's wat they did.

We, on the other hand, were cavalier, a reklessness dictated by necessity, and in which we continued driven, most of us, by a sense that, since we were only postponing the inevitability of our final defeat, only drawing out the process to squeeze out a few consolation dribbles of America humiliation, it accordingly didn't matter a whole lot, even if we were captured. Sometimes Gradi, Mat, Grinning Georgina, Haskell Bacevich and Desai would sit in a room talking for hours, the mouldy wall resounding with our secrets for all the solar system to hear, if only the Americans had known which house to monitor. We phoned one another all the time, on easily accessed channels, to talk about how long it would be before the surrender: one month more, maybe. Maybe two. There were caches: clusters of sea-bred cattle floating freeze-dried in open space, decontaminated by the ambient radiation, roped together with a single tether to which a transp was tied. The provision of these awkward-looking meat-satellites, blak-eyeballed, scuffy-skinned giant slugs of meat, had been one of the few examples of Upland advance planning. From time to time the Americans chanced upon one of these dumps, and confiscated it; from time to time a desperate Uplander obtained the transp and seized the whole lot, trying to hoard it to trade meat for other necessities – water, technology, sex. But the first three people to try that found that it was Upland Irregulars rather than potential traders who answered their obliquely phrased announcements. They disappeared; scoured to oxidised powder, their atoms tipped like cupwater in the sea, to mingle with the winds of the upper atmosphere.

'The caches,' said Gradi, at several meetings, so that her words might pass as gossip amongst the whole community 'belong to all the Uplands; not to any individual uplander. We take from them as we need, and only in emergency.'

She was forcing a collectivity upon this immiscible congregation of selfish billionaires and loners. She could do this only because of the extreme circumstances in which we all found ourselves. From time to time I even wondered if this had been her true motive for driving us so implacably into a war we could never win, precisely in order to generate a climate of such harshness, precisely in order to remove the billionaires from their money, so that she could press them all into something resembling collective citizenship.

'How long, Gradi?' I asked her.

'When the time is right,' she said. But she meant *when I will it.*

'You're pregnant, Gradi,' I pointed out, often. 'You're pushing this whole thing dangerously close to the limit, you know. Shouldn't you make overtures to the Americans now? You'll need to think about transferring down to a groundling hospital pretty soon – there are specialist facilities in Germany that deal with pregnancies that began in zero g. But you'll need to make your peace with the Americans soon. You'll need to surrender.'

She never gave me a straight answer.

Living, this day followed by that day, was appallingly monotonous. We rose in our planes and hovered, kestrels of patience before swooping to our destination. This time it was a poky little three-room house, already crowded with half-a-dozen people: two couples, two single people, all sleeping at irregular hours in bags pinned to the walls like bizarre artworks, or (the material tending to be printed with bright colours) shapeless butterflies. The pressure of so many people in so small a space told in repulsively immediate ways. Unable to afford more sophisticated treatments for the air, the house trailed a ten kilometre line into the upper atmosphere, and circulated the air; but with nine people (for Gradi and Georgina and I joined them) there was too much CO_2 being breathed out to be compensated for by this slender pulse, so old-fashioned scrubbers had to be switched on: noisy, grinding machines that seemed to scrape tortuously through my brain.

A dozen varieties of mould grew on the walls of this house, fed by the moist funk of combined breaths and warmed by our body heat: blak velvety trim mosses, or patches of spekly discolouration that, on closer examination, revealed myriad dark green trefoil particles, or little pads of hairy growth. Spores went everywhere; everybody suffered, even Gradi – rheumy eyes, headaches, bloked noses, sneezes. Phlegm, ejected as the sneezer was pushed bakwards by Newtonian equalisation, stuk to the wall and could not always be located in the mess to be cleaned up afterwards. Crumbs, threads, scraps of paper and plastic, all floated through the air; all eventually made their way to the walls, into bends and crevices. To touch the walls (as a person sometimes needed to do) was to press fingers into a slimy gritty layer, and to come away oilily dirtied.

We played chess, or talked, or watched the screen – mostly, in fact, we watched the screen, because the conversation very quikly exhausted itself, and the chess pieces, greasy with much use, tended to come unstuk from their magnetic squares and float away and get themselves lost in corners and behind objects. The screen was always tuned to EU news stations. From time to time an American ship would pass, broadcasting a disruptive signal and the screen would tingle into a haze of white-grey particles, the voice of the newsreader distorting to whistles, or groans. But these were only intermittent interruptions; the US was haphazard about disrupting our phone and screen communications.

The war occupied the bulk of the news for a week. After the American declaration of victory, the news became bored with us, and other stories pushed to the front: EU diplomatic outrage at the treatment of the Uplands, and particularly the seizure of so much EU citizens' money (the proportion of Upland citizenry was five to one EU/US). But, soon, the approaching new century, with its myriad excited celebrations, was the topic: and after that EU elections approached; and then the Euro Football championship build-up. From time to time the news would revert to us: and any depressed buzz of conversation there happened to be in whichever room we were in would cease. Uplanders who had happened to be trapped downbelow when the war began were frequently interviewed. Klara, my mother-in-law, became a frequent figure: with her wild hair and her restless eyes she was exentric enough, and not yet sixty she was still physically attractive enough, to make good television. There were deeper lines in her brow, and she had recently acquired a mole on her chin, like an old crone – a raised circle of pale pink with a plastiky look about it, one more piece of evidence of her animadversion to the benefits of pharmakos. But these badges of age in fact, and perhaps counterintuitively, only made her appear more real, more human and therefore attractive. She spoke only to the one theme: the great crime committed by the Americans against her family – against her, and therefore against Gradi, and therefore (it being universally assumed by now that Gradi symbolically embodied her people) against the whole of the Uplands. Klara dilated upon this crazy theory with such passion and detail, to any interviewer prepared to put a camera in front of her face, that it became something of a fixture. The Americans even issued a formal denial; they refuted the damaging accusations made by and so on and so forth.

By late January there was, officially, no more war and we figured very rarely in the news. 'The real war-zone,' Gradi said, on more than one occasion, 'isn't up here: it's in the courtroom'. But even the various legal news channels rarely mentioned us; since the lodging of the US victory announcement there had been very little legal action. Some groundstuk Uplanders, whose money had been frozen by the Americans, had lodged suit to try and free up their money; but this was a fairly half-hearted strategy. A few exentric individuals had weighed in with personal suits, pro-Up or pro-US, adding to the detritus that washes up and down on the wide surf-beach of the Law. But the courts were waiting for the real business – for Gradi's official surrender, which would unlok the flood-gates.

The people with whom we stayed often pressed Gradi on precisely this point, 'I'm not used to the hunger, the actual physical hunger, Gradi,' said Ustinov, when we stopped for five days in his spacious house. And it was true, his skin was draped loosely about his large bones now, like pale leathery robes. 'You see I've never experienced it before, in my life, and it's much harder than I thought. I've lived that whole life as a wealthy man, and never known hunger. I'm too old to turn ascetic now, Gradi – when will you announce your surrender? Make it soon, draw a line under this suffering, and let me get my people to fly me up some chiken, some salted trout, caviar, real red cabbage in vinegar—'

'Stop!' I squealed like a whiny child. 'You're making my mouth water.' And it was; drool was seeping out through my lips and glazing my chin.

'It won't be long now, my friend,' said Gradi. 'Soon. I'm just waiting to – to *time* it *right.*' She looked corpse-like, her body upsettingly distorted – the shoking plumpness of her waterballoon belly and the extreme thinness of her arms, her legs, the suked-in cheeks. She was continually nauseous and often sik. She barely slept. There were violet leaf-shaped patches under her eyes all the time. But she still manages to conjure energy and charisma, as if from a limitless store, whenever we hauled ourselves through the door of a new house, a new place to stay for five days, or three weeks, or a single night. 'Hello, hello! It's excellent to see you again, John' (or) 'Nan-Shan' (or) 'Deborah' (or) 'Mohammed' (or) 'Jukes' (or) 'Gallano, my old friend' (or) 'Parky', or whosoever it might be. The brightness of the eyes, the carefully focused interest, the sense she always managed to generate of doing, of futurity, possibility, change, excitement – all those things. As she got iller and thinner it became more of an effort for her to do this; but she still made that effort.

Everybody had had the Americans through, in their lumine red-and-white suits, with their guns out and primed. Some Uplanders showed, with shy pride, bruises on their cheekbones or foreheads, where they had objected noisily to this intrusion and floated too close to the troops and been batted bak with a telescopic baton, jak-and-boxing out suddenly to wak them with its plastic tip. It was poor resistance, but it was better than acceptance.

We stayed for four days at the Islamic retreat *daru'l-ridzwan*: twelve serious men of various ages in white clothes gone grubby with unchanging wear. Their hostility to the Americans had overcome their distaste for the billionaire's play-republic with its immodest female president. Gradi wrapped her head in a shawl and acted a part of perfect restraint. 'They came in here,' said the Imam, an elderly man with a trailing beard called Avram, 'without courtesy or respect. They rummaged through everything and disarranged the pages of the holy Qur'an. They knoked many of us with their punching stiks, and aimed their guns.'

'They are,' said Gradi, 'scared.'

This was the first time I had heard her say such a thing. It startled me, but the Imam nodded sagely. 'They are looking for you,' he said, inclining his head towards the unself-declared President. 'The longer they go without finding you, the more scared they become.'

When we left the *daru'l-ridzwan*, the Imam gave us a scroll on which was written, in willowy Arabic script, the first line of the declaration of American independence.

يولد جميع الناس أحرارًا متساوين في الكرامة والحقوق. وقد وهبوا
عقلاً وضميرًا وعليهم ان يعامل بعضهم بعضا بروح الإخاء.

It is very hard to know how to describe the smell of this war. Smells grow old so much more quikly than do the people who create them. A stiff, cabbagy-rotten stench that never left, that seemed to lodge insinuatingly inside the nose itself. The tart, metallic smell of the fabric of the house; the purply-green stink of old sweat, unwashed flesh, the softly gagging smell of food rotting. Not that many people allowed food to go off, since we lived in various degrees of starvation.

More acute than the shortages of food and water, than the itchy sensation of clothes worn without change or wash for weeks at time, than the oppressive sameness of all the different houses, loaded with weary hostages to Gradi's will, imprisoned as was I in her sheer stubbornness of mind – worse than any of this was not being able to talk with my sons. Gradi's reasoning was that the Americans had certainly loaded the screens and phones in Helsinki and France with their most sophisticated locating devices; and that as soon as Hope or Sol answered my call two Quanjets and a dozen Marines would storm whichever house we were placing the call from. I knew she was right, but this didn't stop me growing increasingly furious with her for depriving me of my boys. Oh, they were neither of them *mine*; but this fact had ceased to gnaw at me. Hope peered at me with Mat's eyes; and every guest or passer-by who complimented me on how *like me* my son was touched nothing but a gentle melancholy inside me. People were less likely to compliment me on perceived similarities between myself and Sol, for he was a singular-looking little boy who bore surprisingly little resemblance either to me or even to Gradi; as he grew older he acquired a purer Eastern look, short dark hair, brooding little face, canny little eyes. But they were still my boys. I had hugged them when they hurt themselves or were sik; I had changed their nappies – or, at least, I had been present when servants had changed their nappies. I had taken them out for ice cream, or walked in parkland with them whilst they whizzed past on their powerbikes. I had sat with Sol in the ambulance all the way to hospital, where doctors had fixed his broken leg. When we look at a tree we give no thought to the provenance of the conker from which it grew; we care only for the way the trunk has risen straight as a solid geyser, the way the foliage spreads itself to accept the photonic gift of the sunlight. The way I saw it, if these boys were not strictly mine at birth, then I had made them mine during the process of raising them.

I achieved a degree of peace; but Gradi's third pregnancy unsettled me again. Because, after betraying me (as if she could help it!) with Mat to conceive Hope, and with Liu to conceive Sol, she had enacted a more complex betrayal for her third child and ensured, with her tenacity, that it was fathered by me. The conception happened during that period of three months of intense travel and activity, as she went from house to house in her land readying her people for the coming storm. She insisted I come. She insisted we sleep together. She even managed a perfect imitation of insecurity, luring me in to physical reassurance. As the wind blew sparks out of the wings like electric bubbles and the sky outside grew darker she leant in to me and said, 'We make love so rarely these days.'

I blushed. I had not expected this. 'I'm sorry,' I blurted.

'No, my love,' she said, putting her arm round my nek. 'I'm not rebuking you, I know that kind of thing can be difficult after so many years of marriage.'

'It was difficult on our wedding night,' I said, more severely than I intended, 'if you remember.'

'But it's been better since.' This sounded feeble to her, so she added, 'Much better, really', which qualification (of course) made it worse.

'Off and on,' I said, to try and agree. My blush had sunk inward, and I was feeling that chafing sensation in the chest that signifies swallowed anger. Why was this making me angry? Perhaps I had grown so used to disappointment that I was disinclined to surrender it? At least a person knows where they are and wat to expect with disappointment.

'I want to try harder,' she told me, facing me directly, 'There's a new pharmakos, a married-love concoction, that—'

'I've *already* had a pharmakos for my sexual drive,' I blurted out. This sentence came out much louder than I had intended and my blush roasted again on my face.

Gradi looked actually shoked. I had never before, in all our years together, admitted this fact to her before: this fact from my life before her.

'You have?'

'It was years ago,' I said, hurriedly. 'It was before you. Only, these sorts of pharmakos, they root in the brain pathways, don't they? I don't know if it's possible to combine two of them. I mean, not into the same physical system – like the sex system. They might throw off unforeseen—' I stopped speaking.

Gradi was looking intently at me. There was a nakedness in her eyes that I had not seen for many years; and perhaps I had never seen it before. Behind the calculation and political charisma and judgment as to how to play people, there was this almost child-like innocency of astonishment.

'You never told me!'

'It never came up,' I gruffed. But then, immediately, I corrected myself; the nakedness of her gaze was warming me a little; I blushed. 'No that's not it, of course,' I said. 'I'm ashamed of it. That's it. You always seem to inhabit yourself so powerfully, with such effortless command. It makes me feel inferior. I mean, I mean,' I added, speaking more rapidly, 'in a bad way – of course, I feel inferior to you in lots of ways that are right, proper, you're Artemis and I'm happy to be your acolyte, you're Gradi, I'm just an Uplander. But there's a place inside a man that reacts very badly to being diminished. I have no doubt it's a ridiculous caveman thing. But—'

At this point she kissed me, tenderly on the lips, and leant away again. Tears threatened at the bak of my eyes. In that moment all my buried and impacted resentment just melted away; as if this was the single moment for which I had been waiting. Sleeping beauty woken by a kiss. 'I love you!' I cried. 'I love you!'

'And I love you too, Paul,' she replied. I think that was the only time, in all our married life, that she said the phrase that way, just straight out as a flat statement without qualifier. It filled my heart.

'We will,' I swore. 'We'll make love more often! Let's make a child together – let's make a baby.' I had never known her so open to me, so guileless and unprotected. My prik was stiffening then and there in the plane.

'Another one,' she said. 'Very well. But, Paul, wat *was* your pharma-kos?'

'Wat?' I asked, stupidly, distracted by my increasing seizure of desire.

'You said you had a pharmakos treatment for your sex drive – tell me about it. When was it? Wat was it for?'

'It was when I was a teenager,' I gabbled, eager to exploit this sudden intimacy. 'Years and years ago. I'm sorry I never told you about it. I should have told you about it.'

'But *wat* was it?'

'It made me hetero.'

'Really?'

'The doctor was rather surprised, actually,' I said, trying to remember interesting details I could tell her about wat was, actually, the dullest of medical interventions. 'He asked me twice to confirm that this was wat I wanted. He said that most people came to him for the opposite – straight men who wanted to be gay men, and took the pharmakos to lodge their minds that way. Men who were having too little success with women, and who believed they were going to increase their chances of getting sex. That sort of thing'

'I'm sure it would. Would increase their chances, I mean.'

'Or, if not that exactly,' I went on, driven by the strange new dynamic that had blossomed between us, to be as precise and truthful as possible, 'then at least to simplify their sexuality. Male homosexuality is really preferable to male heterosexuality in many ways. It's a less conflicted, more straightforwardly *male* sort of sexuality. Prik, prik, you know? Anyway, the doctor told me he had a dozen men wanting to be oriented homo for every one who wanted to opposite. But I wanted the opposite.'

'Why?'

'Oh—' and I grimaced. The pressure to continue this rigorously truthful communication was starting to bow down my words. How to explain it? 'It was complicated. I think I wanted to escape myself a little bit.' I tried to remember. 'I think that's wat I wanted.'

She kissed me again.

That night, in our own house in the hurtling Uplands, we made love – this was the first time for several months. We shared a sleeping bag, and clutched one another like swimmers, and went through the slightly unsatisfactory buking and wriggling of zero-g sex. We shared the same sleeping bag every night for two weeks. This was when our third child was conceived, and he (the early scan revealed he was *he*) was mine, he was my blood and genes.

*

That was many months before, in the late autumn of 2099. Now it was February in the year 2100, and still Gradi had not relaxed her will. She was holding out for something, although she would not tell us wat. Why should she bother telling us? It was all happening in her mind, a spindle strung on the spar of her will, that was all. Increasingly, people, exhausted and starved and unhappy, pressed her. 'When's the surrender coming, Madame President?' asked Aziz, in his fantastically messy and ramshakle house.

Gradi simply hung there, immovable as a planet; and as her legs and arms grew thinner and her face seemed to shrink, it was the absolute pulchritude of her swelling belly that was increasingly coming to define her physical presence.

Mat was there too. Even he, the most loyal of Gradi's immediate staff, had begun, grumpily, to press her to name the date by which the collective misery would be over – which is to say, to challenge her. He had taken to reading the Qur'an over and over: an English-language translation, not the original. Whenever asked he still insisted he was an atheist; but his repetitive reading was puzzling. I remember one time in particular, for reasons that will become apparent in a minute. There were six of us in Aziz's house: Gradi, Mat, Aziz, myself, and two women called Casta and Jocelyn. We had shared a meagre meal of pasta between us. Mat had sulkily floated over to the seam of wall and ceiling, where he piked crumbs and fragments and examined each of them in turn to see whether they were edible or not.

Casta, a short woman shrink-reduced by hunger to an infant's frame, was talking to Gradi. She had Upland-pale skin, I remember, and large denim-coloured eyes, very striking eyes, variegated blue-grey rings that looked worn and tired in her round pale face. Her bone-blonde hair had grown out from its practical close crop over the six months of the siege into an unwieldy dandelion frizz. She spoke nervously, chatterly: 'Everybody is talking about the surrender. When the Americans came through here last week, that's all they were asking. They kept saying "wat's she holding out for? Wat's she hoping to gain by holding out?" I couldn't answer them.'

'Yes,' called Mat, from the ceiling. 'Wat *are* you holding out for, Gradi?'

'Madame President,' said Casta, trying to reframe Mat's question in a more respectful manner. 'Wat I mean to ask is—'

'Your *people*,' said Mat, speaking over her, and pushing himself away from the wall with one leg to float down towards us, 'are curious as to why you're delaying? Your *people* want to know wat your plan is. In fact,

Gradi, your *people* need to know that you *have* a fuking plan – that you're not just making this up as you go along.'

Gradi fixed placid eyes on Mat and his miniature rebellion.

'We were just in Ustinov's house,' Mat announced to the whole room. 'Gradi and I.' I'd been there too, but Mat didn't mention that. 'Ustinov and Gradi here spent three hours cloistered together, talking about . . . wat were you talking about, Gradi? You and he? Could you tell him wat you're doing, wat you are *playing* at? Him and not us? Did you talk to him because he was clever enough not to put any of his money in dear-departed Bran's Upland Bank, so he can still command funds? Is that why you treat us so cavalier, and keep him so close to your planning?'

'Mat,' said Gradi, in a quietly commanding voice, 'be quiet.'

Mat glared at her, but stopped speaking, and shortly he returned to the ceiling to hunt for crumbs.

There was a very awkward silence. Gradi, sighed and, cradling her floating planet-belly with both hands, she started speaking:

'Wat you all must try harder to understand,' she said, in a brittle voice, 'is that wars are won in the lawcourt. That's one place where we can salvage something from this wrek. The US have all the advantages, but they have miscalculated in one respect. They prepared, legally I mean, for war, for victory and for my surrender. By not giving them this last thing we compel them to maintain their blokade. That means that, legally speaking, we are under siege. Do you understand the significance of *that*?'

Everybody was looking at her.

'There hasn't been a siege since the twentieth century. And sieges haven't been a regular part of warfare since the middle ages. Downbelow air power and heavy ordnance make it impossible to withstand military assault; walls get knoked down, citadels get occupied. The last siege was Berlin in the 1960s. Or perhaps Stalingrad in the 1940s. There's not even legal consensus on *that* point, on which was the last siege, never mind on the proper legal protocols for siege warfare as such. Which means that, we have something for which the Americans have not been prepared. Nobody knows how the Belligerent Court will play this. *All we have to do*,' she said these last words with a kind of desperate emphasis, 'is to hold out long enough to establish that *we have been besieged*. Then we have humanitarian grounds, shaky legal precedent, room for manoeuvre.' She was lying, of course; but I didn't realise that 'til later. 'Enough,' she snapped, as if overwhelmed by our idiocy and dislocalty, 'I'm going to sleep.'

Later, with everybody asleep, Gradi and I zipped ourselves into a wall-bag in the bak-room by ourselves. She seemed distracted, so I hugged myself against her bak. 'People are only anxious that this period of suffering be over,' I whispered, like a supplicant. 'That's why Mat blew up in there.'

'He lost it,' she replied in a distant tone. 'I expected more of him. I won't forget this – that he lost it. At the crucial time.'

Unsure why I was defending Mat, I said: 'it was only in front of you and me, and a couple of other people. We're all loyal, it won't go any further.'

'That's hardly the point.'

We were silent for a while.

Then, tentatively, I said: 'We should talk, though, Gradi. We must, surely, be – you know where.'

'Be? Where?'

'We must *be* at the outside limit of this time period. I understand wat you said earlier, about the legal case and everything. About being under siege. But even so.'

Gradi laughed humourlessly. 'That stuff about the siege – that's not it.' Her voice was grim. 'That's nothing. The US have a hundred senior officers in their Corps Legal who'll tear that case to pieces in seconds.'

'Yes? So wat did you . . . ?'

'They'll say we're occupied, not besieged, and evidence the fact that American soldiers can pass easily from house to house. It won't last three days in court.'

'But if that's not the thing . . .'

'Georgie thinks we can go somewhere with it, but I think she's being optimistic.'

'Georgie?'

'She's my military second-in-command.'

'She *is*? I didn't know.'

'Lots of things you don't know, my love.'

Her condescension of tone piqued me. 'Look,' I said. 'There's no need to be like that. Nobody has been more loyal than me. I've laid my entire life at your disposal – all my money, my time, my,' I couldn't think of the word, so I said, 'obedience. I didn't know we still *had* a military command of any kind. There doesn't seem much point in having one. You didn't tell me?'

'Top secret stuff, Paul.' She sounded sleepy. 'Bran showed how easily the Americans could get inside us.'

'Alright,' I said, my tom-tit masculinity asserting itself. 'This is enough, right here. We've reached the final line. In fact, we crossed it a month ago – three months ago. Christ, Gradi, you're pregnant! With *my son*. You've had four months, more, of zero-g pregnancy. It's a miracle you haven't lost the baby already. I daresay he'll be born with some pretty problematic malformations. So, so, it stops, now. Why are you holding out? Wat are you waiting for? Is it just a kind of leader's stubbornness, a refusal to admit that you're beaten. We've all been beaten. Call the Americans, say wat they want to hear, then let's get you to a downbelow hospital for the remainder of your pregnancy, and once Joshua is born—'

'Oh, Jesus,' she interrupted, with a harsh sort of laugh. 'You *named* it?'

'We *talked* about this. I told you I liked Joshua. Joshua is a good name.'

'Oh, Jesus,' she said again.

'It's gone far enough. You can't stay up here indefinitely. We've been luky so far, but you could miscarry – no, strike that, you *will* miscarry if you spend many more weeks in this starvation zero-g environment. We're stopping this now.'

'We haven't been luky,' she said.

'He's my child as well as yours. I get an equal say in wat happens.'

'You say we've been luky so far, but we haven't been luky,' she repeated. This paused me for a moment. I tried a different approach, wheedling a little. 'You've achieved amazing things,' I said. 'You've held this nation together through nearly half a year of extraordinary times. You've stood up to the world's superpower pretty much single-handed. But—'

'It's dead,' she said.

I heard these words, and understood them, but for some reason the understanding did not mesh into the gears of my brain. It was still rattling along with its pointless chatter. 'Once you surrender,' I said, 'all that will mean is the process of negotiation will begin, all the legal stuff. And that'll take years.'

'Felt it stop moving, stop kiking and so on, days ago. I can feel it's motionless, not alive, I can feel it inside me, motionless and dead. Thirty, forty hours ago, maybe, it happened.'

There was a strip of cloth pinned over the porthole as a makeshift curtain. The rectangular border of this shape glowed with the inevitable, frequent dawnings of Uplands, the regular forty-minute gush of light escaping over the lip of the world. Crap caught all around the porthole glowed and threw off elongated shadows. The net of the cloth caught a draught of light in its close web and glowed.

'Are you sure,' I said, in a low voice. My chest was a creakily empty birdcage, not a boombox. I could barely swallow.

'I've been getting these—' and she shuffled in the sleeping bag as if itchy, 'cramps and, little tikly cramps. I think my body's about to expel it.'

'It,' I repeated, in an accusing tone

'I'm sorry you pegged it as *Joshua* in your mind, Paul,' she said, in a level, chilly voice. 'If I'd known you were thinking like that I would have discouraged you. That's liable to make things harder than they would otherwise be. It's – unfortunate.'

'He's dead?' I said, stupidly.

'It's the Americans,' she said, but without heat. 'It's another casualty of,' but she broke off.

A hope fluttered feathery inside me. 'You can't be sure. It could just be sleeping. You don't know he's actually – dead, dead. We need a doctor. That guy MacWhirr, that Scottish guy, he was a doctor. Let's pik out his transp and go over to his house, get him to look at you.'

'It's inside me,' said Gradi, as if that said everything. Then she said, 'I'm tired, I'm sleeping.'

I still didn't believe it even when, with exhaustion challenging will-power, Gradi went into labour. Except that I did, really. I denied it to myself. Casta and Jocelyn attended her, in the bak room; and although the rest of us were forbidden from watching, I kept opening the door and looking inside. I looked for a few moments, and then withdrew in disgust, until agonised curiosity overwhelmed me again and I looked once more. Casta tried to catch as much of the mess with a pair of sheets, but zero g is a triksy medium and the walls were sloshed with blood and matter. Though dead, Joshua was a large size to push out; and though Gradi had had two children already her birth canal was unyielding and her muscles were sluggish. In the tiny house every howl and grunt was audible. Every single terrible yawp. Several times she screamed, and the scream wobbled as if modulated by a wah-wah pedal.

Mat turned up the volume on the screen. France-EU was playing Italia-EU in the semi finals of the EU Cup. With unpleasant irony, the swelling cheers of the football crowds seemed to grow after one or other piercing shriek of pain from my wife, as if moking her suffering.

It occurred to me, stunned and miserable as I was, that Gradi might die too. To die in labour seemed egregiously medieval: like the siege warfare that Georgie (*Grinning Georgie was her military second-in-command? When had that happened? Why not Mat? Why not me? Shouldn't we at least have been asked?*) was planning to use as legal leverage when the courtrooms finally opened up to the cases. Wat if she died? Who would succeed? There was no succession. She had nominated no *dauphin.*

Then it was finally over, and pale Casta opened the door and flew past with a bloody bundle of sheets in her arms, stuffing the refuse straight into the porch and shutting the door. I watched from a side window as the convoluted sheet, more blak than red in the vacuum outside, partially unfolded, like stiff paper, as it floated away rotating slowly.

Gradi was asleep, but exhausted. She had lost a great deal of blood, and the house's precious supply of water was at her disposal. She drank, she slept, she drank. I still didn't believe it.

After two days Gradi insisted on moving to a new house. One advantage of zero g is that it makes it very easy to move invalids: we slid her through the air, through the door of Aziz's house, into our plane and up into a high, slow orbit. She dozed, starting in her sleep with little clonic jerks. We waited.

I sat up front, staring through the down-angled windshield at the whole world, all of it. From time to time a miniature shape moved with unnatural rapidity across the arc of the world, sweeping its path clear of absconding Uplander jets. It can only have been a Quanjet.

Gradi muttered something in her sleep.

Mat had come to sit next to me. I looked at him, an unashamed long look. I had known him for many years, had worked with him intimately in the creation of a new country, and had never had a prolonged conversation with him. Who was he? But if it came to that, who were any of them? They were like those advertising automata that litter the streets of American and EU cities, chattering phrases they don't understand at anybody who approaches close enough.

He sat there now, looking drawn and thin, his sharp Malay features sharpened by that graphics programme that hunger runs called *whittle.* His hair, unwashed, was starting to clot together into dreadloks. 'I feel terrible,' he told me without preliminary. 'I know it was a function of the zero g, her losing the baby I mean, but I feel almost responsible. I mean I feel terrible that I – well, you know.'

'Wat?' I asked, quite unable to see wat he meant.

'The day before I'd lost it, I'd ranted at her. I mean, maybe it had nothing to do with – wat's happened to her. But I can't stop blaming myself for—' he stopped speaking, but almost eagerly I supplied my own silent conclusion to his sentence, *for effectively killing your child, Paul.* How little desire I had to talk to this man. Living in close proximity to anybody is like constantly handling a fragile piece of paper – some paper with antique value, an old literary manuscript or legal document. Perhaps you don't read the paper (as I had rarely spoken to Mat). But you have it always about your person. We had experienced extraordinary things together, Mat and I – the attak by that rapist and Gradi's lethal reply; the execution of Bran, the first traitor of the Republic, a hundred other things, he and I had been shoulder to shoulder. Yet I neither knew him nor liked him. The constant pressure of fingers and thumbs on the paper reduces it to shreds, rubs the ink away and eventually degrades the fabric of the parchment itself. I looked at Mat. He had long ceased to be a real person, a full human; he was just Mat, only a thin matrix of habit away from becoming some kind of blank simulation. I wondered how his death would affect me, but instead of indifference I found, in my heart, a sudden little kik, something approaching delight. From there it was a short step to starting to imagine how he might be killed; lingering over fantasy details, over wat I would say, over how I would lean in to push the knife—

'She is strong,' he was saying, glancing over his shoulder at Gradi.

'She is that,' I said, noncommittal.

'I mean physically strong. But of course she is the other – she has a strong will. Those two go together, I think. If I were religious I would say she had a strong soul.'

'Great soul,' I said in the same blank voice.

'Wat I mean is that she'll return to health soon. It is barbaric, wat has happened in this house. We should have been in a hospital facility; instead of which she might as well have been in a Neanderthal cave. But she'll recover. She's strong.'

'Wat if she doesn't?' I asked.

This made Mat's cheeks darken; a blush connoting either shoked anger that I would say so unfeeling a thing, or else embarrassed aknowledgment that his own thoughts had been running along those very lines. For a minute we neither of us said anything. The sun went behind the earth in a glory of rays, like an illuminated engraving, and then into a more impressionist blush of colour, and then darkness.

'Who takes over, if she does pass?' I asked, puzzling myself as I spoke by the strange choice of words I have, half-unconsciously, employed. Passed?

Mat considered this, staring out the window. When he did speak it was not immediately obvious in wat way his comments related to the question I had asked.

'Before I met her,' he said, 'I had only encountered the concept of *will* in an abstract sense. I studied philosophy, you know, at Paris XIV. There's a lot of philosophy about will – Schopenhauer, Nietzsche, that sort of thing. They say it's important. And even political philosophers. And I thought I understood wat they meant. But until I met Gradi I really didn't. Left to its own devices the early American Republic would have divided into two separate nations, and probably into three or four, but Lincoln said no. His will dammed that force up, kept the nation together. That's how the historians read it anyway. I'd never really believed it.'

He cast a shy, almost flirtatious look in my direction, and then fixed his eye out the window again.

'But that's Gradi, isn't it? It's her *will* that we not give way to the Americans. Without her we would simply have given way, immediately. Indeed, without her there probably wouldn't be a nation at all. She is will.'

This little lecture unnerved me. Mat had studied philosophy at university? This was news to me: I'd thought of him, when I'd thought of him at all, as just another rich boy, somebody filling his time and spending his money by indulging a passion for life in the Uplands. But, it occurred to me, he had intellectual pretensions.

'You make her sound like a Nazi,' I said, to show that I too had studied a little history. I pronounced this as if it were an English word, *nahsi*. As soon as I'd said it I realised I'd got the pronunciation wrong. Mat didn't correct me. Perhaps he knew no better than I.

'I'm not saying she's a *tyrant*,' he replied, looking over his shoulder at her sleeping form with exactly the twitchy paranoia a party apparatchik would look at a tyrant. 'She's not that. But she's sometimes – I don't know, superhuman.'

And with that I realised that Mat's love for Gradi was different to mine. I loved her as a personal goddess, as muse, as the huntress-queen; mine was the love that mediated precisely my human emotions. But *he* loved her as the idealised force of history itself, as Will, as the spirit of the people incarnate. I despised him as a fool. But, at the same time, I despised myself, since he and I were the same individual – I wonder if you can understand that? He was defined almost wholly by his relationship to her; and I was defined almost wholly by that same relationship, and as a mathematical expression this reduced, straight-forwardly, into an equivalence. We were male-shapes given substance only by Gradi's regard. I despised everything. I even hated her, emotion that startled up inside me at odd moments and overtook me with its vehemence.

We piked up the transp we were waiting for, and cheking that our stretch of sky was clear, for the moment, of Quanjets we made our way to a four-room house.

Georgie was there. Her grin, her famous grin, had become a rather desperate, unpleasant feature. I remembered our first encounter with her, in that shared house with its floating and micturating cat, its mess and student-digs feel. She had come very far since then. She had hardened, and her grin had hardened too: now it emerged like something frozen on her face, and stayed there only long enough for it to thaw and vanish. She had, it transpired, spent more time travelling even than Gradi and I. 'I'm not sure there's a corner of the Uplands to which I haven't been in the last few months' she boasted wearily.

I was amused at the notion of the Uplands having corners. This, let's be honest, is the least *cornered* land in the history of the world. Gradi said, 'Good good.'

The two of them talked, at length and in detail. I started listening to them, but my mind could not focus. I found myself watching the action of Georgie's lips, the action of Gradi's lips, the chewy, pursing, smiling, circling motions, the liked-by-tonguetip, curling, tapping-together, holding-apart varieties of the movement of their mouths. The sounds these mouths were making became almost an irrelevance. If a whole language can be created only out of the movement of deaf people's fingers, then surely a whole soundless language could be created out of the motion of people's lips.

I was in a state of shok, I think. The thing that surprises me about it is how well I was able to function, despite the depth of it. I went through the actions of life, day by day, waiting, watching the news. We watched France-EU beat UK-EU in the football, that celebrated Euro final match in which eleven goals were scored; and it occurred to me, in some thinking part of my head very far from my face, that the crowds in the Paris stadium were wholly absorbed in that match: that for those ninety minutes those teams and that ball were the most significant thing in the cosmos to them – that even those who supported the Uplands in their continuing siege (and many in the EU did support us) then all thoughts of us were squeezed from their heads during that time. It seems inconceivable, monstrous somehow, that all of us living and dying only a few miles above their pumpkin heads could be dismissed from their thoughts by a game of football. Our life was so intensely experienced, minute-by-minute, our misery was so acute, we most of us had that child's belief that the whole of the universe must be infected by it, even if only to a degree. But that's not the case, of course. People would file into football stadia, or settle down to watch a performance of *Hamlet*, or turn on their screens for the latest instalment of *Sea Farm Family*, or any 3nimation, or concentrate on cooking, or making love, or their jobs, or scratching themselves, or clearing a reluctant and maddening piece of grit from the lining of the eye, or adjusting the settings on their smartcloth coats for rain, or fingering a cut on the scalp caused by tripping and stumbling against a piece of furniture, or reading, and the evanescent thoughts of Upland suffering vanished completely from their heads. This, it seemed to me, was beyond comprehension.

In my misery I became looser-tongued. Gradi, who slowly recovered a percentage of her strength and her vigour (more than fifty, I'd say) sometimes asked me: 'Are you alright, Paul? You seem very contemplative.' And where before I would have replied with some studied blandness, as befitted my role in the marriage, now I startled her with: 'You married me only for my money, I think – you married me because I was wealthy, and you needed money to get up *here*.'

I think I was quite deliberately trying to hurt her feelings in saying this. It was a poor and passive sort of aggression, I'm sorry to say; and Gradi had spent a decade perfecting precisely the political skills needed to turn away a sharp rebuke. She was able to intuit exactly my present blend of resentment and self-pity, and (for I baited her several times with this observation in the aftermath of her miscarriage) reply appropriately – as it might be:

—'Don't be silly, you know how close is the connection between us. It's lasted this long, hasn't it? I'd be lost without you – you're my anchor' which would scurr my self-pity in a little typhoonic swirl, and leave me teary-eyed and holding her and babbling about how much I love her. Or,

—'Have you' (spoken in a gruff, accusing voice) 'been storing that resentment up *all this time*, and not spoken about it before? That's a slap in the face to me, Paul. That's not loyal.' Which would act as an astringent and stem my complaints. Or,

—'Right,' (with a laugh), 'and the gender balance in the Uplands is – wat is it? Eight men for every two women, most of the men super-rich, and one or two of them *even better looking* than you, my love, as if that were possible' (with another sly laugh, and a chuk under the chin) 'and I could have any one of *them*, yet I chose you – for your money?' The comical incredulity of this might even coax a smile from me. Because, of course, she was correct: any heterosexual Upland man would have been powerless before her, should she have decided to claim him as her partner. The half-year of siege had only enlarged her in the collective Upland perception. As our misery increased, increment by increment, the more people chafed and gossiped and blamed the stubbornness of Gradi for prolonging the inevitable capitulation, the more we nevertheless found ourselves relying upon her. Everything else that had acted as orientation in our lives had been stripped away, so we clung more tightly to the one thing we still had. Take riches from the rich, and wat is left? Before the war, and speaking as a wealthy man, I might have said, nothing. But I discovered the truth was otherwise: without money the wealthy man becomes a creature defined by the money-shaped gap inside him, the hole-locus of all desire; he becomes a man in whom *wanting* is very much more intensely present. It is that wanting that is the key medium of the politician. Do you think Gradi didn't know this?

We passed from house to house, Gradi's health slowly improving. And, as if some darkest point had been encountered and passed and overcome, the mood of the Uplanders we encountered improving as well. At Ustinov's house for a second, or perhaps third, time, we found the old Russian in heroic spirits.

'I shall thank you, Gradi, today,' he boomed, as we floated through his doorway. 'Thank you for taking away my wealth! I see now how much it was a parasite upon my soul – without it, I have rediscovered myself!' His eyes burned with this new pleasure, asceticism, the one novelty his pleasure-weary body had not experimented with before, a thing that at a stroke validated all his old self-indulgences in one heroic action of self-denial.

'You're welcome, old friend,' replied Gradi.

Then there was the plague. No, that's too absurd a way of putting it. We had regressed, in our hurtling cells, into the Middle Ages. I'm sure all of us had paid for that marrow pharmakos that protects the body against virus, in watever manner those pharmakoi work – those little gene-inflecting concentrations of organic matter that grow in a thready knot in the relevant part of the body, dictating the cellular manufacture of x or the cellular growth or inhibition of y. But of course, unlike drugs, pharmakoi cannot simply be stored in a cabinet and brought out at need; they need professional placement, they need to be adjusted to the specifics of each body before insertion. Even if we had had the supplies, and the medical personnel, in the Uplands, we would not have had the machines. And so we regressed to a more primitive humanity. Some disease, a three-quarter virus perhaps, bypassed our pharmakos, and spread quikly from Uplander to Uplander. In one sense we were fortunate that these diseases were not more deadly than they were. Everybody learns at school just how many assassin viruses there were in the twentieth century, the flu that killed hundreds of millions at the beginning, the sex virus that killed as many at the end. We suffered from neither of those skull-crossbone diseases. Our illness made us feverish and sik, and turned our eyeballs blood red, and muddied our urine; but only a few people succumbed fatally to this; older, weaker folk. Most of us suffered for a week, and then recovered. Gradi did not even get sik. I don't know how she avoided it, given the continual restlessness with which we passed from house to house, avoiding the Americans.

It meant that opening the door of a house was like as not opening a hatch into some sewer-like space, mephitic, the air rotten and warm and sometimes so foul that the lungs rebelled in coughs from having to breathe it. This was not the stench of disease as such (although the infected tended to sweat a stiky, rotten-meat-smelling sweat during the hottest part of the infection); it was that those who were ill were unable to perform even the most rudimentary housework.

Then I fell ill myself. It seemed, at the time, simply the logical summation of my despair: my mind had collapsed, and so my body followed. I floated in a perfect distillation of agony for long days, unable to sleep for more than a clutch of minutes at a time but never exactly awake either. My eyesight dimmed. My mouth felt crusted over inwardly with dry scales, my fingers seemed to my disordered senses grotesquely large and elongated, as if the forearm that led up to my palm had been surreally replicated, five-fold, at that same palm's other end, although, when I peered at the digits they looked normal enough. I hitched myself to a wall fastening, and watched the lozenge of sunlight slide over the floor and up the wall opposite me, making its twenty-minute dash, pausing for twenty minutes and reappearing again at the start point. In my confusion I think I forgot that I was in the Uplands at all. Perhaps I believed I was in the France house, lying on a bed, and watching not forty minutes but twenty-four hours with each of these passages, such that *months* seemed to pass in a delirious stasis of misery. I was living according to geologic rather than human time, watching the parallelogram of light move away from me and up the wall before fading, only to be reborn in a swift swelling illumination as a square on the floor again. After an indeterminate period of time I was grasped, not unkindly, and floated through the room and through the door into a plane, to be jostled by acceleration, and shuffled through into a new house. For a while I was aware only of my skin's clamminess, in a misty vagueness.

Finally I began to recover my health. I was first very thirsty, and then, as my wits restored, extremely hungry. I devoured such scanty rations as I had and begged like a child for more. There wasn't enough food, but perversely even without a full or healthy diet I became strong again.

We were in the house of a loyal Uplander, a man called Rorik. It was a three-room string, with a (and these were increasingly common in Upland houses) transparent thik-plastic pod at the far end in which a variety of vegetables were being grown. The Americans, on their periodic searches, made sure to trample out anything they found there, the better to starve us into submission; but it seemed that in the bright Upland sunlight and the zero-g plants grew surprisingly rapidly. I ate real cress, bitter little carrots so orange as to be practically red, a soup made from some variety of algae whose name I cannot remember but which tasted tart and strong and filled me up. Gradi was her old self, inexhaustible, as good-looking as Jekyll and strong as Hyde. Rat-tat. *Bang!*

'Things are moving along,' Mat told me, fidgety with excitement. 'It's very much all coming together. At last!' he cooed. 'At last! Gradi was telling me – it's almost time!' So I knew that Gradi had finally judged the moment right to approach the Americans. I was so exhausted, so depressed, it meant very little to me.

'How long has it been?' I asked her directly, during our first time alone. Myself and Gradisil alone together! 'I think I lost trak of time there, for a while, whilst I was ill. How long has it been?'

'The siege? Nearly nine months.'

'You knew, didn't you?'

She didn't answer this. I meant, and Gradi understood perfectly: you knew when the war started that you would hold out for this length of time, nine long months; and you knew that this would cost you your pregnancy, but you judged that a sacrifice you were prepared to make. For why? Only to hold the Americans at arm's length for this period of time, so that post-war legal discussions would be marginally advantaged? The cinder in my heart had come alight at this, and my resentment at the death of 'my son' (oh) in the service of this fuking political game-playing roused me. My murdered son (oh, oh). She could tell I was angry, even as I floated there sullenly.

'It'll soon be over now,' she offered, as if to placate me.

'*This* part of it is over,' I retorted, 'is wat you mean. But *it* will not be over – it will never be over for you, will it? This phase ends, but you're going to continue the war some other way – aren't you.'

She didn't need to confirm the rightness of this judgment. It was, really, self-evident.

'So,' I pressed, weary and angry at the same time, 'wat now? Do you contact the Americans and ask for a parley?'

She nodded, very slightly. Then, an almost incredible admission. 'I know it has been hard for you.' She never said anything like that to me before. 'I'm – grateful that you've stuk by me.' That didn't sound like her either. Perhaps it was her acting the role of concerned spouse. Or, then again, perhaps it sounded, to my ears at any rate, almost like a plural vous, not a tu, *that you, of all people, have stuk by me.* I pondered it for a while. How to answer it? Something like: wat else could I do? Did I have the force within me to escape your gravitational pull? I didn't say anything.

Failure, when it is finally embraced, is a more complex and more deeply human experience than success. Any success is only a postponement of later failure, after all, for otherwise we'd all live forever in endless delight. But it is the *prospect* of failure that is the so much more debilitating thing than failure itself. Entering the house of failure, as we finally did, was in fact a refreshing thing. It was almost a sense of reconnection with the essential business of being human. And we realised at the time, just as, looking bak, the observation seems unavoidable to me: that there was something monstrous about Gradi's will-power, her insistence on holding out far longer than she needed to do, regardless of the cost to herself or to others. The house of failure was the place at which this monstrosity finally assumed its normal shape again.

sixteen. Slater

Surrender

It's the 'we need to talk' that passes between international players. It's the yada-to-yada of nation-state affairs.

Nine months after the declaration of American victory Slater is flown High Arc to DC. It is mid-morning in the eastern US. He is escorted from the plane into government buildings by an honour guard, the moment captured by official cameras. He walks a long beechwood-lined corridor. At the far end his friend Colonel Philpot is waiting, sitting patiently on a slotted beechwood bench outside a large double door. 'Congratulations, Slayer,' says Philpot.

'Wat you doing here, Philp?' Slater asks.

But Philp only nods him to the main doors, and together they walk, through the portal, onto the deep soft pile of purple carpets into which the crest of the President is woven, a deadening of step. The Vice-President is there, and General Niflheim.

'You're promoted Colonel, Slater,' says the Veep, without preliminary. 'Colonel Philpot will be your new aide, and act as your liaison with me.'

And so, after more than a year of saluting Colonel Philpot and keeping his raillery within proper military bounds, Slater is suddenly Philp's equivalent in rank and his de facto superior. He has been expecting a promotion, but the suddenness of this startles him. 'Thank you, sir' he says, loudly. 'Thank you!'

The far wall has nine screens on it, tuned to nine different TVs. All of them are news channels, and the only news is the Uplands war.

Through the bay doors a path leads away, flanked by at-attention guardsmen daffodils, quivering slightly in the breeze. The apple tree in the lawn bulges with cottony blossom, as if its soul has returned to it. The sky is water blue, water clean. Colonel Slater, and not yet thirty. *Colonel.*

310

'She wants to meet,' says the Veep, and for a moment Slater has trouble dragging his attention bak to the room. People will say of me, he thinks to himself, that *he had a good war.* He can't stop himself smiling. Colonel Slater! Fuk! 'I'm sorry, sir?'

'Gradisil. She's made the usual advances through diplomatic channels. Course she's jittery, afeared we'll simply imprison her. She doesn't seem to realise that our situation is now legally triksier, now that so much time has passed since the victory declaration. Nevertheless a meeting is a good idea. The surrender has not been accepted yet, and that's the crucial legal rubicon – wat I mean is, when that happens the whole legal flow will begin. You go, you take Philpot with you. Meet with her.'

'Where?' says Slater. 'US, or EU?'

'Up, of course,' says General Niflheim, almost crossly. His big, lumpy face is looking reddened, a little scorched; less than healthy. Slater half-wonders why he doesn't get his facialist to prescribe him something to make his skin less florid. He almost wonders why Niflheim is being so crosspatch. But he can't think about these, because the glory of Colonel Slater is filling his mind.

'In the Uplands,' he says. 'OK.'

'There'll be a run-around,' says the Veep. 'They've asked that you carry no gun and no personal transp. It's to be a face-to-face, and they don't want to give her position away. Like I said, they're being suitably paranoid.'

'It's urgent,' says Niflheim, again with an undertone of wrath. Slater tunes in to this ire, but cannot imagine why the general would be angry with him. Or is it this mission? Does he think this mission is a bad idea? Why doesn't he just say so?'

'Urgent, like the general says,' confirms the Vice-President. 'You're going straight to a Quanjet and straight up. To a house, thence who knows where. But they've promised to get you bak within the hour, so you'll be coming down to me early this afternoon to tell me wat – she – *says.*'

'Am I to . . . excuse me, sir, but am I to negotiate with her?'

'Wat's to negotiate? She's the President of the Uplands. We've beaten her fair and square in open war. That's the intro and main portion and postscript of the whole story. That's all there is to say. I'm assuming she wants to meet with you to surrender, in actual fact even if not in so many words. She'll want terms. She's only got one thing to negotiate with, and that's herself; she'll want something in return for handing herself over. Listen to wat she wants, concede nothing, come bak down and tell me.'

'Sir!' Slater salutes.

'Now, this is crucial, Colonel. We're flying the best Colonel-Legals we have up from the EU arena right now. They'll be prepped and ready for their trips Upland this very evening. If she offers to surrender *don't concede anything.* Wat I mean is, of course, she will offer to surrender, and your job is *not to concede anything.* Tell her that we'll send a team to accept her surrender. The transition to the *proper* post-war legal protocol is . . .' he shakes his head with a sour expression on his face to convey just how vital this is. 'No schoolchild errors, Colonel. Don't be triked by her offering, say, unconditional surrender. Don't say anything that a lawyer might subsequently use in court to argue that the US accepted her unconditional surrender. You follow wat I'm saying?'

'Absolutely. Perhaps somebody from the Legal Corps could come along, to . . . ?'

'She says no, no military lawyers. She just wants you and Colonel Philpot, the two of *you,* asked for you both by name. Which makes me suspicious. I think she's insisted *no lawyers* because she wants to try some half-assed wordgames with you, try and trik you into an admission of liability. The meeting will be recorded, so just watch your words. Hell, *I'd* like Legal with you,' booms the Veep, 'just as *you* would. But these are the terms on which we get her. Reel her in slowly. General Niflheim assures me that you are a man with a cool enough head to handle this. He has the greatest confidence in you.'

Slater glances at Niflheim, who nods in confirmation, although his face carries a concentrated expression of pure contempt that, did he not know better, Slater might think was directed at him.

Up, salute, snap-heels, and through the big door.

Outside, in the beechwood-lined corridor, Philpot falls into step alongside the new colonel. 'See?' he says, with a mischievous grin. 'Colonel Slayer, my man, sir. How it feel?'

'Good,' says Slater, beaming. 'Only, wat crawled up Niffy's nose and died? He seemed pretty pissed, despite all the good news and cheer and all.'

'Haven't you heard' says Philp, sombrely. 'He's dying. Some cancer or some other cancer. The problem with all these pharmakos everybody is taking all the time nowadays is that they make you look and make you feel just fine, so when a cancer comes it can spend a long time stewing inside you. I heard that every single organ in his body has metastasised cells in it. Months to live. Only months.'

'Fuk,' says Slater. 'That's hard. Still – *Colonel* Slater. That has a nice ring to it, don't you think?'

The Quanjet is parked on the Presidential runway, and Slater only has time for short call to his wife on the way to the craft. 'Darling, you won't believe my news.'

'Wat news won't I believe?'

'Will you believe, I wonder, that you're now Mrs Colonel?'

'But I was so fond of my old surname.'

'Seriously, Marina, I just heard – it's promotion.'

'Why that's wonderful news, my love,' she says, her fine features folding into a pretty smile at mouth and eyes. 'Wait, I'll get the kids . . . you can tell them direct.' Her face leaves the screen, and Slater is instructed to turn off his phone and board the craft before she returns. Already, even in this luminous moment of triumph, the worm of anticlimax is starting to stir. So it's over, so we won, and wat next?

Unlike a tried-and-tested Elemag plane, and despite the fact that they've been being flown for two decades now, Quanjets are still classified as *in development*. Accordingly, both Slater and Philpot must remove their uniforms and clamber into spacesuits before launch. 'But my suit is at Fort Glenn,' Philp complains. 'This one's too big for me.'

'It's regulations sir,' says the Corporal-Pilot. 'In case of accident.'

And they strap in and the plane sweeps down the runway in regular flight, and climbs over the eastern seaboard in regular flight. Philp fidgets in his seat, unhappy in his spacesuit, which doesn't fit quite right. Slater peers through the window at the ground sinking away below him. 'Don't you never get tired of looking out of airplane windows?' asks Philpot, grumpy in his ill-fitting suit.

'I don't suppose I do,' replies Colonel Slater, letting his eye rest on the view below him, receding below him, the faceted running bulge and dip of the Appalachians, the morning sun stroking their eastern flanks; the moon-coloured clouds clumping and stretching through clear air over the mountains; the sheer clarity and depth of deep air. Halfway into the flight the Quanjet fires its engine, and flight becomes much more rapid. In minutes the window is blak.

They park at a small civilian house, hurtling through the hurtling Uplands, and are greeted by two depressed-looking natives. There is a smell of sour milk in this house, and too much detritus is floating through the air; papers, crumbs, kit, a sok. It has the air of being seedy, a house defeated.

'Your *suits*, gentleman,' says one of the Uplanders. She was more than drug-thin. Indeed she looked actually half-starved: her cheekbones making two sharp ^s on each side of her long ↓ nose, her eyes bulging like gobstoppers. 'I take it,' she said, 'that you have your own personal transponders, in these suits? Please remove them. We'll keep them here, under the watchful eye of your pilot and his second officer.'

They do this. Both the Corporal-Pilot and his second have pistols in their hands; they are floating together by the porch door, watching carefully.

'Are you carrying weapons?' the second Uplander asks Slater and Philp. He is similarly thin, with an unpleasant red moss pattern of broken bloodvessels in his eyeballs.

'We are not,' said Colonel Philpot. 'Care to frisk?' He holds his arms out.

'That won't be necessary,' says the woman. 'Please come with me.'

'Are we going straight to meet Gradisil?' asks Slater.

The woman, leading them out, does not reply.

The Uplander plane is small, and in a poor state of repair compared to military craft. There are bare wires poking through holes in the wall. The door, in the nose, is manual release, and the handle is very obviously bent. It takes the starved-looking woman several goes before the nose gets heaved shut, and then she has to apply a long strip of putty-style sealant to the gap, presumably to preserve cabin pressure. She straps herself into the pilot's seat almost listlessly. They break away from the house, drift briefly, and then power up the Elemag and angle down, piking up speed.

'Do you have a name?' Slater asks.

She does not reply.

There's a hiatus.

Um—

'You'd *think*,' Philp complains, shortly, 'that they could have got a suit that fitted me better than this one. It's not like I'm an abnormal-size guy, or anything.'

They fly on in silence.

'So,' says Philp, after long talkless moments have passed. 'Marina pleased about the promotion?'

'Oh?'

'You called Marina, I saw. Told her about the promotion? She pleased?'

'Sure is.'

'Of course she is, the *old lady*, of course she is. You're luky to have Marina, Slayer. You're a luky guy.'

'I'm a luky guy,' Slater agrees.

'Wat I mean, she's beautiful. And hey she adores you—'

'And Daria,' says Slater, smiling loyally.

'Sure,' says Philp, nodding. 'That's right.'

The talking dries up. It seems as though there's nothing to say. The body of the plane throbs with the weird action of the Elemag.

Eventually Philp says: 'so, we're finally going to meet the great Gradisil. Finally meeting her face to face. The gre-e-at Gr.'

'I guess so.'

'Grr-grr. Meet her face to face. I'll confess I'm excited.'

And they are silent again, as if they really have nothing to say to one another. After so many years!

There's the gathering pull forward of deceleration as the plane climbs.

With a worryingly heavy bump the plane doks at another house. The anonymous pilot leans the mass of her leg against the release lever, and squeezes the nose open. There is a burst of breeze, and crumbs and grit is suked past Slater and Philpot's faces. 'Maybe we should put our helmets on,' Philp jokes.

The air pressure settles. 'In there,' gestures the pilot.

Slater wonders whether the pilot is coming too, but it seems not. He leads the way, with Philpot floating behind him, through the nose and into a spacious and almost entirely empty room.

'Finally getting to meet the famous Gradisil,' says Philpot cheerily. 'Hey, I'm almost excited.'

But Gradisil is not in the room. Nobody is in the room, and it is almost bare of furnishings except for a screen tagged to the wall halfway down.

'Wat's this?' Philpot asks. 'Is this a staging-post? Who is it will be taking us to the real rendezvous?'

Slater hand-over-hands to the screen, examines it. There's an on-button. He pushes this.

Gradisil's face on the screen is immediately recognisable. 'Hello Lieutenant,' she says.

'Madame President,' says Slater, smoothly, floating bak a little so his face isn't filling the camera. 'Actually I've recently been promoted.'

'Colonel Slater,' says Philpot, offscreen.

'Congratulations,' says Gradisil, gravely. 'It's a well-deserved promotion I'm sure.'

A shudder runs through the room. It is the door being shut. There is only a small porthole window in the door itself to give a view of the outside, and after Philp has pushed himself and swum over to this he reports angrily: 'Hey, she's disengaged. She's flying off.'

Slater takes the situation in his stride. He sighs. 'Madame President,' he says, trying for a stately and slightly disappointed tone of voice. 'Wat is going on? This is not a smart play on your part, Madame President.'

'I'm sorry about this, Colonel.'

'You intend to hold us prisoner? This won't achieve anything, I'm afraid. The war is over, and I'm afraid you lost. This sort of kidnapping is not an act of war now, it's merely a criminal action. You're merely opening yourself to prosecution.'

'We do not intend to hold you prisoner,' says Gradi. 'I am sorry about this, I really am. I was just looking you up on USUP web. You have two children, I see.'

Slater has that sensation of sudden insight, that static-electric sensation in his scalp, that tumbling sensation in his torso as if he were about to fall. I'm sure you've had that sensation, that numinous gleam of sudden realisation, the peek into the imminent future. Suddenly Slater *comprehends*. 'Philp,' he calls, his voice loud in the small room. 'Put your helmet *on now*.'

But Philpot, at the door, is slow. 'Wat?'

Slater has pulled the helmet up from its poket at the upper-rear of his suit, pulled the smart plastic up and over and fastened it at his collar in front of his chin. The flaps fold down, and he fumbles with the buttons. '*Philp*,' he urges, his voice muffled now. '*Do* it.'

'That won't do you any good, I'm afraid, Colonel,' comes Gradi's mournful voice. 'I truly am sorry. It's nothing personal.'

The left flap is fastened, and the right is almost there when the door to the room explodes. The whole far wall explodes, and it's *bang* and it's *whsh*. Flash of white-orange light. There's the briefest of blazes, a cupola of fire that swallows Philp and dashes hungrily at Slater, but is suddenly inverted, suked away as the air that feeds it vanishes into the nothingness outside. Slater is yelling. He feels his body yanked and twisted, a wet rag that some muscular force is trying to wring dry. He is shouting, his voice inside his helmet is very large in his ears. His hands are ungloved, and the catch on the right side is not properly fastened, although the smart-plastic has sealed the side and front flaps to make his helmet a clear dome with two creases in it running bak of shoulder to front of shoulder. But the catch on the right needs to be fastened, and he needs to – get – his – gloves – on – he is *not* properly suited up for spacewalk.

The room bukles and spins.

Adrenalin gives everything a weird clarity and precision. He sees the whole length of the room wobble and flex, and the sheared chunks of the far wall vanish twinkling into the darkness with extraordinary rapidity. He is falling along the throat of the room, and he forms the phrase in his mind, with exaggerated exactness, *my hands are ungloved.* He wonders how tight the elastic seal at his wrist is. He wonders if he will be able to get his hands into the gloves, which are flapping like pennants on the suit sleeves as he is thrown forward.

But no sooner has he started to wonder this than the room has vanished from around him, and he's tumbling head over heels, or heels over head, and his naked hand in plain vacuum reaches up to the right of his collar and cliks the button closed.

The primary sensation he is aware of is as if he has plunged his hands into ice water. The fingers are puffy and unresponsive, like the fingers of a very very old man. Like, he thinks, the fingers of a dying man.

No.

And then his hands have gone numb, and he can't feel anything from the wrist down any more.

Get the gloves on, he thinks. Get the gloves on. The phrase has its own lolloping rhythm. *Get* the gloves *on. Get* the gloves *on. Get* the gloves *on.*

His left hand, working like a leper's hand, nudges and manoeuvres the right glove over his right hand. He pushes, he pulls, feels the rasp of fabric against the skin of the fingers. He strains his hand into the glove, strains in it, and then reflexively tries patting his wrist to secure the fit.

He is aware of sensation returning to his right hand. The way he is aware of sensation returning to his right hand is that it hurts, is that *fuk,* it hurts. The fingers all feel broken. They throb, and the skin burns, and the slightest movement hurts.

I wonder, he thinks to himself, if I'm in pre-shok. I wonder if this sense of mental calmness will soon be overtaken with panic, or actual shok. Before that happens, he thinks, I must get my left glove on.

He reaches round with his right hand, makes clumsy grasping motions, but every flex of each finger joint is agony. Closing his grip hurts in a dozen places, and unclasping the hand hurts in a dozen different places. And he can't seem to find the glove.

The world is right there, immediately before him, an enormous gleaming balloon, rotating impossibly about his head, spinning its vast airy curve round and round and round.

Can't find the other glove. He reaches, he reaches, he reaches, his

317

breath is desperate in the enclosed space of the helmet. Where is the glove?'

Stop this.

Stop.

Stop this. Be calm. Calm down. It must be there somewhere.

With his gloved right hand he works systematically around his wrist, ignoring the pain of his hands. He finds the short cord by which the glove is tethered to the sleeve, but there is no glove at the end of it. This takes a moment to sink in. It has fallen off. *Fuk*, that's not good. He's lost it, and that's not good. But how *can* it have fallen off? This is a USAF suit, made to the highest standards. Calm, and be calm, calm, think.

Slater thinks. His breath scurries and rasps inside the helmet. Perhaps the glove snagged on something as he was suked out of the exploded house. Perhaps it was ripped off. It hardly matters how. Wat matters is that he has no glove.

This is not a situation for which he has been trained.

The whole enormous balloony Earth twirls and twirls about the axis of his head. His head has become the axle-point of the spinning cosmos.

He raises his left hand and holds it in front of his helmet. The hand is blak, like it has been dipped in dye. Is that bruising, he wonders, a total bruising around the whole of the hand? Or is it frostbite, a freeze-dried hand? There's the vaguest throbbing numbness somewhere in the centre of the palm. Perhaps it's not quite dead yet. But then it won't be long. Won't be long before the hand is dead.

Won't be long, Slater thinks, before I'm dead too.

Got to get my breathing under control, or I – will – [*puff*] – hyper – [*puff*] – venti – [*puff*] – late. Late as in the late Colonel Slater.

He centres himself. He has to think through his options. He has to set his transponder going, wait to get piked up. But he has no transponder, of course; he surrendered that to the skinny woman.

This is such a stupid play for the Uplanders, he thinks. That cadaverous Uplander waiting in that house, with the Corporal-Pilot and his second officer pointing guns at him. When he and Philp do not return they'll take him into custody. I guess he doesn't mean anything to the Upland cause. But this is a crazy play. It's plain terrorism; it'll only result in a military crakdown. Perhaps that's wat Gradisil was angling for.

Not angling with *my* dead body, he thinks. Not if I can help it.

But he can't help it. This, he knows.

The first question is: has he been given a right-hand or a left-hand suit? The odds are on the former, but it's possible it's the latter. Also, it is hard to tell when his fingers are so sore-numb. But he can just feel the nubbins of the control inside the glove; so at least it's a right-hand suit; and that's something.

Slater applies pressure, and the Elemag fibres charge, and his rotation slows, and his rotation stops. All those filament fine lines of force through which he is hurtling and spinning. With his fingers he conjures a weak Elemag field out of his suit, meshes with the invisible contours of his environment, orients himself. The world has stopped circling his head, like a cartoon of an astronaut hit on the head with a comedy mallet. It steadies on his right hand. He wobbles, a little. His battery is too weak properly to manoeuvre himself.

He looks around. He can hear his heart drumming, inside the seal of his suit. Wat can he do now? There's nothing he can do now.

seventeen. Paul

When I was a boy, in Amiens, I was sometimes scared by the trees in my parents' garden. Isn't that the strangest sentence I have written yet? Don't you think it is?

My parents' house was an extensive estate on the outskirts of town, and to step through the bak doors was to walk across a stretch of warm-breed grass, perhaps thirty metres, and then into the broader, more old-fashioned reaches of garden and meadow, which in turn led down to a stream, the border of the estate, whose water moved with an insolent slowness. There were trees all over the gardens, but in particular there was a phalanx of trees that lined the warm-grass, a living wall separating the greenhouse to the right from the view out of the bak door: a dozen sentinels, twenty metres tall, standing in a line.

The trees were not scary in winter; on the contrary they looked poor, beggarly, like the skeletal phage-plaguers who camped out down by the old cathedral, hoping like medieval peasants for divine intervention to cure their horribly man-made ailments. Nor were the trees scary during the height of a summer's day, plump and self-satisfied in their bulging greenery, riddled with birds like a shaggy dog with fleas. But there were times, especially at dusk, when they were blakly silhouetted against a sky in which light and dark were indifferently mixed, when they would move with a more than vegetable urgency, and would thresh the air like giant serpents. Then I was actively scared. The strange thing is that I often sought out the fear that this created inside me – which was a very real fear, panting, sweating, staring, a terror that filled me with rabbity panic. Sometimes it would be too much and I would flee from the bak of the house altogether, run all the way up the stairs to my room. But sometimes I would lurk there, whilst the huge shadowy things lurched and hissed at me, and I would let the fear pass through me and through me, like a kind of metaphorical vomiting. Finally, when I could bear it no longer, when the giant trees seemed to becoming more and more agitating with inchoate Brobdingnagian rage towards me, I would break and run, the fear flushing suddenly into pure adrenalin.

Of my father I remember little, except that he was tall and slender, and rarely in the house. With the blitheness of childhood I simply accepted this as part of the way the universe was structured. I didn't miss him; I had Mama. My mother was the most beautiful human being I ever knew; the first person whose physical loveliness intruded on my otherwise wholly inward-looking life. She was a small woman, but perfectly proportioned, with the most beautiful face I, as a child, had ever seen: her eyes perfect almond-shaped, with two mirror-image tiks in the far point of each of them, lined with make-up blak, like Maria Callas. Her body was a pillowy aggregation of spheres and ovals, with a gorgeous sweet-like smell to her skin. There was no happier experience to me as a boy than to fold myself into the embrace of that body. I was struk by the enormous disparity between my own body and my mother's. Specifically I liked to touch myself a great deal in the bath – I don't mean only my genitals, although there as well, but my whole skin; running individual fingers or a stronger pressure of both palms, over my chest and stomach. There was something ineffable about the beauty I found in my own torso. My legs less so: they seemed skinny and somehow irrelevant, as if they were marginal; perhaps because removed from the core of my being, my face, my chest. But the fascination I found in my own skin was intense enough to be unsettling to me, even at that young age.

The way the breeze that touched my face, and the breeze that pushed through the weave of my shirt to touch my shoulder and chest, felt so differently, although it was all the same breeze.

I'm rambling – wat about the war? Wat about the assault? With the counterattak, Gradi was suddenly galvanised into becoming a war leader, no longer a partner in the world with me, her poor cukolded, passive, moneybags husband – no, nein, non – now moving purposefully through a world of her own making. I was so depressed that I barely noticed; exhausted by my illness, caved-in mentally by previous events. I stayed with this Uplander or that, in this or that strange house, and did nothing more than go through the motions of eating with mashy teeth, and watch the screen (the news stations suddenly enormously interested in events in the sky), and sleep.

The key to her counterattak had been co-ordination; and with a simple innocency that baffled the less child-like Gradi had arranged this in full view of the enemy. She had employed, indeed, the most puerile code of all. The night before the attak, she had phoned her dozen key military people, one after the other. As each of their faces appeared on the screen, she had said to them: 'I shall speak to the Americans tomorrow; tomorrow afternoon I shall meet their preliminary representatives at five pm EU standard to talk about surrender.' And the code was this: *for* surrender *read* counterattak. I daresay there's never been a simpler code in the history of war, and yet it was a code the Americans failed to break. As simple as that: the intricate discussions over the many months of the siege, the location of caches of hardware disguised as space junk floating in orbit, or hidden in plain view bolted to the side of houses (but taken for piping, or ice), the various strategies, the grander plan, all this was primed. Her message was the first glimmer at the fuse's end.

That day two senior US officers flew up to, they thought, receive Gradi's surrender. At 5 pm, EU standard, the house they were in was blown up. Simultaneously two EleMag ships came rolling silently down from high orbit and fired old-fashioned firework missiles at the large rotating space station the US had only just finished building. This was too large a target to be destroyed by the home-made weapons at our disposal of course; or so the Americans thought. Its great circle of corridors and rooms was heavily armoured on the outward side. Dart lasers were positioned to pik off debris that might knok holes in the fabric; but they were tuned to objects of a particular sort, the size of discarded screws and bolts. There *was* a missile-cannon located in the hub, but it was not in a state of readiness at the time of the attak – and since there were two ships on the attak run, it wouldn't have made much difference even had it been. The assailants fired at the hub, hitting it three times.

Here is the simple truth that Gradi had grasped, which was the core of her strategy: any pressurised container in a vacuum is effectively two-thirds bomb anyway. It takes very little, once the wall is pierced, to destroy it completely. Breaking through the wall itself will often be enough. And as soon as the central hub area of the US station was ripped away, in tendrils of glinting metal and plastic, the complete structure was doomed. It continued to spin, of course; but without a central structural lok the ring began to deform under these unusual pressures. Where external attak would not have been able to penetrate the armour, internal stresses broke the constitutive segments of the ring apart from one another, a process that gathered momentum with its increasing destruction. There were, I believe, nearly 400 soldiers and officers aboard at the time of the attak; and of them precisely 11 survived, because they happened to be in an EleMag plane doked at a porch when the attak was launched.

It was ill-fortune rather than any defensive action by the Americans (troops who had long ago given up – if they had ever possessed – the belief that Uplanders could fight at all) that destroyed one of the attaking Upland planes: the cokpit window pierced by a chunk of debris from the disintegrating station, pilot and co- killed. But the other plane got away, dropping into a low fast orbit, spinning round the world, and then climbing out to drift, all engines off, as just one more piece of occupied flotsam, amongst the many thousands in the Uplands. The Americans, preparing for our surrender, were not even patrolling the escape routes downbelow with their previous thoroughness.

Fort Glenn was also attacked, by three planes. But it was a sturdier platform, and although several chambers were pierced and casualties inflicted, the Fort survived. Two Quanjets were stationed there, and both were launched: one Uplander plane slipped away, but the Quanjets, supple and rapid as eels in water, dogfought and destroyed the other two. Two other sites were attacked; an old EU Station now used for storage by the US, with a skeleton staff; and the main polar relay satellite.

Over the many months of American house-to-house searches, a man called Harrison Gow had been assembling an AI map of US procedure. Gradi later said that she was by no means certain the Americans would be so predictably systematic – that if *she* had been in charge of the Occupation she would have randomised the house-to-houses through-out the Occupation. But, after a two-week period of random searches the US settled into a distinct pattern. They did not proceed one, two, three, of course; but they did move according to a determinable grid and Gow's skill – working like an old-fashioned amateur, with limited computing power and patchy data, phoned in by only those house-holders able to contact him – was to scan it. His AI map meant that Gradi knew which houses were due to receive their latest visit from the Americans. Gow only just had it ready by May (had we had it earlier we could have saved ourselves a lot of anxiety as we fled from house to house); but it was ready in time. It meant that Gradi was able, with some hurried shuffling about, to remove certain unreliable (because lily-livered) Uplanders from their houses and replace them with people prepared to fight, and perhaps die.

This aspect of resistance did not go as straightforwardly as it might have done. A dozen planes were in flight, carrying armed teams to a dozen houses. Half of these turned bak from their missions on hearing the paniked news over their comms that Forts Freedom and Glenn were under attak. Of the half dozen who carried through their orders, only two were unprepared for resistance: having doked immediately prior to the counterattaks, they came through the doors as they had done hundreds of times before, and were gunned down. Uplanders pushed through into the American jets and fought with the remaining crew. Both jets were taken, with only one Upland casualty. In the remaining four planes, crews were jittery with anticipation, lodged in porches, opened their doors and shouted warnings through rather than simply entering, shouting 'Show yourself, put your hands first through the hatch, come in, you are inside our firing arc!' and so on. These battles were more hectic. Uplanders fired blind through the door, but this is a poor way to hit targets; American return fire was heavier and more devastating. Some Uplanders rushed the door, or threw bombs along the weirdly straight trajectories that are characteristic of zero g – crazy desperation, since to blow up one ship is to blow up two when the two are linked together. It is hard to think oneself into these four fierce little firefights; except to know that, at the end, three times as many Uplanders were dead as Americans, and the US were still in control of those four planes.

After all those many months of confinement in the Uplands, after spending day after day after day in Mat's company, I had only one further conversation with him, after which I was never to see him again.

I was moved from house to house. I had no idea where Gradi was, but people would fly in, ask me politely to accompany them, and passive as a caged bird, I would go with them. We were no longer taking the long way from house to house; any plane in the sky was a potential target, so we hurried journeys, minimising transit time, diving precipitously and then climbing up with deceleration that sometimes bruised my ribs against the straps holding me. I did not know why I was being moved from house to house, and did not ask. I was content to be a passenger; or, indeed, a mere piece of cargo.

In one house, walls greasy with sweat and mould, detritus floating everywhere, three exhausted occupants, I met with Mat. He was hanging on the wall watching a craked but still functioning screen tuned, of course, to a news channel. There was a pervasive smell of burnt vegetable oil in the house, mixed with sour old milk, and a sharply acidic coppery stench that scraped the sinuses and was perhaps from some overheated piece of equipment. I took up a place on the wall next to Mat, and watched the screen with him in silence for a while. The three householders passed to and fro in front of us, fretful and worn-looking, speaking broken phrases or peeps of conversation, their skulls shrink-wrapped in ill-looking skin, their eyes fever-bright.

Eventually Mat spoke, without looking at me: 'I had no idea this was coming,' he said.

'You think I did?'

Mat sniffed derisively through his nose. 'You are Gradi's – wat's the word the English had, once upon a time? You're Gradi's consort.'

'She has several consorts,' I said, without rancour. However much I despised him we at least shared something: two men, possessed of certain gifts, wealthy men by the standards of the downbelow, yet both men essentially zeros, in themselves nothings that only come into importance when placed after the 'I' of Gradi.

Mat sniffed again. I realised that his sniffing was not an affectation: he was suffering from a head-cold, with a pressure of gluey snot in his nose and ruddy, scratchable eyes. 'They're saying,' he said, after a while, 'that this is our tet offensive – the newscaster used that phrase just then, in an interview with the Finnish president.'

'Finland? Wat does Finland say? My sons are there.' As I spoke this a voice in my head reminded me that neither of those sons were mine; and that, indeed, the father of one of those cukoo children was hanging right next to me. But they were my boys. The sparkle of fury that flushed through my head, dissipating as a blush and a sense of weariness (wat did it *matter*? They were still my boys – wat did *anything matter*, after all?) meant that I missed Mat's reply.

'Still,' he was saying, 'wat's a tet offensive?'

'You're asking me? I don't recognise the phrase,' I said.

'*I* don't recognise the phrase. Isn't it French? You're French, aren't you?' The ludicrousness of having spent a large fraction of ten years in close company with this man – of having shared my wife with him – and after all this time him asking me a question like that, as if we'd only been vaguely acquainted; for some reason this infuriated me. Not that I cared wat Mat thought about me. But still. Piqued, I replied in a reedy, insistent voice.

'Come on, Mat, you speak French, I know you speak French.' And then, to ensure the point was made. 'We've known one another long enough, after all.'

'Don't feel I know anybody very much,' Mat replied, in a preoccupied tone, his eyeballs shimmering left to right, left to right, as he tried to follow some complicated newsinfo graphic on the screen. 'Isn't it "head"?'

'Tête means head,' I confirmed.

'It's some historical reference, I guess.'

We were silent together for a long time. The news broke off for commercials.

'She . . .' said Mat, eventually, and said nothing more than this one word for several minutes. We both knew to whom *she* was referent.

I knew wat he was going to say; so I said it for him. 'She was planning this from the very first; planning this but not telling us.'

'Didn't tell you *or* me,' he agreed, tacitly catching the tone of aggrieved fraternity between us.

'Told Georgie, I hear.'

'Georgie.' Mat shook his head.

After a while I spoke again: 'She,' and again, although we had just been talking about Georgie, the non-specific female pronoun clearly meant Gradi, 'she waited all that time, the whole period of the siege. She planned it all out. She knew how long to wait, to lull the Americans into false security, and . . .'

For the first time Mat became animated. 'Oh no,' he said. 'Oh no, it wasn't *that*,' he said, as if this were a crucial point that I had misunderstood. 'It was for our benefit.'

'Our benefit?'

'I mean to say, for the benefit of the Uplands as a whole. It was a period of coming into being of our nation. That's why she did it. Wat bound us together, this village-sized population of billionaires and space-obsessives? Nothing, we were all, each of us, all wrapped up in our own selfish world. Wat gave us common cause? Wat bound us together? Well, she orchestrated this . . . experience. And it has bound us together. We're a nation now.'

'We were before,' I said.

'No. But now we are. Before, we were lots of people addicted to money. Now the money has been cold-turkeyed out of our systems and we've been given a much more potent drug instead. If we win,' and his voice caught, as if even he – detached, knowing, alienated – could not help the surge of excitement in his breast at – *the – very – thought –* 'then it'll take root and grow through all our souls.'

'If we win,' I repeated, meaning to sound dismissive, but also caught up in the luminous possibility. 'Do you think we can win?'

'If she had just surrendered, and the Americans had chopped and ordered the Uplands according to their convenience, then the idea of this nation would have withered, and the various billionaires would have fallen bak into their selfish ways. But if she can knok them down,' (as if Gradi were a muscular prizefighter in the ring and the entire American air force a single flabby contender) 'particularly after they made us suffer so much for so long – if she can do that, then she will make something out of us. She, single-handed. She'll be a god to us, and we'll be her people – one people because her people.'

In a smaller voice, I asked 'Do you think she can win?'

'The news, I mean, OK, it's EU news, but the news – the news thinks there's a good chance. They're saying that the Americans have never received such a shok in war. This is a new kind of war, you need to remember. It's a battlefield that's never really been tested.'

'There was eighty-one.'

'But,' said Mat, animated suddenly, 'that's the point, that wasn't a real war, the Europeans capitulated almost *immediately* then. There wasn't any hard fighting. And at the end of last year, *we* simply lay down and let them roll over us. We didn't give them any resistance either. But when the fighting starts, they begin to see how vulnerable an army is up here. In vacuum, in nothingness, it's a triky place – there are no strongholds up here, because a medium-sized hole in *any* structure will rip it to shreds.'

'Applies to both sides.'

'But there's the point! Because we're not vulnerable the way they are. Their forces are concentrated in two main forts, and a few storage bins. We've knoked one of those forts out already, and the other is looking more and more precarious – once we've taken Fort Glenn out, wat are the Americans going to do? But we, on the other hand, we're not concentrated the way they are. We're spread through thousands of houses. I'm sure the US will destroy a number of those houses, but – wat are they going to do? I mean, they could conceivably destroy every last house in the Uplands, but then that wouldn't be war, that would be genocide, and a whole different legal situation.'

I revolved this perspective in my head. 'We haven't,' I pointed out, searching for flaws in his logic, 'knoked out Fort Glenn.'

'Not *yet.*'

'But even if we do, they could just build a new one. Theirs are all the advantages of money, population, access and so on.'

'Yes, they could build a new station, and they might do so, if their national pride and outrage at prospective defeat goads them. But if they do we'll just knok it out again. Wat they *can't* do is occupy the Uplands the way *we* have, spread over thousands of houses, because that was decades of slow accretion. Time has been on our side.'

I pondered. 'They could capture Gradi,' I said. 'Or kill her.'

'They could do that,' said Mat, in a gloomy voice. 'They'll try that, yes, they will. But they can't guarantee to do that.'

After a long pause, I said: 'She was planning this the whole time. She knew she would wait this long before counterattacking. She let people think she was planning to surrender, but she had no such intention.'

'She's far-seeing,' said Mat.

'She knew it would cost her the pregnancy,' I said, my voice catching. Then because it sounded obnoxious in my own ears to talk about the death of my unborn only son in terms of *cost*, as if it were simply a matter of a greater or lesser expenditure of *money*, I restated: 'She knew that the child would die.'

'She was prepared,' said Mat, speaking slowly now, with a weird soothsayer clarity of tone, 'to sacrifice the child to the larger aim, oh that's very *her*. Very much *her*.' He was proceeding carefully now, testing the ground to see how I might react – rage, tears, despair, he didn't know and neither did I. 'I'm sure she thought about it very carefully. But, in the end, I guess she decided that making a nation was,' he havered, coughed, wiped his eyes, looking blearily at me sideways, 'was, I mean, that it outweighed the life of a baby, a *fetus*, I mean to say.'

This went straight through me like a blade sheathed in my chest. Outweighed? These conventional phrases, which come almost unthinkingly to our tongues, unpak into unsettling complexity of implication. Mat was saying that the birth of the Uplands *outweighed* the birth of my only biological son. The metaphor was one of sheer density, as if the fatter man was more worthy than the thinner. It was almost insultingly literal: on this side of the beam *all these people*, tens of thousands of them, and the hundreds of thousands who would come after and call themselves, proudly, Uplanders – so many, such a weight. On the other side, only a frail unbreathing body, no larger than a skinned rabbit. The woman Casta flying past with a bloody bundle of sheets in her arms. Wat kind of balance was that? Except, again, the literal notion was undermined by the facts of Upland life, because all of those thousands, in a perfectly literal sense, had no weight at all. I could feel my face was blanched, colourless.

Then Mat said: 'I don't mean to be cruel. The loss of the fetus is a shame, but you've got two sons. I mean—' and he stopped, seeing my expression.

I glowered at him, and, then, unexpectedly, my rage snagged, caught, and dissolved in a great gush into tears. I was crying. He didn't mean to be cruel. He had one son with Gradi, and Liu (wherever he was, in whichever American holding facility) had one son with Gradi, and I had none at all. It was unfair. I was crying for the weightlessness of all of us, up, as we were. The tears were crying through me, falling from an infinite height and drawn towards a depth infinitely distant beneath us, the whole cosmos a fall of atoms.

'It's *her*,' I said, as I sukked my tears bak into my throat, drawing a great shuddery breath, and then another, and fought to get a grip on myself. 'You don't mean to be cruel, but *she* does. She doesn't care.'

'Oh no,' said Mat, inspired with earnestness of a sudden, as if this were the most important thing in the world, and it were an utterly vital thing that he communicate it to me: 'you're wrong. She does care, about many things, even about us. Wat is alien to her is pity. She just doesn't do pity – or more precisely, she thinks of pity only as a weakness. Her essence is as free of pity as any I've ever known. That's the secret of her success. No,' he added, more contemplatively, 'I don't mean success. That's the secret of *her*.'

eighteen. Slater, a death

Slater floats. No: he *hurtles*, and *soars*, only feels as if he floats – and no – in fact he doesn't even feel floaty, he feels as if he is motionless and the world is revolving over his head. Slater wonders wat is going on in the world and over it; or perhaps *wonders* gives the impression of a fanciful or meandering mind – he tries, rather, flexing his mind like a muscle, comprehensively *to work out* the balance of likely *possibilities*. Gradi has tried to kill him. She succeeded in killing Philp. Why did she do it? He considers the possibility that it is the overture to a more concerted counterattak against American occupation. But no ruler would be so rekless, surely? That the war is over is more than American propaganda. Any strike the Uplands could make, especially after half a year of hunger and privation, would be feeble; American retaliation would inevitably be swift and overwhelming, shoking, awe-inspiring. If the lion has settled its jaws about your head, a dentine coronet with the points inward like a crown of thorns, and yet is gracefully declining from crushing your skull, then you do not pinch the lion's belly with your thumb and finger. Or so it seems to Slater.

But wat other explanation for the attak? Gradi presumably hopes to demonstrate, by assassinating two senior officers, that she can still hurt America. But she must know that, although America will respond with righteous anger and pride, that America will not in any meaningful sense be *hurt* by these two deaths? Angered, perhaps; but it is no gash in the multicellular people-behemoth occupying those spacious spaces between the western and the eastern shining seas; it doesn't even amount to a tickle, to an inconvenience. Perhaps it was mere spite on Gradi's part. Perhaps – and this thought seizes him suddenly, almost excites him, since it flatters his sense of self, even in extremis as he now is, to think that the great politicians of the world consider him at all – perhaps she had a personal animus against him. Perhaps it was murder, not assassination. Wat had she said? *I'm sorry about this, I was looking you up on USUP web.* Had she been monitoring him, like a webstalker?

Was there some reason, obscure to Slater but real enough to have actual consequences in the world, that may have made her hate him? He can't think of it. His mind goes round and round. His body is making literal this figure of speech.

His orientation is such that the whole world is above his head, and his feet seem to slide forever over an infinite, blak, frictionless floor. He puts his head bak. Clouds are lying over a sea gleaming coppery-yellow that shines from the action of the now oblique sun. The cloud cover has the stylishly ragged-edged quality and much of the apparent texture of high-quality art paper, heavy rough-weave cartridge carefully torn into broad leaf shapes and lain overlapping one over the other. He passes into the dark side, and the tinselly glitter of nightside illuminations sparkle above him, moking the much wider and purer enstudding of actual stars in space beyond.

He flies on, unhoused, through the sterile vacuum and through all the darkness. There is no sensation in his left hand now; although the bone of his left forearm has a chilly ache running all the way along it up to the elbow, as if the marrow were a channel for the inhuman cold of the Uplands outside.

There is only one hope for him, as he knows: to be seen by somebody, and collected in a plane. It would need, obviously, to be a USUF jet, and preferably a Quanjet, to be able to manoeuvre safely close enough to him and draw him in. But there is perhaps the possibility that a good samaritan Uplander might rescue him. He weighs the pros, the cons, trying to tense his mind into a properly disciplined and rigorous and *military* frame. He's still a soldier. This is how he works best; not thinking wildly or free-associating, but meditating methodically.

Pro: he is wearing a brightly visible suit: the red stripes glow like raked over embers and the white stripes gleam like neon when the sunlight hits them. If someone is looking for him, in the right bit of sky, then he won't fade into the bakground.

He thinks, studiedly, searching for other pros. They are elusive.

Pro: when the USUF discover their people have gone, they will come looking. Leave no person behind, as the motto goes. But as soon as he considers this thought, a con pops up: they won't if they're being suddenly overwhelmed in counterattak. Maybe hundreds of troops are dying. Maybe they'll just assume Philp and Slater are dead too. And as soon as one con has presented itself, more follow.

Con: even if the USUF do come looking, they'll have no idea where he is, not even of the location of the house from which he has recently been explosively ejected.

Con: the Uplands are vastly more enormous, and vastly more empty, than any space on the Earth. It would take an army of thousands, combing carefully through the billions of cubic kilometres of nothingness, *years* to be sure of locating Slater. Entire houses go missing for months when they slip the leash of recorded transp signals, and are usually only relocated by chance.

Con: Laking all relevant equipment, he has no means of communicating with anybody.

Con: He is improperly suited, his hand probably dead, and who knows wat chill, or deadliness, might not be creeping up his arm.

Con: He is wearing only an emergency suit; and it is not even his usual suit. He does not know how much air or water it contains, but must assume the answer is little.

All these cons point to one conclusion. He is going to die up here, soaring over the heads of everybody he knows, round and round, a man unsheathed. In a sense, he thinks, he has been pinned to the upper branches of the world-tree and left to die of exposure, which gives his death an ancient and primitively pagan bitterness. Wat was the name of that figure who was exposed, pinned to a great tree with wooden wedges, until he died? Slater can't remember. He ponders. Who was that, wat was his name? Jesus Christ, of course, but he doesn't mean him. The pagan figure.

He comes round the corner of the world and the sun emerges in its splendour, the splendour it wears every day and every night regardless of humanity's attention or inattention; indeed, not only careless of human observation but actively hostile to it. Burn out your eyes! Bright white focal point, look away, mauve afterimage, hanging as insistently in the centre of vision as a bothersome fly in the summertime.

So Slater looks away from the sun, his eyes instead settling on the Earth, and an extraordinary intensity of copper-coloured sea down there. A fat peninsula of land is visible in the midst of this, but because of his unusual orientation it takes him a moment to identify it. Florida. The atmosphere is almost wholly cloudless which means that the sunlight burns uninterrupted off the seas west and east. Indeed, the molten spatterings of orange lakes and watercourses in the middle of the land are precisely the same copper colour and intensity as the shining waters of the Atlantic and the Gulf of Mexico, which gives the landmass a curiously flattened, floating quality, as if it were a moth-eaten wafer laid tentatively over a truer, purer, gleaming red-orange medium.

Being in the sunlight again, he feels warmth in the centre of his blakened hand. Not all dead in there, after all. The suit he is wearing is designed to reflect away a good proportion of the direct sunlight, and has a cooling grid to deal with excess internal heat. His face visor is that place where the heating effects of sunlight is most felt, and even that is minimal. But his exposed hand, blak and heat-absorptive, is burning. He is glad the nerves are dying inside this flesh, or it might be painful.

He thinks of another con: he has no timepiece. He has no idea how long his orbit is taking him. Were he able to time the respective sunrises he would be able to determine if he was going faster, which in turn would mean that he was spiralling downwards and would presently begin to burn up; or slower, which would mean he was floating away from the world. Burnup: a quik death, he thinks. Quikdeath. His mouth is set so firm, his lips closed so tightly, it looks like a healed scar in his face (if only he could see what it looks like!). The alternative is an endless looping round and round, until his air is exhausted and he asphyxiates. He contemplates this for a long while, encouraged that, even in this extreme situation, he has at least this one raw set of alternatives: choke or burn. It's a false encouragement, of course. If he is hurtling faster and faster then there's nothing to do but prepare for a fiery consumption. The choice is not actual; it is only an opportunity to prepare the mind. Which of the two is less obnoxious, death by heat or death by air-lessness? The latter has the advantage that it must extend the period in which he carries on living, simply hanging in the Uplands, which minutely increases his already minute chances of being spotted by someone – of a plane scooping down and slowing on the upward trajectory to nudge up against him. But the former is surely the pre-ferable death, a glorious immolation, turning one's porous, friable body into a splendid meteor to scratch the skies above humanity with brief light. Photonic apotheosis. This train of thought reminds Slater of his friend Philp, with a guilty awareness that his own predicament has crowded this other out of his mind. He realises that he does not know whether Philp died in the fire of the explosion, or whether he survived being ejected into the Upland vacuum and died because he had no helmet on. Experiments conducted decades ago had thrust pigs into the nothing of space to see wat happened to them; and recovery and examination of them afterwards showed a particular pattern – the vacuum having suked the lungs empty of air, of course, but also tended to suk the contents of the stomach into the throat and mouth to spatter in space, such that the desperate lungs, working to draw air bak into themselves, instead inhaled vomit, stinging and poisoning until asphyxia shut the startled brain down. Pity those pigs. Not a pleasant way to go. Philp went into the nothingness without his helmet. Pity him.

He looks again at his hand, holding it close to the visor of his helmet. The naked skin has gone purple-blak all over, and when he looks more closely he can see myriad minuscule beads of red-blak at the base of each individual hair. There's no sensation at all. He taps it with his gloved left hand, and then grasps his wrist and knoks the fingers against his faceplate, but this gives him no sensation apart from a distant jarring in the bone, sensible in the elbow rather than the hand itself.

He pulls his knees up, and wriggles in place, star-kiking clumsily, pulling himself in again, trying to see how far he can reorient himself. The Atlantic is over his head, blue as heaven and streaked with spoorlike trails of cloud. By shuffling and lurching, he starts to swing himself about his own solar plexus. The world slowly hinges about a wobbly axis, inching in uneven increments until it is beneath his dangling feet. Somehow, that feels more natural.

The line of the terminator is fast approaching, improbably jewelled with diamond lights on its far side. Was that quiker than before, that orbit? Or did he just lose trak of time with all his wriggling about? If sunrise was above Florida he must now, at sunset, be over Russia, or thereabouts. *Zdravstvuyte apofeoz!* The lit land just west of the terminator looks parched and hay-coloured beneath its salty, frothy layer of intermittent cloud. Oh but the world, so full of wonder, draws his eyes. The house of the days, the beautiful days, the locker in which all the nights are stowed, the cabinet in which are arranged *almost* all humanity; a cabinet of inexhaustible delights. He stares. He really ought to be looking in the territory of the Uplands itself. He ought to be scanning for houses, or planes. He looks about and about, twisting and wriggling in situ to rotate himself through a full turn. He can see only stars. Some of these stars are probably houses, but he cannot tell which. In the landscape-less topology of the Uplands an astronaut dwindles to a dot at four hundred feet; a house recedes to a mere point of illumination at twice that. He would need to pass within a few hundred feet of a house, or a plane, to see it clearly, or – the more he thinks of it, the more impossible it seems – to be seen by it. And even then, wat? He has no idea of his relative speed: he might go shooting bullet-like past a house; or it might shoot past him. And even if he saw a house, wat should he do? He has no means of attracting anybody's attention short of waving his arms and legs; and even if somebody were close enough to see that they would as likely think he was a tumbling corpse as a live human being.

The sunlight winks out behind the pregnant-belly line of the horizon. Slater looks down again at the scintillated darkness of the globe. There is nothing he can do.

The sensation in his hand dies again. He feels the cool on his face, although his suit preserves the temperature differential.

He looks forward, to where the knife-like edge of the atmosphere gleams a vast thin arc of blue-tinted rainbow as he hurtles towards the sunlight again. And then he is out in the light again, and the sky over the western Pacific is filled with little dappling clouds like a school of white-silver fish.

It occurs to Slater that he ought to prepare himself for death, but he has quite literally no idea how to go about such a task. He is not a religious man. He believes in no god, no soul, no afterlife; and yet the thought that the long, uninterrupted stem stretching from his childhood to now could be snapped off abruptly is very difficult for him to hold in his head. It is not an impossible thing to conceive; he can, by concentrating, fix it in his mind, this notion *I am going to die*, but it slides out of thought without even indicating its departure, and he finds himself in the middle of a train of unconnected thought. The mind is unreceptive to the idea. It is like holding a bar magnet north-down over the north pole of a stronger magnet: with focus and a strong wrist it can be done, but if the attention wanders it slides frictionlessly away.

He thinks of the last conversation he had with his wife. He wishes he had some way to contact her. If she were up here she'd at least be able to pray, or something.

At least I'll die a colonel. This thought makes him laugh, briefly.

He imagines that his wife has secretly been deceiving him, has had her pharmakos reversed and is again flopping in the intensities of bipolar religious faith under the lubricious ministrations of her preacher-man. Perhaps she will pray to God for him, which would at least relieve him of the burden of doing so. His habits of strategic thinking have rendered him incompetent at singlemindedness. It has for too long now been his job to consider all angles on a question, to forestall objections, to plan for immediate victory over the Uplanders to considerable resistance by the Uplanders. Which means that, in extremis, his brain nags with his counterfactuals, wat if there is a god, wat if you go to hell for your atheism?

Wat if he dies, but his soul remains trapped inside this suit, circling forever cold around and round the world, endlessly frozen?

Wat if time slows for consciousness as death approaches, such that, hurtling through the atmosphere and burning, seconds stretch to minutes, to hours, to decades of fiery agony, the sequence unspooling like $x \to x^2$?

Wat if he lives? But obviously – not.

Wat if death is not a blankness, or an altered consciousness, but no consciousness at all; neither thing nor nothing, an actual point beyond which it is meaningless to talk of Slater? This he has always believed to be true, if anybody had asked, but now that he comes to think of it he cannot find it in his mind. Trying to speak about the impossibility of language, or a fish trying to conceive of a medium other than the water in which it swims. Or, no, that is not right, for there are media other than water, even for a fish's mind (gasping and flipping epileptically on the quay under the pitiless sun), where there is no medium in which his mind can exist except life. But the bar-magnet slides effortlessly away, and he finds himself thinking about wat time it is in Florida right now, whether the kids are at school right now, wondering wat Marina is doing and thinking.

It is night again, below him, in Russia. He is definitely speeding up.

He fumbles with the controls in the right glove, unwilling simply to plunge into fire. He needs more time to think through the implications of wat dying means. He's been a professional soldier for more than ten years and he has always assumed that he was ready to die, if his job demanded it, though naturally he would prefer to live given the choice. But now that he is facing the actuality, he discovers a deep-seated revulsion in his heart to the notion. Perhaps, he told himself, he could manipulate the suit to bounce him higher into orbit, slow him down, head himself for a slow cooling. It dawns on him that the cold and dwindling air might just put him to sleep, where plummeting into the atmosphere would plunge his acute consciousness into agony.

But as soon as he has had this thought his spirit revolts against it. It is, he recognises, cowardice. He's going to die either way, so he can at least ensure that he does not die a coward! Dive in, dive in. That's the way to do it.

The suit can generate only a small EleMag field. He pushes the finger buttons in various combinations, experiences a series of lurches and physical shuffles, an anapaestic trill of tremors, a sensation, very slight, of deceleration in his stomach.

He has studied the discipline. He passed the army exam on EleMag physics, in the top fifteen per cent as it happens. As he comes into the sunlight again he knows that on this side, under the pressure of solar wind, the lines of force emanating from the world's pole and sweeping down to the world's opposite pole are squashed together, giving more resistance to the action of an Elemag action. He knows, similarly, that on the nightside the lines are tugged bakwards into an invisible wake, which gives that medium a different feel. This close to the Earth the difference is not as pronounced as it is further out, but it is different enough to be palpable.

He sweeps into the sunlight again, and tries the finger buttons. The reaction is a little more pronounced. He feels the tug in his stomach, and unexpectedly, flips about in a pirouette. He pushes the buttons again and flips round about.

He *thinks*. Electromagnetohydrodynamics. He knows it is a relatively weak interaction, but he also knows that it doesn't need to be very strong to have usable effects. In a plane, with powerful motor generating the sculpted force, it can haul considerable mass up through the air and through vacuum. A single-person suit could never achieve such effects, lifting a body up into space; but perhaps it could – he think of it like this – act as a small paddle thrust into the flowing water. It might break his motion a little, it could slow him.

He wishes he knew how much juice there was in his suit battery. Nobody had expected him actually to go out into vacuum wearing this suit; it had been a mere matter of regulations to dress him in it. Would the ground staff have properly cheked all general-use suits, making sure the battery was charged fully before each signing-out? He thinks, on balance of probability, not.

But then again, he thinks: wat else is there to do?

He pictures again, as he flies towards the terminator line again, the world-tree itself: a vast willow, with a central trunk that pours branches out in all directions to bend and flow downwards. Willow leaves, with their silvery undersides, like colored parchment schematic cutouts of minnows pouring from some spout and seeking the cold waters again. There is a huge willow by a pond at Macquarie's, a leisure outlet not far from his Florida home, where he sometimes takes the kids, and he thinks of it now; he can almost see this tree swaying uncertainly in the breeze, looking more rooted to the pondwater with its many drinking-straw tentacle branches than to the ground.

He is passing at ninety degrees through the slap and thrum of all these branches now.

He squeezes the finger buttons again. The deceleration is slight, but palpable.

If he had some *plan* – or some way of mathematically modelling wat he was doing. But there's nothing.

By trial and error he finds the optimum pattern of pressure to call that gut-sensation, that slight stress in his stomach that indicates slowing down. Press, press, press, and he slows. His heart is shaking at his ribs. It occurs to him that he should try and control his breathing, that he doesn't know how much air there is in the suit, but he can't prevent these vast gulping suks of air.

Suddenly he is very excited indeed. Maybe there is a way—

But this is a much less tolerable position in which to be. He is more scared of his sudden access of hope than he was of dying. Of course he is still dying.

Tug, and he slows. Tug, and he slows. The Earth is in darkness beneath his feet, like a footstool, and he is flying towards the dawn line again, he can see the great curve of dawn lying over the world.

He has a vision of himself standing, motionless (as if there were such a thing as motionlessness!) miles above the Earth. To orbit is to fall towards the Earth and endlessly to miss the horizon. Then, that tug in his gut, slowing some more, he becomes aware of confusion in his thinking. Geosynchronous satellites are standing still, are they not? Yet they're clearly not, they're hurtling at tens of thousands of kilometres an hour. How can something be standing still, as if at the top of a giant pole, and yet hurtling faster than a missile? It baffles his brain.

It occurs to him that his air might be running out already – so soon – and that he is experiencing the early stages of hypoxia. He *knows* all this stuff; he studied it. He's lived and worked in the Uplands for many years. How can it be a problem?

It's not a problem. It's relative. It's the central stem of modern physics, from which all the branches emerge, this understanding that everything is relative to everything else. That's the answer. Although, thinking about it some more, he's not sure how that answers his problem.

The world has swollen. Directly beneath his feet is a dappled expanse of closeweave cloud, like an oblong carpet stretching over Europe and Atlantic. Occasional irregular circular gaps in the coverage resemble primroses. Slater tweaks the controls, pulsing that tug in his gut, and considers this display. Its beauty seems very acute, very vivid, to him: he is surprised that he has noticed so little beauty in his environment over this last year. His mind has been on other things. The optical impression is such that the cloud cover can be read as blue flowers against a white ground, or else as a white fleece dotted with flower-shaped gaps that display the blue beneath, which (of course) is wat it is. But, to his delight, he sees that he can flip from one way of looking at it to another: the duk becomes a rabbit and switches bak as easily as mentally counting. Blue-on-white, white-on-blue, and soon he has passed over the clouds and is heading towards the line of darkness over

Russia again. He tries to remember the Russian he learnt at school, but only a few words remain. *Chort!*

Squeeze, slow, squeeze wobbly-slow, squeeze—

Chort is Russian for devil, he remembers that from somewhere, one of his various language classes. The recollection sets in motion a non-specifically metaphysical series of thoughts. It has never occurred to him before, but does so now, that perhaps life itself needs a ground against which to be perceived at all, in the way that the line of a drawing only *is* a line because of the blank white paper against which it is formed. Has his own life, unbeknown to him, existed only as a series of marks placed on a revealing medium, some substratum or plenum upon which all life is, somehow, inscribed? It's a mystical thought, and makes him heady, unless that's the hypoxia. And anyway (he thinks) it can't be right. We see a drawing of a tree on paper in the same way that we see the lines of a winter tree against the sunset sky, blak bands and strands piked out by the red-gold glory behind: but the tree exists when seen from any angle, against any sky, or even in the blakest night. The tree just is, whether we see it or not.

Spurts of deceleration. He seems to have been over the nightside longer than before. Perhaps these little spurs of invisible energy are indeed snagging against the transparent branches, slowing him, slowing him.

The arc of haze of the world seen face on is a little fatter, blue tingeing into almost invisible long threads of rainbow intensity on its outer side. The arc itself is straighter.

His fingers are starting to cramp. He gives an overlong squeeze, and for some reason, some invisible kink in the lines of force through which he is spurling, he tumbles forward, spinning over and over. More squeezes, and he rights himself. There are startles in his eye, retinal flashes as if his tumble involved him hitting his head, which of course it didn't. He cheks again, and the flashes are from below. He is over a night-time stormcloud that is shorting its jags of lightning into the Siberian ground below this shroud, and also, equal-and-opposite, puffing short-lived blotches of bright electric light into the upper atmosphere.

He tries to think slow, slow, as if perhaps the patterns of electrical impulses in his brain might even interact with the branches of the world-tree and slow him down further. He is rather taken by this thought, and then doubly pleased that the *thought* about his *thoughts* can only add to the drag he is creating. Think more complex thoughts! The sheer craziness of all this makes him laugh aloud. He's going crazy, with the isolation, and his craziness is manifesting itself as a huge enthusiasm for the approaching death. Bring on the fire! Into the fire!

Will to stand still. Squeeze, squeeze, a series of irregular shakes and heaves in his gut, as the dawn line below him seems to be creeping more slowly, more slowly.

The world has crept up on him. The horizon line is perfectly level now, or near as damniny. It lies like a weighty bar separating the tiklishly bright and diverse world below from the enormous obscurity above. It gives the cosmos a craked, bipolar look, two sides of the same thing separated by a rainbow chasm and on their own terms indistinguishable, as if (blue-on-white, white-on-blue) the world is an immense globe of flawless blak oil above him, and the heavens are a quilted confusion of blue and tan, grey-green, white, yellow and shine, below.

He has no audience for his journey, even though he is flying angel-like over the heads of the busy people below. He thinks: for whom am I laughing? Who is watching me? Nobody of course. The eye is a tiny central circle of blak vacancy moated about with the beautiful bicycle-spoke colours of the iris, radial barcode lines of blue or brown like craks in glaze, and round that the fat glistening white of the eye that bespeaks the fat glistening globe of the eyeball itself. But the Eye of the Cosmos, if you'll, if you'll indulge me in, the Eye of the Universe is all blak vacancy and nothing more, nothing at all.

The line of darkness that indicates where the dusk is seeping through the city streets below him, where the fields and forests are darkening before the night, that line is approaching noticeably more slowly than before; he can actually see the extent to which he has slowed (squeeze, slow, squeeze, slow). He is also close enough, now, to see that it does not constitute a sharp line, like a diecast plastic shield being slid over the curved surface, but is instead a frayed blur from light through purple-grey and purple-blak to darkness. To one side he sees the bright-lit hills of the central EU, the white thorn-shapes of mountains glinting white-pink in the sunset, the little irregular patches of urban sprawl amongst the hills or between myriad tiny rectangular agricultural fields, looking like the scabs grown over grazed skin. Moving his gaze minutes, an inch east, over this living map, he sees the negative: light cities on a blak ground instead of the reverse – bright clusters of lit-glass dust clumped together against a dense volume of darkness. Yet even in the darkness Slater can see gradations, a dusky variety, bruise-coloured, grape-coloured, redwine- and coal-coloured, crowblak and holeblak.

340

His heart is still doing its desperate, rapid, pump-thrust. It is working so strenuously, Slater wonders whether it isn't thrashing his blood to foam and bubbles in his vessels. Squeeze with the fingers, slow, slow.

He moves slowly over the line from day to night. He moves slowly.

Longer pressure on the finger-button produces relatively stable deceleration. He is slowing. The wasteland of darkness below him moks the night sky with its dribbles and scrabbles of random light, spatters of luminous fluid here and there gathered into mini-pools at the location of cities. It's not a patch on the real constellations. It laks the amplitude and the random harmony.

Even though he is round the bak of the world, away from the boiling sun, he is aware of warmth in the soles of his feet. A spark, lazy as a spectral bumblebee, drifts out from his toe and floats up past him.

This, he tells himself, is the beginning of the burning. He has nothing to lose now, except the life in his bloodstream and lungs, the skittery constellations of electrical linkages and decouplings in his brain that simulates thought – nothing at all that isn't already lost. Two more sparks, five more, flitter from the soles of the suit. Heat, convecting through his exposed dead blak hand, creates a wan, unsettling sensation of heat in the bones of his left forearm.

He squeezes all the fingerbuttons. He flips over, feels a surprisingly powerful kik in his stomach. He no longer cares about his orientation, it is all over anyway, so he simply pushes as much resistance to the electromagnetic medium as he can. He yearns to stop dead, like a baseball at the zenith of its trajectory, simply to hang there suspended on nothing except the infinitesimal stretch of a moment. It's impossible, of course.

He keeps the pressure on; his suit's field suks its tiny wake in the giant invisible, impalpable fluid. He wonders: would *spinning* slow him more? Might it maximise his deceleration? Perhaps not – for his mind is incapable of making even approximate calculations or conceptualising or thought-experimenting. Thought, as such, has been burlied out of his skull by the sheer exhilaration. Diving into cold blakness that would, paradoxically, miraculously, soon metamorphose into a consuming fire. The thought of his body disassembled into constituent and carbonised atoms and raining softly down like dust upon the sleeping people below produces an almost exquisite sense of metaphysical pleasure in him. There are worse ways to go. This, he thinks, is wat it must be like to become a god, transformed into something radically different and durable but most of all *infinitely disseminated*, something that the ordinary mortals crawling over the face of the earth will breathe into their lungs, and rub into their eyes in their efforts to rub the smuts away: to become dissolved in the cells and bloodstream of millions.

There is a great lurch, as if he's been hit by a plank. He jerks bakwards, and feels his stomach contents rise and hammer against the throat-sphincter holding them down. His feet twitch, kik, but not because he has willed them into movement. Wat was *that*? It's like he flew into something.

The sensation of warmth inside his forearm is growing, and is no longer pleasant. There is a glow somewhere immediately below his legs – his head (as he topples) – his legs again. The blak Earth and the blak vacuum swap places in his line of sight with clokwork regularity. He can distinguish sparks flying past his visor with the colder, distant stars, shards of reality, splintering and flapping away under the impact he is making. He keeps the pressure on the fingerbuttons.

Cutting into—

A second soundless bang, and a nek-craking lurch bak and around. He's no longer tumbling, he's hurtling bakwards, he's facing the way he came and is shooting bak-first. His arms and legs are out, at 90-degrees to his body, tuked into his trail, and he flitters like a shuttlecok. Everything is blak, except for the jarring epileptic fliker of random lights. Then, with a sharp blak smell (which must be inside the suit) the pressure in his gut is released. Has his EleMag net given out? It must have given out.

He is falling now, spine-first. His legs and arms are pulled irresistibly in front him, tuking into the slipstream of his bakward plummet, four tugs on four marionette strings, until they are all parallel with one another. Collapsing continually bakwards, his limbs trailing after him, down into the void. Won't be long now, he thinks. He thinks that. His vision of a rapidly receding and infinitely lengthy tunnel.

With willpower, and straining his muscles, he pulls his hands towards his face. His right hand is still there, but twitching his fingers has no effect. The stench in his suit is making him cough.

He finds he cannot simply fold his left arm in to bring the hand to his visor. For some reason the elbow will not simply flex, the muscle is sluggish, the suit fabric has somehow stiffened or frozen, he doesn't know why, he can't think why. It's hot now.

He drops the left arm, pivoting it at the shoulder, down towards his hip, levers it out into the slipstream, and tries to bring it up. He is choking, gagging and coughing, although the suit's inner systems have purged the contaminant and his vision is clear. Perhaps his air supply is now at this moment giving up. Becoming exhausted. The little slab of hardware that stores and circulates and scrubs the air is woven into the bak of the suit, and is enduring the worst of Slater's re-entry friction, so perhaps that has something to do with it. It hardly matters now. His lungs spasm, gulp air, and he pulls his left hand round and up, and holds it in front of his visor.

The hand is glowing, like a blak and heated coal. There are no fingers on it any more. As he watches, with a dream-like marvellousness, tiny flames suddenly fliker into life upon it. He is burning, burning, *o lord* – actually on fire. There's no pain, it doesn't hurt. It dazzles him. He holds his hand away from him, and it flares brighter. Down he plummets, his arm a flame-tipped brand.

Something in his eyes stops working. He's gone, he's under.

He dreams, and whilst he experiences the dream, immersed in it, he is simultaneously aware of the fact that he is dreaming, and that this may be the last dream he ever has. He's in an Upland room with Gradi and the Vice-President, but it's an impossibly long room, there's something from earlier in the dream, or from another, related, dream, which he can't remember, and this bothers him. Gradi is explaining how fireworks operate. He turns to look at the Veep, but whichever way he turns he sees Gradi, as if she nips in front of him, or perhaps as if there are many Gradisils. But just as he sees that one of the Gradis is actually Marina in disguise, just as he is about to demand of her wat she is playing, the dream

stops—

Is this wat happens when people die in their sleep? Do they begin a dream which then shears off, incomplete, with nothing to follow and no consciousness to worry that the strands were not woven together, as the waking sleeper often does, rising from bed and stumbling into the bathroom thinking all the time *wat was that*? It is a sort of Russian-roulette dream that will end, Slater knows, not because his alarm clok has chirruped, but because the consciousness that attends the dream has ceased to be. The pistol has six bullets in its six chambers, it's just a question of when the finger squashes the trigger bak to—

Shh. There is a great shushing. A giant is trying to hush him to sleep. It is a waterfall, he is trapped on his bak in a waterfall which is pressing an enormous weight of fluid constantly against his faceplate and front. That's not right. The faceplate is pressing against his face. That's not right. There should be a space between his nose and lips and the plastic of the faceplate.

It's grey, the colour of predawn.

The faceplate has a split in it. He can't be sure wat he's seeing; it's not easy, even opening his eyes. But he opens his eyes, and it takes him several moments before he realises that the gash in the sky in front of him is a line in the material of his visor, and not the veil of the sky itself rent across.

He's been sleeping the sleep of the hypoxic, but something has woken him. Perhaps this powerful headache. This ache, ow, in head, ah-ah. Man, that's *bad*. Or, now that he gathers himself enough to notice it, perhaps this spread sense of soreness across his bak, his shoulders. It occurs to him to chek his left hand. He holds it up in front of his face, but it doesn't seem to be there. Be there.

There is a crakling noise from his faceplate, he doesn't know wat that is.

Suddenly he is very awake, very awake, adrenalin is lurching and sparkling through his bloodstream. Fuk. He is in air. He needs to think quikly. He thinks: *I must think quikly*, but the quik thoughts do not come. He had slowed himself in orbit, slowed himself to a point where he was indeed simply standing on nothingness sixty miles above the Earth, and then he fell – down. He tries to see past the big gash in the centre of his vision, he twists his body, which stings and groans in painful complaint. He tries to sit up, as if he is on a bed, and then laughs at the stupidity of it; for he is in no bed, he is cushioned all around by rushing air.

He pulls his mind bak, hand over hand as if hauling in a great wet sea-rope from some vortex: those jumps over the Mojave, part of the basic training. Remember to remember those. Stepping over the metal lip of the plane's square open ass into the burlying air. Falling; remember falling. Slater had developed this little trik, of slipping the catch off his mind, letting his gears spin free, so as not to be thinking about wat he was about to do. Otherwise he wouldn't have been able to do it. It wasn't a fear of heights, exactly, since unlike being on top of a tall building there were none of the usual visual clues as to height, it didn't, actually, *feel* as if one were high up – it was a non-human perspective. But his brain knew that wat he was doing was dangerous, and that orderly part of his thoughts disliked that: the pull-down menus in his mental map behind which were stored, methodically and according to proper protocols, all the facts and probabilities of living: all the fatalities and serious injuries of people who had stepped out of planes, just like this one, wearing one of these parachutes (centuries-old technology upon which nobody seemed to have improved). He had read all the books.

He knew that terminal velocity of an average man, averagely laden (for, counterintuitively, the terminal velocity of a fat man is greater than that of a thin man) is about one-hundred-ten miles per hour, before the parachute is deployed. Laking a parachute, this means the average man's body (averagely laden) will hit the ground at one-hundred-ten miles per hour. Slater's instructor, those years ago, had explained it in these terms: imagine standing on top of a groundeffect train travelling at that speed, wind in your hair, it's even exhilarating, except that you're still standing there as the train sokets into a tunnel. The train goes in, but like a toon you are left behind, flattened onto the overhang of the tunnel. Would you expect to survive such a collision?

He wriggles, and his skin complains. The pain sharpens his mind, fills him with swear words. Is that crakling noise *coming* from his skin?

On the other hand, terminal velocity means that you'll hit the ground at that speed whether you fall from a thousand feet, or, as in Slater's case, from a third of a million feet. It will still be fatal. The height below which most fallers survive but above which most falls are fatal is thirty feet. His instructor had told him that. Slater can recall his instructor vividly, Captain Sheridan, a tall man with short-cut sandy hair, flat cheeks, eyes like willow leaves, bony wrists and long, rather scholarly hands in constant motion as he explained aspects of parachuting. Thirty feet is not much. One full general died after falling from a military jet, and it was still on the ground. He had been waving from an open door, and lost his footing, fell through just enough of an arc to break his nek.

The noise of rushing air is so complete, so immersive, that Slater can only become aware of its full intensity by actively concentrating on it. Belatedly he becomes aware that the air is touching his skin. There are holes in his suit, like cigarette burns. With his one hand he reaches behind him and fumbles at the mothwork that heat has done upon the bak of his suit. Looking down his front he cannot see similar damage on the front.

He tips himself forward, is falling face down. The cloud thins.

Breathtakingly, the grey dissolves away around him, like salt in clear water, and the world reveals itself. It is terrifying and beautiful, two apperceptions that often go together. The sun is very low, resting on the furred horizon like a drop of wine on the rim of the sky's upturned wineglass. The world below is misty, with occasional jaggy prominences rising above the opacity. He looks for snow; a snow-banked mountain flank upon which he might – just conceivably – land, upon which he might obliquely roll and not die. But there is no snow. The fog is thiker in some places than others; where it is less opaque he can see green hills, with the tessellated press of many different kinds of roofs. He looks to the horizon again; the line is fuzzy with trees. He looks down again, and sees the towers of a suspension bridge priking through the silk undulations of the fog layer. That means a river, a major road, a built-up area.

This is no good at all. Houses, roads of stone, these are bad things on which to land. There might be a river, but to hit water flat at a hundred miles an hour would be exactly the same as striking concrete. He needs to slow—

The flaw in his vision, this crak running down the middle of his vision, is quivering. Perhaps it is about to give way.

His training tells him to roll four-point, ankles, thigh, hip, shoulder, to distribute the deceleration. As if that's going to make a difference at the speed he is going. The biggest fist in the solar system this side of Jupiter is flying towards him at over a hundred miles an hour.

There's not much time to thing. Not thing, think. But even if he had all the time in the world to think, his brain isn't much help. His skin is burning, and with a half-reflex, half-cunning motion of his right hand he fumbles at the catch that releases the fastener down the front of the suit. His gloved fingers are too crudely plump to effect it. He reaches over with his left hand to unfasten the right glove and realises, after long fruitless seconds that he has no left hand, none at all.

He knoks at his visor, but his hand flies away like a ball bouncing on stone. The wind takes it and flaps it up in the air, over his head somewhere. This won't do at all. This will not do at all. He pulls the hand bak down, but the muscles feel stretched and weary, the tug gone out of their elastic. It takes active willpower to pull the hand bak down. With more focus he knoks at the faceplate again, trying to get inside. With one or other of the repeated, rather frantic little blows the crak spreads and a huge noise of wind fills Slater's ears, chills his face. He thrusts his hand in at the space, bumbling over his own face, forcing the hand to the side by his right ear to give his teeth the purchase on the tag that released the grip at his wrist. It doesn't seem to want to – something, presumably adrenalin, is giving Slater a renewed mental clarity and sense of urgency. The noise of the air is very large, very loud. He bites down.

He pulls, and his hand slips out of its sheath naked in the freezing uprush. Almost at once he starts to lose sensation in his fingers' ends, which is triky because it's a delicate operation to find the frontal-tag, the thumbnail-sized stiff button that must be rotated three times counter-clokwise. He fumbles at his chest. The ground is coming towards him at a hundred-ten-miles-an-hour. The wrist of the glove, its hand still in his faceplate, is flapping like a propeller. It slips, and the bikering noise increases in volume, and then it is gone, whipped away to fly through the air.

Briefly, Slater gets a blurry glimpse of the ground hurrying indecently towards him. He tries to pull apart the front of his suit, but the tag needs another twist before it will unbukle. This is all crazy. Is it possible to – there it goes, and the seam unzips smoothly down, and—

(//uurgh//) the whole of Slater's suit inflates with ice-temperature air blown in at pressure. His sleeves go stiff, his trouserlegs go stiff, the wind's deathly cold intimacy reaches round to the small of his bak. The little wormholes burnt into the bak of the suit vent just enough air to keep the suit inflated. He can feel himself yanked upwards, as if a cord has been pulled, but it does not seem to slow him very much, because—

and he goes into the mist. That's the end of him.

nineteen. Poodle-hoops

The American media give little time over to reporting the counterattak, in part because it coincides with a much more public-fascinating brouhaha concerning the subcutaneous technical augmentation of several key pitchers' arms in the World Series, the putative legality or illegality of this, wat it means for the future game, and so on. The deaths of US servicemen *is* news, but the US media spin it according to governmental feed: terrorist action, under control, outrageous assault, the very fact that you can imagine just the sort of thing the media say shows how easily these interpretations fit into human pre-conceptions. Meanwhile, after five pitchers admitted to 'MA', or Muscular Augmentation, the Southern States become the first major league team to pay for their key *hitter* to be similarly beefed up (*metalled* up would be more like it). 'The Courts are sitting on it,' said SoSta manager Vinny Shenin, 'so we decided to act. They can sort the legal out later: this is the future of baseball. Right now we got our sights on the Alaskans.'

> Two runs crossed the plate, a scoreless tie broken, the game not even four innings old, and the stands above the Southern States dugout began to tremble, then shake, then earthquake with the aggregate excitement of the crowd. For all we reporters knew, GWB Stadium was about to come apart at the seams – but it neither alarmed nor annoyed us. It may have been the most beautiful thing I ever saw.
>
> 'Words can't describe it,' SoSta center fielder Bryan Synagog said. 'This is the most thrilling baseball I ever seen. The game has crossed into the twenty-second century. The future is ours'.

Like partygoers so wholly focused on getting to their party to have A Good Time they don't quite register wat distressed Mom on the phone is telling them about Dad in hospital dying, actually dying now, storing it away 'til later when they'll be prepared to hear those words, and be

348

sorrowful *then* – just so, these media indulged the story. It had been coming to the boil for many months. Military kerfuffle and niggle was the second lead, but all eyes were on the GWB Stadium. And then, like those partygoers, America woke the next morning guiltily hungover. News feeds started siphoning EU reports: for the EU had dropped all other stories to cover this one thing, this Upland counterattak. It was the end of American domination.

Finland-EU was the first officially to recognise the Uplands as a new nation, self-determining and under the presidency of Gradisil Gyeroffy. It was hot-headed defiance of America, and for three long days the rest of Europe held its breath whilst the US corpus diplomaticum blustered and raged. But you don't invade a country for diplomatically recognising another, even another with whom you are at war. And besides . . . and besides . . .

In the US the story filled a day; and was demoted again to second lead after twenty-four hours, because a better story came along – a major-league soap star revealed that he had been conducting an incestuous sexual affair with his own brother. The revelations came after the screen star (he hid a secret actual name, rumoured to be the unappealing *Krolik*, under the screenname Gentian de Koch) had ended the relationship, as a direct result of the spiritual guidance of the Church of Christ the Green Man. De Koch gave a press conference at which he confessed that it had been a pharmakos adjustment to his sexuality that had provoked the long-term sinful relationship, something he and his brother had freely decided upon as part of a twisted desire to explore the territory on the far side of taboo – neither of them previously being gay, or intrafamilially inclined. This Church (116,000 registered members) was pushing its campaign to have pharmakos outlawed, as meddlesome perversions of divine design, whether gay or straight.

For a day this was the main lead; and it spilled over into a second day when the celebrated names of US popular culture pushed their pro- or anti-pharmakos lines to myriad reporters; and into a third day when many of the anti-pharmakos speakers were decloseted as hypocrites who maintained their seductive flesh or career-enhancing sex lives through pharmakos, pharmakos and nothing but pharmakos.

Then, *out of the left field*, as the phrase goes, ('*Words can't describe it, baseball has crossed into the twenty-second century*') something happens to push Gradi's counterattak up to the position of prime lead in all US news outlets, and it is this: the President himself, Daniel Veen himself, corners his Veep and two senior military men in a non-secure room – a hospitality room in a sports facility called the Lion Center, as it happens

– and speaks certain inflammatory words. His raging, his swearing and, alas, the projection of a certain quantity of spittle from his fast-working lips, are all captured on an unnoticed camera located on the wall, and of course immediately sold to the news. This is a side of the President that few have seen before. He has always presented himself as scrupulously courteous, religious, pious, controlled, calm, patrician. But here he is so angry he cannot keep his eyes open, as if anger above a certain level becomes narcolepsy. He is so angry his cheeks go purple-red, and he trembles visibly like a palsied old man.

'This fuking *woman*, you told me you'd have her in fuking *custody* by the end of last year, and now she's fuking throwing *roks* at my *caravan*? Fuk her. Fuk her EU-sponsored *ass*. Why isn't she dead, Johan? Why did you *fuking* promise me her corpse and then leave her alone to fly fuking planes and explosives' (for some reason the president drew this last word out enormously) 'at my troops? We've gone, Johan, General, from one single casualty to *over five hundred*, you want to tell me how that has happened?'

And as the Veep begins to try and answer the President's emphatic questions, he is interrupted by Daniel Veen continuing his tirade.

'I absolutely ref*use*, I refuse, I will not be *put on the same level* as this fuking woman by the international media. She's in charge of fewer people than a fuking *small-town mayor*. I *will not be seen* to be butting heads with this woman, I won't be seen *negotiating*, Johan – with this woman, as if any small-town mayor flies on the same level as the *President* of the United States.'

'Small-town mayor', is one phrase that, excerpted from this rant, will haunt the administration afterwards (there is another, which we'll come to in a moment). Had the US suffered militarily at the hands of a major world power that would have been one thing: but for the entire US air force to be defeated by a nation literally no bigger than New Bedford, Massachusetts, or Big Timber, Montana, or Milledgeville, Georgia – well, *that* reflects something worse than defeat on America. That reflects ridicule. The President knows it will diminish him. People will stop thinking of him, as they have been doing, as *Big Dan Veen*, and he will begin to assume Lilliputian size, proportionate to his Blefuscan antagonist, this tiny half-Euro, half-Japan woman.

And then, destined to become even more mokingly famous than 'small-town mayor', is the President's parting shot. This is something that will simply leap from the idiom of the screen media into popular consciousness, perhaps because it chimes with the irrational ludicrousness of the whole circumstance. The Veep, sombrely, tries to reassure his

President that 'I don't need to say how sorry we all are, sir': but at this piously conventional expression of beta-male subordination, the President, Big Dan Veen who has become shrunken, shrieks like a parakeet: 'it's poodle-hoops, Johan,' he cries, and sweeps from the room.

This is the phrase that occurs and reoccurs in myriad media contexts over the following weeks. Nobody is quite sure wat it means, precisely, beyond (obviously) indicating that the President considers this whole matter insultingly absurd and demeaning, incompatible with his dignity as President of the world's only superpower. But *poodle-hoops*? Is it some phrase from Veen's childhood, or some frat-house slang? Is it gibberish conjured on that spot from his subconscious? (in which case, wat did it signify? Dogs? Hula? Food? Piddle? Whores?). The oddity of the phrase eclipses even the President's ill-chosen repetition of the word *fuk* in American disapprobation. Indeed, having committed so thoroughly to red-blooded obscenity throughout most of the speech, the Prez would have done better to have concluded with a straightforward expletive, 'It's bullshit, Johan' or 'It's fuked up, Johan.' As it is, the preceding torrent of *fuks* makes the conclusive 'poodle-hoops' seem not only coy but, worse, dishonest, effeminate, even a little deranged.

The American news media produce, in refluxes either sober or satirical, these two phrases over and over. 'Small-town mayor.' 'Poodle-hoops.' To have one's face slapped by a small-town mayor, when one owns the largest face in the world! To have become caught up in the poodle-hoops of some piddling military adventure, to conquer mere vacancy a hundred miles over people's heads – and for wat benefit? It was absurd. Absurdity must be coursed to its source, and President Veen stands suddenly revealed as the fountain of all corroding American absurdity. Poodle-hoops? *He* is poodle-hoops.

A widow stands in the Media Square, Washington DC, with a holographic placard on which spectral letters spell out: *my husband died in your war, Veen; is* that *poodle-hoops*? There are dozens of virtual gatherings, and several virtual riots, including one that swamps the East Coast BookTalk web with violent posts and aggressive linkage, collapsing it under the sheer virtual weight of bodies, and seventy per cent of the attendees are anti-Veen, anti-war.

Pundits argue that the twenty-second century was doomed to be the century of American decline. Why are we tangled in this absurd war with a small-town mayor? Wat does that make Veen? *Another* small-town-mayor, that's what. We used to be the world's ultra-power; now we're a thousand houses and a regional walmart. Small patches of worn grass, a baseball diamond, dust sinking down.

351

Visuals represent the tactics of the Uplanders. Phrases start to echo through news coverage: brilliant, audacious and courageous to describe the Uplands. Doomed, hubris and over-stretched to describe the American programme.

Uplanders and their supporters feel the throb of new life in their cold dead bodies. We are *not* dead. We are not *dead*. It is not *we* who are dead.

Suddenly, in a gaggle, other EU nations scramble to recognise the Uplands diplomatically. Finland-EU now looks prescient and politically astute rather than rash. A dozen other countries open negotiations with a view to establishing relations. This completely changes the legal situation. Two-thirds of the suits filed by the US Corps Legal are made redundant by the new status of the enemy territory. Military lawyers scrabble and scurry to assemble new paperwork, to submit to the Court. But it is now that the many Upland sympathisers, some of them actual Uplanders trapped on the ground by hostilities and eager to get bak up, begin their legal counterattak. Representatives sue the US for every single civilian casualty. One suit disputes the term 'territory', used ubiquitously in all American legal documentation to describe the Uplands, on the grounds that vacuum and emptiness is not territory; three judges agree that this suit has *grounds* – which is to say, it is not shuffled into the *minor* or the *vexatious* files, but rather moved to the front, green-lit for further discussion. And if it is adjudged meritorious then the whole US legal assault will crumble. But just as the US start to marshal a complex and expensive series of countersuits, the Upland legal team hit again. More than thirty separate suits are filed that describe the events of the last year as 'a siege' – something with only antique legal precedence, and which therefore threatens to unpik the whole elaborate web of US legal work. The US Corps Legal is faced with the very real threat of having to start all over again *ab initio*, and moreover to do this without the guidance of the senior officer who oversaw the initial legal assault, Slater himself. All is chaos. The Veep, taking personal charge of the collapsing campaign, receives report after report reiterating the general point: it's chaos, sir. They've out-manoeuvred us in court sir. With limitless money and lawyers we might still – just possibly – reclaim the legal initiative, but it'll take a year minimum, that's minimum. Sir.

Satirists and cartoonists take to portraying Veen as (a) a poodle with tiger-like hoops of colour, perhaps red and white with stars circling a bewildered and purple poodle-head, or (b) as a skinny elongated human form stretched topographically out into hoop, feet lodged in mouth, circling the large canine form of Gradi herself, not unlike the rings of Saturn. One columnist notes that the size of the USA (x million square kilometres) is trivial compared to the much larger size of the Uplands (x billion cubic kilometres). 'We know which small town is the smaller.' 'If this is so important a war,' asks Aqua Taurus, the West Coast commentator, 'then why did Veen delegate it to his Vice-President? Why not take *personal* command?'

Gradi sits in front of a phone to talk to American media from some anonymous location. She is wearing a shirt on which is written the phrase Small-Town Mayor. She cradles in her lap (oh *rare!*) an actual poodle, around whose poodly waist a hoop-ish circle has been tied. It's witty. It almost doesn't need the warm smile on Gradi's face to establish it as the iconic wat-me-worry image of the year.

Aren't you worried, ma'am, that Quanjets are circling the blakness all around you, seeking you out, hoping to kill you? They've been trying for a year now without success, says Gradi. *Aren't you afraid of dying?* Of course I am, says Gradi, but any soldier fighting for a cause in which they truly believe sets that fear aside. *And wat cause is that?* Freedom, says Gradi, immediately, losing the smile and creasing her brows just enough to indicate seriousness.

The President stands next to his Veep, standing in the strong wind at Arlington, saluting two flags: the Stars-and-Stripes, and the military colours of the USUF, silver sphere on purple ground. The pennants wriggle on their poles like the wind shaking crumbs out of a pair of gaudy tablecloths. But he's looking old, and worse, he's looking small-town.

The military are paralysed. They put every plane they have in the air, flying as many from Fort Glenn as they can, and lifting the remainder from the ground (*regardless of expense*, thinks a forlorn Jon Belvedere III). But nobody has the nerve to order massive retaliation, with the massive loss of life that would result. The legal situation has not been properly prepared, so such an assault is enormously risky; and modern war-makers are massively risk-averse. War-makers apart from Gradi, that is. So the planes do little but fly-by. One or two high-profile raids on specific Upland houses, carefully preplanned, legally prepped and covered by high-calibre cameras for later media dispersal, capture two dozen Uplanders. These people are described as 'prominent' Uplanders, but nobody downbelow has ever heard of them.

Then there is a second wave of Upland attaks. Four Upland planes come sweeping silently through the silent medium, accelerating from a high orbit to a low one on trajectories that are plotted to pass directly through Fort Glenn. The defences of that base – considerably augmented since the counterattak – fire fusile projectiles in a grapeshot pattern to puncture the skins of any illegally approaching spacecraft. But, once again, the Americans have underestimated the Upland military strategy: for although all four planes suffer multiple depressurisations and one pilot is killed outright, these are all suicide missions, *kamikaze*, horatii-at-the-bridge. They plough on through the flak, and crash, one, two, three, four, into the main fabric of the Fort. They are loaded with explosive material instead of passengers, and when the bursts from these meet the rushing oxygen paked into the pressurised Fort it kindles, instantly and briefly, with panel-shredding force. There is no fireball, as might happen inside the atmosphere; but there is a wrenching glitter of debris flung in all directions. Only one single blok from the many out of which Fort Glenn was assembled retains its internal atmospheric pressure, clamping airtight doors; and it is sent spinning on an elliptical orbit whose closest approach heats its skin and drags it into terminal decline. It burns up, a fireball visible over much of Western Russia.

This total loss – one hundred and two personnel, two (doked) spaceplanes, all the hardware and other *materiel* – at the cost of only four Upland pilots' lives, heaps humiliation on the already prominent mound of ludicrousness. With this act, Gradi seals her fame in the EU forever. Crowds, delighted at this blow against the power that had cowed them for two decades, gathered not only in virtual space, but actually – floking together in spontaneous dancing masses in town-spaces and fields, and providing the authorities with certain problems in maintaining social order, and clearing up the mess afterwards. People chanted *poo!-dle!-hoops!* in delirious unity. The US condemned as terrorist the suicide-bombers who had taken the lives of so many American heroes, and Upland lawyers immediately filed suit for defamation, libel and criminal slander against the US both for 'suicide-bombers' and 'terrorists'.

Another meeting between the President, the Vice-President and senior military staff, is not accidentally or illicitly recorded. It takes place in one of the most thoroughly debugged and secure rooms on the planet; and it concerns the options. Wat are our options? Veen asks. He repeats the question.

Militarily, the options are wide open, Mr President, sir. The military staff, including a very worn-looking General Niflheim, assure the President that they can still launch into space without difficulty – launch from ground bases, it is true, but the beauty of Quanjets is that they can fly from anywhere on the planet straight to orbit, sir. At your order, Mr President, we can start a series of raids that destroy the Uplands house by house. Pik it clean, Mr President, house by house, until the Uplanders surrender unconditionally.

But the Legal staff look very uncomfortable at this. The legal situation is very complicated, sir, they say. If you start a systematic house-to-house destruction policy it's going to lay us open to suits alleging genocide – suits it'll be *very hard* to defend against. ('Impossible, more like,' opines one Officer-Legal, sotto voce but perfectly audible). That will cost the States billions, perhaps trillions: there will be suits from every family member and friend of every dead Uplander. There may well be reparations, punitive fines. It would be crippling.

'So give me military targets,' growls General Raduga. 'And I'll fight against military targets.'

'But that's the whole point,' says Eksreher, a General-Legal. 'It's hard to identify *any* military targets in the Uplands – any legally unambiguous military targets, I mean. Apart from planes actively attaking US forces. Those are legitimate targets, we'll shoot them down for sure.'

This does not seem to satisfy General Raduga.

'Politically speaking,' says the Veep, Johannes Belvedere, looking grim, 'this whole escapade is costing us kudos, it's vampiring kudos from us. I mean, both as a nation and an administration. EU is in open revolt against our influence. The rest of the world is delighted, frankly, at our dilemma. My opinion: anything that smaks of genocide would cause such damage to our standing in the world for which no conceivable benefit from winning the Uplands could possible compensate.'

Everybody looks at the President.

'So,' he says, under half-closed eyelids, his lips straight, his expression an enigmatic opacity. 'I guess the question is.' He breathes in. 'If we launch a fightbak, killing houses and their occupants, we need the Uplanders *to capitulate right away.* If they do that, we can gloss the houses as military targets – fight that out in court. If not-too-many Uplanders die then the genocide word doesn't get bandied. That way we win. But – *but* – but if the Uplanders hold out until the bitter end, then it all comes unravelled for us: legal and political disaster, accusations of genocide, ultimate defeat, resignations, prosecutions.'

Nobody disagrees with this presidential assessment of the situation.

'Lawyers,' mutters General Raduga, for like many military men he cannot quite believe that the strong muscles and iron talons of the army can be smothered by this anaconda thing called law. Lawyers object?

Shoot the lawyers! Except, except, wat nobody needs to rehearse in this meeting for its knowledge is so common, the world legal superstructure is actually the American legal superstructure swollen to globalised dimensions. To dismantle it America would have to unpik its own fabric of being. There's no way round it.

'It'd be a gamble, then,' says President Dan Veen. 'The unknown is the lengths to which Uplanders will hold out, even if they're dying steadily. How long will they hold out?'

'They'll give in almost immediately,' asserts General Raduga, and then looks around as if defying the others to disagree with him. 'It's a gamble worth taking. They're at the end of their tethers, sir. One push from us—'

'I disagree,' says General Niflheim.

He speaks.

Everybody looks at General Niflheim. There is his desert lichen skin, his eyes overmoist, almost brimming, like a pool after heavy rain, in which like strands of lurid weed many red capillaries are visible. Everybody knows of his cancer diagnosis, his approaching death, and his weird metaphysical proximity to death gives him a shamanic aura. He has, after all, lived for much of the last five years in the Uplands. He knows the Uplands, he's virtually a native. Homo planetensis. The altitude at which he has lived, with its reduced levels of protection against solar radiation, has indubitably contributed to his cancerous state; which is one more reason for attending to him. He's paid the price for his knowledge. He disagrees, which reminds some in the room of the old saw, that there's no discourtesy in saying grunt to a pig.

'You disagree?' prompts Veen.

'I think they'd hold out to the very end, Mr President,' he says slowly. 'I think they have heart, now. This last year or so has toughened them, got them used to hardship, danger. Got them used even to death. They got something bigger'n themselves to live for now. They'll know that by holding on they'll be hurting us. They won't care about the cost to themselves. Most of them won't.'

The President stares long at Niflheim, as if reading every line on his old and dying face as a hieroglyph. There is an electric silence in the room. Then, with a palpable sense of history pivoting, that vast yet silent weight shifting just enough to swing the whole teeter-totter inverted pyramid of everything into a new orientation, he draws his eye away. Is this the way it goes? Do you know? It's an undecided thing, whether history is actually the agglomeration of myriad individual acts of will and motion, little people contributing little to it, Great Folk contributing much, such that the whole narrative is the heap of all these parts? Or whether History is a force in its own right, relatively independent of individuals, like gravity? People prefer to think it's the former, because that gifts their actions with the potency of significance; but maybe it is the latter; maybe history is Force and Economics and War and Religion and nothing to do with the things individual homines sapienses want. Did President Veen have the power – I'm not speaking constitutionally, I'm speaking in terms of History – to order his troops into genocide, to pik the Uplands clean of humanity, to force that narrative to obtain against all the forces pulling in the other direction? You may decide to think, no. And if the individual cells in a plant, growing, were gifted with individual consciousness, wouldn't they think *yes, I struggle and strain and my individual action, combined with all my fellow cells, slowly builds this stem as we reach upwards?* The strenuous, self-splitting wrench of pulling in two the central braided cord that lives inside you, of pushing half your fluids and half your chemicals into a second version of yourself, and then sulking through the pain of regrowing yourself and your budded-self to a dual version of the original – all-consuming, effortful, surely (you think) important? Surely of the *greatest* importance? But perhaps a different perspective is truer, that the tree grows according to the universal logic of trees, not according to the will of a million individual cells; that a tree grows up unless some calamity specifically prevents it, and even then. They say as the twig is bent so the tree grows, but that's a lie. I exhort you to try the experiment. Bend a twig over, and then settle down to watch, cheeks on palms, elbows in the dirt, through the months that follow. This is wat you will see: first on the far side of the bend small new twigs sprout, like the fibres from old potatoes' eyes; then the strongest of these stiffens and hardens and becomes the new stem, restoring the vertical line. And so the tree grows up, as trees always do, regardless of the failure of a disk of cells, and the seemingly terminal setbak. This is how it must be; humanity must grow out from this conker we call world and into the solar system as a whole, just as the tree must grow up; and only active prevention, or disaster, can stop it. Political leaders have the power to inflict misery on many, and even essay genocide, which turns the *many* to *most*; but they don't have the power to change the larger currents of history, rant as they will.

President Veen is not going to order genocide.

There is disagreement in the room but it is already being carried along the lines of flow of inevitability.

'Then,' says Veen, on an indrawing breath, 'I guess diplomacy—' and he is turning towards the Vice-President as he speaks.

'Hit them hard now,' Raduga interjects, hurriedly. 'All I'm saying, say, why *don't* we? – hit them hard, that we set out – exterminate *all* the br— the enemy, quikly. Let Legal sort it out afterwards. Wat's done is done, and if we depopulate the Uplands entirely I don't see how they could . . .'

But the debate about possibilities has moved past him now. Belatedly he realises this and stops speaking. He is sweating a little. He blinks his eyes, blink, blink, blink.

'So,' says the President. 'Wat deal should we hope for?'

'They'll want,' says the Veep, 'absolutely uninterrupted access from the ground to the Uplands, and a cessation of house-to-house searches. For that I think we can get the right to build a new Upland base, free from attak I mean, and I think we can manage to avoid giving up our claim entirely. We can probably get commercial enclave status. We can also keep most of their money in legal limbo for several years, that's a given. It'll be a compromise.'

'It'll need to be a compromise we can spin as victory,' says the President, in a weary voice.

This is so obvious a point that nobody bothers to agree with it. But the Veep adds, for the benefit of everybody, 'We need a longer-term strategy. The Uplands, watever treaty we agree, the Uplands are in our sphere of influence. In the longer-term we need to think of ways of advancing American interests up there.'

'Well, the first thing to do,' says Niflheim, rousing himself, 'is to take out Gradisil. Grab her at the first opportunity – take *her* out of the equation.'

This produces a general murmur of agreement.

Slater

Slater is flown up in a Chinese military transport, and transferred to a US military transport in midair, through one of those newfangled ponto-tubes. Both planes follow a computer-coordinated falling trajectory that create zero g which facilitates the transfer of his mostly inert corpus. Once this human cargo is loaded, the US transport disconnects and slides up into a high trajectory to rise to a programmed peak, so as to fall gradually towards the southeastern corner of the USA, its destination. Slater, strapped face-up on a medical gurney, is settled into his new transport. A medic attends to him.

This medic is a great mass of muscles in military scrubs: a close trimmed hairdo, a nek thiker than his head, that tight look in his face that comes with years of intensive physical training. But his hands are expert, even tender, as they settle Slater into his tech-pallet; and his bleached-blue eyes have an approachable slant to them, catching their patient's eyes as if to share the sly understanding that all this medical suffering can actually be a shared joke.

'Where am I going?' rasps Slater. 'Where are you taking me?'

'They should be taking you to the Smithsonian as an exhibit of the marvellous in the modern age, you want *my* opinion.' He plugs Slater to a monitor with a cable no thiker than a nerve. 'You mind if I put some music on? I work better with music on. Just the radio, you know, just pop songs. OK?'

'Watever you like,' breathes Slater. The distant white-noise hush of the plane's engines is soothing, and otherwise it is silent in the plane. Slater's feelings on the subject of music are entirely neutral.

The medic reaches over to his side and pulls a holographic button out of the air. The music comes on, the ether-thin soprano of Arnault Lariviere, this year's big star:

> Qu'est ce qu'ils savent
> de la'amour?
> Et qu'est ce qu'ils peuvent
> Comprendre
> de la'amour?

That swirlingly uppy-downy melody line that had helped the song climb the invisible rungs of the popchart to its apotheosis as number one, il primo, un, une. French is this year's language *en vogue* for pop songs. The medic is working his way over Slater's left-arm stump, shining some sort of diagnostic light-pen onto the flesh. As he works he is half-singing, half-humming, *de la'aa-aamour*. 'Wat happened to me?' Slater asks. 'I remember falling. I don't – how did I get here?'

'Short-term memory a bit jangled is it? Twas quite a knok you received.'

'I fell.'

'That you did.'

Slater thinks of adding, I fell through the aquamarine sky with my left hand blazing as a torch, but hesitates. It would be uncharacteristic of him to speak so purply. He's not sure, even, where the impulse came from.

'Where are you taking me?'

'The facility at Newport. In the Panhandle.'

Slater considers this. 'A military hospital?'

'No, a dinosaur theme park, of *course* a hospital. It's the new facility, I'm sure you heard of it. Not far from Tallahassee. Now, *on* your side, please, I want to take a look at these Chinese spinal inserts.' He helps Slater to roll in the pallet, and taps at the four metallic pads inset into this wounded bak. 'These are pretty good,' he says, shortly, and with a reluctant tone of voice,

'I remember falling. Mist – and I tried everything I could to lose speed. I used the EleMag coils in my suit to—'

'I *love* this one,' enthuses the medic, gently repositioning Slater on his bak. The song has changed. A spiky, rather jittery drum loop swells with piano-percussion and distant, rather eerie top-end wail, rising and falling, and a layered-over guitar thrum that is delicately stinging. It was a hit last year, but has already acquired that slightly stale intimations-of-mortality stain of the old-fashioned. The vocal is split between three singers:

> *Senshuraku wa tami wo nade*
> *Medeta kere, shakuson, shakuson!*

Japanese was so very much *last* year's vogue in singing in pop. The medic doesn't sing along (perhaps he doesn't know the words), but he waggles his head from side to side with a joyous expression, and tries to follow the intricate drumming with his right thumb against the palm of his left hand.

'I don't really remember wat happened after I went into the mist,' says Slater. But he is not really trying to remember. He'd prefer it if the burden of narrative was taken by somebody else. An exterior perspective would perhaps fix wat he has been through, make it more solidly real.

'Hit a tree,' says the medic. 'First of all. It flipped you about, which is a luky thing. Then you hit a cow.'

'Hit,' Slater repeats, stupidly, as if still trying to wrench his mind round it.

'It was a pet, actually-factually. I heard it was a purple fur-shagged yak-like beast, one of those genengineered creatures that they make nowadays. It b'long a family, was just standing in their garden, probably asleep. I don't know, I didn't see the cow, I only heard.'

'Did I kill the cow?'

'Put it this way. If you were a cow, and a man dropped on you from sixty mile up, you'd expect to live? The fortunate thing is you were flipped over by hitting the upper foliage of the tree in their garden, so you hit the cow back first. That broke some ribs, and tore up your skin some, but all that's fixable. Much more important is the topography of the inside lining of the skull. I can explain why that's important. The bak of the inside of your skull is lovely and smooth and curved, and the perfect shape against which to decelerate the wet-suet of your brain, if deceleration become necessary. On the other hand the *front* of the inside of your skull is jaggy and spiky, full of inpointing thorns of bone and dangerous holes, especially in the area of the nose and the eyes. Decelerating in that direction tends to impale your soft brain on the iron-maiden spikes, and kill you. So you were luky to get flipped about.'

'Luky,' says Slater. 'I—' But there's neither verb or object to attach to that pronoun in his mind right now, and the sentence is not completed.

'Course, falling on your bak has certain other difficulties associated with it. You broke four of your vertebrae badly enough, although there are things we can do with those. Wat we can't really do anything with is your *left* hand.'

'It was on fire.'

'Fire.'

'Where did I land? I was over Russia I think. I remember passing over the terminator, seeing the little lights in the blak like glitter.'

'You landed, Colonel, onto a small town in China, in the province of Ch'ueh, town called called K'an. We just piked you out of a Chinese transport in mid-air. You don't remember that? You don't remember Chinese medical personnel treating you, loading you in that plane? I'd better look inside your head, I think, see if your brain's still there.'

'I think I remember that.' But it's very hazy.

The next song is in English.

> *Wore out my shoes walking, on the eighth day*
> *Come over mountains and down into LA*
> *In Autumn too many leaves just broke their stalk*
> *And the worn-out rain pooled on the sidewalk*

The transport, passing the apex of its trajectory, begins its descent. The sensation of coming down is very gentle, but it claws in Slater's belly and primps memories out of the shok of his mind. He gasps, and clutches at the side of the pallet as if that can save him, his eyes widen a little. But by the time the medic sees his distress, his internal flush of adrenalin has carried him up to a mini-peak of alarm, and then pushed him over the lip into the consequent trough of exhaustion and sleep.

He wakes only when he is being unloaded from the plane, and wheeled through the open air. This is Fort Newport, where Slater will be nursed bak to health. The air is warm, and smells of growing things, of clean vegetation and a pleasant taint of sea-air. Slater can see that he is being moved towards a wide three-storey building very white in the Florida sunshine. Behind this, reaching a long way up, are many trees. They seem positively dripping with bright green foliage, like crashes of verdant foam, a mighty wave frozen in the process of engulfing the settlement. And the blue sky is a bank of colour above them, and it is *more* than blue, a brilliantine, photoshop, flawless blue. Everything is neon-ish and hypervivid, almost at the point of being hurtful to the eyes, not because of its brightness (although it is bright) but simply because of the brimming fullness of its *realness*, of wat the philosophers call its quiddity, the marvellous glamour of ordinary things in ordinary conjunction. That so much intensity of affect can be milked from simple things just because they are real – just buildings, just trees, just sky – strikes Slater with such force of revelation that tears come to his eyes. He can't remember the last time he cried, but he is crying now, at this plush beauty of ordinary things: weeping stupidly, brine flushing down the sides of his face.

The medic is still in attendance, and leans over him now. Slater doesn't know the medic's name, and, since the guy will leave on the plane that brought him, he never will. But the medic knows him better than most. 'No shame in crying,' he says, bringing his face close to Slater's. 'No shame at all.'

'I don't know why I'm crying,' Slater rasps.

'Glad to be alive,' says the medic, firmly. 'Reason enough.' Yes, yes, even Lucifer can feel glad to be alive, still to be thinking, even in his broken body.

A swift slides downwards through the air, wags its wings and soars up. *How art thou fallen from Heaven O* – round and round, throwing O-rings about the world. That's the Uplands, isn't it? A whole world of people who fly forever.

twenty. Paul

And so the war ended. There was a peace treaty that was, in essence, a declaration of Upland victory, although the (two fingers) 'V' word was not used anywhere in the documentation. That didn't matter. Uplanders, living with the bright eyes and hectic complexions of people for whom exhaustion and privation have become witches' familiars, were suddenly free to fly home again, if they chose. The treaty was signed by Gradi, but not sitting in the same room as President Veen. She did not trust the Americans, she said – she said this publicly, frequently, on any media that interviewed her. 'It'll be hot for me for a while,' she said. 'They'll want me, they'd like that – imprison me. You'd never see me again. I think I'll stay out of the way of American forces for a while longer!' So Georgina and Ustinov flew down to Paris to collect the treaty; they flew it up, it was transferred between half a dozen planes, and eventually (the camera on her) Gradi signed. The treaty was flown bak down, signed by the Vice-President, and that was that.

The complex process of post-bellum legal negotiations and tidying up began. New suits were filed, alleging breaches of protocol and demanding reparations, on both sides.

The jubilation was enormous in the EU, and in other parts of the globe. There were street parties. There were thousands of virtual meetings. Apparently – I didn't see any of it myself. In common with the majority of Uplanders I did not avail myself of the immediate post-war opportunity to fly downbelow. I was scared, in fact, of the prospect of walking under the influence of a full g, afraid my shins would snap like wax tapers. During the long indolences of the siege we had, almost all of us, kept up with the elastic exercises of leg-push, leg-pull, of bak stretch and arm-heave – after all, there had been little else to do. But springs and elastic are no substitute for the immersively bowing force of gravity itself. With vaguely virtuous ideas of upping the exercise routines and preparing myself better I postponed my return, even though my children were waiting to see me, and importuning me to return on the frequent phone conversations we were able, finally, to have with one another.

But I held bak, for reasons that were not altogether clear to me. In retrospect it is clear that I was grieving the death of the son I did not have; and that the physical presence of the two sons I did, the two boys who were mine (who were not mine) would have been too astringent an irritant to my soul. But I distracted myself with exaggerated memories of the oppression of gravity. Besides, Gradi had a sort of Upland victory tour to embark upon, travelling from house to house, addressing rooms filled with alarmingly hyper-happy Uplanders – looking as ill-kempt and cadaverous as tramps but possessed by an almost religious fervour aggravated to near-mania by the delight of victory at last after long months in which the only certainty had been the certainty of defeat. They chanted her name so loud, so long, with such perfect rhythmic co-ordination that the meaning drained from the word and it became as random a sound as the echo of surf sounding against the smooth curved interior of a coastal cave.

> *Grah-di, Grah-di!*
> *Grah-di, Grah-di!*
> *Grah-di, Grah-di!*

I asked her: did you know all along that we were going to win this war?

'Know,' she said, in a twisty voice. 'I wouldn't say "know" is the right word.'

'I thought we would lose,' I said. 'I thought it before the war started. And when it did start I thought we *had* lost. I thought it was just a matter of time.'

'Nobody seemed to figure,' she explained, glibly, as if this was something she had said many times over to many people (as it probably was) 'just how vulnerable these big US bases were. Pressurised canisters in vacuum – a little jab would explode them. Nobody seemed to consider that *we* weren't in the same predicament.'

'So you knew,' I said, speaking very low, very quietly. She sensed something in my tone, and her body language settled down, began mimiking the depressed hunch and inward curl of mine. 'You knew,' I pressed, 'that the counterattak would be devastating.'

She paused before replying. 'We had to time it right,' she said, eventually.

'And the best part of a year went by—'

'It was the time necessary to lull the Americans into a sense,' she

364

interrupted. But then she changed tak: 'It served several purposes. It bonded us, as a nation. Those Uplanders who lived through that time have been changed by it, because of the suffering, turned from individuals, selfish and rich, into citizens of something larger. It involved pain, I know, but when you're giving birth to a new nation there are bound to be labor pains—' and she stopped speaking, because that, of course, was my point.

I opened my mouth to speak, but she knew wat I was going to say, so there was little point in my saying it out loud, so I shut my mouth again. You, Gradi, decided not to fight a war pregnant, or with a new baby. You, Gradi, waited until the child in you had died, and only after that did you strike bak. The timing of your pregnancy, Gradi – which is to say, the life of my only child – was an inconvenience to your political nation-building, so you sacrificed the child. Did I make an effort, in myself, to surmount my resentment and forgive her? I did not. It was all part of that same spiritual lethargy, which is sometimes called depression, which had filled me toe to crown. I was pressurised with it, as if it kept seeping out of my bones and inner organs, bloating me with misery. I lived with that stuk, agonised sensation of a pressure waiting to be relieved in some great bursting-out, although it did not come in the Uplands. Instead I lived on in that crepuscular state, eating, sleeping, watching the screen. I accompanied Gradi on the first few of her victory visits to the interminable succession of crowded, dim, malodorous halls, but I suppose it became obvious to those around the Leader that her grey-faced, glum-faced husband floating silently in the bakground was doing nothing more than weakening the more general mood of triumph. I was not asked to cease my attendance. I just stopped going along with her.

Much of wat happened even in the Uplands, then, struk me only at second hand. It is true as far as I know that there was a delighted influx of those Uplanders who had been trapped downbelow by the war, together with a press of excited groundlings whose imagination had been captured by our heroic struggle against the superpower and wanted to move up – to be part of Gradi's clean new style of nation. I did not meet these people personally, although the EU news media celebrated them as new pilgrim-emigrants, leaving compromised terra for a better life in the sky.

It all meant very little to me.

Finally we flew down, Gradi and I, to the strip outside Helsinki. Re-entering gravity was much harder than I had anticipated, even though, in the pessimism of my depression, I had anticipated wat I thought the worst. But this was continual bone-pain, and the crushing asthmatic inability to breathe properly as if my lungs were swaddled with metal hoops. It was that dispiriting inability to do so much as lift a hand to my face to scratch my itchy nose – to struggle pathetically with the hand ten centimetres above the armrest as if trying to break the cord that holds it down, before eventually giving up and letting it collapse bak down. Pphhh. We rode in chairs, slotted in the passenger section of our energCar, bak to the Helsinki house to find our sons waiting for us in the front room. They were both rather oddly still, as if not knowing wat to make of us. They had not seen us for the best part of a year, and during that time their intermittent but real, physical apprehension of father and mother had been supplanted by the virtual figures of *Gradisil* and *Paul* who appeared in the news media (Gradisil appearing a great deal more than Paul, of course). So they did not know to whom to address themselves; their fleshly progenitors eclipsed by the more real light-and-information simulacra that haunted screen media and virtualities.

I am trying to anticipate the sorts of questions you might want to ask me, since this antique medium is not one that permits exchange between compositor and audience. But I am also trying to give you credit. The obvious handful of related questions – *at wat point did you decide to betray Gradisil? Was there a proximate cause, a trigger that pushed you over the edge, or was it a longer-term build-up of resentment? Did you not think of us, when you did this? Did you approach the Americans or did they approach you?* – are in fact trivial variations of the more essential question – why betray Gradisil to the Americans? – and that is a question that concedes its banality and pointlessness as soon as it is asked. Can you really think of an answer to it that will satisfy you? All betrayal is the same quantity. Faced with sexual infidelity, the wounded husband will ask the wife 'did you think of me when you were with him?' The only acceptable answer (though few realise this) is *yes – I only fuked him to get at you,* because this leaves us free, if we are strong enough, to believe that we still occupy the important parts of our lover's mind. But the truth is always no, the unspeakable no; the truth is always I was so caught up in my passion with him, I had no thoughts except for him and in fact hardly any thoughts at all. That's the acid of betrayal. It is not to do with losing unique possession of the lover's body; it is to do with a much more primal terror, of being ignored. The impossibility of coming to terms with the fact that her mind is elsewhere than where you are. And that is why betrayal, to the betrayed, always feels so monstrously unequal. For I *could not* put my mind elsewhere than where Gradi was: she was the whole circular horizon of my life, the sun rose and the sun set and never left where she was. I thought about her all the time; I still do. But the pain was understanding that this complete location within the love object was not reciprocal. Gradi was kind to me, and even sometimes I suppose loving, but only when she was reminded that I existed.

Of course, in another sense, the more specific questions are truer to the heart's experience of being betrayed. Wat haunts the mind of the cukolded man is not the windy philosophic generalisations about *the importance of being true* and *the wikedness of living the lie*: it is the horrid specificities: it is the eagerness with which she got onto all fours to allow him access; or the precise way she lifted her knees up to her shoulders as she lay on her bak; or the crumpled, gasping expression of ecstasy she surely adopted underneath his pounding body; her kissing him *right there*, or begging him to slide his tongue forcefully into her *just there*. It is the plague of details that collapses the mind. I fretted and wept over the specifics of wat Liu and Gradi did in their fuking; and fretted and wept over wat Mat and Gradi did in their fuking. But I endured it, because I knew in my heart that neither of these men had supplanted me in Gradi's heart; on the contrary, their positions were precisely as precarious as was my own, and strange to say, there was a certain miserable consolation in that fact.

But the Uplands themselves, the *idea* of the Uplands, was a different sort of rival. I think I had fooled myself into thinking that it was as much my dream as Gradi's, a new nation that was a new *sort* of nation, and so on (and so on and so on and so on). But I didn't really care. No man, I'm tempted to suggest, can ever really care for something as non-specific as nation. Men don't live and die for ideas. Men are simple creatures; we fixate on individuals, and measure our triumphs in individual terms (I have fuked *this many* individuals, I can see from their faces that *these* individuals esteem me). Women may be different. Wat might we say? That they are better tuned to the hazy indistinctness of futurity, because they carry inside them fleshly kernels that need to be seed-bedded in that realm? They think with their hearts of abstracts like home, land, nation, the various manifestations of the nest they crave hard enough to construct for themselves. This flirts with essentialism, of course; but although pharmakos can swap straight for gay and gay for straight, which is just a matter of taste, nobody has yet concocted a pharmakos that actually interchanges male and female, and I don't believe they will, for this is not taste but essence.

I walked with callipers, dolefully shepherding my boys to the park to play, sitting exhausted with the physical effort on the park bench. Gradi was more knoked over than I had ever seen her, she spent a week in bed. Klara was there, beaming and exentric with a sheer happiness I had never seen before. 'I'm proud of you!' she cried, more than once. 'You took on America and you defeated them! I'm proud of you!'

Wat happened next, after an indeterminate length of time, is that I was approached by two American agents. Helsinki was, suddenly, verminous with Americans in that summer and autumn, immediately after the victory. This was the summer of the elongated negotiations between US and EU, held in Paris, from which city many Americans decided, despite the distance and lak of obvious touristas appeal, to 'pop over' to Helsinki. In fact the main tourist attraction was Gradi herself; so much so that she was compelled to move out of our house altogether, and instead took up a ground-based version of her Upland house-to-house existence. She stayed with a number of different friends, in Finland-EU and Russia-EU, and soon she was commuting, on a deliberately unpredictable schedule, between the ground and the Uplands once more. 'This,' she conceded in one of the few conversations à deux we had during that time, 'is harder than the war, in some ways. The really crucial thing is not to lose the momentum. There isn't the intense US pressure there was during the war.'

'Which is a good thing,' I tried.

'You can't make diamonds out of coal without *pressure*,' she bounced bak, beamingly. 'And now the only person who can keep applying that pressure is *me*.' She was explaining why she had to return to the Uplands, without me, so soon after touching down. I didn't fight it. Wat should I resent?

So she flew up, like a monkey rattling expertly up through the branches of the tallest tree, up to where the sky goes cobalt, and purple, and blak, and she was turned into her screen image, beaming into the camera lens and talking fluently about her new nation, her new kind of nation.

We still had gawkers outside the Helsinki house, even though it was very publicly known that Gradi was not in residence. Finnish authorities erected a fence, but I didn't much care one way or the other. The days laked a sharp enough leading edge to separate themselves one from another in my grey brain.

And then, abruptly (it seemed to me) it was summer. Scrub had become grass, green as money and much more communal. Flies dangled from a million incredibly slender threads and swung their endless pendulum trajectories in the air. The winter (where had it gone so suddenly?) had shrunken to a perfect circle of ice and transformed itself into the sun, fat and white in the sky, the blue-grey depth, the Atlantic swell of blue; and the heat was coming not from that pale disk but seemingly from the air itself, from all around.

I would take the boys to school, for they were now of school age. To be honest (and if I am not honest then there is little point of these memories) it was rarely I who took them to school: Kirsi did, or else Kimoko Hahn, a slender but muscular bodyguard we hired on our return to Finland. But on occasion I grew so weary of the indoors that I would walk the pavements to the nearest Anglophone school. After seeing them off at the gates I might sit in a coffee shop and seek to compensate for the slakness of my mood with caffeine.

One morning, in the late autumn, a woman approached me: slim-bodied, dark haired, with tiny, precise features of the sort that looked prettier in photographs than they did in real life. She asked 'Do you mind if I sit with you?' in an East Coast US accent, and I was so habituated to my misery that I could not think of a way of brushing her off. So she settled in the seat opposite me and nursed her latte in silence for a while. Then she sat bak, rather too obviously selecting gambit number eight (or watever) from her mental palmcomp, and said:

'I could pretend to be an innocent tourist and start up a con-versation,' she said, setting her features into an expression that almost managed *ironic-pleasant*. She smiled at me. Had she studied flirting at the State University of New York her play could not have been more obvious. I looked for a while at her face, and thought to myself that I must be a blank page in watever file American Intelligence kept on the Uplands if *this* was wat they thought would be likely to seduce me. There was no heat emanating from her white-rose skin, her mint-blue eyes, her complete calmness in the face of the enemy sitting opposite the table.

I cleared my throat. 'You obviously know who I am.'

'You've obviously guessed who I am,' she countered, and hazarded a smile. It was the smile equivalent of a chord combined of C, D flat and G sharp. I did not believe her – I don't mean believe wat she said, I mean simply, believe in her.

'Wat do you want?' I asked.

'Just to talk,' she said, leaning in a little. It occurred to me to wonder how far she had been briefed to go with me; to wat extent actual intelligence operatives resembled their screen imitators – physical seduction? Drugs? Money? It was too absurd even to contemplate. I couldn't believe I was in this situation. I sniffed.

'You're really not interested in me,' I said, sounding sulkier and more resentful than I intended. 'Really, you're interested in Gradi, and only her.'

'Do you want me to be interested in you?'

I swallowed. 'That's a little over-obvious of you.'

'Gradisil is an interesting woman,' she said ingenuously. 'But then again' (the smile again) 'you're an interesting man.'

'No,' I said, 'I'm not. I'm dull, far too dull, to be of interest to you, and too dull even to betray Gradisil. That's how dull I am.'

'Betrayal?' She pushed her top lip up and squeezed her thin, proportionate nose into a series of waxy wrinkles. 'You're not reading me right. That's not wat I want to talk to you about – at all. Look, there's somebody I'd like you to meet, right here, right now.'

I stood up. I hadn't even tasted my coffee; it was still cooling. I had *comme d'habitude* over-estimated the amount of muscular effort required by the action of 'rising from a chair' under the soggy omnipresence of this oppressive gravity, and I ended up bouncing ridiculously on my heels. I wished I had a witty rejoinder with which to sting the smile from her face, but I could think of nothing.

'Paul,' she said as I left; not entreating, or wheedling, but simply saying my name. I walked out. I walked along Bulevarden in a daze. The fashion for advertising automata had only just reached Finland, a decade out of synch with the rest of the consumerist world; so the boulevard looked strange, busy with pink humanoid figures bustling and bowing and spouting their pre-recorded spiels in the universal language of advertising, *Why not visit Florida where tourists are welcome? Discovered by Ponce de Leon in the early sixteenth century, it is – Not all vatgrown and seacultured foodstuffs are revolting! Talk to me for further information on an exciting new development in food technology and – This season's 'must-have', tailored books, sensitively crafted by the finest AIs, the classics of literature are now available with yourself and your loved one written in, replacing the original characters, including physical description and bakstory details – Midget toys, guaranteed safe for all children, why not ask me about – Pharmakos can't solve everything; ask me about Dr Nik's Traditional Drug Remedies from the twentieth century – Have you tried the new hydrodynamic telephones? Ask me about their new features –* and so on. Their voices were modulated and pleasant, and the programmed gestures timidly imploring. In France, where they had long since ceased to be intriguing novelties, passers-by did more than ignore these dolls, with their candy-pink and chocolate-brown complexions and lit-up eyes: they shoved past them, cuffed or kiked them, and some people went out of their way to assault them, punching and wrenching them, pulling off their heads. To watch the Finns treat these machines with startled courtesy was peculiarly touching, and rather saddening; because, of course, the machines no more deserved courtesy than did any piece of advertising. I felt disgust inside at the stupidity of this: the same human failure to distinguish the valuable from the valueless. People who reflexively blinker their minds to the sufferings of millions of human beings but who will expend prodigious energy on the discomfort of their pet dog. People who believe their car is alive 'in a practical sense'. Anybody, in fact, who prioritises an ideal which is actually nothing more than a externalisation of some inner yearning or regard onto an outer figment, over an actual: anybody selfish enough to devote their precious human empathy and love and passion to anything inert at all. You can see, of course, of whom I was thinking. For wat is more inert than the idea of a nation?

'You ran out on me,' said the agent, into my ear, with a dripping purity of enunciation.

'You really think,' I said, louder than I meant, and speaking more rapidly and less in control than I wanted, 'that you can insinuate yourselves into my head, persuade me to betray my wife and,' but I couldn't bring myself to say 'my country', since it had dawned on me – there, at that time, in that moment – that I had no country, especially not the Uplands, which was merely a sort of nightmare location existent only in Gradi's mind. So I ended up just repeating, 'You really don't believe you can insinuate yourself into my affections with this 3nimation-style spy-school shit.'

The law was that advertising automata could speak only if people approached them. In practice this approach meant that anybody who walked within a metre of them prompted their voiceboxes into their chatter. I took several strides, trying to walk away from the American agent, and passed by a 150cm manikin, which cooed at me *Real flowers, gentian flowers, delivered to your door! Ask me about the—*

The agent was at my side, matching my steps. 'If I had nothing to offer you, I'd hardly be so bold,' she said.

'Offer *me*?' I said, looking down at her. 'You think I'm interested in . . .' Wat? Nothing again nothing. Trailed off again.

'Paul, come bak to the coffee shop. There's somebody there you know, waiting. Guarding our coffees! Come and meet him.'

I stopped walking. I felt abashed. It suddenly occurred to me that I had not been treating this person properly, as a human being. I had been guilty of wat I deplored, projecting my own resentment onto the shape she made in my line-of-sight, taking her as only a more sophisticated automated manikin. I rebuked myself, and on the upstroke of this purely internal adjustment felt a tremor of sensual possibility. They had been clever: they had not sent a woman who physically resembled Gradi, that would have been too crudely obvious. But there was a certain likeness in this person, in terms of physical appearance only, a quality of self-containment, of dark-haired neatness, that did appeal to me. I had a flash of wat it might be to have her body, naked, underneath mine; of her face pressing itself into the curve made by my shoulder and nek, of my own climactic pelvic vibrato. It can be hard to keep that sort of day-dreaming from one's mind as one talks to attractive women.

'Who's waiting?'

She knew better than to tell me straight away. Instead she led me bak along the Bulevarden, and bak inside the steamy low-ceiling kaffe-shoppe, and there, at the table, was Liu. I hadn't seen him for a year, not since an American military patrol had chanced upon him in the besieged Uplands and carried him away. He looked better than I did: stronger, happier. And he smiled too, as I sat at the table. He started talking, but wat struk me most, as I lifted the mug to my lips, was that my coffee had not gone cold. I felt as if I had returned from the land of where the wild things are, to find my mug still warm.

You won't be interested in most of my conversation with Liu; or if you are, then I must disappoint you. I won't tell you; it's an intimacy I do not wish to violate. Meeting him again, after a year or more, I was less surprised by his conversion to an American cause than I might have supposed. 'It was seeing her on screen,' he told me. I didn't need to ask him whom he meant by *her*. 'It's a very different experience to being with her, in the flesh. I don't know how to describe wat it's like being in a room with her, the charge of it, I mean like electric charge. The charisma, the buzz. I don't need to tell you.'

'No need to tell me,' I said.

'But seeing her on the screen I came to see her as a, well, fraud. If I state it so bluntly it sounds kinda crude, but you need to understand I came to this realisation over several months.'

'Did your, um, hosts,' I asked, nodding at the still nameless American woman sitting beside us both, 'encourage you to, er . . .'

'My name is Lucette,' she said. 'We did nothing to Liu here, except supply him with wat he asked for.'

'It's true,' he confirmed.

'Of course you'd say it's true,' I pressed. 'I mean, if they had done . . . something.'

'It's a misunderstanding of pharmakos,' Lucette put in, 'to think it can be used to alter consciousness, to brainwash or turn people into zombie-loyalists. Surely you know better than that, Paul?'

I smiled weakly at her. 'Science keeps making new breakthroughs,' I said.

'Come come,' she chided. 'You had pharmakos to alter your sexual preference, didn't you?'

I thought of registering surprise that she knew such a secret about me; or perhaps outrage that she was sharing this detail with Liu, and anybody else in the shop who might have been eavesdropping. But instead I say, 'That's got nothing to do with anything.'

'I only mean, did it alter your brain? Did it change the way you think? No, of course not. There's no such thing as a bioelectric pharmakos; it's just hormones, moods, just the mindless organic cellular processes.'

'She's right,' said Liu. 'I don't mean about the pharmakos – I don't know anything about that, that's not my field of knowledge. But I know that they didn't do anything to me, apart from give me access to lots of screen reports and leave me to think about things for a while.'

I looked at Liu Chuanzhi and tried to remember wat he had been like before. He had been in the bakground at first, following Gradi like a pet hound as we all did. Then his star had risen as Mat's had waned, and he had spent much more time with Gradi – attending her personally, going off on trips and missions *à deux*. But even in this period, his glory, there had been a vacancy about him. His heart-shaped flat-fronted face with its pharmakos-perfected skintone, his mouth precisely as wide as the broad nose just above it. His dark eyes then, I had sometimes thought, were indices of an inner emptiness, twin blakholes. Now, in this coffeeshop, his eyes no longer looked empty or hungry. On the contrary they looked glisteningly filled, like blak olives glazed in oil. His whole face was fatter. His whole manner was more contented.

'You look happier,' I said, eventually.

He nodded, and then he said: '*You* don't.'

I almost laughed aloud at this.

'I shall tell you both something interesting,' said Lucette, spreading both her hands on the table. 'When we – I mean the United States of America – decided on going to war with the Uplands, one factor which influenced our timing and our planning . . . do you mind me talking like this?'

She was looking at me. 'Not at all,' I said.

'One factor was our knowledge that Gradi was pregnant for the third time. We, I mean our intelligence service, smart people sitting in committee, thought that this pregnancy would be a constraint upon her. We thought,' (and she was watching me intently as she said all this) 'we thought that she would have to sue for peace after a month or so – at the latest – in order to fly down and complete the pregnancy on Earth. The alternative was that her child, I'm sorry, I don't mean to upset you,' (but of course she did), 'but the alternative was that her child, your child, would die. We didn't think she would allow her own child to die in order to—'

'OK,' I said, gruff. 'You don't need to labor the point.'

'It's a question of whether politics is more important than your own family, your own child. Isn't it?'

This was a fatuous thing to say, and ill-judged on the part of Lucette. If I hadn't already been so deeply implicated in this whole business – if I hadn't already betrayed Gradi a thousand times in my thoughts – I might have walked out at this point, in protest at the crudity of her approach. But I didn't. I scowled. I sat. We talked some more. It continued growing upwards, my beanstalk betrayal.

We talked for half an hour. 'All we want is Gradi, and that only for a brief period of imprisonment. We'd take her to America, try her, lok her up for a year, then let her go. That would be enough to . . . serve our purposes.'

'If you want her so badly,' I said, 'why don't you grab her from here? She's down here, Helsinki, pretty often. It'd be an easy thing, bundle her in a car . . .'

'That's not going to work,' said Lucette, briskly. 'The whole political situation is very delicate. We're in complicated negotiations with EU right now, it's all happening right now in Paris. A kidnapping would be . . . legally bothersome. We might be forced to give up Gradi after taking her. It might jeopardise – no, it *would* jeopardise the talks. It's too risky. But if we took her in the Uplands . . . that's a different sort of territory altogether.'

'I don't know,' I said. But I was expressing practical, not ethical, reservations.

'There are ways of arranging it,' Liu insisted. 'It doesn't have to be tomorrow . . . months may pass. We'll set up a meeting.'

'She'll insist on safeguards. It wouldn't work.'

'That's fine. We'll meet. Tell her we want to talk. Let her lay down watever safeguards she wants. We'll set things up.'

When I came to leave, walking stiffly out with a calliper still on my left leg, I asked. 'Wat shall I tell her about today?'

Lucette spoke eagerly, almost excitedly, about the most efficient method of lying. It occurred to me, watching her, that this may have been a topic on which she became physically, even sexually, excited. A very slight blush, like the pale pink that marks the petrified lips of a sea-conch, was visible in her cheeks. 'The trik with convincing lying is to keep it absolutely as close to the original as you can. When you next see her, tell her – do you know when you will next see her, by the way?'

'No.'

'Never mind. When you *do* next see her, tell her that you met me. Give her my name if you like. Say that you were approached by the American intelligence services. Say that we tried to turn you to our side, although, of course, don't tell her that we succeeded.' This seemed presumptuous to me. I was not turned; on the contrary, I had turned *them*, was using them as a tool for the purposes of giving my one, solitary, dead son his chance at swordplay in the light. But I did not interrupt. 'Tell her that we said we want a meeting, a negotiation. Leave it to her to determine how to make that safe.'

I wasn't really listening to her at this point. I was recalling a dream I had had a week or so before, in which I had rolled over in my bed (I was in my bed, dreaming that I was in my bed, except that my dream bed was larger and sheeted in red silk) and come upon my son; he was a slippery little fish of rubber, a fetus with closed eyes, but he had opened his mouth and started crying when I rolled onto him.

twenty-one. Slater

Marina drives up by energCar from Titusville, leaving the kids with Elizabeta. She does not fly, although it's a four-hundred-kilometre journey, because she doesn't like to fly, she's never liked that business of being disconnected from the living earth. She drives the first few hundred klims, telling herself that it will get her there more quikly, but in fact in order to have something to concentrate upon, to prevent her mind from wheeling with anxiety about her husband. He is the only husband she has ever had. But by the time they get onto route 10 Marina has had enough of the intense concentration. She flips the car to automatic, and stares out of the window, smoothing at one hundred kliks past the great artificial swamp, in which blue herons, as elegantly bodied as hand-turned glass vases, pek and pry, or rise up in floks like dark litter in a strong wind. The swamp, in its flatness, recedes in every direction like a virtual landscape, a mathematical plane.

At Fort Newport she is kept waiting for half an hour in the front lobby, before a military nurse, a trimly bearded young man, takes her through to her husband's room. He is lying on his bak, spinal-plates plumbed into the techne of the bed. There's a screen in the ceiling he can watch if he chooses. His eyes swivel, and he smiles.

'Hi, love,' he says. He doesn't get up.

Her sloping tumble to the ground is interrupted by the chair at his bedside, which collects her hips between its upholstered arms. 'Oh God, look at you,' she says, and then: 'Oh God, look at you.'

'Not too bad,' he replies, as if she had asked how he was feeling, as perhaps he had expected her to. 'Considering wat I've been through.'

'They won't tell me *anything*,' his wife sobs. 'They said, told me, you'd crashlanded in *China*, But why did you choose China?'

He gurns, thinks how to answer. 'It chose me,' he says.

'We've never been to China! Did you go to China on military mission, on time?'

'Mary—'

'And *why* did you crashland? Did your plane *go wrong*? Darling, I was worried. This uniform rang at the door, and he told me . . .' But she gives up this sentence, and tries to convey, with the sheer intensity of her gaze, wat has been so oppressive in her mind. She tries, almost, to beam the state of her emotions directly into him tele-empathically, like that character from the TV show that Alice watches every weekday afternoon, wat is it called? She can't remember wat it is called. But she wishes that instead of the clumsy impedimenta of words she might be able to run a cable from a port at the bak of her skull directly into the port at the bak of his, so that he can immediately understand how unendurably massive has been her anxiety, her resentment and even her despair, how she has wanted to scream, and felt nauseous from waking to sleeping such that she's wanted to do nothing but sleep.

Slater, in his raspy voice, says wat any husband would say in these circumstances: 'It's OK, my love,' he says. 'Don't upset yourself,' he says.

She shakes her head. 'I don't understand,' she says.

'I came down without a plane,' he tells her, in his rough voice. She has to lean in closer to hear him properly. 'Wat? Wat?'

'Seriously – it's the truth. I was in orbit in nothing but a suit. I didn't even have the glove for my left hand. I used the EleMag coil in the suit to slow my velocity, and then slipped down through the air at – barely – less than burn-up temperatures. It's so crazy I can hardly believe it. I can hardly believe it and I lived through it.'

She cannot process all this at once, and so she fixes on one detail. 'You were in empty space without your spacesuit glove?'

'That's right. Everything happened at once – did they tell you how I ended up there?' His voice is like unplaned wood.

'They haven't told me *anything*,' she repeats.

'Well – you've been following the war on the screen news?'

'It's horrible,' she sobs. 'It's terrible. They've had dozens of widows – any of them could have been me! I can't watch it, it's so terrible.'

Slater thinks how to judge wat he has to say to match his wife's mood. 'I ended up in space, outside any plane, just me – I was thrown out, as part of the Upland counterattak,' he says. 'And I didn't have time to put on my glove.'

'But can you *go* in space without gloves? Is that allowed?'

Slater smiles. 'It's not advised, no.'

'Didn't it hurt your hand?'

By way of reply he fishes his left-arm stump, sealed in its plastic bandage cap, out from underneath the bedclothes. He holds it up, and his wife stares at it for long minutes without saying anything.

'Not too handsome, I know,' he says, a little anxiously, seeing the undisguised upset on Marina's face. 'But they'll fit me with a machine-hand. Some of those are very life-like, you know. They haven't come to try and fit me yet – not yet, anyhow.' There is a hollow moment in the communication between them. The expression on her face has not changed. He says, 'Say something, love, you're freaking me out a little. It's not so bad, is it?'

This jolts her into shaking her head, and mumbling, 'I'm sorry my love, it's all just been, it's just all been, it's just *all* been such a shok. Your poor hand! At least you're not left-handed. They'll fit a prosthetic? That's alright. Oh I'm sorry, how selfish I'm being, how are you? Are you OK?'

'Not so bad,' he said, smiling with relief at this more conventional wifely responsiveness. 'I watched the hand burn up, right in front of my eyes. That was – something.'

'Oh my poor love, did it hurt?'

'No no,' he says, 'never. It was all numb, down to the marrow. It was just – spectacular.'

'But why did it burn?'

'I guess I, I guess it gotten itself heated up pretty high when I was falling. It was black from the depressurisation, bruising, so it absorbed the heat. I guess coming fast through the atmosphere, it got heated.'

She thinks about this. A strange, dislocated expression is on his wife's face now, and he doesn't like it. He tries to fish up a more reassuringly loving face from the depths of Marina's mind with the hook-on-line of saying 'Love, are you *feeling* OK?' But the expression of almost cringing stealthiness which comes over her instead is painful to him.

'I'm fine,' she says. 'Don't *you* worry about *me*.'

He is sterner-voiced. 'Wat *is* it, Marina? Wat's on your mind?'

'Look,' she said, getting a red-bound notebook, the size and thikness of a wad of banknotes, from her jaket poket. 'I made some notes. I wanted to talk to you about this, but you were . . . up there.'

'Talk about wat?'

'I was in the garden, a week ago. It was beautiful, it was a beautiful morning, and I was just drinking a little coffee, and there was this bird . . .'

'Bird?'

'I don't know wat *kind* of bird,' she said petulantly, perhaps piqued at having been interrupted. 'A blak creature, with a shiny blak beak like a great blak thorn. It flew down and then settled in the tree, in the garden – the elm, you know?'

'So there was a bird . . .'

'It spoke to me. I mean, it made its cawing noise, its *graa-graa* and its *o-a-o-a* noises. But I listened, and then it suddenly kinda cliked in my head.' She pauses, and looks at her husband's pillow-propped head to chek he is following wat she is saying. 'It's really crucially the . . . thing,' she goes on. 'I mean, I know birds can't talk, leastways not talk like human beings, no?'

'No,' he says, firmly. 'Mary . . .'

'But if that's so then how was I hearing the words? Somebody, some . . . *thing* . . . was speaking through the bird. I did a screen search and birds have been considered creatures of omen in a thousand cultures. I wrote down wat I heard.'

'Mary—'

'I know, I know,' she says, urgently, 'but before you start at me, just have a look at wat I writ.' She opens the notebook at the proper page and places it in his one remaining hand, where it perches, not unlike a bird itself, headless with two rectangular wings.

<u>The bird in the tree over my right shoulder says:</u>
gra

open-up	go-way
o'en up	run (a)way run
o-a, o-a	you are—I know—you are
right-right	away away aroo
	go where? is?
	go there!
	beware—go
	wore, ware, woe

Slater contemplates this. 'Marina,' he says. 'This is – is this a joke?'

'Joke?' She is offended. 'No!'

'All these words, these are in your head, not in the bird. You know? You hear these words in the birdsong the same way that people pik constellations out of the sky. The constellations aren't really there, it's just the pattern-making bias in human consciousness.'

But these are not the terms on which she wants to discuss this matter with him. 'I wanted to talk to you about it right away, and I called your base, but they said you were away on active duty, and it was classified, and so on. But it seemed so urgent, and when I turned to look at it it flew away.'

'Marina . . .'

'It was warning me, don't you see? It was telling me to go away, to get out, to get away, but where?'

'Calm, love. Don't get over-excited.'

'But then I got the news about you – your news. Don't you think that confirms it? Don't you think that's more than a coincidence?'

'I really don't, no I don't.'

This doesn't register with Marina's jitterily monomaniacal mind. 'It says to go, it must mean both of us, but where should we go? Go where? After we talked about it I decided that . . . I know you won't be angry with me, my love. I've only seen him a few times; but it makes – oh, *such* a difference.'

He understands. She has been bak to the Pastor. She has had her pharmakos neutralised. The sensation inside his head is an almost exact analogue to the sensation he has already experienced in his gut upon falling from sixty miles. This is terrible. Blotches, like monstrously exaggerated semi-transparent bacilli or bacteria, float across his line of sight. His head feels larger than it did before, or else much more massy, almost like a bowling ball. His limbs feel similar, like rolls of dense cloth. 'Mary,' he says, his voice still raspy but stronger. 'Have you been bak to see the Pastor?'

She doesn't answer this directly; it's self-evident. Instead she says, 'He wants me to tell you that love is a universal, that if you love me and God loves me, then this is the same thing, from the perspective-point of eternity, isn't that a beautiful thought? There's only love, like drops of water in the ocean so if you love me and God loves me it's impossible for you and God to be on different sides of the . . . uh.' She falters before the shrunken fury of his face.

'Is he in the car? Did you drive with him all the way up from Titusville?'

'Of course not!' she says, blushing. But, just as Slater thinks, with a ridiculously disproportionate spurt of relief, that she is at least sparing his feelings, she adds, 'He's an important man, I couldn't coop him up in a car for hours and hour,' and he realises that in fact she has been sparing *his* feelings.

He closes his eyes.

*

Had he the power of prophesy, wat might he see? That his recovery will take longer than the doctors anticipate, despite the excellent spinal knits generated by the specialist pharmakos? That his artificial left hand will give him pins and needles up and down his arm whenever he tries to pinch its fingers together, in some obscure neural-feedbak glitch that the medics can't quite eliminate? That his wife, once again in thrall to the overwhelming mental stimuli of God and Devil will leave him, tearily, convinced in some way she cannot quite articulate (because to articulate it would be to reveal its illogicality and puerility) that by falling from heaven, burning as he fell, her husband has changed from being a Warrior of Light into being a devil, Miltonic, melodramatic? He can't see these three things. Nor can he see that however earnestly he will try imploring her, rotating systematically through begging, yelling, weeping, reasoning, insisting, bak to begging, she cannot be dissuaded. She will not try to take the children, because her two-thirds-cancelled mental pharmakos has not relinquished its hold on her mood entirely, and therefore she feels (in herself) irrational, guilty, even a little stupid at the decision she has made. But, sinner though she is, she owes a greater duty to her immortal soul, a thing that belongs to its creator and not to herself. It's inconceivable to remain married to a man God has – in the most elaborate way possible – revealed to be a devil, even if you love him. So she follows the bird's advice and runs away. But there's a truth here, which Slater will, only very slowly growing uncrippled, come to grasp, something along the lines of (although not precisely) 'I will die, therefore I am'. It's a triky business.

twenty-two. Paul

My betrayal cheered me, perversely. I became less depressed, more energised; I had something to live for, to live *towards*. Gradi noticed the difference in me, and encouraged me (or permitted me, which perhaps amounted to the same thing) to accompany her. 'We've got a few months of post-victory euphoria,' she told me, 'to lay down some of the structures of a properly-functioning nation. We need structures about which to congregate. I don't mean literal structures – although, in the long run, it wouldn't be a bad idea to put up a few public houses, a public water supply for individual use, a town hall, maybe a – but I mean to establish the principles of Upland citizenship. No taxation, that's a given. Though Gallano thinks we can top-slice some of the money the Americans seized when we get it bak from the courts, establish a modest treasury. I'll need a treasurer.' Was she asking me to be treasurer? That would be a high prestige post in the new Upland republic, although the fact that Gradi had executed the previous Upland chief banker with her own hand might reduce the number of people eager to put themselves forward.

The new stars in Gradi's political firmament were: Georgina, Ustinov, Gallano. Mat and I had waned, become little more than pasteboard figures to fill out the bakground of screen shots and publicity opportunities.

Why did my betrayal cheer me? Sometimes Gradi's sheer charisma would inspire me again, and I would start to believe in the possibility of a glorious future for the Uplands, houses that swim forever into new dawn after new dawn. It occurred to me that I could have taken a senior governmental position, become a world political player – except that, now, it was only a matter of time before my betrayal became known to the world and instead I fled not only the Uplands (for who in the Uplands would suffer a Judas such as I to live there?) but also the Upland-friendly EU, ran into an exile and an entirely deserved obscurity. Nevertheless the fact of my betrayal cheered me. Why was this?

It was because I had a secret to nurse: I had a reason to get up in the morning, I had something worthwhile to hide from Gradi. Given the previous dynamic of our relationship, with my complete passivity and openness to her, this presented me with a series of interesting challenges. Every morning I greeted Gradi, shadowed my usual scurrying thoughts with a sinister, thrilling, mendacity. It was just dangerous enough to be exciting (for, after all, it was treason) but not so dangerous that it threatened my fundamental peace of mind. Because whilst Gradi was now Gradi the Victor, vanquisher of the USA, forger and fuehrer of the Uplands, she was still (of course) my Gradi, the same girl I had met more than a decade before – penniless, desperate for anybody who could help her with the financial necessaries to lift her into the Uplands. And then, although I permitted myself to be persuaded by her expert advances that she really did love me, that it really wasn't just my money, it was less my vanity and more the sheer delight a parent experiences with a clever child – how well she played me, how sensitive and perfectly judged her advances were, thinking to overcome my resistance when in fact I had loved her almost from the first time I had seen her, and wanted nothing more than to be overcome. Had she uncovered my treacherous scheming wat would she have done? Shot me, as she had shot Bran, the first traitor-Cain of our new world? It's a counterfactual, so the case can be argued. But I don't think so. She was no sadist, she took no pleasure in hurting or intimidating people, she wasn't like that. Of course, she was, as Mat had said, free from the debilitating pity that mars most people's will-to-power, but that's a different matter. I believe she would have forgiven me. I believe, in fact, that I was, obscurely, doing wat she wanted me to do.

I nursed my secret, feeding it tenderly and swaddling it about with carefully spun-out half-truths. I told Gradi I had met with the American agent Lucette, who had wanted to set up a meeting; but I didn't tell her I had met with Liu, which would have piqued her curiosity too much. I told her I could meet this agent again, and Gradi, thinking herself sly, briefed me with a complex series of proposals for her.

I met Lucette in Helsinki aquarium, surrounded by the spooky sheer walls of deep blue behind which both real fish and genengineered faux-poisson circulated and circulated and never grew tired of their circulation. In the big tank sharks jerked their heads and fanned their tails to cool the water and moved coolly on, orienting their peaked heads and 2-D eyes on blue vacancy, and then on more vacancy, and blue vacancy again, and always swimming towards it without arriving. Squid, lying sideways, shuddered their horizontal way through the water. Small fish fled in shoals that moved with just-slightly-out-of-synch singleness. I sat on a bench and Lucette sat next to me in the aquamarine light, and I said to her: 'I don't want Gradi to be harmed.'

'Of course a lot depends on how we might want to define harm. Deprivation of a person's liberty might be termed *harm*.'

'You know wat I mean.'

'Do I?'

'Yes.'

'And wat *do* you mean?'

'It's physical harm. I want a promise from you, from America, that Gradi will not be killed, or physically injured, or I'm pulling out of this altogether. I mean it.'

Her smile looked ghastly in the blue light; blak lips craking slightly to reveal mauve teeth. 'I think it's too late for pulling out of this altogether.' This did not reassure me. 'But I'll happily give you that kind of assurance, Paul. Gradi dead is no good to us. Wat – Gradi the martyr? Do you really think that's wat we want?'

I was silent for a while.

Gradi set up a meeting with the Americans, together with Aleks Smouha, the Finnish ambassador whose career had flourished egregiously on the fame of being the first diplomatic officer to talk to Gradi – though that meeting, many years ago, had been fully hole-in-the-wall and clandestine, Smouha anxious that the Americans not find out about it. But that didn't matter now; now everybody celebrated Smouha's incredible prescience. We met the American representative – a plausibly official looking young man, in a smartcloth suit of purple and a tie that displayed the latest Market and Sports scores. He was, I suppose, an agent, although he acted the part of diplomat so perfectly that the two roles seemed indistinguishable.

We flew up. We flew down. Gradi toured her kingdom, and was greeted as a hero in every house. She made speeches.

The problem with establishing a new country – establishing a new kind of country – is that revolution is exciting, and winning wars is exciting, but politics is not *exciting. Day-to-day politics may be essential, but it does not inspire the heart. But we must guard against this! Without this essential day-to-day politics the Uplands will be stillborn. Everything we have worked for, and suffered for, and fought for, and some of us died for, everything will be lost. And I'll tell you my truth – the possibilities that politics opens up for me are the most exciting I have yet known. The possibility of a land genuinely free: for our citizens are wealthy enough,*

*and our infrastructure needs are non-existent enough, for us not to need
to levy taxes; and our space is large enough to welcome as many incomers
and immigrants as there are people on the planet below, provided only
that they build their own houses and arrange their own transport; and
our spirit is strong enough, and the independence we have fought for is
vital enough for us to need no police force or army – except that every
Uplander is dedicated to policing this freedom and defending it against
attak, except that every Uplander will defend his or her fellow citizens
from any person or persons who seek to interfere with their liberty. This is
the dream I am following, the utopian gleam that tempts me onwards. If
this is politics, then who dares call it boring?*

She really had all those triks of political rhetoric down pat: those
modulated repetitions, those Gettysburg-Address touches of heightened
vocabulary and diction. Was this the last speech she made before the
end? One of the last, certainly.

'It's important,' she said to me, 'that we meet the Americans on our
own turf. We need to assert our independence. It would be too easy,
having broken the American hold over us, to fall into the comfortable
embrace of the EU. I know they're keen to grab us.'

'You think so? They seem to have their hands full digging their moat
between the US and themselves.'

We were talking outside the Lutheran cathedral in Helsinki; sitting on
a bench, with two security guards (at wat point did Gradi start hiring
security guards? We had never needed them before the war – or during,
for that matter) standing a little way behind us, hands on weapons. The
boys were running down the hill towards the market at the foot, and the
two of us were sitting on a bench. There was a very attractive view over
the bay, the hammer-point sun coming down towards the anvil of the
horizon with tender slowness to our left. The sunlight was the color of
pale whisky.

'America and the EU have history,' she said, as if this were necessarily
a bad thing, like typhus or slavery. But in her vocabulary, of course, it
was. A key reason the Uplands gleamed so hopefully in her mind was
that it was free of *history*. History is the shape of a drug-addict's career;
it is that thing that makes it so difficult for him to break his addiction.
History is habitude.

'We could,' I suggested, as if this were something I had thought up
myself, and not something Lucette had told me to say, 'arrange a meet
at Gallano's.'

She contemplated this idea. 'Maybe,' she conceded.

I rushed in with all the cautious prophylactic strategies with which Lucette had primed me. 'We'll have them fly up, frisk them for transps, transfer them to another plane, or maybe two . . .'

She laughed. 'You think they'll go with that, after wat happened to their two senior officers?'

I laughed too, although I had to pretend it, little gulps of simulated hilarity. I nearly said *they'll go for it, absolutely*, because I knew from Lucette that they would. But instead I inserted some conversational filler, a lumpish misdirection. 'Wat was the name of the one who fell – fell all the way down, didn't burn up and didn't dash himself to death on the ground, or so *they* say.'

'So they say,' she agreed, still laughing.

'Wat was his name?'

'I guess it's so outlandish a story that it may be true,' she said. 'It would be a bizarre story to make up from scratch.'

'They'll go for it,' I said. 'The Americans I mean. We can play the USA off the EU. They'll fall over themselves to establish proper diplomatic links with . . .'

'Sure,' she was saying. 'Sure.' But she wasn't really listening to me. She was gazing off into the distance, as if the broad, beaming stretch of water, upon which the sunlight was sketching innumerable luminous bars and crescents all linked and chain-mailed together in fleeting motion, was futurity itself. Everything is possible in a land without history, a genuinely-genuinely new land. And here were the boys, labouring energetically up the hill towards us.

As we walked away from that conversation I felt an elation build inside me, that I had once again managed to preserve my secret inside me. That was my challenge, every time I spoke with Gradi, simply to keep that hidden thing. It was inside me, my own growing baby nurtured in my own unfaithful betraying flesh, and for those months (it lasted very many months) all my love and loyalty became focused on it. I practised my deception; I thought through everything I said before I said it. I prepared my verbal spontaneities.

How many months? Almost a whole year. It was autumn again before the end came. Autumn, the season when the trees bleed in a flutter of ragged 2-D corpuscles and thereby diminish themselves. The danger was in my interludes of weeping; they were the one thing I did not seem to be able to control, because I did not properly understand them. We rode the plane Upland, and as the sun bloomed in explosive brilliance round the world's shoulder I would find my eyes inexplicably full of tears. I would control myself through a difficult conversation with Gradi, and afterwards we would talk about wat we wanted to have for supper and tears would spatter from my eyes to float in zero g.

It mattered very little, in the longer run. It was just puzzling to me.

And so we took our final flight together, the last time I was ever to be with her; a plane crowded with excited Uplanders and immigrants. I sat wrapped in myself by a window, whilst Gradi worked the crowd. I had told her that we had another meeting at Gallano's.

'You're sure?' she asked. 'You're *sure* they want to meet? I met with them not long ago.'

'Yes,' I said.

'It's kosher? It's a real meet?'

'It's concessions, that's wat I heard.'

We doked, and took another plane. Gradi brought only one guard. She went everywhere with a guard these days, but it amounted to very little. Too little. We flew, and I insisted on piloting – something I rarely did. But Gradi's suspicion was not awakened. She was staring out through the windscreen at the world-sized shield on which was carved, in perfect detail, shiny landscape and shinier sea, billions toiling and resting, laughing and crying. It was all there. The sun was bright with Upland brightness, the brightness that groundlings never see, since the air that is their medium is closer to smoke than purity. Our sunlight was hard as chalk.

I swept down, and hauled up to slow outside a house. With clumsy camouflage the Americans had moked it up to look like Gallano's; it seemed to me a pitifully clumsy attempt at disguise, at any rate, but Gradi did not look alarmed. Her guard was smiling, chatting with her. I nosed into the porch, and pulled the nose open, and called to Gradi, 'I'm going in. Are you going to stay in the plane jawing all day?', and slid through the exact middle of the doorway. The space I entered was crammed with military men and women; they hung on the walls, pressed against the ceiling and the floor. All had guns, all pointed towards me. I was expecting it, but even so I almost yelped with terror. I slapped a hand over my mouth, and floated on through.

The guns did not follow me. I was not their target.

Part Three
HOPE

one

The clouds have dressed themselves as blak as dominatrices and are applyiŋ their whiplash lightniŋ to the compliant naked baks of the hills. The humped horizon moans and grumbles its shameful pleasure. But is this weather to fly in? Safe? I don't think this is weather to fly in. Breathe that: you know wat that is? Ozone, it's the stink of static. That cool breeze blowiŋ in from the storm front, washiŋ over this whole airfield. See that frizzy border between the lower line of the clouds and the ground? – that's rain, hard as the fiercest *douche*-settiŋ, falliŋ over kilometres and kilometres of land simultaneously. That's hurryiŋ through the sky towards us.

'We'll be up above that in no time,' says the pilot. And Hope nods, smiles, bustles up the stairway into the plane. His smile says I trust you, but his heart says this is it, this is where I die, struk by lightniŋ, broken by the big wind, snapped from the plane like a pistachio from its shell to tumble to extinction. Worry sinks, a nauseous pebble through the gloopy fluid of his guts. His eyes itch, but he knows from experience not to rub them, for that makes them much worse. He doesn't want to die, but the accumulative pressure of this morbid inevitability is growiŋ with every single day he stays alive, every single minute. This intense sensitivity to the prospect of his own mortality, the constant tikle on the skin of his soul, has become much more pronounced since he became a parent. To die now is not only to collapse his own consciousness to nothing, it is to deprive his kids of a father, his wife of a husband. And now he is goiŋ to trust himself to this flimsy winged tube as its pilot tosses it into the maelstrom, and then – who knows how battered and leaky afterwards – engage its Elem and ratchet it up into vacuum, where it can explode, or depressurise and choke them all, or perhaps simply lose power and drift into a burn-up trajectory. He is aware of a clamminess under his armpits, and he moves his arms, slowly but unmistakeably chiken-like, to try and dissipate it. He is at the top of the stairs. He duks through the oval door to enter the plane.

There are a dozen other people on board, all already settled in their seats. Hope stows his bag in his compartment and straps himself in; but the pilot, eager to run on before the crashiŋ aerial wave of that storm front, has already started the plane, they are already rolliŋ forward. They're moviŋ along the runway.

Through the window the air is purple. The grass beside the concrete strip is wriggliŋ and shiveriŋ, each individual stem fightiŋ its tether to try and get away, to fly off, before the crashiŋ roll of the storm descends. Hope peers anxiously out of his little porthole: the curviŋ roof of the terminal, the hangar beyond, a single plane sittiŋ forlorn in the open air, the scrub land darkeniŋ as the clouds progressively roof the whole area over. It seems, somehow, intensely sad. Hope shuts his eyes; he uses his fingers to do this, to weigh the eyelids down, his thumnails standiŋ in for the coins of the corpse with which the ferryman must be paid.

'Horosho, OK, gentlemen and ladies,' announces the ferryman (*pilot*, I mean) over the speakers. 'This is your *Konduktor* speakiŋ. We'll soon be—' there's a lurch, a hiccough, and the grindiŋ noise of wheels-over-concrete is blotted into the sensation of frictionless onward motion '—oy-oop, *there* we go, in the air now. We'll be runniŋ on a little to avoid those *nubarrones*, the – pardon me whilst I search for the English word, the, in other words – those thunderous clouds, behind us. Then we'll swoop round. Once we're over the weather and we engage Elem we'll be in space in less than a half of an hour. Settle down enjoy the flight.'

Hope tries his meditative mantra to try and calm his poor little fish-on-the-riverbank heart. He repeats, silently to himself, his personal mantric phrase. Repeats it, re-repeats it. I can't tell you wat his phrase was, I'm afraid; it's an intimate secret, one he has told neither his wife nor any of his four children. There's little point in you knowiŋ, either. It is ineffectual, it does not calm him. It almost never does. He opens his eyes again, and hazards a look into the desperately threateniŋ sky. The ground is barely visible; the light has darkened and thikened, taken on the colour of *chocolat-au-lait*, scrubbed across with shreds of cloud that whip past the window. There's a camera-bulb flash of lightniŋ that dips the porthole, momently, in white, but that only makes the darkness, which immediately reasserts itself, seem darker. Hope cranes his nek to see whether he can see behind the plane to the lightniŋ, forked or sheet, but the perspective is not right.

'Wilfrid Laurier,' says the man sittiŋ in the seat across the aisle.

'I beg . . . ?'

'—my pardon, it's not necessary,' says the man. He is speakiŋ with a

392

southern-states American axent. His face is broad, composed of round-nesses: boyish round cheeks, pluggy round nose, round blue eyes. He's well dressed. He smiles like a professional smiler. 'Worried by the storm?'

'Not at all, not worried,' says Hope, untruthfully. 'I've flown with this pilot before. He's very good. Pablovich.' (He pronounces this *pebble-of-each*, which is how his interlocutor, confusiŋly for him, hears the phrase). 'I chek the UpAir schedules, I always chek to see when he's flyiŋ, and book accordiŋly.'

'Very wise, I'm sure,' says Wilfrid Laurier. 'And, I didn't catch your name?'

'Billetoi, tikets,' says the tiketman, who seems to have popped up from nowhere: a diminutive fellow, perhaps no more than seventeen years of age, dressed in the UpAir uniform of purple and canary. Wilfrid Laurier has his tiket instantly at the ready, but Hope has to pull his bag down from above, rummage and scrabble and eventually find the plastic square lodged inside the covers of his book (it's a copy of *The Red Top Hat* by Olga Repnin). 'Thank you', says the tiketman, sarcastically, moving on to the people further down the plane. 'Billetoi, tikets, please.'

'It always seems a crazy thing to me,' says Wilfrid Laurier, tukiŋ his *billetos* bak in his jaket, 'to ask for tikets after the plane has taken off. Wat would they do if my tiket weren't in order? Chuk me over the side?' He laughs, a surprisingly low-pitched, rather mournful sound.

Hope, scrabbliŋ to return his *billetos* to his bag, and rearrange the riotous objects contained therein to some sort of order, and prevent his own jaket from twistiŋ round into a knot somewhere at the small of his bak, says 'They'd mark your account, take the money together with a retrieval fee from . . .' But, of course, Wilfrid Laurier knows this, and Hope knows that he does. It occurs to Hope that he is missiŋ a possible opportunity. He really should do better than this. Who knows but that maybe this Wilfrid Laurier is a billionaire, who might fund Hope's plans outright – and alright, OK, *that's* unlikely (since he's flyiŋ coach, after all, where if he possessed that kind of wealth he'd have his own jet), but maybe he works for a company that – or an individual who – or maybe he's friends with somebody who might – or any number of possibilities. All Hope needs is the *one luky break*, an investor suitably far-sighted, and then not only his fortunes but the whole future of the Uplands would be changed to . . . But his train of thought is interrupted, hijaked, he can't find his thum. He tuked it inside the inner poket of his bag, but it's not here now. Without his thum he can't do the presentation he needs to – no! This is disastrous! This is awful! The whole trip will be ruined, the presentation will be – stupid, stupid *man*! How could he *be* so stupid? He must have lost it, perhaps it fell from his bag as he was scurryiŋ up the steps to—

But here it is, tukked in the folds of his smartcloth tShirt, itself underneath his copy of *Alice Through the Camera's Eye*. He blinks the sweat from his eyes, grins at his own foolishness.

'Forget your sleep-puffer?' enquires Wilfrid Laurier, in a kindly voice. 'You do need one of those, if you're planniŋ on sleepiŋ up there, otherwise the carbond'oxide can pool around your head whilst you sleep. But don't worry, they sell them most places. They definitely sell them in the hotel.'

'It's alright,' says Hope, brightly, sealiŋ the bag and hoikiŋ it bak up to its overhead slot. 'I know all about the puffers. I've been up before.'

Wilfrid Laurier nods encouragiŋly. 'Often?'

'Pretty much. I'm sorry, I'm beiŋ rude. My name is Hope Gyeroffy.'

'Hi there, Hope Gyeroffy, call you Hope? OK?' says Laurier, reachiŋ over the aisle to offer his hand for shakiŋ. 'Good to meet you.'

The plane banks, enters a lengthy curve.

It's that awkward moment, one which Hope has never yet quite deduced how to negotiate. Does he introduce himself fully, *My name is Hope Gyeroffy, I'm the eldest son of Gradisil herself* – does he say that? He risks, then, the possibility that he simply won't be believed, that his companion (whomsoever he, or she, might be) will think he's a crank or a fantasist or a delusional type, or, wat is worse, will think that he is speakiŋ in fatuously metaphoric terms, ah, how true for are not all Uplanders, in a sense, children of Gradi? But there's a risk associated with reticence: for wat if he strikes up a friendship or a relationship with this person, and they later come to learn the truth? Won't that look odd? But why didn't you mention this before! You're the son of only the most famous Uplander in . . .

'Goiŋ up on business?' Wilfrid Laurier asks.

'Yes, in a manner of sp— yes.' Hope laughs, fidgets in his seat. 'Why else?'

'Well, most of *them*,' says Laurier, turniŋ his head and takiŋ a leisurely look at the rows of seated passengers behind them, 'are goiŋ up on servants' contracts. Workiŋ the hotels, private houses, that sort of thing.'

'Really?' says Hope, followiŋ Laurier's gaze. 'How do you know?'

'I was chattiŋ with them in the terminal. They're a group, altogether; they been hired as a job-lot by Bruslot.'

'Brusl . . . ?'

'The, that's the company that specialises in providin labour to the Uplands. There's a high turnover of staff, they can't work their workers for too long in the xero g without makin them ill. Bruslot. You not heard of them?'

'I have to admit, I . . .' He smiles, he shakes his head. 'You don't work for them?'

'Bruslot? Christ, no!' Wilfrid Laurier's brow creases. 'Hey, don't mean to offend you. You mind if I swear?'

'Not at all.'

'*I* work for MakB. That's for whom *I* work.'

'The junkfood—' Hope starts to say, with, alas, characteristically blundersome clumsiness. 'I mean,' he gabbled, tryin to undo his faux-pas. 'The restaurant, the chain of . . .'

'It's alright, nobody would claim we were *hoch-cuisine*,' says Wilfrid Laurier, but though he smiles there's something about his eyes that suggests it's not alright, that he is offended.

'I'm an idiot,' says Hope, frankly. '*Junk* is so insultin, I really didn't mean – actually, I eat MakB all the time, really.'

'You do?'

'I have 4 children. We're always goin into a MakB. MakkiB my eldest calls it. So you, you're flyin up on, wat? Company business?'

'We're openin our first Upland franchise,' says Wilfrid Laurier with some pride. '*It's* in the Worldview. It's a very handsome set up. We've had to design special ovens, special broilers, to cook the food – xero g, you see.'

'I suppose so.'

'I'm flyin up to arrange something, make some things OK for the openin, next week – big media *spazm* planned, a jamboree. Are you stayin in the Worldview?'

'For two nights only.'

'A shame – you'll miss it. It'll be something worth seein. We got a *celeb*. A *real* one, none of your pop singers. And we like to think,' Wilfrid Laurier continued, leanin bak against his seat and beamin at nothing, 'that it'll make something of a splash in the newscreens, the celeb-shows, the gossipblogs, something of a spazm. Say, how well you know the Worldview? You stayed there before?'

'This will be my first time.'

'Really?' Laurier leans forward again, lookin canny and askin as if hopin to catch him out, 'but you said you'd been Upland before?'

'Yes, many times. But never before to an American – uh, facility.'

'A hotel's hardly a facility,' Laurier laughs. 'Hey, we're not so bad.'

'We?'

'Americans, you know. You might *be* an Uplander yourself, I don't mean to offend you, I know that a fair few Uplanders don't own their own planes these days. Do I got you pegged right?'

'I'd call myself an Uplander,' says Hope, nervy. 'Yes.' He always feels a fraud sayiŋ this, although he has as much right to call himself this as anybody.

'So, first time on American territory, yeah? Well, well, it's been 30 years since the war. More than 30 years. I've yet to meet an Uplander who carries a grudge. You don't carry a grudge?' Without waitiŋ for an answer, as if takiŋ the answer for granted, he continues, 'Besides, the way I like to think of it: there's never been a case of 2 nations, both of which have MakB restaurants on their – soil, I was goiŋ to say, let's agree on *in their space* – there's never been a case of 2 such nations ever goiŋ to war. The conclusion? Easy. MakB prevents war! Not that I'm sayiŋ there's something magical in our patties, or our VegeBox cooked in its copyrighted marinade, of course not!' This is startiŋ to sound like the sort of prepared speech trotted out in front of investors' meetings, or to senior managers of companies in negotiation for ancillary rights. 'It's just that. Trade makes more sense. Than fightiŋ. There are more trade outlets in the Uplands now than there's ever been. It's a new frontier for the hardworkiŋ businessperson.'

'Well,' says Hope, a little thrown by the earnestness of this speech. 'Quite.'

'Are you even old enuff to remember the war? You don't mind me askiŋ.'

'No, don't mind you ask – actually yes. I mean, yes, I do remember the war. I was just a kid, and watched the whole thing on the news, downbelow.' He thinks about addiŋ something else, about his family, about Gradi, but he doesn't.

'The,' says Wilfrid Laurier with mighty emphasis, *thuh!* Then he says 'Tea', and Hope understands, a beat too late, that he is sayiŋ *Thir-ty Years* with a deliberately exaggerated rhetorical flourish. '*Yurrrs,*' he concludes, with a shake of his head. 'It's a devil of a lengthy time. That's my point.'

'I quite agree.'

'I know it still lives on, but as *history*. Yes? I'm dedicated to makiŋ the most of the future in the Uplands. There's no point in gettiŋ bogged into the past. The possibilities—'

With a miniature electronic yawp, followed by a hum, the speakers come on again. It is the pilot speakiŋ. 'Gentlemen and Ladies,' says Pablovich in his Tartary-axented voice. 'In one moment I shall be enjagiŋ the Elem, please strap.' The communication ends abruptly.

'I'll tell you wat,' says Wilfrid Laurier, sittiŋ bak properly in his seat and sealiŋ his waist-strap. 'We're gettiŋ a celebrity to open the franchise – it's a first for MakB, this Upland outlet, a first for world trade and the eatery business, so we've pushed the boat out. Do you know who we've got?'

'I've no – I mean, I don't really—'

'The man who fell to Earth himself! Colonel David Slater himself! That's one of the things I need to do, I'm his corporate liaison. He's booked in, luxury suite, company's expense. I got to meet him, make sure he's tuked in nicely, give him his speech. We want him to learn the speech.'

'You don't say,' says Hope, but his attention has wandered. The pilot's announcement of the imminency of Elemag has rekindled his terrors. It's one thing to move through the air, supported on the broad wings, cushioned safely above and below by atmosphere. It's *quite another* to slip from the air in which so many heavy things (those galleon-shaped clouds, those great glintiŋ curves of multicoloured steel we call rainbows) are supported, into *nothing at all*, nothingness, vacancy, emptiness. That's not right. It offends his common sense, even though that very anxiety makes Hope feel like a religious bigot, *if Gawd had intended us to fly into space he'd have furnished space with good cleanly air* – and, he realises, he is not fittiŋ the smartcloth seal of his seatbelt together, he is holdiŋ one end of the strap in one hand and scrabbliŋ at his own groin with the other. He disgusts himself. He is fearful and disgustiŋ. He tries to cover his own incommotion with a laugh, but he's not fooliŋ anyone. He is blushiŋ rose-colours, both pink and scarlet, in his face. There is sweat comiŋ out of him. He is a leaky hessian sak masqueradiŋ as a man. But then, with a whine of the motor firiŋ up and that distinctive sluggish lurch, the plane piks up the Elemag effect and starts to climb. Hope looks through his porthole again. The air is blak, but the ghost of the lightniŋ still clings, in miniature spectral form, about the edges of the wings, flutteriŋ up in shiniŋ stars.

At least we're up above that thunderstorm now.

'So wat's *your* business?' Wilfrid Laurier is askiŋ.

Still tryiŋ to get his breathiŋ properly under control, Hope removes his eyes from the porthole. 'I'm meetiŋ,' he says. 'I'm meetiŋ the representative of an—'

But Laurier isn't really interested, that's very obvious. 'You like it up there?'

'—an American investment corporation, representiŋ a – sorry?'

'You like it up there?'

'Yes,' says Hope, surprised at himself. 'I do. You?'

Laurier is all puzzlement. 'Me?'

'Do *you* like it up there?'

'Do I? You kiddiŋ? I love it! I wish we'd won that fukiŋ war – no offence, *I'm* only jokiŋ, but then it'd have been stars-and-stripes amongst the stars. Man, I'd have planned to retire there, if that had been the case. Do I *like* it up there?' Laurier seems disproportionately amused by Hope's banal enquiry. 'You kiddiŋ? I *love* it up there. It's a river of diamonds. *Une rivière de diamants.*' Something in his manner makes Hope think he is deployiŋ this gaudy metaphor not to express the poetic beauty of the Uplands but rather its enormous and as yet untapped financial potential.

He seems to be asleep now, this hideously hearty American, with his pharmakos-toned skin and his blue smartcloth suit. Hope doesn't want to wake him. He tries to read one of his books, glanciŋ round guiltily at the other passengers, most of whom are absorbed in screens. Readiŋ a book is a pretentious affectation these days, like weariŋ spectacles, or speakiŋ Latin; and Hope cannot shake the sense that, perhaps, he's doiŋ it as a kind of pretentious performance even for his own benefit, as if he is tryiŋ to convince his sceptical innerself that he is more intellectual than in fact he is. His eyes, drawn by the fearful possibilities of the porthole (the wiŋ has come off! Elem flight has been revealed to be a collective hysteria and now the madness has worn off! A rogue flier is loomiŋ up to crash into us – we're-goiŋ-to-*die!*), finds it hard to concentrate on the words on the page. The book is *The Red Top Hat.* The ghastly Dr Blagovo has been murdered. A huge hammer has crushed his skull, a hammer so heavy that only a circus strong man or a professional body-builder could ever have wielded it (the story is set in 1922; Hope isn't sure about the prevalence of professional body-builders at that time). A dozen people have the motive to kill the sinister doctor, and flashbak scenes (how *very* twentieth-century) reveal that he was blakmailiŋ them all, burstiŋ in upon them in the commission of some sinful or criminal act with his ludicrously egotistical cry 'I am the Doctor!' But which of the twelve suspects is the owner of the titular *chapeau,* the clue indicative of their guilt? The problem is not enuff to keep Hope reading – indeed, it so happens, he will never finish this particular story (the answer, in case you care, is that the culprit is the one person too diminutive and weak to ever have lifted the hammer; and the twist is that, standiŋ on a stepladder, she pulled it from a high shelf and it happened to land head-onto-head on the wiked Doctor standiŋ below). Hope watches the porthole. The world is visible there, and then, with a clik and a burr, the speaker comes on, and Pilot Pablovich announces to his passengers that dokiŋ at Hotel Worldview is imminent.

Later, as he floats out of the door and into the hotel's spacious porch, with its barndoor-sized portal closed fully to enclose a space large enuff for 3 planes simultaneously, his attention is distracted again. He tuks his feet into the dragalong and is gently hauled, with all his fellow travellers 2-by-2 in a line behind him, along to the chek-in. A small crowd is there, gathered round, waitiŋ, perhaps, to greet various disembarkees. Hope, holdiŋ his bag, slides underneath the 3-D Worldview logo, its O alternately an eye and a schematic of the world. Then his tiket is cheked, his national accreditation and his reservation, and he fits clumsily a snap-twang harness to his shoes. There's an announcement: a second plane is dokiŋ, haviŋ flown up from American ground, and the waitiŋ crowd becomes more excitedly agitated. So it seems that this crowd has actually gathered to meet a traveller from this latter flight, a celebrity no less. Hope loiters, to see who it is – and it is, as he suspected, Colonel Paul Slater, holdiŋ his artificial hand (indistinguishable from his fleshly hand) up to greet the gawping crowd. Celebrity does that. But it is not this American folk hero who snags Hope's eye, not at all. Instead, it is a much less famous figure; tall but gaunt, sandy hair cut short over a slightly bulbous skull but standing up as if charged in the xero g, leaniŋ forward into an elasticated stride, seen only from the side, but unmistakeably the man whom Hope thinks he is. There isn't time to slip passage into a different groove in the floor and snap-twang over to him to double chek, to ask his name; he's gone, he's through a door and away, followiŋ Slater and himself followed by an anonymous third. But Hope doesn't need to double-chek. He doesn't need, he doesn't *want*, to meet the person in question. He knows.

He can hardly believe it.

He disengages the elastic from its groove in the floor and floats to one side. He needs to get to a phone. There goes Wilfrid Laurier, marchiŋ past, calliŋ out, 'Hi, Hope' as if he is announciŋ to the world the height of his aspirations, and addiŋ, as he moves past, 'See you later'. Hope is still gawpiŋ. He scrapes his toes along the floor to propel his floatiŋ self to the side, where several hoods perpend. Inside is a public phone, and

Hope chatters the number into the grille in so agitated a manner that the AI has to ask him to repeat it. He gets through, the connection is made, and his brother answers. 'Sol,' says Hope. 'Sol Sol Sol. I've seen him – he's here.'

Sol looks out of the screen at him. The implacability on his brother's face, the simple refusal to be moved, to become agitated or excited, that is *very much* Sol; that's him to a T. His face remains impassive. 'Who's *he?*' he asks, plainly. 'And where's *here?*'

'*Here*,' says Hope, lowerin his voice – absurdly, because, the least secret thing about this place is its name (the O in Worldview is an eye now, blue as Wilfrid Laurier's) 'is the Worldview, you know it? The American-owned hotel. *He* is Dad.'

Sol is nodding slowly. 'And you're sure?'

'And,' says Hope, noddin along, 'I'm sure.'

two

Sol is comiŋ now – flyiŋ over. Flyiŋ straight here as soon as he can connect with a plane that's booked-in. 'Are you sure?' Hope frets on the phone. 'It'll cost just comiŋ inside. It's not like a groundliŋ hotel, they charge you for just steppiŋ inside the lobby here.' He is babbliŋ, and Sol knows it, and he knows it himself. 'It's not like downbelow, course it would cost a lot lot more to park a private plane. But—'

'There are several hotels downbelow that charge people to step into their lobby,' Sol replies in a factual tone of voice. But, of course, the hidden burden of Hope's communication is not factual, but freighted with symbolical anxieties. It is not like downbelow in that, once you're in a house you cannot simply step outside. If you discharge a handgun into a twitchiŋ, weepiŋ, elderly body, then up here you cannot simply throw the weapon in the river and run over 3 fields to where your car is parked. Kill a man and you're stuk there. Knowiŋ this, but also knowiŋ the tectonic implacability of his brother's will, Hope feels only squished and pressured and horribly overwhelmed by everything. Why did *he* have to be here? Of all places? Why did Hope have to glimpse him?

Hope is clutchiŋ at reasons for Sol not to fly over. 'I'm booked into a single – it's nothiŋ more than a tube, you know, it's not a room. There's no way we could both fit in there.'

'Change your bookiŋ,' Sol orders, in his grey voice. 'Extend your stay, and book us a double tube. Book us a *room*; we'll probably need a *room* – a suite.'

'Alright,' said Hope, miserably. 'But it may not be possible. The hotel is pretty full; there's a do, a thing, a happening, MakB is openiŋ a junk-outlet. There are celebrities here.' He cannot stop his mouth runniŋ on. 'Slater is here, that guy who fell all the way through the—'

'Do you think that's why *he* is here?' interrupts Sol.

This had not occurred to Hope. 'I don't know. I suppose it could . . .'

'Here's wat you need to do,' says steely-voiced Sol. 'You need to chek the schedules of flights *out*.'

'Out – and in?'

'No,' (said scornfully) 'Just out. They won't let you see passenger lists, but every time a plane is scheduled to fly out you need to go to the embark-lounge, just wait there, see whether *he* comes in. If he does we'll need to hire a taxi-plane to fly us down to follow him. Listen to me, brother – are you listeniŋ? Good, because we cannot let him go. We may not get an opportunity as good as this again – do you understand?'

Hope's problem is not that he doesn't understand. Hope's problem is that he understands too well. They've been put into a suddenly enormous velocity by fate, both of them. They're freefalliŋ towards the ground like the celebrated Slater once did, at a hundred miles an hour, at terminal velocity and the ground a flat pan of concrete miles wide. It is the inevitability of it all that causes fibrillations in Hope's heart muscles, sweat, trembliŋ. He cannot bear to contemplate just how horribly, fatally inevitable it all is. It's such an elaborate way to commit suicide. He thinks of sayiŋ this to Sol, right now. But wat would be the point in sayiŋ it? Sol would simply repeat that they'll never get so good a chance again – their quarry confined in the spacious but nevertheless finite topography of the Worldview rather than roamiŋ the endless Cartesian plane of the world below, in who-knows-wat location in the midst of enemy territory. It's true, it's right, but how strongly Hope wishes it weren't.

'Wat are *you* doiŋ there, anyway?' asks Sol, his face showiŋ its first expression (a slightly crumpliŋ of the brow to indicate curiosity) in place of his usual mask-like self-control. 'Are you there for this junk-food openiŋ thing?'

'No! *I'm* talkiŋ to a potential investor.'

'Oh,' says Sol, the crumpled brow smoothed again, his uninterest in his brother's plans insultingly obvious. 'It's your old-time thermometer thing.' Hope closes his eyes. This is Sol's joke, or, more accurately, this is the closest Sol ever comes to makiŋ a joke – with all the corrosive implications of laughter, of lettiŋ one's-guard-down, of common humanity that jokiŋ would carry with it. He had made this joke ('huh! it sounds like the action of an old-time thermometer!') right at the beginniŋ of the project, when Hope first told him 8 years ago, shortly after the legal papers had been filed and Moving Mercury Inc had officially come into beiŋ. 8 hard years, duriŋ which time Sol had made not one single expression of interest. Every time Hope mentioned the project Sol made the same joke.

'My meetiŋ is tomorrow,' gabbles Hope. 'I'm booked in 2 nights, in case there's a follow-up from the, um, potential investor.'

'Book for a week.'

'And pay for it – how?'

Sol snorts. 'You can't afford a double room at a hotel for a week? Your interplanetary corporation isn't generatiŋ much income, then.'

'It's not an *investment corporation*,' replies Hope, stung into crossness by his brother's attitude. 'Investment is just the—'

But the phone call is over, the phone connection disintegrates into the swirliŋ logo of North American Screen Telephonies Inc. That's that.

Sol is comiŋ under a pseudonym. He will come on a public flight, rather than pay the cost of private parkiŋ (which of course he could afford – Sol has not lost *his* money, as Hope has: but if he flew in his own plane it would betray his true identity, and that might alert authorities to the danger for Paul Caunes; or might have consequences later on. After the deed. Hope doesn't like to think of that, the deed, the deadeniŋ, deadly deed).

Hope spends a frustratiŋ half hour tryiŋ to get his reservation altered, because, you see, something has come up, a colleague is comiŋ to help him with his presentation to – yes, yes – and more time as well, further days, yes? The clerk is not used to dealiŋ with customers face-to-face, and seems nonplussed, but the arrangements are made. The fact that Hope is prepared to take one of the largest double rooms on the top storey smooths his path; that's mucho money, mucho. It seems that the openiŋ of a junk-food outlet, even in space, is not so enormous a media opportunity as Wilfrid Laurier made out. The hotel has many empty rooms.

Hope's head feels overinflated, as it always does when he comes up to xero g. It'll take his body a night to adjust. The blood which gravity usually pools in his legs is now distributed perfectly evenly throughout his vascular system, overfilliŋ the veins and arteries of his upper body. But it does give him wat they call the drinker's window. He fits his elasticated walkers into a slot and snap-twangs down the entrance corridor to the main atrium.

All his years of comiŋ to the Uplands, he has never before visited this 10-year-old luxury hotel; and so he is as agog as any first-time Upper to come into this vast open space, reachiŋ hundreds of metres up (or *along*, or *down*), lined with bars and boutiques and eateries all the length of its cavernous shaft. The twin central lines, in constant motion up and down respectively, gently drag visitors through this space that looks, to Hope's still ground-adapted perceptions, like a cathedral-tall tower stretchiŋ dizziŋly up, through which fly angelic people in blue and green and red and white. He tells himself not to be foolish; it's just a very large house, with lots of rooms of varyiŋ sizes, from bee-cells to whole expensive suites, and a few shops to tease more money from visitors. He snap-twanged his way across the floor (or wall, or ceiling) of this blue-steel, plasglass atrium, headiŋ towards the bar on the far side of the podium in which the two cables, with their feathery hand-holds like sprouts on the central stalk, sink into the infrastructure.

'I'd like a whisky,' he says to the barman – and that's right, an *actual* barman, in a blak and white suit with elasticated sleeves and leggiŋs, waitiŋ behind the bar! That's how luxurious the Worldview is. He presents Hope with a globe-and-straw, cliks the panel on Hope's proffered chip (but Hope's thum is not pressiŋ against the proper place on the plastic and so the procedure must be repeated), and smiles at his customer. Hope hooks himself onto a seat, and watches the comiŋs and goiŋs in the hotel atrium.

'Up here on business, sir?' the barman asks. 'Sort of business are you in, sir?'

Hope looks at him. 'Assassination,' he says, glumly.

'That so?'

But this is too close to the horrible truth. 'No, not really. I'm the director of a company. It's a company called Moving Mercury.'

'That so, sir?'

'I'm lookiŋ for possible investors. It's really the biggest project humanity has ever contemplated.' But why is he selliŋ the project to a *barman*, of all people? He shifts gear. 'You don't happen to have two hundred billion euros to invest, do you?' He is tryiŋ, with this mild joke, and with a lopsided, hook-shaped smile, to draw the barman into his dank world; conversation, the shariŋ troubles, directionless talk. He sips the whisky again. Many people don't like drinkiŋ whisky from globes. The argument goes that the odour is a significant component of the flavour and with a globe you can't smell anything. But Hope can still taste it, and it still tastes to him of russet and amber and the colour of rosé wine in sunlight. His blood-filled head registers the incipient intoxication.

'It's interestiŋ you should talk about money,' says the barman, comiŋ a little closer. 'Because with HighHouse Incorporated you can own your own little piece of the Uplands, for as little as *eight thousand euros* a month – that's on a share-scheme model – for individual ownership it's a little pricier, but we can cut you a deal with AmAir to arrange a cut-price season-tiket for flights up. Eight thousand euros a month – that's less than the hire purchase of a new energCar! Why not ask me about our special terms for first-time buyers . . .'

Hope, distracted and a little detuned, mentally, by the alcohol takes as long as this to work out wat a more observant (or, more precisely, wat a less self-absorbed) man would have noticed immediately: the barman is not human, he is an advertisiŋ automaton. Hope takes a closer look. They are certainly gettiŋ more lifelike, but the face still has the texture and shade of plastic, the movements still don't quite inhabit the physical idiom of real people, the lips aren't quite mobile enuff. He tries to remember wat the protocols are for shuttiŋ them up. ' . . . all the freedom and the splendour of an Uplands house, the perfect getaway when gravity is gettiŋ you down . . .' 'I'm not interested,' Hope says, loud and clear; but the thing keeps talkiŋ and it pops into Hope's head that he needs to repeat this phrase 3 times. With European automata it's enuff simply to turn your bak. '. . . and all for less than the price of an average city rent in . . .'

'I'm not interested!' Hope cries. 'I'm not interested! I'm not interested!'

The barman (bar*thing*) retreats, shuts up, though with a wounded expression that must, Hope realises, have been programmed by its designers for no other purpose than to wound the feeliŋs of punters who decline the machine's pitch. That seems mean-spirited, somehow. Hope doesn't dwell on it.

Two powerfully built women, both dressed in suits of deep blue across which larks seem to flit in an endlessly pouriŋ flok, are approachiŋ the bar; but they've been stopped by Hope's raised voice. They hesitate, look around; do they want to share a bar with a shoutiŋ idiot? But the other bar is axessible up the central dragline, and the blonder of the two shakes her head. Hope cringes a little inside. He is horribly conscious of makiŋ a fool of himself in front of women, and most especially attractive women, as these are. As they settle themselves with their knees hooked under the bar, he angles his face down. They're both splendid physical specimens, they really are. One of them has her hand restiŋ on top of the other's, on top of the bar. The barman cliks 2 globes (of wat? Wine? Beer? Fizzee? It's not possible to tell) onto the surface before them, and leans in. Are you ladies up here on business? Wat sort of business are you in, might I ask?

Hope tries to take surreptitious little looks at the 2 of them. Very attractive, very. A couple, he estimates, together, well-off, perhaps business as well as sexual partners. Savvy, too: they dismiss the barman immediately he starts up and fall deeply into a murmuriŋ conversation with one another.

Hope risks invitiŋ another automated sales lecture by orderiŋ a second drink. Why not? Get drunk, sure. All this blood overfilling his head, until his body rearranges the pressure, it delivers alcohol to the loci of consciousness quiker than usual. Sol will be here in hours, and then they'll both be dippiŋ their hands in blood, scatteriŋ blood like miniature planets and stars through the space of this hotel so why not? The drink comes, and the sales pitch does not come, so perhaps the thing's software protocols do not permit him to approach a customer whom has instructed him thrice to desist.

The women are chattiŋ to one another. He thinks to himself: *if only they knew the murder that is in my heart!* But this is false; the murder is in Sol's heart, not his. All there is in his heart is the guilt. Sol gets all the assassin's strength of will, and he gets all the guilt, that's the properly familial distribution alas, always has been like that. It's only fair that these quantities be shared out, he thinks to himself, which (of course) was one of his father's mantras. It's only fair. You've had the toy for an hour, you must let Sol have it now, it's only fair. Share and share, that's wat it means to be part of a family. The women are chattiŋ to one another. Hope looks again. It has occurred to him before, on comiŋ into the uplands, that xero g, by removing that sense of one's cok and balls as weighty pendulum excressions, works as a mode of virtual castration. Your genitals no longer tug at your abdomen, or rub and pull at your trousers. As the blood pressure rearranges itself they tend to shrink, and as the gravity is removed they become rather floaty and insubstantial. With his left hand Hope, surreptitiously (everything he does in his life is surreptitious) slides his left hand between his thighs, rubbiŋ a single downstroke against his crotch. It's still there, the disgustiŋ worm of it. How revolted these women would be if it were drawn to their attention! Hope's heart is pulsiŋ more rapidly. He withdraws his hand, rubbiŋ an upstroke rub against his crotch on the way out, and usiŋ that hand to unsnik the globe from the bar and raise it to his lips, all in one smooth motion. How revolted these women would be, this decent, well-presented loving partnership of women, if *it* were drawn to or forced upon their attention. Hope imagines their ire. He imagines the disdain, the dismissal, himself apologisiŋ, he imagines himself stretchiŋ out his long and disgustiŋ body before them as nude as the Moon, as open as the sky itself. He can almost hear their disgust, the *uh!*s, as they exchange shakes of the head and sour looks. The lacquered xero-g-proof blonde sculptured hairdos that look so sharp-edged and handsome. The unyieldiŋ blueness of the eyes. But perhaps they'll know, on some level, that he is *with* them, that he shares their revulsions. He can almost see the taller of them slippiŋ her shoe off, and graspiŋ its heel to raise it, club-like, and bring it hard down upon—

He finishes his globe with a slurp. The whisky, the empty stomach, the extra pressure of blood in his head, it's all dizzyish and intoxication-esque. Time to go, before he makes a fool of himself.

He reconnects his feet to one of the many paths in the floor. He has made a decision, notified himself internally with a *Well!* – well, since he's got a room now, at absurd and deflatiŋ expense, he might as well *use it*. Since he's already spent 3 times wat he'd planned to spend, out of the fortune which, once substantial, he has managed over 15 years to dissipate entirely in his flibbertigibbet Mercury project – well (says the whisky) he might as well spend even more. Spend your own money, and the pile of your money gets smaller. But spend *somebody else's* money and the pile gets *bigger*. Isn't that a curious observation? Of course, it's *the other guy's* pile that's swelliŋ, not yours, but that hardly matters, we're all 1 under the solar eye of God, after all.

The snap-twang thing is much harder to negotiate when you're a little drunk. He makes his way across the enormous atrium, to an AI information point. 'I require,' he speaks into the grille with exaggerated precision, 'a *female – heterosexual – prostitute* – right away, right away, can you recommend . . . ?'

'I'm sorry sir,' comes the chirpy-voiced reply. 'That service is unavailable at this present time.'

'Hi there, Hope!' says somebody. It is Wilfrid Laurier.

'Well,' says Hope. He tries, mentally, to pull the string at both ends, to try and tighten the knot of his concentration, but it is hard. 'Howdy there.'

'Settled in?'

'Actually, yes, I'll tell you,' says Hope, feeliŋ an axess of volubility, 'I decided to upgrade my room, I've changed my bookiŋ from a tube to a double room with a window, and I'll be stayiŋ for a little longer too, so perhaps I'll be here for the openiŋ of your—' He cannot, momently, remember wat it is that Wilfrid Laurier is openiŋ.

'I couldn't help overheariŋ,' says Laurier, leaniŋ in, 'and I just wanted to say to you that, well, not to put too fine a point on it, I could arrange for you to—'

Hope really doesn't know wat Laurier means. He really doesn't. It does not occur to his brain to connect his enquiry at the AIpoint with Wilfrid Laurier. He can't compute wat Laurier is sayiŋ, he doesn't understand at all, and then he does understand, in a sort of rush. 'Oh no, oh not necess – no that's alright.'

'Nothing illegal,' says Wilfrid Laurier, beamiŋ. 'I'm talkiŋ legit, top-of-the-range, hetero, eager workers with pharmakos-enhanced libidos. There's 3 of them workiŋ here. The hotel, I happen to know, is in legal dispute with them over the rights to their advertisiŋ, which is why the AI is so unforthcomiŋ, but I'd be happy to arrange an introduction—'

'If you'll excuse me,' says Hope, with ridiculous and maladroit hauteur, 'I need to go and place a phone call to my wife, who is downbelow with my 4 childrens. Childs.' He wobbles off, snap-twang, snap-twang, the alcohol arraŋiŋ the atrium lights inside the jelly of his brain as impossibly beautiful and eye-dazzliŋ constellations of sparkles.

three

That night he sleeps very poorly, partly because of the weightlessness and partly because his conscience is doiŋ the thing that bad consciences do – *worryiŋ* him, *troubliŋ* him, *prikkiŋ* him, like a medic performiŋ the biopsy that confirms a diagnosis of cancer. Or, no; cancer is not severe enuff a malady for Hope's state of mind; something much worse. I fall upon the thorns of life, I bleed. I can't sleep. I'll get up.

It's a large room; tall, broad – although of course small enuff compared to the average Uplander's place. But the average Uplander doesn't have axess to the atrium, the gym, the 2 bars, the shop, the hyperdenominational chapel, the medical officer and so on. But Hope is painfully aware that, cubic-metre by cubic-metre, it is one of the most expensive hotel rooms available to the human consumer. He floats to the window. Above this portal is the winkiŋ Worldview logo, and beneath it the glisteniŋ 3D legend *32 dawns every day* projected, he discovers by runniŋ his thum around the rim of the window, from a nubbin on the top. There's a similar message over the door: *Remember Your Sleep Tube!* and underneath in smaller letters *Worldview Inc Are Not Liable for Customers Who Omit to Wear Their CO_2 Dispersers.*

Lookiŋ through the window he sees the great curviŋ whale of the Earth drift up and float in front of the sun, snuffiŋ its glare into a saint's-head spread of shards of beams, and then nothing at all. He looks for the Moon, but he can't see it. It has always troubled him, obscurely, that the Moon still goes through phases, here in space. But it does. He also used to expect it to look somehow bigger from space. But an object a quarter of a million miles away does not increase in perceived size just because you have moved 60 miles towards it. The deeper truth is his desire, of course; not the physical universe. His desire is that he wants this land, his mother's own land, to declare its incommensurateness with the clumsily heavy world below. But the truth is it's a land pretty much like any other land. That's the way of all new things; they seem radical and strange, and then you live with them for a day and they are folded into the continuous tapestry of the ordinary and the already known.

He takes breakfast in a coffee parlour, and then makes his way down to the lobby to await the arrival of the next charter flight: this one from the Uplands to the Worldview, a much smaller plane than the Up-Down charters.

And here is Sol, compact, moving with the ease of somebody very familiar with xero g. He is looking at the crowd as he walks towards it, scopiŋ each member with brisk, appraisive, *I-could-snap-your-nek-like-a-breadstik* looks. No smartcloth for him; blak trousers and top, like a 3nimation ballet-fighter. 'Brother,' says Hope, steppiŋ forward and feeliŋ double shambolic and ill-coordinated.

'We must talk,' replies Sol, omittiŋ, as is his way, all pleasantries, all how-are-yous, smiles, handclasps or shoulder-slaps.

'Come to the room I have booked,' says Hope. 'My room – our room, I mean.' It really is as if Sol's alarmiŋ self-possession bleaches all sense of rightful possession from Hope's consciousness, as if he cannot have anything just to himself whilst his brother is there.

'It may be bugged,' says Sol, snap-twangiŋ onward. Hope tries to keep up. 'Let us talk in the atrium.'

'Then people may overhear,' Hope points out. 'Passers-by.'

'Let them.'

'But that doesn't make any sense. If you're worried about people buggiŋ the—'

'That would be special services, buggiŋ. If passers-by overhear, they're just passers-by.'

'We could still get arrested,' hisses Hope, as the two of them move out of the lobby and into the atrium. On his second day in the Worldview Hope finds that he is now unimpressed with the place; habit has shrunk the atrium into the proportions of a large glass shed; but Sol, for whom this is his first sight, cannot conceal a fliker of admiration crossiŋ his face.

'Nobody will arrest us,' he says, runniŋ his gaze up the crystal length of the structure.

'You shouldn't be so cavalier,' frets Hope. 'This is an American hotel, it's not the regular Uplands. This is American territory.'

Sol makes a *ptch!* noise. 'They're here on sufferance,' he says, grandly. 'We *permit* them to be here in the Uplands. American territory? It's all our territory, and they rent this space from us.'

'Nevertheless—' Hope starts to say.

Sol completes the sentence for him with '—nothing. I'm a member of the Upland government. This is our land, not theirs. I refuse to be cowed in my own nation.'

'Upland government,' Hope repeats. 'Like there's anything as organised as an Upland government. But Sol has spotted the bar at which Hope had, the previous day, beheld the handsome couple and drunk 2 whiskies. 'Here,' he says. 'We'll talk here.' He strides with improbably speed and has ordered 2 beers by the time Hope, awkwardly tryiŋ to get the rhythm of calf-muscle, thigh-muscle, tip foot *up*, angle foot *down*, into an optimum onward-moving arrangement, stumbles into the bar area. Sol is at one of the tall-stalked tight-headed mushroom-shaped tables. Hope sniks himself in.

There is music playiŋ in the atrium, a long piece by Dog Lyre that sounds like birdsoŋ, quivery and frou-frou, and might even be mistaken for a recordiŋ of downbelow birds if it weren't for the fact of a kettle-bell percussion runniŋ alongside the semitone warble of the melody; and the fact that the words *Today's Music: Dog Lyre's New Suite, Shoal* are circliŋ the rim of the atrium in unmissable spring-green projection. People are driftiŋ in and out of shops.

'Do you know which room he is stayiŋ in?' Sol asks.

'No,' says Hope, fretfully. 'No, no. How would I know that? I have to tell you,' droppiŋ his voice into a more conspiratorial register, 'this represents spectacularly bad timiŋ. I've been angliŋ for this meetiŋ – today's meetiŋ for months. I've finally got an in. Months of work – years. This is a real possibility, real investment might come out of this, it could be a lifesaver for the project.'

'Your project,' says Sol, blankly. He appears to be retrieviŋ information from some deep-buried database inside his compu-mind. He says: 'You're still devotiŋ your life to the Moving Mercury thing.' He doesn't phrase this as a question, and doesn't inflect the words, but Hope cannot miss the rebuke in his words.

'At least I'm not *devotiŋ my life*,' he snaps bak, louder than he planned, 'to tryiŋ to act out the fukiŋ *Oresteia* in real life.'

Sol blinks, pauses, and then relaxes his face into a smile, his first since comiŋ into the hotel. The smile is more emoticon than emotion, but it is, perhaps, a gesture towards a more human sort of interaction. 'Brother,' he says, 'did I ever tell you? When you first accused me of that I didn't know wat the *Oresteia* was. Afterwards I went to look it up on my palmcomp, but wat I typed in was *Rose Tyler*. I got two dozen companies run by people with that name, fictional characters, all sorts.' He lifts his beer, drinks, and then leaves the globe hangiŋ not far from his head, with the ostentatious ease-with-xero-g of the long-term Up-lander. 'I'm sorry it's a bad time for you, brother,' he says. 'But you can see that we have to seize this opportunity . . . can't you?' When Hope says nothing to this, he carries on, 'You've spent 15 years on this project . . . will another few days really—'

Years of frustration push the followiŋ words out of Hope's mouth: 'You've never believed in it, you've never seen the potential. I'm not doiŋ this for my own benefit, I'm really not. I'm thinkiŋ of the long-term future of the Uplands. I'm moved by my matriotism, and from where I'm sittiŋ from a truer love of the Uplands even than you. If Mother were alive she'd be right behind me.'

'Mother was the most practical human beiŋ ever born,' contradicts Sol. 'She was always concerned with the here, with the now, not with some far-distant cloud-fantasy like—' He immediately reins himself in. 'I didn't mean that, brother. I don't mean to be insultiŋ. But you have to axept that there are more pressiŋ things right now than—'

But Hope's pitiful little dander is up now. 'You talk about Mother as if you've known her for decades,' he objects, querulously, holdiŋ his drink in both hands like an orb of royal state. 'Sol, *I* barely remember her, and you're 2 years younger than me. You don't remember her. She's just a name, she's just a *reputation.*'

'I don't believe,' replies Sol, primly, 'that there's anybody who has spent longer researchiŋ or readiŋ about our mother than I.'

'That's my point. That's not the same thing as knowiŋ her.'

'Her blood is in me.'

'And me too – but apart from that you might as well be any Upland-infatuated groundliŋ, if you're sayiŋ that. I wasn't 10 years old when she—' he is goiŋ to say *died*, but the truth is they neither of them know for how long she lived after her capture by the Americans, so he alters it to '—was taken, and it's not as if she was a constant presence in our childhood for those first 10 years. It's not as if we saw much of her – be honest.'

'She loved us,' says Sol, mask-faced.

'I'm sure she did, brother. But she was certainly an *absentee* parent.'

'She had,' says Sol, his voice startiŋ to quiver dangerously, 'some rather important things to attend to duriŋ those early years . . .'

'I know, so she gives birth to a nation but she was shit as a mother.' But, even for Hope, this is too much like blasphemy, especially here, inside a buildiŋ that is hurtliŋ through the spacious territory that some of her more ardent followers have taken to calliŋ Gradiland, this nation she forged out of her own will. So Hope crumples his face up and shakes his head and says, 'Sol, Sol, Sol, why are we arguiŋ about Ma? Let's not go bak over all that. You know I love her as much as you do. She's as much my mother as yours.'

'You say you love her,' Sol says in a voice that counterpoints calmness with plangent unhappiness, 'yet you're prepared to let *him* go free, just because you're worried about some meetiŋ with some billionaire American.'

'It's not like that. I just think we need to talk about it,'

'We've talked about it ad nauseam.' This is true.

'He,' says Hope, 'is our father, after all.'

But they've been over and over this, between them, over the years. Sol, who has spent a certain amount of time in Russia, replies 'He is an *obmanshchitsa.*' This word means 'deceiver' or 'betrayer'.

Hope lowers his head. 'It's just that you talk as if he shot her himself. You talk as if he actually pulled the trigger. He wasn't personally responsible for the SWAE, after all.'

'Trace the cause and effect bak, and the whole chain starts with his betrayal. Besides – besides, who believes that? About the SWAE? I mean, who believes she truly was SWAE?'

'Who knows?'

There's a short silence, which is to speech what vacuum is to matter.

'Is there really a chance,' Sol asks, perhaps genuine, 'that this investor will bak your scheme? Do you really think? Doesn't seem likely to me. An *American* investor? Why would he advance the cause of the Uplands?'

'Because it will make him rich.'

'I assume he's already rich.'

'Yes, yes, I don't know,' sighs Hope. 'It'll require a different pitch to the usual. Usually I pitch to rich Uplanders, and I play up the contribution it will make to creatiŋ an independent and wealthy nation. But you're right of course, the matriotism line is hardly goiŋ to convince an American billionaire. I'll have to think of something else.'

'It doesn't sound like the matriotism line has persuaded any Uplanders either,' says Sol.

'You're right, of course,' Hopes repeats. 'It isn't that they're not matriotic – they are, generally. They just like the Uplands small and quaint and the way they remember them. They can't see the bigger picture.'

Sol unsniks himself, leaviŋ his globe of half-drunk beer hangiŋ in space; and Hope cannot stop himself thinkiŋ *that's probably the most expensive beer on sale in any bar, and you're not even goiŋ to drink it.* But

Sol has lots of money, enuff not to think about things like that. He didn't invest *his* entire fortune, and more, in the dream of shuntiŋ an entire planet across millions of miles of space. 'Are you goiŋ?' Hope asks.

By way of reply, Sol says, 'Give me the key.' And as Hope hands over the whimsically key-shaped chip, he adds, 'I need to chek out the room. I need to – store some things there.'

'My brother, the terrorist,' says Hope, half to himself, and is distracted by the motion of several people away to his left. One of them, he realises with a rustle of annoyance, is – yet again – the clownish Wilfrid Laurier. He catches Hope's eye, and waves to him, fiddliŋ now with his feet, readyiŋ himself to leave his table and come over to, wat? Be introduced to Hope's brother? Talk up MakB? Try to pimp him some first-class prostitution? But Sol, with the insolent ease of the show-offy Uplander, has discarded his snap-twangs altogether, and, haviŋ visually ascertained which level the room is at, has pushed off like a swimmer and is floatiŋ a bullet-line for the entrance to the circular corridor of that level.

'Hi,' says Laurier, arriviŋ. 'Was that a family resemblance I noticed?'

'My brother,' says Hope, lookiŋ after the planetary body in miniature Sol has become.

'I'm sorry I missed him. Hey, I wanted to invite you, officially, to the openiŋ; but your brother, hey, he's welcome too!' But Hope is not listeniŋ. He is heariŋ in his mind Sol sayiŋ 'I mean, who believes she truly was SWAE?', and wonderiŋ about it, and worryiŋ about it.

'I'm sorry,' he says, to Laurier, 'I'll have to catch up with you later – I've got to go give a presentation now to a potential investor.'

four

SWAE is an American acronym, shot while attemptiŋ escape; and as he prepares his presentation for Malet, Hope finds his imaginatively-enhanced memory strayiŋ bak to where he had been when he heard the announcement that Gradisil Gyeroffy had thuswise been killed. It was world news. Every network had carried the announcement, and it had generated a maelstrom of commentary and outrage. The fact that there had been no details meant that speculation was suked into the news vacuum. Had she been swaed soon after her capture by the Americans in '02? Had it happened shortly before the announcement in 2115? Had it happened at some time in between those 2 dates, and the US had delayed announciŋ it, knowiŋ that it would create global outrage? Hope had been at college, in Bern, when the news swamped the news outlets. Sol had phoned him at once, from Uppsala, and (in effect) ordered him to fly straight there. Which, of course, Hope had done; the 2 brothers actiŋ their roles, active, passive. Hope found Sol in tears; the only time in his whole life that he had ever witnessed that sort of moisture on his brother's face. Sol was drunk too. Sol drank all the time, and had done so since his early teens, but Hope had never before seen him actually drunk, as he was that one occasion. He had sworn a grand oath, like a screen villain, raisiŋ his arm and waggliŋ his twig-like fingers at Hope and sweariŋ *by my hands* that *he'll pay, he'll pay, just let me take his life and die myself.* The next day Sol made no reference to this outrageous promise, and Hope chose to believe that it had been the alcohol speakiŋ and that his brother had no memory of makiŋ it.

But, no. Sol had actually begun orientiŋ his life around the brown-dwarf stellar intensity of Gradi's death. He decided, moved by nothing more than the intuition of grief, that the announcement of SWAE was a lie, and that Gradi had been cold-bloodedly executed by the US, perhaps years before. This helped focus his grief. But it was easier for Sol than for his brother. Hope, at 24 had been a shallow and self-obsessed individual, and he knew it – a life constrained like a geisha's foot by money and indolence, an upbringiŋ that had done nothing to channel his excessive sensitivity and self-indulgence into a healthful version of adulthood. He despised himself most of the time, even as he continued in the self-oriented grooves of his life. But even at 24, Hope had possessed enuff insight to realise that Sol was seiziŋ on this announcement with the sort of savage glee that is not incompatible with genuine grief. Years of hazy uncertainty about the fate of their mother had, finally, precipitated out into something that admitted of action, of *movement towards*. He had a purpose in his life. This had not been the effect on Hope's life. Indeed, it had been 2 further years before he had, in conversation with various individuals whose names history has recorded, chanced upon the Moving Mercury idea.[1] They had wanted him to act as a figurehead for the project – Gradisil's eldest son, the Upland Bonny Prince, a minor celebrity. At first Hope had been happy with beiŋ merely a figurehead; but soon an osmotic process had steeped his dreams in the idea itself, and he had taken a more and more active role in the movement. He had used almost all his money – and a very large sum had devolved upon him upon his mother's death – in buyiŋ a quarter share, and then a half share, in MM, and in fundiŋ various necessary research exercises, AI virtual projections, hardware mok-ups and, of course, travel. Where his brother had fixated on killiŋ a single individual, he had become psychologically addicted to manoeuvriŋ a whole world to bring long-term prosperity to the Uplands; but both of them had been propelled, the pool-ball strikiŋ the pool-ball and lurchiŋ it into smooth motion, by the death of their mother.

And wat of that actual death? The event has been dramatised by a number of EU screen dramas and 3nimations, and, as has been the case for many of the memories a child should have of his or her parent, the fictionalisation has overwritten the reality. That this is so has been the been the bane of Hope's life; there has even been an art-house screen drama made about this facet of the existence of Hope and Sol, the way the sheer fame of their mother has meant that real memory has been overwritten by ersatz. Which means, in turn, that when Hope thinks bak to Gradisil's demise he sees it as a montage of dramatic angles, the rain-vexed landscape (had it even been rainiŋ when Gradi was SWAE?

---

[1] Three uplanders: Zhenia Allen had died in 2127. Farmer Pictus had sold all rights in his percentage of the idea to Hope in 2129, after finally growiŋ tired of the long period of frustration at the slow pace of project development; he went on to copyright certain ideas to do with undersea habitation. John Church had vanished in 2130 – a not uncharacteristic action for him, but one which left his percentage of the rights in the idea in legal limbo. By 2131, where we now are, Hope was the only main partner left from the original 4. Meanwhile prolonged financial drought had reduced the MM permanent staff to only 3 people, and only one full-timer.

Who knows?) the desperate dash across an open space, the small dark woman runniŋ literally for her life. Maybe it had been nothing like that. Who knows? Rat-tat, *bang*.

He generally prefers 3nimations to screen dramas. At least 3nimations use actual images of Gradi, brought bak to melodramatic life by the powers of information processiŋ. Some of the dramas he had seen have employed actors who resemble Gradisil very little, which is, to say the least, distractiŋ to her son when it comes to embellishiŋ the scant actual memories of her he has in his head.

Hope is waitiŋ now, in the tightly curviŋ corridor outside one of the Worldview's most expensive suites, for Malet's staff to allow him axess to the great man. He is nervous, nervous. He has had a dozen meetings like this over the last decade and a half, and none of them have brought results. It is very hard to continue believiŋ that MM will ever come to fruition. Very hard, and the effort of tryiŋ to keep faith with the project is exhaustiŋ and crepitates in his head. He's frightened of failiŋ; but then he's frightened of everything, so it is not failure particularly that torments him.

The door opens, and a woman floats out. Her head is shaven, a white ground upon which myriad little blak dots are visible, giviŋ her skull from a distance a grey, crepuscular sheen. There's a firmness, a razor-steel quality to her eyes, her mouth is set in a level line, and her body is clothed in tight thik cloth that reveals her sinewy figure but no detail – it is enuff to brew an erotic reaction out of the anxiety, the memory and the sense of powerlessness in Hope's head. That absurd, jak-in-box reflex, that Pavlovian erotic twitch. He hates himself for it. Get a grip, keep your thoughts steady. 'You can come through now, Mr Malet is waitiŋ,' she says, and Hope must apply the bromide of his own will-power to his suddenly perky erotic imagination. Why does it surprise him that a man of Malet's wealth would employ handsome women?

'Thank you.'

The leather strap whisks down flikeriŋly in his mind, to purify the texture of his skin from pudgy into gleamiŋly hurtful, *you – bad boy—*

He pulls himself through, hand-over-hand.

The decor of the Worldview emperor suite is haut-moderne, spacious, aquamarine walls with vermilion inset holopattern and a long strip of window providiŋ a spectacular sight: the world, the sky. The net-line of the world's horizon has gathered all the land and ocean and all the litter of cumulus and everything into a neatly demarcated arc at the bottom of the view; above is nothing but the rippleless sea of blak immensity. Light in the room means that not even the stars are visible.

'Mr Malet,' says Hope, his left hand on the wall, his right reachiŋ forward. He's floatiŋ a little higher than Malet, who has his feet fixed in the middle of the floor and looks as if he is standiŋ. 'I'm so pleased to meet you,' says Hope.

'Mutual,' says Malet.

He is a handsome man, regular features set proportionately in his oval face. The top of his head has that towelliŋ texture of thik hair close cropped. His eyes are a startliŋ, bright, pharmakos blue-green, the colour of pigeons' breasts. He wears the same sort of clothing as his assistant; an almost monkishly understated outfit for so wealthy a man; indeed he and his 4 attendants are giviŋ out a slightly ascetic, cultish vibe. Hope tries not to be distracted. Malet smiles, applyiŋ the considerable pressure of powerful will to bend slightly upwards the iron rod of his mouth.

Rather than float, rudely, in mid-air in front of this wealthy and powerful man (funny how the little social protocols seem to have developed spontaneously in this new land) Hope hooks an arm through a strap and settles himself against the wall. There are 3 people in the room, apart from the aristo-faced Mr Malet: the woman who had shown Hope in and 2 others, both male, both shaven-headed, both weariŋ the same outfits. It looks almost cultic. Hope beams at them, runs his right hand over his scalp. 'I feel a bit over-hairy,' he says, offeriŋ the observation as a way of lighteniŋ the mood, 'in present company!'

The mood does not lighten.

'So, Mr Gyeroffy,' says Malet. 'You want my money?'

'Not all of it!' says Hope, and laughs. But why is he tryiŋ the joky approach? It's clearly not appropriate; clearly not goiŋ to work; clearly he should—

'Pitch,' says Malet. 'Please – feel free. Pitch.'

'Let me tell you wat my company plans to do, Mr Malet,' says Hope, in a soberer voice. 'Let me tell you of wat your investment could mean for—' and this is the point, usually, when he would say *the Uplands*, but that's not goiŋ to play here, in the American hotel, with this American trillionaire, thrice the cover-star of *US Wealth*, so he substitutes, 'all humanity' and hopes that there's enuff species-pride in Malet's handsome head for the worm to nuzzle in there, the meme to fix itself. He looks to the man immediately on Malet's left, whose shaven red hair has grown bak just enuff to give his silver white scalp a rusty look; and then to the man to *his* left, with skin the colour of sherry and oil-blak eyes, a thoroughly Brahmin look about *him* to be sure, *very* handsome. He does not trust himself to look at the woman. He needs to keep his wits focused on the task. 'Is there an input for my thum?'

The redheaded man takes the thum and slots it into an expensive lookiŋ screen. Images pour out upon it, and Hope slips into his lecture, the familiar words settliŋ into their familiar grooves. As he speaks them they assume hypertext transcendence in his memory, each sentence overlaid with specific images from his decade-and-a-half of floggiŋ this shit all over Europe and the Uplands. He remembers sittiŋ in uncomfortable pepperwood chairs in some ancient buildiŋ in Eŋland-EU, or presentiŋ before the polished steel tables of a Romanian corporation, or floatiŋ in larger but far seedier Upland rooms than this – a multibillionaire called József in a green-painted pod-shaped house; a consortium of extremely wealthy breakaway Catholics and their Pope (one of 14 rival Popes) in a spare 7-room mansion; tryiŋ to present to an ancient man called Ustinov, whose skin cancers were beyond even pharmakos, and who had expressed interest but turned out only to want to reminisce about Gradi; or a dozen other occasions when piquant aspiration had soured to disappointment in the space of half an hour.

'Mercury is a world we know little about, even in the 22nd century – even as we start to spread through the solar system' (which is a reference, of course, to the American base on Mars, as if *that* means anything) 'we still pay Mercury no attention. Yet it's a fascinatiŋ world. Its diameter of 4 thousand and 80 kilometres' (all the facts and figures are right there, they haven't gone away) 'is a little over a third of Earth's, so it's small. At 3 point 3 times 10-to-th'-23 kilos, its mass is only 5 *per cent* of Earth's, so it's really very small. But do you know wat the surface gravity is?'

Look expectantly at your audience. Replies tend to vary from polite *do tell* to *how-the-fuk-would-I?* Malet only raises one eyebrow.

'Nearly *half* Earth's gravity!' says Hope. 'Point 4 gee. Point 4! The Moon is pretty much the same size and only pulls point 1 6 gee. Mercury's density is very close to Earth's, 5 and a half grams per cubic centimetre. Do you know why?'

'I feel you will tell me,' says Malet. He is bored. Hope needs to ratchet it up.

'The inner planets are roky worlds,' says Hope, speakiŋ more rapidly. 'Roky mantles with iron cores, like the Earth. Some iron from the core has got mixed in little ripples through the rok, for instance in the Earth, which is wat miners dig out, but most of it is far below, inaxessible, in the core. But Mercury – Mercury is pretty much all iron. *All iron!* Nobody knows why; but the roky mantle has been almost entirely shuked off. It may have been a catastrophic collision that knoked it all away, or maybe it's been blown off by the solar wind – the pressure of that is pretty intense that close to our system's lighthouse bulb.' Now, when Malet is lookiŋ his most bored, now the killer. 'Mr Malet, it's the greatest concentration of iron in the solar system. It's the most enormous resource, the most stupendous natural resource. And for the person prepared to—'

'Yes,' says Malet, and for a moment Hope thinks the great man is agreeiŋ with him, so he surges on: 'and here, in the Uplands, is a land cryiŋ out for that resource, limitless iron to build houses, planes, superstructures, billionaires happy to pay you to provide the materials with which the Uplands can be transformed . . .'

But Malet says 'Yes,' again, and Hope understands that it was punctuation, a full stop, not encouragement. So he stops.

Malet appears to be thinkiŋ about it. His Indian (or Pakistani, or Bangladeshi, or Kashmiri, or Independent Republic of Mumbaian, or watever he is) assistant shifts himself through the air, bringiŋ his mouth close to his master's ear.

'Right, Mr Gradisil,' says Malet, and Hope does not correct him. 'I'll tell you the problem I have. You say, move the iron here, in bulk, a planet-sized lump of it, sell it to the Uplanders for ambitious Upland construction projects,' he holds out his right hand, turns it over, turns it bak up, a dumb-show for *and so on, et cetera, kai ta loipa,* 'fine. Here's an investment niggle I have: those projects are the sorts of things governments buy. I don't mean to insult your nation, Mr Gradisil—'

'My nation?' interjects Hope. 'Ah but Mr Malet, wat *is* my nation? Is it a—?'

Malet waves this aside. 'But I don't see that the Uplands *have* that kind of government. There's government of a sort here, sure, a very loose, chimerical government, 2 or 3 prominent people squabbliŋ over who gets to be called the official heir of your mother. But there's not a public works department, you know? A taxation system whose revenues could be . . .'

Hope feels the sale slippiŋ from him. A rekless sense of abandonment comes to him. Interrupt the big guy, why not? 'I'm goiŋ to stop you there,' he says, tryiŋ to judge the proper level of loudness. Malet's eyebrows slide up his brow; not used to beiŋ interrupted. 'I don't think you're gettiŋ me, Mr Malet,' says Hope, firmly. 'You're right about the rhizomatic nature of governance in this land. If this were the 55th state of the USA then I'd probably be pitchiŋ to a government department in the first place. But it isn't. This is about free enterprise; and wat I'm offeriŋ is a focus, a premise, for a massive engineeriŋ feat that will do *more* than bring a saleable resource into this territory. Much more.'

Malet breathes in, breathes out, waves his hand in front of his mouth to dissipate the gas. 'Go on.'

'It's the moving of Mercury, as much as the seizure of this enormous lump of saleable iron – it's the *moving*, Mr Malet, that is the attraction for an investor such as yourself. It's gainiŋ a leverage share in the idea, the technology. It's makiŋ you a master of the universe. It's so that future generations will look bak,' (he's extemporisiŋ now, but the spirit is in him, he feels on *fire*, the words all *flow*) 'history will look bak and say, *Malet! he reached out his arm and laid his right hand upon a planet and moved it*. That's wat we're talkiŋ about. The resource – yes, that'll offset the initial investment, that'll set up a 20-year timetable for retrieviŋ the initial money, after which it's all profit. But that's not the half of it.'

Everybody in the room is lookiŋ at him. Is this wat his mother used to feel, addressiŋ little cadres of followers in hurtliŋ tinpot rooms in the early days of the republic? It's a rare feeliŋ for Hope, an addictive one.

'Yes,' says Malet, and this time it's a prompt. Hope pulls a bigger breath into his lungs, and sets about explaining how he will lay an arc of wing over the sunny side of the planet, and how that will move the world, the whole of the world.

'The actual arc,' says Hope.

'Arc?'

'The arc of wingfront, on the sunny side of the world. The arc need not be the full 24-hundred kilometres of daytime planetary stretch. About half of that area, a little under 14-hundred kilometres, would be laid; and even then the installation would be a dotted line: 5 hundred metres of front, and a gap of about the same, repeated over and over.'

'So 7 hundred klims. Still a long stretch of – wat is it? Cable?'

'It's not the cable that'll be the expense,' says Hope. 'We can use regular cable, spool it up, fly it there, unspool it. It'll need a ceramic sheath, or it'll simply melt in those temperatures, but that's not the expense either. I mean, it'll melt anyway, but it'll retain conductivity inside the sheath. The problem is the one and a half thousand generators, each of which will need to be heavily shielded and heat-resistant, and fitted in place. That's where the project takes on,' he searches for the right word. 'Takes on epic dimensions.' He is startiŋ to feel tired; haviŋ passed over the little hump of excitement, and after last night's lak of sleep, but he pushes himself on, summons a little more sparkle. 'But it's doable.'

The Indian assistant interjects: 'How do we get the materials down to . . . ?' The question hangs.

'It's all part of the development strategy,' says Hope. 'Every feature has been planned. Gettiŋ there isn't hard, it's downhill all the way there after all. We've planned a kind of solar parachute, to guide the descent into Mercury orbit.'

'Also quan?'

'Everything is quan.'

'And the US military are . . . ?'

Hope peps up again; this is an important point. 'It's old technology now; it's half a century old – more. Now it's perfectly true that the US have, that your government have developed newer more efficient forms of quantum wingfront, and that's top secret. But the basic principle, and the original models, these have been public domain for a long time. We don't need the most up-to-date model for wat we're proposiŋ. It's not the nuance we're lookiŋ for, it's the brute, the brute force of it. Listen: this is a world that is beiŋ continually blasted by the most intense solar wind in the system. It's already the most ion-scarred world in – all we need to do, really, is nudge it a little, a little push with the wingfront and it will shift. We'll be pushiŋ it uphill, but it'd be like helpiŋ – imagine a baseball sittiŋ on top of a powerful fan, the fan is blowiŋ but just with not quite enuff force to lift the ball, and all we're doiŋ is fixiŋ a thread and giviŋ it the littlest . . . of hoiks . . . or a better way of thinkiŋ would be, we're fittiŋ a peak to the ball, adaptiŋ the ball into an aerodynamic shape that . . .'

They're all still lookiŋ at him; they're all still interested. This is startiŋ – he cannot dare hope, but – this is startiŋ to look possible.

'At the moment,' he says, 'all this immensely valuable resource is stuk in the least hospitable place in the solar system, pressed against the ragiŋ-hot cheek of the sun itself. We *can* reach down and pull it up here. You can, Mr Malet. *You* can do this.' It's close. He can almost feel the money pouriŋ from Malet and into the project. 15 years!

Malet breathes in again, breathes out. 'And these parachutes . . . ?'

'The? Oh, ah, that's just the—'

'Tell me about them.'

He thinks. 'They're not the most significant detail of the . . .'

'Mr Gradisil,' says Malet. 'Let me tell you about myself. Let me tell you about the vision I had.'

Vision is good. Hope feels the mood is positive enuff for him to try this: 'That's why I came to you, Mr Malet, because you are a man of vision. It's no secret that I have tried to raise funds for this project amongst Uplanders, and it's no secret that they've been too blinkered to see through to the possibilities. But you, Mr Malet, you're the first non-Uplander I've approached, and it's precisely because you have vision.'

Malet, who listens patiently to all this, says: 'I don't mean that kind of vision.'

Oh.

Something is wrong here.

Hope keeps the anxiety off his face, inclines his head, 'I'm sorry, I misunderstood.'

'I'm not a mystic, Mr Gradisil,' says Malet. 'I don't believe in God. But I have had a vision. Venus, Mr Gradisil. Venus.'

'The planet?'

He doesn't dignify this with a response, but instead says: 'You've told me some interestiŋ things about Mercury, things I didn't know. Let me repay the compliment, with some facts about Venus. Same size and density as Earth, a little closer into the sun, a hell-world. Temperature varies from a minimum of 2-hundred-30 Kelvin to 7-hundred-and-77 Kelvin. The average temperature is 737. The atmosphere is 96 per cent carbon dioxide. The clouds are made of sulphur dioxide. Sulphuric acid falls as rain. At ground level there's no wind, whereas the cloudtops are ripped by winds of 3-hundred-50 miles an *hour*.' He's relishiŋ this account of *Dis*. He's grinniŋ. 'Now there are volcanoes on Venus, spewiŋ CO_2 into the atmosphere, but this is a world entirely without tectonic activity. Tell me, Mr Gradisil, how can this be? How can you have volcanoes without tectonic activity?'

Wat on earth is this guy talkiŋ about? Hope says: 'I don't know.'

'Very well, here's another question. A million years ago Venus was like a steamier version of Earth. There were oceans. There was plenty of genetically-mutatiŋ sunshine and radiation. There must have been life.'

'OK,' says Gradisil. 'I'll confess I'm not sure I see where this is goiŋ.'

'So my second question is how did we get from there to here? From Eden to Hell?'

'I don't know.'

'No. I didn't know either, and I didn't care. I made my fortune in tradiŋ and developiŋ pharmakos. My horizon was the human body. Then I had my vision. Never before in my life, and not since, has this happened to me. Something communicated with me – I don't know, exactly, how. I certainly don't know why. But they did.'

'They?'

'Venusians.'

Malet says this with so straight a face that Hope, lookiŋ intently at him, decides not to laugh, even a warm we're-all-in-the-joke laugh. Can he really believe this? 'I'm afraid,' he says cautiously, 'Mr Malet, that I don't – quite—'

'It's a lot to swallow I know,' says Malet, blithely. 'But understand this, Mr Gradisil. I'm not askiŋ you to follow me, or even to believe me. You only need to understand that, haviŋ spent 3 decades only makiŋ money, I am now driven to move sunwards. The American government isn't interested; they think there's nothing on Venus to interest them, nothing but hell. But I know – better—'

This is terrible. Hope can feel that his smile has become fixed and unconvinciŋ, but – fuk. He had no idea. There's really no end to the madness of the very rich. This guy is clearly not goiŋ to sink his billions into MM. This meetiŋ is a dead end, just a chance for him to rehearse his craziness in front of a blinkiŋ, grinniŋ audience.

'One thing I would say,' Malet is goiŋ on. 'It doesn't need a vision to realise this truth.'

'Truth?'

'That there must be aliens, Venusians.'

'Must be?'

'The volcanoes are not volcanoes, they're heat transference portals. That's why they're arranged so regularly, and how they've come into beiŋ without tectonic activity.'

'Transferriŋ heat from?'

'The interior of the planet, of course. Increased solar radiation, abundant water, life *must* have evolved quiker on Venus, must have reached sentience, intelligence, much earlier than on Earth. They're ahead of us. They abandoned the surface of their world – who knows why. Pollution, natural disaster, some other reason. It doesn't really matter. They went underground. They constructed this enormous series of vents to transfer heat from the centre of their world up and away, to make their underground kingdom liveable, the ideal temperature. They've been doiŋ this for as long as – who knows how long? But it's turned the surface of their world into hell. But they don't care about the surface, they've perfected their society underneath the surface. Wat other explanation is there?'

He has stopped. Wat to say? 'It's an interestiŋ,' Hope says. 'An interestiŋ—'

Malet smiles very broadly. 'Mr Gradisil,' he says, 'please do not be alarmed. And do not be self-conscious. One advantage in beiŋ as wealthy as I am is that you need no longer care wat people think of you. You, for instance, are thinkiŋ that I am a little insane. I don't care wat you think. And wat's more, Mr Gradisil, you shouldn't be thinkiŋ that. You should be thinkiŋ *will he fund my project?* That's all.'

'That is indeed wat I am thinkiŋ, Mr Malet. That's why I'm here.'

'I am interested in your ideas for quantum parachutes to negotiate the steep downhill towards the sun. And I'm interested in your plan to move an entire world.'

Hope breathes in. On the wall, the screen is still cycliŋ its images and charts.

'Well, Mr Gradisil,' says Malet. 'I'll tell you. I will present your case to my management board. I shall present your case – positively.'

Hope takes in a breath, and releases it. He didn't see that comiŋ. 'That's excellent news,' he says, stunned. Then, with more feeliŋ, 'That's excellent news – you're goiŋ to fund the project?'

'I am very interested in your project Mr Gradisil. It seems to me to be financially plausible. It seems to me a high-profile project that can only enhance the reputation of my company. And perhaps more importantly, it seems to me an opportunity for engineeriŋ on a planetary scale – something to impress the Venusians. They have already achieved this level of engineeriŋ capability. We need to show them that we are on a level with them before we make contact.'

Hope has the strenuous sensation of blood pumpiŋ in his skull, sketchiŋ a coil-shape. His skin is serratiŋ into goosebumps all over.

'I'm sorry, Mr Malet, can I just confirm . . . ?'

'You've done it, Mr Gradisil,' booms Malet, throwiŋ his arms wide. 'You've convinced me. You've done it.'

five

His head is still slightly swollen with excess blood from arrival in the Uplands, which makes it hard for him to distinguish between the physiological and the metaphysical sense of cranial enlargement. Fifteen years of disappointment, the shatteriŋ of his entire fortune, the loss of the 3 partners who had first proposed the idea until he stood alone, the ridicule of his friends, even of his brother – and now, at the last gasp, the project is to be funded. It is to come off. Hope cannot believe it. He tingles with an undescribable thrill.

It is goiŋ to happen. The things he had used to prettify Malet's ego, about posterity regardiŋ him as a god, as somebody who reached out his hand and moved an entire world, this is the secret ambition in his heart. His mother helped give birth to a new nation – fine, but hundreds of human beiŋs have managed as much on the ground, from Solon to Stalin. *He* would move a world, and none have done this before.

He is, to use one of Paul's phrases, as happy as a marriage bell. He's not used, in fact, to this sensation of happiness. It is almost uncomfortable; like a sort of thin pain in his chest, the expansion of gas in an awkward corner of his torso. He floats, rather than usiŋ the snap-twang, along the corridor away from Malet's room. He emerges at the top (the bottom, the side, it hardly matters) of the atrium, close to the great transparent dome with its dartboard framiŋ of panes of weave-glass. There's the whole world through the glass, and he – it is absurd that he has never been struck by this before, or perhaps not absurd but a pitiable reflection on the misery of his life in the Uplands – is on top of the whole world. He stares at it. Zhenia gave up all hope of this ever comiŋ to fruition long before she died. At least she kept her despair to herself; Farmer harassed and harassed Hope with his loss of faith in the project, badgeriŋ him into surrenderiŋ a second massive chunk of his fortune in order to buy the crabby older man out. And John disappeariŋ, probably suicide. All of them had given up, but he, Hope, had endured, and it was endurance, it seems, that won out. He'd beaten them all.

He can't believe it.

Through the atrium's dome the world is dark, acned with little nodules and rashes of light. But the sun is just around the corner, because the arc of atmosphere huggiŋ the blak horizon is alive in its blueness, intensely and purely blue, like the crown of lit-brandy fire on a Christmas puddiŋ. Oh happy day!

A confident tourist launches himself towards the floor (the ceiling – the other end) of the atrium without utilisiŋ the comfortiŋ tug of the central line; and he flies, with that giddy spry Peter Pan-ness, straight along, the look on his face a delight purified by a residuum of primal fear at his fall. And *that is life*, Hope thinks. That's the purest kind of happiness there is. He launches himself, like this flier, from the walkway and skims through the air down (or up, or along). He has got to call Véra. He must tell her, first away. Her and the children.

There are ways of patchiŋ one's mobile into the network that supplies Upland-groundliŋ traffic, but it's absurdly expensive. Although of course, he can afford it now! When the deal comes through, he'll have plenty of money! But, then again, it wouldn't do to tempt fate – to throw money away too lavishly, and so he makes his way to the far floor and then along to the public phone hoods. His soul is thrummiŋ.

The call takes about a minute to be connected.

'Véra? Véra?'

And there she is, on screen.

'My darliŋ I have wonderful news,' he booms, like an actor pro-*jec-tiŋ* a line to the very bak of a great atrium, and his elation is so intense that it even obscures, from himself, how unlike him, how inappropriate to their wounded marriage, this mode of speakiŋ is – almost as if he is mokiŋ her Russian ancestry, with actorish unselfconsciousness, the world is *my* stage, listen to *me*, dare link wander fool knee ooze! None of that matters now. The primal curse of a woman, which is to marry a man mainly for his money, and then for that money to vanish, would shortly be undone, he would return the charm to their life together, *he* would. The magic word spoken. The end in sight.

'I've spoken with the investor I mentioned . . .'

'This is MM again,' she says.

'Yes, it's MM.' Of course! Does she not know that's wat he's doiŋ in the Uplands? Did she think he'd gone off to gallivant?

'And?'

'Véra, but this guy's goiŋ to bak me. He's a bit wako, but he's goiŋ to throw all his money at me. It'll be the change for us all. It'll mean money, it'll mean the project is goiŋ to finally come off.'

'Sol was in touch.'

'Sol? Yes, he's here, he's come up here to be with me.' Sol? 'Why did he get in touch with *you*?'

'He says you've discovered your father. He said you've—'

'Shsh! Not on the phone – the phone may be—'

Véra looks crossly out of the screen. 'Don't snap at me Hope. I'll not talk to you if you *snap*.'

'Véra . . .'

By alludiŋ directly to Paul's presence, and Sol's intentions towards him, she had found the only way to spoil the elation of gettiŋ bakiŋ for MM. Sol was intent on killiŋ. But that would ruin the deal – it could hardly do anything other than ruin it. The whole business with Sol had, he understands, been pushed out of the currents of his mind by excitement, by the prospect of money, by the possibility that he could turn 15 years of failure into a glorious world-changiŋ success. But Malet will hardly give money to a murderer, to an assassin, a father-killer— 'Véra,' he says, and, stupidly, there are tears prikiŋ at the bak of his eyes, for fuk's sake, *tears* – it's the simple frustration of it. To come this close to success after all this time! And then to have it snatched away at the last moment! It's intolerable, it cannot be tolerated. He cannot tolerate it. 'Véra,' he says, 'Véra, wat did Sol say?'

'He said that he was goiŋ to the hotel you're at. Is he there?'

'Yes he's here.' Hope can't believe he is cryiŋ now. Somebody should punch him to shut him up! He's nearly 40, and here he is cryiŋ like a child. But it's so unfair! He blinks and double-blinks, tryiŋ to clear the water from his eye. It doesn't, in the xero g, roll down his cheeks, but it bulges out, and bell-shaped blobs separate and drift away, propelled by the paddle-action of the eyelids.

'He said that he was goiŋ to *collect* you, that the whole MM business was history now. I'll confess I was pleased to hear it, Hope. It's suked you dry. It's taken all our money. You need to move beyond it.'

His skin is prikliŋ with his tearfulness. 'But it's finally payiŋ off! This guy is goiŋ to bak the project – there will be lots of money now. I know it's been hard, but it's all comiŋ good now!'

Véra looks suspicious. 'You sure? This wouldn't be the first time you've . . .'

'This guy's real! I mean, he's a bit exentric, he's got some pretty waky ideas. But he's wealthy, he's real, and he's keen.'

'Hope,' says Véra. 'Are you *cryiŋ*?'

'I've got to go, love, I've got to go talk to Sol.' He hangs up, and the abrupt termination of this conversation with his long-sufferiŋ wife acts, obscurely, as the trigger to a full sobbiŋ outflow of tears.

six

He gets his emotions under control, hangiŋ in the air faciŋ a wall, near one of the barcode-like fan grilles from which faintly-scented fresh air pulses gently. Every wipe of his overfull eyes spills pearls and uncut diamonds of brine into the air, to drift away into the general space, ultimately, perhaps, to be suked into grilles set in the walls and disposed of, or perhaps recycled. Hope needs to speak to Sol. That's the crucial thing now. He has to make Sol understand that his deal has come through; that the whole revenge plan will have to find another venue.

He makes his way up (or down) through the atrium, round the curviŋ corridor at the top, where the tall, spacious, luxury rooms and suites are located, and to the door. It looks like a downbelow hotel room door, that's how lavish it is. Hope doesn't have the key; he gave that to Sol, so he knoks. Knok-knok.

There's a pause, and then the door opens, Sol lookiŋ out furtively. 'Come in,' he says. 'I've discovered something.'

'Sol,' says Hope. 'I've got something to tell you.'

Sol ignores this. 'I cheked the manifests. He's—'

'How did you do that?'

Sol looks blank. He doesn't like beiŋ interrupted. 'Wat?'

'How did you chek the manifests? They're not public.'

'I haked the – it doesn't matter. It doesn – the important thing is that he's not here under his real name. He must be travelliŋ under a seudonym.'

'That's unsurprisiŋ,' says Hope. 'He's hardly likely to come bak here to the Uplands and announce to the world who he is. Even on American territory.'

'That's the second time you've said that,' said Sol, with his peculiar sternness of voice. 'I told you before. *They* don't own territory up here. This is *our* territory. This hotel, all their trade, it's all on our sufferance.'

'I don't care,' says Hope, as earnestly as he can manage. 'Listen to me Sol: the meetiŋ today went well.'

'I'm delighted for you.'

'It went very well. They're goiŋ to bak me. Malet is goiŋ to fund the project. Fifteen years of my life, which I had begun to think must be wasted years, will not be wasted. Everything I've been workiŋ for – it's validated.'

Sol's face has assumed its mask expression. His thin face. It's not puffy as Hope's still is, his is a true Uplander's skinniness, the tight places where his skin snags on the bones beneath, the glassy blonde lids of his eyes, the eyeballs themselves shiny like polished stone. Hope must make him understand how important this project is (was). He must at least try. 'Sol,' he urges. 'It's been my whole life. We can't wrek it now. It's been,' he repeated, his voice falteriŋ at the feebleness of simply reiteratiŋ the statement, 'my whole life.'

'Wrek it?'

Hope suks in air, blows it out, too aggressive an exhalation to be a sigh. 'We can't kill Father here, not here. We'll have to – postpone it. If we kill him here then it'll collapse the deal. 15 years!'

'I'll tell you how it seems to me,' says Sol, and he is speakiŋ in a low yet forceful tone. 'Fifteen years is shit. It's been twice that since *he* betrayed Mother,' (that way he had of utteriŋ that single syllabic personal pronoun, pressurisiŋ it with such significance and loathing) 'since *he* killed her, he's had 30 years of sweet life with that partner of his, the other traitor, liviŋ in American luxury. That weighs heavily against me, that's intolerable to me. Do you understand? For 30 years we've not been able to get to him, and now here he is, and we cannot let him slip away again. Wat – another 30 years? You think it would be fair to let him live on for another 30 years? He's 68. He'll live at least as long as that, if we don't punish him. We must punish him now. The time is here. My brother, are you really sayiŋ – think carefully, and answer me: are you *really sayiŋ* that we should let him just go?'

Hope has an intimation of the impossible vacuum chasm that exists between himself and his brother, and it makes him despair.

'I'm just sayiŋ.'

'Fate has donated him to us,' says Sol, with infuriatiŋ certitude.

'No, Sol,' he says. But he cannot advance on those 2 words, he cannot think of a clearer or purer way of registeriŋ his feeliŋs. 'No, Sol,' he says again.

Sol betrays the facial webwork of annoyance. It looks odd on his usually hypercontrolled visage. 'Wat do you mean? Wat do you mean, *No, Sol*? Wat does that mean?'

'I mean—'

'You aren't challeŋiŋ the facts?'

'He's our *father*,' says Hope. This is a desperate strategy; this is ignoriŋ a decade and a half of intense if intermittent discussion between the 2 brothers, weariŋ away the sinew connectiŋ sons to father with the unbluntable flint of justice, of righteous anger, of the death of Gradi herself. But Hope can't think of another argument. 'We can't fukiŋ murder him, he's our father. It would be—' but, first with an *umm*, and then with a furious *ach!* he must admit he can't think of the word, can't remember the term, and so finishes lamely, 'the Greeks had a word for wat it is.' Then, repetition to cover the lameness of this: 'He's our *father*.'

Sol has smoothed the web of lines out of his face, and taken refuge behind the mask again. 'I can't believe you're tryiŋ that line of argument,' he says, levelly. 'He betrayed our mother to imprisonment and death. Have you forgotten that?'

'He's our father,' Hope repeats, stubbornly.

Sol places his right forefinger in at the outside corner of his right eye, and his left forefinger in at the outside corner of his left eye, and just holds them there, as if holdiŋ the eyeballs in, or perhaps as if meditatiŋ. He speaks, again in a level, controlled voice. 'This is the most selfish thing I've ever known you to say. Of your many, that's the worst. You're sayiŋ this to preserve a business deal you have just made. Think of that! Just to preserve some money-grubbiŋ deal. I don't care for how much, or for how long you've been planniŋ the deal.' He released the fingers, and 2 pads of whiteness sit momently at the outside of his 2 eyes, until the blood seeps through the skin to fill them again. 'The truth is, you're puttiŋ your profit before justice.'

'Oh,' says Hope, genuinely stung. He's really wounded by that. 'Oh,' he says again.

'I don't wish to talk of this further,' says Sol, becomiŋ pompous. 'If you truly value profit over justice for our mother . . .'

'How can you say that?' retorts Hope, and, for the second time in an hour, tears are threateniŋ to pour from his eyes, smokiŋ the baks of the eyeballs with an acrid little flame. He dabs his face into the crook of his right arm. 'I loved Mother more than . . .'

'Prove it!'

This is impossible. 'Sol, you're not listeniŋ to me,' says Hope, without hope, and Sol proves the bleak truth of the assertion by immediately launchiŋ into some lengthy disquisition, not all of which his brother follows, about some immensely powerful nerve agent, some toxin, presumably the assassination weapon. But instead of followiŋ these ins and outs Hope's focal length grows long, and Sol's face becomes furrily blurred, and the background comes into sharp relief, and he watches 2 elderly but well-preserved hotel guests tryiŋ and failiŋ, tryiŋ and failiŋ, tryiŋ and *succeediŋ*, to hook themselves into the downward line, and descendiŋ through the atrium with delighted expressions on their faces.

seven

They spend the night together, in their expensive double room, brother and brother. Night is merely a convenience of the hotel's timetable, of course; it's night every 40 minutes up here. But people must sleep, and so for the first time in decades the 2 brothers go to bed in the same room. Hope tries again to raise the subject of his meetiŋ with Malet. He tells Sol about it, tries to get him to see how crucial a breakthrough this is. 'It'll change the Uplands – it's the chance for the Uplands to break through. Think how we'll be with a whole world-sized lump of iron as a raw material! We'll become a superpower.'

Sol is watchiŋ a news-channel, only half his attention on his brother. 'It's a beautiful dream, brother.'

'It can be made real.'

'That,' says Sol, noncommittal, 'will be a great day when that happens.'

'But we can make it happen right now, with Malet's money.'

Sol snorts. 'He doesn't sound like a very reliable investor.'

'Wat do you mean? He's a trillionaire.'

'All that stuff about Venusians? He's wako.'

'Exentric,' corrects Hope, over-loud.

'Wako.'

'And even if he has his exentricities, but that doesn't matter, that's not the – his money isn't wak, even if *he* is.'

'I wouldn't be so sure,' says Sol.

At this the conversation fails between them, and soon after Sol falls asleep. By the time Hope falls asleep in turn it is much later, and when he wakes he is alone in the room.

It's another day. Sol, already up and dressed by the time Hope wakes, tells him that he is goiŋ down to the lobby to arrange for a taxi-plane. Groggy with sleep Hope does not interrogate this statement further, although obviously this is the getaway craft, which must mean that Sol is planniŋ to commit the political murder sooner rather than later. But

433

Hope doesn't want to think about that, and turns his face to the wall as his brother leaves.

He has to get out of the room. He doesn't want to think about it. He pulls himself out of the sleepiŋ bag and pulls off the CO_2 disperser; he moves about, turns his body into a process of circulation. He tries to distract his mind, but his thoughts keep returniŋ to his brother. His brother is driviŋ him beyond sanity. Just the presence of him, with that implacable bronze-hard will of his, that remnant of his mother in him. Why, Hope wonders, didn't I get those genes? Essence of Gradi. So that essence went to Sol, and I got . . . wat? Here's a window, lookiŋ out (says the slowly circliŋ legend) upon the oceanus noctis, although he doesn't know wat that means. He's at the end of the corridor now, where it gives way to the atrium. Here, Hope pauses. He looks along the length of the atrium, sees people risiŋ and sinkiŋ on the central lines, sees some of the more adventurous guests flyiŋ directly through the air. A young couple, 2 beautiful young men, arm snaked in arm, drift over to Hope's window and look out. 'See!' says one to the other. 'You can see the comet!' Hope can't see anything, and neither can the second beautiful young man, until his companion fingers the smartglass to magnify the image, and there it is: its head no bigger than a bright star, its tail a narrow-apexed triangle of misty white. It looks, to Hope's eyes, like an icicle hangiŋ horizontally in the sky. Ominous. Hope has that gastric discomfort, that sensation of fear in his gut. It's all leadiŋ inevitably somewhere bad.

He doesn't want to be thinkiŋ this way – he'd prefer not – so, so, turniŋ to the atrium again, and Hope begins systematically to scan all the facilities. He is thinkiŋ of where would be a good place to visit, to take his mind off things. The bar at the top (or bottom), the other bar at the bottom (or top), and at various interludes in the space in-between two shops, the MakB outlet, which of course is yet to open, a coffee parlour, a high-price communication shop.

Coffee. So Hope pushes, flies, grabs and pulls himself down to the coffee shop. And there, inside behind weave-glass sittiŋ with his long legs hooked under the table, talkiŋ to somebody – no, not to just *somebody*, but to David Slater himself, the celebrity himself – is Hope's father. He's right there. Hope thinks: if Sol were here, would he hurl himself inside, stab him through the heart himself, make a speech about betrayal and freedom . . . Wat would he do?

Perhaps it is not so surprisiŋ that 2 men, both stayiŋ in the same hotel, a facility from which it is not possible to step outside, will bump into one another after a few days; but to Hope it feels like destiny.

He enters. He hasn't seen his father in 2 decades. There are still those butterflies in his stomach; or perhaps those crawliŋ, tikliŋ sensations are pupae, maggots, worms. The shop has an oval walkway, forever circliŋ around its tables, on which moving surface are little rubber hooks designed for ease of feet insertion. Hope toes one of these, and rolls around to the bak of the store, where his father is sittiŋ right there, talkiŋ to David Slater (of all people!) as if it were the most normal thing in the world to be speakiŋ with this celebrity. His wife left him, Hope recalls, because she decided he was Lucifer, or rather the Devil. Wat a strange thing – never to have met this man before, yet to know such intimate details about his life.

He's here, and his father is here.

Hope steps off the walkway not far from their table, floats in space. Who's it? Slater has cloked him in the corner of his eye, and is lookiŋ round. The man's a celebrity, he's used to being approached by strangers, and his face has adopted a blandly distant expression, sign your flimsy? Have my picture taken with my arm round your girl? Talk to your mother on the phone for a second? Sure, sure. That slightly over-earnest facial settiŋ, like a visual correlative of the bored sigh. His right hand is old, the skin stretched and a little thin-lookiŋ, despite the best that pharmakos can do; but the left hand, in its waxy pinkness, is forever young. It will not age.

'Dad,' says Hope, and looks past the suddenly puzzled face of Slater.

'My God,' says Paul. 'My God, is that you, Hope?'

'Dad,' says Hope again.

Paul looks aghast, just for a moment, but then he looks astonished; then he looks delighted. It is this last expression that upsets Hope the most. He half rises from his table, but his knees are sniked under there and he sits again. 'My God,' he says, again, 'wat are you doiŋ here?'

'Hi Dad,' he mumbles. He is nearly 40 years of age, and yet to stand in front of his father reduces him chronologically to his teens again.

'Hope, wat are you *doiŋ* here?'

'Dad, yeah.'

'Wat are you doiŋ *here?*'

There's a danger that the conversation between them will resolve into nothing more than this, Hope sayiŋ *Hi Dad* and Paul Caunes sayiŋ *My God, wat are you doiŋ here?* over and over, round and round, orbitiŋ forever; but David Slater intervenes.

'Paul, this is your *son*? Fantastic – fan*tas*tic to meet you, sir. It's an honour. Won't you join us? We're just haviŋ a coffee, jawiŋ, just hangiŋ out, and you're very welcome to join us.' Each wrinkle in his handsome face marks the place where the parchment of the skin has been repeatedly folded and folded in one or other beaming, smiling, asserting, positive expression.

Hope hooks his toe into the underside of the table, pulls himself down, grabs with his hands and settles himself on the stool, all without takiŋ his eyes off his dad. He looks so old. He knew, of course, that he was old, but somehow Hope didn't expect to see him lookiŋ so old. His hair, a little too long for xero g, floats frizzily; his skin, though pharmakos-preserved, looks thin, tiny wrinkles unmissable like craks in the glaze of his face. His long body is thin, starved, pauce, which emphasises the gangly, slightly dyspraxic flow of its motion. His elbows and knees, underneath the cloth, must be like knots in rope. It's been 15 years. 'So,' says Slater. 'Since you guys are too stunned to – you've not seen one another in a while, I guess?'

'No,' says Paul.

'Well, sir, allow me to introduce myself. My name is David Slater.'

'But I know who you are,' says Hope, and Slater inclines his head in slight aknowledgment of his celebrity. 'I didn't know you knew my father.'

'We've been friends for a long time.'

'You haven't answered my question,' presses Paul, lookiŋ at his son intently. 'Why are you here? In this hotel?'

'I'm meetiŋ,' says Hope. 'By which I mean to say, I have met – I have a company, and I've had a meetiŋ up here with a potential investor. My company is involved in puttiŋ together a very large project, bringiŋ a massive new resource of iron to – I needed, we needed investment money, and . . .'

'When's your meetiŋ?'

'It was yesterday.'

'Really? And how did it go?'

Is this the sort of conversation one should have with one's father, not haviŋ seen him for 20 years, haviŋ parted then on poor terms? Is this the way to talk to a man you are conspiriŋ to kill? 'It went very well. It's Malet – you know of him?'

'Of course! But he's rich! He's super-rich. And he's investiŋ in your project?'

'He's bakiŋ it entire. It's goiŋ to save the project, the company.'

'But this is fantastic news,' says David Slater, loudly, beamiŋ. 'Fantastic. Maybe we should float on down to a bar and get some champagne?'

'Sure,' says Hope, without takiŋ his eyes off his father, and immediately upon utterin that single monosyllable, its sibilant collapsin into a hum, he thinks to himself: *wat am I doin*? He does not know why he came here into this coffee parlour to confront his father. How has he slipped into this sociable-friendly mode? There's an answer of course, and it even occurs to him, but he doesn't like it. It probably has to do with a sort of masochism of the spirit, something Hope has had cause to register within his psyche on several previous occasions. The killer that maintains a healthy self-esteem and psychological balance is the killer who objectifies and denigrates his prey, as alien, vermin, a stain, a problem, nothing more. That way the process of eliminatin another consciousness does not stik its cactus-skin in your throat as you try to swallow it. But *get to know* your victim, humanise him, and you *will* do yourself psychic damage when you murder him. This is not because no-man-is-an-island-all-are-parts-of-the-same-continent, although some have thought so. Rather it is because the process of empathy in the homo sapiens mind depends upon a sort of clonin, or xeroxin, or overlayin of one's own self-identity on the symbolic version of the other; and that once one has done that with another human, killin them means, unavoidably, killin a part of yourself. And yet, knowin the implacability of his brother, and knowin how implicated he is himself in this same murderous intent, Hope has still elected to introduce himself to his father again.

Or he could warn him – get out! Get away! Your other son is murderous towards you . . . But those words don't come.

'Sure,' says Paul, smilin at his son. 'It's so good to see you again! I mean, I know a lot of water has flowed under a lot of bridges . . .'

'And a lot of clichés have been clichéd,' laughs David Slater, scratchin an itch on his brow with his artificial finger.

'That was a long time ago,' says Hope, and it sounds in his head as if somebody else is speakin. Wat is he doin? How can he *say* that? It's not a long time ago. It lives in a continuous present in his mind. How could it not?

'It is,' says Paul, noddin, lookin sombre. 'I guess time is a great healer.' But Hope thinks how wrong this is: time is what adds gangrene to a fresh wound. How could anybody think elsewise?

'I guess,' puts in Slater, seeminly a bit giddy with the buzz of this reunion, 'I guess cliché is a great conversational aide.'

Paul waves his right hand at Slater's face, flikin his fingers as if dismissin him as a tiresome buzzin insect, but he is grinnin, it is all a joke.

'How's Sol?' he asks his son. 'You seen him?'

'Yeah,' says Hope, and then stops himself before he can add *He's here in the hotel*, which would be a stupid thing to say for many reasons.

'He alright?'

'I'd love,' says Hope, and he tries to pull himself together. 'I mean, I would love to catch up. I'd really love to catch up. Why don't we have supper together? I mean I don't want to interrupt your coffee together right now.'

'It's no interruption,' says Slater beamiŋ. 'It's wonderful to see you. You must feel free to join us. In fact, I insist upon it. Paul has told me so much about his wonderful sons, and I absolutely relish the opportunity actually to meet one of them.'

But Paul reads the sentence differently, as containiŋ within it the sentiment: I'd like to talk to you, Dad, alone, without this third party overheariŋ. And he says, 'Sure, sure. They do excellent food here, right here . . . why don't we meet here this eveniŋ, say 7?'

Hope, rather too abruptly, nods, agrees. 'Later' he says, extricatiŋ himself from the table and floatiŋ upwards. 'Later.' But later, he thinks, Sol may have shot you through the heart with a wireframe bullet, Father, and you will be gushiŋ your life into a million dissipatiŋ globes and beads of red.

eight

Hope floats around the atrium in a daze. Here's the main viewiŋ window again; the handsome young couple have long moved on. Why is the world composed of handsome young couples, all happy and bonded, except for him? Véra's contempt for him is so complete that she will no longer even indulge her anger and his craviŋ by beatiŋ him, instead inflictiŋ the punishment which, despite its intense painfulness, no masochist can bear, that of ignoriŋ him. The maggot is inside his brain: maybe he will change that by finally committiŋ a crime that removes him utterly from the congregation of axeptable humanity, by murdering his own father. Better to be despised by the whole world than be nothing at all, surely. He's already committed the crime in his heart, he's a worm. He's revoltiŋ. He revolts himself.

Through the window: the gleam of impendiŋ sunrise around the curve of the Earth looks like a golden scythe, ready to harvest the latest crop of stars. There's the Plough, the Big Dipper, the peaked-cap, the trapezoid house with a trailiŋ air-line, the net, watever you want to call it. There's wasp-waisted Orion. There are the Pleiades glimmeriŋ, poured out upon the blak velvet bakdrop. And there is – but, no, because here is another swift sunrise, one more of the hundreds of swift sunrises that bathe the Uplands every single month, and the light dazzles his eyes, pouriŋ over the lip of the world like an upward shower of rain.

He asks himself this: can he cut his own father off from this world of beauty? He can't. It's not as if Gradisil was shot *by Paul* whilst attemptiŋ to escape custody. It was all woven out of the red threads of war and the aftermath of war. Justice does not apply. That's not the right way to think about it.

He goes bak to the room. He must tell Sol that he cannot do it, spill the blood of his own father, it's impossible. He rehearses this phrase in his mind; spill the blood, spill the blood, and his agitated mind becomes distracted by the illogicality of this phrase, this cliché, as if his father is a cup brim-full of blood, and the slightest nudge would cause the treacly

439

red to come gloopiŋ down over the side – here is the door to the room. He is about to open it, when he remembers that Sol isn't in there, that he had gone down to the lobby to arrange for a taxi-plane to get them away. Gettiŋ away seems the thing that will happen at the very end of time, shortly before the cosmos is crumpled up like a sheet and stuffed in the blak hole of endiŋ. Paul will be dead, Hope's company, his dreams, the plan of supplyiŋ the Uplands with an inexhaustible supply of raw iron – all will die. After that? The possibility barely exists.

Should he go down to the lobby to confront Sol there? Or perhaps the thing is to stay in his room for a while, to get his thoughts together. His hand is on the doorhandle, when he hears a voice behind him.

'Mr Hope Gyeroffy?'

It is Wilfrid Laurier, yet again, pesteriŋ him. Hope can't believe it. It is a most provokiŋ thing. 'Yes? Wat?'

'I want to have a word, Mr Hope Gyeroffy.'

'This is not a good time, Mr Laurier.'

'A word, Mr Hope Gyeroffy.'

Hope tries to conjure a spark of rudeness from his mild soul. He shuts his eyes, and tries to generate a performance, to act the role of Sol – fuk off, leave me be, go away. Go away. Go! But it's hard, it's not in the grain of his character. 'I'm afraid I can't talk now. Perhaps we can get together for a drink another time, Mr Laurier.'

'I know,' says Laurier, 'that you are planniŋ to murder your father.'

'I haven't got time,' says Hope, panikiŋ now and fumbliŋ at the handle to his door. 'To talk to you now.' But he is only sayiŋ the words to try and drown out the crash inside his head, the *he knows*, the *how could he possibly know?*

'We have to talk, Mr Gyeroffy.'

Hope takes a deep breath and turns bak. There he is, this ridiculous businessman, this MakB junior executive or watever he is. There's a point at which comical becomes just fukiŋ *tiresome*. 'Wat do you want?' he asks, hoarsely. 'How do you know that?' He rethinks this. 'Wat on earth leads you to think that I would – how *dare* you accuse me of so monstrous a—' But there's no heat in this. 'I'm,' he adds, but he doesn't know wat he is.

'We can talk about it in this corridor if you like,' says Laurier, louder than necessary; and there are people floatiŋ about further along, hand-over-handiŋ themselves round the curve, comiŋ and goiŋ. Talkiŋ about it in the corridor is obviously a very bad idea.

'Blakmail?' barks Hope.

Laurier smiles. 'I don't work for MakB, Mr Gyeroffy. Of course I don't. Did you really think I did? Didn't you wonder why I kept bumpiŋ into you, why I was always hangiŋ about you close enuff to overhear those careless conversations with your brother?' There's a gun in his hand. Despite the blip of fear this generates in Hope's mind, he is almost excited to see it. He's spent so long in the EU, he hardly ever sees guns; the device carries the associations of screen thrillers, not of reality. 'I work for the US government, Mr Hope Gyeroffy,' Laurier is sayiŋ. 'I'm an agent. Paul Caunes returns to the Uplands, that's a PR coup for us, particularly when he's got his arm round the shoulders of an American hero like David Slater. Paul Caunes shot by Upland agents – worse, murdered by his own bloodthirsty *sons* – that's a PR disaster. You didn't think we'd deploy agents to prevent that eventuality?'

'You want to hustle me into my room to shoot me?' says Hope. The sentence seems removed from his sense of real life. Even though he speaks the words, and realises how likely they are, he still isn't as scared as he should be.

'You'd prefer I shoot you in this corridor? Open the door.'

Hope does as he is told. He's startiŋ to feel alarmed, something finally shiftiŋ inside him like a tectonic plate and reformiŋ the usual coastline of anxiety that defines his soul. There's something in the— 'Look,' he says. 'Look. This is all wrong.' The sensation of fear, like alcohol into a drunkard's blood, is almost reassuriŋ, almost pleasurable. Hope is sweatiŋ.

Laurier shoves him with his free hand and Hope flies straight bakwards into the room. That 3nimation action-hero style of fightiŋ, where a blow from an impervious fist sends the villain zippiŋ bakwards through walls and pillars, only here made real.

Laurier is inside the room, the door shut behind him, a quik glance into every corner – almost furtive – to chek they're alone together. Then he tugs out a thumnail camera, bips it to his lapel, and says to Hope, 'A quik confession.'

'I've nothing to confess!' bravadoes Hope, lookiŋ around rather desperately.

Laurier simpers. 'Hope Gradisil,' he says, in an insinuatiŋ tone, 'you have the guiltiest conscience I've ever come across, and I've been dealiŋ with criminals and vagabonds for 20 years.' Hope thinks: *did he really say vagabonds? How strange.* His mind won't come straight. He can't think straight. 'You've had a guilty conscience all your life,' Laurier is sayiŋ. 'You think gettiŋ talked into planniŋ a murder by your sycho brother makes you guilty? No, *that* is just one more thing pulled out of the witches' broth of your bad conscience. The guilt doesn't depend on that at all. It's all bottled up. It's the pressurised container of liviŋ a life as Gradisil's fekless son, never matchiŋ her achievements, never liviŋ up to wat she managed. You'll feel so much better when you jab a hole in the side of that absurd existence, really you will. You'll feel so much better – I can't begin to tell you.'

'You'll shoot me,' says Hope, quavery.

'Not if I have your confession. I won't need to. But if you're stubborn, and don't talk, then maybe that'll be my only option.'

'I don't know how to confess,' says Hope, although he has to drag that statement up from somewhere surprisingly deep inside him. Once it's said, though, he sees how true it is. There's a profound truth in it, in fact.

'Just start talkiŋ. I'm not jokiŋ; you'll feel like a migraine you've had all your life has been simply whisked away. You'll feel better.'

And Hope almost believes him. He can sense the granules of truth, like grit in honey, within Wilfrid Laurier's speech. And, who knows? Maybe he will start doiŋ what the man has told him to do, confess, only he sees something that Laurier can't see. His head is frazzled, which is why – although he knows (obviously!) that he shouldn't look up – nevertheless he looks up. Looks up. His line of sight is a giveaway, and Laurier follows it, looks up as well. But by then it's too late. Sol, wedged across the corner of the ceiling to give himself purchase, brings a dagger down, and there's a wet teariŋ sound and the side and front of Laurier's nek splits open in a spectacular fluid firework of red baubles. The windpipe is not cut right through, there's still a patch of cartilage at the bak, or something like that (Hope's mind is disarranged, his sense of the way bodies fit together suddenly unclear), but Laurier can't scream, it's comiŋ out as puffs of air at his throat, turniŋ little circular globes of blood into myriad oval baubles, waftiŋ the spray of red into tiny tourbillons. The gun in Laurier's hand discharges. Lukily it isn't pointiŋ directly at Hope, or that would have been messy.

A wire bullet embeds itself in the wall. Official USA ammunition, fired, missed.

Sol has pushed off and he flies, he flies along the ceiling, like Peter Pan tryiŋ to catch his own shadow, except that wat he is actually doiŋ is tryiŋ to avoid the billowiŋ and expandiŋ cloud of red drops already splotchiŋ dully into the wall. He pulls himself down, grabs Hope, and yanks him out of the way of the scarlet steam. 'Outside,' Sol says, in a surprisingly calm voice. Surprisingly calm. But, then again, Hope isn't panikiŋ either. It all seems weird. He has one of the sleepiŋ bags off its hook, and is usiŋ it as a kind of shield to push through the mess of floatiŋ blood to the door, open, outside into the corridor, bundle the sheet bak through, shut the door.

There they both are, on the other side of the closed door. There they both are, in the corridor.

Hope can't quite bring his thoughts into mental focus on wat has just—

'You've got some on you,' says Sol, lookiŋ disapproviŋly at Hope's shirtfront. Hope looks down, and there is a little red-on-white star map there, some Sirius-like larger dots, some little distant clouds of galactic haze. It is only by lookiŋ down that he can see that his own hands are trembliŋ. He feels removed from his own hands, but they're wobbliŋ like flaps in the gale. It's Parkinsonian, it really is. He feels removed from his own trembliŋ hands. He wants to share his simile with his brother. 'It looks,' he says, 'like a red-on-white star map, cartography of our destination,' but in speakiŋ he realises that his own voice is trembliŋ too, so wobbly indeed that it's actually quite hard to hear wat he's sayiŋ.

Sol has pulled off his own jumper. He is weariŋ a blak tShirt underneath. 'Wear this,' he says handing him the jumper, and then helps Hope's wibbliŋ hands to manoeuvre the too-small top over his head, down his torso, coveriŋ the evidence of their—

'You killed him,' he says to his brother.

'I heard the 2 of you outside the door,' says Sol. 'So I got myself up on the ceiling. He scoped the room,' he adds, grabbiŋ Hope's wrist and pulliŋ him. 'But he's used to workiŋ downbelow, I guess, as an agent I mean. He's not used to chekiŋ the ceiling as well as all the walls. He was thinkiŋ 2-dimensional. Come on, come on.'

They go round the corridor and out into the atrium, and as before – as if nothing had happened – people were throngiŋ it, moving to and fro, goiŋ into and comiŋ out of shops. There are human bodies dispersed through the space, just as there were, a little while ago, or was it a long while ago, separate monads of blood dispersed through the space of the hotel room. 'We have to go away,' Hope says to Sol, and his voice, though low, is steady. 'We need to get away now, now, now.'

Sol is scanniŋ the atrium. Hope knows, telepathy perhaps, wat his brother is lookiŋ for.

'I was just with him,' he says. 'He's in the coffee parlour. I was just with him.'

'I know,' says Sol. 'I saw you, on my way bak up from the lobby.'

This is the moment to say *we can't kill him*, and to say that with enough force to make the statement true, but somehow Hope can't work the words out of his pukkered little mouth, this *turdus* of a sentence. Sol has him again by the wrist, and they are both flyiŋ straight down. Hope thinks: wat did he do with the dagger? Then he thinks: the thumnail camera is on his lapel, it will have recorded everything. This panics him. They should go bak, but obviously they can't go bak to that room in which particles of blood must now, surely, have interpenetrated every single cubic centimetre of space. Then, the thoughts tumblin fast through, he thinks: but the image will not be of me committin murder, only of Sol, and now they are at the entrance to the coffee shop, and Paul is there, and Slater is there, both chattin genially away, now eatin couscous with those little xero-g spoon-sivs. This is the most disorientin of all, for now Hope must compact into his brain the fact that it is only a few minutes since he was here, sittin with them, and that in those tiny little minutes, bug-like in size compared with the leviathan years, everything has changed. It belongs to a different world, and here he is again, before it has had time to alter.

Hope tries once again to tell his brother that they cannot murder their own father. This time it comes out, but in a strangulated and altered form: 'it's a crazy, is crazy, not to – we can't do it here, not in here' he says. But the words seem, simply, redundant. Events have changed things. Everything has changed now.

Sol is inside the coffee shop. Hope has this same sense of hurtlin towards something implacable, a rok wall say, or freefallin parachuteless towards fields of flat concrete; this is a feelin that he has had before. It's like some kind of primal scene. Paul is lookin up, and his face is registerin that his *other* son is also here, a contorted hey! no! well! expression that is more fearful than it was when he greeted Hope, because – well, because he knows his sons, and he knows the difference between Sol and Hope, and he knows from which of them the greater danger is likely to come. But he's still happy to see his younger son, despite even that. Of course he is.

Hope pushes off, flies through the air, snags his hand on a ceiling bar to pivot and angle himself down. His father, startled at this sudden movement, relaxes. Both his sons are here, so it's alright, it must be. Surely Hope will act as a restraint upon the wilder possibilities of Sol's rage. But as David Slater turns towards Sol, perhaps to introduce himself, the younger man jabs him with something. Hope emits a high-pitched noise, pure scared alarm, thinkin this is another knife-stabbin, like the slaughter of Laurier in their hotel room; but it's a diffuser needle, and Slater's skin is not cut, his life not taken. Instead something strange happens. He freezes in mid turn. Hope sees that Sol has injected him with some sort of neural paralysin agent: Slater is stopped in the act of turnin, and of reachin out with his left hand to hold the table, but the oddity of watever agent Sol has introduced into his system is such that his prosthetic hand is not frozen, but rather trapped in some loop of stimulus so that it turns the palm down, turns it bak up, turns it down, turns it up, whilst the rest of his body holds itself with exaggerated stillness.

Paul Caunes starts to move his head to take a look at Slater, his expression just on the point of startiŋ to cramp into distrust, and in a counterpoint move that is balletically mirror-matched to his father's Sol turns and jabs him as well. There is no fuss. Paul simply stops moving. The other customers in the parlour do not seem to notice that anything amiss has happened, although several heads are turned in their direction, drawn by Hope's precipitous entry, and by the odd tikiŋ of the left hand of Slater (Say! Isn't that – you know, wat's his name . . . ? The guy who . . .).

'Wat have you done, have you killed them both?' asks Hope, although as he speaks he knows that Sol has only paralysed them.

Sol, characteristically, doesn't answer the question asked of him. Instead he says: 'Take his elbow. I need you to help me take him.'

'Are you crazy?'

'I can move him by myself, of course,' Sol says, slippiŋ his hand between Paul's torso and left arm, 'but with 2 it will look more natural.'

'Wat are you doiŋ?'

'There's a private plane in the porch,' says Sol.

'A taxi?'

'Private plane.'

'You think you can simply carry the body through a busy hotel, through the lobby and out into the porch without anyone noticiŋ? Don't you think somebody'll see that you're luggiŋ an unconscious body . . .'

'You're thinkiŋ like a groundliŋ,' says Sol. 'Take his right elbow.'

Paul's eyes are still open.

Sol says 'It's easy', and so it proves; they move easily through the coffee shop and out into the atrium. They carry Paul's awake-lookiŋ body between them – it's a little stiff, but not implausibly so. They move through the lobby and nobody stops them. It's all part of the dream-like, vividly dissociated procession of events. There is a man, or there was a man, whose job it was to prevent exactly this sort of kidnappiŋ; but his blood is spattered through the 3 dimensions of the hotel room on the top floor.

They're in the plane. The hatch is open, and Upland hands are helpiŋ pull Paul Caunes inside. They're inside the plane and the hatch is closiŋ now.

nine

Hope says, 'I can't believe we just did that' as the plane pulls away from the Worldview's porch, haviŋ paid a leaviŋ fee that Sol – with an actiŋ skill Hope did not know he possessed – called 'exorbitant, a scandal, I've half a mind to compose a message of complaint,' passiŋ himself off as a typically grumpy Uplander rather than as the kidnapper and assassin in the commission of his crime that he actually was. But they pay, they leave. They drop down into a lower orbit and put the world between themselves and the hotel. They pull up. Hope keeps repeatiŋ: 'I can't believe we just did that'.

Hope is introduced to the 3 Uplanders in the plane: their names are Hopson, Brok and Twain, 2 of them are male and 1 female, 2 of them are white-skinned, with the sunless bleachiŋ of complexion that comes of repeated lengthy stays Upland; and 1 has skin the colour of bran. They are all delighted, energised, so pleased to meet you Mr Gyeroffy, sir, to meet the eldest son of Gradisil; they all greet Sol as an old friend. But Hope takes none of it in. All he can do is look at the static floatiŋ body of his father, and repeat: 'I can't believe we just did that, I can't believe we just did that.'

'Believe it,' says 1 of the 3.

'We pulled him right from under their noses,' says another.

Paul twitches, shudders all the length of his long body, and makes a sort of low bark. He flaps his arms, tryiŋ to rub his eyes but instead flailiŋ, throwiŋ his limbs into a series of peculiarly modern-dance-like postures. This motion starts to shift him in space, rotatiŋ his body very slightly.

'He's comiŋ round,' says the first of the 3, Hopson, Brok or Twain, Hope really wasn't payiŋ attention as to which was which.

It takes Paul 20 minutes, and several lengthy swigs on a globe of water, before he is able to communicate properly; and even then there's a sluggish calm to him that doesn't seem appropriate in the circumstances.

'So,' he says. 'I wondered, when I saw Hope in that coffee shop, whether something like this was afoot. I wondered.'

'You should have made a bolt for it then,' says Hope, sulkily.

Paul doesn't say anything. For long minutes nobody says anything.

'Well, you've got me. Take me to a house, lok me in the porch, open the outside door. So why are we waitiŋ?' asks Paul. He seems oddly calm.

'We're assembliŋ a meetiŋ, puttiŋ the word out so that people can have their say,' says Sol in a colourless voice, not lookiŋ at his father.

'Why bother?'

'Bother? This is justice, father,' says Sol. That word, that *father*, is like a little dart of electricity into Paul's body; he jerks, minutely but visibly. 'The Uplands are *almost* free of laws, but we are particular about treason, and we have forms to follow.'

'You're in the government, of course,' says Paul. 'I saw that on the news channels. Bravo.' Sol doesn't reply to this.

'How can you be so blithe about it?' asks Hope, bitterly. 'Dad, you do know wat this will mean?'

'You think I don't?'

'Dad, there's goiŋ to be a heariŋ, a sort of court, and you're goiŋ to have to energise yourself if you want to defend yourself.'

'Defend myself against wat?' asks Paul, with all the appearance of an elderly person not entirely sure wat is happeniŋ.

'Against the charges. Don't sit there so . . . so . . .'

'The charge is treason,' says Sol, still without lookiŋ at his father.

This interruption is too much for Hope. It's so typical of Sol, talking right through another person. 'I was *talkiŋ*,' boils Hope, decades of compacted irritation forciŋ through; he flaps his right hand, he scowls at his brother. 'I was right in the middle of talkiŋ and you just—'

'Boys,' says Paul, mildly, just as he used to do. 'Don't bikker.'

There's a silence at this. This is too too weird. The three Uplanders, Hopson, Brok and Twain, have on their faces a uniquely strange expression, compounded from equal parts of embarrassment at beiŋ privy to this family quarrel and delighted pride at their axess to this, the remnant or relict of Gradisil's own family – traitor husband, hero sons.

'Father,' says Sol, after a pause. 'It's murder.'

'Whom did I murder?' Paul asks, lookiŋ round absently

'Don't be facetious,' says Sol.

'I'm serious.'

'It's treason,' says Sol, 'and it was tantamount to pulliŋ the trigger.'

'It's Gradisil I murdered, is it?' Paul asks, innocent-seemiŋ.

447

'Dad,' says Hope, wantiŋ this conversation to stop.

'You know it,' says Sol. 'You killed her.'

'You're beiŋ silly, boys,' says Paul. 'Gradisil is unkillable. She's more alive now than I am; more alive than most people. She's impermeable. I know you care, boys, and I'm proud of you for that. I know you loved her. Do you think I didn't? But I *knew* her, and you never did. She's not a figure susceptible to bleediŋ. She eats up death and digests it as her food. She's—'

'Be quiet now,' says Sol. 'Be quiet now, Dad.' He pulls himself up and floats over to a phone, bleepiŋ quietly in the corner of the plane. 'Time,' he announces, and 1 of the interchangeable 3, Hopson, Brok or Twain, scurries to the pilot's chair.

They drop down, and axelerate; they pull up and slow down. It's all ball beariŋs rolliŋ around the frictionless lip of a massive cup, getting faster nearer the bottom, slowing down as they rise up. Hard-times, heart-times. Paul floats quietly, his arms crossed. Hope presses his face to one of the plane's windows, tryiŋ perhaps to catch a glimpse, actually to see, this fabled land, this Nova Americana, this empty world, this homeland, motherland, this new utopia, goodplace-noplace. But all there is nothingness, of course; the empty medium in which things can be, but not beiŋ itself. Is that so different from any other landscape?

Yes, Hope thinks. Yes. Here I am, and I am the Great Isolato. Perhaps this is my true place, a land in which no sound and no heat and no liviŋ matter can pass over the blak fields outside each hermit's house.

They have just grabbed Paul Caunes, ram-stam. He still can't believe that it has happened. It has been Sol's impetus that has pushed them, or dragged them, into this circumstance: he is the force that has pumped up through the broad hollow stem to fountain in green and iridescent at the top.

'So, Sol,' says Paul, with a father's easy intimacy with his son. 'Wat will you do when this is all over?'

This touches a sensitive spot. 'Don't worry about me, Father,' says Sol, not lookiŋ at him. 'I'll be fine.'

'You see, I'm not sure you will,' says Paul. 'As your dad I am naturally concerned for you. If punishiŋ me has been your project for so long, I wonder wat you'll do to give your life direction and meaniŋ after I'm—'

'I'm a member of the Upland government,' interrupts Sol fiercely. 'I'm happy to dedicate my life to the buildiŋ of my nation, Paul. Once I have undone the damage *you* did, Paul.'

Hope looks over at his father. There is the slightest of blushes rougeiŋ his old cheeks, and he is fixiŋ a steady, pained gaze on the wall. That Sol could so easily cause their father pain makes Hope, obscurely, angry. It takes him a moment to locate the reason why, but it comes to him at last. Sol wants revenge because he thinks that it will confirm his mastery of his own pain. He's not so foolish as to believe that it will dissolve the pain away entirely of course, because of course it won't, but he believes, consciously or subconsciously, that enacting his revenge will register a refusal to be passive in the face of sufferiŋ. He sees it as an assertion of agency in the face of hurt. But this is the difference between the 2 brothers. For Sol pain is only something to be mastered. Hope has a less illusioned relationship with pain. He sees that it can never be tamed, it will always command humanity, and the best thing to do is axept it, to revel in it even. It seems to Hope clumsy, even vulgar, to include their old father in these games; although, of course, for Sol, mastering the father is all part of mastering the world as a whole, bending suffering around his own lines of force until it is squeezed into rainbow delight.

The plane doks, nosiŋ into the porch of a great barrel-shaped hall of a house, 4 times the dimensions of a standard room, with ordinary-sized rooms attached at various places. Hope has been here before; the Central Hall of the Uplands, the nearest thing this dislocated, hurtliŋ, individuated nation has to an official buildiŋ, a centre of government, watever the downbelow equivalence would be. There are 5 planes already doked there.

Paul, still twitchiŋ, murmuriŋ something indistinctly, is pulled through the hatch and into this big space; and inside are 20 people or so. When they see Paul comiŋ through they let out a great cheer. It is a properly 3-dimensional crowd, distributed along the floor, up the walls, through the interveniŋ space, all faces wide with genuine delight and excitement. We have him! These are the real Upland zealots.

ten

In theory, as many Uplanders as feel themselves personally involved or aggrieved are entitled to turn up, address the accused, exhort their fellow citizens towards one variety of punishment or another. In practice, numbers are limited to as many planes as can fit in the multiple porches of this space; although by crammiŋ into shared planes the large hall could easily be filled to burstiŋ. In this case, the apprehension of Gradi's former husband and betrayer, numbers are also compromised by the suddenness of the seizure. It is only now beiŋ announced on the news channels.

[[*in a bold, guerrilla raid Upland forces have seized Paul Caunes, former husband of Gradisil Gyeroffy, from the American hotel Worldview. There are reports of at least one fatality in the raid. Caunes is wanted by many Uplanders on charges of treason, and attempts have been made through a variety of courts over the last decade to extradite him from his home in the United States. Colonel David Slater, who was present duriŋ the raid, said this to reporters earlier:*]]

The 20-or-so who greeted Paul with such whoops of lynchaphilic happiness were the people contacted directly by Sol, or contacted directly by the people Sol contacted. They assembled as quikly as they could. The garishly triumphalist mood is fuelled less by bloodlust, and more, strange to say, by a kind of nostalgia, and almost tender fascination with the history of the young country. Few of the people in this hall are old enuff to have personal memories of the war. For them – as for her sons – Gradi is a legend, not a real person. The excitement is partly to share a house with somebody, Paul, who knew her so well, so intimately. It should not surprise you, this starstruck yearniŋ to lay hands on relics of the Great One. If, let us say, one of Gradi's coats came up at auction (and all manner of detritus from her private life is sold off in a dozen auction venues every year); and if, let us say, you had the funds to buy so substantial a relic – perhaps you would press the garment between two sheets of crystal and display it, or perhaps you would donate it to one of the Upland historical museums established in the EU. But before you did that you would take the artefact out of its protective wrappiŋ and, in the privacy of your own home, you would try it on: slip your arms down the cloth tubes that her arms used to fill, strike a succession of poses in front of the mirror. Touchiŋ the talisman of Gradi becomes a way of approximatiŋ yourself to her. This is true of human bodies to precisely the same degree as it is true of other objects. The man who obtained Eva Péron's embalmed body, who told the world he was keepiŋ it for his nation, wat else did he do, when he was first alone with his acquisition, but strip it, pore over it, frot himself against it? Only it was not the body that excited him, even though perhaps he thought it was; it was his own symbolic investment of psychological energy.

In the case of Paul Caunes, here he is, and he is still breathing, pantiŋ, lookiŋ around at this hostile crowd with fear on his face. He is lookiŋ, in fact, like a fish with a frown (to employ one of Klara Gyeroffy's favourite idioms). Like a fish with a frown. But because he is an object with such an intimate association with Gradi herself, these people revere him as much as they hate him. This involuted knot of passions means that many of them would eat him, if they could; to internalise this symbolic connection with their beloved founder; to punish the man they hold responsible for her death. And this is something Paul knows.

[['I have been good friends with Paul Caunes for 10 years or more,' says Colonel Slater on the news channels; 'I am horrified and appalled by this development. For many years he felt himself to be exiled from the Uplands that he loved, because of the hatred of a handful of fanatical fundamentalists. He agreed to come up again, to attend the launch of a new restaurant inside the Worldview hotel, in part because he believed that this hotel is American territory, and that he would be safe. He has been betrayed by murderers and kidnappers.']]

The trial is filmed by a dozen different Upland cameras, and it is as ragged-edged and as intermittent as any Upland trial has ever been. Sol is first accuser. 'There's little point in him tryiŋ to deny his treason. He handed Gradisil to the Americans, he was personally present when this happened. Immediately after he fled downbelow, and took up residence on enemy territory. He had pharmakos treatment for his sexual orientation and lived as a couple with Liu Chuanzhi, until this latter's death 2 years ago.'

'I don't deny any of that,' says Paul. For this he is cheered by the crowd; it is not clear exactly why. Perhaps they take this to be bravado.

'Well,' says Sol, lookiŋ less triumphant than perhaps he might. 'I say the punishment for treason is death.'

'I don't want to die, though,' says Paul. 'I'll tell you – and believe me, I've had a long time to think about this, liviŋ as I have been doiŋ in exile downbelow.'

'Exile!' scoffed somebody, from the far side of the hall.

'Of course, exile! Why wouldn't I say exile? I was an Uplander before I ever met Gradisil. She married me, in part, to gain axess to this land, in which I had a house – before any of you in this room were born! You think I was happy to leave here? No. Why else would I take the risk of returniŋ, comiŋ bak up, makiŋ myself vulnerable to beiŋ snatched by—' and he concludes this sentence not with words, but with a meaningful look in the direction of his 2 sons.

It is very quiet now.

'I've thought about this a great deal, and I realise now that, although I thought I was betrayiŋ Gradi – more, that although I tried very hard to betray Gradi – the fact is I did not. I could not, I was just a tool. Gradi used me, expertly, to arrange exactly wat she wanted to arrange. None of you knew her, but I knew her very well. I knew her as well as any human beiŋ in history has known her, although that's not very much. She cared for one thing only, and it wasn't me, or our sons, or any other person, it was the Uplands, it was this nation. She cared only about bringiŋ this nation to birth. She engineered the war to that end, and she engineered her own betrayal by me, her capture by the Americans, her death – do you think,' and he is growiŋ more agitated now, speakiŋ more fiercely and rapidly, 'do any of you think that she had the slightest qualm about dyiŋ? Of course not. I knew her, and I tell you that death held no terrors for her. If she thought her imprisonment by the Americans would bind the nation she created together, then this is wat she would orchestrate. She thought that by dyiŋ a martyr she would provide a focus around which her new nation could aggregate. She was right in that, as she always was.'

He stops. For a moment nobody speaks. Then a confused series of shouts break out, from 3 or 4 different people: 'Traitor!' 'Tryiŋ to wriggle out!' 'Blame Gradi for her own death?'

'Stop,' yelled Hope, in a sort of agonised blurt. 'We don't have to execute him! We could imprison him.'

Sol shouts, 'Brother, brother, he killed our *ma!*'

'I don't want his blood on my hands!' cries Hope, and there are tears pearliŋ out and away from his eyes. 'It's already wreked – I've already been ruined! I've spent 15 years pursuiŋ my dream for the Uplands! I just – I just got fundiŋ for.' It's hard for him to talk, his chest is heaviŋ. 'And now that's all been yanked away from me! And here I am, with my brother. And here – now you want to take him away, because – but he has confessed his crime. He knows it. Why couldn't we just . . .' And at this point the sentence is lost in Hope's hubbub of cryiŋ.

This nudity of emotional pain shoks the hall. Nobody says anything. Then, from the bak, somebody cries out: 'He's right! The Uplands should be more than an eye for an eye!' The room erupts in shoutiŋ.

'No! That man is *personally* responsible for Gradi's death . . .'

'Why? Why did he . . . ?'

'Lok him up!'

'We could exile him—'

'Throw him out the door – exile him in vacuum.'

'He must die!'

'No!'

'Justice!'

'Wait,' calls a tall young woman. 'Everybody stop yelliŋ. This is Sol and Hope's call. They're the ones most closely harmed by – this man's actions.'

The room is silent again. All gazes are directed at Sol and Hope, the latter twitchiŋ in space with the shuddery convulsions of his chest, and surrounded by a mucusy halo of shed tears.

'We brought him here,' announces Sol, in a firm voice. 'He confesses the crime. We must ensure that justice is done.'

'No,' says Hope, in a smaller voice.

'I'm not talkiŋ about revenge,' says Sol. 'I'm talkiŋ about the best thing *for the Uplands*. One thing Gradi saw clearly was that it takes blood to fertilise a new republic, as it always has. We are a young country. The branches of our nation-tree are still growiŋ. Wat we do now – wat we do today – will have the *greatest* resonance for the way our nation develops into the future.'

'Then why not,' says Hope, masteriŋ his sobs, 'establish the principle of forgiveness? That's a good principle for a growiŋ nation, isn't it?'

'Nations are not people, to turn the other cheek. If another country makes war upon you, you do not surrender, you do not forgive them, you don't axept your defeat passively – you fight. Fight, fight, fight. This is wat we are doiŋ here today. We are assertiŋ the strength of our nation.'

'Yes!' yells somebody; and then somebody else cries, 'That's it!'

Paul is lookiŋ at his own feet, floatiŋ beneath him.

'We choose, here, now, for our nation's future. Which is it to be? Justice? Or forgiveness? Because we cannot have both.'

Through his bleary eyes, Hope watches his brother with some amazement. He has never seen him so fired up, moved with such oratorical eloquence. Gradi's genes do come right, at the right moment.

'Justice is the seedbed of freedom,' says Sol. 'From forgiveness wat grows, except weakness? And which direction do you want the Uplands to grow?'

There is another general acclamation. This, after all, is the reason everybody has assembled.

Hope tries one last line. 'I still have one question. I have one question for him.' The babble and whoopiŋ does not still, so Hope repeats loudly 'One question! One question!' until he has the room's attention.

'One question,' agrees Sol.

'I want to know why, that's all. Want to know *why* did you hand Gradisil over to the Americans?'

'Yes,' says Sol, for this is a question on which many commentators have speculated, and on which Paul himself, in his rare media appearances, has always refused to be drawn.

And this is the moment when everybody looks at Paul Caunes. He draws air into his tired old luŋs, and blows it out again. 'It wasn't me,' he says, again. 'I was just the device that Gradi used to get wat she wanted. Wat she wanted was you – all of you, all Uplanders – united. That's wat she got.'

This is an unsatisfactory reply, and the derisive and hallooiŋ uproar that greets it does not abate for a long while.

There is no point, says Sol, actiŋ with his mother's firmness and pitilessness, in postponiŋ the sentence. They grabbed him ram-stam, let them execute him ram-stam too, make their example now, in front of a dozen cameras. Paul is taken to the Central Hall's main porch by his 2 sons, and he is pushed, not aggressively, into one of the sections: the one on the far left, as it happens. Sol is lookiŋ at his father with a fiercely passionate expression on his face that, in another context, would read as an especially devoted form of love. Hope, on the other hand, is cryiŋ: he can't seem to stop. All these tears! Already his hungry conscience is gobbliŋ at the large thought that, had he asserted his case more aggressively, had he commanded the crowd with powerful oratory –

454

instead of blubbiŋ like a child – then maybe his father would be spared. But it hardly matters now.

They have a hand on each elbow, Sol the right, Hope the left, and all this is beiŋ recorded for all posterity and the edification of subsequent generations of Uplanders. The old man's perfect passivity has an unpleasantly saintlike aspect to it, and a few in the crowd cannot resist tryiŋ to lower his dignity a little by flikiŋ little dabs of – well, it is difficult to say wat, chewed paper perhaps – which travel with the impossibly straight trajectory of xero g to stik to the strand of hair liftiŋ and floatiŋ from the bak of his old head like stringy seaweed in a tidal flow. The 20 people in the crowd follow, most of them still filmiŋ. Their names are now as famous, amongst the Uplands, as the signatories of the Declaration of Independence, or those Englishmen who put their signatures to the warrant for the death of Charles I. And they're eager for their names to be so known; it's their chance for history to register them. None of them think that the future holds any criminal action against them, for rushing through the execution of this one man. Why would they? You need a speck of blood at the root of the new nation-tree. Who can deny it? An old man pushed into a very literal nothingness; that's fatal very quikly, and then the body falls with acceleration into the hot embrace of the atmosphere and is purged, cathartically reduced, scrubbed to constituent atoms. Perhaps Paul, contemplatiŋ this fate, was even rather gratified by the prospect of this.

And here is the moment. He's pushed, not violently, into one of the segments of this multiple porch. The old man is agitated now, because the imminency of real death, real chill and asphyxiation, is not something he can quite banish from his mind. 'Hope,' he says, pulliŋ a thum from his trouser poket and straight-line tossiŋ it, almost casually, to his son. 'You asked why. You asked me why. That says why.'

'Wat's this?' Hope asks, surprised.

'I wrote a memoir. It was after Slater had his success with his; I thought to write one as well, so I did. But nobody has seen it. I couldn't bring myself to publish it. It's on that.'

Hope looks at the thum. 'What you want me to do with it?'

'I'm sorry,' says Paul; and in later years Sol will choose to believe that he is sayiŋ *I am sorry I betrayed Gradisil, sorry that I betrayed you my boy.* But Hope will come to very different interpretation of his apology, will believe him to have been sayiŋ, *I'm sorry I gave this account to you to read, my son, for I know how upsettiŋ you'll find it. I had hoped to keep it from you, but in the end I was too weak to die without leaviŋ my version of*

455

events. They could either be right. They could, perhaps, even both be right.

'I'm sorry,' says Paul. That's wat he says instead of goodbye; for this is the moment that the inner door is pulled shut by an implacably determined Sol, and with barely a shudder (for this Central Hall of the Uplands is so large a structure) the air and the organic matter inside the sealed space is ejected into the vacuum which is the fields and hills and valleys of the Uplands itself.

.

chronology

2043		Klara Gyeroffy born
2063		Gradisil born
2065	Treaty of Tenerife ends first US-EU war	
2072	'Short War'. Destruction of Paris. Peace of Madrid	
2075	Klara Gyeroffy appointed EU envoy	
2081	US seizure of EU houses in Uplands (sometimes known as 'first space war')	
2088		Gradisil marries Paul Caunes
2091		Hope Gyeroffy born
2093		Solidarity Baldwin born
2099	First US-Upland war	
2102	Gradisil apprehended	
2115	Gradisil declared SWAE	
2131		Death of Paul Caunes

Acknowledgments

To thank: Simon Spanton; James Lovegrove; Roger Levy; Rachel Roberts; Justina Robson; Gillian Redfearn; Ariel; Keith Brooke; Avraam Kawa; Charles Kinbote; Steve Calcutt; Brian Green; Julie Green; Sophie and Brian Coughlan. Tony Atkins read a portion of this manuscript and made very helpful comments. The observations on the erroneous nature of the saw 'as the twig is bent so the tree grows' in Part II is adapted, although not quoted, from Les Murray's 1990 poem 'Experiential'. I am greatly indebted to Wikipedia, in which invaluable resource I consulted various articles on the magnetosphere, electromagnetism and Maxwell's equations. I have also made use of Ira H. Abbott and Albert E. Von Doenhoff's *Theory of Wing Sections, Including a Summary of Airfoil Data* (Dover Publications 1959).